Lisa Carey grew up in Brookline, Massachusetts. She attended Boston College; later, while working on her MFA in Writing from Vermont College, she worked as a bookseller. She went to Ireland to research her first novel, and ended up living there for five years. Her novels have since won numerous awards and been translated into a dozen languages, as well as being optioned for film. Lisa lives in Portland, Maine, with her husband and son, and returns to Ireland whenever she can.

You can discover more about the author at www.lisacareybooks.com

THE STOLEN CHILD

May, 1959: St Brigid's is a remote island off the west coast of Ireland. It is barren and its small community is dwindling. But according to rumour, it is a magical place, home to a healing well. Two sisters, Rose and Emer, have resisted the call of the mainland. Rose is beautiful, blessed with love and many children. Emer is unlovely, and worse still, cursed by the strange currents that run through her fingers. When an outspoken American named Brigid arrives in search of a miracle, she is initially shunned, as the islanders keep their secrets close. But as the months pass and Brigid carves out a place on the island and in the sisters' lives, a complicated web of betrayal, fear and desire culminates in one shocking night that will change the island, and its inhabitants, forever . . .

LISA CAREY

THE STOLEN CHILD

Complete and Unabridged

CHARNWOOD
Leicester

First published in Great Britain in 2017 by
Weidenfeld & Nicolson
an imprint of the Orion Publishing Group Ltd
London

First Charnwood Edition
published 2017
by arrangement with
Orion Publishing Group Ltd
An Hachette UK Company
London

A catalogue record for this book is available
from the British Library.

ISBN 978–1–4448–3459–8

Published by
F. A. Thorpe (Publishing)
Anstey, Leicestershire

Set by Words & Graphics Ltd.
Anstey, Leicestershire
Printed and bound in Great Britain by
T. J. International Ltd., Padstow, Cornwall

This book is printed on acid-free paper

For Liam and Timothy,
who don't hold back any love.

Author's Note

The Stolen Child is a work of fiction. While the inspiration came from true stories of evacuations of Irish islands like Inishark and the Blasket Islands, St Brigid's island and its inhabitants are imagined and not intended to represent any real place or people. Any mistakes are mine, either out of ignorance or artistic licence, and I apologise for them in advance.

Come away, O human child!
To the waters and the wild
With a faery, hand in hand,
For the world's more full of weeping than you
   can understand.

   'The Stolen Child', William Butler Yeats

Part One

ST BRIGID'S ISLAND

I will arise and go now, and go to Innisfree,
And a small cabin build there, of clay and
    wattles made:
Nine bean-rows will I have there, a hive for
    the honey-bee,
And live alone in the bee-loud glade.

'The Lake of Innisfree', William Butler Yeats

Prologue

May, 1960

The day of the evacuation, the first of May, 1960, dawned cloudless and still, weather so fine the islanders said it was stolen.

St Brigid's Island perched like a jagged accident above the water, all grass and rock, no beach to ease the passage of a boat, no harbour to shelter it once there. Twelve miles west of Ireland, at times nearly impossible to get to and just as deadly to try to leave. It was the whim of the wind and the swelling sea that determined who landed there and who was let go. The islanders were apt to say it was not the weather at all that decided such things. Something else, they believed, turned the world to suit itself.

So they said it was stolen, that morning's passage, from the good people, the fairies. They did not give such gifts, or lend them. Someone must have tricked it out of them. The islanders muttered their gratitude at the same time as they crossed themselves, in the name of their saint, against it.

Had it not been the day they were scheduled to leave, the women would have put off their chores, set chairs outside their houses, and turned their doughy faces to the sun. Lashing rain and gales had battered the island for most of April, the sort of weather that abandoned them.

Many had speculated that this day would not come at all — that it would be put off, perhaps until midsummer — and the thought of another month like the last few set the women gasping at the ends of their sentences with disapproval and fear.

Two sisters, twins who looked more like strangers sharing the same bed, noted during the night exactly when the weather let them go. Emer breathed deeply, the invisible band that gripped her neck and tethered her loosening enough for a sigh. Rose pressed her lips together, too angry to allow a breath of concession. She had nothing packed. The other women had been ready for weeks, but she hadn't even brought the crates in from the shed.

Rose got up and stirred the hearth, feeding dry rushes to the orange spots of heat that had crouched waiting beneath the ash during the short night. The same fire had burned on St Brigid's Island for generations, some said since the time the saint herself had lived there. Glowing clumps of turf were buried and reawakened; whenever a new house was built the first fire was brought over on a neighbour's spade. Evacuation or no, Rose would not be the one to extinguish it.

By dawn the boats were already there, anchoring out from the island because the rocks and current made approaching the slip impossible for anything larger than a currach. Four boats — the mail boat, two fishing trawlers and a Galway hooker — all piloted by men from the mainland and the neighbouring island. Rose, watching from her doorway, grumbled over the attendance.

'Sure, when we're leaving, the vessels come out in droves; if only they'd been so keen in February.' She heard the slight change in the silence of her sister. As though the mention of February had actually stopped her breathing.

A dozen men rowed in, along with the priest who had been essential in bringing the evacuation about. More men than had stood on that island in years. They shared a pipe together before starting the first load. All day long families walked their belongings down to the quay, the borrowed men carrying dressers and bedsteads roped to their backs, the women lugging baskets of linens and dishes, the children gathering cats and hens and cattle and ushering them towards the water. The dogs bullied sheep into cramped, panicked flocks that huddled in the currachs. The cows and the one bull were made to swim, as well as a donkey, tied by their necks to the back end of a currach, their eyes huge and shining white with panic. One girl put her cat into a cast iron pot, tying the top down slightly off-kilter so there was a slit to let the air in and the wails of protest out. Then, every once in a while, a nose, a paw with claws extended. Soon every covered pot on the island held a cat or a duck or a hen and they lined them up on the grass, like a parade of badly tuned instruments, to wait for their turn on the boat.

In the house above, Emer and Rose moved, barely speaking, through the morning routine of breakfast and chores and getting children ready.

5

Since there were plenty of children, this took until the sun was high above the boats waiting below. The children ran back and forth from the quay to the house, reporting on whose family had loaded what, whose cat was in a pot and who was arguing about what to bring and what to leave behind. Rose's oldest, Fiona, told them that Jimmy Moran, eighty-six years old and the only male left on the island over the age of eleven, was refusing to leave. He was parked on a kitchen chair outside his door and was striking with his cane the knees of anyone who tried to get in.

'The old fool,' Emer said. 'As if they'd let him stay.'

Rose stiffened. 'That's grand,' she said. 'Coming from you.'

Emer narrowed her one eye. The memory of the other eye was hidden under a brown leather patch. She opened her mouth to say something further, but Rose turned away.

Emer, who had her own house down the road that she no longer lived in, had only one trunk, which had been packed for weeks. She was leaving the rest to the birds. Rose, who was more likely to want to bring everything, still hadn't packed a bag, and was washing the breakfast dishes and putting them away in the press as if it were any other day.

'Will I put the delph in a crate?' Emer said. Rose gave her a look that was enough to stop any further suggestions.

Emer went outside. Their mother was propped on a stool against the stone house, one limp arm

6

tucked beneath her breasts, her head covered in wool as though the sunshine and sea air were insults she needed to guard against.

'She'll take her time about it, sure,' she slurred, the left side of her mouth as useless as her arm. Emer ignored her. Though her own opinions often leaked out of her mother's half-paralysed mouth, she refused to commiserate. Only Rose had the patience to answer her any more.

Emer walked the two cows and their calves down the road to the water. The man who took the rope from her did so with caution, taking care, as they all did, not to brush against Emer's hand.

In the early afternoon, when a man from the boat told Rose it was time — hers was the last house to go — she nodded at Emer, and they began to collect things. It was all done quickly; within an hour a house that had seen life for two hundred years was empty. Their mother rode down on the last donkey, led by the men, like a tired child. Rose stayed behind, sweeping at the cobwebs and dust blossoms that had appeared when the furniture was moved. Emer, who had walked the children down, came back up with one of the babies on her hip and found her sister feeding the fire from the pile of turf on the hearth.

'Rose,' Emer said, not trying to keep the sharp annoyance from her tone. 'What does that matter now?'

'*No fire, no sun, no moon shall burn me,*' Rose muttered, the incantation of Saint Brigid that children were taught to say, lighting a fire or climbing into a boat. It was meant to protect them.

'It's a little late for that carry-on,' Emer said. She left her sister, going down to the water to wait with their mother and the children.

Rose washed the floor, wiped down the windowsills and polished the thick glass of the tiny windows. 'No lake, no water, no sea shall drown me. No arrow of fairy nor dart of fury shall wound me.' She fed the dust and dirty rags to the fire with tears running down her cheeks, swiping at them as though they were something not related to her, like a bee too close to her face. She cleaned and cried and burned what was left, and when the house was spotless and the fire was as hot as it could get, she blew her nose and stood in the open doorway. She took the Saint Brigid's cross from where it hung on the wall, woven from rushes last February by a woman she missed more than she cared to admit, and briefly imagined igniting it in the fire and touching the flames to the thatched roof. The fire would make short work of the dense straw, it would leap from one roof to the next, and feed itself long after the boats were gone. From their new council houses on the mainland, in such fine weather, they would be able to see that fire, burning on top of the sea.

If she must go, she thought, why not leave the whole place ablaze?

But she was a sensible woman, a mother, a sister, a guardian to the fragile leftovers of her family. Emer was the one who could get away with setting fires, burning hope away with her hands, like a possessed, grief-stricken witch. But Emer was done with all of that, and Rose had never been allowed.

She nestled the cross in the basket instead, along with the last treasures she found in the secret crevices of the house. She put on her good coat, usually worn only to Mass. In its pocket she slipped her kitchen knife, the tool every island woman kept at hand, as the men had once carried their spades. She said three names softly and closed the door.

She saw women gathering in the graveyard, nestled in a promontory above the quay, a patch of jutting purple stones, the first and last thing you saw when pulling a boat into or away from the island.

Rose wouldn't bother with that.

She walked the long road instead, up north to the cliffs, past the clocháns that had stood for centuries, solid as beehives mortared with honey, since the time when the island was a convent of loving virgins. When an island of women alone was a pilgrimage to God rather than a death sentence.

There was too much to remember here, at the cliff's edge, where even on a calm day the wind skinned her ears. The memories licked like fire at her throat, her groin, her heart: screaming to save her sister, lifting her skirt for a lover, building fires to cry out for help in the darkness. She could not separate the love from the terror. She listened for the trickle of water she knew ran quietly beneath the grass, a holy well hidden where few would think to look for it. She half expected to see a fiery-haired woman with a red dog at her heels, coming to seek the water. But that woman had left the island already, following the same watery road as those who had gone before. They had trickled away, for storms, war, emigration, careers, to a handful of souls, and today was the last day people would ever live here.

The story was that Saint Brigid swindled this island away from a king. He agreed to give her for free whatever land she could cover with her cloak. When she unfurled the blue fabric, the wind carried it in every direction, until it grew and spread and darkened itself over the entire island. The king, angry at being codded, warned her that the place was rotten with fairies, called 'good people' only to placate them, for they were anything but good. Brigid, the story went, only smiled and said: 'That will suit.'

She wasn't a Christian saint, but a Celtic one — born in the doorway between two worlds, named for a goddess, suckled on the milk of fairies, ordained as a bishop — she was a woman who feared nothing, with both God and the good people on her side.

Now the islanders were being given a village, on the mainland, for the price of leaving this story behind.

The same cove that once protected the nuns, isolated them in devotion, was a curse in the modern world. A dangerous inlet that was not a real harbour, a rocky hollow and narrow cement quay where men risked their lives pulling a boat in. Or they used to. Now there were no men to risk it. Now they were only women, save old Jimmy Moran and a few young boys. Women not willing to pretend they had the strength of saints any longer. This evacuation had been coming for almost as long as they'd fought against it. They asked the government for a harbour; the government gave them a cul-de-sac on the mainland instead.

On that last walk down, down the green road that had been carved by nuns and trampled by the bare feet of children, Rose turned her mind. Now that she was packed, she would go without once looking back, let the fire go out, leave the holy water in the ground, not carry it with her in a tiny vial as the other women surely would. She would busy herself making her new council house, with electricity and a water tap and gas cooker and a toilet and a key for the front door, into a home, and be kind to her sister, who seemed not to care that they were losing their entire lives because she had already lost far more than the boats could take away. She would build a fire in her virgin chimney, the hearth so small it was meant only for pleasure, and light it with a match.

Rose didn't think that morning's weather was stolen. The fairies wanted them gone as much as Emer did. Even Saint Brigid had abandoned them. They, too, had had enough.

On the last run, the mail boat brought a reporter from Galway, who snapped a few photographs for the sensational story that would appear in the weekend edition. He took pictures of the women kneeling in the children's graveyard, and one of Jimmy Moran being carried, chair and all, down to the boats. The photograph that made the front page, and was used afterwards whenever the subject of evacuated Irish islands came up in the news, was one of Rose and Emer, sitting in a currach, each holding a baby in her lap. Both of the sisters wore the traditional island head covering, brown sheep's wool knitted into a tube, which could be worn over the head to block the wind, or draped as a scarf on finer days. The wool was knit in a continuous circle, a spiral, so once you put it on, it was impossible to lose it to sea air or the hands of needy children. It was said to be the same head covering, the reporter wrote, that Saint Brigid knitted for each of her new postulants.

With this wool draped over their heads, their hair hidden, and in black and white, which smoothed Emer's complexion and dulled Rose's, you could see a physical resemblance that was rarely there when you looked at them in life. The set of their jaws perhaps, the worry lines, deeper than they should have been for women still young. Though they had always been opposites, in the photo they were reversed; Rose, who had always been sunny next to Emer's dark scowl, looked snuffed out, while Emer, who had spent a lifetime being asked to smile like her prettier sister, was lit from within, glowing, as if something had just been whispered to her, handed to her, stolen and then returned. As if Emer, the one who was bringing nothing, was the one most looking forward to the future. As if, the eagerly dire reporter suggested in his article, leaving the island might put to rest all the terror and sorrow that trying to remain upon it had born.

1

The Yank

May, 1959
ONE YEAR EARLIER

The Yank arrives on the first day of summer, with the pigs. She comes in Festy's boat, which has to drop anchor and wait for the island men to row out in a currach. They hand her over the side along with the mail and two squirming sacks. Rumour has it the Yank has been waiting on the mainland for two weeks, staying in the room above Oliver's bar as the last of the spring storms battered the quay and made it impossible for anyone to approach the island.

Emer's son, Niall, has been watching the quay all morning. His father and uncle rowed out early to purchase this year's piglets. Every May, during the festival of Bealtaine, which marks the beginning of the summer, each family on the island gets a new pig. They are raised into the autumn and slaughtered one by one over the winter, so fresh meat can be shared between them. Pig day was a favourite for Emer and Rose when they were children, and now it is her son's turn to be excited.

'They're in,' Niall comes running to tell her, though she has already seen it from the window. 'They're helping Festy bring that Yank.'

15

'*Amadan*,' Emer's mother hisses from her perch by the fire. Fool. No one responds. Their mother is used to complaining to the air.

Emer, who has been peeling potatoes at the kitchen table, slips her small knife in the pocket of her apron and dries her hands. Normally, Emer would send Niall down alone, to avoid Rose's husband, and the other islanders who avoid her. But she wants a look at this Yank. She wants to know what sort of woman she is, coming here all on her own. Americans, the islanders know, are used to modern conveniences that St Brigid's Island is not able to provide. Emer wants to see for herself if it takes something more than a fool.

Niall runs back outside, twirls downhill in the sunshine, then circles back for his mother to catch up. Emer should call in the other direction to Rose, invite her to come along, but she walks quickly to keep up with Niall, without looking back. No women will be clamouring to meet the Yank, she knows. They'll keep their distance, wait to see if she is staying a decent stretch. Emer wants to meet her first.

Emer is tall, like most St Brigid women, sharply angled and awkward, nothing soft to ease the protrusion of bone. She keeps her dark hair trimmed to the length of her jaw and banished behind her ears. Her skin is decent enough, sallow, with olive tones left over from Ireland's collusion with Spanish pirates. As if reinforcing that theme, she wears a calfskin patch over a stolen eye. Beneath the patch is the fat worm of a keloid scar that seemed to widen long after the

16

rest of her stopped growing. The eye she has left is striking, always wet, lipping over, like a dark blue stone sitting at the bottom of the water, far too deep to reach.

They say Saint Brigid pulled her own eye out, to repel a man sizing her up for a wife. When he was gone, she popped it in again, and her beauty was restored. No one dared propose to her after that. The fairies took Emer's eye, but the one they left suggests she is capable of doing something similar. Of ripping away what is precious should you look at her the wrong way.

The men have rowed out in two currachs to meet the boat, transferred all the Yank's bags and trunks, and are hauling her up on to the quay, one man for each arm, grunting and apologising. She has a fierce lot of bags and wooden crates from the shop in town. Piled on the quay along with all her things are supplies for the island that hasn't had a delivery in three weeks: mail, flour, sugar, tea and tobacco, and two sacks which are bulging and emitting the muffled squeals of terrified baby pigs. Niall skips over to them and nudges the lumps in the brown fabric with his bare feet. Emer stops just before the stone quay, to look at the Yank from a distance.

The young men are already taken with her. Rose's husband, Austin, and his cousins, Malachy and Michael Joe, are slagging her about the pigs; apparently she sat down on one of the bags on the way over. She seems able for it — hooting at their jokes, throwing her head back with a big American laugh. She isn't bothered by them grabbing her around her long arms and jostling her breasts as they settle her on the quay. Her hair is loose and frantic with wind, auburn with streaks of fiery red, the curls springing every which way about her head like they are trying to get away. She is wearing a massive yellow jacket and matching trousers the men are praising as American genius. ('Won't that stay bone dry in a wetting rain, now.') She pumps the hand of old Jimmy Moran too fast and eager, not seeming to realise that he would prefer a simple nod and wink of welcome. She catches sight of Emer and smiles, revealing dazzling white teeth, so Emer is forced to step forward. She holds her hand out as Emer approaches, and Emer hesitates before taking it.

'I'm Brigid,' she says, pronouncing her own name wrong, hard on the last *d* instead of softening it to barely there. Emer takes the woman's hand and wraps her fingers around the palm.

Nothing happens. Brigid seems to have no aversion to Emer's hand. Instead of Brigid pulling away first, it is Emer who lets go. She doesn't do what most strangers do, look back and forth indecisively between Emer's remaining eye and the patch over the other. She looks at Emer straight on, as if both eyes are still there. Brigid's eyes are auburn and match the darker streaks in her hair. Even after Emer lets go, she can still feel the woman's palm, pulsing, relentless, like a child chanting the same demand over and over again. Emer flushes and tells her name.

Brigid makes her repeat it twice. *Ee-mer*. She

18

is not only loud, but asks other people to speak up, as if she is slightly deaf. Most Americans are like this.

'Brigid and Mary be with you,' Emer mutters automatically.

'Everybody keeps saying that,' the Yank booms. 'My mother used to say that too. When I was little I thought it was about me, but then I found out it's about the saint.'

Emer gives no response to this. She makes no effort to nod and smile while others are speaking, or fill awkward pauses with chatter. *Like talking to a stone*, islanders say about her.

Niall skips over to them.

'Mammy, may I have my pig now? Austin says I can choose. I want a spotted one.'

'Where have your manners gone to?' Emer says. She often chides him in front of others, out of an attempt to appear herself. She is a different person altogether when they are alone.

Brigid winks at him. 'What's your name, handsome?'

'Niall,' he says. He has to say it twice, *Nye-l*, then spell it.

Brigid holds her hand out and he takes it. Emer has to quell the instinct to stop him, to prevent her son from touching her at all.

'Look at those eyes,' Brigid croons. Emer crosses herself quickly. Brigid notices, flicking her eyes quickly back to Niall.

'They're a fairy's eyes,' Niall says, mimicking what the islanders say about him. The outer ring is a cloudy, feverish blue, the inner area, around his pupil, as orange as a hot ember. Emer can be

19

feeling her worst, cold and damp and scatter-brained and trapped, hating the island, Patch, her bright, smiling sister, her sullen, crippled mother who divides her time between Emer and Rose's house, and she only needs to look at Niall's eyes and the burning settles her right down.

Where he got these eyes, however, she can't think about for too long or she forgets how to breathe. He didn't have them when he was born.

'It's only an expression,' Emer attempts.

'I have fairy ears, myself,' Brigid says, hauling her hair back to reveal them: cold-reddened, protruding a fair distance, slightly pointed at the top. 'Wanna trade?'

Niall beams. This is the sort of teasing he is used to; the Yank wins him over instantly, and Emer isn't sure she likes it.

'Mammy?' Niall nags.

'Go on and choose your pig, then,' she says.

Austin unties the sack and holds it open for Niall, who sticks his head and arms right down into the screaming pit. He emerges with his hands full of squirming pink and grey flesh, and tucks it into the front of his jumper, crooning and stroking it until it settles against his small chest like a contented baby.

The men whistle and hoot at Brigid to get moving, they've loaded as much as they can on to the donkey and are carrying the rest. Niall joins the procession, walking next to Brigid. The piglet, a spot like coal dust around its eye, falls asleep. Niall twirls around and winks at Emer, daring his mother to follow them.

20

'What will you name it?' Brigid is asking. Emer walks just behind them.

'We'll slaughter it come autumn.' Niall explains this kindly, a bit condescending, as if Brigid is a child and he is the adult.

'Can't it have a name in the meantime?' Brigid says.

'You might name it Rasher,' Emer says. No one responds to this.

'How old are you, Niall?' Brigid says. He looks at her oddly, this is not the way they ask in Ireland.

Emer translates: 'She wants to know what age you are.'

'I'm six,' Niall says. 'Today.'

'Is it your birthday?' Brigid beams. Niall nods. 'And I didn't bring you a present.'

That's when Emer realises that her husband is not among the men hauling her gear.

'Where's Patch?' she asks Austin.

'He'll be along later, sure.' Austin evades her eye.

Not likely, she wants to quip. He's at the pub and won't be back for three days, not until his brother bodily collects him.

Niall has run ahead, but he circles back to bestow a curative squeeze to her hand. He knows what it means that Patch is not there, but it doesn't bother him, beyond regretting that it bothers her.

'Were you named for the druid Brigid or the saint?' Austin calls out to the Yank.

'What's the difference?' Brigid says.

'Some say there isn't one.' Austin is flirting

with her. He wouldn't speak to her at all if Rose were around.

'The first Brigid was a druid goddess, daughter of the original fairy race of Ireland.' Austin, who finished secondary school, is showing off now. 'The one who lived here was a Christian nun. Some think that it was one woman who changed camps when it suited her.'

'Even Britain is named after her,' Niall adds.

'I didn't know that,' Brigid smiles politely. 'But I think my mother just named me after this island. Because she missed it.'

Emer makes a quick gasping noise in her throat, a noise particular to island women, a noise that makes Niall look up and wonder what has his mother so peeved.

They make their way up the west road. Brigid is explaining to them how she wrote to the priest to say she was coming to live in her uncle's house after Old Desmond died, but they all know this already. The priest's housekeeper couldn't resist such gossip and told them months ago. Desmond's is the last cottage before the road ends and only sheep paths continue up and around to the cliffs. The view from one side is of the open Atlantic, from the other, the house looks out on the mountains of Connemara and the neighbouring island, Inis Muruch, which has four times the population, the priest's house, a church, a shop and a pub and gets mail delivered year round. No one has lived in this house in the year since Desmond died, unnoticed for long enough that the body had started to turn. He hadn't spoken to another islander willingly in forty years.

Emer watches for the Yank's reaction as they get closer. The house looks no better than derelict, whitewash worn away to grey stone, one window broken into a circle of jagged teeth, thatch on the roof half-eaten away, wrens rising in commotion as they approach. When Austin halts the donkey in front of it, the Yank stops for a beat and blinks, but presses on, stepping over the fallen stones and crushed barbed wire of Desmond's wall. The men mutter and apologise, prop the door open to let in the air, reassure her she'll have it sorted in no time, unload her belongings and pile them neatly inside. They scurry off like startled mice, promising to bring down a load of turf, leaving Emer and Niall alone with the Yank in the house. It smells of damp that has been let to win, urine and the old, bitter man that died inside it. If she were that Yank, she'd walk straight back to the quay. She imagines she sees a dip in the woman's broad shoulders, a weary release, as if the state of the place is a last straw. But Brigid puts her hands on her hips, which are square and strong on top of lean legs. She is almost as tall as the doorway, taller than most of the men who hauled her things up, though St Brigid men are not strangers to being towered over by women. She blows a stray cluster of red curls away from her eyes. It bounces up and back like a live, opinionated thing. Her complexion is as bright and as varied as her hair, milk-white cheeks giving way to a wave of auburn freckles across her nose. She might be Irish, except for the teeth.

23

'Well, this is even worse than I thought,' she says blithely, taking off the yellow costume and pushing up the sleeves of her equally mannish but more familiar woollen jumper. Though Emer hates to clean house, as her sister, mother and husband can attest to, she can't really bring herself to walk away. Women are expected to do such things, just as the men were expected to unload her belongings and take off for another chore. Emer suspects it is no different in America. There is something about this woman — her resolve seems to border on desperation — that fires up Emer to help. She wants to see what she might do next.

Niall goes back outside to let the pig run around on the hill behind the house. Within a few minutes he has taught the thing to play a version of tag.

Emer and Brigid open three of the four windows, pick the last one free of broken glass. They sweep out the cobwebs and mouse droppings from the cupboard, clean the ashes from the hearth, and start a new fire with the turf Austin brings back in the donkey's creel. For luck, Emer knows they should borrow from another fire to start it, but she doubts the Yank knows or cares about this, so she uses a whole box of damp matches that Brigid brought from the mainland to get it lit. Emer tells her how to bury the fire at night and dig out the embers in the morning so the fire will never go out and no more matches will be needed.

'My mother used to do that,' Brigid says. 'There's a chant you say, about Saint Brigid.'

24

'No fire, no sun, no moon shall burn me.' Emer's recitation is quick and without feeling.

'That's it,' Brigid says. She jerks her head, as if flicking aside an unpleasant memory like one of her curls.

Niall comes in to check on their progress. He has found a bit of rope and fashioned a lead for the piglet. It trots beside him happily, the screaming emigration over the water in a canvas sack wiped for ever from its mind.

'What about Saint Brigid's well?' Brigid says. 'The holy well the island was named for. Is it nearby?' Brigid says this casually but Emer can tell she is holding her entire self in check awaiting the answer. There is that feeling from her hand again, a pull, a frantic grab, though her face remains prettily detached.

She's come for a miracle, then.

'The island was named for the saint, not a stream,' Emer says. 'You'll hear a lot of nonsense about what she could and could not do. But there's plenty of wells,' she says. 'You won't want for fresh water.' Niall, who has been trying to get the piglet to sit on command, looks pointedly at his mother.

'Take that creature outside,' Emer says, to stop his tongue. They don't share the well with outsiders. Not any more.

She sends Niall out for ordinary water. He takes the job on like a game, cheerfully bringing them the bog-stained liquid and pouring the dirty buckets into the dyke when they've used it up. If Brigid can hear his chattering, the back and forth of a half-invisible conversation, she doesn't say so. Perhaps she thinks he's talking to the pig.

Emer marvels at the groceries, luxuries they only see on a holiday: store-bought milk, butter and yogurt, white sugar in a paper bag, sliced bread and potatoes scrubbed so spotless they look sickly. Rashers sliced thick and ready to fry. Chocolate, currants, soap wrapped like a gift.

'I guess I wasn't thinking,' Brigid laughs uncomfortably. 'I was expecting a fridge.'

'We haven't been given the electricity like some places,' Emer says. She shows Brigid the low, dark shelf where she can store the perishables.

'I'll bring you milk and butter until you sort out a cow,' Emer says. 'You can buy mackerel from the lads at the quay. They set aside some before selling the rest on the mainland.'

Brigid nods and smiles, taking it in as if she's lived on a remote island in Ireland before and it's just a matter of remembering how to do it. There's a tension to her smile since she asked for the well, a tight crack in her face.

'Are you from New York?' Niall asks when he whirls in again. He has tied the pig outside and it squeals painfully for him.

'No,' Brigid says, 'Maine.' She has to explain where this is. She ends up saying it's above New York and below Canada.

'What's it like?'

'Like this,' Brigid says gesturing to the sea. 'Rugged, rocky coastline. But with trees.'

'Like a forest?'

'Yes. We call it the woods.'

26

'Have you got fairies in it?'

'I used to make houses for them,' Brigid smiles warmly now. 'Don't you?'

Emer is glaring at him with one cold eye.

Niall sees this and shrugs.

'Em,' he says. There is a pause where all they can hear is the pig still crying for him. And for a beat longer than is comfortable, Niall is gone. His pupils contract, making the fiery ring around them look larger. Emer darts towards him, alarmed, but it is over quickly, he pulls himself out of it, where often he needs to be hollered at, or shaken. Still, it is a few painful seconds before he speaks again. 'We've tree roots in the bog,' he says, as if there was no pause at all. 'They're massive.'

Brigid smiles, but Emer can see that she noticed. Noticed his absence, and Emer's reaction. She probably thinks he is simple.

Emer tells him to go outside and silence the pig.

'Is he your only child?' Brigid asks when he's gone, and Emer sets her jaw.

'He is,' she says, ready to defend herself.

But Brigid only nods, as if this answer is acceptable.

'You must have had him fairly young,' says Brigid.

'I'm twenty-three,' Emer says defensively. Brigid chuckles and shakes her head.

'I'll be forty in February,' she says. Emer forgets for a moment to hide her thoughts, letting her mouth hang open in shock. Her own mother is forty-two and looks ancient compared

27

to this tall, glowing, barely wrinkled woman.

'I'll take that as a compliment,' Brigid says.

'Are your children grown?' Emer asks.

'Haven't had any.' She says this casually, not even looking at Emer, as if she might just change her mind and start a family next week. But that smile again. So tight it has begun to quaver.

That's what she wants the well for. The stories were that Saint Brigid used the water to heal sick children, or to revive barren wombs. The islanders guarded it, though there was no evidence that it still worked. Emer could discourage her. 'They tried it on my eye,' she could say. 'I lost it regardless.' But she holds her tongue.

Emer says she needs to go, so they walk outside. Brigid squints out over the view, the mountains on the mainland, the sea like a calm blue walkway pretending as though it never tries to trap them in rage.

'It's beautiful,' Brigid says, but she doesn't mean it. Emer sees it in her face, in the set of her shoulders. Looking at the sea brings her something other than peace.

'What was my Uncle Desmond like?'

'A bit touched,' Emer says. Brigid doesn't need to ask what this means, like most Americans would.

'Did any of them come back?' she asks Emer. 'Of my mother's family? Anyone before me?'

'No one comes back here once they've got away.'

'Why not?'

'Can you imagine a more desolate place?'

28

Emer scoffs. Brigid raises her eyebrows.

'We're to be evacuated,' Emer blurts. 'The priest on Inis Muruch is trying to get the county to give us land in town. We'll have new houses, council houses.' She almost pulls out the planning sketch the priest gave her, which she keeps in her apron pocket, of the council houses, painted in cheery pastels, concrete paving around them. But she decides against it, when she sees Brigid's face.

'Sounds like you want to leave,' Brigid says. Emer shrugs.

'We'll be gone by the time Niall is seven, please God,' she says.

'What's happening when I'm seven?' Niall says, coming around the side of the house, piglet in tow.

'Whisht, you,' Emer says.

Brigid shakes her head, as if she can shake Emer and her pessimism right off her like she does her curls.

'Well, I've come to stay,' she says. Emer says nothing. Let's see how long you last, she thinks, with no phone, no electricity, no doctor or priest, no newspaper unless the weather permits it, and weeks on end with no contact whatsoever from anyone but the same people you've seen every day of your life.

'Mammy!' Niall calls. Both the Yank and Emer turn to where he is pointing.

A dog is crouching in the weeds to the side of the house, a low growl in its throat, the skinny red body arched as if to run or attack.

'Mind that dog,' Emer says to the Yank. 'It

won't take to anyone since Desmond died.'

'I'm supposed to mind it?'

'That means be careful of it. The lads drowned her litter before you came. Couldn't catch herself though. Too clever for death, sure.'

'How cruel,' Brigid says.

'You won't say so after she's bitten you,' Emer says. Just like a Yank, she is thinking. Fussing over dogs as if they are children.

'Sure, she's only a mongrel who couldn't feed her pups,' Emer adds, for Niall's sake. Despite what he says about slaughtering the pig, he is on the touchy side about animals as well.

Brigid goes inside and comes out with a plate and two of the precious store-bought rashers. She puts it just below the stone wall. The pig squeals. The dog looks at the pig, then the plate, and growls low in his throat.

'That's a waste of good rashers, that is,' Emer says. Niall laughs and jumps up and down, clapping his hands.

'You're like Saint Brigid,' he says. 'Giving bacon to the dogs.'

'She's not taming lions, for pity's sake,' Emer scolds.

'Thanks for all your help,' Brigid says. She has learned to direct her smiles to Niall already. He's the one who returns them.

'See you tomorrow,' Niall chirps. Emer takes his hand. She has to pull to get him to turn away from Brigid and start walking home.

The pig trots beside them, stumbling every once in a while on the uneven ground. Niall's hand is in hers. She squeezes it lightly and rubs,

30

milking the comfort. He leans briefly against her and she allows herself a quick brush of her lips against his glossy ink hair. She mutters an endearment in Irish: *A chuisle mo chroí*, and he whispers it back. She never lets others see this sort of thing, but there's no one watching now but the pig.

They walk the long way round the field to check on the sheep. Niall sings softly, as he often does while walking, to himself or to something else, Emer is never sure. The pig seems to join in, squealing and grunting the same rhythm.

The wind is gusting when they round the cliffs, and the pig stumbles. Niall picks him up, buttoning his jumper around it once more.

'I like the way she talks,' Niall says. Everything he says to Emer is a thread from one long, uninterrupted conversation.

'Do you now,' Emer mutters.

'Is Brigid our cousin, Mammy?' he asks.

'She's not. Desmond was no relation to us.'

'Is she our friend, then?' he says hopefully. Niall hasn't started school yet. When he does, he will be related to every child in his classroom. The concept of friends is as foreign as the Yank herself.

'Would you like her to be?'

'I would,' Niall says. 'She's lovely.'

Emer bristles, though she has been thinking the same thing. Thinking how ruined she must look in comparison.

'I'd say she's fond enough of you,' Emer says.

'Her smiles have frowns in them,' Niall says.

'And what do you mean by that?' Emer says,

31

but she already knows. It was in Brigid's hand as well. Emer couldn't put anything bad into it, there was so much pain already there. Still, a charge comes off her, as lively and invading as the copper glint of her hair. Emer finds herself thinking ahead to tomorrow, and the next day, of the moments between chores that they might find a way to see her again. Chance a greeting from that fiery hand.

'Will you not tell her about the well?' Niall says.

'I won't. And don't you go blabbing it either.'

'Auntie Rose says it gives you babies.'

'Your Auntie Rose could do with fewer herself.'

The wind turns and assaults her with a whiff of the pig at her son's neck.

'That thing is ripe,' she scolds half-heartedly. 'And now you will be as well.'

'Sorry!' he laughs, letting go of her hand and running ahead to chase the sea birds. When he runs to the left, towards the cliff, he vanishes from her limited vision. Her neck grows tight and she yells for him to mind himself. She misses the days when she still carried him everywhere, bound to her chest with a woollen shawl, and she didn't have to rely on her faulty vision for vigilance.

'Mammy, can I bring the pig in the house?' Niall says. 'So he can sleep by the fire?' Emer grunts but knows she will let him. Her mother has gone to Rose's house, and there is no sign of Patch returning. No one is there to remind either of them not to get too fond of something that will only be taken away.

Inside Emer's mind, she still sees with both eyes. The image of Brigid's bright new face burns there now. With the wind from the cliffs screaming memories into her ears, Emer can't decide what she is feeling. There is a striking similarity between anticipation and dread.

2

Mongrel

It takes three days, all the rashers, and half a chicken before Brigid gets the dog to come in. Most of the dogs on the island look like some mix of sheepdog — long dirty fur, black or brown patched on white, chunks missing from their ears and tails. Brigid's mutt is an auburn shorthair, with the long face and droopy, apologetic eyes of a hunting dog. She moves the plates of raw meat closer to the back door each day and on the third day it is sitting there, haunches tucked in tight, trying to make itself as small as possible. She holds the door wide and moves aside. The tail wags once, then it looks at her again, eyes as auburn as its fur.

'Well, come on,' she says and the dog half trots, half wriggles inside, excitement almost bending it in two.

She leans down to run her hand over the sleek head. The smell almost gags her.

'Boy do you stink,' she says. The dog wags its whole body in agreement.

She takes down the metal dish tub and pours water from the enormous black kettle, warm on its hook by the hearth, and adds a squirt of dish liquid. She has to lift the dog into the tub, but it freezes and lets her. The dog stands, tail between its legs, eyes rolled so far sideways the whites are

34

shiny with panic, while she pours the water over its back and shoulders, soaps and pours again. She knows how to do this. She has bathed grief-stricken women and tense newborns, coiled into themselves, unwilling to let go and return to or enter the world. This dog requires the same firm consolation of her hands. One leg is crusted with dried clots of blood. The stomach is a slack pouch, nipples extended, raw and empty. The memory of puppies still in her skin. Brigid croons and speaks softly to it while she massages away dirt and blood, and the dog doesn't take its eyes off her. When she rinses it a third time and the water at its sinewy ankles is brackish and foul, she uses the one bath towel she has to dry it off, then folds it into a little mat in front of the fire. The dog turns around six times in a tight circle, then lays down, curled up as small as she can get, her chin touching the base of her tail.

'I don't believe you've bitten anyone,' Brigid says, pulling each of the ears through her hands like she's smoothing the pigtails of a child. 'No one who didn't deserve it.' She dumps the water outside into the drainage ditch that lines the road and by the time she returns the dog is deeply asleep, not even stirring when she pulls the rocker up so she can share the heat of the fire. She makes more tea — the amount of tea she drinks here has quickly climbed to the unfathomable, she drinks it like she once drank water — and eats some brown bread with butter and marmalade. She cannot be bothered to figure out how to cook on the open turf fire, so she spreads things on the bread Emer brought

35

her and calls it a meal. Soda bread, butter and jam, brown bread, butter and smoked fish, brown bread, butter and a soft egg. She is afraid to eat the unrefrigerated meat and used it all to seduce the dog. She swallows enormous vitamins with glasses of lukewarm milk from Emer's cow.

She rinses her mug, plate and knife with the last of the water. She pokes at the turf fire — slow-burning clods of earth which often, if the wind is wrong, fill the house with smoke — and buries the red nuggets with ash. In the morning, they will still be there. Fire seems to last longer here, like the sun. The sun doesn't fully fade until midnight, the twilight stretching on for hours, and comes blaring up again at four a.m. Her sleep has been riled by all this daylight. Though she covers the windows with sacking, she still senses the light, and there is a part of her, a child she remembers from a long time ago, that seems like it is sitting up in bed all night, eyes wide open, hair tingling with fear, listening for the moment it is safe to get up again.

She goes into the bedroom, changes into her chilled, slightly damp nightdress, laying her clothes on the trunk for the morning. She gets into the low bed and burrows under three blankets and the eiderdown bedspread she auspiciously purchased in Dublin. After a minute she hears the dog get up, stretch, and click its toenails along the floor, pausing at the door to the bedroom. She folds the covers back in a triangle of welcome and it climbs in, turning once and flopping down so Brigid is spooning its back. She covers it up with the blankets and smiles at the thought of Emer, with her lyrical voice that is punctuated with disapproving noises, telling the islanders that the Yank sleeps with her dog.

She came here planning to keep her hands to herself. She wants to be finished with touching, and everything that gets smothered and resurrected between fingers. The dog is a nice compromise. It warms the bed; she can stroke it because it expects nothing more from her hands.

★　★　★

The first time Brigid shakes Emer's hand, she knows the girl is trying to put something inside her. Brigid can feel it, something stronger than the grip of her palm, which is weak really, passive, the sort of handshake she despises, someone presenting their hand but unwilling to contribute any pressure to the exchange. The jolt is not what Emer is trying to insert as much as the resistance Brigid is able to muster, as if whatever Emer is handing out, a dark uneasy germ, has met its match in the calluses on Brigid's palm. It cannot penetrate her, and Emer, who doesn't meet eyes easily, widens her one eye in surprise.

'You won't try that again, will you?' Brigid wants to say. But she doesn't need to. Emer takes her hand and its intentions and buries them away in the pocket of her apron. Her fist bulges in there, balled up in anger at the defeat.

They're not unfamiliar to Brigid, hands that do damage. Her own parents had them, and used them frequently enough.

37

The men on the boat won't even admit the well exists, let alone tell her where it is. They speak Irish on the row over, hard, guttural and lilting, her mother's secret language in the mouths of these rough, thin-lipped men. She knows it wouldn't be wise to let on that she understands them. She lets them speak about her and around her, not catching it all because though they called it a calm day, the wind is still there, relentless and mournful, right at the entrance to her ears.

'She'll not be long if she's looking for a miracle,' one man says.

'She's quare enough,' the other man says. 'Like all the Darcys.'

'She'd better be hard as them, as well,' the man replies.

Her stomach drops a bit, as the currach rises high on a wave. This is where it began for her mother, the hardening, the carapace, the shell she had needed to escape, and then survive. Brigid hasn't come here for that. She's been so many places already that required her to be hard. She wants this one to crack her wide open.

Once she is settled, the men on the island are helpful and friendly and wink a lot, until she mentions the well, and then they evade her eyes, drop their voices even lower than usual, mouths barely moving, dismissive mumbles lost in their beards or the wind. Some of them blush, as though she has asked something improper, or feminine, like where she might purchase sanitary napkins. Others smile, cock their heads and look delighted, as if she is a child and keeping this secret from her is an enjoyable game. This is infuriating, but she can't afford to anger or insult them. She is not sure how this magic will work, but she may need one of these men in the end. She sizes them up with this in mind. Austin: handsome, seems intelligent, but she is suspicious of him. He held her hand too long, and left a film of oily sweat she had to wipe on her trousers. Malachy: sweet, dim, solicitous, he might fall in love with her if she is not careful. Festy, the mainland man who runs the mail boat, who told her without preamble, as if they'd known each other for years, to send word when she was ready to leave, seems the least complicated. Imagining having to decide between these options leaves her anxious and slightly repulsed. She did not come here for a man.

★　★　★

She searches for the well every day, walking the island in the mornings after breakfast, at midday which stretches on for longer than it should, no shelter from the merciless sun, and in the bright evenings, up around the west road past the cliffs and down again by the east end. The dog accompanies her, taking the lead, bounding in front along the green road. Half the houses are abandoned, thatched roofs long since decayed, spiky weeds and wild flowers growing as high as the walls inside. Occasionally she sees women in the occupied houses; if they catch her eye they will nod and cock their heads, but then look away, not inviting her to talk. They are nothing like the Irish women she met on the mainland, who called her 'Pet' and were eager for conversation. Here the women keep to themselves, or at least keep themselves from her. She catches the names they use for her, which she knows from her mother mean 'blow-in' and possibly 'madwoman', she can't be sure. The men call happily as she goes by, often stop and talk to her for longer than she would like. They wear the same woollen coats in the fields and on the water and marvel over the Grundens oiled canvas jacket and overalls she brought from Maine. She is not sure why she is accepted by one gender and snubbed by the other, but since she came here to escape the complications of women, she is not complaining. Though she does wonder, do they avoid her because she is a blow-in, or because her mother was not?

She climbs narrow paths made by sheep to the highest point of the island, where circular stone buildings sit abandoned by a sheer drop to the sea, listening for the trickle of fresh water beneath the earth. She turns over stones, squats down to smell the ground, plunges her fingers into boggy soil that leaves a stain she can never fully remove from beneath her fingernails. Everything is wet here, even on dry days the very earth is soaked to the core. She has found seven wells so far, not man-dug holes but natural crevices in the earth, marked with circles of purple rock, one so deep it has slate steps leading into it and a tin dipper held by a chain nailed into the earth above. She drinks from every one of them, trying not to think of land run-off and primitive latrines and disease. She gulps the cold liquid, clear or bog-stained, and waits to feel something, but they are just wells. None of this water can come close to addressing her thirst.

Though she is not overly fond of nuns, she prays to the saint as she trudges the steep hills, where slivers of slate layer with dirt that crumbles if you step on it at the wrong angle. She whispers to her as she investigates small coves, pocketing cowrie shells while following the rivulets in sand, the veins where freshwater runs to meet the sea. She recites the fireside chant of her mother, the prayers she once muttered in obligation as a girl. She calls her own name over and over as she lies on swathes of moss so varied and intricate they look woven by tiny beings. *Saint Brigid, hear me. Saint Brigid, have mercy on me. Saint Brigid, save me.*

She doesn't really know what she is doing. She is not familiar with the magic she is looking for, and isn't sure if it is a saint she is calling to, or something older and darker, the sort of spirit that makes islanders cross themselves in fear. She didn't even know where this island was, or that it shared her name, until she received that letter from the solicitor. All her mother ever told her of this place were stories she didn't intend to be taken as true. Stories of fairies and changelings and enchanted water and the superhuman strength of threatened children. Brigid wasn't even certain the well from the stories was real, until she saw the reactions it caused in the shifting fishermen and awkward, bitter Emer. They don't want her to find it, and this fact more than anything lets her know that it is her answer. Being so close fills her with an almost unbearable anticipation, she wants to scratch the eyes out of every local who mutters and looks away and pretends not to know what she is asking for.

She calls the dog Rua, which she remembers means red-haired. She says it over and over when they're walking, until the dog learns to bend her ears to the sound.

★ ★ ★

After ten days, the women still won't speak to her, beyond a murmured *God Bless*, or a *Soft day*, a phrase that apparently means 'it's raining, again'. Most merely nod and look away before she can speak. Their children come closer but then giggle and run away if she tries to talk to them, or look blankly as if she is speaking a language they have never heard. They run back to their mothers and Brigid feels the familiar remorse, the stab that occurs whenever she witnesses the thoughtless gestures that occur between mother and child. The swift easy lift of a toddler on to a hip, the blind swipe to clean a nose or cheek, even the yank of an arm to warn of danger or disobedience. A mother's hands are not careful, they don't need to be. They are efficient, harried, solid, quick, and tender extensions of the bodies that are poised to react, with their strong arms, thick middles, full breasts. Mother's bodies are not their own. The happiest ones seem to have forgotten what it is like to want themselves back at all.

The patient anticipation she came with has surrendered to a frantic anxiety. She barely sleeps, she walks the island until her legs are on fire, until the sky darkens with charcoal and the rain soaks through every layer of clothing and claims her skin. She turns over boulders, rips at bracken and heather, and, during one violent hail storm, crawls into a strange, child-sized hut of stone to weep and fall asleep, holding the warm consolation prize of a mongrel dog. The dog whines as if she knows exactly what Brigid is grieving, and presses her body right into her middle, as if she can fill the void for her. Brigid wails a visceral, unselfconscious keen, enormous inside the hive of stone, while a part of her waits to cry herself out, hoping that no one but the dog can hear her above the cliff wind.

She cannot find it on her own.

If she keeps this up, she will go mad. She has ripped her arms bloody on nettles, her pants have worn down at the knees. She hasn't bathed in too long and when she squats looking for water the smell between her legs assaults her. She has tended to women who let themselves go like this, who smelled like they were rotting from somewhere inside, because to freshen up was to start over and they couldn't bear that.

She needs to calm down. She won't find it this way. It's hidden, it's a secret they don't want to share. She is acting like a child, she could ruin the last chance she has by exposing such blatant need. She must behave like the mature woman she is, deliberate, methodical yet gracious, not some teenager who grasps at chances because she still has some vague hope that adulthood will be so much easier than being a child ever was.

She hasn't laid eyes on her mother in almost thirty years, but now she hears her accent daily in the words of the islanders. When she dares to remember herself that young she is now reminded of Emer, a needy, barely grown girl who is an adult already whether she wants it or not.

When she goes to sleep that night, she dreams of Matthew, of his long, slender, feminine hands on her body, caressing her belly as it swelled and emptied over and over again. Her darling, guilt-ridden Matthew. She was a child when he fell in love with her, and he tried to make up for this crime for the rest of his life. He died after failing again and again to give her the only thing she wanted. If she does not find this well, she will have let him die for no reason at all.

She wakes early the next morning and takes her tea outside to watch the mountains. She is almost forty years old, but she is no longer racing against time. It is not her body she must rely on, her only hope is a miracle, or a curse. She doesn't care which one. She wanted to do this alone, she imagined that being here would be similar to her childhood, where there was no one but herself to rely on. A place so quiet she could have conversations with the rocks, the trees, the sea, and no one would hear them. But this place has no trees, and they won't let her find it alone. She will go back to her original, less attractive plan, to the exhausting bright conversation, to flirting, to pretending she has come to be a part of this place instead of merely taking from it.

She looks at the cottage, derelict, the weeds grown high as the miniature windows, yellow lichen eating its way through the stone. The roof leaks so furiously when it rains she has to move her bed to an odd angle in the centre of the room to avoid it. She will ask Austin and Malachy about their offer to repair the thatch. The next time Emer comes by with bread or milk, though she is exactly the sort of desperate girl Brigid has vowed to stay away from, she will invite her inside. She has seduced what she wants out of people before, though she no longer has the same enthusiasm for it.

Instead of searching for the well, she spends the morning heating buckets of ordinary water, for herself, for dishes, for her underwear and the filmy sheets. In between batches, she tidies the place up; she has neglected the inside of the house as much as herself. She squats in the lukewarm tub and lets the water slough off the layers of her first weeks here. In her mind, she makes a list of the things she will need to turn this abandoned nest into something resembling a home.

Neither of them is in any condition to welcome a baby.

3

Changeling

Saturdays have always been bath days. On Sundays, if the weather allows, the islanders all go over to Inis Muruch for Mass, so Saturday is the chance to wash the week away. Even if the weather looks fierce, and Mass unlikely, children are washed of their sins regardless.

The Saturday after the Yank arrives, Emer heats bathwater for Niall, then herself. Her husband is still 'on the tear', which is both a relief and an embarrassment; when he does arrive he will need three times the bathwater to wash it away.

Niall has never whinged or resisted baths, but sits happily playing with the soap while she scrubs and rinses his body with a gentle touch no islander would suspect of her. She knows every inch of him and cannot imagine a day when she won't, so though he is old enough to bathe himself, she has never suggested he try. Niall has never felt anything but love come out of Emer's hands.

Emer's own ablutions are rough, quick, she doesn't like to linger over her body, which is like a girl's, strong but too thin, without the curves men admire on Rose. Even after pregnancy, she shrunk immediately to her former bony self. Aside from breastfeeding, Emer's body hasn't

46

participated in much pleasure, nor been the object of any desire. Sometimes Niall will peek around the curtain she fashions over twine to ask her a question (the notion of privacy still baffles him), and gaze at her small breasts as if trying to figure something out. Then the fiery ring in his eyes will grow and she'll have to bark at him to leave her be. She worries, when she sees that ring in his eyes, that he is remembering something far more dangerous than suckling milk.

Once they are both bathed and dressed, they walk up the road to Rose's house, Niall's pig trotting alongside him, so Emer can help bathe their mother. Rose's oldest girls, Fiona and Eve, are outside feeding the hens. They call Niall over to them. Emer doesn't like to let him out of her sight for long, but Fiona has a head on her shoulders, and can be trusted to yank him back if he starts to drift away. The other girls are too young to be of use, and Eve seems to have nothing but wool between her ears.

Rose bears her children in litters of two, all girls with her red-gold hair and the names of Saints. She is currently working on her fourth pair of twins in eight years, during which she has always been pregnant or nursing or both. That many pregnancies without a break makes other women look knackered, but Rose looks better with each one, as if the babies are adding something to her body instead of taking it away. 'More's the pity,' they say on the island, 'that her sister has only the one.' There is a rumour that Emer is barren, that something went wrong during Niall's birth in the hospital on the mainland. Emer started this rumour.

Rose has just finished up with the toddlers, Clare and Cecelia. She sends them outside with Teresa and Bernadette, who are six, and instructions to comb their hair.

'Emer, pet,' Rose says brightly. 'The day's fine enough, is it not?'

'It's lashing over on the mainland,' Emer reports. 'It'll come our way if the wind changes.'

'Where have *you* been?' their mother slurs. 'You went missing and Rose had to come collect me.' Rose pours the contents of the kettle into the metal tub, then adds a bucket of tepid water.

'Is Patch home, Emer?' Rose deflects.

'Not yet.'

'Useless bastard,' their mother mutters.

'Language, Mammy,' Rose chides, but she winks at Emer.

'Austin says you wasted a whole day settling that Yank,' her mother says. 'He had to milk your cow, you could hear her keening from the field.'

'Austin wasn't bothered, Mammy,' Rose says.

Emer moves over to her mother's chair and begins to take her hair out of its pins, too quickly to be gentle, and her mother bats at her ineffectually with her better arm.

'What's she like, so?' Rose asks. She lifts their mother under the arms and supports her standing, so Emer can pull down the woman's skirt and remove her stockings and bloomers. Her mother's thighs are like strangers to each other, one heavy and pocked with cellulite, the other loose skin swimming around bone. Her pubic hair has shed away in the last few years,

48

and what is left is as sparse and colourless as the hair on her head. Rose removes her top and woollen undershirt. Clodagh stopped wearing a bra a long time ago.

'She's like most Yanks,' Emer replies. 'Bold.'

Together they help their mother shuffle the few steps to the bath, guiding her useless leg over the metal lip, and lowering her slowly into the murky water. Emer takes charge of her hair, while Rose starts soaping her limbs with a scrap of flannel.

'If she's at all like her mother she'll put your heart crossways,' Clodagh slurs.

'Oh, hush,' Rose chides, pouring water over her hunched, soapy back. 'You didn't know any of them besides Desmond.'

'I know the stories. Changelings and whores and good men twisted to evil.'

'Leave the stories, so. I want to know about the actual woman.'

'She's here for the well,' Emer says. Their mother makes a noise like she's amused. Emer pours the rinse water too sloppily over her head and her mother ends up sputtering and cursing her, wiping at her good eye.

'Poor thing,' Rose says. 'Did you tell her, Emer?'

'I didn't.'

'I don't see why we keep it secret,' Rose says.

'We can't be giving away our miracles,' Emer imitates the thick accent of an older island woman.

'Nonsense. As if Saint Brigid herself would be so stingy!' Rose says. She accompanies this with

49

a quick sign of the cross that inspires an eye roll from her sister. 'It's not as if you believe in it. And you're not the loyal one. Why not tell?'

Emer shrugs. She didn't keep the well from Brigid out of loyalty to the island or belief in the legends or anything so grand. The longer Brigid looks for it, the longer she will be there. Emer already wants her to stay.

'She'll bring us nothing but sorrow, sure,' their mother says. 'She'll want to change things. Yanks always do.'

'There's no panic,' Rose quips. 'We're able to stand a bit of change. Isn't that so, Emer?'

'Will you not get me out of this tub,' their mother says. 'I'm after freezin' me arse off.'

They lift her to a standing position and Emer holds her steady while Rose swipes her dry with a ragged towel. They get her dressed again, pushing the useless half of her into sleeves and leg openings while her working side pushes itself, knocking into them without apology. Even Rose, viciously bright-minded, looks knackered after wrestling their crippled mother into clothing. They've been caring for her most of their lives, physically since her stroke the year they were twelve, and though she grows weaker each year, her temperament hasn't eased at all. A woman almost as angry at life as she is at her inability to leave it. Emer is often tempted to use her hands, to press all the anger she has at this woman into her ruined body, but it would only create more that she and her sister would be required to tend to. They plop her clumsily back in the rocking chair and empty the tub in the ditch.

50

'I should call in to her,' Rose says, visibly relieved to be finished with this chore. 'I've a fresh batch of scones.'

'Don't bother,' Emer says, trying to sound nonchalant. 'She won't invite you in. She's as batty as Desmond was.'

Niall and Fiona come inside, announcing that they've seen Brigid with the dog, walking up over their Uncle Aidan's back field.

'Can I go say hello to her, Mammy?' Niall asks.

'No,' Emer and Rose say together. Rose will say that Emer fusses over her only child too much, but even she knows there are places on their island that Niall should not be let to go alone. Their Uncle Aidan's back field is one of them.

'Stay with your cousins in sight of the house,' Emer says, and Fiona takes Niall's hand and leads him, dejected, outside. Rose looks out the open top half of the divided back door.

'Poor woman,' she mutters. 'What do you suppose she's after?'

'I didn't ask her,' Emer says.

'Do you not think it's a baby?' Rose says.

'You think every woman wants a baby,' Emer scoffs. 'And she brought no man with her, so I'd love to see her manage that.'

Rose smiles, caressing her own belly, just beginning to swell with the latest pair.

Austin comes in then, and Emer blushes. He looks so hard and handsome in the small house usually full of women and children. He drops a bloody lamb leg on the table.

'Did I miss your bath, ladies?' he jokes, and Rose grins, and before he can steal a kiss, and send their mother into complaints of impropriety and Emer into a hot rush just being close to it, Emer walks out on the lot of them.

She shades her eyes from the fierce sun and watches the Yank trudging up a steep green hill. Emer has watched her every day, on the road, on the cliffs, across the bog. Every stone Brigid turns over has a memory attached to it, every place she looks is already lodged beneath Emer's uncomfortable skin.

★ ★ ★

Their mother wasn't always like this. She was once as young as they were, a dark beauty their father would grab in the middle of the kitchen, sending the children out of doors for an hour. She doted on her husband, and on their older brother, Dónal, her first child and her only boy. Boys were the only true children on the island. Girls were just small women, expected to behave before they could even speak. If their mother wasn't glaring at five-year-old Emer and Rose in disapproval, she was nodding at them with a sort of solemn recognition. The girls were there to help her; her son was there to please her. Until he died.

Her husband and son were taken by the sea in a storm that claimed twelve, half of the island's able men. Island women were rowed to the mainland to identify the bodies, laid out on palettes like fish at a market. The boy's body was

52

never found. His coffin was laid empty in the graveyard.

For a month their mother refused to leave her darkened bedroom, where she ripened daily in the bedclothes, the vinegar smell of her an onslaught when her daughters opened the door to bring her tea. Then she rose one evening, put on her scarf, and brought them to the cliff.

★　★　★

Emer knew something was wrong while strapped to her mother's back, wrapped too tightly in a damp flannel shawl — she was five and far too big to be carried this way. Rose was made to walk beside them, cheerily enough, until it began to rain and she asked their mother where they were going.

'There's none of our sheep this way,' Rose said. They were following an old narrow sheep path, barely the width of one of her mother's calloused brown feet, up over the hills of grass and gorse and heather and dead wild flowers.

There was nothing in this direction but the cliffs, where the wind was so strong the birds dove and rose without needing to flap their wings, wind that got in your ears and bruised your brain. No island child was meant to go there alone.

Their mother didn't answer, just changed hands, pulling Rose behind her like part of a set dance. Rose met Emer's eyes, and looked daggers at her. Emer turned her head. She didn't often help her sister. She preferred to slip away,

53

or put a face on as if she didn't fully understand what was being asked of her. This was why the islanders said that one twin got more than her share of brains in the womb. They said this in front of them, as if Emer was not even bright enough to understand the language. She obliged them by blinking at such comments. Not scowling, but not smiling either. She didn't smile the way her sister did. She got less of that inclination in the womb as well.

Emer, her ear pressed against damp wool, could hear her mother's heart beating, quick and rushing, not from the walk — their mother walked up hills all day — but from some excitement. Her heart was hammering with this thrill and every few minutes it skipped, and Emer recognised this as something she had felt before in herself, this skip that was like a little interruption of dread.

They crested the last hill and the ocean appeared in the distance; she couldn't see how close it was because of the sheer drop that was the cliffs.

She meant for them to go over it. Emer knew this. Heard it like a short, brutal sentence through her mother's back, though it was not said aloud.

Rose struggled to get her hand free. 'Let me go, Mammy,' she said, but all Emer could hear was the tone of it, words blurred by wind. Her mother's voice, booming inside her chest, was clear.

'We're almost there.'

Rose had given up walking and was trying to

pull her mother back. Their mother leaned over to lift her, but Rose was writhing, slippery, impossible to catch, like a fish leaping about on a boat. They moved closer and closer to the ground in this struggle and finally their mother laid right down on top of her, upending Emer, pinning Rose down under bosom and belly. Rose began to cry.

'It'll be done soon,' their mother said, and the last word was swallowed with a sharp inhalation of breath. It was the same musical gasp all the islanders used, to indicate agreement or horror or finality, much like the way her mother's heart skipped, a pause you could get lost within.

Emer could see the cliff edge from her perch on top of them both, how it looked just like any swathe of thick grass, how deceiving it was, you could put your foot forward sure there would be something beneath it and fall straight into rock and water and wind. The birds would sweep away from you, no help whatsoever, they would barely look as you fell right through. That was where they were headed, over that edge, and Rose, crying, raging, pinned to the ground, knew it now.

'I won't, Mammy!' she screamed from underneath her mother's soft weight. 'I won't allow it! I won't! Emer!' Her mother tried to muffle her voice with pressing hands, when that didn't work, she put her mouth on Rose's in a crushing kiss, like she could swallow the noise. It had no effect. 'I won't go, Mammy, I won't.' It sounded like her throat was ripping on each won't, like such determination would permanently scar her voice.

'It will be done soon,' their mother said again, but the assertion was missing. Emer could tell that her mother thought it sounded wrong now, this phrase, when it had sounded almost reasonable a moment ago. 'Please,' she said instead, and Emer heard it through her chest like wind. 'Please, Rose.'

That's when Rose spat in her face. Their mother rolled off her in shock, and Emer, jostled and dizzy, expected her mother to strike. She had seen it before, the rough red hand rushing at her sister's lovely cheek.

Rose was holding a knife. She'd taken it from the pocket of her mother's apron, the small, wood-handled paring knife that all the island women kept near, given to them as girls, their age revealed in the wear of the blade. Their mother's blade was not as worn as her face; she was only twenty-three years old.

'You'll leave us, so,' Rose said, breathing heavily from the effort of screaming. 'You'll leave my sister.'

That was when their mother began to cry, pressing her face to the wet ground, keening with the same raw wail as the day she buried an empty coffin. Rose watched her with a look of superior disgust.

Emer was whispering, so softly it sounded like no more than her breath. Whispering encouragement, but not for her sister.

She turned her head, her damp hair catching in the fibres of her mother's back, and saw the clochán, a beehive of stone with one small opening. The ruins of Saint Brigid's abbey were all over their island, and the children liked to play in them. Emer had never seen this one, completely intact, perched on the edge of the cliff like an offering.

Emer saw a hand. A hand coming out, not from the clochán, but the air. It pried its way from nothingness and hovered there, wriggling its joints as if shaking off sleep. Then it pinched its fingers and pulled the scene of wind and grass and grey sky aside, like a veil. A curtain that looked exactly like the world. The hand was attached to a woman, who ducked and stepped through the opening she had rent in the sky. She was dressed all in white, robes of fabric whipping in the wind like untethered sails. Her hair was as orange as flames leaping above her head. She reminded Emer of the stained-glass window in their little church, which portrayed the rising soul of Saint Brigid. The woman looked right at Emer and smiled, and Emer knew she was not a saint. Her teeth were too sharp. A saint wouldn't smile like that, Emer thought, when it was quite clear she knew exactly what Emer was thinking. A saint would have come to help Rose, not stood there grinning wickedly in destructive collusion with Emer. In her other hand she was clutching some sort of fabric or pouch, blue as a jewel, and she held it towards Emer like a gift.

She didn't point the woman out to Rose or to her mother. She didn't want to be told, as she was quite sure she would be, that only the clochán was actually there.

She closed her eyes, counted to three and turned back again. The woman was gone. All that was left was the beehive hut and the wind and the knowledge that everything she saw could be as thin as that veil.

They sat by the cliff's edge, sliced by rain and wind, Rose holding tight to her mother's trembling hand, kinder now, now that she had won, the knife hidden in the pocket of her small dress, ready to help. Emer was still strapped to her back, her burning eyes closed, her whispering, which was fierce and fast only moments ago, gone, as if her little voice was the only part of them that managed to throw itself over that edge. She didn't know if anyone, other than that woman, heard her during the last moments. For while her sister screamed and saved them, Emer had been murmuring encouragement into the warmth of her mother's neck. 'Go on,' she had whispered. 'Go on, go on.'

For a long time, Emer would think this day was the beginning, that it defined her, that she alone had inherited her mother's pervasive, bitter despair. That Rose would be the fighter and Emer would give up, let the worst of it, the strongest things, pull her over, and it would be like this time and time again, so surely they would grow to depend on it and design their lives to fit inside. Emer would see things her sister never could, but they wouldn't save her. They would only mortar her more immutably in herself.

Even after she had Niall, which banished for ever the option of merciful cliffs, she would refuse to forget how she let herself be pulled towards a death of wind and rock and sea, not from giving up so much as to see what would happen if she let go.

★ ★ ★

After Mass on Sunday, Rose sends Austin to the mainland and he comes back with Emer's husband. After nearly a week of drinking in town, sleeping it off in fields when the pubs were closed, Patch needs Austin to help him walk up to the house. Emer stands outside her doorway, ready to collect him, and sees the fiery-haired shadow of Brigid above on the green road, dog at her heels, looking down on Emer's embarrassment. Emer almost raises her hand in greeting, but clenches it in her apron pocket instead and turns her eyes to her fetching brother-in-law and his foul-smelling failure of a brother.

Patch avoids her gaze, but she can see he is sober enough, just too knackered to walk on his own. Austin brings him into the house, sits him down on the hearth bed, and ruffles the dark head of Niall on his way out. He doesn't look at Emer either.

'Hello, Da,' Niall says, out of obligation, but his eyes go to his mother, gauging her mood. She manages a smile for him, and a wink, and gestures that he take the pig, sleeping by the fire, outside before Patch gets his bearings enough to notice it.

She heats water and draws him a bath. Patch undresses behind the curtain and drops his clothes to the stone floor. She scoops them up, turning her head and trying not to gag at the

59

smell. She takes them outside and scrubs at them angrily in the washbasin, watching Niall run around giddily with the pig. Once the foul chunks and smears and a tinge of cosmetics have been washed away, she hangs it all on the clothes line. She wants to stay outside long enough that she doesn't risk seeing him in the bath. She does the milking, since evening is coming on, though the sun is still high in the sky. Mass today had been full of questions about the Yank, and since Emer was the only woman who had spent any time with her, she had got a lot of attention. Away from her island, Emer is a bit easier to talk to, as long as they stay away from her hands. She is always sorry to row back home.

When she finally goes in again, Patch has finished, and put on his spare trousers and flannel shirt, combed his long hair, the leached colour of dried turf, and shaved the week's worth of dirty whiskers from his neck and face. He sits at the table, avoiding her eyes, holding on to a mug of tea tightly to disguise the tremor of his hands. He looks young enough, still. Emer has a flashback to a less ruined version of his face and their first awkward, dogged kiss. She hasn't kissed him, or anyone, unless you count the small willing mouth of her son, in five years.

'Will you have a bite?' Emer says roughly and Patch nods, so she slices some cold chicken and heats it up with the leftover spuds, adding a dollop of butter and pinch of sea salt. When she puts the fire-warmed bowl in front of him, he leans away to avoid an accidental brush with her hands.

'*Go raibh maith agat*,' he says, *Thank you*, his voice rusty from little use. As she turns away, he adds, so softly she almost doesn't hear him, '*Logh dom*.' Forgive me.

'You're all right,' Emer says, with a smidgen less vehemence than her normal tone.

Emer is not fond of her husband. He is a daily reminder that she plays second fiddle to Rose, married to the better brother. She resents his failure to follow through on the few promises he has made. But this is not, she knows, entirely his fault. He has never fully recovered from the time when he was still willing to put his hands on her and be touched by her in return. The few times her husband entered her was enough to turn him off the whole business, even though she tried, for a while, to touch him in other ways.

Every person on the island, except Rose and Niall, stays away from Emer's hands. Even strangers can sense something in her, beyond the scowl and the plainness, which makes them shy away. As if standing too close to Emer is like choosing to grasp the hand of a fairy and be pulled into the dark, boggy, merciless ground.

★   ★   ★

Emer never forgot that hand. As a girl, she looked for it in all the places on the island where children were forbidden — the fields where corncrakes nested, the green road which rose past Old Desmond's house, a cluster of ancient piled rocks by the cliff side. In any of these places, they could be stolen, snatched away, a husk of a child left in their place. They would live in an eternal world of gluttony, lust and dancing, and they would never see their families again.

Emer went to all of the forbidden spots, looking for that woman, the curtain to another world. She wanted to fall into her clutches, be stolen away. Lose herself. Like the stories of women and children who fell under the world and refused to return, leaving a fairy changeling in their place.

The cave which hid Saint Brigid's holy well also harboured a shelf carved into the walls of the cliff that held one heavy rock — *an clocha breacha*, the cursing stone — left by the fairies and linked to tales of murder and revenge. Emer went there, but refrained from actually touching the stone. She didn't want to accidentally kill herself in the process of being saved.

It was two years before the hand came back for her, in the bog. It was turf-cutting time and the whole island was at work, children and women outnumbering the men, who had either drowned or left the island in search of employment. At seven, Emer and Rose ran the household. Their mother had crawled into her grief and would not budge. If she could not die, she refused to live either. She left the house only for Mass.

Emer was slicing the earth into floppy dark logs and laying them in rows to dry. When the smallest hand imaginable came poking out of the bog wall — a hand the size of a newborn's but with long delicate nails iridescent as oyster shells — and handed her a knife, Emer didn't scream a warning as a sensible child would have, but took the knife eagerly, a little disappointed when it made the hand sink away.

She used the knife, with an engraved silver handle much finer than any she'd ever seen, to slice away the turf, and the amount she cut was much more than what she was able to do before. Only Rose noticed her sister's sudden fervour for the chore and the expectant flush on her normally pallid cheeks.

Later, when the hand came back and Emer set down her knife to hold and caress and tickle it, Rose snuck up behind her, picked up the blade, and lopped the fairy hand off with one swipe. There was a squeal of angry horror that only Emer could hear, and the stump of wrist, clean as a sliced turnip, no blood or flesh or anything so messily human, pulled back and closed itself off in the earth. The little hand rolled to rest at Emer's bog-stained feet and shrivelled upon itself, curling and shrinking and turning whitish green, until it resembled nothing but a loose clump of lichen. When Emer tried to lift it, it crumbled in her fingers and left a fine green-grey dust on her apron.

'What did you do that for, Rose?' she cried and stood up to face her sister, stomping her feet like a toddler in a tantrum. Later, in the loft bed they shared at home, Rose would apologise, spooning herself into Emer's rigged back, and whisper how she would never, ever let her be stolen away. But in the moment, in the sun-warmed bog, a fairy blade glinting in her hand, Rose said, 'Don't be a fool,' and walked away.

She didn't even want to know what the knife could do. She marched straight up the cliffs and tossed it over, scattering a flock of birds from where they'd been hovering within the wind of the sharp cliff's sides. Emer was sure that Rose, who had no idea what it was like to desire something else, to *be* something else, even if it was deformed and threatening, had ruined any chance of her being invited under the ground again.

★ ★ ★

The bees tried next, when she was nine. In a high back field that belonged to their Uncle Aidan stood a tree stump left from another time, when the island was covered in enormous oak trees, before they were cut down, burned and ultimately swallowed into the bog. The stump was so wide around that two children couldn't circle it, five feet tall, a forest of moss and purple thistle on top, and deep inside the hollow base lived a writhing colony of honeybees. Their Auntie Orla used turf to smoke them into a trance, and gave tiny jars of honey as Christmas presents. The honey was a luxury, and never offered to children unless they were ill, when a dollop was set on their tongue to cure a swollen throat or cough. Children on the island longed for sickness so they could be given a taste of that honey.

Only Rose and Emer knew what it was like to gorge themselves on it. Not even their Auntie Orla had ever swallowed more than a judicious

64

teaspoonful. Emer let it dribble from her thickly covered fingers into her sister's waiting mouth.

Emer could lull the bees more effectively than the sweetest turf smoke. Rose would stay back, lying in the spongy grass, while Emer approached the log, the bees growing quieter the closer she got, the hum subsiding as they dropped off to sleep. She would dip a jug into the opening — dark with crowded, furry bodies — picking off the small corpses that had sacrificed themselves to the sticky sides. The honey was amber brown and flecked with bits of comb, lost bee legs and ancient chips of bark that stuck like crisps in their teeth. It tasted like the scent of wild flowers and was thick enough to chew. They scooped it into each other's mouths, giggled and sighed and lay down, because they could barely stand up with such sweetness coursing through them. It was dishonest and gluttonous and a little bit lustful, all things they'd been raised to avoid and confess as sin, and, to Emer's surprise, Rose didn't call on Saint Brigid for help to resist it. Emer loved what the honey did to her sister, normally so sharply tuned to what was safe and what was right. Rose didn't hear the threat, as tangible as the magic blade of that knife, buzzing underneath.

Emer felt the difference one day as she leaned in, as if the bees were only feigning sleep, as if every fuzzy body were just closing its eyes and waiting for the cry of *Now!* before they came awake and snatched her.

What Rose saw was this: her sister reaching in and being pulled, yanked with a force that seemed merciless, a gulping swallow that left no

65

regret about what it might leave behind. She leaned into a space only large enough to fit her head and shoulders and disappeared as if she were stepping off a cliff. The bees rose in a swarm of angry victory, and Rose ran screaming and crying over the fields for help.

All Emer saw was the little hand. The one her sister had sliced, grown back, slightly smaller, like the severed arm of a starfish. A little hand coming out of the honey, ready to pull her away. She remembered nothing after that moment of decision, where she chose the cruel promise of that hand and, as she did so, felt the bees wake up, or rise from pretend slumber, and cheer callously as she was yanked under the world.

She wasn't gone for seven days, or seven years, like the stories told. She wasn't even gone for an hour. By the time Rose's hysterical crying was deciphered and the women ran up the fields, aprons whipping up at them, their hair wild with maternal ferocity, Emer had been spat back up again. She lay on the rough grass, her throat puffed up to the width of her face, her eyelids ballooned shut, her mouth a smear of bruises. Bees fell out of her nose and mouth and she coughed and retched and tried to answer the worried questions of the women who lifted her. They carried her back home, bees shedding behind like husks of dead skin. She was wrapped in flannel soaked with holy water, and the men rowed the doctor over from the mainland when it was clear that her breathing, the way it kept catching, then stopping, then starting again, was not quite right.

The doctor calmed her wheeze and removed hundreds of stingers, properly, so no more poison was poured into her. He wasn't there when the infection began in her left eye, and by the time he returned and discovered it, despite a visit to Saint Brigid's healing well, it was already too late. She was taken to the hospital on the mainland where a surgeon removed her ruined eyeball.

When Emer came home from the hospital, the place where her left eye had been sewn tightly shut, she tried to see if she'd been changed in some other way. But all that remained from being pulled under the world was a thick, buzzing band of anxiety that gripped her neck, a swarming that would follow her into adult life. It was as if, instead of stealing her, the beings under the ground had taken a good long look, flipped her over, then decided, as the human world had, that she wasn't much to fuss about, and sent her back. She was not a changeling after all, but simply Emer, dipped into a pool of bees and found not sweet enough to keep. Expelled, rejected by the very world she so longed to abduct her. She would never be invited again. All that would stay of her trip below was the brown circle of leather held over the memory of her eye, and the power to make others feel as ugly as she did. The good people had left some fire in her hands, but it did nothing to warm her.

★   ★   ★

All these years after her trip beneath the world, darkness still rises up in Emer like water filling to

67

the top of a well. It swells up from deep inside her, forming a thick, immovable plug that settles in the hollow of skin below her throat. Every time she looks in the mirror she expects to see it there, an ancient, gnarled fist waiting for the chosen moment to unfurl. People's faces make it rise, and bright sunshine, a bee snarling inside the cup of a flower, that unbearable millisecond between when she calls her son's name and he answers her. Life threatens daily to close her throat.

She puts it into people. She folds their hands inside her own and presses and something bites into their souls. Her hand can reach into them, find where there is a doubt or a guilt or a fear, a small hole in their fabric, and catch it, pull and widen it, until someone who was feeling just fine about their day or their life or their choices will be almost doubled over with a hopelessness, a yawning weight that makes them question their former happiness. It only lasts a few minutes, but afterwards, for days, or weeks, they will shudder at the memory of that place underneath who they believe they are. Women who have birthed children liken it to labour, a contraction of pain in the mind that is only bearable in retrospect, when it is all over. People like Emer's mother find the feeling familiar, and assume it comes from their own grief-laden hearts. Emer drags them under the water and pulls them back up just when they've forgotten how to breathe. It doesn't make her feel any better, but it does, while she grips them, make her feel less alone.

It doesn't work on Rose. Emer tried for years, when their bodies developed (Rose's prettily and

Emer's in an embarrassing, odorous, hairy way), when Rose was praised in school, or noticed by a boy, or laughed with other girls in a way that made Emer suspect it was at her expense.

Emer despises her sister. She hates Rose for loving her. 'She's not as bad as all that,' Rose will say, when others criticise her. Emer can see that Rose will never really see her, will never believe the worst, will stand beside her whether she feeds her stolen honey or tries to strike at her with the fire of her hands. Emer knows this is some sort of blessing, unless of course it is a curse, that this person who will always love her is the one who knows her least of all.

Niall is the only true antidote. Only with her child are her hands able to soothe rather than repel. The fairies she once invited terrify her now. She has gone from a girl begging to be stolen by something dark and exciting to a mother who must guard her child. All she has wanted for years is to leave the island and the good people far behind.

But then the Yank resisted her hands. Unlike Rose, who just can't be penetrated, or Niall, who diffuses it, something came back from Brigid's hand, a response that burned Emer's darkness away like dried moss tossed on a turf fire. There was strength in there, alongside the need. Brigid is damaged, but not easily harmed.

The Yank, true to her mother's gloomy predictions, has already changed things. Now Emer is thinking less about fairies and evacuations than she is about what might happen if Brigid's hand touches her again.

4

Nesting

May, 1959

It's not until Brigid decides to fix the house up that she notices so much is missing. She has been drinking tea out of the same cracked mug, eating off her only plate — thick pottery with a sponged pattern of red, bell-shaped flowers. She often licks the one fork and knife clean instead of bothering to wash them. The sheet on her bed is worn thin and stained with a man-sized yellow sweat blotch; she has been using her rolled-up fisherman's sweater as a pillow. At first she assumed this was the austerity of her bachelor uncle, but then she wonders. According to Malachy, this house has raised generations stretching back centuries. It must have sheltered women and children and all the necessary accessories that go along with them. What happened to it all?

In the narrow, catch-all drawer of the kitchen press, she finds various treasures: a bank passbook, a Mass card with the names of what she assumes are her grandparents, various handwritten receipts for the purchase and sale of sheep and wool, a fountain pen and a bottle of clotted ink. A brown envelope with a neat stack of birth certificates, school reports, confirmation and communion cards. A white envelope with an American stamp on it, a short letter written in careful schoolgirl's cursive.

Dear Desi,

I made it to America I live in Maine now, in the northeast, where it snows in the winter and some trees lose their leaves and others don't and are like dark green giants that walk over the land. My village is by the ocean and the men here trap lobsters and catch herring just like they do at home. When I first arrived I lived in a boarding house for girls, but now I have a husband. He is a lightkeeper and we will be moving to his first posting this spring.

I miss the fuchsia and the mountains the sheep, even the corncrake. It makes me sad to think I will never see them or you again To think of you alone in that house now, all of us gone. I wish you would consider emigrating yourself.

I won't be able to post much from the lighthouse, as its very remote but I will write you often and send them all together in large parcels when I can I hope you can find someone to read them to you.

I have a baby girl. I named her Brigid. She looks how I imagine Mam must have looked, with furious ginger hair. She is a great comfort to me.

Your loving sister,
Nuala

After reading this letter, Brigid looks all over the house for more, but that is all. She goes back to bed in the middle of the day, the worried dog

71

pressed to her aching middle, and cries for her mother with a freedom that seems childlike, except she never allowed herself to cry that way as a child.

★ ★ ★

'Most of it was stolen, I suspect,' Emer says when Brigid invites her in for tea and asks about the lack of necessities. She opens Brigid's press and finds it bare of anything but long, spindly-legged spiders and their cotton candy webs. 'People help themselves when a house is abandoned.' Brigid has a brief image of shawl-laden women flapping down on the place like vultures. 'I can ask around, bring some of it back.'

'That's all right,' Brigid says. She should have guessed. Her mother told her about stealing from the neighbours. Running around the island in the dark, ransacking abandoned houses for tea crumbs and sugar. They were that poor.

'Your mother was the youngest?' Emer asks.

'I don't know,' Brigid says.

'The one who went to America on her own?'

'Yes,' Brigid says. Though her mother didn't tell her directly, she believes something ugly and unforgivable occurred here. Something that should have made Brigid wary of crossing that water at all.

'Did she tell you what it was like?' Emer asks. Brigid cannot meet Emer's eye.

'She told me fairy stories.'

Emer makes a gasping sound in her throat and

for an instant, Brigid is in a dark, dirty kitchen with her mother. It is the same noise, the noise she thought was her mother's own: a gasp of surprise and agreement but also despair, humour superimposed on to dread. Emer's phrasing, her accent, the hard glint of her eyes, all of it brings her mother back like a slap to the face.

'You'd have to look long to find love in this house,' Emer says. 'Ten children, and their father drank, and hit them more than was prudent. The mother died in childbirth. The children were sent to the orphanage on the mainland, all of them caught fever and never left. Desmond was the eldest, he stayed to care for the old man and the baby, your mother. She was the only one to get away.'

She wonders if that is all that Emer really knows. It's a hard story, but it's only the surface. Nothing about what her mother could do. Brigid had worried that people would know, and she would be driven away. But apparently it has just become a simple story of poverty, and the failings of the human world.

Brigid looks at Emer now, who shifts a bit in her chair.

'Have I shocked you? It was a hard place. Still is. It's not the saint's paradise they write about. She left us to our own defences a long time ago.'

'No, I'm not shocked.'

'Desmond was the last of them. There's none of yours left here.'

No family, no crockery, the furniture pulled apart and the place ransacked. Barely a chair left behind. The memories of whatever happened

73

here smothered like the fires they bury at night.

'Everyone's wanting to know why you've come,' Niall says to Brigid. Emer looks daggers at him.

'You're not the only ones who can keep secrets,' Brigid says, winking. He beams, but Emer narrows her one eye in warning.

* * *

Emer returns something to her every day. Plates, bowls and mugs in the same spongeware pattern, three caned chairs and a bedside table, thick cotton sheets bleached white by the sun, mismatched cutlery, a washing board, cast-iron pans. Delicate, cracked lace doilies far fussier than Brigid would ever use. An apron like all the island women wear, a smock she must pull over her head and fashion at both sides of her waist. Emer always carries a small knife in the front pocket of this apron. Brigid finds a similar knife in the deep back of Desmond's drawer, the wooden handle worn to the soft curves of another woman's hand, the blade narrow from generations of sharpening. She finds it useful to keep in her pocket, for cutting the wild flowers she collects on her walks, or clearing away nettles looking for the origin of a bubbling spring. She still looks for the well, but with less furious desperation. She is waiting for the right time to ask again.

She hopes the answer will be given to her, the way Niall brings her a canvas sack filled with stolen belongings, as if they are gifts.

74

Another week passes before she finds out about her cows. Emer has been bringing her fresh milk, and one day Austin is there, stopped on the road talking to Brigid in her doorway. Emer comes up quietly, behind him, as if she hopes she can slip by without being seen.

'Howaya keeping, Emer,' Austin says, nodding. 'Niall.' A little wink for the child, but his eyes avoid Emer.

'Austin,' Emer says, with more disdain than should be able to fit into one word. He is a handsome man, but Emer doesn't seem impressed. Niall hands Brigid the jug of milk he's been sloshing up the whole road.

'Thank you,' Brigid says. 'I just drank the last of it.'

'What are you getting milk delivered for, when you've a cow up in that field?' Austin says. Brigid is confused, but Emer shakes her head, and glares pointedly with her one eye.

'I suspected as much,' she murmurs when Austin has gone.

She walks Brigid up over the field and they speak to Michael Joe, who behaves as though she's known all along that she has cows and he's been waiting for her to collect them. She is apparently the owner of two brown cows and a calf, and Emer and Niall help her move them over to the field directly behind her house. Emer tells her to leave one cow separate for milking. Brigid hasn't milked a cow in years and finds she enjoys it, resting her forehead against the cow's thick side and pulling down the warm teats. The cow always seems grateful, she lets out a sigh when she empties her. Other than that they are blank, boring animals who seem forever to be chewing. They look at her as she approaches them, every time, as if they've never seen her before in their lives. They remind her of the island women, who still will not give her much beyond a nod, an occasional, grudging enquiry into her comfort that is not meant to be answered.

A week later she is told about her sheep. A dozen of them, grazing in the neighbour's field, mentioned casually again, by Malachy as she chats with him at the salt house where she buys fish. Again, presented to her as if they've just been babysitting until she got around to collecting them. Then there are the hens and a rooster brought up a few at a time by the men who have been minding them since her uncle died the autumn before. She vaguely remembers the solicitor mentioning livestock, but after packing up and settling her life in Portland and making the journey she had forgotten it all.

'They'd have kept them for themselves,' Emer explains. 'Like anything else left behind. Only they're fond of you.'

And so all the things that have supposedly been stolen from her are being handed back in spades. She takes it as a good omen.

Emer brings over a churn and teaches her to make butter the consistency of ice cream that she eats with a spoon. The eggs from her hens are exquisite. The bright orange yolks cling to the brown bread like golden gravy. She rediscovers the steel cut porridge of her childhood after a delivery from the mainland, and simmers it over-night on the fire, dolloping it with the ice cream butter and shaking a brown sugar crust on top. She loves eating by herself, no one to answer in between each delicious mouthful. On foggy days — her favourite weather because of the shroud of stillness and mystery — she cannot see the sea or the other houses and she imagines she is the only one on the island. She chews and swallows in pure silence, listening to the old, familiar longing gurgling deep inside the well of her soul. The yearning to have someone growing inside her again, so she is no longer alone.

*   *   *

Most of the time, she is not alone, though she does not invite the company. She is called in on every day by grinning men offering to help rebuild her house or tend to her growing herd of livestock, and the strange fosters of Emer and her little boy. Emer is both grumpy and eager, a girl desperate for a friend who pretends she can't be bothered. She looks like a twelve-year-old tomboy: tall as a woman but thin and underdeveloped. Her face is at times pinched and angled as a furious fairy, but when she thinks only Niall is watching, it softens. She is so uncomfortable in her body it's almost painful to watch her; she will yank at her clothing and scratch as if the material, or her very skin, is a constant torture. Brigid has already seen that no one touches this girl, no one but her son. The men, who already squeeze Brigid hard enough to pinch around her waist when she says something that amuses them, never put a hand on Emer. Her one eye is a sharp, angry blue, startling, gorgeous and lonely next to its shrouded mate. Her lips are so full and dark they look bee-stung and she gnaws at them, hungry for something she's never had.

Brigid remembers girls like this, so lonely, so miserably self-conscious they can't see that they're not as hideous as they imagine. She always had a weakness for those girls.

Emer finds a way to see Brigid daily, bringing her stolen goods or following her on a walk, her manner slightly put out, as though Brigid needs her company and she will oblige, when really, Brigid can tell, it is Emer who needs someone. The boy is lovely, an antidote to his mother's shadowed disposition, flitting about her like a firefly in the darkness. But he lives in another world. She's heard him talking to it. It is not necessary for him to seek out company. He could take or leave all of them, she gets the impression, aside from his mother. He is always coming back to her, to touch her hand, her skirt, to press his face to her side. Like he gains some comfort, some grounding from the contact. They whisper in Irish to each other, thinking Brigid won't understand them. *A chuisle mo chroí.* You are the pulse of my heart. It is an endearment, Brigid remembers with a chill, meant for lovers.

One day as she walks the cliffs she meets Emer

and Niall and asks them about the stone huts, ten of them in varying stages of decay, the intact ones shaped like beehives, that sit empty and resolute, facing the onslaught of the open sea.

'Saint Brigid built them,' Emer says in her quick, unfriendly voice. 'For her postulants. She was the only woman ever ordained a bishop, because she rattled the priest by making fire come out of her hair. Usually it was only men who were given monasteries.'

Niall, no longer afraid of the dog, is leaping around her, trying to get Rua to run with him and his pig. Rua, clearly unused to such play, sits next to Brigid, leaning against her leg, waiting for their walk to resume.

Emer tells Brigid about the abbey, how each clochán housed two women, each nun had an *anam cara*, a soul friend, who was their partner in everything. They copied the Gospels over and over in Latin and Irish, then illustrated them like the Book of Kells. They worked the land together, tended the animals, prayed together, slept on one palette to absorb each other's heat. The women chose their partners and had a ceremony to celebrate the commitment. They were meant to spend their entire lives together.

'Like a marriage,' Brigid mutters.

'Like all nuns, they were meant to be brides of Christ. But he wasn't much help with the cattle.'

Brigid wonders if Emer even knows she can be funny.

'Pretty racy,' Brigid says. 'For nuns.'

Emer blushes, glancing over at Niall.

'A lot of them came here for cures,' Emer says.

79

'Brigid was said to have healing in her hands.'

'So I've heard,' Brigid says. Emer blushes, hard.

'Sure, it's all nonsense,' Emer scoffs. 'People still come here, like yourself, looking for holy remnants, looking for miracles. There's no miracles on this island that I've ever seen. Not Christian ones, anyways.'

She's not a very good liar, Emer. She can't look at Brigid as she says this, and her voice is much more animated than she ever allows. Plus her son's open mouth is a dead giveaway.

'People believe a lot of things if they need to,' Brigid says. Emer shrugs, opens her mouth to say more, then decides against it.

Instead she announces that it's time she and Niall were after the sheep, and they leave Brigid and her dog alone by the cliff's edge.

Brigid runs her hand over the low crown of a beehive hut. The clocháns are meticulously round, the stones angled gradually to form the roof, no mortar visible to hold them together. No windows, just a small arch to crawl inside. When Emer and Niall have disappeared down the hill, she sits inside the one still fully intact, which is thick-walled and perfect shelter from the abusive wind of the west side of the island. Rua crawls in after her, leaning warmth into her side. She isn't crying as much any more, and her nightmares have eased. She tries not to beg, she tries very hard to be serene, to sit in the silence after a question waiting for an answer. The sea and wind sound far away and harmless inside this mound. Little caves of inspiration.

Wombs of penance. She imagines small women inside, with only quills and pots of ink and piles of vellum, ripe and naked under brown cloaks, sure of their love and wanting for nothing.

★ ★ ★

In the shed behind her house, which Malachy has restocked with grain for the hens, the milking pails and stool, and various tools she will need to start a garden, she finds a collection of skulls. They are lined up in descending order of size — sheep, dog, rabbit, vole — on a shelf within the thick-layered stone wall. Behind the skulls, a pile of sun-bleached bones. She wonders if this was a child's collection Desmond couldn't part with or if that grown, lonely man wandered the island looking for death the way she looks for a miracle.

In the damp corner of the shed is a dirty tarp she pulls at, thinking it will be a temporary covering until the men can patch her roof. Underneath it she finds a diligently wrapped parcel, another waterproof tarp, then oilcloth, then softer, cleaner flannel, each layer closer to the object that waits underneath.

A cradle. Hand-carved from driftwood soft and weathered by salt and wind, a pattern of limpet shells affixed round the edges and across the curved head. The bottom is carved like the hull of a boat, and it is darker there, water-stained, as if it has spent time at sea. Brigid's mother once told her that this was how she got her to sleep as a baby, by lying her in the rowboat and tying it to the dock with a rope long enough to let it sway in the dark water. It was the way, she had said, that all babies in her family had been lulled, with the music of the sea as their lullaby.

Brigid brings the cradle inside and puts it next to her bed, and when she wakes in the night she reaches down to run her fingertips over the mountain range of limpet shells, like crenellations on the fortress of a royal child. She rocks it a little before she turns over, puts her arm around the warm dog, and falls back to sleep.

It was wrapped so meticulously, hidden in that shed, as though someone had stored it with the intention that Brigid find it instead of the thieving neighbours. As if her uncle had known that it was the one thing in the house she might actually need.

5

The Lightkeeper's Wife

1927–1933

There was a time, before it all went cross-eyed, that Brigid's mother was a soft pillow of flesh and a lilting voice that climbed into bed with her, pulled the covers over their heads and told fairy stories. She told them in Irish. It was a secret language, hardly anyone spoke it any more, her mother said, not even in Ireland. Her stories were about heartless creatures who stole babies and lonely women for their own amusement. For Brigid, the more terrifying the story, the better. She liked a story that made her forget to breathe in the middle of it.

One of her favourites was about a mother who was stolen.

A woman was passing a fairy ring and stopped to listen to the music. She was pulled under the ground and an identical version of her, a changeling, was left in her place. Only her children could tell it wasn't her, and no one believed them.

The new mother played cruel tricks on the children, starved them of their dinners, pinched them black and blue, laughed like a braying donkey when they cried that they missed her. The father preferred the fairy wife to the old one, whom he had often struck when he'd been drinking. This new wife spoiled him, giggled and flirted, kissed him shamelessly in the middle of the field, not caring who might see. It wasn't long before the mother was smugly round with a new baby.

But when a baby girl was born, the mother died. They lived on a remote island, far from any doctor or priest, and complications arose. The fairy may have just decided to abandon them, having had her fill of human life, but refused to return their real mother at the end.

The children did not grieve her; as far as they were concerned, their mother had been dead for over a year. But the father raged over the loss. He got viciously drunk and tried to drown the baby in the well. No matter how long he held it under, the baby just seemed to wait, her eyes wide open and shining up from the dark water, holding on to breath for as long as was needed, refusing to die.

The father ended up drowning himself, falling off the cliff and being battered against the rocks, though no one was sure if he took his own life out of grief and guilt or sloppy stupidity. The children were sent to the orphanage on the mainland. Only the oldest boy stayed; he was twelve and able to tend the farm. He wouldn't allow them to take the baby. He fed her milk from the cow and wore her tied to his chest with an old woollen shawl of his mother's.

She grew into a girl, half-fairy half-human, who had the power to heal in her hands. She eased the pain of childbirth, lifted the fevers of children expected to die. Some of the islanders knew that she was the child of a changeling, others believed her power came from the holy well her father tried to drown her in. It was the same well the nuns had once used, saving the cauls of children born with the sac intact, filling them with holy water, to heal the barren wombs of women. No one cared much where it came from, pagan or Christian, as long as it was helping them.

When the girl was fourteen, there was a baby she could not save. She put her hands on it, but it had already died before it came into the world. The islanders who had called her a saint when she could help, called her a devil when she couldn't. They planned to punish her in the old ways, to burn her and see if she could heal herself. She was gone before they could try.

Her brother never revealed how she got away, no boats had come or gone on the island, she disappeared during a day when the sea raged them into seclusion. Some said she had thrown herself over the cliff, others that she had gone back under the ground to where she had come from. She

*was never seen, or heard from, on the
island again.*

'Where do you think she went?' Brigid would
ask her mother breathlessly, whenever she
finished this story.

'I think she swam,' her mother would whisper
in their little cave under the covers. 'I think she
swam until she couldn't swim any more and
found herself all the way across the sea.'

So many of her mother's fairy stories ended
badly. Brigid liked the ones where they got away.

★   ★   ★

Brigid's father was a lighthouse keeper. The
lighthouse was on an island, ten miles off the
coast of Maine, two acres of layered grey rock,
one side shorn down so steep it looked like it
had been broken by something in anger. Stalwart
pine trees grew between the cracks to form a
miniature forest. On one corner perched the
tower, painted white and splattered with yellow
lichen, and set behind it, a white brick building
with a red roof, two rooms meant for one lonely
man. Instead it sheltered Brigid's small, painful
family, three people shaped by isolation,
shadowed between the dark sea and a constant,
revolving warning of light.

Brigid and her mother were not supposed to
be there. Such a lighthouse would normally be
run on shifts, by men who returned to their
families on the mainland for weeks at a time. But
it was such an unpopular posting that when her

86

father offered to take it on full time, so he could devote every spare minute to his painting, a hermit artist on an island out at sea, the state was eager to give it away. He was fed and supplied by boat, paid a salary he didn't spend, and left alone. Brigid was told never to show herself to the fishermen that passed by and greeted her father with three pulls of their bell.

'Am I a secret?' she asked him.

'A treasure,' he winked.

Her father called her his deckhand, showed her how to polish the individual prisms of the Fresnel lens, layered together in a beehive of glass the size of a child, the light they were there to keep. A history of the lens was kept in a leather-bound book, each prism was numbered, every chip or discolouration recorded. There were multiple notebooks involved in his job, for logging boats, radio transmissions, tides and weather. Brigid loved to climb up the perilous wrought-iron spiral of stairs, her father's enormous shoulders just behind her to break her fall. From the top of the tower you could see for miles, and the reflection of sea and sky and the angles of honeyed light trapped in the amber glass lens made Brigid feel, when they were up there, like they had climbed into another world. He painted her like this, a girl looking over the sea, her hair the same colour as amber sunlight cupped in the deepest crevice of the lens.

By the time she was seven, she could tie any knot her father asked for, trim the wick with precision, knew the colours of his oil paints better than any art student he'd had. She could bait and set back a string of lobster traps, though he hauled them for her, since she was small enough to be crushed if they fell in the boat. She knew a lobster was big enough to keep without the measuring gauge, and could spot an egger before they opened the parlour.

'Always throw the mothers back,' her father said. He taught her to notch their tails with the sharp end of the gauge, so the next lobsterman would recognise the breeders. 'The ocean needs them more than we do.'

These were her parents, Silas and Nuala: peculiar, intense, zealous. Their love was not consistent, it was as mercurial and varied as the colour of the sea. It depended on the angle, which portion of the glass you looked through, whether they were tender or severe. They took turns with her, because when the two of them were in the same room, she, and everything else, tended to fade away.

It was like they set the room on fire. They were both struck by the same fever that flushed their cheeks and glazed their eyes. They touched whenever they could, her father often grabbed her mother in the middle of some chore, to kiss her neck, press her against the counter with a teasing growl. He would stand in the doorway to tell her he had fish for dinner, and she wouldn't appear to listen, instead she would reach out and put a hand on his forearm, as if she'd never seen it before. He would look at her hand, and lose his words. They closed themselves in the bedroom in the middle of the day, or her mother padded barefoot out to the lighthouse at night, and Brigid grew up with the sounds that accompanied these sessions; they were as familiar as the moaning of the wind and the sea.

They loved each other too much, Brigid thought, when she was old enough to analyse it. They couldn't see through the fog of it. It possessed them. '*Is tú mo chuisle*,' their mother often whispered to him, and she would hold his hand so his rough palm cupped her jaw and the soft spot at her neck. *You are my pulse*. They were in each other's veins.

* * *

She began to hear something other than love at night, voices rising in pitch and intensity, like a harmless wind escalating to a concerning one. A thump that didn't belong, a clatter, a shocked silence, a sound that could have been a cry. She stood by the door, feet bare, nightgown billowing from the draught that came in underneath. The lines of light around the door edges encircled her, framing her inside a dark rectangle, her hand on the cold brass doorknob, gripping but not turning it. In the bedroom, within that illuminated rectangle, she was still safe, and what was happening outside of it might not have been real. She would stand until her hand on the knob had fallen asleep, the fingers full of stabbing glass pins, then she would let go and get back into bed and will herself to sleep beneath the dark weight of the covers.

There would be detritus to further confuse her in the morning: a green bottle with a silver ship on the label, her father's evening drink, so potent it made Brigid's eyes water if she got too close to the open glass, half-full the night before, would be empty and lying sideways on the counter. Shards of shattered glass hastily gathered in the dustpan but not emptied into the wastebasket. Once, what appeared to be a small, jagged bone lying on the porcelain drain, which on closer inspection she decided was a tooth. Her mother too ill to get out of bed, something wrong with her that couldn't be named.

Blood, sometimes. On a dishtowel, a handkerchief. A dark painting of it on the seat of the outhouse. She asked her father only once, when her mother didn't emerge for three days and he brought her tea and took away armloads of darkened sheets to be scrubbed in boiled seawater. Some rags he didn't bother soaking but he fed directly into the cast-iron stove.

'What's wrong with Mam?'

'She'll be all right,' he said, but he wouldn't look at her.

Something had fallen out of her, Brigid thought. Something she had wanted to keep inside. Like the tooth, only worse. She didn't know what it was. She didn't want to know.

Once she heard her mother screaming, accusing him, weeping about a baby. There had never been a baby. She imagined this was how babies were made: by drinking fire and bleeding and lying in your bedroom until a new, dark being was formed out of it all. But a baby never came.

She helped her mother after she emerged from

these bedroom sessions, though she much preferred her father's chores. Her mother showed her how to make dense boulders of brown bread. No matter how many times Brigid did it she could never remember the steps involved and could not make bread herself, she forgot key ingredients, the baking soda, the salt, or let the whole thing burn black in the stove. She knew her father's paint hues and the chips on the lens prisms by heart, but couldn't cook a simple meal. 'Your memory is choosy enough,' her mother said. She wasn't angry, she merely sighed and gave her something less complicated to do.

Sometimes she thought her mother's face looked a bit lopsided, one cheek puffed out as if she was storing food in it. Or she moved too stiffly, carefully, as though trying not to spill something hidden in the walls of her back. Once, Brigid walked into the bedroom just as her mother lifted her blouse above her head, and saw a livid green and purple thing on her back that looked more like something alive than a bruise. Later that night, when she was asleep, Brigid pulled the sheet back to look at it again. Her mother's slight, spaghetti-strapped nightgown was thin enough to see through, but even in the bright moonlit room she couldn't find the mark. It was gone.

*　*　*

She was nine the first time she saw him hit her. The yelling was loud that night, insistent, as if they'd forgotten their usual attempt to hide it. Later, when she thought about what finally made her open the door, she decided it was hearing her own name, her mother called it out, like a warning. She opened it in time to see her mother's flailing arms and wild hair, see her hurl a glass and watch it shatter by her father's head on the stone wall of the chimney. See the look of angry terror behind her father's dark beard, the huge, gulping steps he took towards her, his hand, the enormous stone of his fist, driving at her face, so decisive and blunt that Brigid thought for a moment he was trying to knock something out of her, whatever invisible thing that had possessed them both. But it wasn't that. It was merely this, her tender, powerful father hauling his arm back and punching her mother, on purpose, in the mouth. The crack it made, the sound of the bones in his hand meeting the flesh of her face, was a shameful sound, something private, that she should not have been allowed to hear.

'Fuck,' he yelled, livid, guilty, frightened, like the time he dislodged three prisms from the lens and they shattered and he had to radio to ask for their expensive replacements. Furious at his own careless stupidity. As if he meant to caress her and misjudged the pressure of his hand. Then he saw Brigid, standing in the dark doorway. His shoulders dropped even lower, he could not meet her eyes. 'Shit, shit, shit,' he moaned, punching the wall this time, hard enough that Brigid heard something else crack. He left the house, tears carving thick pathways down into his beard.

Brigid padded over to her mother, who had slid down to sit against the wall, unable to move, her eyes closed, leaking tears. She squatted down and reached a hand out to the pulsing hot mess that was the lower half of her mother's face. She wanted to fix it. But her mother opened her eyes and shook her head. She let go of her own mouth to stay Brigid's hand. Her front teeth were dark and pressed in at an angle that was not right. Her lip was split so deeply it looked like a fish sliced down the middle and splayed in two.

'Don't,' her mother slurred. 'Leave it.'

She would learn later why her mother left the bruises. She wanted to leave all the comforting to the one who was to blame.

'What's happened to Da?' Brigid whispered. He looked possessed, as if some dark beast had dragged him under the sharp rock and left behind a monster who used fists like he intended to break her mother in two.

'It's only the drink,' she lisped through the blood and split flesh and fear. 'It's all right.'

'Oh,' Brigid said. She was dumbfounded.

It made no sense. The silver ship drink that made her father glassy-eyed, heavy-lidded, and sloppy, also turned his fists into punishing stone?

Though Brigid had been angry at the idea that they were hiding something, once she found out what it was, she regretted ever being curious. It was no longer possible for her to go back to being the girl in the nightgown who listened to noises, but had not yet made the mistake of opening the door.

It didn't happen every day. Or even every week. Months could go by where all that passed between her parents was the familiar foggy-eyed desire. Had it been constant it would have been easier to hate her father. As it was, she both loved him and feared him as though she had two fathers. Two fathers on shifts like lighthouse workers, appearing to relieve each other just at the moment the other reached a breaking point.

Her father apologised with paintings. In the lighthouse room that was his studio, there were stacks of her naked mother, lying down, looking out of the canvas with a dark, feverish happiness. After he hit her, he painted her wounds.

Brigid watched through a round, dirty glass window as her father used his brushes to heal what he had done. Eventually he put down his brushes and came over to her, he would cry and she would kiss his tears away, and that was when their bodies would come together, together in a way that Brigid, through the thick dirty window, couldn't fully understand, but she imagined it was something that grew between them and all they could do was hold on tightly, like they were being pulled by a current, until it let them go.

They both became something else. It was as alarming and as hopeful as if she had watched them transform into slick-skinned animals and flop into the sea.

Later, when her father was up in the tower, Brigid looked at what he had painted. He painted the bruises on to thick, ragged-edged paper he seemed to keep just for that purpose. There were heavy black folders full of renderings of wounds as they changed and healed and faded. He could capture the exact red of her blood, then the darkening to black as it crusted and healed. He painted scars with the detail of beautiful features. Just as he had a recording of every ship that passed, every barometer reading, the nightly position of the moon, every wounded prism, he had a painting of every injury he had ever given her. It was some sort of penance, the way he recorded it. Soon after he was finished apologising, her bruises disappeared, as if his remorse was all they had been hanging around for.

★ ★ ★

Brigid was ten by the time they found out about her hands. She was helping her father in the oil house, watching as he emptied hot oil into a drum, and a spill glugged over and grabbed him. Her father swore, clawing at his trousers, trying to rip the fabric away.

Brigid went to him, her hands reaching for the dark spot on his thigh. He tried, not gently, to avoid her and when this didn't work, to bat her away. 'Nuala,' he barked, her mother's name, then 'you,' as if he couldn't recall her name at all. Backing away from her, he tripped on a toolbox and in the instant of backward sprawl he was helpless, and before he could stop her it was over.

She put her hands on his thigh, spread them

95

wide to try to cover the oil. For an instant, the pain he must have felt when it spilled racked her, but that was merely an entry, a trip over his pain into what happened next. There was a pulling sensation, heat rose up her arms and through her shoulders and into her head and then crashed down into the trunk of her body, like a wave on a rock. The oil on his thigh evaporated, the hole it ate through his trousers was still there, but the skin underneath was now tender and pink and hairless, like a sunburned child's. Either her father didn't feel the relief of pain yet, or it was merely his instinct, because he hit her. He knocked her off her feet just at the moment where the pleasure of removing the fire was at its peak. He thumped a hard hand to her chest and sent her reeling backwards, where she banged the back of her head on the rough cement wall. For a while, until the opportunity occurred to do such a thing again, Brigid believed that the sickness that followed this — vomiting until nothing was left but her body heaved anyway, three days of a fever so high her parents fought openly about whether to radio the coastguard — was because her father had hit her, and not because she had healed him.

It had only ever been something she had done to herself, playing with matches in her cove by the woods, burning her fingers then drawing the burn away, the same way she played with adding twigs and shells to the fairy houses she built, an experiment of magic and nature. She pulled the burn away and it felt good and that was all she knew. She'd kept it a secret because of the

96

feeling it brought. The loosening, building, mind-evaporating hum was something she didn't want either one of them to know about. It didn't make her ill, but if she did it too often, it did exhaust her. Her father's burn was the first real wound she had ever tried to heal.

While she was still recovering, she waited for an apology, some indication that he was grateful or full of remorse. But he never came in; it was her mother who tended to her when she was ill.

Her father came to find her in the woods when she was better. Since the time when she first saw him hit her mother, his eyes were always pointing somewhere else when he was talking to her, or unfocused, as if he was purposefully blinding himself to what was in front of him.

'Does your mother know?' Brigid shook her head. She liked to answer her father in gestures, because it forced him to flick his eyes in her direction.

'I think it best you don't tell her,' he said.

'Why?' Brigid said.

'You know why,' he said. Brigid shrugged again, forcing her father into eye contact. 'She might think you're touched. She might want to do something with it. With you. Understand?'

'Yes,' Brigid said. He was lying. Her mother knew more about these things than anyone. She told her stories of just this sort of magic. But though she felt a pull of guilt, Brigid liked having a secret with her father. Like the secret language with her mother, or the secret of the penance paintings.

Secrets meant you were loved.

97

For months after she first healed him, her father avoided drinking from the ship bottle. He didn't want to cause an injury, Brigid thought, that his daughter might be obliged to heal. But then the violence seemed to build in him, as if there was a ceiling on the loving ways he could touch her mother, and when he reached that, he needed to do something else. He drank, he hit, he apologised.

One night she heard her name called out like a curse by her father. As soon as Brigid came out, her father fell to his knees and started to cry.

'Help her,' he said. 'I went too far. Something is broken.' Brigid laid her hands on her mother for the first time, but it didn't work.

The attempt came rushing back at her, like a deliberate slap in the face. Understanding, then revulsion followed. Her mother opened her eyes, challenging her to tell, but Brigid never did. She pretended to heal her mother's broken bone, but she didn't do a thing. Her mother healed herself. Nuala had the same secret inside her hands that Brigid did. Most of the time, Brigid realised, she chose not to use it. If she healed herself, her husband would have nothing to apologise for.

Brigid saw it now. Despite years of being battered, her nose broken, cheekbones and ribs cracked, wounds splayed open like mouths across her face, her mother didn't have a mark on her. She was as flawless and lovely as the young girl Silas had first painted, first captured into this violent spiral that neither of them

98

seemed able to leave. She had healed all her scars, even as she stayed and asked for the wounds.

★ ★ ★

Her father had always spent his nights in the lighthouse, drinking large thermoses full of coffee, so he could continue the conversation of light between the tower and passing ships. Brigid still slept in the bed with her mother, where she had once listened to fairy stories of women stronger than any of the evils that threatened them. Her mother had less and less to tell her these days.

'Why do you let him?' Brigid said once, and her mother stiffened. 'You're stronger than he is. Why do you let him hurt you? Why do we stay here?'

'You wouldn't understand.'

Brigid said nothing, but her silence demanded more.

'I was a girl when he found me. I was in trouble. He saved me.'

'What trouble?'

'It doesn't matter. He's a part of me. Like you are. You don't choose who you love.'

Something resonated in Brigid then, she wanted to scream and rage and insist that this was rubbish. That she wouldn't fall for it. She would choose whom she loved, or she would not love at all.

'But he hurts you.'

'Not in a way I can't bear.'

'We could leave. We could swim away, like the stories.'

'Just because I'm strong enough to leave, doesn't mean I want to.'

'That doesn't make any sense.'

'It could be worse. It could be a lot worse.'

But Brigid doubted that.

'There are other ways to be hurt,' her mother tried. 'He only uses his hands.' Her mother paused. 'He *can't* hurt me. Don't you see? Any more than he can hurt you.'

'But he has,' Brigid said. 'He does.' Her mother stiffened, held her tighter, pretended she didn't hear.

She fell asleep before Brigid could ask the question she most wanted the answer to. She whispered it anyway.

'Are we real?'

She didn't know what was true any more. The story they were trapped in or the ones her mother no longer told.

★   ★   ★

When she was ten, Brigid wanted a changeling baby. In her mother's stories, babies were stolen from their cradles, a fairy left in their place. Other babies were given to women who couldn't grow one themselves. Fairy children, lent to the world, had a foreign loveliness and fire in their eyes. On her mother's island in Ireland, there were places known as entrances to the fairy world: green roads, the ancient stump of a tree, a cave in a stone cliff by the sea. Places where

100

children could hear music and laughter and a pull to something that would swallow them away. Where something else could be born.

Brigid set up sites on the island where fairies might hear her request. A circle of stones in the woods where she built fires and burned and healed herself while waiting. A cave down by the shoreline that was swallowed at high tide but dark, wet and promising at low. An old oak tree whose trunk she could not fit her arms around, which she surrounded with a colony of fairy houses made from bark and pine needles and shells and moss.

There was the chance, she knew, that she would be stolen instead. The instant she passed through bark or damp mossy ground or stayed in a cave until the sea swallowed her, she planned to gorge herself, eat and eat from whatever she was offered, drink goblets of fairy wine until it ran down her chin, eat beyond the point where she felt she might be sick, to make sure that there was not the slightest chance she could ever be returned.

Either way, stolen child or fairy gift, Brigid would no longer be alone.

★ ★ ★

Her mother's hands shook her for a long time before Brigid relented and opened her eyes. The first thing she saw was the blood. Her mother had smeared it on the sheet and the doors and the walls. There was so much blood Brigid assumed it was coming from her, but she pulled her out of bed and outside, barefoot over ice and

101

rock, murmuring, 'Hurry, hurry,' even though they already were.

Inside the studio was a mess. The fight was an epic one. Smashed glass, ripped canvas, they had broken and torn and shattered it all. More blood than Brigid had ever seen. Streams of it, puddles, smears, soakings, blood like spilled and wasted paint. Blood leading in an ungraceful sweep to her father, still and curled up in the corner, where he'd pulled himself then stopped. Brigid didn't want to go near him, she wanted to turn around and go back to bed. But her mother was still holding on.

'I hit back,' she said, pulling Brigid along. 'I hit him too hard.' Brigid's bare feet warmed on the bloody floor. 'I can't fix it.'

The fire iron was still where she'd dropped it. His head was a mess, the blood as dark as his hair but glistening, weighing down his curls as if he'd just emerged from a deep and oily sea. It pooled beneath him black and so thick she could tell it was already cold.

'Right there,' her mother said, pointing to an indentation in his skull, a broken pit behind his ear. There was something in there, in that pit, something besides bone and blood, something neither one of them was ever meant to see. An entrance, Brigid thought, an underworld.

It was not something Brigid could put her hands on. Her mother forced her, pulled her down to her knees in the blood and pressed her daughter's hands to the pit and begged her to close it. Nothing happened. There was no heat, no rush of pleasure, there was nothing inside him that she could get a grip on. He was gone.

'He's not in there,' Brigid mumbled.

'No. Nonononono.' Her mother paced the round room in her bare feet, leaving bloody footprints in a spiral, swearing and crying and mumbling to herself. When Brigid tried to talk to her, she looked as if she didn't know who she was, or what language she was speaking. She looked like something other than a mother, like the changeling that had replaced her who could not figure out how to leave.

* * *

Part of Brigid was relieved when nothing happened. When she put her hands to her father's head and found it empty. The relief opened a throat constricted with guilt. Though she would have saved him, though the reality of her father dead — the father who had once held her hand and shown her how to polish light — made her want to fall into darkness herself, not saving him meant that they were free. It meant that someone would come in a boat and take her away and it would be better than being with the fairies because she could escape and still live in the world. She thought her father dying would break open the trap that was the three of them.

But her mother decided to stay.

'They'll take you away,' her mother explained. 'I'll go to jail. Is that what you want?'

'I'll tell them,' Brigid tried. 'I'll tell them it was his fault.'

103

'Look at us,' her mother said. 'There's not a mark on either one of us. No one will believe you.'

Brigid stopped arguing. She was only a child. None of this had ever been her decision.

It wasn't hard for her mother to pretend. They left his body in a cave that was walled off by enormous boulders pushed in by the sea. The boat still delivered supplies and thought nothing of leaving the wooden boxes on the dock. They had never liked Silas, who was gruff and impatient with small talk, so they dropped things in a hurry to avoid him. Brigid knew how to run the lighthouse, how to log the boats and punch in the Morse code at the appropriate times. How to pull the enormous bell three times in greeting to a passing boat, each ring a bigger lie. Her mother burned stacks of sketches in the stove, annihilated images of her broken, bruised body, swallowing them with flame. She refused to listen when Brigid said they could be used as evidence. She alternated between periods of energetic destruction and collapse, taking to her bed and not leaving it for days, weeks at a time. She had hallucinations, open-eyed dreams where she grabbed Brigid's arms and tried to warn her of something.

'They'll burn me,' she said. 'They're waiting with the fire irons. They'll burn me and kill the baby.'

'There is no baby,' Brigid would insist, and then feel guilty that such pragmatism sent her mother into a fresh episode of tears.

Brigid ran the lighthouse by herself then,

signalling the boats, manned by those who knew nothing about what was happening underneath the light. At some point it occurred to her with a rush that they could be here for years before anyone came. They could be here for ever, two women who could barely meet eyes or speak, having murdered the only thing that bound them to the human world.

★ ★ ★

One summer morning, Brigid was swimming in the cove when she saw a sailboat. She was halfway to it before she even realised what she was trying to do. She swam so hard she forgot to pace herself, and the sailboat moved quickly out of her sight. She swallowed water, couldn't keep her head above the waves long enough to cough it out, swallowed more. She panicked, struggling. She felt something large and warm brush against her legs. Suddenly, she was not afraid. It was so easy to stop struggling. To believe that falling beneath the sea would save her. This is where the fairies have been all along, she thought, as she felt a small arm circle her neck, and heard a whisper that seemed to come up from the water. *Brigid*, the watery voice said in the secret language, *mo chuisle*. My pulse.

She woke on the shore, coughing and vomiting seawater in a violent gush. She lay for a long time, her bruised and scraped body heavily alive in the sand. When she felt strong enough, she walked back to the water. She lowered herself in a tide pool and watched the blood, sand, and all the hopes she'd had for being stolen lift off and swirl away.

★   ★   ★

Later that night, in the bed they shared, Brigid's mother said simply, in Irish, 'Don't ever try that nonsense again.' When Brigid didn't answer, her mother put an arm around her waist, pulled her in tight.

'Don't give up on me,' she said into Brigid's neck, moving her hair aside. 'I don't know how to start over again. But we'll figure something out.'

Her mother had been the one to rescue her. Not to save her, but to chain her there. Trapped in a story worse than any fairy tale she'd ever been told.

Brigid stopped wishing for a changeling. Once she imagined that her mother was the brave fairy girl who swam herself across the sea, now Brigid thought the story was about her. She knew exactly what it felt like to be that fairy girl, an accident born from the blasphemous joining of worlds. She couldn't escape this life any more than she could hurt herself.

It wasn't just happening to her or around her, all of this darkness. It was part of her.

She couldn't bring a baby into all of this. She imagined it slipping away, like newborn seals that had to be nudged back up the rocks by their enormous, aggravated mothers.

It would have nothing to hold on to.

★   ★   ★

When Brigid was eleven, the state decided to renegotiate with her father, and though her mother forged his signature on letters requesting an extension, it was denied. Three young coastguard sailors, eager to prove themselves, arrived on the island expecting to talk down a madman, but found instead two wild-eyed, emaciated women and the bones of the lighthouse keeper rattling around in a cave of sharp grey rock. Nothing magical saved them. The world that Brigid thought had forgotten them merely stumbled in.

In town, the police pulled a confession out of her mother as easily as a needle drawing blood. She was sent to Saint Dymphna's Asylum, from where, it was well known, no woman ever left. They weren't sure what to do with Brigid, who wouldn't say a word. She was as tall as a grown woman, with wild, fire-coloured hair and a look on her face that made the adults required to help her extremely uncomfortable. In the end, Brigid was sent north to an institution that bore her name, St Brigid's, run by a group of Irish nuns who had a reputation for reforming the most damaged and bold of wayward girls.

Her mother had told them her father had abused them both. That was why she had killed him, because he was hurting their child. Brigid didn't learn this until later. Somewhere in the shuffle of policemen and social workers and doctors, Brigid and her mother never said goodbye. Brigid was left to wonder alone, until she grew tired of wondering any more, which one of them — the mother who had stolen from her, or the mother who had saved her — was the one she should remember. The fairy or the saint.

6

Bonfire

June, 1959

On June 21st, the longest day of the year, the older children come home from secondary school for the summer and the whole island gathers to meet them at the quay. Five teenagers looking taller, filled out, and more interested in each other than they were the year before.

There are only eight families left on St Brigid's Island. Someone is always leaving, uncles, cousins, classmates waving from the mail boat in their good coats, mothers keening after them as if at a funeral. They leave for jobs and wars, for marriage and school. For life. Only six men are capable of lifting the heavy boats and working the hard land of the island, and Rose and Emer are married to two of them. The rest are women or children under the age of twelve. When children turn twelve, they leave. They go to the mainland to attend secondary school and they only come home during the summer. By their first summer home, they are already different, already gone.

Rose and Emer are standing on the grass hill that looks down on the quay. Emer can't help fidgeting, she is eager to get up to Brigid's, where she spends most days, with the excuse of

109

helping her fix up the house — but Rose and Emer never miss this.

'Seems like it was only last summer that was us,' Rose whispers to Emer, squeezing her arm affectionately.

You mean you, Emer thinks, trying to pull away, but Rose is used to this and ignores it, threading her arm through Emer's elbow and holding tight. The side of her belly against Emer's arm feels obscene. Her bump has grown quicker than ever this time, and the men have been slagging Austin, saying it's probably quadruplets. Emer would find this mortifying, but Rose has never been embarrassed at her own body.

The teenagers, like the Yank, have to be handed down from the big boat into a currach; Austin and Patch row out to them. Emer can see Austin greeting the only boy with a shoulder slap and a whispered comment that flames his ears. The girls he hands down sweetly, with a wink, like they are his own. Patch keeps the boat steady, avoiding the greetings, he is known for fierce shyness around women and children. They angle the currach into the cove, timing between waves which could upend them, and at the slip they lift children up to where their mothers have been waiting months to get their hands on them.

'Look at the face on Oisin,' Rose says to Emer.

Oisin is the pimple-faced son of Malachy and Kathleen. He is getting on so well that there is talk of him having the points to study medicine.

'What are you on about?' Emer says.

'Himself and Deirdre are trying so hard not to

110

look at each other they're practically falling off the quay. Those two have been busy this winter.'

'Don't be crass,' Emer says, shifting uneasily as she does at any mention of romance or sex.

'I'm only observing.' Rose smiles.

'Oisin can do better than Deirdre,' Emer says. 'She won't last long in the city.'

'He'll come back here, so he will,' Rose says. 'To be the island doctor.'

'And who will pay him for that?' Emer says.

The island isn't funded for a doctor, or a priest, a lighthouse or a new harbour, not even for electricity or a community telephone. The government would rather give them a new start. They want people off the islands, so instead of Inis Muruch, where they have relatives, they are offering a cul-de-sac of eight brand-new houses on the mainland. For reasons she cannot wrap her mind around, no one wants to go but Emer. You'd think the government was trying to burgle them rather than give them new houses when you hear Rose voice her opinion on it.

Rose makes her way to the quay, to hug and fuss over these children as if they are her own. Austin reaches out and pinches her rear, she laughs and slaps him away, delighted. He grabs her for a kiss. Emer looks away. Their public displays of affection have always sickened her.

'Howaya, Emer,' a few of the teenagers say as they walk past, avoiding her eyes. She nods at them. Her husband walks up the road to their house without a glance at her.

Niall is already up at Brigid's house. He has no time for the return of the prodigals. He

111

doesn't care about these teenagers any more than Emer does. But neither does he have her desire to feed off the feeling they bring home with them, the broad, fresh faces that are a little unfocused, a little absent, as if half of them has been left in another, better world. It fills Emer with jealous rage, but she can't help coming to see life rise off them like smoke, just the same.

★   ★   ★

Emer and Rose grew up assuming they would leave, leave the island, leave Ireland, because that is what children did. Old women crossed themselves any time they passed the quay, remembering all the children the island had lost to the world. Emer looked forward to the day she would leave for secondary school the way she had once anticipated being stolen by fairies. It was the only hope she had of escaping the treeless three-mile stretch of bog and rock. Of escaping herself.

The summer before they were due to leave for secondary school, their mother had a stroke. She collapsed in the kitchen and when she woke, she couldn't move or speak, so the doctor was rowed over. Auntie Orla explained it to the girls when the doctor said she would need to go to hospital. Rose broke down in the loud, dominating sobs that always required attention. Emer raised her voice above the noise to ask if it was a 'fairy stroke', the illness said to affect those who were being stolen, still halfway between this world and the underground. She asked with such a gleam

112

in her eyes that her Auntie Orla crossed herself. 'Stolen child,' she muttered as she turned away. Emer didn't flinch. She'd been called this before. She still wished it were true.

Their mother came home with one half of her face frozen, a useless arm curled like a broken wing to her breast, and a deadened leg that seemed to weigh as much as the rest of her, the foot turned permanently inward. The way the paralysis pulled her mouth made it look like it was half-open and ready to scream.

This was one month before Emer and Rose were due to leave for school. There was no discussion. Their mother could not be left. Everyone on the island could barely feed their own families. There was no one to take them on the mainland, or in America, where some other widowed families went. Their mother's three brothers had all been killed fighting for England in the war. Even if they'd had a place to go, their mother declared, she would never leave the island. Not with her baby boy still in that water.

Rose and Emer were already used to the chores. They milked the cows, fed the calves, did the laundry and the cooking, and dug, alongside the other orphaned children, endless rows of potatoes in September. As girls they had ridden side by side on the donkey creels full of turf, now they led the donkeys themselves. They carried knives in their aprons, knit circular scarves to protect their heads when they went out to tend the animals. But after their mother's stroke, it was as if they became women, as hard and old as their mother in a few months. Emer, at least.

113

Rose maintained some callow girlishness. She continued to go to the island school whenever she could. Emer announced loudly, whenever she set off, that she was wasting her time.

It wasn't long after this that Emer started her monthly bleeding. Her cramps were like water breaking on to rock, constant, unbearable. So much dark, clotted blood fell out of her that nothing could staunch it, not the thick flannel folded between her legs or the modern sanitary napkins, coveted and few from the mainland, which had to be tossed, like most rubbish, into the fire. Emer bled through them all. After one humiliating accident in the church pew, during a Christmas when the boys her age were home from school, she stayed near the house for the first week of every month. She had headaches that felt like bees swarming in her head, that made her vision vibrate and sunlight unbearable. She added these to the growing list of things that locked her away and let her sister get on without her.

Rose's blood, when it started the next year, was dainty and spare, a pink stain on a cloth that could be rinsed clean and forgotten, or thrown on a fire without threatening to smother it.

'Mind yourselves,' their mother slurred. 'A man can put a baby in ye now.'

'Wouldn't that be the straw,' Emer scoffed. But Rose smiled and winked at her.

★ ★ ★

Two years after their mother's stroke, the island teacher convinced Rose to go away to school

114

after all. She never thought to make such a suggestion to Emer, who had stopped showing up altogether. One of them would have to stay on the island with their mother, and Emer was the obvious choice. When Rose tried to ask Emer what she thought about this, Emer acted so disinterested that Rose was hurt.

'I'll stay if you want,' Rose said.

'Sure you will. Don't you always do what you're told?' Emer said.

Emer refused to speak to her for the rest of the summer, but Rose left anyway.

It was the longest winter of Emer's life. There was storm after storm where they couldn't leave the island for weeks at a time, and Rose couldn't come over to see them. She didn't even make it for Christmas, celebrating the holiday with the family she boarded with in town. Emer and her mother sat silently in front of the tough goose whose neck Emer had wrung with a pleasure that startled her. The few times that Rose was able to get over, that autumn and again in the springtime, Emer was barely civil to her, cruel, distant, angry to the point where she often imagined slapping her sister's face hard enough to leave an ugly mark and a betrayed expression. She had never wanted her hands to suck happiness out of someone as much as she wished they would out of Rose.

At Easter, when they were working in the kitchen together, peeling potatoes and making bread, Rose tried to reach across the floury table and grasp Emer's hand.

'I know how difficult it must be,' she

115

whispered, so their mother couldn't hear. Emer dropped her knife in her apron pocket, put her shawl and headscarf on and walked out into the fields, leaving her sister, who somehow managed to both be self-effacing and get everything she wanted, alone with the dinner half-prepared.

★ ★ ★

Rose only lasted that one year. Her first summer home from school, the weather so fine that the bleak winter seemed like someone else's memory, she told Emer she wasn't going back. She'd fallen in love with Austin Keane, eighteen years old and finished with school in Galway. For years everyone assumed he would get the points to study medicine, but he refused to take the exams. He was moving back in with his mother and younger sisters, to fish and work the land like his father, who had drowned at the same time as theirs, before him. He and Rose both believed that staying on the island with their families was more important than any academic or worldly ambition.

'Got into your knickers then, did he?' Emer said when Rose told her this. Rose ignored that.

'You can go now, Emer,' Rose said, her eyes so bright with possibility Emer found herself wanting to poke them. 'Go to school on the mainland, if you want. Mammy can live with us.'

Emer acted as though the suggestion were ludicrous. Rose was confused and spent a good deal of time trying to convince her. Telling her about Galway, and how much there was to do

116

there and the bookshops and the train to Dublin. Emer lost her temper eventually, snapping at her sister's pretty face.

'Sure, you're only disappointed for yourself,' she said. 'I won't go gallivanting about to make you feel better, or be made to pay for it later when you've ten children and no hope of getting away.'

Rose went cold then. She would go cold, if Emer pushed her enough, she wasn't all sweetness and warmth, even if Emer was the only one who knew it.

'I'm sorry Austin prefers me, Emer.' And just with one sentence, that was how Rose would do it. Emer could rage and insult her and whinge, but Rose, eventually, would cut her down with one retort. Because she knew, and had known all along, how Emer felt about Austin.

He had held her hand once. The summer she was thirteen, at the St John's bonfire. Austin, just home for the summer from school, had fumbled in the dark for Rose's hand, but got Emer's instead. She was so shocked and delighted by this she forgot about what her hand did to everyone by then. Austin yelped, pulled his hand away and swore to himself in the darkness. Rose, standing to the side of Emer, giggled at the swearing, and that was when Austin realised his mistake. Emer felt him shudder to himself, shake it off and guzzle stout he'd nicked from the keg, as if he needed fortification against the cold dread that had seeped from her hand.

But for the breath-holding second before she ruined it, Emer lost herself. She let go in the wet darkness, buoyed by the flattering pressure of

Austin's hand. In that instant it wasn't like watching Rose, it was like being Rose. As if she had stolen from her sister the assurance, dense and impenetrable, that she was wanted.

Emer didn't go. The subject of school on the mainland never came up again. She told herself she was staying to spite her sister. She remained out of a vague hope that was more like fear. Fear that, were she to leave, without her sister beside her, she would be as ugly and cruel and paralysed as the mother that obliged them to stay behind. And that no one would dare to reach out for her hand ever again.

★ ★ ★

In the field behind Brigid's house, Niall is running circles with the pig and dog, whom he has taught to play keep away with a sun-bleached sheep femur he found in the garden.

'Seems like a big morning,' Brigid says, gesturing to the quay. She is sitting outside her door on a kitchen chair, like an old island woman already. She looks tired, Emer thinks, and it occurs to her that Brigid's energy isn't as deep as it appears. It can run dry.

'It's just the children coming home,' Emer says. 'It puts them all in a tizzy.'

'I can imagine.'

'There'll be a ceili tonight at the bonfire,' Niall says. He has run over panting, the pig standing to attention nearby, bone in his snout, grinning with victory. 'For St John's Eve. Will you come, Brigid?'

Brigid grows still. 'Should I bother?' she says casually, but it sounds breathless.

The island men have checked on Brigid daily, but the women have barely spoken to her. They will be friendly tonight, Emer knows, forgiving, with the children home and the two barrels of porter they came with. It would be the right moment to be introduced, when they are feeling loose and grateful enough to give strangers their time. They won't give her the well, any more than Emer, even though Brigid seems to think the longer she stays the closer she gets to being told. The eager desperation Brigid barely holds in check rattles Emer, as if it is she, not what she knows, that Brigid is so taken with.

Emer shrugs and pretends the question barely interests her.

'If you care for that kind of thing,' she says, turning her blind side to Brigid's questioning eyes.

Niall comes in when they're making bread to announce that Fiona and Eve are coming up the road. Emer's hands freeze in the mound of flour.

'Who are Fiona and Eve?' Brigid asks.

'My nieces,' Emer says.

Brigid walks outside to meet the girls, who have had their Saturday baths and their red gold hair plaited and are wearing their best clothes for the bonfire. Fiona is carrying a plate of freshly baked scones.

'My mother wanted to welcome you and say she hopes to have a chat at the ceili tonight,' Fiona says. 'She couldn't get away as she's bathing the babies. The plate is yours as well.'

119

Fiona looks to Emer like she might jump out of her hair ribbons, she's so keen.

Emer hadn't asked Rose if she had any of the fuchsia pottery from Brigid's house, but the other women who begrudgingly handed over their pieces must have told her.

'Thank you,' Brigid says. 'Won't you come in, girls?'

She makes tea and puts out the plate of pink and blue sweeties she keeps ordering from town because they are Niall's favourites. Fiona looks around the cottage with such probing interest it borders on rudeness. She sits straight in her chair and accepts one of each colour sweet and nibbles daintily at them. Eve, just as pretty but on the shy side and as a result, fiercely boring, takes a whole handful and gobbles them greedily the same way Niall always does. Then she looks like she regrets eating them so quick, because she has nothing to do while her sister leads the conversation.

'Are you from New York?' Fiona asks Brigid.

'I'm afraid not,' Brigid says. The men asked her this as well. *Everyone*, she has said to Emer, *wants me to be from New York.* 'I'm from Maine.'

'Oh,' Fiona says, with no attempt to hide her disappointment. 'I'm going to New York someday. I want to be an actress.'

Emer gasps in amused disapproval. Fiona flicks a glare in her direction, and continues.

'I saw a film once at the cinema in Galway with your woman, Marilyn Monroe. She's brilliant. I do the recitations at the Christmas concert on Muruch and my teacher says I'm the best in the class.'

Rose would be mortified. Though she is proud of Fiona, who has top marks, she wouldn't allow her to be so boastful, so bold. And she certainly wouldn't encourage any nonsense about New York. She's hoping Fiona will be the island teacher. For the most part, Fiona pretends to like her role as her mother's right hand, she cares for her siblings and takes on the endless chores without complaint. Only Emer noticed, when Rose announced the new twins at Easter, Fiona go pale and still, like she had just been told she was pregnant herself. She is the only one of Rose's children who has no fear of Emer. Emer suspects if she tried her hands on the girl, she would flick her right off like she does everything else.

'But, Fee, no one comes back to visit from New York,' Niall says.

'You could come with me,' Fiona dares, and Niall backs away from the table. He moves to stand next to Emer and puts his small hand in hers. Emer grasps it tightly and tries not to smile.

This is one thing she has that Rose does not. None of her girls are as devoted as Niall. They can't be. As soon as they are old enough to walk away from her they do it, without turning back to check if she is watching. There isn't enough of her for any of them to cling to.

'Will you go to New York, too?' Brigid asks Eve politely, who looks at her blankly for a moment, then blushes and shrugs.

'She just wants to get married,' Fiona scoffs.

As if that's not the only option available, to the both of them, Emer thinks.

'Are you married?' Fiona says, bold again.

'Not any more,' Brigid says. But she gets up and puts more water on before Fiona can ask what that means. Fiona looks so enthralled by this she nudges her sister, who glares at her, still angry at her slag.

'I might not get married,' she whines. 'I may take the vow.'

'You're only saying that so Mammy will swoon over you,' Fiona whispers. Eve tries to kick her, but Fiona dodges this at the same time she darts her hand out and pinches her sister hard.

'Girls,' Emer warns.

Fiona catches Emer's one eye and looks quickly away.

Brigid comes back over with a fresh pot of tea.

'Tell your mother I look forward to meeting her,' she says. Emer clenches her hands into fists. The girls leave as quickly as they can, they start giggling as soon as they are far enough down the green road to believe they are free to do so. They are carrying Brigid's message, and with it Emer's dashed hopes, as heavy and easy to give away as that plate full of scones.

★ ★ ★

Rose married Austin when she was fifteen, with a three-day-long party on Inis Muruch, and they moved into his mother's house until he could build them their own. Emer was left alone again with their mother. After their honeymoon to Dublin, Rose blushed whenever her new husband was nearby. It wasn't embarrassment; the blush was connected to some hot expectation. Emer could tell Rose was always wanting to get him alone, and he her. They rarely managed it. They lived with his mother and his three sisters all in the one little house. Emer had seen the old women cluck and shake their heads at the way they eyed one another, even in church.

'Will you mind the way you look at him,' Emer said to her once after Mass when they did it again in full view of the priest. 'You're making a holy show of yourself.' Rose laughed at her.

'It's no sin to admire your own husband,' she said.

Emer learned one day what these looks were all about. She was walking to the cliffs to check the sheep and heard something coming from the clochán. Someone was breathing quick, as if they'd been running and were trying to catch it, but also broken, as if they were afraid. For a moment, Emer thought it was the fairy woman. But then she heard another breath, deeper, with a rhythm, like an animal that knew how to sing a song. She recognised Austin's admired voice even when it wasn't using words. Emer knew that she should turn around and go back down the hill. These were not noises that she knew, but she knew that they were private. Even as this thought formed, she was crouching by the clochán, going right for the small hole in the stone that she knew was there. She peeked in, needing to see what it was that had so changed her sister's expression.

Emer watched them for a long time, until she had to slow her own heartbeat and breath, lest they should hear her through the stone, then she crawled away through the bracken, wet from the damp ground and the slick well she hadn't known was inside her.

Emer had never imagined that the chores of marriage, and of making babies (she knew the basics of it but hadn't realised there were such options), could be anything like what she witnessed that day. That you could be taken away by someone, snatched and filled up and adored, stolen by someone else's hands and mouth, without once losing yourself.

★ ★ ★

Emer married Austin's older, less attractive brother the summer Patch came home from Dublin to help Austin fix up a ruined cottage into their new house, and Rose was swollen with her first set of twins. They were thrown together, Austin having written him at his sister's request, after Rose suggested how fitting it would be that they marry brothers and their children be closer than cousins. Patch was studying for the lighthouse service and about to get his first posting. It could mean, Rose assured Emer, living all over Ireland. Often wives and children were set up with houses in the nearest town, so the men didn't have to travel far on their weeks off.

Emer and Patch barely had to participate in a

124

courtship before they were engaged. It happened around them, like weather, the swirling wind and rain of opinion, the insistence of others that they fall in love causing them to feel dizzily aroused.

'You're not as senseless as some girls,' he said once, as though trying to convince them both. He only resembled his brother when he smiled, which wasn't very often. In that way he and Emer were a perfect match.

By the time she wondered at the wisdom of it, it was done already. There was no trip to Dublin, no weekend on Muruch, just a simple ceremony in the small island church that had no pews; women brought their milking stools, men stood round the edges. The priest hurried off immediately for fear of the weather turning. Their mother stayed the night with Rose to give them a honeymoon. Rose had done Emer's hair and make-up, taught her to shave her legs and armpits, lent her a nightgown. Even Emer had been surprised at how well she looked in the glass.

Patch barely glanced at her, blowing out the candle before quickly stripping his clothes off and climbing into the bed. He smelled strongly of soap, and she had a brief image of his mother scrubbing him clean in a kitchen tub for the occasion. There was the same grunting, and heavy breath, and a pain she hadn't expected, but that passed quickly. She waited to feel something like what she'd witnessed in her sister. There was nothing. Only a friction that quickly became unbearable, then a grunt from Patch and it was over. He was almost asleep when she spoke up.

'Would you not put your hands on me? Or your mouth?' She knew it was a mistake the moment she said it. The whole bed stiffened along with him.

'Are you hurt?' he said. She said that she wasn't. 'Then what are you on about?' He looked as if he regretted the whole thing. She had been careful to keep her hands to herself, but still he looked a bit like someone who had just clasped her palm, and been pulled down into despair. He turned away from her and was soon asleep.

The first few times she tried to move underneath him, to think of Austin's voice and her sister's catching breath, but there was nothing, only that crowding friction, then wetness from him, then the feeling that she'd been emptied, and would never be full of what her sister had. And the look on Patch's face, as if it were something like revulsion that propelled his groaning release.

Then he left for his first appointment, Fastnet Rock, a lighthouse so desolate and remote there was no possibility of her going along. She was left alone with her harpy of a mother, calling out criticisms with grating persistence. It was as if she had never been married at all.

The first time Patch didn't come home when he was due, Austin had to travel to the mainland, drag him out of the pub and row him home. It wasn't the first time, it turned out, just the first time since their marriage. He'd lived away from the island so long, no one had known but Austin.

'You'd think Austin might have warned us,' Rose said angrily when they were back. They

126

stood in Emer's doorway watching Austin half carry him up the road. Rose had two babies strapped to her chest in a way that allowed her to nurse them and do the chores at the same time.

Emer went wordlessly inside. She was pregnant, the goal of marital fumbling successfully attained, and had already given up on the fantasy that she might feel anything more for her husband than she felt for anyone else.

★   ★   ★

Patch wanted to name the baby Padraig, after himself and his father. Emer named him Niall, and gave her husband his second name, though grudgingly. The boy was born on the first of May at the hospital on the mainland, small and big-eyed and silent, with wrinkles like a worried old man lining his forehead. He wasn't able to eat. The first time she put her nipple in his mouth, it flopped right out, as if he hadn't the strength, or the interest really, to keep it in there. Her milk came in, her breasts swelled and burned, and though he rarely cried, he shrieked when she tried to feed him. He fought it, balling his little fists and twisting his neck, and her milk leaked like tears down his cheeks. The nurses tried to show her how to do it properly but each of them gave up when, after touching Emer, a rush of hopelessness overwhelmed them. The doctor was consulted, but he just seemed embarrassed by the whole thing. He suggested tins of baby formula, which was thick and beige and vile-smelling; Niall swallowed it only once before being sick and never opening his lips for it again.

There was a nurse who only came at night, an old woman with Connemara in her accent, who watched and waited through all the fuss. She came to Emer's room on the third night and, whispering in Irish, showed Emer how to pinch and knead just behind the nipple to get her milk out into a jar, then dribble it slowly into Niall's mouth. Once he'd tasted it, he started gulping, as if it had taken him three days to realise that he'd been hungry all along.

'My own mother was the midwife on Inishturk,' the nurse said. 'Don't be telling the doctor what I show you. They think the old ways are no better than witchcraft.'

She pointed underneath Niall's tongue, where a little cord of glistening tendon held him so tight that even when he cried, it could not extend out of his mouth. She took a small scalpel from her white pocket and before Emer could say anything, she thrust it into his mouth and flicked, once, with a sound that made Emer lose her urine into the already bloody clothes on the bed. She hated herself in the next moment, for not even thinking to move her son away from a madwoman with a blade. But Niall didn't cry, just looked at them both and yawned, a small swirl of blood collecting in his mouth and staining his drool pink.

'That'll sort him,' the nurse said, and Emer just held him closer, grateful that he didn't seem hurt, angry that it was no thanks to her. The next time she put him to her nipple he didn't scream.

He didn't suck, but kept it in his mouth, and she kneaded like the nurse had shown her and he swallowed a few times, sweet, loud swallows that let rush a joy through her like nothing she'd ever felt. A lot of it ran off down his cheeks and into his neck. He grew tired and let his face fall away. She worked the rest of her milk into a bottle the nurse had placed close by, and poured the formula they thought she was giving him down the sink.

She brought him home to the island, fed the tins of formula to the calves, continued to express her own milk into a tiny porcelain jug with a fuchsia blossom painted on the side. Their best jug, the only delicate thing they owned. She fed him from the lip of this jug, decanting sips into his eager little mouth. He was like a man with a pint of stout, deep swallows with pauses for sighing.

At the end of his first week, during a night feeding, he turned his head away from the jar. Her breast was exposed from expressing the milk and he latched on to it with such force and precision she jumped a little at the shock, but he held on. He was suckling. She could tell the moment it happened that he had never done it properly before, the tug that went all the way up her breast and beyond, as if he were intent on swallowing her whole self, body and soul, into the gaping hole of his mouth and throat. She began to cry, heaving sobs that she tried to control because she was afraid it would distract him and he would forget what he was doing. Patch woke up because her crying shook the bed, rolled over and looked at her, puzzled and a little wary. He'd never once seen her cry, and she had never taken well to direct questions.

'Are you well, then?' he risked.

'The baby's eating,' she said.

'That's grand so,' he murmured, confused. Patch hadn't watched any of it, he'd looked away when any fuss around her breasts seemed to be going on, so he couldn't imagine why a baby eating would suddenly make her cry.

Emer spent the next week in bed, Niall nursing almost constantly night and day. Rose came by with toddlers trailing by her side, the next set of twins heavy and round beneath her apron. She baked them bread, milked Emer's cows, tidied the house, churned butter, swept the hearth and kept the fire up, left a plate for Patch for his tea and brought another plate to Emer's bed. Emer did nothing but watch the baby drink, as if he'd never get enough, and for once she was grateful for her sister, who asked nothing but seemed as proud of the sight as Emer did herself.

'Isn't he a dote,' her sister would murmur, and Emer would hold the baby up to nuzzle his neck, hiding the flush of love that flamed over her face.

★   ★   ★

When Rose's second set of twins were born, when Niall was six months old, Emer went to see her in hospital. She asked for the nurse who had helped her, whose name was Bridie, because she wanted to show her what a strong mouth he had

130

now. None of the nurses knew whom she meant. She asked every staff person who came into Rose's room, until Rose told her to stop. She was exhausted by the birth and had no energy for Emer's prodding anxiety. The secretary at the front desk looked through the books and told her there was no nurse named Bridie from Inishturk and there never had been.

Emer went home to the island with Niall tied tightly to her bosom, her neck swollen with dread. There were stories about babies who couldn't eat, who fairies fed with their own milk and thus laid claim on them. 'Some children the fairies save,' her mother had said when she saw Emer expressing her milk. 'But you're only let to have them seven years. Your brother was one. That's why he was took into the sea. His time was up.'

'Ridiculous,' Rose said later. 'The old fool.' Despite everything she'd seen, Rose seemed to maintain a naïve, optimistic attitude towards anything that smacked of an underworld. As if it could be tidied away where it would no longer bother them. Most islanders pretended the same. It would never do to say you believed in such things out loud. It was asking for interference. Instead they gripped their rosary beads and called on saints and parcelled out holy water and fire, as if this were any less foolish.

Emer had been too drugged by this new ecstasy, this swoon that happened every time Niall pulled milk from her, to care what her mother said. None of the fairy world had come near her since the age of ten. But six months later, thinking of the imaginary nurse and Niall's strange eyes — they had developed a ring that looked like burning turf in the middle of the stormy sea blue — Emer's old desire to be taken was replaced by a fear that part of her, the only part of her that had ever been lovely, had already been claimed.

Emer told Patch she would not have any more babies. She told him something had gone wrong during Niall's birth, something inside her that would never heal (he looked away at that, the thought of anything inside her too much for him) and that if he came to her again and got her with child it would kill her. If it occurred to him not to believe her, he didn't say so. She thought he might be relieved. Emer knew what sex with her was like for him. Once she realised there would be no pleasure involved, she had stopped holding her hands back. When he entered her, and she pressed her palms lightly to his back, Patch was seized with a feeling that was similar to when he passed from happily drunk to miserably so. A weight bore down on him, a weight of misery he couldn't hope to escape, misery he could not stop from thrusting into until his release. The way he kept drinking past the point where it felt good any more. Once she'd known she was with child he had willingly backed away. When his young wife sat him down and told him they would never again have relations, he agreed with a nod and went out to the fields. If she didn't know him she might have wondered if he had even heard her. He found what he needed elsewhere, off the island on his tears, she knew this. They never spoke of it.

This was how Emer assured that no other babies would force her to take her eyes off this first one. She couldn't afford to be distracted. She'd seen how divided Rose was with multiple children. How early they wandered away from her, and Rose was often soothing the accident of a toddler while trying to nurse an infant. Emer couldn't risk this. Constant vigilance was required to hold on to Niall.

She never left the baby alone. If she was forced to go out to the cows or the well she tied him within her shawl or left the fire iron across his cradle like a prison bar. Until he was three, she dressed him like a girl and never cut his long dark curls, a tradition the islanders had abandoned, not remembering that the fairies preferred boy babies. She kept all the superstitions she once scoffed at or purposely broke during the time she wanted to be stolen herself. She buried a piece of burning turf in the ground in the hope that he would live, like the stories told, for seven hundred years. She brought him to Saint Brigid's well, the holy well that was kept secret by the islanders, said to cure illness and infertility and protect babies' souls. She didn't believe in the power of this well — if it were true she would have two eyes — but she did it anyway, just in case. She avoided the raths, didn't walk down the green road past Desmond's house but went around by the field instead, squirted the first release of the cow's udder into the dirt to appease the creatures under the ground. She crossed herself and glared blame at anyone who dared to admire him aloud. 'Don't overlook a child,' it was said on the island, for the compliment would render it vulnerable to snatching. Any time Niall was ill she didn't sleep, but sat up beside him drenched in her own terrified sweat, her neck pulled so tight she had to lean forward to manage each breath.

She let Rose put a woven Saint Brigid's cross over his cradle, and finger a trinity of holy water on his forehead. But Emer didn't trust Saint Brigid any more than she trusted the fairies. Her stories were so odd and warped with pagan magic and prediction — a druid prophesied that she would be born neither in the house nor out of it, and bathed and suckled on the milk of a red-eared fairy cow — she almost seemed worse.

The fairies wanted Niall, she was sure of it. They had left something in her, she was tethered to them, like a debt, and Niall was the payment. His fiery eyes, the way he could hear things no one else could, he seemed half-gone with the good people already. The memory of that fairy nurse, sliding her knife into his mouth and kneading Emer's milk, was enough to make her heart go crossways. They could come after you in the most unlikely places.

For years Emer held out hope that Patch would take them off the island. Take them to another part of Ireland where there was a lighthouse and a town and the land held no memory of what she owed it. But Patch made a bollocks out of all that. Drank on duty and let the light snuff out, causing a fatal collision of vessel and rock.

It's the evacuation Emer has pinned all her hopes on now. Perhaps, if they all leave and give the island back, the fairies will let her go. Instead of using the land and the sea to reach out like a long arm and drag her back every time she almost gets away.

* * *

They've been preparing for the bonfire for weeks, all the island rubbish collected from where it has lain in their gardens for the last year and moved to the field next to the small church. Furniture broken or rotted with damp, cardboard and paper, plastic containers, building materials, fence posts, weeds and old fishing nets, an old rotted door with a ship's window at the centre. Once, the fire was used as a religious ceremony for burning broken rosary beads and old scapulars, but in later years it has become the easiest way to rid themselves of modern rubbish.

Emer puts Niall down for a rest after tea and wakes him again at eleven. It is still dusk, grey-blue sky clinging to light that lasts for all but a few hours this time of year. They walk up the road and stop in to collect Brigid. When they pass Desmond's hay field, a piercing croaky cry rises out of the night silence. Brigid is startled.

'It's the corncrake!' Niall says, and starts calling back to it, imitating the repetitive raspy calls.

'I've been wondering what that was,' Brigid says. Niall tells her, as if he's conducting a schoolroom, that it's a bird, which only comes to the island in the summer, and croaks until it convinces a female to settle down underneath the nettles . . .

'It'll keep you up all night if it decides to nest there,' Emer says. 'We had one in our field last summer and I nearly went mad from the racket.'

'It does sound like an alarm clock you can't shut off,' Brigid says. 'But I've always slept through mine.'

'What's an alarm clock?' Niall asks. Brigid laughs and explains.

Emer can't stand the corncrakes. They cry all night, rhythmic sirens that pierce her brain, and she can still hear the echo long after dawn when it finally rests.

'Nana says they're the voices of fairies that have failed in their mischief,' Niall says brightly. Brigid chuckles, but Emer crosses herself.

The men are coming across the fields with torches; Emer can see the fire moving at the level of their heads. The torchbearers, who have brought the fire from their own hearths, converge on the pile and light it all together, their individual fires rushing towards each other's with a whoosh of paraffin oil. The men gather round the barrel of porter they rowed over that morning from the mainland. They have brought their own pint glasses from home. They call out friendly greetings to Brigid, who smiles easily at them.

Brigid seems to make a decision then, looking at the women gathered together, handing out sandwiches by the fire. She walks over before asking Emer and sticks her big hand out to Rose, bold and Yank as she can be.

'Thank you for the scones,' she says, and Rose beams as if they've been friends for ages.

'Brigid and Mary be with you,' Rose says to Brigid, and then their mother is offering her working hand, and Kathleen and Nelly and Margaret and Geraldine, and their aunties and cousins and grandmothers, and the next thing Emer knows they are all smiling and laughing. They ask if she is sorted in the house, as if they haven't ignored her and begrudged the time their husbands have given her for the last seven weeks. Emer stands back from it all. The children are lighting sticks and throwing them into the air. The teenagers are gathered in a clump, devising plans to pinch drink when the men aren't watching. She could have told Brigid weeks ago that this reception was only a matter of time, that as soon as it was clear that she wouldn't give up after a week, all she needed to do was approach them in their own territory. Mass would have done. They were harder to reach than the men, and kept to themselves more, but they were polite enough once you knew them. She can see the look of approval flitting between the wives. Brigid is sound enough. Not a hint of the mad family she came from. They can put aside the stories and stop wondering if she means any harm. She will never become one of them, she will never be far from suspicion, but they will let her believe she is.

Emer had wanted Brigid to herself. With one handshake, she belongs to all of them, and Emer finds herself on the perimeter again, dropping there naturally, like a coal spat aside and burning apart from the fire.

Halfway through the first barrel of porter, Malachy takes out his fiddle, Seamus the squeezebox and Michael Joe the bodhrán and the music starts up, jigs and reels and hornpipes, women and children dancing in the flickering light of the fire.

Then they start hooting and demanding that Austin sing. Emer backs away, sitting down on a wall away from the heat of the flames. She can't stand too close when Austin sings. He has a low, powerful voice that every generation of men in his family is known for. Emer hates her sister the most when she thinks of the moments Rose has that voice to herself, late at night in the darkness of their bed.

Patch's voice, when he chooses to use it, is high and grating, often so unbearable in the house that she fakes one of her headaches to get him to stop talking. He is happily drunk like the rest of them, but he will be the one to keep drinking when the others are done, keep drinking as long as he can still swallow. He will sleep outside, by the withering bonfire. He always does.

After twelve verses lamenting the Irish emigration to America, Austin asks Brigid to give them a song, and instead of blushing and waving them away, as Emer expects her to, she obliges.

A stór mo chroí, when you're far away
From the home you will soon be leaving
'Tis many a time by night and by day
Your heart will be sorely grieving
The stranger's land may be bright and fair

138

And rich in its treasures golden
You'll pine, I know, for the land long ago
And the love that is never olden.

This leaves Austin hooting and smiling as though he's poured her out of the keg himself. The women fall all over her again, praising her voice, which is tuneful, if rough. *Ah, go on, you're a great woman, altogether.*

A stór mo chroí. Treasure of my heart. One of the many endearments Emer shares with Niall that are meant for lovers. She wonders if Brigid even knows what it means.

The jigs and reels start up again, and the islanders take turns leaping over the edges of the fire. Brigid has a go, using her long legs to clear the flames with power. Emer has never jumped through, not even for luck before her wedding. Islanders say you can tell a couple's future by the way the flames leap. Austin and Rose made the thing blaze after them like a roar of approval before they were married. Emer imagines had she and Patch gone through it, the fire would have sputtered out in disappointment, or worse, lighted her up like a dry stick, as the dolt of her fiancé stood by and watched her eaten up into the summer night's air.

Emer is so preoccupied with watching Rose and Austin and Brigid, she forgets about watching Niall. She sees the other children first, giggling and pointing at something on the other side of the fire.

Niall is walking towards the bonfire. Not to light a stick or jump over the edge, but as if he means to enter straight into the heart of it. His eyes are flashing, the same colour as the flames that reach to fold him in. Emer is too far away to grab him herself, so she screams.

Everyone stops what they are doing and looks at her, when she meant for them to look at Niall. Only Brigid seems to know why she screamed. She steps up quickly to Niall and, knowing better than to touch him, just puts herself between his determined eyes and the fire and says his name softly. To Emer's surprise he stops, looks at her, his pupils pulsing as he tries to focus on something other than what he was seeing in the fire.

'May I have this dance?' Brigid says and Niall blushes, mumbles a no thank you and hurries to Emer's side. Now they are all looking at both of them, women tsking and men shaking their heads, and Niall presses his face into his mother's middle, trying to hide.

'I'm sorry, Mammy,' he says. She squeezes him tight, not trusting her voice to sound kind. Emer would like to put her hands on everyone, to grip them all until they can feel what she feels, until they are pulled into the dread that rises to choke her every day. But she has to keep her hands soft to stroke the hair of her son.

As soon as Niall learned to talk, Emer quizzed him mercilessly, asking him if he heard the fairies, heard the music, saw the lights. He was so eager to please her that he often said yes, he could hear music. When she appeared alarmed he said he hadn't heard a thing, and they would wind each other into a frenzy with Emer barking questions and Niall trying to answer what she wanted to hear. He'd end up in tears and Emer would feel like she was being choked by the grip of her fear.

She would have to stop herself then, from lashing out, from shaking him silly, so afraid he would be stolen from her that she was almost willing to hurt him if it made him understand.

Now that he is six, he knows the correct answers, or at least the ones that make her eyes stop spinning in her head. He knows the rules. Never take the food they offer. Don't be tempted to dance to fairy music, but run away, run as fast as you can in the other direction. Run to your mother.

'I will never go with them,' he has said, so many times, a small hand placed into the tension of his mother's forehead. All he needs to do is put his hand there and the headaches that once plagued her for whole days vanish in an instant. Only he can make her smile, wiping the look of pure terror away from his mother's face. But he can't take away the fear she has every day, that it will be her last day with him.

After a time the ceili resumes. Austin, a bit worse for drink now, is dancing slowly and shamelessly with Rose, who smiles as she closes her eyes and rocks against him. The older women say a few prayers for the crops and drop in a headless statue of Brigid and a plastic rosary that burns blue. The men will spread the ash over the fields in the morning, and will sober up in time to do it, albeit without moving their heads too quickly. Except Patch, of course. He won't recover for days.

Brigid comes over to stand next to Emer and Niall.

'So, what do the women have to say for themselves?' Emer asks. Brigid's jaw tightens.

'I've been invited for tea,' she sighs. They dodged her questions about the well, so.

As a consolation, and because she feels grateful for her quick reflexes with Niall, Emer tells Brigid to take some of the embers for her fire.

'When you move in or build a new house, you light the fire from a neighbour's or with the midsummer embers. Every fire on the island is said to come from Saint Brigid herself. We never let them go out. It brings luck to the house,' Emer pauses, then adds dismissively, 'so they say.'

'Is it the superstition that bothers you, or the optimism?' Brigid says, but so quietly to Emer that it is like a secret between them, rather than ridicule.

Brigid takes a tin mug from one of the women. Emer sees what happens next, and though everyone else is standing there, she seems to be the only one who notices. Brigid scoops a serving of glowing embers out of the fire. She fumbles a bit with the mug, drops some coals and picks them up with her bare hand and puts them back in. Not quickly, like someone avoiding a burn. She grips her palm around bright orange coals and holds them like they are nothing. Then she starts, and looks up, as if she has forgotten herself and is worried someone has seen. She looks straight at Emer and freezes for a moment, waiting, to see if Emer will react.

Normally, at the hint of anything so otherworldly, Emer would snatch her child and run in the other direction. But the fear that usually grips her neck is not there. Instead there is a little thrill that blooms larger when she sees Brigid wipe her fingers on her skirt, and the fingers come away clean, rough from house and farm work but not even slightly burned.

They walk back together, a mug of glowing midsummer between them, Niall half-asleep and stumbling, resting his face against her hip. When they say goodbye, Emer, in an unaccustomed gesture, can't stand the suspense, so she reaches away from Niall to squeeze a goodbye into Brigid's free hand. It is the same temperature as her own, the fingers bony, the skin a bit looser from age, calluses on the edges and softness at the centre, a hand just as disappointing as any other she has touched in her life.

Her neck tightens at the thought that she has been seeing things, inventing magic where it doesn't exist. That she and her son are alone in this, after all.

Then Brigid squeezes her fingers, and winks at her.

7

Beehive

July, 1959

Once the house is sorted, Brigid builds the hives. She asks Malachy in June, but by the time the timber and wire and tools arrive, July is half-gone. She builds the hive herself, impressing the men with her easy wielding of hammer and saw. She's done this before. She sands and paints the outside, carves inverted handles into the sides. She takes a lot of care, the men say to her, building a useless box. She smiles and ignores them, and assembles frames around squares of wire netting. Ten of them fit snugly together into the box, sliding in on perfectly spaced, painstakingly sanded grooves.

She makes a special trip off the island to collect the bees. She doesn't trust the invisible handoff that brings her everything else, from tools to towels to soap to books, to ferry something so precious and alive. She imagines it being left on the pub counter for two weeks, which happened once to her bag of apples. It costs her a small fortune to be driven to an apiary outside of Galway and spend the night in a hotel. The next day, she holds the buzzing cage wrapped in brown paper and string on her lap for the lift back and the currach over. Malachy

144

and Michael Joe row her the entire nine miles back to the island. The dark waves out at sea toss them so high in the air that when they finally fall it is as if Brigid has lost half her body in the process, the middle of her hooked by the sky as the rest drops back down to the plank seat. She hugs the cage with one hand and the seat with the other, trying not to dwell on the image of it flying overboard, dark water gulping down her precious box of life.

When she walks to her house, the newly painted yellow door beckoning all the way uphill, Brigid is not surprised to find Emer and Niall waiting for her. They come almost every day the weather allows it, so much that she often welcomes the torrential days where she can hear herself think again in her own house. It doesn't seem to occur to Emer that Brigid might crave solitude. Now that she has been to almost everyone's house for tea, Brigid knows there is no one on the entire island besides her who lives alone. People live with their children, their parents, their grandparents, their widowed sisters. Beds are flattened and full, siblings grow up sleeping to the rhythm of the others' breath. She has already deduced from Niall's comments that he and Emer sleep together, Patch banished to the hearth bed, a cushioned corner made up in every island house, for extra children and in-laws, right beside the fire.

Brigid still sleeps every night with the dog. Emer discovered this once while tidying the bedclothes.

'Ach, the dog's been in this,' she said and

Brigid made a crack about doing what she needed to keep warm. The look on Emer's face was as bad as if she'd said she was having sex with Rua. Niall was delighted and tried to sneak the pig into their bed the same night, which Emer tossed back outside with a squeal.

He has a way with animals, Niall does. The pig, which he has named Cabbage, half the size of the dog already, follows him everywhere. He can milk the most resentful cow, hypnotise sheep into submission when his father needs to sheer them. While Brigid gets pecked gathering her breakfast each morning, her hens allow Niall to pick them up, and they nest in the crook of his arm, cooing softly while he strokes the retracted feathery mound of their necks. He pockets their small, warm eggs as if they are jewels. Fur-matted cats hopping with fleas follow hopefully behind him on the road. And Rua, who still distrusts every other islander, especially Emer whose disapproving eye sends her tail curling between her legs, will actually play with Niall, play with the clumsy abandon of a puppy who has not yet been kicked.

This affinity for animals goes along with Brigid's general impression of Niall, that he is otherworldly, not fully with them, one ear half-heartedly listening to people while the other is attending to a world no one else can see. He is more than dreamy and self-absorbed. For much of the time, Brigid feels coldness around him, an empty pocket of air, as if he is not there at all. As if the life inside him has gone somewhere, and what is left is only pretending to be a boy.

146

She wonders if Emer knows the cause of this, but hasn't yet tried to ask. It is clear that something about him distresses her. She is always calling Niall back to her side, as if too many minutes away from her risk him not returning at all. Niall hasn't reached the age yet where this will bother him; he is still happy to reassure her.

Brigid is already too fond of Niall, but Emer is more difficult to relax around. Though she is used to Emer's one-eyed scowl of disapproval, her greeting today borders on hostile.

'We didn't know you were going over,' Emer says.

'I didn't know I needed to report my every move to you,' Brigid says. She keeps her voice light and winks at the boy. Niall has knelt down to kiss the face of Rua, who met her at the quay, wiggling herself into a frenzy, but now looks beaten down by Emer's tone. Niall tries very hard to make up for his mother.

'You might give a person a bit of warning,' Emer says. 'That dog of yours followed Niall home and howled at the door to be let in.'

'Did you let her?' Brigid looks at Niall. He grins. Emer grunts disgust. But she is deflating now, getting hold of herself. She backs off when she thinks she has gone too far. It's these moments that affect Brigid the most — watching this caustic girl try to make herself more likeable.

Brigid goes inside and puts her precious parcel on the table. Emer comes next, then Niall behind her. Brigid notices again how the two of them are like Irish weather in a room, ominous clouds followed by unexpected sunshine.

The fire and the kettle are already on. No one knocks here, they just call and poke their heads in if the top half of the door is left open for air. If Brigid's not home, Emer will let herself in anyway.

Emer sets about making tea. The parcel on the table begins to vibrate and buzz, and Emer's face grows white and pinched, her one pupil swelling with fear.

'What in the name of Saint Brigid is that?' she says hoarsely.

'Bees,' Brigid says, pouring fresh milk into her tea with a satisfying plop. 'For my hive.'

'That's what you went to town for? Were there not enough creepy-crawlies here for you already?'

Emer is not letting the package out of her limited sight.

'I haven't seen any honeybees,' Brigid says.

'There used to be,' Niall says. He has been encouraging the dog to jump up and put her paws on his shoulders, so they can dance. Emer snaps her head around and glares at him.

'Who told you that?'

'Auntie Rose.'

Emer makes the island gasp and silences herself with a large swallow of tea.

'Will you have honey, then?' Niall asks Brigid.

'That's why I got them,' Brigid says. 'Honey is the great cure-all. It'll save us from the winter colds.'

'Doesn't seem worth the work,' Emer says.

'Well, I have to keep busy, don't I?' Emer looks

away. She has remained stubborn about the well, but Brigid still pushes, even when she isn't asking directly.

'May I help?' Niall says.

'You won't go anywhere near those bees,' Emer says suddenly. 'If you do, I'll tell Himself to take the belt to ye.'

There is silence after this. Clearly this is not a threat she uses often by the betrayed look on Niall's face. Brigid is a little disorientated, hearing Emer refer to her husband with the same mocking, disrespectful title Brigid's mother once used for her father.

'It's safe enough,' Brigid assures her. 'There are ways of hypnotising them, with smoke. I've never been stung and I've been doing it for years.'

Emer stands suddenly, scraping her chair back. Brigid is sure she is going to leave, to storm away in a rage that will remain unexplained, dragging her disappointed but loyal son behind her. Good riddance, Brigid thinks. After a few days off she is wondering why she puts up with this snarled-up fist of a woman at all. As if she is fighting an invisible set of arms, Emer lurches forward, knocking into the table, then plops back down in her chair. Though she is clearly furious or, Brigid thinks, terrified, something inside her cannot leave. She reaches for her tea and drinks it down, one long swallow, for strength. Brigid and Niall stare at her, as if waiting to see what some invisible puppeteer will make her do next.

Brigid feels a pull of guilt, as if her own arms

are yanking the strings. She came here intending to escape this sort of thing, this confluence that she doesn't invite but grows like a weed in the space that reaches between herself and other women. Emer needs something from her, something that Brigid is no longer willing or even able to provide. Not to another adult. She wants a baby, but instead she has these two misfits, hanging around and not telling her how to get it.

Niall comes over and puts his hand on Emer's forehead, swiping the palm across like he's wiping moisture from her brow. Then he leans in close, touching his forehead to hers. For the first time Brigid sees her smile. It fades quickly, it is not something meant for anyone else to see. But it is gorgeous, it transforms her, she looks more like her son than anything like herself. Something tugs on Brigid, low in her belly, and she has to look away to stop it from pulling her any more.

She pours more tea, and Emer nods slightly at the consolation.

*　*　*

After tea, Brigid heads out to her handmade hive to release the bees. Niall, at the instruction of his mother, climbs up on the stone wall, so he can see what she's doing without getting too close. Emer keeps an eye on him from even farther away, leaning inside the back door, the bottom half of it shut tight.

Brigid sets the cage down on the ground. She has taken the paper wrapping off and can see the bees now, clustered in the corners of two mesh windows. She lifts the outer and inner cover off her hive. She takes three frames out to create a gap and lifts the travel cage, thrumming with what feels like fire, and begins to pry out with her knife the sugar can that plugs the opening. It moves up with difficulty, anchored by sticky wax. When she finally lifts the can, bees spill out the edges of the hole calmly, as if they can't even fly. She reaches her hand inside the writhing hole and pulls out the small wooden box, no bigger than a tin of tobacco, covered in a thick coating of bees, like it has been dipped in them.

'These are the queen's attendants,' Brigid calls up to Niall, shaking them gently off into the hive. Now she can see the mesh circle and the queen bee inside. 'Right here is a plug of candy that the bees will slowly eat through to let her out.' She removes the wax on one end of the cage with her knife and uses it to secure the queen's box to the side of one of the frames. The bees are starting to wake up now, to fly and buzz and swarm around her. The majority of them are still clustered together, intimately swarmed, crawling all over each other in massive clumps of what has always looked to Brigid like love.

She turns the cage over and gives it a few sharp shakes, and bees shower in as cleanly as flour into a bowl. She hears Niall draw his breath in wonder. A few vertical turns and thumps to empty the inner corners, then she replaces the frames, swipes the edges free of stragglers before putting the inner cover on, then upends the sugar can on top of the escape hole. She explains

151

to Niall that this will feed the bees until they have built their combs, until they are settled and the queen is laying eggs and the workers are divided and given their duties.

'There are three types of bee,' she says to Niall. 'The queen, the female workers, and the male drones. The drones are only for fertilising the queen. They don't do anything else. They can't even sting. It's the women who rule the bee world.'

Niall nods, but it seems like he is not really listening to her. His eyes are unfocused, like he's turned them off. He is listening to the bees. She sets another wooden box on top of the sugar can, and then the outer cover, the top of which she has covered with shiny metal, to pull the sun. She walks away to let them settle in, a small cloud of anxious guards circling the box, painted in the same deep yellow she used to transform her door. Most of the bees have stayed inside, snuggling down into their new home. She thinks of one of her first nights on the island, curling up with the heavy cotton sheet and pillowcases that Emer returned. She had hung them on Brigid's clothes line, so that although they were slightly damp, they were infused with fresh sea air and sunshine.

One little rebel tries to sting her as she walks away. But it changes its mind because, as it lands on her neck, it is overwhelmed by a feeling of dopey peace and forgets its intended attack. She brushes it gently away and it flies back to the hive. She wasn't completely honest with Emer, she still gets stung. But she has grown immune to it. It is a pinch, nothing more, the swelling and pain that follow for others hasn't happened to her since she was a girl.

While she explains to Niall how she will harvest the honey, Emer makes fresh bread at the table, with such violent arm movements the dog retreats outside to avoid her. She looks as if she's trying to calm herself down after witnessing some violation. Brigid watches Niall go over and put a hand on her arm, which helps her to calm her jerky movements and take a breath and let whatever is trapped inside her — anger and misery and fear — move to the edges, like the outer ring of disturbed bees, so that her core can get on with its work.

★ ★ ★

Over the next week, Niall finds ways to come alone to see the bees. It is not easy for him to get away from his mother, Brigid knows, she is the nervous, hovering type. He convinces her to let him bring his father and uncle their midday meal — bottles of tea wrapped in woollen socks, scones and thickly buttered brown bread, boiled eggs wrapped tightly together in a cloth parcel. There is too much work now, at the height of the summer, for the men to come home for lunch. He promises to sit and eat with them, but instead leaves the food and walks the wrong way to Brigid's house, while his mother is occupied with Rose and all of his girl cousins. Brigid always has candy for him, and a lovely concoction of warmed milk and honey, so sweet it leaves a pleasant ache in his mouth.

She brings him to the hives and pulls out the frames, showing him how quickly the workers have established their hexagonal wax city, where they separate the jobs of tending to young from producing and storing food. Niall's effect on the bees is similar to her own — he soothes them into sleepiness. Neither of them needs smoke to hypnotise the bees into submission, even while taking honey. Brigid knew this already about Niall, that he would be safe and useful, and that Emer had no need to worry. Still, he makes her promise not to tell his mother. She does this easily. She has been accused before, because she is not a mother, of taking children too seriously. Of keeping their secrets, as though she were a child herself. It is not childishness, but longing that compels her. She can pretend they are hers, for as long as it takes to tell a secret. Just as she is distracting herself with this exercise in life — helping bees make a home so they can make more bees and flowers — Niall is a distraction from the urge she has to go back to crawling across the wet ground howling with need. Niall is a great help to her, another pair of hands for the tricky pulling apart and putting together of the intricate puzzle of the hive, and he calms her down. His mother, Brigid thinks, worries too much.

★ ★ ★

They have the hive open when Emer catches them. She runs all the way there, after Fiona reports that Niall is not where he is supposed to

154

be. In fairness, Rua tries to warn them, but they don't stop to notice her slinking, whining performance, too entranced by the humming, sweetly fragrant bees. Amidst them, it is impossible to hear the back door or the squelch of Emer's bare feet across the damp grass. Brigid notices the bees' reaction before she even sees Emer there.

They start to swarm. Lifting out of the hive in massive sheets, forming, by some complex communication of pheromones, a single-minded cloud. It hovers above them for a moment, awaiting instructions. Brigid thinks they are leaving, because the only time she ever sees this behaviour is when the hive gets crowded and the older bees decide to move on to let the younger bees flourish. Niall looks up at the cloud with a distracted smile on his face, cocking his head as if trying to decipher something beneath what Brigid realises, too late, is an angry thrum. The dog barks. Emer shrieks her son's name.

Then he is gone, swallowed whole by the swarm, which has morphed to resemble the shape of a boy. Emer is running to him.

For a beat, Brigid thinks he will be all right. She thinks they have covered him with the same sleepy silence that they sometimes cover her hands. Then Niall begins to scream.

Emer is trying to wipe the bees off him, like sluicing water from hair after a swim. Any part of him she uncovers is quickly swallowed up again. Brigid, knocking her aside, ducks and pushes her shoulder into his hips, bending him in half and lifting him off the ground. The bees are stinging

155

her now. She runs for the well, a thick stream of water that runs over rocks and collects in a stone pool, before falling off a small cliff to the ocean. Not the well she's been hoping to find, but large enough to submerge a bee-covered boy. She lays him down in it and holds him under the flow by lying down on top of him, the icy water seeping through her shirt to assault her breasts and stomach. The bees rise again, what is left of them, making their way back to the hive. The rest, dead, a thousand of them, float in the water and cling to Niall's clothing like black and yellow moss.

When she pulls Niall from the water, he is already swollen, his neck huge, his lips deformed, his breath an inefficient desperate wheeze. Brigid lays him on dry rock, opens his mouth and clears it of the bees that have made their way inside.

'What's happening?' Emer says. The sound coming from Niall's throat is horrible.

'He's allergic,' Brigid says and she shakes her head at her own stupidity. 'Did you know he was allergic?'

Emer is beyond answering her, she is reaching for him and Brigid loses patience, knocking her away for the second time. Brigid spreads her large hands over Niall's throat.

It is painfully familiar, the pull that ransacks her, the distinctly sensual rupture she had sworn she would leave behind.

Then she is being sick quietly onto a cluster of bright yellow lichen, and Emer is holding Niall, wet and shaking with fear, his lips and throat and face back to a reasonable size. Niall holds his bare arm out and brushes stingers, which gather like wet stubble into clumps he flicks on to the grass.

'You said you wouldn't let any harm come to him,' Emer says, when Brigid has stopped retching.

'I'm sorry,' Brigid says. She looks up expecting daggers, but the way Emer is looking at her is not what she expected. Another thing she'd thought she'd left behind.

'Some touch,' Niall says, smiling and pulling Brigid's gaze away from his mother's, inserting himself between them, clean as a knife.

The three of them sit for a while, until the bees that are left settle down, until Niall and Brigid begin to shiver from the wet weight of their clothing and Emer, no longer in a frenzy of buzzing fear she arrived with, suggests tartly that it is time they go inside.

★   ★   ★

Back at the house, they won't leave. Brigid is spent, irritable, she wants to be alone. But they hover around her, Emer makes her a plate of smoked fish and brown bread and heats water for more tea. Niall rolls around on the floor with the dog. Brigid wishes briefly that the bees had attacked Emer — the one who angered them, she is sure of it — instead. And that she hadn't interfered.

Emer sits down across from her, watching her eat. She is deciding whether to say something.

157

Brigid silently encourages her not to.

'They took my eye,' she says.

'Who did?' Brigid doesn't want to know this, but she can't back away now.

'The bees,' Niall says.

'No,' Emer says. 'The fairies.'

'I'm sorry.' Brigid doesn't know what she's supposed to say. She is not hungry now and she is suddenly so exhausted she wants to push her tea aside and put her head right down on the table.

With a quick, whispery argument, Emer sends Niall out to fetch water, reminding him to stay away from the bees. She watches him from the small window.

'That's what I have,' Emer says. 'What those bees tried to do. It's in my hands.' Brigid doesn't want to talk about Emer's hands. She doesn't even want to look at them.

'It can't touch you,' Emer says. 'Same as with Niall.'

Brigid feels hot, like something is rising out of her, it's all she can do to keep herself in her chair. Part of her wants to stand up and knock this girl over, the other part wants to clench her vicious hand and lead her into the other room, press her down on the bed. She never should have let them in.

'They say your grandmother was taken.' Brigid refuses to look up, but she is listening. 'By the fairies, like. Your mother was the child of that changeling. Her own father tried to drown her and she washed back up again, good as new. They called her a witch. The islanders said it, there was some test they had, and she passed. Or failed, depends on how you look at it. She left the island as a girl, got away from them and nobody saw how.'

Brigid can't swallow any more. There is something, large as life, lodged in her throat.

'They say she couldn't die,' Emer says. 'That's the story about her. That she was touched by the fairies and was immortal because of it.' Brigid flinches thinking of the bruises and cuts on the flawless flesh of her mother. A lifetime of attempts that were healed, one by one.

'Oh, she died all right,' Brigid says. 'Eventually.'

Emer comes back from the window, sitting down across from Brigid. She puts her hands on the table between them. They both look at them. Work-roughened, red and peeling, but still, underneath that, they are as young as a girl's. They don't have the loose skin of Brigid's, youth starting to let go its tight grip on bone. Brigid puts her hands in her lap, pressing her fists, an old habit, to the lowest, emptiest part of her belly.

'If you've the healing in your hands,' Emer says, 'what do you want Saint Brigid's well for?'

But Niall comes in and stops them from sharing any more.

★ ★ ★

Brigid has a recurring dream. In the dream she stands in front of a mirror and sees in her reflection something she never sees while awake. An absence, a mildness, which smoothes her features and makes her young, younger than

159

she's ever been, because even as a child her face was burdened. In the dream her face has no fear, no regret, no desire. Absence and peace. Despite the warnings of her mother, and now Emer, Brigid believes that this island is where she will find her dream face, a peace that has eluded her for her whole life. That with enough tea and turf and walking in wind that screams in her ears, her face might settle into the one from her dream, where she is no longer torn apart by feelings of others, free from desire and all its disappointments. Where the slack failure of her belly might smooth away and leave her, where the memories of what she took for years, from countless women who trusted her and laid back while she pulled them inside out, will fade into the mild, blameless blue of ocean and sky. Where what she has been can disappear so the thing she wants has room to become. She crawls into the stone huts of nuns and thinks of their sacrifice, their letting go, those who lived with nothing and cherished it. She'd like to be empty. She'd like to be emptied of it all and feel as if she is full. She'd like to make room for what she wants to come next.

But now what came before is beginning all over again. Now the islanders will know what she can do and will expect it. Now there will be so much coming into her she will not be able to be empty and receive the only thing she truly wants. Now another damaged, deadened girl has felt a promising twinge in her presence and is looking at her hungrily, wanting Brigid to show her what it means. And Brigid won't be able to resist.

8

St Brigid's Home for Wayward Girls

1933–1936

Every one of the Sisters sounded like Brigid's mother. They had emigrated as an entity, an exodus of Brigidine nuns from Connemara who came to Maine to start a Home for Wayward Girls. The rumours about why they were there were thick, layered by years of speculation in the minds of their imaginative charges. That they had once been wayward girls themselves, that they'd all had babies, and if you lifted the dark folds of their skirts you would find the evidence, skin that had been stretched then vacated and left not quite the same. Once the evidence of their shame was taken away, they were given habits and made to care for the next crop of impregnated girls as penance. Some thought that the nuns were the babies — that they'd been born to unwed mothers in Ireland, raised by nuns and expatriated to do the same; shame, beat and leave hopeless a whole new generation of sinful girls.

This was suggested during a dorm room discussion, voices rising from the thin, squeaky cots. Every ten minutes the door would open, Sister Margaret would say, 'Whisht!' with the same vicious impatience as Brigid's mother once

161

did. It only shut the girls up for a few seconds.

'If that was true,' a girl named Mary said, 'what happened to the boy babies?'

'Priests.'

'Drowned.'

'Eaten!' The voices came in quick succession out of the darkness.

'There weren't any boys,' a girl said. 'Everyone knows those babies are always girls. That's how God punishes you.'

'Of course there were boys,' a girl named Jeanne said, dismissively. She had a grainy, mannish voice. 'The boys get adopted by rich folks in Boston. They go to Harvard. Then they knock up their girlfriends and send them back here.' There was a silence as everyone digested this.

Jeanne had stringy brown hair, a bald patch worn above her forehead where she couldn't stop pulling it out. One eye and cheek were given over to a wine-stain birthmark, and the saturation of colour changed with her mood. She smoked cigarettes and had fat, wormy scars on her arms from when, rumour had it, she had once tried to kill herself. She was the same age as Brigid, twelve, but seemed old before her time. Brigid hadn't had the nerve to talk to her yet, but Jeanne often caught her staring, which left Brigid hot, confused and mortified.

All the girls in this dorm were either too young or too lucky to be pregnant, they were here because they were orphaned or molested or abandoned. Not unwed mothers or adoptable babies, but unwanted and in-between.

162

'Why do the *boys* get adopted?' someone whined in the dark.

'What are you, some sort of retard?' Jeanne said, and Sister Margaret came in again, whishting, and this time they settled down, not so much out of obedience or sleepiness but because they were too discouraged to continue the topic. In the silence, Brigid could still hear them all, a roomful of girls, turning fact and fiction over in their minds, the same way their lean, underdeveloped bodies flipped like fish between the stiff sheets.

★ ★ ★

Brigid had never gone to school, never done a callisthenic or purposeful exercise, never ridden a bike or counted money. She'd never had a friend. Unlike the girls who had come from farms, she had not handled horses or cleaned out stalls, and though on the island they'd once had hens, they refused to lay eggs for so long her father had just wrung their necks. Their milk, sour and smelling of urine, had come from a moody little goat that submitted to her mother's hands with a look of pure disgruntlement. Brigid was a terrible cook, she couldn't sew a stitch, and she had never seen a mop.

At the convent she was expected to work. Clean and scrub and wring until her hands were cracked and bleeding from the harsh soap and hot water. Overnight, alone in her bed, she ran healing fingers over the skin, until she realised that if the nuns saw you had smooth hands they

163

made you do even more. So she let the raw cracked skin form into calluses that dirt could not escape from.

Before breakfast they worked, after breakfast they had school in their scrubbed out class-rooms. Brigid could read but had no concept of what to do with numbers, so she often ended up grouped with the six-years-olds. After school were exercises in the cold yard, jumping jacks and running in circles, tennis against a cement wall. Then more work. Dishes, laundry, toilets, floors. Cleaning was a never-ending process, much like the purification of their souls. They would never be pure, but they were expected to attack the tarnish daily. Prayer was an astringent, prayer and penance, like bleach and scalding water. Kneeling on stone for so long it felt as if your kneecaps had shattered under the pressure and you could barely limp back to your dorm. Lashings, given not so much as a punishment for rudeness or shirking but as a lesson in the graceful acceptance of pain, girls' backs ripped into ridges that would heal and form a shell they could bear their life upon.

Once a week, in the early hours before an interminably long Mass, the girls lined up in the pews of the chapel and went behind the altar to confess to Father Hanrahan. He came on Sundays only, up from Bangor, and seemed equally uninterested in the nuns and the girls. It was said he was only there for show, that every such place needed a priest to maintain the illusion that someone was in charge. He spent five minutes with each girl. He tried to glean something, anything, out of Brigid, she suspected at the prompting of Mother Superior, but she remained as monosyllabic as she'd been since arriving. 'If you don't let it out, my child,' he said once, 'the sin will fester inside you. It will eat your soul away. Let it out so God can forgive you.'

'Yes, Father,' she said, but she didn't volunteer anything.

He eventually sighed and gave her handfuls of Our Fathers and Hail Marys, prayers she didn't know, and traded her for a more malleable girl, one who liked to try to shock him or another who burst into tears over her own unworthiness. Brigid kept her soul locked up tight.

★ ★ ★

Most of the other girls ignored her. She didn't try to get attention, wasn't vying for the roles of rebel or saint, hardest worker or cleverest student or basket case. She worked at being invisible, and they allowed it. Only Jeanne could not leave her alone.

'I heard your mother murdered your father,' she would say when they were scrubbing in adjacent stalls in the bathroom. 'How did she do it? Did you help?' The other girls stiffened with anticipation when they heard the cruel things Jeanne said to her. But Brigid, who had grown up with parents who sometimes spat the worst things that came to their mind, ignored her. Jeanne was worshipped by most of them. She cursed readily and creatively. She was known for alarming sessions in deserted broom closets and bathrooms where she would wrench something violent and luscious out of another girl's body, something most girls, especially the young ones, had barely suspected was there, and leave them limp and wondering when she might do it again. Most of the girls, the ones of a certain age where something was happening that no one bothered to explain, watched Jeanne with breathless hunger, wondering when it would next be their turn for the few thrilling moments in a bathroom stall, trapped against the cold tile wall, Jeanne's hands working on them until they could barely stand up. The lucky ones were captured by her in an empty dorm, or in one of the offices with leather sofas. If you met up with Jeanne and there was an available surface, something you'd never even imagined would happen. She would lay you down and do something that later the girl could barely explain, something that left their faces fired with shame and revisited delight.

Brigid, when she heard these whispered rumours, late at night in her hard, exposed bunk, turned over and pressed the pillow around her ears, trying not to think about Jeanne's huge, chapped, angry mouth.

★ ★ ★

At St Brigid's there was a separate floor for the pregnant girls. They came when their bellies were no longer easy to hide, and left after the baby was born and given away. They had their own schoolroom, which wasn't used very much, the idea being that if they could read and write there wasn't much use in bothering after that. The lucky ones would still get to finish school, or get married, but most of them would end up doing alternate versions of what they did now, laundry, scrubbing other people's waste off toilets, boiling up tasteless, filling meals for large crowds. The younger girls rarely got to see them, because their sins were so garish and alive, bellies like enormous blisters underneath their frumpy uniforms. The littlest girls, before they were unceremoniously told how it all worked, thought there was something contagious about the swollen stomachs, that either you could become engorged yourself if you were touched by them, or that the broken morality that landed them there could seep into you, and eventually cause you to make the same life-ruining mistake.

What Brigid noticed most about these girls, when she glimpsed them move, not so gracefully, through the hallway past their classroom, was that they weren't girls any more. They were not much older than she was, the youngest swollen belly belonged to a girl of thirteen, but the babies inside them transformed them into something else. The lewd jut of the belly, the small gestures that surrounded it, hands placed without thought on the top, or slid underneath like a ballast, showed that whatever child the girl had been before had been swallowed up by the new one growing inside.

They were supposed to be a warning, these girls, trapped by their sins, lonely for their families, not allowed to keep their babies. Brigid couldn't get enough of them. She volunteered for jobs that gave her glimpses, sweeping the hall near the room where they sewed, their enormous forms wedged between their chairs and the frantic sewing machines. She washed windows so she could watch their halting, unbalanced exercise in the yard. She lay in her cot at night, rolled up her itchy nightgown, and ran her rough palms over a child's flat chest and belly, closed her eyes and imagined a swelling, a growth, a body full of something else, something that was, mercifully, not her. Like the changeling she once begged for, not from the ground, but forged from the very soul that desired it.

When babies were ready to be born, the doctor's car came and stayed the night. The doctor often took the baby away with him, a basket in his passenger seat permanently there for this purpose. Only occasionally would a couple come to St Brigid's, young, healthy, ridiculously happy people that took the baby and left behind a foul mood. No one liked such blunt happiness displayed in the corridors of St Brigid's, least of all the nuns. It didn't belong, and left everyone fantasising about things they'd sworn to leave behind.

Sometimes, the baby died. The nuns always said that this was a blessing.

★ ★ ★

Jeanne was the first girl Brigid healed. She was known for getting the worst of Sister Josephine's whippings, a masochistic nun who would stop

168

only when a girl begged forgiveness, because pure stubbornness meant she passed out before ever giving in. She liked to pull up her nightgown and show her scars to new girls, just for the satisfaction she got from the release of their lip, the tremble, the tears when they realised, with a glimpse of her ugly back, what their life here would be like. She had tried it on Brigid when she'd first arrived and the other girls had gaped at how easily Brigid, who had barely spoken to anyone, laughed.

Jeanne paid her back for that laugh two weeks later. She and Brigid were cleaning the dormitory bathroom and Jeanne attacked with no warning, a punching, kicking, hair-pulling dervish. Brigid didn't hit back, but did what her mother used to, made herself as small as possible to minimise the damage, and waited for Jeanne to give up. By the time she did, the white tiled floor was brilliant with blood. A kick had made it through to her nose. Sister Josephine pulled Jeanne off her and dragged her to her office for a caning, and Sister Margaret, a gentle but ineffectual nun, gave Brigid a cloth for her bleeding nose and walked her to the infirmary. Sister Margaret cleaned the blood off Brigid's face with astringent and hot water, but found no wounds or bruises underneath. Since she wasn't injured, she sent Brigid along to be caned as well. When Brigid arrived at the sister's office, two other nuns were carrying the unconscious Jeanne to the infirmary.

Sister Josephine hit her twice, two hard, slicing blows, before Brigid said it was enough and that

169

she was penitent. The nun was surprised, sure Brigid would be the stubborn one, let one more fly before sending her on her way.

She watched the corridor until Sister Margaret left the infirmary for afternoon prayers, then stepped in to find Jeanne lying on the cot behind a white screen. Jeanne was so occupied with stifling her convulsive sobs that she didn't hear Brigid come over to her. She was lying on her side in only her underwear, her back pulpy with scars and fresh lashings sliced through them. There was so much there, so many times she'd been hit or begged to be hit again, that Brigid realised, as she reached out to touch it, how hard Jeanne had worked to build up such armour. She was sorry that she had laughed at it. The whole time Jeanne had been hitting her, Brigid had been waiting for this part, the part that came later, the penance.

Jeanne turned her head at the first touch, but before she could react, throw her off, sit up and try to fight her again, Brigid put one hand on her back and the other she brought to Jeanne's mouth, crossing a finger over her lips that asked for promised silence. She spread her fingers out over the bloody gashes, closed her eyes and pulled. The heat came out pulsing, angry, and coarse, so different from the quality of her own wounds that at first Brigid thought something was wrong, and that she would not be able to do it. Jeanne's wounds lashed out at her, pulling the places in her body not in one long slow climax, but in quick wallops of pleasure, so that by the time she was done and the wounds were gone,

Brigid felt not peaceful like she usually did, but unfinished. She used her hands, hot and full and still tingling, to turn Jeanne over on to her now painless back. Jeanne's body was caught in the middle of a metamorphosis. Girl with woman half-emerged, with lean, childish hips and hard, swollen lumps of breasts that poked up with the same angry defiance as her face. Footsteps in the hallway startled them both, Jeanne pulled the white sheet up to her neck and Brigid reeled back, overcome with nausea, and Sister Margaret came in to find her vomiting in the white sink.

★ ★ ★

That night Brigid lay awake, her heart bonging, waiting for something to happen. She saw Jeanne get up, slipping soundlessly through the shadows, and she counted to sixty before getting up to follow her. Jeanne went to the infirmary, and when Brigid arrived there she found the girl already lying naked in the same spot they'd been interrupted. She thought of her father and his studio and the apologies she never got, and reached a hand out to touch her. Jeanne's back arched, she closed her eyes. Brigid lifted her nightgown above her head and climbed on to the table and pressed into another girl all she had once wanted pressed into her. They opened their legs and mouths and hands, and what Brigid once imagined growing between her parents grew between them, for a terribly long time, something that cracked her open and never went away. Even after it was over and they were hastily

171

dressing, worried about nuns patrolling the hall, it was still there, waiting impatiently for the slightest touch before it would swell again and take them over.

Later that night in her cot, when Jeanne came to slip under the covers with her, it was as if they had never let go, as if they had been pressed together for the hours in between, waiting for the right moment to begin to move.

★ ★ ★

In the summer, they worked outside. They sunburned until their skin peeled off in swathes, leaving a lighter imprint of freckles underneath. They planted seeds, watered, weeded and picked what grew from them. They milked cows, stole eggs from angry hens, and tended the bees: a whole city skyline of tall wooden hives with drawers that needed two girls to pull them, heavy with the honey the nuns sold to the town market. They weren't meant to taste it, but they did, feeding each other fingerfuls when no one was looking. Brigid got used to the sound of bees behind everything she did, a dizzy buzz urging her through chores, towards the next moment she and Jeanne could steal alone.

They found each other every day, capturing slivers of privacy in a place where their every move was watched. Lying down in blueberry fields, standing against giant oak trees in the woods. Brigid loved to watch Jeanne's face, the way her birthmark darkened and the cruel mask fell away, as she lost herself to Brigid's hands.

Jeanne called it making love. This name made sense to Brigid. She had waited for love but now knew it had to be made, sometimes by ripping something apart and sealing it back together again, or pulled out of someone the way they were learning to pull clay into the walls of a cup. You built it, with fire and clay and honey and skin. You made love. They hid this because they were supposed to, but not one bit of it felt wrong.

★ ★ ★

The first time she bled, a year after arriving, when she was thirteen, she was no longer naïve enough to try to heal it. You couldn't live with twenty girls, half of whom had entered puberty, and not know that at some point blood would begin to drip under your dress. The nuns said it was a punishment for being a woman, but some of them, your first time, would let you lie down for the afternoon with a hot brick. Jeanne was shocked when she found out the holes in Brigid's reproductive knowledge. Though she had breasts now, Brigid, breasts that grew so quickly she needed a larger dress every month, breasts as soft and welcoming as Jeanne's were angry and hard, and her period, she had missed some important information somewhere. She believed that now that she was bleeding, Jeanne would be able to put a baby inside her. Jeanne felt almost bad about shattering the delusion, but not bad enough to be gentle about it.

'You moron,' she said. 'You need a boy for that.'

It was a while before she learned that Jeanne didn't have all the facts either. But even when she knew it was from a boy, she still wanted it, wanted a baby growing inside her with the same longing that drove her to press her hands into wounds, or her mouth to Jeanne's chapped lips. The longing to be rescued. It seemed, in the short time she'd known about it, exactly what she was meant to do. She was dejected when Jeanne first told her. There was no part of her that desired to do with a boy the things she did with Jeanne. Other than the priest, Brigid hadn't seen a man since the doctor that dropped her off. There was another doctor, one who slipped in to deliver the babies, but they never saw him. Apparently she would need a boy, at some point, to get what she wanted. She hoped to find the kind that quickly disappeared, like the ones who had abandoned the girls at St Brigid's, while their babies were still growing.

Jeanne thought she was crazy. No one except rich, married women with nothing better to do actually wanted to have a baby. It ruined you. It stretched your body and then ripped its way out, they'd all heard the screams. Sometimes the girls even died while it tried to get out. Even if they lived, no one was allowed to keep it. The babies were carted away and the girl was left leaking blood and milk and ruined for any sort of normal life where you could live happily ever after. Jeanne had heard of girls who had survived the birth, left St Brigid's and had gone on to kill themselves after all.

Yes, there were those who did it on purpose to

snag a particular boy. But often that backfired, like with Jeanne's cousin Myra who was awaiting her due date upstairs, and then you lost the boy, the baby and your life. It just wasn't something a normal girl would *want* to do. She was so vehement, Brigid stopped talking about it, but the fantasy continued in her mind. Her belly grown hard, full of blood and flesh that was not hers, but was more a part of her than anyone could have been. More a part of her than her parents, who had been too caught up in their dance of brutality and forgiveness to love her, more than this rough, desperate girl who seemed to want to be violated to match what was happening in her mind. More than any of them, a baby would be the closest Brigid could come to love. She imagined it like stealing, more of an abduction than a creation, but once you'd got the baby, there was no chance of another world taking it back. Not if you held on tight enough.

That she was a child herself, planning on having a child, never occurred to her. She hadn't felt like a child in a long time. She wasn't even sure she had ever been one.

★　★　★

Jeanne was taken from her bed the night her cousin Myra went into labour. Something was wrong. They wouldn't have come for her, thought Brigid, awake and listening from her cot, if everything were going to plan. Jeanne hadn't even seen her cousin since the first day she'd arrived, when the Mother Superior had

175

allowed them a brief reunion visit in her office. Jeanne told Brigid that Myra had talked the entire time about her boyfriend, who was going to come and get her as soon as he saved up enough money.

'She's an idiot,' Jeanne summarised.

A few hours later, Brigid was woken again by Jeanne's familiar hands, and she could tell before she opened her eyes that someone was with her. The hands were tentative, tapping at her as if they'd never touched before. Brigid opened her eyes. Mother Superior was there. She instructed Brigid to put on a dressing gown and they went out to the corridor.

'I'm not sure why I'm allowing this,' Mother Superior said. 'But Jeanne seems to think you have an ability to help. Do you, Brigid?'

Brigid glared at Jeanne. She had promised not to tell anyone. She didn't want to do it any more, now that she'd found other ways to share her body.

'Yes, Mother,' she said, wishing, not for the first time, that she was just a normal child with no idea what to do except cry for help when encountering someone else's pain.

* * *

Even when her father died, there hadn't been this much blood. It was everywhere, smeared across the floor by the panicked soles of the nuns, burying the doctor up to his elbows, christening foreheads like dried up dabs of muddied ash. It came out of Myra like

176

something being washed in from the sea, clotting into enormous sacs. Brigid imagined if you broke one apart, you'd find a baby hiding inside. But the baby was still in Myra. Stuck.

Brigid was led up to that space, the space between Myra's legs that was the centre of so much panic, even the doctor, tired and out of ideas and fed some lie about Brigid's mother being a midwife, was stepping aside to let her in. Myra was in too much pain, screaming, thrashing, struggling to close her legs which were held open by two blood-spattered and terrified-looking nuns, to even know that Brigid was there. Someone poured something clear and stinging over Brigid's arms.

Somehow she knew what to do. She put her hands on Myra, first one and then the other, as easily as if she were sliding them into wet clay. Myra stopped screaming. She whimpered, like someone whose pain has backed off, but the memory of it is still spilling over. The blood stopped gushing out, though this was hard to tell because of all that was already there. The baby had ripped places that Brigid sealed even as she reached for it. She felt the small hard joints, an ankle, a knee, the heel bone of a miniature foot. The leg pulled away from her, curling in on itself like something afraid. The baby was hiding, no intention of coming out, holding on, willing to let her mother bleed to death before leaving the only place that was safe. Brigid held on to it, letting her healing hands soothe a baby that was not injured, only afraid. She slowly turned it around so she could cradle the head, fists clenched to its chin, and gently, with no pain for Myra and a silent promise to the reluctant baby, she pulled it, long and slimy and covered in a white, waxy crust that beaded away blood, out into the harsh white room. Instead of handing the baby to the doctor or one of the nuns, Brigid stepped forward, laying it on the bloody sheets draped on Myra's still massive belly. The baby curled back up again, like a rubber band snapped back into shape, and stopped crying, as if that was where it belonged. Before they pulled her away, while she sealed the last rip in Myra that her own hands had helped make, Brigid saw the look on Myra's face. The pain had been gone for a while, as had the fear of dying. As soon as Brigid had first touched her, Myra knew she wouldn't die. But the way she looked at that baby, as if it were just as horrifying as the wobbly clots of blood that came before it, made Brigid want to snatch it back, hide it in her nightgown, run away. Apologise for exposing it to this in the first place. Myra closed her eyes and turned her head and let the nuns, once the doctor pulled Brigid away and cut the cord, remove the baby from its place on top of her, as if its weight meant nothing at all.

★ ★ ★

The doctor was not like she'd imagined him. Brigid had never seen him up close, only the form of his shoulders and hat as he was rushed in and out to deliver and remove these little lives. She had assumed he was like the priest, old and

178

craggy-faced and revolting, without a hint of kindness, but his face was young, open and feminine, with the large, barely blinking eyes of a deer. His lashes were long and wet and it was clear that he had not yet in his life needed to shave. He came and stood next to her while she washed her hands in the enormous sink, watching the blood fade to pink, form a whirlpool around the drain and swirl away. He held a hand up and she thought he was going to touch her shoulder, but when she cringed, he put it down on the edge of the sink.

'It's easier when they don't want to hold them,' he said.

Brigid said nothing. She was looking at his hands, delicate, smooth, with long fingers and only the slightest thickness at the knuckle. They could have belonged to a woman, or a child.

'Can you take out your own eye as well?' he asked. 'Then put it back, like your namesake?' She looked quickly at him, before she could stop herself. Then back at the sink, but she could feel a smile stretching.

'Of course not,' she was blushing.

'I'm not one to question miracles,' the doctor said. 'So I won't ask how you did that.' His voice was light and high, a voice she imagined, had she ever met any, might come from a boy. 'But I'm going to insist that you do it again.'

She didn't have to answer him, because she started gagging and a nun led her quickly to a bathroom. She was allowed to sleep the morning away in the empty dorm, where Jeanne visited quickly before running off to mop the floors.

'He took the baby with him,' Jeanne said.

'I know,' Brigid said.

The doctor was wrong, Brigid thought. It wasn't that the girls didn't want to hold them. When something is stolen from you, it is sometimes easier to act like you never wanted it in the first place.

9

Ink

August, 1959

Emer can't stop thinking about Brigid's hands. The long fingers, slender except for prominent knuckles that move like stones beneath her skin. When she pulled that poison out of Niall, Emer could feel a loosening in her own neck. Normally a late sleeper, now she is up before dawn counting the hours until it will be proper to stop by, just to be near them again.

Emer catches Brigid by surprise, out back trying to move her stubborn cow. Seeing Emer without warning, combined with the frustration at the cow, makes her face go dark, it looks fed up for a moment before she can rearrange it into a welcome. Emer is used to this face. Her mother gets it, Patch, Austin, and even, though she tries to hide it, Rose. Emer is not greeted with joy by anyone but Niall. She makes people start, cringe, slink away. If they are unlucky enough to brush against her, she makes them wonder why they bother getting up in the morning at all. Even the people who are supposed to love her dread being alone with her. She is already worried about the day that Niall first looks at her this way. The Yank doing it hurts even more than she thought it would. With

181

Brigid, Emer wishes she could be someone other than herself.

She helps Brigid with the cow, and Brigid asks her in for tea, the obligation that Emer relies upon. Now that she is friends with Rose and other island women she will have even less energy, Emer is sure, to put up with her alone. But she is already bound by the custom of offering tea.

This is new to Emer, trying to make a friend. She's not very good at it.

'Why aren't you married?' she says, cringing at how it comes out, like an accusation. She stirs milk into her tea and tries, if not to smile, to at least straighten her face into something neutral.

'I was,' Brigid says quietly, not looking up.

'Did you run away from him?' Emer says. 'Is that why you came here?'

'No, Emer,' she says. 'He died.'

'Car crash?' Emer says. She has heard this is how loads of people die in America.

Brigid sighs, pressing two fingertips against her temple. 'Cancer,' she says.

Niall has been trying to dance with the dog and the pig, encouraging them to stand on their back legs. Brigid allows his pig inside now because it is as well behaved as any of them, though it can't really manage to stand on two legs. He stops now and looks at her.

'Poor Brigid,' he says. The dog and pig sit neatly, waiting for their next instruction.

It is so much easier for her child to speak to people than it is for Emer. How little time he spends, no time at all really, thinking about what

182

he is going to say. It is the sort of ease that she hates in other people, like her sister, or Austin, or Brigid herself.

'Could you not heal him?' Niall says. 'With your hands, like?'

'Nope,' Brigid says, a catch in her voice that she coughs her way through.

'Why not?' Niall says.

'Hush, Niall,' Emer scolds him, even as she feels grateful for his nerve.

'Some things are too dangerous,' Brigid says quietly, 'to get my hands around.'

Emer allows herself a quick glance at Brigid's hands, tightened to whiteness around their mug. And it happens again, the pull, so strong it is like being accosted, a longing that has flared up in her, ever since she saw what Brigid can do. A vicious need, so sinful and foreign and unthinkable that it makes her dizzy. She is not even sure that what she wants is something that women do. She imagines, over and over again, like the fantasies of Austin that once looped in her mind, Brigid laying those hands on her.

★   ★   ★

Rose has Brigid over fairly often now, for tea, and though Emer is always invited along, she hates these afternoons, she suffers physically every time Brigid smiles at her sister.

The islanders are all taken with Brigid now, they like her big American laugh and her quirky hobbies and her expressions of respect and gratitude. She is constantly complimenting

183

them, praising them, as if what they do mindlessly every day is actually admirable. Emer thinks she lays it on too thick, and is amazed at how they all fall for it. Still, no one will tell her where the well is. No matter how fond they get, she will never be one of them.

Their mother is the only one Brigid hasn't charmed yet. Clodagh doesn't speak to her, just sits out of the circle in her rocker, crocheting with one hand and looking up every so often to glare her disapproval. Brigid smiles at her, and pours her tea.

Rose's girls, of course, adore Brigid. Clare and Cecelia sit on her lap and try to feed her their porridge and she makes them laugh by pretending to gobble up the offered spoon. Fiona and Eve mimic her accent, borrow her busily patterned scarves, bite their lips until they think their mouths are as red as Brigid's. Rose's girls have always steered clear of Emer, and everyone on the island knows better than to hand her a baby. This has always suited Emer just fine, but watching Rose's girls fight to sit next to Brigid makes her want to pinch every one of them off their chairs.

'What did you do in America?' six-year-old Bernie asks her. 'Were you a film actress?'

'Certainly not,' Brigid winks at Fiona.

'Are you somebody's mammy?' Teresa adds, and Brigid's smile stiffens.

'No. I was a midwife. My husband was a doctor. He took care of babies.'

'Like Saint Brigid?' Fiona says.

'I thought she was the patron saint of

184

midwives, not one herself. Nuns don't usually have babies.'

'Do you not know the stories?' Rose asks her. Rose has an annoying loyalty to the saint, and prays to her with the same ignorant fervour, Emer thinks, as a woman fifty years her senior. She raises her girls on tales of Brigid's miracles: hanging her cloak on nothing but a sunbeam, blessing cows to give endless amounts of milk, offering her well to two lepers to bathe in, and, when the first cured won't help the next, cursing him ill again. Even the toddlers know how to pray over the fire at night, smooring it in her name.

'Saint Brigid leans over every cradle,' Rose likes to say, whenever someone has a baby. Emer hates this expression. She believes that something else, something prayer has no power over, hovered over Niall's.

'Emer told me about the convent,' Brigid says. She looks at Emer then, so intensely Emer has to look away. 'She said nothing about babies.'

'Well, first it was only the nuns, for the isolation, and the peace, to finish the scriptures, that sort of thing. She brought her postulants here and built those clocháns and lived on not much more than sea air.'

Rose pours tea into Brigid's just emptied mug and continues.

'They had a reputation, mind, for healing, even now Brigid is the patron saint of childbirth. Some say that girls came here, when they were in trouble, and had their babies. And Brigid let them stay.'

'There's nowhere in Ireland you could do that now,' Emer explains.

'True enough,' Rose says. 'A girl gets pregnant nowadays they send her to the laundries and sell her baby to rich Americans.'

'Little pitchers,' Emer warns. The girls are listening, rapt. Rose dismisses her.

'Not that we'd do that here, not in donkey's years,' she says. Their mother lets out a snort of laughter. Brigid looks over, but Rose and Emer ignore her.

'There's nothing shameful in being a mother, sure,' Rose declares. 'It's what God wants for us.'

Emer looks quickly between her sister and Brigid, a vice grip on her neck.

'It's not God who makes those little whores open their . . . ' their mother starts, and Rose interrupts her, loudly suggesting the children run outside to play. Brigid actually leans over, puts a hand out and pats the woman's arm. Their mother is shocked silent by this. Eve, pouting, ushers all the little ones out the door, but Fiona stays.

'Some say it's how she found her soul friend,' Rose says. 'Darladuach was one of those girls; she and Brigid raised her baby together. Darla was so devoted to Brigid that when Brigid was on her deathbed, she laid down and asked to die along with her. They say she died a year later, on the same day, the first of February, of grief.'

Emer had forgotten this part of the story. She remembers now how she felt the first time she learned it at Sunday school. The picture in their book was of a dark homely woman standing like

186

a child at Brigid's side. It had reminded her of how she felt standing next to Rose.

'Why did they leave?' Brigid says.

'I expect they hadn't the strength to carry on after that. Some stayed, they say, and had sons who grew to be men and married the daughters and that is where the island families come from. The fire that Brigid kept, the eternal fire that the nuns guarded so it would never go out, is the same fire we have in our hearths today.'

'And her well?' Brigid says. 'Didn't she leave a healing well behind?'

'Wouldn't you like to know?' their mother taunts.

Rose is blushing, realising she has gone too far. 'Och, that was all a long time ago now.'

Emer is holding her breath. She thought perhaps Rose would tell her where the well is. But, true to island tradition, she is keeping it to herself.

'Some say she wasn't a saint at all,' Fiona pipes up. 'Only a fairy queen disguising herself as a Christian when it suited her.'

'That's enough of that talk,' Rose scolds.

'Others say there wasn't any magic to her,' Emer adds. 'It's just a story of women who wanted to get away.'

Brigid looks at her for so long that Emer feels heat rush from her face all the way down to her lap.

'I know the feeling,' Brigid says.

★ ★ ★

Brigid's next delivery, happily lugged up the road by Malachy, who is so taken with her he is ridiculed by the other men, is art supplies. A wooden case of pastels with more colours than Emer has ever seen laid out like precious, edible things. Bottles of coloured ink and long, delicate brushes so fine they look like they might prick like a pin. Rectangles of charcoal that leave smudged fingerprints on everything Brigid touches, as if she has dipped her hands in the ashes from the fire.

'Are you an artist?' Niall asks, excited, when he sees the tools spread out on the table. The sheets of paper are thick and soft and jagged at the edges, and there are sketchbooks that he flips through delightedly, each and every page identically blank and waiting.

'I like to draw,' Brigid says. 'Though I'm not very good at it.'

But of course, she is good at it. She draws the dog first, smudges of charcoal, shadows and lines that seem random, until a recognisable figure emerges. She draws the pig, capturing in a few strokes the expression of the thing, though before she drew it Emer didn't realise it had an expression.

Other days her drawings are not realistic at all. She draws odd mutations, Niall's head on the pig's body, her own fiery curls on the dog's. She renders them quickly and adjusts them to make Niall laugh. Sometimes they do it together, she will sketch a face and Niall will finish it off, putting wings and a stinger on himself or trousers on the dog.

'You don't have to let him scribble and ruin things,' Emer says, but Brigid laughs this off.

'We're only having fun,' she says. Emer thinks, if she could draw like that, if she could use her hands to translate lines and smudges into life, she wouldn't want anyone to touch it.

Whenever she draws Niall she gives his eyes fiery concentric swirls that look like they are moving, turning in circles on a white page.

One day, Emer is fussing about Brigid's kitchen while Brigid is trying to draw.

'Oh, Emer, sit,' she sighs. 'Pose for me.'

'I wouldn't know how,' Emer protests. Her heart is hammering so hard she's afraid it is audible.

'There's not much to it other than holding still,' Brigid says. 'And you're driving me batty moving around so much.'

So Emer sighs and shrugs, hiding the thrill that courses through her at the thought of Brigid's hands drawing her. She imagines Brigid taking the charcoal and smudging it across her skin, like smothering a fire, dousing the hot anticipation that crawls all over her. Desire so strong it has lipped over into pain.

It's backward, having someone look at her so intently. So purposefully. Instead of what usually happens, eyes glancing at her and running away. Niall comes in and out with the dog and pig, checks Brigid's sketchbooks and nods, serious as a man.

She does not see any of Brigid's drawings until the end. What she had imagined, during the hours that Brigid's eyes studied her, was ugliness; bad posture, awkward limbs, a puckered pocket of skin where there was once an eye. She thought the drawings would be as disappointing as looking at herself in the mirror. When she finally sees them, she is suspicious at how pretty she looks. In the charcoal sketches, her torso is long and graceful, her neck and clavicle look like they belong to some other woman. Her face is absent of the clenching she sees in the mirror, not smiling but looking at least as if it eventually might. Her dark hair covers her patch so it looks like merely a shadow, her good eye is lovely, the lashes longer than she knew.

The ink drawings are stranger. In them her figure is recognisable, but instead of shadows and cross-hatching she is composed of furious swirls, swirls of what look like fire, then water, then air, some of them bumping into one another in the junctures of her body and creating a storm. In her middle, curled like an infant but taking up more space, is a version of Niall. He is half-boy, half-pig, a frightening deformed creature except for his face, which is beautiful. In the storm that swirls about her body his eyes are the only fixed and steady spot, the only place in the drawing where you can comfortably look. He stretches from her groin to her neck. There are whorls of dark water in her neck and her hands. But in her middle, where Niall is, the blue lightens to silver, like the colour of sun on the sea.

'What is that supposed to be,' she scoffs.

'What do you think?' Brigid says.

'Queer enough,' Emer says, and Brigid laughs. Emer feels suddenly cold, like she's been wrapped in something that was ripped away.

'It's like you're drawing inside me,' she says quietly.

'Yes,' Brigid says, and Emer wonders if she understands. She doesn't mean that Brigid is interpreting her. What she means is that Brigid's pens, her ink, her coal-smudged fingers, seem to be reaching down inside Emer herself, reaching for something as deep and as secret as what she has spied on, what she had stopped wishing to find. And that something inside her is rising up, begging to meet Brigid's hands.

★ ★ ★

On a calm day, they take a picnic to the cliffs, spread a blanket on the grass between the clocháns. Emer and Brigid eat scones and drink tea while Niall and the dog and the pig chase after birds. Emer hasn't spent this much time outside since she was a girl and has lighter streaks in her dull hair and a colour to her face that her sister has told her is handsome. It's not just the colour, her expression is a bit softer. Not so chiselled. Once, walking by Malachy in the fields, he said, 'If I didn't know better I'd say Emer was smiling.' This of course made her scowl, but she couldn't bring herself to hate him for it. Because Brigid winked at her.

They are like this since she started posing. Easier. Brigid smiles when she sees her coming up the road, instead of sighing and reaching for the kettle. Occasionally Emer cracks a joke and makes Brigid laugh and those moments are so satisfying, Emer wants to grab at the air between them and swallow it, so that she can feel this friendly, this loose, this enjoyed, all the time.

It is as though the drawing has softened Emer, as though a new version has been inked on top of the old. Right on to her skin. She has even posed nude for her — Emer, who can't undress in front of her own sister without turning away. She lay naked on Brigid's bed and felt drunk with the cheek of it. Looking at the drawings afterwards, she is mortified at the jolt of longing she feels from the curve of her own breasts.

Even Emer's mother notices the change in her, and says, if she catches Emer smiling to herself, 'Aren't you making a holy show.'

Lying in the grass, listening to the wind rise and fall and the birds' wings flapping against it, Brigid's pen scratching at paper, and Niall laughing at the animals, Emer almost falls asleep. Then something yanks her, as if she is falling and instead of hitting the ground she is caught by a rope, and suspended, jarred and bouncing in mid-air. Anxiety surges at her neck and she leaps up, looks for Niall, barks at him not to get too close to the edge.

'He's all right,' Brigid says. Not dismissive, she is reassuring. 'I'm watching him.'

Emer flushes, embarrassed and awkward again. She can't think of a graceful way to sit back down, so she stands, letting the wind whip her hair loose from its place behind her ears. She can see that Brigid has been drawing her again, drawing a peaceful, pretty woman stretched out in a bed of grass.

'What is it you're so worried about?' Brigid says.

Emer considers not really answering, as Brigid brushes her off when she asks too much about her life before or why she is here.

'Boys are prone to scrapes,' Emer tries.

'He's pretty careful,' Brigid says. 'You're not worried in the moment, though. You're worried all the time.' She flips back in her sketchbook to a quick ink drawing of Emer's face, eye closed. Though at first glance she just looks to be sleeping. Brigid has done something with her eye, with her mouth, that gives off flashes of pure anguish, which then fade away, as if the picture itself is moving in and out of a bad dream. Emer looks at this drawing for a long time.

'When he was born he wasn't able to eat,' she says quickly, afraid she will lose her nerve. 'A woman helped me teach him and she wasn't, well she wasn't real. Wasn't human.' She glances quickly at Brigid, but she doesn't look like Rose does when she tries to talk of this, ready to placate her. She just looks like she's listening, really listening, with no contradictions lining up behind her eyes.

'I think she means to come back for him. They'll try to steal him, the way they took me, but they didn't want me. They try all the time, they tease, pull him partway. If I get him off this rock, if I get everyone off, before he's seven, I think maybe they'll leave us alone.'

'Why seven?'

'Seven years is how long they give you. Before they take them back.'

'You think he's a changeling.'

'He's mine. But a part of him belongs elsewhere. It does not live in this world. They want the rest.'

'That's why you want the evacuation,' Brigid says. 'Because you think Niall will be taken?'

'You can see it, I know you can.'

Brigid is quiet. She is thinking.

'Why do you have to get everyone off?'

Emer shrugs. 'I can't see any other way.'

'You could leave. If you wanted to.'

'Please,' Emer says. 'I'm not you.'

Brigid seems like she's going to argue with her, but then stops. She knows Emer is right. Brigid is a woman with no ties, with money of her own, with the American notion that running away is always possible. The box of who she is wasn't already lidded and sealed long ago.

'I don't think they'll take him, Emer,' she says. Emer notes, even as she opens her mouth to argue, that Brigid doesn't bother to say they don't exist.

'You don't know. You haven't been here long. Some say they drove Saint Brigid away. That they took some of her girls, and she, the most powerful saint in Ireland, couldn't do a thing about it. When you cross them, there is no mercy. You'd be better off if you took them seriously yourself.'

'It doesn't help anything. All this fear.'

'What would you know about it?' Emer can't hold it back, the crying, and her voice is bending

194

around it. 'You don't know how I am afraid. It's not like fear for yourself. Not at all. You've no children, so you can't know.'

'I'm no stranger to the kind of fear that strangles you, Emer.'

Emer can't stand that, she turns away, tries to stifle a sob as it rises, as loud and inevitable as the wind.

Emer is facing the cliff, the drop her mother wanted her to take, the drop into sea air and wind that she wanted too, until she had Niall, when she no longer wanted it, though often she feared she would end up like her mother and throw them both off. She misses it, that blasphemous desire, that promise she kept to herself that she could take everything away, that she could destroy something completely, instead of a little bit at a time with the misery that comes from her hands. She doesn't have that any more, that out. Now that she has Niall she is no longer alone with herself in the darkness. His light is insistent and it never wanes. He is like Rose on that wet hill, screaming at her daily not to go. She has no hold on the earth without him.

Brigid comes up behind her. She has never touched Emer before, but she moves in until her front is pressed against Emer's back, her strong arms have slipped underneath Emer's crossed ones, and she is hugging her. Emer leans back into her, feeling like the wind might knock them both over, wanting it to, wanting to fall and have this woman, every strange and promising inch of her, press Emer into the ground.

Emer is breathing too fast, and Brigid holds

her tight and tries to calm it down.

'You're his mother, Emer,' she whispers, her breath a welcome relief at Emer's tight neck. 'You're a horrible crank to everyone else,' she laughs, 'but you're everything to him. He's not going anywhere.'

Though Emer fears she might be pushed away she can't stop herself. She turns around, rotates within the cave of Brigid's arms, so she is facing her, so their hips are pressed together, their breasts, their arms wrapped so tightly you can no longer tell who is holding on to whom. They are exactly the same height. Brigid's mouth is right there and though in one minute Emer will think she imagined it, there is a pause, a lingering of Brigid's eyes on her lips that makes Emer's mind flare with the image of kissing her, open, wet, endless kissing of the kind she has never tried, until it falls back into the realm of impossibly wrong.

Brigid gives her one last, fortifying squeeze, turning this into something else, like the patting hand of someone who is already walking away. She steps back and the wind rushes in between them again. Niall comes running into view, laughing and being chased by the animals, just in time to miss it all. Emer sees Brigid looking at him, she tries to smile casually, hiding her real expression underneath. The way she looks at all children. Smiling as if she'd rather be crying because they are not her own.

'Can you help us?' Emer whispers. Brigid looks angry for an instant and Emer takes a step backwards, thinking she has gone too far. But then the anger fades to weariness and Brigid smiles, looking at her but not really meeting her eye. There is something in this gesture that makes Emer go cold and still inside. The avoidance, coupled with the look of burden, it is the thing she puts in everyone, but she isn't trying now. She wants to find a way to reach Brigid. She is tired of pushing people away and still being surprised when they recoil.

But then Brigid nods. 'Perhaps we can help each other,' she says.

Her smile is a miracle. A genuine smile, directed at Emer.

Emer is too grateful, and too worried that she'll take it back, to disagree. The dog comes running up then, jumping on Brigid, and Niall flies into Emer for a hug. The pig squeals and bonks against their legs. And even as Emer squeezes Niall as tightly as she can, a part of her wishes that he'd stayed away for five more minutes, so that Brigid would not have been required to let go.

10

Kidnapped

1936

After that first birth, Brigid was no longer just a girl to them. They were Irish nuns, their order named for a saint who colluded with fairies, and they knew magic when confronted with it. On the outside Brigid remained the same: a thirteen-year-old girl pulled without much kindness through long days of chores. To the nuns, whose lives were not much brighter, she became the promise of something. Proof that what they did was real. They came to her now, when she was sitting in class or sweeping a hallway, and wanted her to put her hand on their arms. Though she had never tried to heal any wound that wasn't physical, none of them believed her. They came away from Brigid's hand imagining a salve had been applied to their soul.

Matthew, the young doctor, who felt no need to argue with useful magic, requested that Brigid be fetched for every birth, even those that promised to be routine. He didn't believe in drugging the mothers because the drugs, even though they stifled the screams, made the process more difficult. He needed them to push, not pass out. He had seen too many babies' heads crushed by forceps, and had radical views of the natural process of childbirth. The nuns, being from rural Ireland, didn't mind these views, which was why he'd ended up with the job in the first place. He had observed Myra when Brigid turned the baby and he wanted every girl he delivered to be given the same balm. Some pain in childbirth was necessary, so a routine developed between them that moved quietly through the delivery room over the long tedious hours that bled into each other at night. If Brigid comforted too much, the natural contractions would slow down, or stop. The girl giving birth either lay on the cot, seizing up with each surge of pain, or walked around, squatting and grunting and making younger nuns blush. The rhythms of it, the build and release, and often the moaning, reminded her so much of what she pulled from Jeanne that Brigid sometimes grew embarrassed, rearranging her posture in the chair where she was supposed to wait until she was needed. When the pains grew closer together and they had no chance to recover in between, Brigid would be called over to touch their writhing bellies. Matthew wouldn't let her ease it too much. They needed the tight bands of fire to push out the baby. Without it, the body, he explained to her, would not know what to do.

These breaks also eased Brigid's own illness, gave her a handle on it, so that, during routine labours, she could push through a vague feeling of fighting the flu. Other labours, she barely managed to hold it in until she returned to her dorm, where she collapsed with chills and vomiting, or a headache that temporarily blinded her.

She did most of her healing in the last moments, when the baby's head was warping the mother's groin beyond recognition, when the space between her hips and the open folds of her vulva looked deformed, studded with poking bones.

Often, at the moment the baby's head finally broke out, Brigid would feel not triumph but something deep and cold and more like failure. As if she'd assisted in some sort of death. There was grief once the baby was out. Even the girls who held their babies and cried and kissed them didn't get to do so for long. The babies pushed their way out only to be ripped away. Brigid often went back to her cot and, spurred on by fever or cramping, cried silently thinking of the worst of the pain, the pain she could not ease, that came the moment that girl and baby, meant to be together, were pulled apart.

Brigid liked to imagine the hospital where Matthew worked, where the process of giving birth was actually a positive one, where there were smiles and presents and congratulations rather than silence and pinched faces and the sneaking around of doctors who brought no relief in their heavy bags. Where babies were the long-awaited reward instead of the last part of the punishment.

Sometimes, after the mother had been taken away to the infirmary to recover, Matthew was packing up, and the nuns were stripping the bloody linens, Brigid would hold the newly

200

bathed and swaddled baby. They were so warm, as warm as the inside of the womb they'd come from. She whispered endearments to them in Irish. My heart, my light, my pulse. She kissed their impossibly soft feet.

She never saw the mothers again. Soon after the babies were out of them, the nuns had them dressed and packed, rags stuffed into their bras to soak up the weeping from their breasts. A car would arrive to take them away — a guilty-looking boyfriend, a stern social worker, or pale, stony-faced parents. They went back to their homes, their high schools, their jobs. Brigid imagined them afterwards, going about their lives, pretending nothing had happened as grief doubled them over like a surge of labour, as their bodies keened from every orifice, blood, milk and tears pouring out of them with no consolation in sight. Nothing could staunch such grief; it would be there, inside both the mothers and the babies, the rest of their lives.

The nuns said the babies were better off. They were being given to parents who could love them. But Brigid had her hands inside these girls, inside their wombs. It was not for lack of love that babies were being stolen.

★ ★ ★

Sometimes while she waited through a labour, Brigid looked at diagrams in Matthew's medical textbook. Wrinkled wombs, flowery fallopian tubes, smooth, serious-looking ovaries. She read that a woman's eggs were inside her from birth.

201

It wasn't a man who made the babies, like she'd thought, but a man and a woman together, the tiny sperm unlocking something in the woman's egg, so it could grow and change and swell until it could no longer be hidden from the outside. The best part, Brigid thought, on those nights when she thought back to the diagrams and Matthew's eager, boyish voice, was not just that she had eggs, but that they had been there all along. On the island with her parents, in the lighthouse where she failed to pull her father's life back, in the orphanage where Jeanne's hands could make her forget herself, all that time, she had been incubating this possibility. This hope.

The need for a man was a technicality. Her baby was already waiting inside her.

★ ★ ★

Brigid waited for the right time, knowing that to rush it was to risk everything. Matthew thought she was only a girl. They developed a rhythm where he no longer had to call for the time for Brigid to step forward, she already knew. They grew to work seamlessly with one another, one encouraging the girl to push through pain, the other alleviating it. Matthew usually stepped aside when Brigid touched them, or averted his eyes. Despite everything he'd seen, he treated these girls' bodies with a modest deference that made a few of them, not to mention a handful of the nuns, want to love him. But they never got a chance to see him and after what amounted to days of pain and relief and blood and defecation and vomit, they usually forgot by the end of it all that they had thought him attractive. They were never to see him again, any more than they were allowed to see the babies he pulled out of them. Only Brigid saw him repeatedly, was greeted by his shy, eager smile, which he gave when the nuns weren't watching and which always jolted her a bit, in a similar but sweeter way to the throb inside her whenever she and Jeanne saw the chance to be alone.

Once, he forgot to give Brigid space, during a labour that was going along fine and started to tilt at the last minute. While Brigid was laying her hands to ease a contraction she felt a jolt of something going horribly wrong. She panicked, stepped back, and he saw it, walking up behind her quickly, putting his stethoscope to the girl's belly, that was shifting, large mounds of flesh pushing their way across and diving down again. Like whales coming up out of the sea.

'It's the cord,' he said quickly. He put his arms on Brigid's, the first time he'd ever touched her, too intent on a solution to be shy or modest about it. He held her arms from behind, told her to quickly, quickly, his breath hot and urgent in her ear, slip her fingers beneath the cord and loosen it from the baby's neck. As she eased the tight band, her hands inside gave the mother another moment of pleasurable relief, and Matthew, still holding her forearms, felt it. She felt the jolt of longing ricochet back to him, so shocking him that he let go and backed away, but not before she felt something grow between his hips and her back, the possibility she had been waiting for. After the birth was over, he packed up quickly, not allowing Brigid time to sing and softly rock the newborn. She barely got it cleaned up and swaddled before, avoiding her eyes, he took it roughly and left with curt instructions to the nuns.

It was three weeks before he returned again. Three weeks where Brigid continued to make love with Jeanne but could no longer lose herself in it. A memory infected her pleasure. She would watch Jeanne's mouth twist and smile, and have to look away, remembering the moment Matthew had glanced at her with a longing that resembled fear.

★   ★   ★

When a nun finally woke her in the night and brought her to the infirmary, her stomach was knotted at the thought of how he might greet her. Or not greet her. He didn't look up when she came in, he was taking the girl's blood pressure, but as she washed her hands and arms and put on the nurse's gown he always had her wear, she could feel him watching her, and when it was time to go over and touch the girl who was yelping, as if alarmed by her own pain, she stood next to him. He turned to look in her eyes and it was a shock how he didn't try to hide it at all but let her see everything, the desire and the shame. Shame, his eyes hinted, that wasn't going to stop him.

It was all they could do to get through that birth, mercifully straightforward and short, only two hours of rapid, biting labour that Brigid barely needed to help. The baby was expelled out with such force, in one great wave of painful joy, Brigid almost dropped him. After the baby and mother were cleaned up, the nun brought the baby downstairs to the new parents who couldn't bear to wait the few more hours it would take Matthew to deliver their child to them. Matthew said something low to the remaining nun and rather than lead her back to the dorm, the nun retired, leaving Matthew with the keys. If Mother Superior had been there it never would have been allowed, but most of the other nuns deferred to the doctor as if he were as infallible as the priest. So they shuffled off and Brigid wondered later if they knew and envied her the soft click of the lock on the door.

He was driven by something that was not gentle, but he was still Matthew, shy and too kind to abuse her, so she had to put her lips to his first, ease him down into a chair, lift her gown and lead his trembling hands. He kissed her cautiously and whispered the words she had waited to hear as a girl.

'I'm sorry.'

It lasted longer than it ever had with Jeanne, longer than a nighttime of labour, longer than her father had mouthed apologies into her mother's bruised and battered skin. It lasted longer than her life so far and still it wasn't over.

She knew what Matthew was feeling. She had felt it inside of Jeanne.

Eventually he let out a regretful moan, shuddered, holding her with a desperate grip, then grew still. What they'd created continued to move through her, new waves breaking just as the last one retreated.

He kissed her for a long time, filling her mouth with gratitude, kissed her with such serious and gentle intent, she felt it reaching below the ocean inside her, deep down to meet the place where something, she was sure, something akin to love had just been made.

★   ★   ★

She lost the first pregnancy quickly, only a few weeks in. Just as she could feel a pop inside her body when her egg was released and began its way down, she felt the moment where the jumble of cells that was her baby let go, loosened its grip, almost playfully, like a child swinging and dropping from a tree limb. It happened when she had her hands on another baby, the one trying to stay inside Kathleen McKenna, and she was giving it the gentlest of tugs to encourage it out. Just at the moment where the baby gave in and Kathleen groaned in relief as Brigid's hands dissolved her pain, Brigid felt her own child slip, fall away, and the corresponding seize of her womb, as if it were trying to grab on to it, a sob of protest that came too late. By the time she got back to her dorm, she had started bleeding, and spent two days examining but finding nothing recognisable in the brown clots she rinsed from her monthly rags.

The next pregnancy was harder to arrange, since Matthew, after the first time, remembered to take precautions. At first he pulled away just at the crucial moment, and it was all she could do not to cry in disappointment. Then there was the time that she managed to hold him down, he was a small man and she was tall and big-boned for fourteen, and when he realised her intention he started to sit up, but came inside her anyway, and was furious afterwards. She told him that it didn't matter, that she'd not yet begun to bleed, but he wasn't convinced and the next time brought rubber sheaths that left her smelling medicinal between her legs. A darning needle prick to each of the sheaths in his stash was enough to guarantee that her body started swelling up again. This one lasted longer, a lot longer, and it was months between labouring girls, months where she only saw Matthew twice, when he came by to help with another girl's miscarriage, and that time the nuns didn't leave them alone, so he couldn't see how taut her stomach had become, tight and stretched like a drum.

She was breaking Jeanne's heart, she knew this, and tried to ease it a bit, by continuing to touch her, keeping their encounters so danger-ous and brief that it was natural that she didn't get a turn. It wasn't long before Jeanne demanded to know why she cringed if she tried to touch back.

'I'm bleeding,' she said. Since they all had their periods at the same time, Jeanne knew she was lying.

Brigid's body ached to be touched but she was afraid for the baby, that Jeanne's rough hands might make it let go.

And then, before she could move away, Jeanne, sliding her hands down, felt the swell of Brigid's lower belly and lifted her dress to look at it.

'I guess you got what you wanted,' she said, and walked away. She stopped trying after that, stopped coming to her in the night or cornering her in the bathroom or leaving notes about meeting by the boiler. One day, when Brigid ran to the bathroom to throw up, she found Jeanne there with another girl, a new girl who looked as frightened as she was thrilled by Jeanne's hands venturing under her smock. She tried to push Jeanne away, pointing at Brigid, but Jeanne just closed the stall door and kept at it, and even while Brigid vomited next to them, she could hear the impatient breath she recognised from when Jeanne reached inside her for the first time.

★ ★ ★

By the time Matthew came again to deliver another baby, Brigid was no longer vomiting and she had traded her dress for a wider version in the laundry room. Matthew tried not to look directly at her when she walked into the delivery room, not wanting the nuns to see the relief and desire flushing their faces. They moved side by side throughout the night, easing the girl's contractions, wiping away blood and faeces and vomit, mostly waiting in the heavily warped time that occupied a birthing room. When the girl's pelvis was distorted with the final drop,

Matthew, listening with the stethoscope, gestured to Brigid to hurry and release the cord strangling the little neck. Brigid reached in but it was harder than usual to find, the baby's head was so large she couldn't get her hands past it to reach its neck. She had to rip the girl a bit, masking the pain, and pull the cord over like a shirt too small for a child's head. Just as she felt it free up, and the baby's head and bruised neck emerged, she felt a fissure inside her, not a letting go this time but a vicious, deliberate cleave. She doubled over with a sudden surge of pain and Matthew stepped forwards to catch the pulpy rush of baby and blood and mucus and cord. In the business of spanking for a cry, cutting the cord, and towelling to find healthy pink skin, no one noticed that Brigid had lowered herself to the floor and crawled away, as if it were all about gravity, and the lower she was to the ground the less likely she was to lose what was inside her. She was a virgin to the type of pain attacking her, and yet it was perfectly familiar the way it rose and peaked and released only to come again harder the next time. It was only when Matthew needed her to stop the haemorrhaging from a placenta that would not detach that he noticed her. There was a lot of confusion as he left his patient and tried to get Brigid to rise and he saw that she too, on the back of her orphan's nightgown, was bleeding. Somehow, Matthew, whispering in his sweet, confident voice, got Brigid to stand up and walk over to his patient, release her placenta and staunch the gushing blood, searing the vessels with the fire of her hands. By the time the girl on the table was all right, Brigid was passed out from her own blood loss, and wouldn't know until later the panic that ensued and the secrets Matthew revealed with his reactions. He sobbed when the half-formed child was expelled from her. It never took a breath. Brigid remembered only the moment when she stopped her own haemorrhaging. She could smell the odour, like new wood being burned, which accompanied the application of her fiery hands. She healed herself, but could not save what grew inside her.

* * *

By the time Brigid woke up, in one of the rooms they gave to girls to recover from the birth, Matthew was gone. The Mother Superior was the one who told her. Given what had fallen out of an innocent girl with no access to men, from now on no doctor would be needed at St Brigid's Home for Wayward Girls. Tears poured silently down Brigid's face.

'He's lucky,' Mother Superior said. 'I could have reported him to the police, had his license revoked. But he agreed to never return here if I let him disappear.' Brigid held herself still, not wanting the Mother to see that her words were like blows.

'I think you know enough now,' she went on, 'to be our midwife. There is no reason we need anyone from the outside. When you are old enough you can take your vows.'

'I'm not staying here,' Brigid said quietly.

Mother Superior grimaced.

'You're already ruined for anything else.'

*   *   *

A month later, Jeanne and Molly found Brigid in a bathroom stall slashing at her wrists, trying to cut quicker than the slices could heal themselves. They led her back to the dorm and laid her on the bed. Both of them, first Jeanne whose body she knew by heart, then Molly, the new girl, softer, pudgy, with a smell as promising as rising bread dough, climbed in beside her, sandwiching her body between theirs, absorbing her convulsions and sobs with the same silent thoughtless mercy that she used to seal open wounds. When Jeanne tried to kiss her, Brigid pressed her lips still, realising too late that what she was grieving for was not only the child that had come out of her, but the man who had put it inside.

*   *   *

She went back to her life of cleaning and studying and sealing up pain, with less hope than she'd ever functioned with before. Brigid was thin enough to appear breakable, and her only desire seemed to be to find ways to go back to her bed and sleep, sleep that never refreshed her but that she clung to like a life rope, not wanting to come fully to the surface of anything. It was Jeanne who gave Matthew back to her. Through a complicated series of communications involving arriving and departing pregnant girls, she arranged it all. She and Molly woke Brigid in the night, which took some time because she slept as if she were holding on to her dreams for dear life. Jeanne hadn't included Brigid in the plan, in case it didn't work, so when Molly told Brigid they had a surprise, Brigid began to cry, lying back down as if the promise had drained her.

They sat her up, Jeanne bracing from one side while Molly wrestled socks and shoes on her like she was a toddler. They draped her arms over their shoulders, and pulled her across the silent dorm into the dark hallway. Brigid's feet began to move, and the more they moved the more she wanted them to, and the next thing she knew they were running, holding hands, Molly and Jeanne laughing softly, delirious with possibility. It didn't matter if the nuns heard, Brigid thought, in that moment, they were three girls flying down polished halls, they were untouchable.

They ran down the stairs and ducked into a classroom, the same one Jeanne and Brigid used to escape from because of the disguised broken lock on one window. The panels of glass Molly pushed went outward, like a doorway. It was so dark, Brigid couldn't even make out a shadow of what she was dropping into. Jeanne helped her on to the sill, took the last second to sear a quick, angry kiss to her lips. Brigid was so numb from months of grief, and confused by the darkness and the plan, that she remembered later that she should have kissed back, thanked her, said goodbye. They held her arms and dangled her over a dark abyss, the window frame

212

pressing pain into her wrists. Then they let go and she dropped, only a few feet but it felt like it might go on and on, into waiting arms. She knew it was Matthew by the way he caught her, confident and shy at the same time, and the smell of him, antiseptic hands and sweet breath, and though she was perfectly capable of walking now, she held on to his neck and let him carry her, whispering apologies into her hair, letting him tell her that she would never again, after her cruel parents and cold nuns and girls just as broken as she was, never in her lifetime would she have to be alone.

They drove quickly through the night, Matthew's car packed with what he had salvaged of his life. Over the next few days, as she realised what he had given up by stealing her, his practice, his license, his family, she would have instants where she lost breath and thought and word. She would feel, simultaneously, like pain blooming into pleasure, pure relief that he had taken her right alongside the terrible thought that he could just as easily have let her go.

11

The Well

August, 1959

Brigid doesn't try to seduce Emer. She tries to stop it. But even as she tells herself that it will end just like all the others — with gossip and shame and another quick move, a packing up of her life to escape the rage of men she steals women from — she sees herself doing it. Sees how she is pulling Emer in, stroking her, tempting her, long before she even lays a hand on her. She thought this might be a problem the moment they first clasped hands on that quay. She always knows, she can recognise the women who will desire her, tell them apart from the ones it would never even occur to.

It wasn't until she healed Niall that Emer started looking at her that way. Something was switched on then, and though she clearly has no experience with women, her want is there, raw and demanding regardless. It makes her clumsier, self-conscious, and awkward, but also more attractive. The flush, the bright eye, the way she looks at Brigid's hands, her breasts, her mouth. She is like no one Brigid has ever met, and yet, in Emer's desire, she sees all of them. Matthew, too feminine to be attractive to most women, who never quite recovered from the guilt of the crimes he committed, and made love to her with a combination of deference and violence that took her breath away. Jeanne, that scarred, hardened girl, awkward and rough on the outside, gorgeous underneath the carapace. All the women since, the women Matthew ignored and forgave because of what he thought he'd done to her, women who felt burdened, lost or unattractive, who did not believe it when men told them they were beautiful. Most of them had never imagined that this was what they wanted, another woman running her hands over every flaw of their body, until they were cured of the idea of their ugliness that had burdened them for so long. Brigid made lonely women lovely, with the same hands she used to mend their open wounds.

At first, she keeps Emer at a distance, pretends she doesn't even know what the girl wants. This seems to make her even more desperate. Her loneliness is so acute Brigid can practically hear it, like a keen that runs just under that sarcastic, vicious monologue delivered in an enchanting brogue.

Then there is the picnic on the cliff where Emer opens up and tells Brigid what she is afraid of. Brigid comes so close to kissing her, to soothing Emer the one way she knows will work, by validating her desire, that the effort not to leaves her dizzy and slightly nauseated.

It occurs to her that she could seduce Emer into revealing the well. But she doesn't want any more casualties from love affairs. She just wants a baby.

She is grateful for Emer's awkward inexperience. Were she bold enough to make the first move, Brigid would be doomed.

After the picnic, they go back to Brigid's cottage and Emer shows her the picture of the council house she keeps in her apron pocket, folded and unfolded so many times it has faded to nothing at the creases. It's an architect's drawing of a modern Irish bungalow, ugly and squat, made of concrete and slate, and pavement instead of grass in the yard.

'These houses aren't any better, Emer,' Brigid says, though even as she says it she knows they are not speaking of the same things. The houses will have heat, electricity, and running water. They are luxurious if you don't notice they have no soul.

'If you want to leave so badly, why don't you do it? You don't need the whole island to go with you. Why doesn't Patch get a posting on the mainland?'

And Emer tells her why, quietly, simply, like a child telling a dirty secret for the first time, of her husband's last posting, where he drank so much he let the light die out and caused an accident on the rocks. He was fired, lost his pension, and would never leave the island for work again.

Brigid says nothing for a while. She wants to give a speech rallying Emer, telling her she is not at the mercy of her husband, but she knows better. Just because Brigid had a husband who wasn't a trap doesn't mean she hasn't known plenty of women who have been tied up and

216

suffocated within a man's mistakes.

'I understand,' she says finally. 'I do. But I don't see it happening. They can't make people leave the only home they've ever known. Not even for central heating.'

What happened to this girl, Brigid wonders, to make her so vicious? Because that's what she is, a tightly wound ball of ferocity, lashing out at anyone that approaches her with those nasty fingers. At some point she decided that if she was going to be unhappy, she would pull everyone else down with her.

'It will happen eventually,' Brigid says. 'You'll find another way, if it's what you really want.'

Emer looks quickly at Brigid, and Brigid can feel that eye linger on her mouth, and on her hands tightening around the mug of tea. Brigid has seen this many times before, watched as a girl's body opens the possibility in her mind. Where the unfathomable turns into a necessity.

Emer can't even imagine saying out loud what it is that she wants now.

★ ★ ★

Sketching Emer starts as a way to avoid repeating all of this. She sees Emer's raw need and thinks she can heal her another way, without complicating it all by touching her. But then she gets caught up. She translates Emer's body into smudges of charcoal and suddenly, despite her promise to remain alone, sexless, an uncomplicated vessel whose only relationship is with a dog, she can't stop thinking about it. She feels doomed. Their course is as inevitable as the sea rising up in a storm. What she wants to do with Emer will feel like healing, like teaching, but she knows that it is more like theft. She won't be able to help but steal every sensation she thrusts upon Emer. She will steal her from her husband and her son and her plans for a better life, and Emer doesn't even know it yet. She will think she is being saved.

Even remembering all the guilt and complication and lying and fear, she can't help but savour the familiar beginnings. It feels so good to have someone want her again that she forgets, for long ascending moments, that this has never, not once in her life, ended any other way than badly.

★   ★   ★

After Matthew stole her from St Brigid's, they drove north through the night to Canada, where they pretended they were married until she was old enough that they could be. Though charges were never filed, Matthew couldn't go home; his reputation was gone, his family disgraced. The first few months were dark and miserable ones for the both of them. Matthew often ended lovemaking with tearful apologies. He begged for her forgiveness.

'Stop saying you're sorry,' Brigid would say, crying that he still refused to believe her, the only person she had ever fully believed in herself. 'You've done nothing wrong. You didn't kidnap me. I came with you.'

They had to move often. In the beginning they

kept moving whenever anyone grew suspicious of her age, they were often asked if Matthew was Brigid's father. Later they moved when the rumours grew thick about the things Brigid did with the women who came to them for help.

They continued to deliver babies. Sometimes for married women who wanted to deliver at home, but more and more, as the war came, for women who were left alone, discovering they were pregnant after their boyfriends had already been shipped to Europe. Women and girls just as scared and abandoned as the ones they had known at St Brigid's. The difference was, with Matthew and Brigid, they were not expected to hand their babies over at the end.

In every town they moved to, they filled their extra bedrooms with pregnant girls, new mothers, and babies. Brigid had never forgotten the pain of those girls severed from their children, so she and Matthew gave unwed mothers time to bond with their babies, nurse them, and decide for themselves. If they chose to keep the baby. Matthew and Brigid helped them find jobs and homes and daycare, if they chose to give them up, which some still did, they helped arrange adoptions with couples who agreed to keep in contact and send the mothers photographs and letters about their children. For twenty years they moved around, first in Canada, later in New England when the memories of their crimes had faded, and ushered women and babies through the first few fragile months of their lives together.

In every place they lived, Brigid got pregnant

and miscarried. Sometimes it would happen in such rapid succession — pregnant, miscarriage, pregnant again — that she felt continuously with child, but never allowed to give birth, never reaching the part where she felt the flutter of life inside her, before it was pulled away too soon to survive. It seemed that healing the girls brought it on, but by the time she tried to keep her hands to herself, something inside her was already broken. More than once Matthew found her curled up amid the blood-soaked bedclothes, her hands pressed so tight between her thighs that she could barely feel them when he pried them away.

'Why can I help them and not myself?' she asked Matthew. 'They don't even want their babies.' But she knew that wasn't true. They didn't want to be pregnant, but they did want their babies. Wanting them and keeping them were often two very different things.

'Maybe it's me,' said Matthew, who felt each miscarriage almost as deeply as she did. 'Maybe this is the punishment for what I did to you.'

Matthew was not a religious man, neither of them bothered with that. But he had been raised Catholic, and he couldn't quite escape the idea that he had sinned by falling in love with a broken girl with magic in her hands.

'Don't be daft,' Brigid said harshly, sounding like her mother or one of those nuns, women with no patience for whinging self-pity. 'It's not *your* fault.'

But she wondered if it might be.

She went to a specialist who told her that, by the looks of things, her womb and cervix were never meant to hold children. They were incompetent.

'How can I fix that?' Brigid said. The doctor looked at Matthew, then back to Brigid.

'We can't fix it,' he said. 'It's not an injury. It's just the way you were made.' He told them to stop trying, that eventually it could kill her.

'Doctors don't know everything,' she said to Matthew, but he made her get a cervical cap and refused to make love without it.

'We have each other,' he said. She didn't tell him it would never be enough.

* * *

Brigid wanted to remain faithful to Matthew, tried to resist the temptation of the girls who lived in their home. But sometimes, after a miscarriage, this resolve would bleed away, and she would fill the empty space left by another baby with the swollen bodies of these women, many of whom had no idea what their hands and mouths were capable of until Brigid came to their rooms, closed the door, and taught them in the darkness. She only chose women who looked at her a certain way, whose eyes lingered on her mouth, who exuded sexual tension even when they couldn't recognise it. These women hadn't had anyone to teach them about such pleasure. It was another form of healing, Brigid told herself, overwriting the memories of unsatisfying, sometimes violent encounters with men. But the truth was, she was the one who needed healing.

221

Every once in a while a girl would confess to her priest or her parents, or her crippled boyfriend back from the war, what had occurred with Brigid in the fevered months of her confinement. That's when they would move, find a new place where no one knew them, and start all over again. Matthew forgave her every time.

Matthew suggested that they adopt one of the babies the women decided to leave behind, but Brigid refused. He didn't understand. He had not reached deeply into their wombs and felt the familiar rip in their souls as they birthed a child they could not keep. It tore the same places as having them born too soon sliced in her. Brigid found loving mothers for the babies they gave up, but she would never be one of them. She couldn't pretend. She couldn't be part of the cleaving and then raise the child as her own. She would remember, every time she held it, that it was not.

★ ★ ★

When Brigid was thirty-five and Matthew fifty, he fell ill. Brigid could sense it in him way before the doctors found it. He had headaches that blinded him for hours at a time, and when she tried to heal them she felt a dark space, like a wet, nasty hole that she could not see the bottom of and didn't want to put her hand into.

It was a tumour in his brain. Though the prognosis was dire, the oncologist was continually amazed by his patient's refusal to die. The mass was inoperable and grew rapidly, except it kept shrinking, despite Matthew's refusal of treatment. It never went away, but got small and then grew again, like a child playing with a balloon.

Nothing had ever made Brigid as ill as reaching her hands towards that tumour. Each time she shrunk it, she ended up in her bed for days with high fevers, body aches, vomiting, dehydration. She lost too much weight, her hair fell out, leaving whorls like birds' nests in her brush. Matthew tended to her; she had no energy left to heal herself. He would lie next to her on the bed and wipe her face with cool cloths, put straws to her lips, murmur his love and apologies as she thrashed and moaned and forgot whole days. When ill, she was trapped in her childhood again, on that island, with people she could not trust not to murder each other.

The last time she was ever pregnant (darning needles work on rubber cervical caps, too), she made it halfway through, the longest her body had ever managed to hold on. Matthew was in the hospital, declining rapidly since he would not let her heal him. If there were even a chance that it might harm the baby, he wouldn't risk it. She could have done it anyway, when he was sleeping, but she waited, crouched around her own middle and terrified. Terrified of losing the first baby that had grown big enough for her to feel moving, and of letting go the only person who had ever loved her without limits. She told herself she could hold on long enough that she could have both of them.

He died the night the nurses convinced her to

go home and get a decent night's rest in her own bed. When the phone rang at four a.m., she knew before lifting the receiver. Four a.m. was a time they saw together a lot. Babies tended to come then, in that timeless space between night and morning, in those moments where even the weariest body got a rush of adrenaline to spur them on. It was also a common time for people to die because they needed that extra surge of energy to finally let go.

After she hung up the phone, she felt something sever inside of her, and a pain worse than anything she had ever felt drove her to her knees. It took only minutes. She delivered a miniature boy on the floor of her bedroom, saw him breathe once, an inhalation that lifted his entire torso, as if he could hold on to it, and defy nature. Then he died. She woke in her own hospital bed, after one of the pregnant girls discovered her unconscious and haemorrhaging, the elfin child in a vice grip in her arms. A doctor she'd never met before, who was younger than she was and so awkward she almost felt sorry for him, told her she'd had an emergency hysterectomy. She would never be pregnant again.

The next year of her life was as unbearable as any that had come before it. She wanted to die but felt already dead. She kept remembering herself as a child, and all the hope she'd had that when she grew up she would be happy. Her life's work had given her glimpses of this, but without Matthew her heart was no longer in it. It didn't seem any better, somehow, being a woman. The world still stole from her the same as when she was a helpless girl.

She sealed herself up just enough to go through the motions. She had occasional affairs with women, but never with men. She painted, she walked the promenade and looked at the sea, sometimes while holding the hand of a frightened girl in early labour. She resigned herself, even as her heart still raged, that it would never be her.

Then she got the letter from Desmond's solicitor about the island and the house. Her mother's stories started coming back to her, of holy wells that gave babies to barren women, and fairies that lent their dark gifts in exchange for the chance to live in the world. Her mother had died years before, in a fire in Saint Dymphna's Asylum. She was no longer there to warn Brigid of the cost of such magic, or to remind her of how badly all of her stories ended.

★ ★ ★

The weather stops changing, for the entire month of August there is rarely a cloud in the endless blue sky. The sun is much stronger than Brigid expected — no trees means no shade — and it remains in the position of high noon for hours. Rua wearies more quickly, seeks out the shore more than the fields, flops her belly down in the frigid ocean for relief. Brigid takes off her shoes and walks in the same water, watching Niall and his cousins splashing between the seaweed-covered rocks. The weather has made all the islanders giddy, it is not just the children who are bright red with sunburn, their eyes manic from the overdose of sunshine. No one wants to be inside. The women bring their teacups and their dinner plates outside and lay out picnics on the meticulous stone walls. They bring their chairs out and knit and peel potatoes and darn clothing, moving their spots around the house with the circle of the sun.

After three weeks of unrelenting heat, the well closest to Brigid's house dries up, the one further up the hill ceases to flow soon after that. Malachy brings her water in large ceramic jugs on the back of the poor, overheated donkey. He says the weather is good for the hay, which they are cutting all over the island to store for the cattle in the winter. Malachy and Austin cut her field down for her, and when they have gone, the hay piled into clochán-shaped reeks in the field, she finds a bird's nest, whorled out of hay into the ground, eggshells cracked and abandoned. Niall tells her it's the corncrake's.

'They might have left a spot round the nest,' he says, shaking his head. 'Now she will have moved on.' Brigid worries until she hears the male again that night. She knows it is the same corncrake. She can now distinguish the corncrakes in their separate fields. Their voices are as varied as people's.

'Has the island ever had a drought before?' she asks Emer the next day. Niall is running circles around the dog and pig, mocking them with a sheep's thighbone he found in a field. He runs too close to Emer, almost knocking into her.

'Would you mind yourself,' Emer snaps. Emer gets irritable with Niall now, she is so caught up in her longing for Brigid. Niall drops his arm, dejected, and Rua yanks the bone from his hand. Emer pulls Niall in for a quick hug of apology.

'Every so often we get a summer like this,' Emer says. 'The last one was when I was a girl.'

'Will the island run out of fresh water?' Brigid asks.

'Saint Brigid's well never runs dry,' Niall announces. 'It isn't meant to. It's holy.'

Emer glares a warning at him, then flicks her gaze back towards Brigid. Brigid is holding her breath.

'We may have to visit that one soon enough,' Emer mumbles and lets, as she does often now, a smile creep into her one eye, burning blue and relentless, like the summer sky.

★ ★ ★

Three days later Emer volunteers Niall to help his uncle and father mend a currach, and asks Brigid if she wants to go on a walk. She's pulling at the collar of her blouse, a nervous gesture Brigid has noticed — Emer hates to have fabric touching the hollow of her throat. Brigid excuses herself quickly and goes into her bedroom to fetch the pouch she keeps under the mattress, just in case.

They walk up the green road, a road that was formed by the tedious work of nuns, with a wall of piled slate on one side, ditches to divert flood, and a dense, level carpet of mossy grass. The road is littered with pellets of sheep dung, some glistening black, most faded to the colour of hard dust. They walk all the way around to the cliffs, which are quiet today, the normal scream of wind tamed by the heat to a breeze.

Emer gets far too close to the edge. Brigid reaches for her arm, thinking Emer's faulty peripheral vision is to blame. But Emer boldly links her fingers into Brigid's and pulls her along.

A hidden path, no wider than a sheep's hooves, steps down into the abyss of the cliff. For an instant it seems they will step off into the gliding sea birds, but then Brigid sees it, how it winds around and down into a hidden cave, a small room carved into the side of the sheer cliff. After a balancing act that leaves her dizzy and wobbling over the drop, they are inside a sanctuary almost half the size of her living room. Carpeted in moss, a natural hearth in the stone-layered earth, at its centre a stream of water pours into a deep well. It is damp in here, cooler than the weather has been in weeks; the sun hasn't passed its peak and fallen west, so the room has been in shadow since yesterday. The sound of fresh water seems louder than the salt waves crashing below. Emer settles herself on to mossy ground and reaches for the tin mug left in a natural shelf in the wall of the cliff. She dips it into darkness and lifts it again, taking a long drink and turning to offer it to Brigid. Lust, which seems to grow stronger every time they are together, rises off Emer like steam. She isn't bothering to hide it now, she lets her hand linger

228

a bit too long when handing over the mug.

Brigid can see that Emer brought her here because she hopes that this will be the place they can finally grab hold of one another, far from anyone who might stop them. She takes the cup offered to her and tips it to her lips. The water is delicious, so cold it hurts her teeth. She empties the cup. It is the kind of water that makes you realise just how thirsty you have always been.

She kneels down, waiting for a sign, waiting for the warmth in her middle that tells her it has worked. But there is nothing. Only more thirst and the burden of what Emer expects next.

'You've heard the stories, then,' Emer says.

'Some of them.'

'Saint Brigid left it. They say the water never ceases to flow, same as her fire. The nuns were meant to watch over it, but once they left, the islanders didn't see many miracles. They used it to bless babies, and soak the blue cloth that is said to be from her cloak, that sort of thing.

'In my grandmother's time, a woman came all the way from America with her blind son. Saint Brigid was known for blind cures, you know, because of the time she plucked her own eye out to avoid getting married.

'She laid the boy down and let the water run over his face. They say he sat up, rubbed his eyes and said, 'Mammy, look at the sea.''

Brigid is quiet for a while. 'That's not the story my mother told me,' she says.

Emer shrugs. 'There are others. Every family has one. Barren wombs filled up, dying children saved, curses of fairies reversed. They say the islanders got worried because every time they let some blow-in use the well it failed them for a while. Some thought we weren't meant to share it. That Brigid herself wanted it only for those committed to staying here. We keep it hidden now. Took the cross away.'

'Why did you bring me?'

Emer shrugs and looks down. 'It hasn't worked in donkey's years. I don't see the harm.'

'Emer,' Brigid says quietly. She is sitting as far away as she can, the font of water between them, but Emer twitches, as if Brigid has just grabbed her.

'Isn't this what you want?' Emer says.

'Yes,' she says.

'I want to give it to you.' Emer is trying to hide her hands beneath her thighs to stop them shaking.

'Thank you,' Brigid says, carefully. 'I'm grateful to you, Emer.'

Emer shrugs, but she is blushing.

'What do you want it for?' she says. The silence is long, all Brigid can hear is water, beckoning, and Emer attempting to regulate her breath.

'I want to have a baby.'

Emer snorts. 'Did no one let on you need a man for that?'

'I need a miracle first. I don't have a womb.'

Emer makes that quick, dismissive noise in her throat. 'That's a tall order,' she says. She gestures to the water, and says, softer now, 'Go on and see, then.'

Brigid takes the pouch from the pocket of her

230

sweater, pulls the stained handkerchief out from within it, and opens the precious package on the smooth slate ledge that surrounds the pool of water. In all her years of midwifery, it wasn't until the end that she delivered a child born with the caul, which promises, depending on who you ask, good fortune, second sight, a lifetime's safety from drowning. The mother had no interest in such superstition, and had let Brigid keep it. Brigid herself, her mother once told her, had been born this way, entirely encased in a membrane that she had to puncture and peel off to pull Brigid, blue and tightly curled, into the world.

The caul is webbed and delicate, so old and dry that when she picks it up and lowers her palm beneath the water, it fills up for an instant, grows and stretches like the memory of a small skull, then breaks up and is absorbed so quickly it is as if it was never there at all. She barely has time to whisper her wish, swallow what she can, and feels suddenly foolish, heavy, burdened by hope she should have let wash away long ago.

'Were you born beneath the veil?' Emer says. For a moment, Brigid is confused, and thinks of the nuns of her girlhood, black curtains of cloth instead of hair. Then she realises that Emer means the caul. She nods.

'Niall was as well,' Emer says. 'Patch and Austin keep it in the currach. It's meant to protect them at sea.'

'It isn't mine,' Brigid says.

'It's in your family, though. Your mother had it. Was she the one who told you to bring it here?' Brigid wants Emer to stop talking. As if her voice, like her hands, might drive away the promise swirling in the water.

'Don't be thinking the caul comes from the saints. It's the work of the good people. It's like asking a priest the way to the brothel.'

A laugh bursts out of Brigid, loud and out of place in the still room. 'I'm not fussy,' she says, 'about where my miracles come from.'

'Some good it did me,' Emer sneers, as awkward and cruel as she gets. 'My sister tried to heal me with this water after my eye went. Miracles don't work for some of us.'

Emer looks miserable, so caught between her two selves, the one who hurts and the one who gets hurt, that Brigid flares at the sight of it. There is something about this cursed, awkward girl that her hands throb to fix. Like a wound gushing blood that she must stop before she thinks of what will happen afterwards. She is suddenly, furiously, aroused. And so her wariness and secrets drowned out, she crawls her way across the moss, and kneels in front of Emer. She kisses her, straight on the mouth, gently until Emer's lips open up, then relentlessly, pushing the grateful girl on to her back and pressing her into the soft ground. Her abandon is instantaneous, the clenched, furious, terrified Emer is gone, and every inch of her is reaching out like hungry flames, begging for the salve of Brigid's hands.

After a while, Brigid reaches up to flick open the leather patch above her eye and Emer freezes. Brigid feels her switch from helpless to dangerous in an instant. Feels the surge of wretchedness that tries to draw her in. She deflects it with her own hand, threading their fingers and pulling Emer's palm, trapping it between their breasts.

'It's all right,' she whispers. The skin beneath the patch is bumpy and purple, a keloid scar raised up and obliterating what were once eyelids, which the doctors in town ignorantly sewed shut. In a better hospital, they would have fitted her for a glass eye. Brigid kisses the horrible spot gently, like a mother pretending to ease the wound of a child. Emer pulls her hand free and reaches for her, arching her hips and pulling her face down and kissing her hard, with teeth, with anger, with everything she tries to blame on everyone else.

Brigid gives her what she wants. She does everything that Emer has been imagining with slow, thorough reverence. She takes breaks to fill her mouth with the painfully cold well water and then let it flow from her lips into every place where Emer thirsts. They make furious love by the ancient drip of water, and Emer surprises her by turning it around, without asking for permission, as so many women have before. She dips her hand in the same water, and reaches inside Brigid, who grabs on, trapping Emer's wrist in her hands so she will not pull away. She watches Emer's face as the pleasure moves through her for so long it is almost painful, like water so cold you can barely swallow it, watches Emer's eye widen in recognition as Brigid's insides seize upon her hand.

Later she will tell herself she felt it, felt the instant life flared inside of her, but really she is too lost in what she has started to notice what the water begins.

12

Anam Cara

September, 1959

'Where are you off to now?' Emer's mother chides. 'Not to that Yank's again.'

'She needs help with the sheep,' Emer replies.

'Would you not have a mind to help your own sister?'

'Rose doesn't need my help.' Her mother huffs at this.

'That woman's turned you cross-eyed. You've no sense at all.'

'I don't know what you're on about.'

'Don't you, now?'

'Would you not leave me be?' Emer mutters. She wants to scream it, to rage like a child pushed to her limit, but it would give her mother too much satisfaction.

She wishes they would all leave her alone. Rose, Austin, Patch, even Niall, or the fretting over him anyway. She misses the days when she could put the fire iron across his cradle, or wind him to her front with a long strip of flannel. When he is out of her sight, with his father, or at Rose's house with the girls, Emer's neck tightens with anxiety, fear rising and swarming in her throat like the memory of those bees. The moment she lays eyes on him, it breaks away.

The possibility of it returning is always there, it crouches, ready to flare again when he runs outside of her limited vision.

Now she wants him to go somewhere else. Just for an afternoon, for a guaranteed hour instead of the few minutes that stretch into one, to wander off and know exactly how long he will be gone, so she can have this possibility, this promise of Brigid's hands reaching for her again.

She hadn't dared imagine that all the time she had wanted her, Brigid had felt the same. The thrill of it, that moment when Brigid moved into the pained space that separated them. It was like being handed the option to become someone else altogether.

★ ★ ★

When Rose and Emer were eleven, there was a young teacher in the island school who taught them about the druid Brigid alongside the traditional lessons about the saint. The druids believed that souls radiated around bodies, and when a person found their *anam cara*, soul friend, it meant that both their spirits began to flow together, like two streams meeting to fill a well. The teacher used this metaphor to partner the children up for studying their sums and spelling. Having a soul friend challenged you, she explained, awakened you to yourself so you could accomplish things you wouldn't have been able to do on your own. They could remove what was weighing you down, like the peeling off of drenched clothes. Saint Brigid had Darla, and her postulants paired off together, because Brigid was not only a Christian saint. She carried with her stories that were more ancient than Jesus.

The girls in the school fell in love with this idea. During their dinner break they gathered behind the stone wall and re-enacted the druid ceremony of friendship. Girls paired off, wound their shawls high around their necks, clasped hands and recited, with the utmost solemnity, 'I honour your path, I drink from your well, I bring an unprotected heart to our meeting place.' They took water from the school's well and sprinkled it on each other's hair and pressed their lips together with the fervour they imagined they would one day kiss boys. Everyone wanted to be Rose's *anam cara*, but since no one wanted to be Emer's — they wouldn't dare hold her hand and they shuddered at the thought of her chapped, angry mouth — Rose always chose her sister out of loyalty. They didn't kiss or bring much enthusiasm when it was their turn, but there were only eight girls in the school, and Rose couldn't afford to insult any of them by not playing along. The lads, who were the ones they were practising for, played football in the field and paid them little mind.

The priest, who only got over to St Brigid's once a month if the weather allowed, sent that teacher packing when word of her irreverent lessons reached him. He was used to island superstition, and thought it harmless, he was Irish, after all. But it was one thing to hold on to whispered, fireside references to the good people, it was quite another to have a schoolteacher confusing the Christian saint with a pagan goddess.

Rose and Emer were both relieved when he put a stop to it. Rose because the whole business had seemed a bit sinful all along, and Emer because watching her classmates tilt towards each other's lips made heat rise so furiously in her throat she imagined that, if anyone dared to kiss her, she would spew fire into their mouths. She despised the lot of them, and she resented that none of them wanted to be her partner; they all wanted Rose, and they blamed her even more for keeping Rose away from them.

She thinks of this the first time Brigid kisses her, pushing her back on to the ground beside the well and letting the holy water pass into her mouth. She had wanted one of those girls to kiss her, hard enough that it would push away the clog left inside her throat by the fairies. Later, when she watched Rose in the clochán with Austin, when she saw what followed kissing, she wanted that as well.

Now she wonders if Saint Brigid and her nuns were devout at all. She imagines them in the clocháns, not only praying and transcribing but also lifting off their habits and pressing against each other, letting themselves drop away into another woman's mouth.

Worship has an entirely different meaning now.

★ ★ ★

Rose invites Brigid over for the Saturday evening meal. The weather is still hot and cloudless, the drought has left the islanders sun-burned and with an unquenchable thirst they are not accustomed to. Such merciless sun usually bothers Emer's eye, but it now seems fitting. The island is as ablaze and longing for release as she is.

Brigid has been to everyone's house now, for tea or a meal or both, she knows every islander's name and can't walk the road without stopping to talk to a dozen people on the way. They all know she was a midwife and have started coming to her with small ailments. She stitches up Malachy's hand after he slices it gutting fish, she sits and listens to women who have unexplained pain, or abnormally heavy bleeding, or urine infections. It seems just having tea with her makes most of the women feel better immediately.

'Are you healing them too, now?' Emer asks, but Brigid denies it.

'Sometimes just listening is enough.'

When Rose complains of a line of fiery pain shooting from her buttock to her calf, Brigid gives her a bottle of fragrant oil and tells her to have Austin massage a spot on her lower back.

'It will be fun for the both of you,' she says, and Rose, though she blushes, smiles knowingly in that way that used to make Emer furious. Now Emer finds herself, at odd moments, thinking of Brigid and smiling the same way.

The only one who won't take help from her is Emer's mother. Brigid suggests that daily exercise, shuffling around with her cane, would do a lot for her aches and, possibly, her mood.

'We're the same age,' Brigid says. 'We have a lot of life left.' Clodagh scorns this.

'Mind your business,' she spits. 'No one invited you into mine.'

Instead of showing offence, Brigid treats Clodagh with extra veneration, and whenever she is over, she repeats Clodagh's caustic comments as if they are useful and she's dying to hear more. Their mother eventually goes silent, as she doesn't enjoy hearing herself repeated.

Dinner that evening lingers on, normal bedtimes blurred by the two bottles of red wine Brigid brings as a gift. Emer is grateful that her husband is getting drunk on the mainland instead of here — he would drink more than the rest of them, more than the two glasses that make her edges go soft. She can't imagine him managing to say a word to Brigid. Austin slags Brigid a bit about the usual things, but is mostly quiet while she and Rose jabber on about Saint Brigid.

'There wasn't a man on the island then. Brigid wouldn't allow it. Only the boys that were born to those unwed mothers. They say she wasn't too fond of them, either. But once they were here, well, it wasn't easy to go.'

'Why not?' Brigid asks.

'She burned all the currachs,' Rose says. 'The original boats she came with, she and Darla set them alight in the cove so they wouldn't be able to leave. They had to wait for a boat to come to them.'

'That's either serious devotion,' Brigid says, 'or madness.'

'It's a lovely spot to be marooned, I've always said,' Rose says.

'I agree,' Brigid smiles.

'That's not what you say in a storm,' Emer quips, but neither woman seems to hear her. Only Clodagh looks her over with that permanent scowl.

Brigid helps Rose put the children to bed while Emer does the washing up. Austin sits with his dirty socks up on the table, right in Emer's way.

'I don't think she's the full shilling,' Clodagh says, when Brigid carries a sleeping toddler into the bedroom.

'Oh, give it a rest, Mammy,' Emer says.

'You can't say a word against Brigid,' Austin laughs. 'Not to Emer, anyways. She's besotted.' Emer whacks at his feet with the dishcloth, then turns to hide her blush. Austin chuckles and moves over to the fire to light his pipe.

Brigid stays late and by the time she is ready to leave, Niall has fallen asleep with the older girls in the loft bed.

'Leave the child here, Emer,' Rose says. 'He's too big to carry any more.'

Emer stiffens and hopes that Brigid, across the room, is pausing her breath in the same anticipation.

'Would you walk Brigid home?' Rose says. 'I'm knackered as it is. Go and help her with the chores we stole her from.'

Austin looks up at Emer for a second, with

something other than his usual polite sweep of eyes. He knows, she thinks, he can sense what she and Brigid are about to do. But then his eyes pass over her and fix on to his wife and that familiar grin creeps up. He has plans of his own. Funny that his smiles still hurt her, even though she is looking forward to someone else's mouth.

Emer and Brigid leave together. It is September and the sun goes down earlier every day. Soon enough the darkness will be far longer than the light. But the breeze is mild, and the stars and moon are unclothed and the road to Brigid's house appears lit up from within. Emer imagines she can hear within their footsteps an echo of anticipation, the thud and shuffle of lust. This is how Austin and Rose once felt, back when they had to walk to secret places where they could touch each other. Emer recognises the feeling though she is still alarmed at whom it is attached to.

★ ★ ★

'It's all right,' Brigid croons, when Emer starts to tremble, overwhelmed by the ache that grows fathomless as Brigid slowly removes her clothes.

It is all too much this time. Her mouth is so large, her kisses huge and wet and gaping, as if they want to swallow her, her hands are hot and skidding off Emer in their eagerness, gripping occasionally as if they are grabbing her back from a fall.

'I've not done this,' Emer says softly, when they are fully naked for the first time, side by

242

side on the hearth bed, bodies glowing and soft and mirrored, one an older version, just beginning to release itself in places, by the light of the turf fire.

'Not with anyone else. No one touches me. Even when they do . . . It's difficult to explain.'

'You don't need to,' Brigid says, rolling on top of her. Emer can barely keep up with what is happening. It's like a new body being born under Brigid's demanding hands.

After it is finished and the fired-up patches that Brigid ignited slowly throb and go out, she grows cold and searches for the blanket by their feet.

'I thought you were married,' Emer says suddenly.

Brigid laughs. 'I was.'

'But you've done this before.'

'Yes, Emer.'

'With women, I mean.'

'I loved my husband. But I had this with women as well. A long time ago.'

'It's a sin, sure,' Emer says.

'So they tell me.'

'Will you leave us now?' Emer says, letting this new fear rush forward, fear that swells with the same urgency as her desire. 'Now that I've shown you the well?'

'I'm not going anywhere.'

'Which man will you get?' Emer whispers. 'To give you the baby?'

And Brigid kisses her in a way that feels almost angry, but Emer wants this so much that she can't stop to question what emotion is behind it. This time, Emer pushes Brigid on to her back. She does not pause and wonder what to do, she has spent enough time imagining it. She is astonished at Brigid's reactions. Delighted that her hands, her mouth, and her body can be so skilful, can pull such violent pleasure out of someone else. Pleasure instead of disgust.

She stays too long; dawn has already come and gone by the time she half hurries away from Brigid's house. She goes the high road, avoiding the quay and the men readying the currachs for Mass. But then she comes across Austin and his dog driving a group of sheep to a virgin field. Before she can help it, she blushes so quick and hard it seems audible, like a gasp in the still, mist-thick air. Austin has the same blue eyes as Niall, and he locks them on her now. He glances quickly down, raking his eyes over her, then back to her face. Emer thinks he can see everything she just did, and his gaze feels both like a violation and a compliment.

'Out for a stroll, Emer?' Austin cocks his head and winks at her.

She walks the rest of the way home burning with anger and embarrassment, furious at being seen, at being ridiculed, but mostly bewildered that Austin's eyes have the power to undo her still.

★ ★ ★

The next week, Emer allows Niall to start school. She had planned to keep him home another year, though at six he is a year older than most in the infants' class. His cousins walk him there in the morning and Emer picks him up in time for dinner. It is the longest she has ever been without him. She walks straight up the road and pulls Brigid's curtains in the middle of mild September mornings.

Sometimes she even leaves in the night-time, when Patch is off on the mainland, Niall sleeping sweetly in her bed. It is like tearing something as she leaves him there, runs over the brackish grass and stone and arrives, breathless, only to have Brigid take her breath even more. Brigid is always happy to see her, and after they make love her gaze cools into gratitude, something that never happened with Patch, who, back when they had relations, finished with a grunt and a shudder as if he'd just done something distasteful. Even with Brigid, though, there is a catch that reminds her who she is. There is an element of torture in it all, an arm thrown over her face, a twisted expression, a clenching of the mouth and eyes that so reminds her of when she inserts pain and doubt into people that sometimes she wonders if it is all a form of the same thing. If pain and pleasure are so closely linked that just the slightest turning can change it. There is violence in love, more than she'd imagined there would be.

She runs home on these nights, terror in her throat, ripping through the damp air as if it is trying to stop her, barging into the house to fall next to Niall and hold him close, kissing his face, pausing at his lips to make certain he is still breathing. Still himself. To see that she has not abandoned everything just to feel something that, to be honest, by the time she arrives home, has faded into disbelief.

There are moments with Brigid — not having to do with lust but afterwards, lying in the bracken watching the clouds move, or walking without touching along the cliff edge, Niall and the pig and Brigid's dog bounding ahead of them — where Emer has a foreign feeling. Cupfuls of time where she feels no anxiety or anger or ugliness or regret. Where nothing swarms or seizes within her and all she is aware of is a still, liquid feeling of joy. It is not the same as the joy Niall lends to her, which allows her to forget herself and delight in him; this happiness originates inside her. The first time it happens she is jolted, as though from an invisible hand, then smiles as wide as the sky before them.

'Will you look at that,' Emer murmurs, and Niall squints at her suspiciously. His mother is not prone to admiring nature.

Everything looks sharper now, the changing colours of moss and heather, the deep, autumn sun that feels warmer because of the chill in the air, and she imagines this is how the island looks to Brigid, looks to anyone who feels this way, like a paradise.

This new bliss of Emer's is so dense she manages to keep it for whole minutes, long dark nights, entire soft days, before she feels the sharp intrusion of fear, the coiling premonition of regret. Such elation, she thinks, must be what other people feel — her sister, her son, Brigid, a group of married nuns — they must grow accustomed to it, and she imagines it is just as easy to be stolen by joy as by misery.

She takes Brigid's hand on impulse; usually they try not to touch in front of Niall. Brigid stops walking and turns to face her, pulling her hand in to hide it behind the flap of her jacket, and pressing it promisingly against her warm thigh. Since their mouths can't meet, they lock eyes. Emer thinks she can see Brigid's pupil pulse in the exact rhythm of her own aroused heart.

'*Anam cara*,' Emer whispers, before she can stop herself.

And though Brigid smiles, and squeezes her palm, something trips in her gaze, the pupil misses a beat, and she looks away, towards Niall and the pets. Emer convinces herself that it is only prudence that makes Brigid not echo this name.

13

Fairy Music

September, 1959

There is a fair amount of back and forth, but in the end, they all decide to go over to Mass without Emer. When she wakes to bright weather, Emer is so sure she is going that the consequences don't register when she feels the heat on Niall's forehead. His face is flushed, and when he opens his eyes they are wet and foggy.

'Oh,' she says, confused. 'Are you ill?' Niall looks at her without much interest.

'I'm only tired,' he says and turns around and falls back to sleep.

She is so disappointed at the realisation — he will have to stay in bed, she will have to stay with him, she will not be going over for a day of music and food and summer visitors — that she forgets to be worried about him being ill. She doesn't even think of it for the next while, during all the debate of who will go and who will stay. Her mother is determined to go and see her cousins back from Liverpool staying at the hotel, and so struggles into her black dress and shawl and sits stubbornly by the door with her cane, refusing to discuss any other option. Patch has an appointment with a man from the mainland about the sheep and does not suggest changing

248

it. Rose, of course, offers to stay. Emer gets irritable then.

'Do you think I can't take care of the one child?' she snaps at her sister, who is all dressed for Mass but has come down to check on her.

'I do, of course,' Rose says, tidying the table rather than holding the blade of Emer's gaze. 'I thought you'd want the company.'

'Fierce company you'll be,' Emer scoffs, 'with those two hanging off you and your face falling over missing your trip to the shops.'

'You're in a bad twist today,' Rose says casually, though Emer can tell she is hurt.

'Go on, then, and stop the fuss. I'm grand as I am. Bring us a packet of crisps.'

Emer turns around, blinking away the burning in her eyes. This is Brigid's first trip to Muruch. Rose and the other wives convinced her to go. Now Emer will miss it.

Of course as soon as Rose leaves, insulted but keeping her smile up, Emer wishes she had stayed. Now her beautiful sister will be with Brigid instead of her.

She watches from the front stoop as they load the currachs. The whole island is going, it is one of those days where no one fears the water. Brigid is at the quay, well turned-out in a colourful skirt and blouse. Emer watches Patch lower her, then Rose and the girls down into the boat. She has a brief, fierce hope that Brigid will ask Patch where she is, and decide to stay behind. But Rose says something that makes Brigid throw her head back and laugh, and Emer turns into her house, closing the door on them all.

It isn't until the day is half-gone that she realises Austin is still there. She goes out the back door to dump the dishwater and sees him walking the fields to the south-east. He holds a spade up in greeting, then stoops to the weeds. Just the sight of his long body and that shock of hair, dark as bottled ink and down to his collar, is enough to fluster her and she forgets what she meant to do next and goes to check on Niall instead. He is feeling better and able to sit up in bed for toast and tea.

When she goes out to hang the washing, the sky has darkened, and she can feel the wind picking up. The sea between the two islands is choppy now, grey and menacing when this morning it was as blue and smooth as the sky. It has happened before, going over to Mass in calm waters and having to stay with their cousins overnight when the weather turns. As a child, Emer loved those emergency holidays, all the girls jumbled together in the hearth bed, pretending to sleep while they snuck glimpses of the adults' smiling faces by the light of the fire. It was completely the opposite of being stuck on their island; there they were stranded in civilisation. Once they stayed for five whole days and Emer cried the morning they'd woken to sun and agreeable sea.

By the time Austin calls in to her, the rain is lashing sideways, the wind so loud in the hedges that she can't tell the difference between the battered branches and the roar of the sea.

'Howaya keeping, Austin,' Emer says, not looking at him, stepping aside for him to duck in through the door. He smells of rain and wind and sheep, of wet clothing and work, he smells so like her own husband that if she doesn't look straight at him, she won't know the difference. Except when he speaks.

'That wind would skin a fairy,' he says happily, and Emer almost laughs. He removes his hat and shakes the water from his collar. 'They won't be back tonight, sure. The sea's walled them over.'

'You'll be wanting your tea, then,' Emer says, moving around the room without looking at him. She sees out of the corner of her eye, teeth flash; he's smiling at her.

'I can feed myself, Emer,' he says. 'I only came to check on you. How's himself?'

'I expect he'll be well over it tomorrow,' Emer says.

'Grand, so,' Austin says, still standing, beginning to turn awkward as even easy-going people do around Emer.

'You might as well eat,' Emer says, 'if you're going to stand there all evening.' Austin pauses, he would clearly prefer to leave. As if Rose is behind him whispering a request, he takes off his woollen jacket, hangs it on his brother's hook and sits in his brother's chair.

They eat potatoes with butter and cabbage and mackerel and wash it all down with milky tea. Emer sneaks a few looks at Austin as he hunches over his plate, his cheeks are smooth from a recent shave, which means he planned to go over to Mass and changed his mind.

251

'Rose asked you to stay behind,' she realises aloud.

'It's no bother,' Austin smiles. She looks away. He is handsome enough with a straight face but when he smiles it is something else altogether. His smile is like a boy's, nothing held back, quick and full and mischievous, and it still does something terrible to Emer.

'You'll miss the session,' she says, clearing the plates to avoid another smile. Austin is usually asked to sing after Mass, he often comes back hoarse on a Sunday night from granting all the requests. Everyone on Muruch loves his singing, and often he'll sing with his father, who has the same deep voice. Every summer there is some visitor from Dublin or Canada who wants to arrange a tour, but it never happens. Emer knows from Rose that Austin never follows through on contacting them.

'Sure, Rose is expecting the album any day now,' Emer jokes.

'Don't be holding your breath,' Austin says. 'I'm only a fisherman.'

''Tis better than being a fisherman's wife,' Emer scoffs.

Austin snaps to attention. 'Do you not think Rose is happy enough?'

'I'd say Rose is delighted,' Emer says. Austin actually blushes.

'Arrah. Pardon,' he says, realising.

'Not a bother,' she says. She pours more tea.

'Patch,' he begins, then he runs out.

'Patch is Patch,' Emer says. 'We'll leave it, so.' Austin nods.

Silence stretches between them. She puts the kettle on for tea.

'Niall's a comfort to you, sure,' Austin says.

'He is.'

'It's a pity,' he starts. She stops him.

'That's enough of that now. I'll not be pitied about being unable for more. I'm not Rose, I don't want a houseful. I like a bit of quiet to think.'

Austin looks at her oddly. This is the longest string of sentences she has ever said to him.

'This island's not quiet enough for you?' he says.

Niall comes stumbling into the kitchen, hair tufted up in the back, rubbing his eyes.

'Howaya, Austin,' he says pleasantly, then climbs straight into his mother's lap without request or invitation. He still does this; Rose usually puts a stop to children in her lap after the next set is born. Emer had hoped he would always do it, but she's realised lately that he has to hunch to fit in the space between her lap and chin. Soon enough it will be like having a man in her lap. She didn't realise how soon she would miss it, the smallness of him.

'Bad dose, eh, Niall?' Austin says.

'Aye,' Niall sighs, snuggling closer to Emer.

'I've the cure outside,' Austin winks. He goes to the door, opens it and picks up a jug of poitín he has left on the stoop. He struggles to close the door again on the wind.

'You're a terrible man altogether,' Emer says. Niall smiles.

'A little scailtin and you'll be in the fields come morning.'

'May I, Mammy?' Niall wiggles around on her lap, excited.

'If you must,' she says. She's never given Niall the spirit-laden punch that children are fed for colds and flu. She has an idea, which contradicts everyone else's, that the alcohol is not good for him. But she doesn't want Austin to leave, so she heats a bit of milk on the coals, pours a little of the strong, clear liquid in it, dabs a spoonful of butter and stirs the sugar in. A squeeze from the last of the lemon she has on the dresser, wondering if Rose will be able to get her another.

'Make the old ones a spot as well,' Austin says. She pours hot water into two mugs of poitín, adds sugar to hers and slices the leftover lemon rind with her knife into two slivers. Austin makes a fuss out of clinking his mug against the boy's, as if they are in the pub. Niall's eyes widen at his first sip.

When Niall asks him, Austin takes a tin whistle out of his pocket and plays a few tunes, one thigh knocking his chair with the beat. Niall gets up for a brief dance, tapping in the old style, but also spinning and laughing. Emer, who never dances, stays stiffly in her chair. In the lamplight, she thinks she can see the fiery ring in Niall's eyes grow larger, and that look of remove, and so she pulls him back on to her lap and feeds him the rest of the mug.

Emer can feel the poitín working on him as he drinks it down, with each sip Niall grows heavy in her lap. When he's done, half-asleep against her, Austin stops playing, takes the mug from his hand and lifts him, walking into the bedroom.

Emer doesn't like Austin carrying Niall at all, she thought she would as he leaned over, that there would be a moment where she imagined that they were married and Niall was his, but it's not like that. It's the same as when anyone pats Niall's head or squeezes his shoulder or asks for a kiss from him. She needs to squeeze her fists to keep from dragging him back. When he was a baby she always made up a reason not to let people hold him. If an auntie grabbed him regardless, Emer would have to sit on her hands, her milk letting down in protest. She feared that those were the moments he was most likely to be stolen: right in front of her, when she let her vigilance be compromised by manners.

Austin closes the door to the bedroom, comes over to the fire, and makes them two more drinks. The rain lashes against the panes, the wind screams and Emer thinks of Brigid and Rose in her cousin's house, bright-eyed and laughing and enjoying themselves. Trapped on the better side. Austin empties his drink in two swallows and makes himself a third, reusing the lemon rind.

'The dog,' Emer says suddenly, standing up. 'Brigid won't be back to let Rua in.' Austin laughs at this.

'That dog is well able to sleep out in the rain,' he says. 'She pays far too much mind to that creature. Just like a Yank.' Emer sits back down. She can't help wincing at the thought of Rua's narrow face, and the way it looks back at Brigid when they are walking on the green road, its amber eyes wet with loyalty.

255

'Fair play to her, though,' Austin says. 'She's able enough.' Emer hides her blush in her steaming mug.

'Sure, she won't make it through the winter,' he adds. And though Emer once said the same thing, the bitter taste of lemon regurgitates into her throat.

'She may surprise you,' she says. Austin looks at her strangely again. She has no poise while taking about Brigid. She almost wants to rip her collar open to let out the heat that even thinking of her stirs up.

'Sure, with you and Malachy waiting on her all the time she has both a husband and a wife.'

'Stop acting the maggot,' Emer says. Women are meant to respond with disgust at such unnatural suggestions. It wasn't until she was with Brigid that she discovered how often men made them. It is like a game between themselves, how crude they can be about women and their intimacy.

'Will yer man in the government give her a house as well?' Austin says. 'Or will you just let her share yours?'

When she was a girl she thought Austin was sweeter than the rest of them. Now he has the same cruel eyebrows and mocking voice as the boys from her childhood.

'You should sign on,' Emer says, avoiding his eyes. 'You'll get the best house with all those babbies.'

'Rose would never agree to it,' Austin says. 'We're just after building the house here.'

It's as if Emer has been struck.

256

'Would you go?' she says incredulously. 'Would you leave the island?' Austin won't look at her straight.

'You've to pay for all those modern conveniences. And the land is desperate. Full of rock.' He seems to get taller suddenly, in his chair. 'But would I live in a place where my every move didn't depend on the swell of the sea? I'm no fool, Emer.'

'Have you told Rose?' Emer says. Austin glares at her, contemptuous.

'Rose. She wouldn't take a castle in Dublin over this place. She'd live here on her own, like some manky nun in a clochán, if I let her.'

Emer remembers the stories Rose once told her about the year she was boarding for secondary school. The teenagers stayed all week in a rooming house in Galway and snuck porter into their rooms and had quiet parties late into the night. The boys would sneak into the girls' rooms and take turns snogging each of them in the darkness.

Rose and Austin would end up in a corner together long after the others had tired of the game and moved on to something else. She'd lost her virginity one of those nights, as easily, she'd told Emer, as she'd first let his tongue between her lips. *I'll not regret it*, she said, even though she gave up secondary school and he gave up university and all those offers from music agents for that first set of twins. For the first time, despite the way he looks at his wife, Emer wonders if Austin regrets it. Or if Rose even asks him.

Austin has stopped talking now, both of them struck silent by what he's dared to say so far. She is not sure why this realisation — that Austin is something other than completely devoted to her sister — makes her heart beat so quickly, with occasional interruption, a skip that feels like both anticipation and dread.

Emer takes a long swallow of her drink. Austin refills her mug with straight poitín now, buoyed by her familiar silence. They drink quietly and, Emer thinks later, with purpose. Until it begins to take effect.

The drink does the same thing to her as an hour with Brigid. She sinks into her body, her limbs loosen, she sits back and crosses her legs, her neck grows long, she runs her hands through her hair. The clenched ball she normally is lets go, unravels and stretches happily, like a waking cat. She is suddenly aware of the wet of her mouth, the heat in her cheeks, the way her chest rises and falls — nothing about her body feels awkward. She smiles, and her smile is not the normal clenched grimace.

Austin likes her like this, she can see it. He has stopped looking at her warily, and started joking with her, slagging Brigid and her early antics with the livestock. When she begins to smile, he imitates Brigid and Rose talking about literature over dinner. Emer actually giggles when he exaggerates Brigid's American accent, making her sound like an old, haughty intellectual. Still, he seems to remember what books they were talking about. She forgets that Austin used to be scholarly. Now he's just a farmer and a fisherman, like the rest of them. He pours them each another drink. The jug appears to be bottomless.

Whenever she laughs, Austin widens his eyes, encouraged, expectant. His irises reflect the candles with little jumps of yellow flame.

'Look at you,' Austin says. 'Smiling like a basket of chips. You've changed altogether. Rose said as much. Has Patch finally copped on between the sheets?' Emer giggles and suddenly they are both laughing so loud and long she is afraid Niall will wake up. But he doesn't, not then.

Another drink — Austin has two to her every one — and she's asking for a song. He obliges, closing his eyes, allowing her to watch his face in the hearth light, without once having to look away. He sings another verse of the song Brigid gave them at the bonfire.

A stór mo chroí, when the evening mist
Over mountain and sea is falling
Oh turn around and when you list
Then maybe you'll hear me calling
The sound of my voice you might hear
Which calls for your speedy returning
A rún, a rún, won't you come back soon
To the one who will always love you?

Austin's voice is like a hand reaching deep inside her. She can't stop herself from looking at him when he finishes the song and opens his eyes. He looks back, really looks at her, she imagines, for the first time in his life. She catches his stare, holds it, pushes it back. Something flashes in there, deep in his eyes. He sees the person only Brigid has seen.

She wants to laugh out loud, at how much she wants him to do this, how inevitable it feels, even though it's the most inappropriate thing in the world, her sister's husband looking at her with lust. She's not shocked, and it doesn't even occur to her to pretend to be.

So when he moves into the dying firelight and mutters *give us a little kiss*, she smiles along with him, like they're children playing at a harmless game. She can see the ring in his eyes now, like a small fiery circle, but tells herself it is a trick of the firelight. She does not hesitate, she does not want to pause and think perhaps they shouldn't. This is what she has always wanted and the drink and the storm and her sister's absence, and her new confidence from Brigid, make it the easiest thing she has ever done. She won't stop to ponder what it is inside her, inside his eyes and that room and the drink, that makes this vile behaviour as easy and natural as letting Niall climb into her lap.

She barely feels the first few kisses, still reeling at the thought of them, then she starts to kiss back, and his lips are as luscious and foreign as his voice. She had expected, with the drink and the pipe and the memories of Patch, that he would taste like a man — ruined — but his breath is as sweet as a child's. Austin cups her face with his rough hands, the fingers, like Patch's, cracked with work and embedded in soil, and she opens her mouth. She knows now

260

from being with Brigid how to step into him, how to press, how to arch her back and show she is willing for more. He grabs her waist and grunts gratefully. She thinks briefly that perhaps he, too, has been waiting for this moment all along. For the time it takes to start it, she believes wholeheartedly that Austin is kissing her for the same reasons she is letting him. *A rún.* My love.

Then it gets rougher. Slightly, like abandonment to passion, then more so, becoming something else entirely. His tongue thrusts deeper than is comfortable. She feels the drink glug up from her stomach. She pulls away to keep from burping in his mouth, and to break the pressure that has quickly moved from tender to rude and demanding, and mostly because she has a brief image of her sister actually seeing them at it, the same way Emer once watched Rose and Austin through a hole in the stone.

'Austin,' she says. 'That's enough, so.'

He coaxes, that voice swooning whispers just at the side of her face.

'Rose wouldn't mind,' he insists. 'She never minded in the boarding house. She shared me with her friends, so she did. Surely she'd share with her sister as well.'

As ludicrous as this is, somehow during his whispering he has half-walked half-pushed her to the hearth bed, which is deep and soft and warmer than any bed in the house. He pushes her down and lies straight on top of her, kissing her into the softness, and her throat clogs in fear. Lying down was not the right thing to do, she can see that, but she isn't sure how she will arrange getting up again. When she tries to sit up, the look in Austin's eyes so unnerves her — for an instant there is no blue left in them, or even darkness, it is like looking into the orange heart of a fire. Though it fades when he turns his head away from the light, the scowl he gives her so reminds her of the way he has always looked at her, that she can't bear it, so she kisses him again. Each kiss takes her further away, like she's caught in a current and it's clear she can't make it back and that she never should have gone swimming in the first place. She's doing this all wrong. She started bold and now she wants to take it back.

She tries to use her hands. She puts them flat to his chest, willing whatever misery is in them to stop this. It doesn't work. Her hands on him are not the horror they usually are to Patch, nor do they stir up the bliss she elicits from Brigid. Something else rises to her touch. She tries to put her hands beneath her instead, but he pulls at one, pressing it to where he is hard and demanding. She wonders briefly if it is her hands making him do this or something else, something that was in him all along, but it hardly matters. She can see now, how impossible it will be to stop, whatever it is.

He pushes her blouse aside and dives at her breast, taking her nipple into his mouth. She inhales sharply, and he takes this for encouragement, and sucks harder. With Brigid this had felt good. With Austin it is horrid.

'No, Austin,' she manages and he looks up at

her, his mouth circled in saliva, loose, lecherous, grinning. As if they have some secret language, as if no is the most welcoming word he can hear. He fumbles quickly, freeing himself from his trousers. He grabs up her skirt and yanks down her drawers.

'No,' she says again, but it only eggs him on. He moves up towards her face and presses his mouth to hers again, hard, not a kiss, more like a gag.

'Hush,' he says. 'You'll wake himself.' She goes cold at this, silent, realising all of a sudden exactly what she has put at risk.

'Austin,' she pleads in a whisper. 'In all fairness. Stop now.'

He gets a look then that does more than disappoint her.

'Sure, isn't this what you wanted,' he says. 'Isn't this what you planned?' He is slurring. She realises, with a drop in her stomach, that he is very drunk, as drunk as Patch after days on the tear. Why did she not wonder, before now, what was in that jug?

'I planned nothing,' she says. She's not sure what he means. Hadn't he come over here?

'Aren't you the one Rose came back here for?' He says between clenched teeth. She is not sure she has heard him right.

She can feel him on her thigh, nothing between them, a hot threat. Like he is holding a weapon there. She doesn't want to move for fear it will puncture her. He moves a hand down and pushes her legs apart. She is shaking now, the muscles in her legs are useless to defend her.

'Austin,' she tries again. 'Don't. Think of Rose.'

That's when he puts the hand to her neck. His hand is broad enough that it fits across the front, the calloused space between his thumb and first finger resting just on the hollow spot that always tightens when she is afraid. He doesn't grip, just holds it ready, and looks her straight in the eyes. His eyes are burning now, they are dark pits of fire, there is nothing left that she recognises. His face is moving in and out of shadow and for a brief, horrifying instant he looks like someone else, something pinch-faced and slightly feminine and she hears, though the mouth in that face does not move, a shrill voice chanting, *go on, go on, go on*.

The decision is left to her. If she moves, or gets up, because suddenly she wonders why hasn't she just got up before now, walked to the door, and told him to leave, the hand will tighten. She knows it as sure as she knows what his other hand is doing as he positions himself between her legs. Whatever is inside him now, whatever she let in here with the drink and the music and her blasphemous desire, has no intention of letting her go.

Later she will remember making a choice, firmly, completely, like the shutting of a door. But in the moment it happens without her consideration. She opens her legs, and lets him, surprised at how easily he slides inside, with none of the discomfort or resistance she remembers with Patch. It used to feel sometimes that her husband was forcing himself into places that weren't meant to open, tight bony places that bruised and chafed and were sore all the next day. Something is bigger inside her now, or gone, and it barely hurts, not even at the back when he thrusts. It seems she is deep enough to absorb it all, whether she wants it or not.

'Ah, you're well ready for me,' Austin mutters and she cringes but doesn't argue with him. This is no longer a body she recognises. The only familiar thing is the vice around her neck, the threat that a movement or word or swallow will crush her. She couldn't care less at this point what happens below, with the threat of that hand focusing everything in her throat. That hand has been there her whole life; the only difference now is that it's attached to something.

It takes ages. Much longer than Patch ever took. She closes her eye and tries to go somewhere else. While Austin is thrusting, driven by something within him, but also outside of them both, unable to be stopped, she yearns to be carried away, like when she was a child, when she could turn her head and see something, a curtain by a cliff's edge, an invitation to another world.

She opens her eye and she sees Niall. He is standing quietly in the centre of the almost dark room. The tears that are running down her face into the bedclothes are also falling on Niall's flushed face. She can't shake her head without Austin noticing, so she widens her eye in warning. Niall sees it, turns around and walks quietly from the room. Austin seizes on top of her then, gripping her neck to the point of pain, then falls down next to her. He leaves one arm

265

draped across her neck and keeps it there for a long time.

There is a terrible moment later on, where she tries kissing him again. Partly she does it to stop looking at him; the face, next to her in the bed, otherworldly, the eyes not yet returned to blue, partly like asking for an apology she won't get, mostly because she wants to turn it all back to the beginning, when it could still have been just a curious kiss. They're far too gone for that. Austin turns his mouth away. He doesn't want to kiss her any more.

★ ★ ★

The next day the weather hasn't cleared and Niall sleeps later than usual with no sun to pierce through the curtains and rouse him. Emer moves carefully around the kitchen trying not to strain. She goes to the privy and wipes away viscous, rank liquid with a cloth until she feels scraped raw. She is fiercely itchy and longs for a bath. Though she expected Austin to slink away once Niall wakes, he stays with them the whole day, mends a few things Patch hadn't got around to — the hearthstone where it broke away, a wobbly table leg — shows Niall how to bait hooks with baby eel wrapped in leaves and mummified with a wrap of string, leaving the hooks on the windowsill until the fishing weather returns. He jokes with the boy, and Niall, showing no loyalty whatsoever, smiles and follows instructions willingly. At one point, while she is tidying up the hearth bed, stripping the linens off to put in a hot

266

wash, one of the poitín mugs rolls out from underneath and falls on to the stone floor and cracks into two thick pieces. She almost starts to cry, the reality of last night coming at her like the pottery has been thrown in her face. Niall and Austin look up at her.

'Mammy,' Niall scolds. 'You broke it.' Austin whistles, mocking his boldness.

The accusation catches her throat and she wants to scream something at him. She picks up the pieces while Niall leans into his uncle and learns a hitch knot.

She cannot tell how much her son remembers about last night or even if he understands it. She wants to ask him, and when Austin goes out to milk the cows, she says, 'Niall?' Her voice comes out strange and angrier than she means it to and he pretends not to hear her. She doesn't have the energy to say it twice.

She makes breakfast for the three of them, then dinner, then evening tea. Austin showing no sign of leaving, like the weather that refuses to lift. It is as though he remembers nothing from the night before, or he has turned it into something else, and believes she actually wants him here. It's like they are pretending that she and Niall belong to him now. She is too afraid of him, of herself, of what still lurks around them in the house, to say otherwise.

She thinks of her sister over on Muruch, past the excitement of staying now, anxious to get her children home, to be crowded in her own house rather than someone else's. Missing her husband. She wonders if they'll pull at each other's clothes as soon as they can, hungry for each other the way that has never seemed to wane, and if she will smell something different on him, some guilt, some remnant of her sister's wet fear.

She wonders also if Brigid will smell it on her, the next time she puts her face between her legs. Whether there will be evidence of betrayal, of that invited assault.

They spend another night alone, sitting at the fire like an old married couple while Niall falls asleep in her arms. There is no more drink, between them they finished the jug the night before. Austin smokes a pipe and minds the turf fire and cleans up the dishes from their tea. Niall's breathing is clear now, his chest has lost the wheeze it had yesterday, his nose crusted rather than runny. She holds him against her, asleep he seems not much heavier than when he was a toddler. No words pass between them for a long time.

For an instant, she thinks Austin is chuckling over some thought in his head, but realises, horrified, that his shoulders are shaking and the broken, the eruptive noise is him weeping. He is crying and trying not to. She looks at him, narrowing her eyes.

'What are you on about,' she hisses, angry and bitter and fully herself again.

'What have we done?' he says. 'This will break her heart.'

Emer almost can't speak over what rises in her throat. 'Neither of us will be telling Rose,' she whispers. 'Have you gone mad?'

'I don't know,' Austin blubbers. 'It won't

happen again,' he promises.

Emer looks away. She is not sure what combination of man and changeling was in her bed last night, but Austin is himself again. He is no longer attractive to her, and she is newly afraid of him, but still, there is a stab of disappointment that he will give her up that easily, with relief really, and that perhaps none of it had been about any desire for her at all. And this, after all, almost seems the worst of it. The way she fooled herself.

'There's something vile in you,' he says in that deep, bruising voice. In a moment he will go away, out into the rain and wind, leaving her alone with the echo of what they have done.

'It wasn't me did that all by myself,' she retorts. But she is no longer sure.

★   ★   ★

In the morning they all come back, the men worse for two days of drink and dancing, the women smiling and full of news and tea and packages wrapped from the shop. Austin pulls Rose out of the currach on to the slip, after she hands him the two toddlers that he turns and passes to Emer. He swings her around in a hug, hiding the look on his face in her neck, and she laughs and pounds his arm, embarrassed but delighted. Really, she's delighted by anything and everything he does and always has been, Emer can see this now. She wouldn't believe anything dark in him, even if it were her own sister who swore it. Brigid, though she hasn't seen Emer in days, slips away in the commotion and by the time Emer looks for her she is halfway up the road with the dog. No hello, no handshake, no hint that later she will make this better, make the last two days go away as easily as a bee sting. Emer is left to follow her family home.

Niall tells Patch, at teatime that evening while Patch is telling her how much he got for the sheep.

'Mammy was taken,' he says suddenly, and Emer stops chewing, the potato growing cold on her tongue.

'What's that?' Patch says distractedly, annoyed at the interruption.

'Mammy was taken. She broke the mug. Austin showed me the hitch. And we made up the eels.'

'Are you ill?' he says to Emer. She shakes her head. Mumbles something about turning her ankle and dropping the mug.

'Show me the eels, so,' he says to Niall. Niall reveals the wilted, reeking pile behind the curtain. Patch promises they will fish with them in the morning.

When she puts Niall to bed that night, he asks her to lie down with him, and he curls with his back to her belly so they fit together like wooden spoons.

'Did he steal you?' he whispers. Emer shakes her head against his hair.

'I'm all right,' she says. 'You mustn't speak of it. I'll be angry if you do.' This is the biggest threat she can think of. He hates for her to be angry, and will do anything if there is the slightest chance of it.

'I won't,' he says. 'Don't use the angry voice, Mammy. Use your other voice.'

'All right, *a chuisle*,' she says. She sings to him softly, he smiles and wiggles around contentedly. He never stops moving, not even in bed, some part of him is always twitching, wiggling, reaching out. She holds him so tight for a moment he complains and she loosens her grip.

'Settle down,' she murmurs. He tries. His wiggling slows to a minimum. He's almost gone.

'Was that even Austin on you, Mammy?' he asks, just before he falls asleep.

Faces rush at her, first Patch then Brigid, one looking like he wants to die, the other aroused, inviting, but still, underneath it, a well of regret. She thinks of Austin's eyes, lit from behind by a consuming fire that was all too familiar. She sees now that there is little difference between the times she has lain with Patch, the secret sessions with Brigid, and this, this violation that isn't one, this cruelty that she asked for, that she invited to penetrate her as surely as she asked for the abuse of those bees.

The fairies came in. She let them in, with the drinking, the music, the flirtation, she left the door wide open. It must have been fairies, or her own cruel hands. It couldn't be Austin, the boy Rose married, who had done such a thing. Could it?

In sleep her son is perfectly, frighteningly still, like his spirited self is gone and left a husk in its place. Niall falls away before she can say she isn't at all sure who it was — a cruel man or a changeling. Or which of them — Austin or herself — was to blame.

Part Two

THE STOLEN CHILD

The host is riding from Knocknarea
And over the grave of Clooth-na-Bare;
Caoilte tossing his burning hair,
And Niamh calling *Away, come away:*
Empty your heart of its mortal dream.
The winds awaken, the leaves whirl round,
Our cheeks are pale, our hair is unbound,
Our breasts are heaving our eyes are agleam,
Our arms are waving our lips are apart;
And if any gaze on our rushing band,
We come between him and the deed of his
    hand,
We come between him and the hope of his
    heart.
The host is rushing 'twixt night and day,
And where is there hope or deed as fair?
Caoilte tossing his burning hair,
And Niamh calling *Away, come away.*

'The Hosting of the Sidhe',
William Butler Yeats

14

Corncrake

October, 1959

Even before Emer tells her about Austin, on the days where their only opportunities to touch are snatched, breathless moments, Brigid spends the nights afraid of what she has risked. She imagines Emer remembering the Catholic girl she is and confessing to her husband or her sister. Brigid was a fool to gamble this way, on an island where they can take the hope from her in the blink of an eye. She can hear her mother's voice warning her not to underestimate them. *The islanders called her a saint when she could help and a devil when she couldn't.*

She will avoid Emer then, engaging Niall, tending the hives, gathering honey or sketching together, so that he won't leave them alone. She watches Emer move from annoyed, to frightened, to dejected, her eye welling up at the possibility that what she came for will not be offered again. Longing rises off her — Brigid feels it because the same thing is rising out of herself — as furious and lustful as a swarm of ravenous bees.

Her desire for Emer surprises her. She hasn't felt like this in a long time. This willing to lose herself, to feel like you have no choice but to surrender to their hands. No matter how hard she tries to keep Emer at a distance, Brigid always gives in, and makes love to her with a violent abandon that frightens her afterwards. As though despite Emer's inexperience, her deep, almost childish need, Brigid is actually the young one, so desperate and manic in love that she is unable to see past the next encounter.

Brigid can see what happened on Emer's throat even before Emer gathers the courage to tell her. Not a bruise exactly, or a wound, but the suggestion of one, a memory, cowering at the hollow in her neck. Something with a mind of its own that waits, deliberating its next move. It has been there since the day they came back from Muruch, after three days trapped on the wrong island, where Brigid was queasy and claustrophobic and yearning for her small cottage, her loyal dog. Regretting what she started with a girl who is a snarl and twisted bramble of longing and bitterness, who can still drag love across Brigid's body in spite of herself.

'While you were away something happened. I did . . . ' Emer changes course. 'Austin took . . . em, we had relations. Austin and myself.'

Brigid's limbs are filling with a heaviness that seems more than physical, and she wants to lie down, go outside and sink into a rough cushion of heather and fall asleep in the sun. But she forces herself to look at Emer instead. There is a long beat where she has no idea what she will say next. She has a cruel instinct to get angry with her. To use it as an excuse to end this affair that has become too much for the both of them.

'What happened?' Brigid says. It all comes out of Emer in a jumbled rush, she skips from end to beginning, from shame to accusation and back again, a story where the motivation, and the instigation, is never fully clear. The truth escapes her, just as she thinks she has grabbed hold of it.

'I didn't intend it,' Emer says. She is fighting tears, her face red from holding her breath, her one eye widened, expanding the socket as if by doing so she can keep the tears from falling out. The first tear will be like a plug, a stone at the mouth of a well, and she will not be able to staunch the flow once it begins.

'It's not always intention that ignites these things,' Brigid says. Emer shakes her head.

'That's not what I mean. I've fancied it for as long as I can remember. But something else happened. I was willing enough. I intended to kiss him. But then something turned and I tried to stop but it was too late.'

'Tried to stop him?'

'Tried to stop . . . ' Emer can't decide which pronoun to insert. The story will continue to warp and change in her mind, as she inserts variations, myself, it, them, us. It will go round and round in her, and she will not be able to halt it by blurting out only one.

'Emer,' Brigid says carefully, because Emer is trapped inside something that requires care. It's like coming slowly upon an injured animal and trying to help it before it bolts. 'What do you mean?'

'I told him not to do it. I told him we should stop. I told him to think of Rose.'

277

'You told him no?' She sees Emer searching her mind, shaking it, trying to find the clean memory through the thick fog of recollection.

'I did. More than once.'

'He forced you.'

'Not exactly,' she says. Emer sits forward, she wants to shorten the space between them so her words won't blow away, so her explanation can be caught and understood. 'Something came over him. Like a fairy stroke. I might have been the one to put it in there.'

'I doubt that,' Brigid bites. 'It's called rape. What a bastard.' But she stops when she sees Emer's shoulders drop even more, and the shaking of the hand she raises to her neck.

How many girls has she seen like this, bent over themselves, as if they can fold in half like a cloth spotted with blood, fold away all the horror and shame and tuck into a drawer within their minds this thing their bodies will never forget. How many times has she tried to have men punished, only to see the girl they violated penalised even more? She is not a fool, she will not suggest that Emer tell anyone, not Rose, or the priest, or the guards, a nine-mile row and a twelve-mile car ride away. She would need Patch, or Austin, or one of his cousins, to row her there in the first place.

Sometimes there were men, men with souls like Matthew but minds and bodies hardened into a carapace that could summon violence, who took care of these things. Who enforced a justice that did nothing to erase the crime. It had its own purpose, this revenge, it gave a grim satisfaction. But Brigid is an outsider here, and does not know the men well enough to even imagine whom she would ask of such a thing.

Emer is pulling at her collar, warping the wool of her jumper away from the invisible weight at her neck.

'I'm sorry, Emer,' Brigid says. She can see that her angry thoughts will only increase the pressure. Emer's throat is perched on the edge, all it will take is a word, a breath, a thin sliver of skin, to bring the weight of a lifetime down to crush it.

'I'm so sorry,' because there is nothing else to say. All the other words will have to be thrown into the fire and forgotten.

It is not until she touches her, until she slides from her chair and kneels by Emer's, and takes the girl's clenched, furious face between her hands, and kisses her eyelid, closed so tight against what she no longer wants to see, that Emer is able to cry. Ugly, thundering sobs that wrack her body like a series of blows, crying that is too violent to completely succumb to.

'What have I done?' Emer says, when the sobbing subsides, and Brigid shushes her.

'Stop that, Emer. It was done to you.'

'It couldn't have been him alone,' Emer says.

'Why not?'

'It's Austin. He's married to my sister.'

'It happens all the time,' Brigid says. 'It's not your fault.'

'There's something ugly in me,' Emer says. Her head is resting on Brigid's shoulder. Brigid puts her hand to Emer's hair and strokes it, pulling it between her fingers, like separating sections to braid the hair of a child.

'Why can't I stop from calling it up?' Emer says, her voice hushed with terror, as if to even ask such a thing aloud is to set something unstoppable, like a flame touched to an island bonfire, used to burn a mountain of discarded life.

'I don't know,' Brigid says. This is not the right answer. She feels Emer stiffen, the angry coiled centre of her getting ready to spring out again. Emer sits up, kisses her, tries to reach beneath Brigid's blouse with her angry, desperate hands. Deep inside Brigid an ache blossoms that feels so like lust, she opens her mouth, and leads Emer to the bedroom. In an attempt to heal, or at least overwrite the memories of Austin, she brings the girl to a whimpering conclusion, but when Emer tries to do the same, Brigid realises that the feeling is not desire, but revulsion, like something deep inside the place where she longs to be sated is screaming at her to stop.

'Shhh,' Brigid says to Emer, gently deflecting her hands. 'We're both tired. Just let me hold you, and we'll rest.'

★ ★ ★

The unmasking of Austin does not surprise Brigid. There was a moment with him that told her, that lifted the curtain away and showed what skulked underneath.

It was after the Lughnasa bonfire, the festival on the first of August that marked the end of the

280

summer and the onset of the harvest, Rose sent Austin to walk Brigid home. He'd lunged at her drunkenly by her front door, trying for a kiss, and she had pushed him firmly away.

He covered his sneer of anger quite deftly with a smile.

'Would you rather one of the women walked you home, then?' he said.

She did not let her gaze drop from the ugly implication in this.

'Good evening, so,' he muttered, after a beat, when he realised that she has no intention of answering.

Before he left he spat, a purposeful, ridiculous gesture, meant to stand, she supposed, for some sort of dismissal, or warning.

Men, she thinks, can be as foolish as boys, too bad they have the power to twist that foolishness into danger. It doesn't help that these women encourage it, that grown men on this island are treated with the same dismissive, devoted impatience they bestow on unruly boys. It's humiliating, Brigid thinks, for the lot of them.

She does not think much more about it until Emer tells her story. She doesn't think a fairy possessed Austin. But she can imagine what Emer's hands might do to a man already poised for violence. She has seen it, saw what Austin was capable of in the gleam and shadows that were created when he turned his head away and spat into the dark ground.

She puts a hand to Emer's neck that day, and pulls just enough of the damage away for Emer to breathe, to hold her head up, to forge ahead, as grumpy and unpleasant and as normally as she can. There is a minimum, Brigid has learned, to what she can heal without getting ill herself. A psychological salve, as long as she doesn't go too long, is safe enough. It will make her tired, but nothing else. She couldn't grab hold of every wound in Emer even if she wanted to. She cannot twist herself so deeply in the coils of Emer and Austin and the fire they have started. She has something much more fragile to hold on to.

★　★　★

After Emer leaves to collect Niall from school, Brigid goes back into her bedroom, too heavy to remain upright. She has been pregnant so many times before that she adjusts to the signs of it before she remembers that it shouldn't be possible. The queasiness that creeps in, so subtle it is a while before you realise it has been there all day. The disconnect in her throat when she breaks open an egg, the subtle turning of the smells of her home from a comfort to an assault. The band of tightness that stretches above her pubic bone, as if a stone has lodged just under the soft mound of her belly. She reaches her fingers below her waistband to see if she can ease the feeling, but it's permanent, it's not going to budge. She feels like this, as if her body has already expanded to make room for something that barely has substance yet, for days before she allows herself to hope for what it means. Aside from generous waist pinches and Austin's sloppy

282

lunge, no man has even touched her since she arrived.

The well has done what her mother promised. It has given her not merely a womb, but the baby as well. She hopes that what is growing inside her is not a fantasy, or a dangerous pact with the darkness that lurks in Emer. She will call it a blessing from the saint, though she has no evidence to distinguish the gift of a saint from the bargain of something that lives beneath the world.

She lies in bed next to Rua and pulls her soft ear through her fingers, making her sigh and stretch and put her thin face on Brigid's belly.

'Shall we have a baby, Rua?'

The dog thumps her tail, willing to agree to anything, as long as she's allowed to lie beside Brigid, her adoration is simple and boundless, unmatched by the damaged humans who surround them.

The corncrake shrieks mercilessly in the field behind her house, repeating his endless warning, frantic that no one will translate the message.

Be careful, Brigid imagines him screaming. *Everything they give you, they can also take away.*

But by now Brigid has her own warning system. The child growing inside her already tells her when it has had enough.

15

Cursing Stone

October, 1959

Emer is adrift. Inside her is a great swell, it has rent her down the middle and now the two halves are moving apart like a body dragged by the current from an overturned boat. Her neck feels pressed for most of each day, her diaphragm is rigid, she has to stop and lean over and pull with all her might to get air deep into her lungs. Most of the time this fails, her breathing refuses to delve below the shallow, and she fears the space will shrink a little more each time, until she stops breathing altogether.

In the days after Rose returned, Emer was wound tight as a spring, jumping at everything Patch and Niall said as if she'd forgotten they were in the room. She spent those days inside, though the weather was fine, because the thought of meeting Rose or Austin in the field, of watching them approach her, was too much to bear. The knock she was expecting on the door never came.

Things do not improve even after it is clear that Austin has not told. Emer tells Brigid because she thinks if she lets it out her breathing will ease a bit. Brigid doesn't seem shocked, or even that interested, beyond an interrogation of

284

blame and a simple 'I'm sorry.' She lays a hand on Emer's neck just long enough for her to breathe for an hour, but when she leaves, the weight comes straight back in, like the sea air greeting her as she steps outside the door.

* * *

Her desire for Brigid does not wane, if anything, it grows, but now it's a desperate, angry desire. Brigid avoids her, then denies it. If Emer comes up behind her, in the field, in the house, Brigid deflects her hands. She makes excuses, Niall will see, or Austin, whom she claims already suspects.

'Let's lay low for a while,' Brigid says. 'We don't want anyone to find out.'

'I don't care if they know.'

'Believe me, Emer, you do.'

'Is it because of Austin? Because I let him touch me? Is that why you don't want me any more?'

'Of course not.'

'Then what is it?'

'I'm just being careful. It's not about you.'

Even before this, every time Brigid reached for her was a relief. The last time they made love before the night with Austin, Emer had been asking about Brigid's husband, jealousy making her tactless, and, as if to prove her loyalty, Brigid seduced her rather than answer.

'Come here,' she'd whispered, and Emer leaped out of her seat and into Brigid's hands, driven by a lust tinged with fear.

285

They did not bother with the bedroom, but dropped right to the floor; the fire beside them burned as hot as the sparks they ignited in each other. At one point, Brigid called out her name, with a yearning that filled Emer to the brim. Emer imagined holding tight and rolling over, rolling them both into the fire with the same abandon as she once fell into a cavern of bees. The fire, rather than burning them, would just make it all last longer. They would never reach the point where they redid their clothes and Emer started to doubt it all, reading too much into Brigid's lack of eye contact. The point when they were two people again instead of the one glowing brand of lust that bound them. She wanted to reduce them both to ash, in the moment when they cried out with the glorious pain of it, at exactly the same time.

This is her fear: that Brigid has discovered that Emer disgusts her after all, that what Emer has learned to depend on — Brigid's hands — will be taken from her, with the same cruel disregard as a fairy withdrawing its promise.

★   ★   ★

In October, all the old things come back to frighten her. She fears for Niall and keeps him home from school for a week after the teacher mentions that he often spends lessons gazing out the window and mouthing one half of a conversation no one else can hear.

'What were you doing?' she asks him.

'Listening to the music,' he says, so casually

that she feels a surge of vomit in her throat. 'I think Austin was playing his whistle in the field,' Niall says. But the men have been at sea all week, pulling the lobster pots.

In the house, Niall is clumsy and distracted. He spills milk all over the new bread, leaves the bottom half of the door open so the pig comes snuffling in. Emer keeps barking at him, and though she apologises she does it again immediately, which makes him look at her with wide eyes and become even more forgetful. Finally, hating the havoc they wreak on one another, she sends him back to school. She regrets it almost immediately. Without him there is nothing in her small, damp, ugly house but herself and what she has done.

When it is her turn to care for her mother, the woman seems livelier than usual and peppers Emer with cryptic comments about Emer's appearance, or Brigid, whom she still disapproves of, or Niall's seeming a little slow, until Emer imagines strangling her with the kitchen cloth or plunging the thinning blade of her knife into the woman's limp mouth.

Seeing Austin is like being accosted. He won't look at her directly, but still she feels his eyes following behind her, watching to see if she will dare tell. Rose is behaving strangely and Emer is paranoid, every short response or look of weary burden makes her sure Austin has finally confessed it all, and blamed her for it, telling her sister that she is a heartless whore. She worries that Rose won't even bother to ask her side. What if Austin declared Emer a liar and told

Rose never to speak to her again, and Rose actually listened to him?

Emer's headaches return with a vengeance, and she spends entire days blind beneath a wet cloth in her bedroom, insisting that Niall stay in the house but also remain silent, which is so impossible for him to do she ends up scolding him, and just that rise in her voice causes her to vomit until she is sure the inside of her head is as empty as her stomach.

'Would you ever untwist yourself?' Patch says one evening, when every mention of Rose or the girls or his brother causes her to knock over a jug or drop her fork with a clang on her plate. Her mother looks at her with a knowing grimace. Niall looks away, preferring to focus on what no one else can see. And Emer realises how impossible that will be, to ever uncoil the fairy threat from the human mistake, to ever untwist what has been done to her from what she has done herself.

★   ★   ★

Brigid is ill. The freckles on her nose leach away, leaving only their outlines, the skin beneath has a tinge of green. She doesn't want to touch Emer, or kiss her, or even talk to her, she wants to lie down in bed with the curtains pulled and eat only dry toast and read poetry and cuddle with the foul-smelling dog. She waves away Emer's offers of help, of company, and grows weary at her insistence.

'I just need to be left alone,' she says. She can't

see that Emer can barely breathe. She won't even look at her. 'Just for a day or two, Emer, would you find something else to do?'

But Emer cannot stop coming over. When Niall is at school she has nowhere else to go. She sits in the outer room, keeps the kettle boiling in case Brigid wants tea, and listens to her being sick quietly, without explanation, into a waiting bowl.

★ ★ ★

Emer sees it one day, when Brigid moves in front of the fire and the light shines through her oversized blouse. The soft pouch of her belly is tight now, stretched and ready as a drum.

Emer goes cold with dread.

'Is that a child in there?' she says. Brigid turns away but not before Emer sees her smile.

'It is,' she says.

'Did the well heal you, so?'

'I believe it did.'

'But who was it put it in you?' She thinks of Austin making Brigid laugh, Malachy bringing back her stolen cow across the sodden fields. The priest, who'd come to her for tea once.

'I haven't been with a man, Emer. Perhaps it was an immaculate conception. Only not so immaculate.'

'That's not funny. Who was it, really?'

'The saint,' Brigid says. 'Or a fairy. It doesn't matter.'

'Jesus wept,' Emer says, and the hair on her neck rises. There are so many things wrong with

289

this she can't even begin.

'What will you tell the women?' she asks.

'Why do I have to tell them anything?'

'You must be joking.'

'Fine. I'll tell them it was that Australian I flirted with on Muruch. He's the perfect alibi. Gone already.'

'You flirted with an Australian? Was it him, so?'

'No. It was nobody.'

'They won't like it, you not being married.'

'This is what I want, Emer. There is no one to say I can't have it.'

I wouldn't be so sure of that, Emer thinks, but she doesn't say it out loud.

'Are you not afraid?'

'Of whom?' Brigid looks defensive.

'Of what that baby might be.'

'I've seen enough darkness to know it's not inside me, Emer. This baby is a gift.'

'They don't give things for free, the fairies. I know.'

'Saints do. Anyway, I'm not afraid.'

There is a silence where Emer digests this. She rewinds to the well, she can't remember anything other than the glorious relief of Brigid's body, the way they used the water to satisfy their yearning. What had they put inside her?

'Is that why you won't touch me any more?'

'Emer . . .'

'You got what you wanted and good riddance to me?'

'I care about you and Niall both.'

'Is that how you get everything you want?'

'Emer,' she almost whispers. 'That's enough.' But Emer can't stop now. She wants it to hurt. 'What happened to the other baby?' she says. 'What baby?' Brigid stiffens.

'Your belly had a baby in it before. Who'd you use to get that one?' Brigid reaches down with the fingers of one hand and presses there, just above the pubic bone, remembering. Her wide shoulders square up. She directs toward Emer such a look of fury, Emer's legs go weak just at the eye contact.

'Be careful, Emer,' she says. Then she turns around and goes back to the fire.

'I'm sorry,' Emer says. She doesn't want this, this fury she is so familiar with, she doesn't want to feel for Brigid the same hatred she feels for everyone else.

'I miss you,' Emer murmurs. 'When can I have you back?' Brigid pretends she doesn't hear. Emer thinks she sees something in her profile, a pained look, a cringe of regret. But what is the pain? Is it from being with Emer, or being without her?

'I'm tired,' Brigid says, raking the coals to prepare to bury them with ash for the night. 'I'll see you tomorrow, all right?'

She won't even kiss her goodbye, but turns her head so Emer's mouth bumps her cheek. Emer walks home through the autumn darkness, her heart banging with a new dread she cannot name.

★ ★ ★

'We saw Austin on the road,' Niall announces one day, entering the house with his father.

'What?' Emer barks. 'Why, what's wrong?' Patch just looks at her, annoyed.

'Don't have a cow,' he says. 'We're off to town when the tide is high. He asked that you stay with Rose for the night, in case she needs anything.'

Because Rose, Emer thinks, is the one we are all worried about.

'I will, of course,' she says.

After he leaves for the quay, Emer packs up a little fish and the morning's bread in her basket, Niall's nightshirt and her own on top, and pulls her cowl over her shoulders. They walk slowly up the road to Rose's house, a ruin renovated by Austin and Patch, whitewashed stone with two bedrooms and a loft in the generous roof. Austin had wanted to put on a new slate roof, but Rose had insisted they keep the thatch. Austin humoured her, though it meant more work for him.

'I like the way the birds nest in it, and the softness of the rain,' Rose said at the time.

'Sure, it's easy enough to refuse modern conveniences when you're lucky enough to have them offered to you,' was Emer's two cents.

Rose is heavily pregnant now, and not as radiant as she usually is. Her face is swollen and carries a sheen of effort. She catches her breath a lot, twitching with the discomfort of being kicked from within. When these latest babies are born, Emer will have to be over here all the time, feeding Austin and the girls, doing the laundry, milking Rose's cows while she nurses the infants in the damp prison of her room. Other women will help, they always do, but for reasons no one can fathom, Rose, after childbirth, relies on Emer the most. How can Emer do it now, when every glance at her sister makes her think of Austin's hand laid like a gentle threat on her neck? How can she look her in the eye when she knows that she asked for it, that she stole him from her sister like a heartless fairy?

At Rose's pine table, Emer cracks an egg into a bowl and sees a deformed, bloody embryo clinging to the yolk. She heaves, so quick and hard there isn't even the time to know it is coming, or aim, so she is sick directly into the bowl beneath her hands, ruining the egg. She clings to the table with terror, and when she dares to look up, Rose is staring at her, a gleam of amusement in her eye.

'Well,' she clucks. 'Something you've been wanting to tell me?'

Emer thinks she will faint. Rose cops on and comes around the table, takes her arm and leads her to a chair.

'Oh no, no no no no no,' Emer chants, thinking she does so in her head, but Rose shushes her.

'It's all right, pet,' she says, and she sends one of the girls to the well to fetch a fresh glass of water. Niall stands like a statue halfway across the room, the same hot fear she feels in her throat throbbing in his eyes.

'Every baby is a blessing,' Rose whispers. 'You'll see.'

'Oh,' Brigid says when Emer tells her. 'Well, then.' She is unable to hide her surprise or, Emer thinks, her annoyance.

'I need your help,' Emer says. Brigid goes pale. 'No,' she says.

'You only have to pull it out of me,' Emer says. She is pacing the floor, Brigid is sitting by the hearth. 'You pull things out all the time.'

'It's not a bruise, Emer.'

'It's more a bruise than anything else.'

'I don't do that,' Brigid says. Emer blinks, as if she is out of focus as well as not making sense. 'What I mean to say is, I can't,' she continues. 'I'm sorry.'

Brigid is quiet for a while. Emer can't understand why she looks so worried. Not sympathetic worry, but nagging fear.

'It wouldn't be the worst thing in the world to have it,' Brigid says gently. 'No one will know it's not Patch's. It would give Niall someone. The way you have Rose.'

'I never wanted Rose.'

'You don't mean that.'

'I do, sure.'

'It could be someone for you, too, Emer, when Niall is gone.'

'Gone? Gone where?!' She has left Niall with Patch at the house but he's no better than useless at the vigilance.

'To school.'

Emer plops on to the chair across from Brigid and drops her forehead in her hands.

'You don't understand.'

'I do understand. I understand what Austin did. I can't undo it. But you're not alone.'

'Have you no notion of what this child might be? I can't risk it. I can't. It could be the fairies, found a way to finally get inside me. To take Niall.'

'It's not a fairy, Emer, it's a baby.' Emer shakes her head.

'Sometimes it's possible to turn things,' Brigid says. 'Sometimes you decide what you will allow to be taken from you.'

'That's how it works for you,' Emer says. 'Not for the likes of me.'

Brigid nods and sits back again. Emer thinks suddenly that she doesn't want Brigid to give up. She wants her to take her hands, keep arguing, keep saying those three words she has never believed before: *You're not alone.* She wants to rewind to the part where Brigid was still hoping to reach her. She wants her to say: *You have me.*

'Will you not leave the island with us?' Emer says, in a breathless flash of boldness. 'We'll go somewhere, to America even, say we are widowed sisters, raise the babies together.'

Brigid looks at her with such compassion, Emer imagines for an instant that she will smile, relieved, and say yes.

Instead she says this: 'I want to stay here. I need to take care of myself now, Emer. And so do you.'

Emer feels like the very floor has dropped beneath her feet. She is overcome with vertigo, and holds her breath until the urge to be sick passes.

'I can't have it. I can't.'

'All right, Emer,' Brigid says. 'If that's how you feel, if you don't want another baby, I think we both know who can do something about it.'

Brigid stands and walks to the table, picks up her knife and begins to peel a small, dirty potato. Emer can see she is angry with her. Emer wonders why she isn't angry with Austin, or Rose, or this wretched island that imprisons them.

Why is Brigid the one who's angry? she thinks. Isn't she the one who offered Emer something else, then snatched it away?

I thought we'd take care of each other, Emer wants to say. But she doesn't want to hear the answer to that.

'I can't hurt myself,' Emer says. 'It doesn't work that way.'

'It's not you, though,' Brigid says. 'Is it?'

★ ★ ★

She leaves Brigid's, pulling at the collar of her blouse until she hears a few stitches rip. The sun is setting in her field of vision like a fire she can't look at. She stumbles blindly up the hill. She wants the screaming in her head to be swallowed in the wind of the cliffs.

She thinks of Austin's cocky grin, and Rose's graceful beauty, and Brigid's lustful confidence, and the girls she went to school with, with their talents and their plans and their pretty skin or hair or figures and how they knew what was lovely about themselves and made the best of it.

296

She thinks of the ones who got away, who can't afford, or perhaps can't be bothered, to come home again. She thinks of the women who stayed, and how they keep having children, all of them, one after another because they can't stop it, nor do they seem to want to. Their lives appear to make them as happy as Emer's drags her down. She thinks of her mother and how cold and finished she was by the time Emer was old enough to recognise her, finished even while she had children she needed to stay alive for. She thinks of when she still wanted the fairies to rescue her, before she became afraid of them robbing her of what she loves the most. She thinks of the few times she went to Galway, before Niall was born and she was still a girl, when she stood still on the busy street and let person after person pass her by, with their clothes and their looks and their plans and their senses of humour, and a destination, all of them, and how she always thought, if I stand here, stand here very still, something or someone will scoop me up and steal me away and surprise me with a life. And no one ever had. The only one who had come close was Brigid. But she didn't give her a life. She gave her a dirty secret, even more useless and repulsive than what Emer had alone.

She thinks lastly of Niall, who before this barely saw her hate, who, with those eyes fogged by visions, refused to look past her adoration of him. He saw her splayed beneath Austin, saw the ugly rutting, and someday he will know what it means. This baby will be like a nail in the coffin of all that. It will put Niall at a distance, it will make him see something, something of what is really her, and eventually he will either avoid her or glide past her like the rest of them. Even if the fairies never take him back, he will be stolen away from her. He will be like all the teenage boys who leave the island for school or work, he will come home wearing the closed face and distant eyes of an Irish man. He will be able to see, after he learns about the world, the way she is, the way she makes people feel when she cradles their hand. She pulls their happiness away. It is really the only remarkable thing she has ever been able to do.

She passes the nuns' clocháns and stumbles along the cliff edge and climbs down to Saint Brigid's well. On one wall, she heaves aside a large slab of slate, revealing an opening that has been worried into the cliff wall, and inside this a basin, which holds one heavy round rock. *An clocha breacha*. The cursing stone. Some islanders say the fairies put it here, as a dark objection to Saint Brigid's healing. Others say it was left by Brigid herself, who had a dark side, a temper, a tendency to hurt and humiliate if she was pushed. Like the poor man she sent stumbling away by ripping out her eye. Or the leper she cured and then infected again when she saw he wasn't worthy. Most islanders don't believe in it any more, but still tell their children never to touch it. The curse can be turned back on you, they say, if it is not just.

Emer has never used it before. She's not even sure how the thing works. But now she wants something big, something that can break open and release what's inside her, so she turns the stone, iridescent with moss, clockwise in its shallow rock bowl, pulling apart the lichen that has grown to hold it there, like roots that when they rip release a foul, stagnant smell. All the faces of the people who are happier than she is, the faces that look up at her with drained patience because they find her such a burden to be around, revolve over and over in her mind and it is not until she has turned the stone three times and stopped that she remembers what she wanted to do in the first place.

Later she will know what she has done. She will remember how she turned an ancient, evil stone to ask it to clear her womb, and what she asks for instead, and is granted, is the power to destroy everything.

16

Coffins

October, 1959

Islanders call them storms that are born in the sea. No warning from the sky, no darkness or wind shift to make the men pull up their gear and head for home. The sky is bright blue and favourable for as far as they can see, and then it is upon them, the wind and the rain and the chaos seem to rise up from the ocean, just like the swells. In storms like this one, in the past, men have told of clinging to their boats and seeing, when they look up, the other side of the maelstrom: beyond the cluster that swallows them the sky remains as clear and uninvolved as the divide between two worlds.

This time, there is no one left alive to describe it.

★   ★   ★

Brigid watches it from her field. Watches the fog descend and the sea rise, in one spot, like the great watery hand of some creature reaching from beneath. They are so close, six men in a single currach, coming home from a few pints on Muruch. She feels like she could walk out herself and pull them in. Rua keeps running forward

300

and back, barking at her to do something. Then the rain and fog hit them and she doesn't see any more. They must be all right: they were not very far from shore, and Niall doesn't come to tell her otherwise. Rua whimpers and paces in the house all night, though there is no thunder to disturb her.

It isn't until the morning, when the weather clears and she sees all the boats anchored out from the quay, that she knows how bad it was. She has never seen so many people come to the island at once.

It is a stranger, a man from the other island she has never met before, who tells her the sea took it all: the boat, the bodies, the heads of families, the last six young men on the island that needs young men to keep it alive. Like the sea itself knew what to take and chose to swallow what would leave the most damage. Patch and Austin Keane, twenty-nine and twenty-seven years of age, their cousins, Seamus and Peter O'Halloran, twenty-four and twenty-one, Michael Joe Cullen, thirty-two, their lifelong friend and owner of the vessel, Malachy Moran, thirty-nine. Six wives, twenty-eight children left behind.

'Stole any hope of remaining here, so it did,' the man mutters.

Brigid walks away from him in the middle of this prediction, up the road to the women who need her.

★ ★ ★

They start talk of the evacuation almost at once. During the search for any buriable and comforting piece of them, through the suffocating cloud

301

of grief and despair that grips the whole island, as thick and untenable as fog, they begin to mumble about it, just one more inevitable thing that will be thrust upon them.

They'll not let us remain now.

Sure, how will we, with no men?

Are you not inclined to pack it in altogether?

'Tis better for the children to be raised on solid ground.

They talk of it at the wakes, in six tiny houses, where off-island men set their glasses on the lids of empty caskets.

Will they not take them on Muruch?

Sure, they barely have room for themselves.

The shame will be in leaving this land. The land on the other side is all rock.

The sea is hard here, all the same.

Only one body is recovered, Malachy's, to put inside the pine. The priest suggests carefully to the widows that they find something, anything, to put inside the caskets. Preferably something light, something that will not roll or knock inappropriately around. Since they all died in the thick jumpers knitted with patterns to identify them, the widows have to find other pieces of clothing, a cap, a nice jacket worn only to Mass, a photograph of the children, a figure carved out of soapstone wrapped in a woollen scarf.

Niall offers to be the thing inside his father's casket. He says it aloud, at Rose's house, amidst a group of women, islanders and visitors from away, who are all so aggrieved they are having trouble remembering whom to comfort.

'I'll be very still,' he says, looking around at

them eagerly, a little excited to have thought up such a creative solution. Emer, who has been tending the kettle, puts it down and walks quickly across the room, scooping him up in her arms, holding him tight as if she can smother what everyone has heard.

What is he on about?

He's a queer one, is he not?

Niall looks around at them, Brigid sees him realise that what he said was terribly wrong. He starts to cry and Emer has to take him outside, past the women she looks at like she might burn them to a crisp.

Children shouldn't be mollycoddled, they end up quare as their mothers before them.

His mother was touched, as a girl, I remember well the stories.

God knows how they made it this long.

'Tis a grave, this place, a watery grave.

★ ★ ★

The funeral procession is attended by Muruch men, who carry the almost weightless coffins from home to church to the graveyard that sits above the quay. During the walk the women wail together, a rhythmic incantation somewhere between a scream and a song.

'What are they singing?' Brigid whispers to the Muruch man next to her.

'Keening,' he says. 'Legend says the druid Brigid was the first to do it, when her son was killed in a battle. It's a horrible sound.' He shudders.

'Yes,' Brigid agrees. 'But beautiful, too.'

Mostly it is familiar. When her father died, her babies, Matthew. Every time a baby was ripped from a mother's arms. A sound she has heard in her heart.

★ ★ ★

They say things about Brigid in the Irish they believe she will not understand.

The Yank is a comfort, sure.

She's no stranger to grief, you can see that.

Brigid takes it all in her stride, she moves among them with the confidence of someone who has been faced with senseless death before. No hesitation, no simpering questions, no 'Is there anything I can do?' As if people in the grips of sudden death can ever take the time to think of what others might be able to do.

She cleans their houses, keeps their fires up, washes the faces and does up the buttons of their children. Brings their eggs in, their milk, their washing forgotten on the line. She brings them enormous jars of dark, thick honey, like something you might spread on a wound. She says very little, as if knowing that her accent might be too sharp, an insult in a cocoon of grief that only someone from this island can understand. She moves through their houses, sweeping and pressing and wiping, and every once in a while, when a contraction of vivid pain rises up in a wife at the thought of her husband or a mother at the thought of her boy, Brigid will put her wide, calloused hand on their back or

304

their shoulder, and clear a little space in the midst of the pain, just enough for them to inhale past it. She can do this much without harming herself or the baby. She doesn't take the pain away, she merely shifts it, just at those moments when it seems too enormous to bear. Coaxes it away from its relentless clenching of their hearts.

She doesn't touch Emer, as much as she wants to. She would like to ease her grief, to apologise for how she ended things, but when she goes to see her, something has changed. Emer spends the days after the funeral in Rose's bed. The children are told to let her be, and move through the house in hushed, tear-stained pairs.

'She lost the baby, poor pet,' Rose confides in Brigid. 'First the lads, now this. She's wrecked with grief.'

'Emer?' Brigid whispers when she goes into the darkened bedroom. Emer, lying in the bed, turns her head as if it weighs more than the rest of her. Her face is so pale it looks skeletal, her one eye blazing with what looks like a fever, or derangement.

'Was it my fault?' she whispers hoarsely.

Poor Emer, Brigid thinks. The girl is grieving, only not in the way her sister believes.

'Of course not,' Brigid says, and she moves toward her, with the intention of sitting by her side.

But her belly seizes up, the baby lashes so violently she feels like it could bruise her from the inside. *Don't* is the word that comes into her head. *Don't.* As if her own child is wailing, but no one else can hear it.

'You'll be all right,' she says uselessly, and she hurries out of the room, out of the house, to breathe the air and calm the maelstrom inside her. Instead, she ends up vomiting violently by the stone wall. The baby has given her messages before, of when to stop using her hands, just like her sickness used to, sickness that varied depending on the wound.

But she has never felt anything like the fear that grips her at the thought of touching Emer. Just a few days ago she could still touch her, though sex was out of the question. Now, the baby won't stand for it. The darkness in Emer's hands, the power that never affected Brigid, which Brigid could once transform into pleasure, is stronger now, or she has lost her ability to deflect it.

* * *

The children can't get enough of her. They follow her around, dirty hands in her skirts, and if she manages to sit down they swarm on to her lap, squeezing to make room for their siblings and cousins. She does not need to hold back for them. She places her large palms on the crowns of their heads and washes the whole of it away, silencing the keening of their mothers, which they hear like an echo that will never fade.

Niall takes to sitting in Brigid's lap, or holding her hand as she walks across the field to gather forgotten cows. Being with Brigid makes his crying subside, where the arms of his mother make it swell up all over again. He is frightened

306

of what losing the men means for his mother, Auntie Rose, his cousins. Niall doesn't want to leave the island, but he has never told his mother this.

'Mammy is ill,' Niall says to Brigid. 'It's like she's gone away.'

'She'll come back,' Brigid says.

'Ah, I know. She wouldn't ever leave me.'

'Of course not,' Brigid says quietly, not wanting to give a turn to the guileless faith of this child.

★   ★   ★

They have the meeting in the school, and old Jimmy Moran, the one man left, stands at the back, out of tradition, though he is so wobbly Brigid makes him sit down at one of the small desks. The only other island men are boys, all under the age of twelve, trying to stand taller than they are. The priest from Inis Muruch is here, and a small, tidy, nervous man from the Galway County Council. He passes around the same picture Emer has of the bungalows on the mainland. Mortared walls, bedrooms on either end. Water taps in the kitchen. Toilets and proper bathtubs. Electric lights, gas cookers, radios. All on a lovely stretch of beach that looks out over the island on a clear day. To remind them, Brigid thinks, of what they have given up. Confirmation of their failure topped off with a water view. They are naming the new village Cois Cuain, which means: safe haven.

The children, excited by the promise of dances

at the hall and a real football pitch, want to go. So do the old women, who are tired and afraid of dying without a priest there to give them last rites. Jimmy Moran calls out that he will die in the house where he was born, and the women roll their eyes and shush him. Emer sits perched upon her little chair as if someone is about to hand her the keys any minute. Though Brigid has helped them, eased them through grief with her capable hands, she feels some of them cringe a bit when she speaks up, as if silently saying that she has very little right to do so.

'Why can't we have those things here? The other island has a telephone.'

'Muruch has three hundred and fifty residents,' the councilman says. 'The county won't allow a phone on an island with less than one hundred.'

'What do you do here, then,' Brigid asks, 'in an emergency? In a storm, or if someone is ill.'

'We build a fire,' Rose answers her. 'A bonfire, on the hill. And hope that someone sees it and sends help.'

'That's pathetic,' Brigid says, glaring at the blushing man from the council.

'Aye,' an old woman says behind her. 'That it is.'

'What about a harbour?' Brigid continues. The council official, who had expected this to be tied up quickly, is starting to sweat, and wipes at his fogged glasses with his handkerchief.

'Wouldn't a proper harbour solve this? A place for larger boats to dock, emergency boats, in a storm, the way they do everywhere else?'

'It's not the government's problem that this island has no harbour. It would cost far more to build a harbour than it would to build these people a whole new village where they will be safe from the whim of the sea.'

There are a few island gasps at this, then uncomfortable silence. Of course, most of them know this fact, have discussed it among themselves. Nonetheless they are surprised, insulted and a little inspired by the rudeness of saying it out loud. By the cheek of it, speaking about them as if they are livestock.

None of them is quite sure afterwards what turns it, that little mistake of the councilman, or Brigid's Yankee confidence, or just the raw grief and weariness of the thought of packing it all up and abandoning their lives. Leaving the sea, which holds within it the bodies of their men that were never found. Somehow it is agreed that nothing will change just yet, they will press on, that they will see another winter of storm and isolation and abandonment through, see how it goes, as if without the men, it will not go a lot worse than it has in other years. They'll leave it so, and talk it over again in the springtime. Men will come over from Muruch to help them finish the harvest, store the hay, slaughter the pigs. They have the money from the sheep, the sale of cattle, the charity of the neighbouring island.

'I can lift a boat as well as any man,' Brigid says at one point, and a couple of women smile at that, including Rose, as if they think they might be able to as well. The councilman shakes his head to show he thinks them ridiculous.

Brigid requests a distress radio, normally reserved for islands with a lighthouse. And, after a whisper from Jimmy Moran, an iron winch to assist them in pulling the boats up. The man says he will see what he can do.

'Lip service,' Jimmy says, loud enough for him to hear.

After the meeting, Brigid watches them file out of the school. Rua has been waiting outside and watches with her, her warm torso pressing encouragement into Brigid's knee. The women's faces are bruised under their eyes from weeks of mourning, the children look like startled rabbits, something inside them is frozen, waiting for the next threat to appear. Rose looks at Brigid with such gratitude, she is momentarily guilty. She is not sure this is the right thing for them. It is what she wants, and she cannot do it alone.

Emer looks as if she wants to spit at all of them, to spit and scream at the mild optimism on their faces, and at her sister, smiling as if this is some sort of victory. Brigid knows her well enough to feel what she is thinking. She thinks that these women are naïve, so easily persuaded they have forgotten, because of a sunny day and an optimistic Yankee, that living here is like being slowly drowned, held down on a rock and left for the tide to come in.

She won't commiserate with Emer. She can't risk the feeling she has now. She has the energy of three women, flashes of pure, expectant joy she has to hide in deference to the newly widowed. She imagines the baby's life coursing in her veins, and knows that she could do anything, that she could run this island like an abbess, embrace a commune of devout women dedicated to their children and to each other, spread the cloak of her healing to include the sea. She wants to stay here, raise her baby amidst these women she has come to admire, on this island she now loves.

'I'm sorry,' she whispers in her mind, whenever Emer looks at her with that one eye, anger and fear and yearning jostling to be first, but Brigid turns away before she allows her remorse to be seen. She won't let Emer's desire to destroy herself get in the way. No matter how guilty she feels.

She has little doubt that this baby will make it. It has carved out a spot and wedged itself in there and will keep it tight and solid as a beehive stone hut until the very end. It will hold on through heavy lifting and work and the small amounts of fire she lets out of her hands to heal. For so many years it was her womb that failed her. Now her womb is out of the equation. This child shrouds itself. It warns her of danger long before she can fall into it. She has already decided that she doesn't care, doesn't care in the slightest, where it came from.

17

Knife Box

October, November, 1959

At the evacuation meeting, Emer barely hears anything, as if she is half-deaf as well as half-blind. She is permeated by liquid fear; it has risen past her neck and filled her ears, wavered into her remaining eye. Everything people say is muffled, like she is under the water and they are still calling from the surface. She is accosted by the realisation of what she has done in the eyes of every single person who dares to look at her.

She is still bleeding, the remains of that night with Austin continue to fall from her womb. It is not the relief she expected. She started something by twisting that stone and now it is too late to turn it backwards.

Brigid moves in and out of her periphery, Emer sees her laying her hands on the women, on the children, and the jealousy which seizes Emer is enough to make her forget to rein in her own. She is so careless one morning, helping braid her niece's hair, that she makes Teresa throw up. Fiona, fearless as Brigid, yanks the brush from her hand.

Emer hopes that, at least, the tragedy will bring on the evacuation. But by some dangerous concoction of magic and determination, Brigid

312

convinces them all to stay. Only a month before, Emer would have been thrilled at the thought of Brigid hanging around this long, and watching her embarrass the men at the church meeting would have made her proud. Now she wants to wring the necks of all the women who praise her.

They will build the houses anyway, the priest assures Emer after the meeting. For when they change their minds. No one expects them to last. Emer is too paralysed by the weight of what she has done to respond to this. She is being offered what she always wanted, but she can't drag her mind away from the casualties she accrued by asking for it.

★ ★ ★

'I wasn't a good wife to him,' Rose says one evening, late, when the other women have gone home, but Brigid and Emer remain. All the children are asleep, snoring through noses clogged by weeping.

'Don't do this to yourself, Rose,' Brigid says. She puts an arm around Rose's shoulders.

'I haven't shown him the bright side of my face in a while. This pregnancy . . . well, I haven't been in good form. He's been acting queer lately, giving out to the girls, barely taking the time to look at me, never mind kiss me. That was never a problem for us, you know. We've always been mad for each other.'

Brigid tries to shush her, but Rose won't stop now.

'We had a row. An ugly one. He said things

and I, I'm ashamed to repeat them. There was a time he got like that with drink, angry and cruel as his father before him. But he never, sure not since we were at school did he ever let that get the better of him. He frightened the girls, this time, he grabbed my arm, I thought he was going to strike me.

'He said he wanted a better life. He said that to me. Austin. Can you imagine it?

'That was the night before he went off with the lads for a drink, and I wouldn't even meet his eye for the time between. I'll not know what he thought of me then. It will never be over, that row, it will stay in my mind the rest of my days. I will never stop wondering what he thought of his life when the water pulled him under the last time.'

Brigid holds Rose's hands through this entire speech, patting, stroking, not shushing, just waiting for her to let all of it out. Emer stands away from them, still as death, keeping her mouth shut tight for fear she will spew out everything.

'Perhaps we should have left like you wanted, Emer,' Rose blubbers. 'If we had done, they'd be alive now. I never imagined living anywhere else. But that was selfish, I see that, because now we're cursed to live here without them.'

She runs her hands over her massive belly, cupping the underside of it. 'He'd have liked a boy.' Emer almost gags, but she swallows it just in time.

'Do you think he was happy, Emer?' Rose asks, her face streaming and raw, and Brigid

314

shoots a look of warning at her. *Don't you dare,* Emer can hear her as if she'd said it out loud. Something grows hot in her then, seeing the fierce look in Brigid's eyes, as if even she, like the rest of them, will do anything to protect Rose.

'That's enough of that,' Emer says. 'Wasn't he as happy as the next fool?'

And though Brigid squeezes her eyes shut and shakes her head, Rose lets out a brief, bitter laugh.

'Leave it to Emer,' she says, swabbing the stream of tears and snot from her face. 'You'll not let us wallow, now, will you, love?'

★ ★ ★

There's no school on the island for weeks, because every hand is needed for the work of getting ready for winter. The children have their jobs — the hens, the eggs, feeding calves and pigs, and, on Saturdays, bathing themselves and the wee ones, and knife sharpening.

This has always been the job of children, the sharpening of knives and polishing of cutlery, and Emer can remember that Rose started it very young, at the age of five, when the knives needed to be kept away from their mother. Niall and Fiona show this to Brigid proudly, taking the knife box, a long wooden board with a cubby of sand, down from its spot by the hearth. They drag their mother's knives against a layer of grit, and their grandmother's, worn thinner than the rest. They offer to do Brigid's and she praises them too much.

'They'll have their own sooner than I'd like,' Rose murmurs and no one insults this with an argument.

When Niall isn't working, he stays close to Fiona and Eve. They were forced together even more than usual when Emer sent him to school, and then during the long keening days after the wake and funerals when she hid in Rose's bedroom, getting up only to change the roads of clotted blood between her legs. Emer was grateful for the distraction then, but now Niall's interest in the girls offends her. Rather than that look of pure relief he usually has when she comes to rescue him from mandatory time with his cousins, Niall looks annoyed when she suggests that it is time to go home.

'I don't want to go,' he whinges, stomping his foot and scowling. He has never behaved this way. Rose's girls have tantrums, tearful rages that subside quickly because their mother refuses to pay attention until they calm down. Niall, Rose likes to say, is a perfect angel compared to her girls. Emer has defined him from this phrase, and herself, often enough.

'Why can't we live here?' Niall says one day. 'You can sleep with Rose and I'll sleep with the girls.'

He is not the first to suggest it. It makes perfect sense — bonding together in the ruins, widowed sisters have done it before. Rose seemed surprised after the first week that Emer went home at all.

Emer hustles him outside, angry, embarrassed, avoiding Rose's eyes that follow after them. On the walk Niall grows meek again, apologetic, taking her hand.

'What are you lot playing all the time?' she says, trying to sound neutral, but it comes out like an accusation.

'We play house,' Niall says. 'I'm the father as I'm the only boy.'

'What does the father do?' Emer remembers, vaguely, playing something similar with Rose. With dolls and wild flowers and broken crockery. She was always the one forced to be the man.

'I eat breakfast,' Niall says. 'Then I go off so I can die. After I die they wash me and put me in a box and cry and we start all over again.'

Emer grows cold with it, the thought of them playing at their own lives.

'Sometimes one of them murders me,' Niall says. 'That's the fun part. Then we get to have a hanging.'

It takes Emer a minute to remember to inhale.

'I don't want to move to the mainland,' Niall says as if this is a natural segue in conversation.

'Why not?' Emer says huskily. Her throat burns.

'If we stay here, I'll marry Eve. If we move, she'll have lots of lads to choose from at school. I don't want to go to school, and Eve doesn't either. We want to stay here for ever, like you and Auntie Rose.'

'Brilliant,' Emer says.

★　★　★

The work they have, now that the men are gone, is the back-breaking sort, and it never ends. In

317

addition to everything they already do all day long, in and around the house, now they have the fields, the sheep, the sea. The teenagers come home from school on the mainland to assist their mothers, and the teachers give them lessons to do at night, which they fall asleep over next to the paraffin lamp. Only one of these is a boy, Oisin, as slight and sensitive and fragile-looking as Matthew.

Brigid organises them. Like some aged, kindly nun, she finds out what needs to be done and rallies them all into doing it. They dig the turf in one frenzied week, the sun still shining like it's summertime, but dipping sooner in the sky. Women and children slicing, tossing, arranging it in rows to dry. There is Reeking Day, which takes three days instead of one, where they exhaust the poor donkey moving all the hay the men cut in August and storing it in sheds or in fields under oilskin tarps. Every last potato, cabbage, and turnip is ripped from the ground. The weather holds, warm and mild, as if giving them a chance to figure it all out before it imprisons them again.

'Who will pull the pots?' Rose asks, and Brigid smiles.

'I'm from Maine,' she says. 'I know what to do with lobster traps.'

On calm days the fishermen from Muruch give them rowing lessons, their faces twisted in disapproval. Brigid's arms are as long and muscular as a man's. She learns quickly which women are the best candidates: Kathleen, Malachy's widow, with broad shoulders and a

318

willingness to push through pain, Margaret, small but wiry, toughened by years of lugging around the overly large baby boys she had by Michael Joe, and Maeve, Kathleen's seventeen-year-old daughter, tall and awkward and thick-necked as an adolescent boy. Oisin, Brigid can tell, is relieved when she doesn't ask him to sign on for his manly responsibility. Within a month, the four women can get a small currach in and out of the water, timing it with the waves, and pull the heavy oars in harmony the mile to Muruch and back again. Brigid decides they will practise this distance and try the mainland, nine miles away, in the spring. Until then, the men from Muruch will bring them whatever supplies they can. They also sell the lobsters for them, after Brigid teaches the women how to bait and set as many traps as they can manage.

All of the island women are aching, calloused, sunburned, muscles and eyes on fire, sweat-soaked and ripe as their husbands once were. Brigid, while beside them, pulling and slicing and rowing and digging, puts her hand out every once in a while to ease the aches. Just enough to make them think they can go on a while longer. She needs to take care with Maeve, who responds to Brigid's touch with such a vicious surge of lust, it often leaves her too confused and ashamed to get anything done.

In November, the time comes to slaughter the pigs. Of the six that came in the springtime, only Niall's is left, one slaughtered in October by Austin, the others traded to the mainland for necessities. Normally, the pigs are killed and shared among the families, one at a time. Niall's pig will be enough for all of them.

Emer does not want them to do it. Cabbage, though not as eager to play, or able, as he was in the summertime, still follows her son on the road.

'Why didn't you sell that one, then, when you negotiated for the others?' Emer argues with Rose.

'Sure, didn't we hand over the pigs we could find,' Rose says. She is irritable most of the time now, with a puss that rivals her sister's, their mother says. 'That creature runs wild.'

'You can't slaughter the thing in front of him,' Emer says to Brigid. Brigid opens her mouth, looking like she's about to agree.

'Are you wanting to protect him from the sorrows of the world, so?' their mother says. 'It's a bit late for that.'

'She's right,' Rose says.

Brigid and Emer look at her, as if an imposter dressed up like Rose has spoken instead.

'I don't mind,' Niall says. They turn to see him peering over the lip of the half-door. 'I knew he would have to go. I want to be there when you do it.'

Brigid looks at him hard, and she can see he is trying to stand tall, and not flinch. She nods.

A man from Muruch explains how to stun it with a hammer, but Brigid merely smiles and ignores his instructions. She has Niall help her instead. He calms the animals, he always has, with his hands.

Rose is too enormously pregnant to be useful.

Emer is there, grudgingly, and Kathleen and Margaret. Niall leads Cabbage into the barn, whispering, scratching behind his ears, the pig stumbling with pleasure and trust. Niall gets it to lie down in the earth and put his enormous head in his lap. He strokes the thing until it falls into a sort of coma, dropping heavily away from Niall's hands. He looks up at Brigid and her knife with tears in his eyes.

'All right?' she says.

'Go on,' he says, moving aside, pretending to be brave.

Brigid drives her knife in at the top of the breastbone, then cuts up to the middle of the neck and twists the way the man showed her. Three women hold the head up so the blood can rush, steaming and thin, into a metal tub. They will use this for the blood pudding. Emer holds the tub steady, looking like she might be sick and ruin it all. Brigid is feeling queasy herself, the stench is overpowering, but she breathes through her mouth and shakes it off. She resists the urge to place her hand over the wound she has just made, and reverse the waterfall of life pouring out.

It takes them all day to bleed, scald, scrape and gut the pig, another day to cut away at joints and pack pound after pound of salt into its flesh. They throw the useless bits to the dogs, except Rua, who paces outside and growls her disapproval. The pig's head is shoved into a canvas bag, just like the one the piglets arrived in, and boiled for days in an enormous pot outside. The whole island has fresh pork for a

321

week; they hang the salted meat in Emer's shed, a gruesome reminder of his pet swinging at Niall's head every time he enters.

★　★　★

Brigid comes to Sunday dinner at Rose's house after the slaughter. She watches Niall pause before he takes his first bite of pork. He closes his eyes, shoves it in, and chews. In that moment he seems more like a child than he usually does. Though still not a typical one.

Emer eats quickly and without small talk. Clodagh's table manners are similar, though her bad arm keeps her from eating quickly. The pork is overcooked, tough, both strong and bland. It tastes like the blood smelled. Brigid feels suddenly close and nauseated in this kitchen, full of turf smoke and pig fat so thick it has settled on to every surface, including their skin. She holds a hand to her lower belly, the swelling of which she is still hiding under oversized shirts, and breathes through her mouth.

'Are the bees all gone?' Fiona asks. 'The hives are so quiet.' Clodagh makes a disapproving gasp. She rarely says a word to Brigid directly, and refuses to be eased by her hands. All of Brigid's attempts have been flung off silently, like she might push her way out of an uninvited embrace. She is a woman who prefers her pain. She has shared, loudly, how mortified she is at having Brigid's dog inside the house. Rua stays by the door, waiting for her to be done.

'They're hibernating,' Brigid says. 'They sent

the drones out to die and the women will stay hunkered down till spring.' She says this before she thinks about how it will sound.

Clodagh erupts then, with an ugly laugh.

'Sound familiar?' she says. Emer looks at her like she'd like to slit her throat. This is how she looks at almost everyone but Niall, so her mother doesn't even bother to turn her head to deflect it.

'Have you had your fill, Mammy?' Rose says, standing quickly and whisking away her plate. 'I know I have.' Her expression is mild, but her voice holds a warning, and their mother darkens with a blush and says no more.

18

Midwife

November, 1959

Rose is supposed to go to hospital a full month before the babies are due, but she keeps delaying it. She says she doesn't want to leave the children, that she has so much more to do with Austin gone, though Brigid has silently taken care of most of it. Whenever she makes plans to go, the weather turns.

'Mind you don't wait until it's too late, Rose,' their mother says. The older women, the ones who still have time to sit down for tea, dip their biscuits and suck at their teeth in agreement.

'You don't want to be having the babies here, in the middle of a storm, no doctor and nothing to ease your pain.'

Rose dislikes the hospital, Emer knows. She hates being put to sleep and not seeing the babies come out. The last time, she had checked in a week early, and said nothing to the nurses once she was in labour. She hid it for so long that by the time it came to push, the young doctor was flustered and confused and forgot all about putting her under. She pushed them out so fast they shot into his trembling hands. Rose believes she can have this set all by herself and still have dinner on the table.

324

'Foolishness,' the other women say, whishting and dunking biscuits with disapproving vigour.

'Island women used to have their babies here,' Rose says.

'Aye. And haven't we stones in the graveyard to thank for it?' The women cross themselves, biscuits in hand, crumbs springing about.

'We'd a midwife then,' Austin's mother says. 'And little choice. It's pure foolishness for someone to choose to have her baby here now. You'd never forgive yourself if something went wrong.'

'Brigid's a midwife,' Rose announces. Emer whips her head around like an animal ready to bite.

A midwife, is she? From America as well.

Surely she trained in one of those posh hospitals.

Ah you're in good form, so.

The women are muttering as one now, slurping the last dregs of their tea, and Rose warms the pot up for them and smiles at Emer. Emer doesn't even try to smile back this time. She can't decide which thing she is most annoyed about. The fact that Rose seems to know everything about Brigid now, or the thoughtless confidence of her sister, who, even after such tragedy, still assumes that what she wants will necessarily go as planned.

★　★　★

A storm hits them the last week of November. Not a day that any man would dare get in a boat, let alone a woman enormous with her fourth set of twins. When her labour starts, Rose is alarmingly chipper, moving about the house with purpose, stopping occasionally to breathe long and slow, and bend, in a way that makes all the girls stop what they are doing, bend and breathe with her. Then she straightens up again, smiles and winks at them and says, 'That wasn't such a bad one, was it now?' and proceeds with her chores.

This goes on all day, Rose's enthusiasm waning a bit as the contractions wear on but don't seem to get either closer or stronger. They are consistent and draining but useless, like a fire that flares and then dies, refusing to light. 'I don't understand,' she whispers once to Emer, sweat beading on her upper lip. 'It's been eight hours. I should be well finished and having a nap.' Emer mutters something dismissive. Her labour with Niall had gone on for two whole days. How like Rose to question when anything is the slightest bit different from what she desires.

Brigid calls in and takes Rose into the bedroom to check her progress, while Emer eavesdrops at the doorway. Brigid says, 'Every labour is different,' and Rose says, 'Not for me.' Brigid leaves her resting and comes to tell Emer that it may be a long time. Emer brings the girls over to her house, leaving them with her mother and Niall, and comes back to Rose's to wait out the labour along with the storm.

In the small house, with the wind howling and rain lashing on the windows, Rose paces and groans and begins to lose herself.

'Something's wrong,' she says, and the next pain stops her in her tracks. She seems to forget for a minute her ritual of deep rhythmic breath and instead gulps clumsily and without success until the siege subsides.

'It's not like the others. Something's not right.'

'Emer,' she says, after the next one. She only has time to say one thing between each pain. 'Get the cloth.'

It's a tradition she hasn't bothered with since the first pair, the blue cloth blessed in Saint Brigid's well, said to be the way Brigid herself eased the labour of the women who escaped to her: with pieces of her cloak. Emer gets it from a drawer in Rose's chest, soaking it from the bottle of holy water Rose keeps on a high shelf in the press. She binds it with ribbon to her sister's writhing belly, and Rose uses one of her fleeting breaks to smile her thanks.

It goes on, and Rose stops trying to speak, or smile. She walks, she stoops, she leans on Brigid. Brigid holds her up, rubs her lower back, murmurs words of encouragement and wisdom. None of it seems to help. A pain tears through Rose while Brigid is holding her, so massive and loud that Brigid is thrown back and away with the invisible force. Rose screams. And for the first time since she's known her, Brigid looks to Emer as if she's not quite sure what she is doing.

'What's wrong?' Emer asks in a whisper, as Rose gives up pacing and tries to escape the pain by lying in a fetal position, with the covers over her head.

'I don't know,' Brigid says.

'Will you not ease her pain?' Emer says. 'She's had enough.'

'Stop asking me questions,' Brigid barks.

She tells Emer to sit behind Rose and prop her up.

'Rose,' she says loudly. 'I need to put my hands inside and feel the baby.'

'No,' Rose says, trying to close her legs, but Brigid is too strong for her. 'No, don't. I can't stand it.'

'I have to, Rose, I have to check something. You need to let me in.'

Rose screams louder than ever as Brigid pushes her hands up inside, feeling around for an answer.

'Something's wrong,' Rose says. 'What's wrong?'

'Shush, Rose,' Brigid says, as harshly as if she were talking to Emer. 'You're all right. You need to push now.'

'I can't. It's not time.'

'It is time, Rose. Push.'

Emer expects a baby to shoot out after a few good grunting countdowns, but nothing comes. A hairy globe of scalp appears and retreats, over and over with each contraction, never making any progress. The pushing goes on so long that Emer can't keep track of the time any more. The storm rages on, so thick with clouds and rain that there is barely a difference between the black of night and the grey of morning. It takes them a long time to notice the dawn.

'I can't, Emer,' Rose says at one point, caught

in the limbo of this child who is no longer in but will not come out. 'I'm going to die.'

'Stop it,' Emer says. 'You're nearly there.'

Finally, Brigid pulls an enormous baby, face up, its features squashed, ugly and covered in what looks like wax. Brigid seems barely interested in this baby, who starts screeching and turns bright red, dumping it on to Rose's stomach, where Emer has to grab a leg to keep it from sliding away on to the bedclothes.

'Keep pushing, Rose,' Brigid says.

'Can't I have a wee rest?' Rose murmurs, trying to look at the baby, so close to her face she can't really focus on it.

'Not now, push. Quickly, love.'

Emer holds the slippery infant on top of her sister as Rose pushes and roars.

Another one comes out, a smaller one, the colour of heather buds, purple blue and not moving and wrong. Not a baby at all, is what Emer comes close to saying out loud.

There are a lot of commands and confusion, and Emer almost loses her grip on the first baby trying to follow Brigid's orders. She wants her to hold the thing for an instant while she quickly binds and cuts the cord, then she takes it away, closer to the fire, with garbled instructions on how Emer is supposed to care for her sister's womb. Something about massaging it for the afterbirth. Emer does nothing but watch what happens next, completely ignoring her sister and her womb and the first baby, whose cord has not even been cut.

She thinks at first that Brigid is going to put it

in the fire. Set it on the hearth like a changeling to see if it's real. It is not even half the size of the first one, with brittle, wrinkled arms and legs and a blue that her sister must not, Emer thinks, be let to see. 'Where is it, Emer,' Rose whispers, exhausted and unable to focus her eyes in the dim room. 'Where's the other baby?'

'Whisht,' Emer hisses, as if silence might stop the horrible outcome from entering the room.

Brigid grabs a shawl from a nearby chair and lays it on the hearth, putting the baby down gently in front of the glowing heat of a turf fire that is never allowed to die. She wipes at the thing with a cloth, massaging its limbs, its tiny chest, clears the mucus from its eyes, nose and mouth with her pinky finger. Then she leans down and almost takes the thing in her mouth, covering its entire face with open lips, and blows, blows, then presses the chest with two fingers, like she is testing risen dough. She waits, blows, presses again. Just at the moment where it is surely too late comes a weak, protesting little cough. Then a thin cry.

Rose lets out a wail in response. Brigid settles the now pink baby in the waiting space in Rose's other arm. She tends to Rose and the afterbirth, all with quick, confident hands, no sign of the panic and impotence that pulled at her face only minutes before.

Once the babies are cleaned and swaddled and introduced to their mother's breasts, Rose can see how starkly different they are. Girls, like the rest of Rose's babies, everyone assumed they would be, it was something of a joke how Rose's body could make nothing but girls. One of them is plump and pretty and serene like every other baby of Rose's, the other, wizened, scowling, not quite sure what to do with her hands, her mouth, her mother's breast. She seems to look directly at her sister latched on to a nipple and opens her little mouth to let out a wail of righteous anger. Her fists are clenched with what already seems like a lifetime of frustration.

'Oh, this one's like you, Emer,' Rose laughs.

What Emer was thinking was that it looked not like a baby at all, but like the wizened, possessed fairy she had grown to expect as a child. As if any moment it might open its mouth and speak in the voice of the underworld.

Rose nuzzles it and pulls it closer, monster or no.

$$\star \quad \star \quad \star$$

'Will it die?' Emer says to Brigid, as she washes her hands and arms at the bucket.

'It was close, but I don't think so,' Brigid says. She lathers between her fingers. 'She's little, but strong.'

'Did you heal it?'

'That wasn't magic, Emer. That was medicine.'

'Is it part of the curse?' It's out of Emer's mouth before she can stop it, and once out, she does not want to take it back. She wants Brigid to know. She wants to be forgiven.

'What curse?' Brigid says, tired, annoyed.

'The curse I set with the fairy's stone.'

331

Brigid looks at her, eyes widening. 'What stone?'

'It's next to the well,' Emer says. 'I . . .'

Brigid sucks her breath in with an island gasp. 'You *didn't*, Emer.'

'I was only trying to clear my womb,' Emer whispers. 'I think I drowned the lads as well.'

Brigid looks like she is battling something ugly in her mind, fighting something that Emer hopes will never win. She shakes her head.

'It's only a baby,' she says. 'Not a curse.' But she won't look Emer in the eye. 'It has nothing to do with you.'

The way she says it, cold, final, removed. Like she's shutting a door. When she reaches for the dishcloth to dry her hands, they are trembling.

*　*　*

There is a moment in every labour where, no matter how many times a woman has done it before, she thinks she will die. Without this moment, Brigid knows, the baby would never be born. It is as necessary as pushing a bucket beneath the surface of a well. Darkness doesn't do its job if you believe, when you are inside of it, that it will ever let you go. It is not something any of them is allowed to remember. Brigid suspects even she will forget it, when her time comes.

For the first five days after the babies are born, Brigid doesn't leave them once. The weather is desperate, the seas raging, wind so loud she can't remember not being aware of it. 'The sort of wind what leaves you deaf for a week,' Clodagh says. Brigid sleeps on the hearth bed, when she can catch a few minutes, but mostly she holds on to one baby while Rose tends to the other.

Brigid tries not to think too much about Emer's sideways confession, she can't. The baby inside her reacted when Emer said it, with jolting kicks that felt like panicked alarm. Whatever Emer has done, Brigid needs to stay away from it. From her.

Brigid wants to hold the smaller baby more than the other one. This wizened, cranky thing that tried to betray them. She told Emer the truth, she didn't heal it. The first baby came out facing the sky instead of the earth, the second with the cord wrapped round her neck. Brigid used only the medical knowledge she had from Matthew, and waited for the babies to emerge. She breathed into the second twin, felt the thing shudder and resist. As if it wasn't a baby at all, but a furious changeling with no intention of giving in. She half expected it to open its eyes and speak to her. But then it cried and became merely a newborn who survived a close call.

Brigid can soothe it better than her own mother can. She knows exactly how to cradle the more precarious lives in her hands. Brigid's baby grows quiet and content when she holds this one to her stomach, reassuring them both.

★ ★ ★

Rose names the little baby after her sister, and the fat one after Brigid. They call her Bridie.

333

There is no natural nickname for Emer, so Rose calls her Wee Emer, and somehow, given to this peeling, wrinkled baby, the name that once sounded harsh and unmusical to Brigid now feels lovely to croon. She is the first of Rose's girls not named for a saint, which Clodagh points out with a complacency that drives Rose to shush her crossly.

Emer is doing all the outdoor chores she can manage in such weather, avoiding Rose, though she follows Brigid with her reproachful eye. She won't hold either baby. Brigid doesn't want to think too much about Emer right now. She feels like someone Brigid knew a long time ago, whom she is wary of, but she can't remember why.

Wee Emer can't eat. Whenever Rose puts her nipple in the baby's mouth, the girl fusses and won't latch on. Brigid checks when the baby wails — this one cries a fair amount, enough that Brigid has no doubt she will be OK — and sees that underneath her tongue is pulled so tight she can't extend it out of her mouth. She disinfects her pocketknife and uses it to clip the tethered membrane, which makes the grown Emer cross herself. Wee Emer stops crying instantly, as if relieved. Brigid shows Rose how to express her milk; there seems to be no end to it, it flows from her whether a baby is suckling or not. 'I'm the Lake of Milk,' Rose jokes, telling her what happened the time Saint Brigid blessed the cows. Brigid feeds the baby with a soaked corner of a cloth until she learns to use her tongue.

Rose tells her the story of Saint Brigid's birth while she nurses the strong baby in bed.

'Saint Brigid's father was a chieftain, and her mother, Broisech, was his slave and mistress. A druid foretold that the child in her belly would be born at sunrise, neither in the house nor out of it, that it would belong to both worlds, and that it would be greater than any child born in Ireland. The chieftain's wife was so jealous that she sold Broisech away to another castle. In that house a queen laboured in the night but the baby was born dead. At sunrise, Broisech bore her child in the doorway, with one foot inside the house and the other outside of it. This baby was brought to the Queen, offered as a replacement, but when Brigid was laid down next to the Queen's baby she breathed it back to life. That was Brigid's first miracle.'

'And you're our Saint,' Rose says, reaching out a hand to squeeze Brigid's.

'That wasn't a miracle,' Brigid says. 'It happens all the time. Some babies take a minute to breathe.'

'Still, I'm grateful to you. And every baby is a miracle.'

'You're more of a saint than I am,' Brigid laughs, and Rose gives her an intoxicated smile.

★ ★ ★

This was always Brigid's favourite time when she and Matthew had the maternity home. All the women were encouraged to stay with their babies, even if they eventually decided to give them away. The first few hours and days stretched to an unfathomable length. They

335

would remember it, Brigid knew, every one of them, as occupying a larger portion of their lives than certain decades. The hushed wonder of the newborn, the warmth, the insubstantial weight, the flaking skin and tiny fingernails, the butterfly flare of nostrils, the pursed buds of their mouths. The way they spring back, after stretching them out to be cleaned, into the tightly curled form they took in the womb. The sigh that emerges when you swaddle them tight, their relief at that familiar cramp. Those first few days after birth are a limbo, a tributary between pregnancy and motherhood, between waiting for life and living it; right in the middle you can step on to a stone where they are the same.

Even Emer and Clodagh can't stain the bliss that soaks that cottage the first few days. They try, with their gasps and their scathing comments, but they are outside of it, harpies who cannot penetrate Brigid and Rose's enraptured cocoon.

Brigid and Rose coo at the little feet and earlobes and fingers, and run a soft flannel soaked in warm water into the fat creases of one and the hollows of another, they lay down with them, skin to skin, naked babies wrapped inside their blouses, letting the warmth they produced when they were inside seep back in from above. When Rose notices her swollen belly, Brigid admits she is expecting too, and holds her breath. But Rose is delighted.

'Was it the Australian, then?' she says. Brigid merely smiles. 'I don't know that we can find him.'

336

'It doesn't matter,' Brigid says.

'No,' Rose sighs. 'I suppose not. We're only women now.'

When everyone else is asleep, in the timeless deep night, they lay next to one another in the bed, a baby on each of them, and look at the thing reflected in the other's eyes. The slow recognition of what they are holding on to, these tiny bodies that are entirely infused with trust. This is why Brigid could not stay away from birth all those years, even when it sliced her with regret. She covets this time. When they are first born, before things get more complicated, you can press your skin to theirs and absorb that faith, as though you, as well, are being held by something that will never let you go.

* * *

The doctor, when the weather finally allows him through, six days after Rose's labour, is furious at the lot of them. He stomps with angry purpose from the quay up to Rose's house. It is the same doctor. Rose tells Brigid, who was there when Emer lost her eye. This, Brigid feels, is enough of a warning.

The doctor hands his coat and hat to Emer without looking at her.

He asks Rose how she is feeling while he polishes his spectacles.

'If I was any better I'd be unbearable.' Rose beams at him. His frown remains.

'Where is this Yank everyone's on about?' he demands. Brigid steps forward, and with her hair loose and her man's trousers, in an old flannel three-buttoned tunic that once belonged to Austin, she can see how she looks to him, bold, with an arrogance not familiar on the island, or in Ireland, an arrogance that is particularly American. She will milk this now, however they dislike it.

'What sort of medical training have you?' he says. Brigid tells him that she trained as a nurse midwife in the States, adds that she has attended hundreds of births.

The doctor makes a dismissive noise at this information. 'Were there any complications?'

Brigid tells him of the long labour and Wee Emer getting stuck up behind the other, cord round her neck, needing mouth-to-mouth and chest massage to breathe.

'How long before the baby began breathing?' he asks.

'Less than a minute, I'd say,' Brigid answers.

'Did you do the Apgar?'

'Yes. A two after birth, a nine five minutes later.'

'Hunh,' the doctor mutters, as if he doesn't believe her.

He examines Rose, then the babies, one at a time, unwrapping them and prodding until they are both screeching at his cold, rough fingers.

'There's not much to this one,' the doctor says. 'Is she nursing?'

Rose can express milk into a jug from one breast while feeding a baby on the other. Not a bother on her, the island women say.

'She is,' Rose and Brigid say together, and he glances up suspiciously. He finishes examining

338

baby Emer and walks away, leaving her frail, angry, yellow-tinged body flailing uncovered on the table. Brigid re-covers her quickly, swaddling her tight in the wool the doctor has cast aside.

He packs up his bag, letting out occasional disapproving gusts of breath, like an angry horse. Every time he does it, Emer jumps.

'Your babies,' he says to Rose, 'not to mention yourself, might have died. There's talk this Yank has persuaded you people to stay here. You, madam' — he waves at Brigid dismissively — 'are taking lives you have no claim to out of God's hands.'

He wrestles with his coat, and makes one last biting remark.

'She'll likely end up touched, that one,' he mutters, gesturing to Emer in the cradle. Then, in the same breath, he remarks how sorry he is to hear about the passing of their husbands. He looks at Emer oddly on his way out, as if he is trying to place her.

Brigid shuts the door hard behind him, as though she means to catch his generous backside on the way out. After the last comment, she expects morose faces, maybe tears, but she looks at Rose and all at once they are laughing. They can barely speak, holding their sides and breathless with it, but Rose manages to get out a few imitations of the doctor's high-pitched, nagging voice — *You, Madam* — which just sends them off again. They wail with laughter and look at each other, mouths open in silent hilarity, gazes focused on the other's wet and dancing eyes.

Emer is furious, Brigid can tell, but it can't touch them, she is as helpless as the men who, were there any left, would be made to stand outside while the women get on with things.

19

Feet Water

December, 1959

There is almost nothing that makes Emer lonelier than the sight of other women laughing. It's like a fracture, somewhere inside her, watching Brigid and Rose laugh together. She thinks they look like sisters. Or wives. Or some other conglomeration — similar to the fantasies Emer had when she was with Brigid — a different kind of family where every adult member is female. Like the ancient society of women who loved each other before them.

She had this once, this affinity with Brigid. It was the first time she understood what it was like to be Rose, or Austin, with their lascivious looks and whispers. But the woman who adored her (she did, didn't she?) now won't look her in the eye. If she comes upon Emer unexpectedly she will flinch, step back, like every other islander. Emer once took grim satisfaction in people's fear of her, but she doesn't want to be dreaded any more.

It is as though someone took Brigid aside and reminded her which sister was the better one, and now she has chosen Rose. All Emer can do is stand apart and watch them laugh. It wouldn't be any worse, she believes, to see their tongues reaching into each other's mouths.

341

* * *

The children go back to school now that the autumn work has subsided, and Emer, avoiding Rose and Brigid, is often alone. One afternoon when she goes to collect Niall at school, she sees all the children have been let out to play. The air is full of the sort of shrieking that accompanies unsupervised children in a school playground. It takes Emer a while to distinguish Niall's scream from the others. It is not playful, but a panicked wail that sounds so like the cries he let out when he was an infant and couldn't eat, she feels her breasts grow heavy with memory. She quickens her pace on the bright green path and tries to distinguish him in the crowd. Niall is off on his own, ten yards from the rest of them, he is howling and throwing stones. The other children are laughing, or shouting back, and Fiona is trying to speak to him softly, but it doesn't seem to matter what any of them are doing, not to Niall who cries and rages at the whole lot, not to Emer, who can see nothing but her child with his face twisted in pain. When she gets to him he looks at her without recognition, no blue left in his eyes, and raises his fist as if he means to pound her in the face.

'Niall!' she hisses, stopping his hand and squeezing a warning into it. 'Niall?' Then his eyes focus and he knows it is her and his face falls into childish tears and she gathers him up. There is a half-arsed explanation of a childish game gone wrong, and a lecture from the teacher about how little he minds her, and a claim from

Eve that he'd gone off in a fit for no reason, but through it all, all Emer can think of is the look in his eyes when he'd almost hit her, how he'd not even known who she was, how he'd been gone, gone somewhere far away.

She has always worried about music, fairy forts, the lull of dripping honey. She sees now how he can be stolen from her, in the bright of day, even while she holds him in her arms. This is what she should have been afraid of all along.

★ ★ ★

It is subtle, the ways he is taken. For moments the boy she has always known will vanish. She'll be speaking to him and look up and see that his eyes have gone together in a squint and is not listening to her but to something no one else can hear. 'Niall,' she'll bark, and it won't reach him, she'll have to practically scream it and grab his shoulder before his eyes will go straight again and then he'll look startled, hurt at her tone, not at all concerned by his own absence.

'I was speaking to you.'

Then he'll get annoyed, as if she is bothering him about trifles.

'Would you never leave me my life?' he says once, his voice as deep and dangerous as a changeling who speaks from the cradle with the wizened voice of an old man.

It happens again in the currach on the way home from Mass. Kathleen, Maeve, Brigid and Margaret are rowing. The wind is strong enough that no one else could have heard it, she can only

343

hear words spoken against the soft space of her ear. She is holding him and he turns his face up to say it, and the voice which comes out of him is not his own, or the fairy's, it is Austin's.

'It should have been you who was drowned.' She stiffens and wonders if he can feel how her heart seems to stumble over itself, to stop beating in shock and then rush to catch up. When they get home he holds her hand up the path, smiling and chatting as if nothing has happened, and spends the evening drawing little animals for her and wrapping them in paper and twine like gifts.

'*A chuisle mo chroí*,' he mimics, just before going to sleep. *You are the pulse of my heart.* She lies watching him for hours, her neck crushing inward, watching his still, blank face as the light fades with the shrinking candle, looking for some evidence of the thing that is lurking inside him.

★ ★ ★

She tries to tell Rose that he is being taken, slowly but surely stolen from her. But Rose dismisses it.

'He's only a lad, Emer. He's after losing his father. The same thing is happening to the girls.'

'It's not the same,' Emer says. There is something between her and Niall that Rose doesn't have with her girls.

'Did you think he'd be that way always, so?' Rose scoffs. 'Your pet? They grow away, Emer. They're meant to.'

'That's not it,' Emer says.

'He's your only one, so this is the first time you're seeing it, but that's all it is.'

'They tried to take me,' Emer insists. 'They're after him now.'

'Those are only stories. You were stung by bees.'

'I was touched.'

'You weren't, so. It's just who you are. Nothing more.'

She says it as if Emer's evil power, the way she can leave people drowning in their own minds, can be chalked up to moodiness or a disagreeable disposition. Rose has seen the same things as Emer, but she seems to believe that her will to dismiss them is stronger than the fairies themselves.

★ ★ ★

It's not easy to get Brigid on her own. If she manages to come up behind her in the field or back garden, Brigid will start, put her hands to her belly and say, 'Jesus, Emer. Don't sneak up on me like that.'

She used to love it when Emer embraced her from behind, she used to lean back and guide Emer's hands to where she needed them.

'Will you help . . . ' she gets out once, but then Fiona interrupts and Emer can't say any more.

Brigid looks relieved, Fiona smug. Before Emer knows it, they are walking back to the house together, and she is alone.

★ ★ ★

On one of the darkest nights of the year, when the sun is gone by the middle of the afternoon, the husband Emer murdered comes home. She is steeping the tea in the pot when the door bangs open with the wind and he is there, massive and dark and wet, taking off his coat and cap and hanging them on the hook, dropping a load of turf into the hearth box. He stumbles around, sniffling from the cold that runs his nose, making noises somewhere between animal and man. Emer is petrified. Frozen in her chair, waiting for the moment where he sees her and remembers what she has done and forces her to her knees with the blame of it. She thinks of what his body must be like after two months beneath the water, white and swollen and eaten away, and knows she will have to touch it, because surely the punishment for killing him will be to resume having sex with him, and this thought starts her screaming. She screams and she screams and it is not until she sees that the hands holding her wrists are small and soft and belong to her son does she stop screaming. It is Niall's face in front of her.

'When did you come in?' she says.

'I'm here all along,' he says. 'I brought in the turf. Didn't you watch me walk in the door?' Emer shakes her head.

'Have you taken leave of your senses?' Niall says. He is so young still, how could she think he'd got bigger, he looks as small as when she still carried him in her arms. He goes to wash his feet in the bowl that waits by the fire for this purpose. His feet are the same shape as they were the day he was born, squat, ugly toes with nails soft enough to bend. When he was a newborn, they were as clean and smooth as the rest of him. Now the nails are caked with earth, the cracked soles stained brown by the bog. No matter how he scrubs they will never be that clean again.

He takes the basin and brings it to the door, flinging out the dirty water, in the island tradition: it's bad luck to keep the feet water in the house overnight. There was an island girl, the story goes, who forgot to do this and the fairies carried her off the same night. She was gone with them for seven years before she was let home. She was returned the same age as when she'd left, still a girl, still in her nightgown, but she had no toes. She had danced them off.

'Come here,' Emer says to Niall, and he obliges. She holds on to him, too tight, he squirms and tries to get away.

'I'm only just in from the cows,' Niall says. 'Not off to America.' She doesn't laugh as he means her to, but clutches him tighter and pretends to believe it, even as she knows, inhaling — she has known for a while now — that the smell of him is all wrong.

★　★　★

'When is your baby due?' Rose asks.

'In May,' Brigid says.

'I hope you'll stay on,' Rose says. 'You've come to mean so much to Emer.' Brigid looks away.

'Oh, it's not easy to tell, but I see it. She never

had a friend before you,' Rose says. 'Folk steer clear of Emer, because of what is in her hands. She's able to rid herself of it, I believe. I'm not sure why she doesn't want to.'

Because she's like my mother, Brigid wants to say. And yours. Sometimes people get pounded so much by life they choose to burn back at the pain rather than douse it.

'Aren't you afraid of her?' Brigid asks instead.

'Oh, Emer isn't able to harm me,' Rose says. 'And even if she were, she wouldn't. Any more than she'd hurt Niall, or you, for that matter.'

Brigid can't bring herself to say it. Can't look into that lovely face and tell it: *Don't be so sure.*

'I must say,' Rose adds, 'I'm glad you're here all the time. You've eased the whole business for all of us, so you have.'

Clodagh, who has been pretending to doze in her rocker, rises to this opportunity.

'Are you not going to ask her who the father is?' she says.

'It hardly matters,' Rose winks at Brigid. 'I don't see him here.'

★   ★   ★

Brigid isn't attracted to Rose, though she can feel Emer's jealousy, as palpable as winter damp in the room. She pities Emer, greedy and vicious and alone, but even if it were not dangerous, she tells herself she is no longer interested in romantic love, or sex. Her baby grows so quickly she feels fuller, more complete, every hour of the day. She has left so many babies behind, the ones

348

she birthed as well as the ones she lost. She does not have to leave this time, after the babies are born. She will stay on and help Rose feed and bathe and dress them, she will be the midwife to the next woman who needs her, she will birth her own baby into this island of women and girls. She will stay here because there is a space she can fill perfectly and without suspicion, because on this island women dance with each other, walk the roads holding on to each other's waists, curl up together on the same beds to sleep, and it never occurs to them to be ashamed. This island was settled by women who lived together, they had ceremonies where they were essentially married, where they bound their souls, and their bodies, for life. Brigid doesn't need a ceremony, and her body is occupied. She would like to be the woman who convinces them to stay.

When she pulled that crushed, wizened, barely human form out of the forgotten crevice in Rose's body, and had to lay it by the fire and breathe life, not magic, inside, she decided she was done with something. Done with the manipulation of women's most tender parts, and the way she used them to fill something that had never been there. The way her father once pretended to apologise to and caress her mother, the way it appeared to be generous and guilty and really all he was doing was consuming her alive. Feeding her pleasure so he could suck it back into himself. Brigid is tired of pleasuring women, and of teaching them how to wring pleasure out of her. She wants that part to be

349

over, had wanted it over when she moved here, but forgot for an instant, tripped a little, when presented with Emer's raw and awkward need.

She is surprised at how cruel she begins to sound when Rose mentions Emer. Dismissive, unforgiving, done. As if rejecting Emer has earned her a film of Emer's disposition, a trail of unease like something left on a stone by a snail.

'I might call in and see if she needs anything,' Rose will say and Brigid will convince her, without even saying it aloud, not to.

She knows the longer Rose leaves her the further away Emer will slip. Brigid's want of this life, this island, is enough to make her cruel. Though she once promised to help Emer, and had wanted to heal her, now she sees that Emer is not something to heal but something to stay away from. Emer could ruin it all. She destroyed her own family, she'll stop at nothing to get what she wants. If it suited Emer, she would reach in and yank Brigid's hope right alongside the bloody limbs of her half-formed child. Brigid will do whatever is necessary — she will turn her sister and her son against her if she has to — to avoid losing this one last best chance she has ever been given at life.

'Leave her be,' she says to Rose, over and over again, and Rose listens, because, Brigid knows, there is a part of her so tired of missing her husband, and a lifetime of being Emer's better twin, that it would like to have someone else carry away the burden of her sister.

★ ★ ★

'When shall we tell the others?' Brigid asks Rose. It has become difficult to hide her growing middle, even behind the yellow waterproof she wears most of the time now. She is nervous about the reaction. Though they have accepted and welcomed her, she has seen before how quickly even women can turn when you dare to betray their ideas of decency.

'I'd be inclined to tell the lot of them at once,' Rose says. 'Keep the lips from flapping, if you know how I mean.'

So they do. On a wet day when the women are gathered at Rose's, their hands roughened with new calluses, from rope and oars rather than knives and churns. Kathleen, Nelly, Margaret, their mothers and mothers-in-law, the grand-mothers and teenagers left at home to tend the smaller children.

'We're expecting a wee Australian in May,' Rose says cheerily, while refilling the teapot. 'I told Brigid we'd all pitch in, of course. I don't want her lifting that boat any longer.'

There is a heavy silence that goes on long enough to set dread thronging inside Brigid. The women look at one another, at her, at Rose, and seem to come to a collective decision.

It's not as if we weren't in the same position ourselves once. Quite a few of us, if you remember.

Don't mind the talk. She's one of us now and we take care of our own.

That's a blessing, so it is. Babbies born after forty are touched with luck.

Won't it be a stunner, that one? With your

complexion and that Australian was an eyeful.

Sure, aren't we an island of women and children now.

They reassure her, congratulate her, ask her what she'll name a girl, a boy. Later, when Brigid is washing up, she overhears the older ones whispering in Irish.

Same thing happened to her mother, don't you know.

That was another time.

How do we know it was the Australian? Kathleen always wondered if Malachy fancied her.

Whisht. It won't help any of us, that talk.

What about the stories? What her family had in them?

They're only stories, sure. She has no more black magic in her than I do.

We wouldn't be here still without her help.

I'm not certain that's for the best.

Rose is. Rose is sure of her and that's enough for me.

She's too fond of Emer for my liking.

Yes, well, she wasn't told any different. She's copped on now, I suspect.

Brigid can't decide if they believe in magic or not. On the one hand they are superstitious, never walking past places where fairies might cause mischief, crossing themselves multiple times a day. On the other they seem pragmatic and dismiss notions of fairies when it suits them. Rose will talk of Emer as if she is cursed and then act as if she is just regrettably sour. They seem to respect some parallel world at the same

352

time as they brush the very idea of it away.

Brigid keeps a few things to herself. Only Emer and Niall know about the healing. The diffusing of grief she does so subtly no one suspects her hands are behind it. If someone cuts themselves or bleeds through blisters she doesn't mend it. As far as they're concerned her hands are just like their own, work-roughened and compassionate. She suspects Rose knows, has guessed, but she is too loyal to say so.

She doesn't tell any of them she understands their Irish. Not even Emer knows that. All these years later, it still seems wise to Brigid to have a secret language. *You never know*, says her mother's voice, still as close to her ear as if she lies on the same pillow, *when you might need it*.

★ ★ ★

December storms strand them for two more weeks. School is cancelled, boats tied down to cement blocks on the grass, women can't even walk the road without hanging on to fence posts and digging the toes of their shoes into boggy ground. It's all Brigid can do to milk the cows, everything else is left to the rain. She wears Desmond's wellies, the toes stuffed with extra socks, and lines them up next to Austin's at Rose's front door. She stays most nights with Rose, teaches drawing techniques to her girls, learns to knit herself a postulant's tube scarf. They watch the stores of flour and sugar and tea sift away, portion by portion, no hope of replenishment in sight. It begins to look as if there will be no Christmas packages, something Rose's girls fear every year, with good reason. Half the time, they explain, Father Christmas does not come. He arrives in January, with a note of apology tied up with the oranges and apples and chocolates that come over on the boat.

Brigid goes ten straight days without a glimpse of Emer, though Niall comes over daily for a visit. On an afternoon where the wind and rain clear to a frosty fog, she tells Rose she will go back to Desmond's house and get the rest of her flour and tea. She walks the road, a brighter green in fog than it is in sunlight, unable to see more than two feet in front of her. Emer is not far behind.

Emer knocks on the door, announcing herself with the desperate pound of her fist. Brigid doesn't open it; she leans on the other side of the door, barely breathing, willing her to go away. Emer once walked in without invitation, but she has reversed to a formality with Brigid, an odd one considering the intimacies that occurred once she let her in. Brigid can imagine Emer on the other side of the wood, as the plans that propelled her up the path grow cold and her face heats up with humiliation. She hopes Emer can't hear her jagged breath, or the inner voice that, despite her resolve, still calls her name out with something like ardour — *Emer, Emer* — even as it begs her away. Emer lingers for a long time, longer than she should, hoping that Brigid will change her mind, then turns and stumbles her way back down the hill.

20

Christmas Tree

When Festy manages to get across from the mainland and bring provisions for Christmas, Niall comes to tell Emer the men from Muruch are pulling into the quay. They have brought a pine tree for Brigid. She asked Festy to get her one to decorate for Christmas. When Emer goes down to the quay, Brigid and Rose are together, smiling and laughing with the men, and the girls are all taking turns putting their faces in the branches and inhaling the smell of pine. The blasted dog is moving circles around them, jumping and filthying skirts with her paws. No one minds her any more.

'Brigid got us a Christmas tree, Emer,' Rose says. 'Just like a storybook. We'll have it inside the house with candles and sweets hidden in the branches. Why don't you and Niall come for tea and help us decorate it?'

'It'll burn the house down,' Emer says bitterly.

Niall is running around on the quay rocks and she needs to bark at him to get some sense, and that's when Rose gasps her disapproval. Rose never has to tell the girls to mind their own bodies. They just do it.

'Ach, Emer,' Rose says. 'Try not to ruin Christmas for the lot of us, would you now.' Fiona and Eve snicker, like women already, squinting at Emer with cruel glee. Brigid is busy directing women on how to hold the trunk of the tree without damaging the needles. Niall becomes interested in carrying it, but doesn't listen to instructions so just manages to poke himself in the eye. He is comforted by Eve and doesn't even look for his mother. And so they all fuss and carry on and walk away from Emer, so enraged by it all that she can't move, her face screwed up and ugly against the wind and sea spray, left on the abandoned quay. Not even the dog, normally compelled to keep the herd together, checks behind them.

★ ★ ★

On Christmas Eve at Rose's house, where everything they do emphasises the absence of husbands and fathers, where Niall is the only male in a throng of optimistic but weary-eyed women, Emer has too much to drink and accosts Brigid in the bedroom.

The girls have their father's instruments out and are screeching out simple tunes on the fiddle and the concertina while the toddlers wallop the bodhrán. Rose has been cheerful and kind to her all night, to make up for the scene at the quay, but Emer can tell she is thinking of Austin. It doesn't help that Brigid notices it too, and keeps touching her, touching her with those hands, which Emer knows from experience ease the worst of it, the worst of you, like shifting something inside just enough to let you breathe all the way. Emer keeps refilling her wine

356

— another surprise Brigid had brought over on the boat — so she can swallow the rude thoughts she'd like to spew at the both of them. When Brigid goes to get some presents from the back bedroom, Emer follows. The musical cacophony is enough to cover their voices, and Rose, nursing two babies at once, will not be standing up any time soon.

She had only planned to talk to her, to tell her about Niall and her visions, but she is so drunk, and Brigid's body so familiar, that she barely thinks as she reaches her hands to her waist. She wants to press into her, to feel again the only good thing she has felt in years coursing through her body. Even if it's only once more, and is taken away again at the end.

But Brigid deflects her hands, slaps them away like they are meant to hurt. She moves quickly, as far away as she can get in the tiny dark room. Her breathing is quick, her stomach under the pretty blouse is swollen, growing larger by the day.

'Don't, Emer,' she hisses, sounding shocked, as if it hadn't happened countless times. As if it's wrong, Emer's mistake, instead of something she taught her to do.

'Just this once,' Emer says. She hears the pathetic begging in her voice.

'It's not going to happen. I'm sorry, Emer. That's done now.'

It's like being kicked in the stomach, the truth, even when you suspect it. Like her skin being ripped away.

'I'm sorry,' Brigid adds, but she has to force it.

The way she is looking at Emer is not sorry. There is no pity there. Only avoidance mixed with an undercurrent of disgust.

Emer's real voice escapes with a barking hiss, she almost spits it.

'Sure, you wouldn't mind if it was Rose?' Emer says quickly. 'I'm not much of a prize next to Rose.'

'Jesus, Emer,' Brigid says, 'I'm not having sex with your sister.'

'Only because she won't,' Emer says. She sees how this hurts, a quick sting, like catching skin with a sharp nail.

'Must you be like this?' Brigid says, and she turns away, so quickly and easily giving Emer her back that the swivel of it forces Emer's breath away.

'You said you'd help me,' Emer says.

'Has there ever been anything in your mind but what you want?' Brigid says.

'And what do you mean by that?' Emer says.

Brigid lets out a little gasp of disapproval, like an old island woman. Her voice has a lilt to it now. It follows the same rhythm as every voice that has dismissed Emer her whole life.

'You'll not spare anyone, will you?' Brigid says. 'Not a soul is safe that stands in your way.'

'That's grand, coming from you,' Emer says.

When Brigid tries to walk by her, Emer lashes out, like some animal inside her has been released. She clamps on to the woman's wrist, the same wrist she held prisoner against the mattress while she teased with the mouth she's just recently learned how to use. She holds it

358

now, prepared to press all the ugliness she has inside it.

'You won't do that to me, Emer,' Brigid says. 'You can't.' But she looks terrified.

Emer can't do it. Something holds her back. She is not sure that it is Brigid any more.

'It's not me you should be afraid of, so,' Emer says. 'They'll swallow you whole, the lot of them. Rose too. When they find out what you are. They'll spit out your bones. They're hateful.'

'No, Emer. That's you. I thought I could take it out of you. But it's too deep.'

You could have, Emer wants to say. *You did*. But she sees that Brigid is gone. Whatever was there between them is now as cold and unwanted as the relations she has had with men before. She had thought there was something different, with a woman. But it turns out to be the same humiliating, violating, dismissive thing in the end.

Emer doesn't know the answer, any more than the rest of them do, Rose or Patch or her mother or even, now, her own son, to why she can't be loved. This is a rejection she expected, but somehow that makes it even worse. To have such low expectations and then to watch, time and time again, as they are realised.

★ ★ ★

She tries to take Niall with her. Something burst inside that bedroom and now her good eye has a blind spot, a smudge at the edge of her vision where there is nothing, as if the fabric of the

359

world is beginning to peel away. All she wants is to go home and be with her son. In the middle of the tree trimming, the gaiety, the music, the first time she's seen him truly laugh since his father drowned, she tries to drag him away. Even as she sees how unfair it is, she can't stop herself. She can't stand to watch him so delighted by the same people intent on making her miserable.

'We'll go now, Niall.' His face falls, sure as if she's hit him with the words.

'The tree's not finished,' he whinges.

'You can't go, Emer,' Rose dismisses her, not even bothering to glance in her direction. 'Your supper's not eaten.'

'We won't be staying for supper,' Emer says. This is such a ridiculous statement, it's not as if there is anywhere to go, any real reason to leave except that Emer can't stand to be there.

'Don't be cross,' Rose says. 'Give the children a hand with the tree.'

'I'm not one of the children,' Emer spits. 'And I've no intention of fussing over that bloomin' tree.' She can feel the room changing, she is changing it, like the calm that comes before a storm on the sea, a stillness that is more about dread than peace, followed by onslaught. Her nieces' fidgeting gaiety has gone still at her language; they refuse to look at her. Niall is looking at her too hard.

Clodagh looks almost delighted. 'You'd easier get a smile off a stone,' she says.

'I'll make tea,' Rose says, looking quickly from Emer to Brigid and back again, hoping for some explanation. Brigid's face is pale, clenched,

360

revealing nothing. Emer feels like her own face is about to collapse, that if she says too much it will let loose and slide right off her, features broken and ugly and lost in tears. She wants to hold on to it, press her own cruel hands to her face and attempt to keep it on. If she cries she will let loose something terrible. She feels a sudden, sharp slice of pain behind her eye, and then a throbbing, like an echo.

'Niall, get your coat. Now.' Niall looks at her for one more disbelieving instant, then he transforms into a small, angry man.

'No,' he says. 'You leave me be.'

Emer grabs his arm and drags him to the door and tries to force him, thrashing and screaming, into his jacket.

'Let me alone!' he screams. 'Don't touch me!' She hasn't had to put his arms in clothing since he was small and she is surprised at how strongly he can resist her, and this angers her more, that his body is big enough to dismiss her. She is furious, but his wailing insults stab her ears so she alternates between wrestling him and pushing him roughly away.

'You're horrid,' he howls and his hurt fuels her. She feels it coming before she does it, her hands on him changing into the ones that are not his mother's. She presses all her embarrassment, rejection and fury into the small arm of her boy.

'I hate you!' he screams. His face breaks, the anger crumples in on itself and the wail he lets out is pure, though it grates on her nerves as if it is put on. She cannot tell if her hands have hurt

361

him, or if he is merely mourning the fact that she actually tried.

She tries not to look at anyone in the room, all of them frozen and staring, but cannot help a glance at Brigid. Because now she's regretting herself and wants to take it back, and Brigid is the only one who has ever let her do this, or at least the only one who hasn't had to, the only one, besides Rose, who waits long enough for Emer to say something good. She wants to lie down on the bed and have Brigid bind up whatever it is that is breaking up inside her mind and sliding away. But all Brigid gives her is one pitiless shake of her head.

Her vision swims in and out, one second she can see them, blurred as if under the water, the next there is nothing.

'Emer,' Rose begins, but Brigid stops her from being saved.

'Let her go, if that's what she wants,' Brigid says, and Rose's eyes widen at the boldness of it.

'Oh, how the mighty have fallen,' their mother sings.

And though Emer could be convinced now — one kind word from Rose and the storm will subside, and she'll accept tea and make herself small and, if not agreeable, at least not insufferable — Rose, her eyes glistening at the cheek of it, like a girl who has traded propriety for honey, shrugs and turns around.

'Let the boy stay, so,' she says. 'No need to drag him down with you.'

Niall, quiet now, looking slightly ashamed, wiggles out of her grip and goes to stand between Fiona and Eve, who each put an arm around him and glare at her with the same pretty, disappointed eyes as Rose. This is such a shock, he has never not gone with her, has always chosen her, when pressed, over everyone else, for a moment she does not know what to do next. She considers picking him up and carrying him home. But she can barely see, and the stabs in her head are converging into an intolerable wave. She thinks she might be ill, seasick from her own pain. She can barely stand straight with the strain of it; she won't be able to carry him now. This is what she has been dreading all along, this moment where her son recognises what everyone else has always known. When he is repulsed by her. How can she blame him? How can she force him? She does not even want to go with herself.

But she does go, slamming the door behind her, trudging through pellets of hail that mix with the rain, and in the five minutes it takes to walk to her house, she is soaked through and shivering and completely, cruelly alone, all the way down to her bones.

When she gets inside, it is all she can do to remove her wet things and crawl into bed. As soon as her head touches the pillow, a dam lets loose the pain and she screams.

She knows what it is people feel when she takes their hand. Their insides cleave, not just for a moment, but all the way through the future of their lives, as if with one touch she can steal away every joy they once dared to promise themselves.

* * *

Niall comes for her, sneaking in quietly sometime the next afternoon to convince her to come for the lamb dinner. She stays in her bed, where she has lain since she left, up only to change the rags of clotted blood between her legs. She doesn't budge, doesn't turn to him, doesn't even open her eyes when he puts a sweet, loyal, frightened hand on her forehead. If he speaks, she thinks to herself, if she hears his voice, she will be able to open her eyes, and rise out of the darkness and smile and love him again. But he gives up just a beat too soon, and later she wonders if he knows this, that his voice will wake her, and if he withholds it, because he is finding out that things are a bit easier all around without her there. He says nothing, and she pretends she is asleep, and they both let their lies be believed. He leaves to go back to Rose's house, and she stays alone, letting it all pass by without her, with no ability to break the ugliness she has begun, and not enough courage to ask someone, her son, her sister, her lover, to help pull her out from underneath the terrible weight of herself.

She has been so afraid of this day for so long, the day her child turns away from her, that she is surprised at how easy it is to release her grip, and let him go.

21

Brigid's Day

January, February, 1960

In January the storms return. Days turn into weeks turn into a month where no one leaves the island and nothing comes to them. They are drowned and forgotten in the middle of an angry sea. They were never given the distress radio Brigid asked for. (They were given the winch, an old, rusty wheel that broke the first time they tried to haul a boat up with it.) If Emer were still speaking to her, Brigid knows she would say: *Do you see now?* But Brigid doesn't mind the isolation in Rose's house. Her belly grows bigger as Rose's babies fatten up and stay awake for longer stretches, turning their heads to follow the movement of the other children. The older girls and Niall play endless games of domestic imagination, twittering like birds in their laughter, distracting them all from the leaden weather. The sun still abandons them every day before five o'clock.

Emer has taken to her bed. For all of January she lays in the feathered box and Rose is the only one who tends to her.

'I don't know what is wrong with her, poor pet,' Rose confides in Brigid. 'Perhaps it's the grief catching up to her? She can't even bear for

365

me to open the curtains. Says the light hurts.'

Brigid says little in response to this, but she offers to take up all the chores except the ones that lead to bringing food over to Emer's and coaxing her to eat. She leaves that to Rose, who she can see will never abandon her sister, even while a part of her would like to be free.

Niall still spends nights with Emer, crawling in to the ripened bedclothes. He comes to Rose's every morning, looking like something in him has been snuffed out, needing the laughter and lightness of his cousins to pull him out of the misery of his mother.

'Why won't she speak to me?' Brigid hears him ask Rose. Rose pulls him in for an embrace and whispers encouragement into his ear. 'You must be brave for her,' she says. 'She will come back to you.'

'I wish you could help,' Rose laments to Brigid.

'I will if you like,' Brigid concedes. But Rose gasps and shakes her head.

'She's adamant. Doesn't want to see you. I don't know what she's on about but we'd best not cross her now.'

And Brigid lets her breath out as quietly as she can, and says yes, that would be the wisest thing, all around.

★ ★ ★

On the eve of St Brigid's Day, the weather lifts a bit, not enough for a boat, but enough so the girls can have their parade without the threat of being blown into the sea. They have made a

Brídeog, a life-size doll version of the Saint, and carry it in front of them like a masthead, skipping the road and giggling, Niall blowing on a dissonant horn. Rose and Brigid walk behind them, infants tied tightly to each of their bosoms.

At each house, the girls knock at the doors and call out together: 'Brigid is coming!' They must call this out three times before the woman opens the door and says, 'She is welcome, she is welcome.' They are let inside to dance a bit, Eve playing her father's tin whistle, the scarecrow saint propped by the hearth as a witness. The widows give them sweets.

Rose tries to steer them clear of Emer's house, but Niall is insistent. They knock, they call out, once, twice, three times.

'Go on your knees and open your eyes and let Blessed Brigid enter.' But no one comes to the door. There is no lamp lit inside, no candle left in the window, no flutter of curtain to indicate that Emer even cares they are there. It is as quiet as one of the abandoned houses they marched by on their way up the road.

'Come along, children,' Rose claps, 'There is pudding waiting at my house.'

She puts an arm around the dejected Niall. 'You're grand, ladeen. She's resting, is all.'

'It's horrible luck not to let the Brídeog in,' Niall says.

Rose has told Brigid that the tradition started as a way of guarding the house against misfortune, particularly death, in the coming year. But now she reassures her nephew.

'Sure, Niall, you're old enough to know, it's

only a game meant to entertain children.'

When they return to Rose's house, the children stay up late teaching Brigid how to weave the Saint's cross from green rushes. They bend the stiff stalks and weave them into a knot at the centre, then out into four arms and tie off the ends. They make a small one for Brigid's baby, to hang over the cradle, and another for her door. One for each of their beds, and the front door of Rose's house. In the morning they will hang them, tossing last year's version, thick with spiderwebs and all that has happened since Brigid arrived, into the fire.

★   ★   ★

The next morning is the first of February, Brigid's fortieth birthday and the feast day of the saint, and the weather releases its grip on them. The women who man the boat walk to the quay, put the currach in and head off to meet the anchored trawler, to collect their post, flour, sugar and tea. Brigid sits beside Rose on a chair outside in the sunshine, enormous now with her miracle child.

They gather together at mid-morning and file into the church, carrying their milking stools, greeted by the priest who hasn't made it over from Muruch since October. The priest says the Mass quickly, blesses the wafers and places them on tongues, occasionally glancing at the windows to check the weather. He is not keen on being stuck here again. He has brought a box of white tapers for Candlemas, which he blesses and gives

368

to each family to bring home, for protection against storms and evil in the coming year. After Mass he hands out treats to the children, crisps and chocolate from the shop, and they spend a good deal of time trading and trying bites of each other's treasures.

Emer is there, out of bed for the first time in a month, her dress hanging off her shoulders like there is nothing inside of it, a face on her that makes even the priest take a wide berth.

'How're you keeping, Emer?' the women mutter, but don't stop or meet her eye. They move on to talk to Rose and Brigid, one showing off her babies, the other glowing in pregnancy. Emer watches while women reach out and press palms to Brigid's belly, uninvited, and Brigid lets them, these same women who were so cold to her when she arrived, she allows them to coo and praise and molest her as if she is related to them. It is a disgusting display, Emer thinks, watching Brigid reveal her huge white teeth, and call each of them by name, pronouncing them correctly now. She seems quite pleased with herself. She has no idea how quickly these people could turn against her. They barely need a reason; one slip and she'll have their backs all over again.

Niall was happy when she emerged and walked to the church holding her hand, but now he is running around and screeching with Rose's girls and has forgotten her again. The priest tries to slide past Emer with a nod, but she snags him.

'How are they above, Father?' she says and he looks none too happy to stop.

'Well, Emer, well enough. Isn't it lovely to see

the sun,' he mutters.

'It'll be lashing again by evening,' Emer says.

'Sure, we'll enjoy it while we're able.'

'At least you're *able* to leave,' Emer says.

'How is the Yank getting along?' the priest deflects. 'It's good of your sister to take her in. Widows helping each other.'

'Is that what they told you, Father?'

'Poor woman, losing her husband while with child.'

'Her husband died five years ago,' Emer says. 'You do the sums and see what sort of woman she is.'

The priest crosses himself quickly and mutters some excuse to get away.

'What did you say to the poor man, Emer?' Rose says, coming up behind her.

'Nothing I'll regret,' Emer says, and walks away from her sister, looking for Niall, pleased to see the sky darkening ominously in the distance. She'd like the day to be ruined for everyone. She has forgotten her candles, but doesn't bother going back for them.

She finds Niall sitting by himself, white as a sheet in the green field.

'What ails you?' she says. He opens his mouth to answer but instead he is sick, spewing crisps and chocolate and Cidona on to her shoes.

'Brilliant,' she mutters, but still she wipes his tears away and holds his hand all the way home. Just as they get there the wind and rain return, knocking the door on its hinges and drowning out the sound of Niall, retching again in the ditch by their gate.

How kind and good Emer becomes when her child is ill. How gently she is able to smooth his brow and know just where to press the cloth, to cluck and sing and shush him. Her hands are a balm, her voice is comforting, not a shrill invasion to the head, a songbird rather than a corncrake.

'It's all right, *a chuisle*,' she croons. She almost welcomes it, the feeling of a fever on his brow, because now she remembers who she can be. She can realise how silly she has been, and get over her temper, and think again of them moving to the mainland, starting all over in a house where they can both forget all that has happened and who she has been.

She lies vigilant by his side, watches him flip around like he's been snagged, in the bed she washed and made up freshly when she decided to rise from bed and seek her revenge.

★ ★ ★

He is sick every half an hour until there's nothing left but foul froth. Every time the pause between the heaving, where his face flames and he cannot breathe or make any sound, and the release seems to last a little longer. Each time she holds her breath, rigid with terror, waiting for the moment it releases him and he comes back to her. Afraid it will be the last, that he will be seized and his body will not be able to purge it again. He will be stolen away just at the point where he cannot even call out for help.

When Emer was sick as a child, it was Rose who tended to her. Her mother was useless when they were ill, she only got angry, as if their sickness were some personal affront. Emer can see this in herself now. By four a.m. she wants to hold him upside down and shake him, to slap him in the face and demand that he stop. She sees now, how much sense it makes to be angry with your child. Angry with them for making you so powerless.

By dawn, so much has come out of him he can't even manage tears any more. The storm has descended fully and she can barely tell when the sun rises, the black fading to a grey so pathetic it seems a waste. His head is so hot to the touch it shocks her, he is writhing with what he calls a fire in his side. When he opens his mouth to moan or be sick she can almost hear the angry venomous thrum of those long-resentful bees. When Rose comes in, Emer throws herself, grateful and desperate, into her sister's arms.

'Get Brigid,' she says. 'They're trying to take him.'

★ ★ ★

There is an old island story that Emer has told Niall, about a mother who was taken away by the fairies, leaving behind her young son. One night, years later, he woke up and saw that she was back, looking like his mother but not quite the same, sitting by a table full of food and drink, a

372

fire dancing in the hearth. She invited him to eat from it. But the boy had been raised to recognise fairy tricks so he refused, and his mother, or what was left of her, went away again.

When Niall first heard this story, he was puzzled. He knows that if fairies offer him food to steal him away, he should refuse.

But what if his mother is the fairy? Shouldn't he gorge himself then? Shouldn't he do whatever is necessary to keep her beside him, even if it is the one thing she has told him all his life never to do?

22

Fairy Stroke

'It's only the virus that's been going around,' Brigid says when Rose rushes into the house, her hair uncovered and shining with rain.

'It's more,' Rose whispers and her face makes Brigid go for her waterproof.

One look at Niall, white and writhing in the bedclothes, and Brigid moves quickly to him, pressing one hand to his head and the other low on his abdomen. She looks up to Rose and Emer.

'Has the priest gone?' she asks.

'He went yesterday.'

'What about that trawler?'

'Have you looked at the sea?'

'Tell Maeve to get the boat out. He needs a hospital.'

Rose is growing colder and calmer the more Emer paces beside her. She speaks slowly.

'With those swells the boats will smash them to death before they can leave the quay.'

'How do you get the doctor here in an emergency?' Brigid says. 'How do you call him?'

'We don't,' Rose says.

'What do you mean, you don't?'

'Where have you been living all this time?' Emer shrieks. 'Don't pretend you didn't know this. We told you. In this weather we're trapped.'

'What do you do, Rose?' Brigid repeats. 'When it's a real emergency? A life or death emergency?' Rose widens her eyes and shakes her head in a subtle but unambiguous movement.

'Could you not just put your hands on him?' Rose whispers.

So, she does know, Brigid thinks. Emer is breathing fast and loud, as though the air in the house is leaking away.

'I can't fix this.' It's too much, she thinks, and something dark yanks at the walls of her womb, as if the baby itself is clenching with fear. 'It's appendicitis. He needs surgery.'

'Saints alive,' Rose says. 'Austin's uncle had the appendicitis. Two winters ago.'

'What did you do then?'

'We lit a fire,' Rose says. 'On the hill above the port. Next to the children's graveyard.'

Brigid looks between them, narrowing her brow in anger. She turns away. They wait ages for her to speak. 'Well light one then,' she says. 'Light a big one.'

Rose goes out the door quickly, the wind screaming inside the moment it is open, then muffled with a slap when it closes again.

Brigid leans over Niall, lifts his shirt to press her hands gently to his side. He moans and curls in on himself like a snail shrinking into its shell. She dips the cloth in the pail of water by the bed and wipes his neck, his forehead, his bright, burning cheeks.

'It will be all right, Emer,' she says kindly, and she reaches a hand out to pull her down to kneel by the bed. She knows Emer has been waiting for a kind gesture from her for a while, but she hasn't dared. Even now, she does it with difficulty, without looking her in the eye.

'They didn't come,' Emer says, her voice barely audible in the whistle of wind against stone.

'What's that?' Brigid says, dipping the hot cloth back into cool water. She turns towards Niall again.

'When we lit the fire for Austin's uncle,' Emer says. Her voice is a hot whisper of dread at Brigid's neck. 'They didn't come.'

Brigid presses Niall's head again with the cloth, hoping that Emer does not see the tremor of her hand.

'Whisht,' she says, like an island mother. 'They'll come this time.'

★   ★   ★

She can't heal this. Just being near him makes the child inside her writhe and dig painfully, as if clawing its way somewhere deeper inside of her.

Don't, that voice whispers to her. *You can't save him. If you try, they'll take me too.*

She remembers stories of the fairy stroke, illness which couldn't be cured by magic because it was driven by magic itself. She remembers Matthew's tumour, how at the core of it was a dark well she could never reach. Niall feels like this now, as if he is being held away from them all, under deep water, and if she tries to reach him, she will drown.

She shakes off these thoughts, like a buzzing

insect. He has an infection, that is all. She will wait for the fire, for the boats, for a doctor. Every once in a while, it was Matthew who had the answer, not her hands.

In the meantime she does what little she can. She uses a cherished blue cloth and cold water to give him an instant of relief, before it boils up in him again.

★ ★ ★

'I'll leave you alone,' Emer is bargaining. Brigid hushes her, but Emer can't hear anything but herself.

'You can have Rose. I'll leave the island. I'll never bother you again. I'll not ask for anything else. I'll tell them to stop the evacuation. Please. Don't let this go on. Pull it out of him. Bring him back.'

'Emer,' Brigid says. 'I'm doing all I can. The fire will work. They'll send a doctor.'

'You can do it. I know you can. Why won't you try?'

And though Brigid gestures to Rose to take Emer away, to give her a cup of tea, to give her a break from the begging and pleading, she shudders at Emer's words.

She is the boy's only hope. Something won't let her save him. She is not entirely sure it isn't herself.

Don't, the voice in her head is her mother's now, her mother's voice that she hears so often these days, coming out of her own mouth. *Don't be a fool.*

Brigid watches the fire from Emer's window. It is as big as the midsummer bonfire, big enough to push against the wind and swallow the rain before it can be doused. It is a signal, and they will keep it burning all night long. She thinks of her father winding the clockworks in the light, feeding the oil, polishing the lenses and the brass work, telling her that each lighthouse has its own particular sequence, its own voice, foghorns as distinct as dialects calling to blinded ships.

She wishes the island itself could make a noise, scream like a corncrake, drone like bees, call out with the desolate keening that comes from every mother who has lost a child. That the magic left in its ground and water, both holy and blasphemous, could rise together in a great cacophonous howl. A noise strong enough to carry Niall on its back across the sea.

She thinks of her mother, lying with their heads on the same pillow, whispering her worst choices as if they are only a fairy tale.

A woman lays on the edge of a cliff,
holding the hands of two children
as they dangle beneath her.
One is her own, the other a changeling.
She cannot tell between them.
She needs both hands to save only one.
Which hand does she let go?

23

Bargain

The women pile broken furniture, wreckage collected from the shore, an old currach that their husbands never repaired. All the rubbish that has collected since the summer goes into the pile. They douse the thing with paraffin to get it to light in the lashing rain. The wind is so strong the fire leans sideways, reaching out in a desperate plea. Oisin, who since the drowning has gone from a boy to a man before he is ready, minds the fire all night, while the other women and children search desperately, going from house to house, shed to shed, looking for something, anything, to burn. By morning they are breaking apart their beds with axes, emptying cupboards and wardrobes and lopping the legs off tables brought to the island for their weddings. They burn the last of the great planks that were washed ashore from the submarine bombed during the war, the roof beams of cottages that were abandoned for America. They burn it all, as though, if they give up every precious last bit of wood they own, if they build the fire high enough, feed it until it sets alight and burns the sky, it might be answered by a miracle.

★ ★ ★

Though Rose tries to ply her with tea and empty reassurances, Emer crawls into bed with Niall and holds on to him, imagining she can draw the fever into her own body, wishing that she had the same ability to pull badness out as she does to put it in. She prays to every good and evil being she can imagine. She does not care where the salvation comes from.

She lowers herself to her knees by his bedside and begs for forgiveness from a God she barely believes in. She wants to cut her own veins, burn sods of penance into her arms. She wants to turn her body inside out and let every bit of ugliness pour away until there is nothing left.

She would put him back inside her. Cleave in two and grow herself back together in a carapace. Never let him come out, eyes wide, hair dark as ink, thick as a man's, glossy and standing like a shock out of his head. The day he was born, he looked at everyone who entered that room as if he had something vital to tell them.

She knows now that all her searching was stupid and pointless, that she inserted pain into people while looking for something she'd had all along. The yearning for Brigid that still consumed her is gone now, as insubstantial as ash lying dead in the fire. Everything she ever wanted was given to her with this child and she never should have tried to have anything else.

They bring holy water, the women do, from Saint Brigid's well. She bathes him in it, pours it over him without thought to what dribbles down, sloshes it in desperate clumsy spurts, and gestures, without looking up because she cannot bear the resigned pity in their eyes, for them to bring more.

She calls to the same fairies she has scorned and blamed. They can even have him, she promises, if it means he will not die.

She remembers a tale where a woman gave birth to an unearthly beautiful girl. A fairy came to her when the baby was still in the cradle and told her the child had been chosen to be the bride of a fairy prince. 'Take the glowing log out of the fire and bury it in the garden and your child will live as long as it continues to burn in the ground.' So the mother did as she was told and her daughter lived for seven hundred years, married seven fairy kings, until a priest overheard the story, dug up the log and doused it, and she fell away to dust.

Emer holds on to her boy, hot as a glowing log himself, and addresses the darkest seeds left inside of her. She will take back every cruel and selfish and hopeful thing she has ever done. Every kiss she gave to Brigid, the invitation she gave to Austin, the turning of the cursing stone that failed to put right her mistakes.

Tell me what to bury, what to burn, what to drown. Tell me what to do and I will do it. I will do anything.

Then she listens, desperate for a whispered musical answer under the screaming disagreement of the wind.

'Mammy,' Niall says. 'Tell them to stop that music.'

★ ★ ★

Emer leaves Rose and Brigid tending Niall's fever and goes out into the storm. She climbs up the cliffs, almost crawling at times when the wind pushes against her, and down into the cave of Brigid's well. Niall has already been bathed in this water, and encouraged to drink it through the same small pitcher she once used to feed him breast milk. It made no difference, but she has come here anyway, to beg.

No fire, no sun, no moon shall burn me,
No lake, no water, no sea shall drown me,
No arrow of fairy nor dart of fury shall
    wound me.
Blessed Brigid, have mercy on me,
Blessed Brigid, wrap me in your mantle,
Blessed Brigid, mend my bones and save my
    soul.

At each repetition the wind grows louder, the rain lashes cold icy bullets into the sanctuary, and Emer continues to pray. To saints and virgin mothers and forgiving sons, pressing the beads of her childhood rosary so tightly she thinks they might pop and turn to dust in her hands. When she can't feel her fingers any more, she lies on the soft ground and lets herself have a moment of shelter from wind and ice and terror. She almost falls asleep there, until she hears Niall's voice, as clear as if he is lying on her pillow.

'Mammy?' he says softly, and then again, shocked, fearful. 'Mammy, get out of there!' She

382

runs home, dropping the futile rosary on the way. She is fooling herself. The only power she has is the cruel kind. God and the women who obey him are of no use to her.

★ ★ ★

Niall has taken a turn for the worse; any of them can see that. They've burned half the island and no one has come. It is only an hour or so before dawn, but the sky shows no signs of letting up. When Emer returns, Brigid isn't even there; Rose kneels in the bedroom with Niall, thumbing her rosary and praying like a mad-woman. The women who are now the island's men stand in the main room, shifting awkwardly in their wellies, their shoulders still wet from the storm.

'Where is Brigid?' Emer demands.

'She's gone back to her house, Emer. She needed the rest.'

'Wrecked from all that she's brought upon us, is she?'

'What are you on about?' says Kathleen.

'Only she's a changeling, is all,' Emer says. 'She has you all under her spell, otherwise you'd know it. She's put a stroke on my boy. The fairy stroke. Sure, the same as her family did years ago.'

'She's done nothing but good for us, Emer,' Margaret says.

'Because it suits her. She has the healing in her hands, did you know? What else do you think she can do, if she's a mind to? Do you not remember the family she comes from?'

Emer's mother, quiet in the corner until now,

raps her cane on the floor so they will look at her.

'That was a bad family, sure it was,' she says. 'Her mother was born of a bargain with the fairies. She was a whore, she laid down with any man who asked. She killed a newborn child, she did, strangled the poor thing as it was coming out of its mother.'

The women stare at Clodagh as if she has just risen from the dead in the corner. 'No one asked me,' she quips, answering the question in their eyes. 'You were all so taken with her.'

Who knew, Emer thinks, that her mother could be so helpful?

'Do you know where Brigid got that baby?' Emer continues. Her heart is thudding with every word she utters, with the power of them, she can feel their minds pausing, looking back, tripping up, doubting their better instincts.

'Sure, it's from that Australian,' says Kathleen.

'Are you certain of that?' Emer spits. 'Certain it wasn't Austin, or one of your husbands? She came here wanting a baby. She was pregnant long before she met that Australian. She told me herself.'

The women shift uneasily at this, and Rose glares at them. Kathleen has gone white, thinking of how much time Malachy wasted bringing trifles to Brigid. Of the jokes the men made whenever they saw her, and the way his face flared up in response.

'Why do you think she drowned the lads?' Emer says.

'Jesus, Mary and Brigid,' Margaret crosses herself.

'Didn't I see her,' Emer says, 'see her go to the cursing stone, turning and turning and then there was that storm.'

'That's quite the accusation, Emer,' Kathleen steps forward. 'Why would she do such a thing?'

'Ask her yourself,' Emer says. 'Ask her why she got rid of Rose's husband where she's so happily taken his place now. It's not natural. She may have been married, but she has relations with women. She could help Niall if she wanted to. She has the healing in her hands. I've seen it. She could pull it out of him. But she won't and it's because she put that badness into him. Because I wouldn't let her do sinful things to me. That is the truth.'

'Saints alive,' her mother mutters, crossing herself. Her paralysed mouth is twisted into a version of a smile.

She doesn't even need her hands. She sets in into the air, the darkness that seeps into their minds, that threatens to drown them, that is so familiar they do not realise it comes from Emer at all. They believe it is something that came from them, and not something Emer inserted like a blade. They can't see it, every loss or rejection or fear Emer has ever felt, gushing out of her in a torrent. She has let it all out at once, all that hatred and misery, as huge as a fabric that expands to capture what it needs.

They take it from her and carry it along. They are buzzing with it, whispering, spitting accusations out like flames. They are enchanted by the same darkness that drives Emer to destroy things. Their eyes grow shadowed, like storm

385

clouds swallowing the sky.

Her father lay down with a fairy woman and Nuala was their child.

They tried to see was she a witch.

They burned her, they drowned her. But she wouldn't die.

They say she swam all the way to the mainland.

We never should have let her child back here.

She bewitched the men first, isn't that always the way?

The women gather themselves in a knot. This is how Emer knows it is serious. It used to be the men that dealt with such things. Men and priests. But they no longer have either.

Who's to say that women can't be as violent and merciless as men? Or fairies. Or God himself.

24

Fairy Tale

Brigid needs to leave. Since she can't go anywhere until the storm recedes — she is as much a prisoner as the rest of them — she concentrates on packing. She regrets bringing so many things to begin with. She has worn the same three pieces of clothing over and over again because it's all that fits over her growing belly. All the items the islanders brought back to her, the copper teapot, the fuchsia pottery hand-sponged by nuns in Connemara, and the things she had the men bring over from the mainland, the sheets and towels, the bright bottles of ink and thick ragged-edged paper, the bees, all of it she will leave behind. She will run away with the turf still glowing in the fire. Emer would say that islanders will steal it all, but Brigid likes to imagine it folding in on itself, walls and pictures and furniture and the skin she has shed into dust for the last eight months, swallowed whole into the earth, the way the bog swallows a tree and then petrifies it. Perhaps it will end up that her house is flipped to the other side, an underworld, where another kind of being altogether will sift through her things with delight.

She packs only clean knickers, her drawing journal, one bottle of ink, the few wee things she has knitted for the baby. A picture of Matthew, the address book with the numbers of people back in America she had thought she would never see again. Her passport, warped from damp that seeped into the drawer she'd stashed it in. Rua lies by the door, curled up, watching her every move, ready to follow.

She can see now how precarious it was, everything she built here, how it could all come to nothing in one violent winter storm. All that matters is saving what grows inside her. The sight of Niall's feverish, doomed face and that useless, continuously fed fire makes her know why this place is Emer's prison. Those summer days that barely got dark, where sea air and sunshine were as nutritious as her daily meals, seem very far away. For months she thought the child within her lived off this island. Now she is afraid it will die if she stays. As sure as she is that the pathetic fire in the graveyard will save no one.

She can't save Niall. And if she doesn't, Emer will never allow her to leave.

Emer bangs open the door without knocking, and Rua skitters away from it. For a moment, seeing her there with wet hair plastered over a purplish, desperate face, Brigid thinks Niall is already gone. But then Emer looks behind her, closes the door and paces around in a frenetic way, which means she's still in the throes of hoping she can turn it all around.

'They're coming now,' she says. 'I'm only a moment or two ahead of them.'

For a second Brigid thinks she means the doctor, the rescue they are hoping for from the mainland. But she wouldn't be here if it was that.

Rua barks at her. She doesn't stop after one or two, but keeps on, relentless, barks over and over until Brigid must lead her into the bedroom and close the door. In there she stops barking, but whimpers, paces and scratches at the bottom of the door instead.

'Who's coming?' Brigid says.

'Your women,' Emer sneers.

'Come to see if I'm a witch?' Emer avoids her eyes.

'My mother said some things to them.'

'I imagine she did.'

'If you heal Niall they'll not harm you. I'll convince them to let you go.'

'I can't, Emer. He needs a surgeon.'

'You're lying about not being able for it and I don't know why. I know you hate me but you love him. Why won't you pull it out?'

'I don't hate you, Emer. I've tried. I can't heal him.'

'You're afraid it'll kill the baby.'

Brigid says nothing.

'That's how you lost the others, isn't it?' Emer says. 'I won't allow you to give up Niall for yours.'

'I can't do it, Emer. I can't. You wouldn't, either.'

'Well you'll try. Or you'll regret it, so. I can't stop them now. You don't know what they can be like. You would if you'd seen what they did to your mother.'

'I know,' Brigid says. A flash then, a girl

moving across the room, in between them, like a frightened animal. She is only a vision, but to Brigid she seems as real as this girl who threatens her.

'You don't know all of it,' Emer says. 'Unless you help, they'll do the same to you. I can make them.'

Brigid remembers meeting Emer for the first time, how she had tried to put this into her from the start, and Brigid had deflected it, but Emer is just coming back with a bigger hand now.

'What did they do to you, Emer, that ever made you so cruel?'

'Am I more cruel than you? You who'd let a child die.'

They stand against each other, neither of them blinks, neither of them gives. They are Brigid and Darla, saint and changeling, lovers and enemies. Neither one will ever back down. This is about more than their hands, or themselves. It's about their children.

A polite knock at the door. No harder than the rain. As if they've only come for tea.

'Don't do this, Emer,' Brigid begs. 'I loved you.'

'You used me,' Emer says, her voice wavering. 'Just let me go.'

'I can't,' Emer says. 'I have no choices left.'

They file in, a dripping mass of them, too many for such a small room. Kathleen, Margaret, Nelly, Geraldine, young Maeve. They look like men, massive in their husbands' wellies and the oilskins Brigid had ordered from Dublin, and reeking of fire and the sea. The skin on their faces has grown so coarse from working outdoors it looks like it wouldn't bleed if you sliced it. And their hands: hands that were never pretty, after a lifetime of housework, hands that held their own knives and cut with them until the blades were worn slim as needles. Their hands are monstrous now.

Not one of them, though each of them has laughed with her, let her hand bleed comfort into their shoulder, looks Brigid in the eye.

'Will you leave us, Emer,' Kathleen says.

There is hesitation in Emer now, as if she sees something she hadn't expected. She who expects the worst.

'Sure, this about my own child,' Emer says.

Kathleen sighs, turning to Brigid. 'Can you help the lad?'

'I can't,' Brigid says. 'He needs surgery.'

'Emer says it's you what put it in him.'

'Emer's upset,' Brigid says calmly. 'And not a little confused.'

'There's been talk,' Margaret says.

'About?'

'The baby, for one. Who really put it in you?'

'The baby is mine alone,' Brigid says boldly. They mutter angrily to one another. Maeve looks her rudely up and down, as if disappointed by the news that she has no man to blame.

'Did you take our men? Was it you brought that storm?'

'I'd ask Emer about that.'

'Emer,' Kathleen sneers. 'She's dodgy enough but she'd not drown her own husband.'

'What reason would I have?'

391

'Maybe you wanted Austin gone. Wanted Rose to yourself,' Kathleen says. 'That's the other talk we've heard.'

Brigid rolls her eyes at that, but Emer can see how frightened she is. Her normally proud shoulders are bent, curved in like the arms that hold on to her belly.

'What are you, some sort of lesbian?' Maeve asks. Two or three gasps from behind, at the concept or merely Maeve's knowledge of such a word, Emer can't be sure.

Brigid doesn't say anything at first, just looks right at Maeve, who flushes. Emer sees it again. How similar they are, the moments before violence and sex. How easily one could be mistaken for another.

'Wouldn't you like to know?' Brigid says then, bold as anything. She looks at Kathleen's hands. She is holding iron fireplace tongs by her side. Kathleen steps forward.

'Stop,' Emer says. No one is more surprised than herself. They hold their breath, waiting for dispensation.

'I'll do it,' she says. Kathleen gives her the tongs and walks back to the huddle of women.

Emer puts the tip into the depth of the fire, grasping a nugget of turf, an orange as deep and fierce as the only colour left in her son's eyes. Brigid looks at her, curious, cold, with just a trace of how she once looked at her flickering at the edges of her mouth.

'I won't hurt you,' Emer whispers into her ear, the fiery whorls of hair tickling her face. Amazing, that in the middle of such terror she can feel that quiver, that weakening, of lust. 'Just go to Niall now and I won't let them hurt you either.'

'Emer,' Brigid sighs, and Emer thinks of the ways Brigid has said her name, with breathless excitement, with humour, with tenderness. With love. Now, her name, two rigid syllables, is said with the same sickened resignation she has heard from everyone else.

'You can't hurt me,' she adds quietly. But still, her hand reaches into her apron pocket to grip the island woman's knife.

That's when Emer puts the fire against her, the very same fire that has burned on that island for centuries, not to insert pain, but to give her something else. A story she was told over and over again, but never really heard.

★   ★   ★

They're coming up the road, her brother says.
What will they do? Will they make me leave?
I don't know, Nuala.
Don't let them hurt me, Desi.
What happened? Why couldn't you save the baby?
I tried. The baby was already dead.
Desi looks at Nuala's hard, round belly and then turns back to the window.
Jesus, Desi says. There's a lot of them.

★   ★   ★

The girl, Nuala, never knew her mothers, fairy or human, or her father, or her orphaned siblings.

393

All she ever had was her brother, Desmond, a boy who was also a man, because he needed to be, for her. They said he was simple. He couldn't read or write, had avoided school altogether, though he could do sums in his head that wool buyers double-checked on paper in disbelief. He loved the island, his dogs, the sea. He suffered people only when he had to, and then, when he was required to be around them, he looked like he was in physical pain. Women, especially, left him twitchy and mute. He couldn't look them in the eye. Men were willing to communicate in minimal grunts and grumbles over weather or the stubborn nature of sheep. He could stand in a field of men all day and never have to say a word. Women asked questions, demanded answers. Only his sister could talk to him, chatter on about whatever came into her head, because she didn't expect him to respond. Her voice was not the same violating noise in his ears. She belonged in his head, just like the wind and the sea.

When she was a baby he had carried her everywhere, strapped to his chest in an old flannel shawl of their mother's. She could remember snatches of this, how the weather, the rain and damp air and wind, couldn't penetrate. She could press her face against the fragrant wool at his chest and none of it could touch her. She was safer than she would ever be again in her life.

★ ★ ★

Go into the bedroom, her brother says.

Don't answer it, Nuala says, stupidly. As if there is any way to bar an entrance with no lock.

They pound on the door, thuds that sound more like boots than fists. He shoves her towards the bedroom and she goes in without a lamp or candle, and stands within the rectangle of firelight that shines around the edges of the door frame.

When no one answers their knock, the men throw the front door open and heave into the room, massive in their layers of wool, clumsy, like seals flopping themselves across the threshold.

Where's the girl, Des?

Leave her be. She's none of your concern.

I'd say she's my concern. That's my grandchild what she killed tonight.

She killed no one. She's only a girl herself.

She's a changeling is what she is.

You didn't mind who she was when it suited you so, says Desi, sounding like a man who talks back to bullies every day, instead of the brother who is afraid to ask for sugar in the shop.

Hold him, lads.

Desi's dog starts snarling then, and there is a scuffle and a canine yelp of pain and a man swearing and then the door is shut and Nuala knows the dog is outside, throwing itself against the door, with nothing to sink his teeth into. The baby flips inside her, painfully, as if it's trying to send a message. *Go*, it kicks, *before it is too late.*

★ ★ ★

395

Healing them had been the way she could make them not afraid of her. Her brother never understood why she bothered, the islanders had been suspicious of them since their mother's death and he was happy to leave it that way. He didn't have the same need as his sister; she needed their love. So she gave them her hands.

She'd always been able to heal her own childish scrapes and bruises, the broken limb of a dog, the burns on her brother from careless splatters of hot pitch while tarring the currach. When she started doing it for the other children, and then for the mothers in labour, she thought she could get love out of them. She felt it, whenever she pulled pain or fever away, along with it, like a gift, their love, clutching her for a moment before it released with the pain into the air. Her brother wanted no part of their neighbours' emotions, their anger and bitter gossip, their romances and feuds, their loyalty and love. Nuala wanted all of it. She gathered it like spilled sweets into the pockets of herself. She touched people not only to heal them but to feel for a moment all that life pulsing through them, love, hate, fear, regret, bliss.

She touched boys, then men. In the hay fields, at the shore, in the empty clocháns. She put her hands right where their want and anger and misery and hope gathered together and begged to be released. She pulled everything they had ever felt out of them, often thought she might shatter from the intensity of it gushing through her. With the men it required more, she had to lie down and let them push themselves inside her as deep as they could get, until they reached a place where she forgot everything except inviting them deeper. It wasn't forced or cruel or ugly, not to her, but what they wanted from her and what she was intending to give were two different things. The men knew it was wrong, even as she didn't. They had not been raised to believe that a girl should invite, or enjoy, such violation. They hated themselves, they confessed through a dark wood lattice to the priest, but went back to her willing hands again and again.

When she told her brother she was expecting a child, Desi didn't ask who it was from, which was a relief. It could have been any one of them, or all of them. He only asked if she'd been forced. When she said no, blushing, he asked nothing else. He got the family cradle out from the shed, the cradle that was said to have come from Saint Brigid herself, hand-carved from the last of the island's oak, to soothe the babies of the women who ran to her, shamed, violated and alone. He polished it up and replaced the missing limpet shells, and she knew he would accept the baby with the same simple devotion he had shown to her. She couldn't wait to hold it. She felt as though she had fashioned it herself, this child, made it out of all the times her hands had grasped at love.

* * *

Nuala! Desi screams when they have their hands on him.

She has a notion to climb out the tiny window,

397

but is fumbling at the latch and thinking there is no way she will fit through it, when one of them enters the bedroom and pulls her roughly out by the arm.

Put your man in there. Keep him quiet.

How am I to do that?

You there, lad, go with him.

Two men drag her struggling brother into the bedroom and kick the door closed.

The men have taken over in the small room; the combined breath of them is making the air thick, fogging the windows. Men of every age, men she has laid down with and others who would never consider it. Boys, expected to be men even though their bodies and hearts have not caught up yet. Some of them can't look at her, others are looking at her way too hard.

What did you do to that baby?

It wasn't my doing, she says. Her voice is shaking, it sounds, even to her, like a desperate lie. *The child came out already dead. There was nothing I could heal.* This was only partly true. She hadn't tried. The child inside her had seized with such terror that she only pretended to use her hands. She couldn't sacrifice her own child.

Your woman says otherwise, the man says. She looks at him. She has seen this man's face warp in a way no one but his wife has.

I wouldn't let a baby die.

We don't know what you are.

I'm no different than any of ye.

One of them is stirring the fire, breaking up the grey and orange logs, sinking the fire iron deep inside it to heat up. This fire never goes out, they bury it and revive it each morning, and have for as long as the house has been standing. Even their mother, the possessed, imposter mother, had never dared to douse the saint's fire.

Hold the iron against her.

If she heals it, she's the changeling and lying about the baby.

If she can't, she's nothing but a whore.

Neither of these options sounds reasonable or even bearable. There is a pause then, where she thinks perhaps one of them will laugh heartily and dismiss the entire business. She can hear the men in the bedroom with her brother, the sound it makes every time they knock his body back to the floor.

The first one to hold her down is a boy she once tugged at with her hands in a cave by the water until he cried relief into her hair. Now he cannot look her in the eyes. She pulls her mother's knife out of her pocket and slashes at him with it, but he grips and twists her wrist until she cries out and lets it go. He holds her arms behind her, driving his knees into the backs of hers to get her to drop to the floor. She can feel his terror, a slim hard threat pushed against her thigh.

Please, she says. *Please don't hurt my baby.*

Another man kneels down hard on her hair, jerking her neck back to stop that plea. They hold her on her side, her belly too big for her to lie on, and use her knife to rip at her dress back, splitting it easily down the seam. She can feel the fire coming off the hearth and off them for a whole lifetime before they actually bring the heated iron to her skin.

The first few times they burn her, Nuala can't stop herself from healing it. The men watch the skin rise up and knit itself back together, the welt of angry burn sinking into her back as if slipping into cool water. Once they see the wounds heal themselves, the fear of it is enough to want to burn her more. The boy continues to hold her down, and the way he holds her feels both like an embrace and an affront. Once, he brushes a calloused, nail-bitten hand across her breast and Nuala lets out a sob and calls to her brother and two men have to look away. It is more intimate, this scene of torture, than any act of lust or abandon they've participated in.

Desi howls through it all, held prisoner in the bedroom, sounding not much older than a child himself, crying her name and the name of their Saint to have mercy on them.

The burning is meant to tell them something. But no one is clear about what to do with the answer so they just kept doing it, over and over again, until the burns no longer heal and her skin begins to act like it should.

You can't hurt me, Nuala says. *You can't hurt me, you can't hurt me. Not a one of you can hurt me.*

She stops healing herself. She turns inward, encasing her child with all the magic she has left, and lets them do it, lets them sear her with all the fear and doubt and misplaced lust they've ever had. This confuses them, they stop, there is a discussion about what to do. Keep going until they kill her? Apparently they've lost the stomach for that. They will wait instead, for the priest to advise them, an authority who can punish or banish her with the blessings of God Himself. By the time they skulk away she is unconscious and her back is burned so deeply that in some places the bone shines through the blackened flesh. The last of them leaves with the morning, they do not have the courage to stay around and see if she will really die.

★ ★ ★

Nuala. It's all right, love. They've gone now.
They didn't hurt me, Desi. They couldn't.
Jesus, Nuala. Your back.
It doesn't matter. The baby is safe.
Her brother holds on to her as she closes the last of their wounds.

The next day Nuala is gone. Her brother never reveals how she got away, no boats had come or gone on the island, she disappeared during a day when the sea raged them into seclusion. Though there is talk of sending Desmond off as well, in the end they leave him alone. He has none of the power they fear and he keeps to himself. Some say Nuala threw herself over the cliff, others that she went back under the ground to where the fairy imposter came from.

She is never seen, or heard from, on the island again.

★ ★ ★

401

Brigid doubles over with the weight of this story, this fairy tale that Emer inserts with fire under her skin. The very same fire.

You were here before, it whispers. Your mother was born in the doorway between two worlds. You began here, you belong to us. We will not allow you to get away.

The air in the cottage is filled with the odour of what she has seen, the smell of fear and turf and blistered skin. It takes her a moment to realise that it is the wound on her back, where Emer has held the nugget of turf, which smells. It doesn't hurt yet. The women have not moved towards Brigid. They are muttering to one another in Irish.

We should have known. She's her mother all over again.

Hold the fire against her. 'Tis the only way to know.

Let Emer do it.

If Emer were any use, she'd have it finished by now.

Emer's right. She stole that child. Stole our men. She'd let the boy die.

Brigid knows what to do. It's an effort to fight it, to refuse to heal herself, but Emer, by giving her that story, has just shown her how to protect the baby. She had the ability all along. She takes what is in her hands and turns it inwards, folds it like blessed fabric around her child. She does not keep any of it for herself.

'You can't hurt me,' Brigid says to them all, without thinking, in Irish. This doesn't help her. They look angry at the very cheek of it, this

402

imposter using their language. They move in, swarming her, pulling at her apron, her hair, their hands are pleas and punishment, raking her for answers. Maeve, who has imagined more than once a woman's hands beneath her clothes, is the first to reach for the tongs from Emer, intending to press fire into her back. She uses them to knock the knife out of Brigid's hand.

None of them have noticed the brightening.

When Rose burst into the cottage to tell them the sky has lifted and they are no longer prisoners, they reel away from their tight circle. Maeve drops her hold on Brigid like a guilty boy with a stone. Brigid is left lying like a child by the hearth.

'What have you done?' Rose hisses. They don't know themselves.

'The boats are here,' Rose says. 'They've come to take Niall to hospital.' All the women but Emer slip away out the door, her grip on their minds gone now, looking as horrified by the appearance of dawn light as they are at what they were about to do. Rose looks at Emer then, as if she might be able to explain it. Emer looks back at her sister, wide-eyed and pleading as a child, for another answer.

'Rose?' Emer says. 'Why did you leave him alone?'

'Shame on you,' Rose says cruelly. And she pushes Emer, who is left with the cooling fire iron, out of the way.

Rose kneels on the floor and gathers Brigid into her arms. She rocks her back and forth and whispers that she need not be afraid as Brigid sobs.

The dog has keened through it all, locked in the bedroom, she howls like a newborn left wet and alone. A cry that is relentless and piercing, with no intention of letting up until it is given what it wants.

Emer backs away, her lack of peripheral vision causing her to knock down one of the kitchen chairs. Her head sings with unbearable noise. She does not belong here. Not with these women, her sister, her lover, not in this house. Not in this world. She should be with Niall. She was distracted by the thought that someone else could save him. She is the only one who knows how. She never should have let go of her life's only vigilance for the time it took to wonder if it was enough.

Emer pulls herself out the door and hurries toward the place where they have already stolen her child.

25

Ceili

Niall is on an island.

It isn't his island, or Brigid's or Rose's or his mother's island, though it is similar. It is a place where every road has two lanes, one trampled by people and sheep and cattle and children, and the other by something else. It is raining here, but at the same time it is sunny, you can feel the warmth dry the drops on your face even as they fall. There is always a rainbow. It doesn't look like something you would want to wish upon.

He thinks there is no one here, but then he sees they are all gathered together, having a ceili around a bonfire. They have lit it on the promontory over the port, the place known as the children's graveyard. As if the celebration itself is an emergency.

Everyone he knows is there, even the men who went on ahead of them into the storm. Austin is playing music and he looks terrible, he hasn't shaved and his eyes are rimmed with red and he can barely get a breath in between all the blowing. He tries to take the whistle away and say something, but nothing comes out. He goes back to the instrument. He has no voice. He looks, Niall thinks, like something else is making him play that whistle. The party has been going on too long.

His cousins are dancing. The little ones cry out about how their feet hurt, but Fiona and Eve cannot stop to help. Niall's dead father comes up to him, soaked to the skin, his trousers dripping puddles into the squelchy ground. 'The arms are hanging off me after that row,' he says. 'Would you put a pint on for your father?'

'I would, of course,' Niall says, but he's not sure how to do this. Everyone seems to be drinking, but the source of it is not clear. When he turns back to ask his father, he sees the man fumbling with his sleeve. He's having trouble with his arm. It seems to be falling off. Niall turns away.

Brigid is there. She is holding his newest cousins, the babies, the fat one and the little elf, and they are nursing from her, latched tight to her breasts. He stares too long at the enormous, dark curve over her nipples and feels his face growing hot with shame. It seems like he's remembering something and looking forward to something at the same time. She lets go of the babies, using both her hands to receive an overflowing drink from someone. The babies stay put, hanging on by their mouths.

Rose is dancing, spinning, laughing, her hair loose and lifting into the air like something trying to fly away. She has a knife in her hand. She is slicing some enormous fruit, he can't tell what, and feeding it straight into people's lips. She twirls over to her husband and straddles him, laughing and riding him like a child playing at horses. Austin cannot stop whistling long enough to receive the dripping piece she offers.

The good people are everywhere, but they are not the strangers he expected. They are his neighbours, his cousins, his auntie and his grandmother. There are no small fairies leading them maniacally around by a leash. There is no one here, except for Brigid, whom he has not known for his entire life.

He cannot find his mother. There was a time when he truly believed that they were one person, tethered by an invisible but unbreakable twine, a band that led from her neck, that pulled him back if he wandered even an inch too far. If her head ached, he knew it, if her neck tightened, he pulled at his own collar. If she took someone's hand and poisoned them he felt as if he had just emptied himself. When that thing that looked like Austin was on top of her, he knew it was inside of her as well. He had felt it, it punctured between his legs and pried, splitting them both in two.

But now he cannot find her, and it is worse than what has been happening lately, where he turns and sees her and she looks like someone he can't remember, not the woman whose love he has always been sure of, but someone he is wary of approaching at all.

The fire is massive; they are burning the whole island in it. Furniture, clothing, doors, cradles, carts, the plough, anything that might ignite has been thrown into the pyre. The islanders are ripping the clothing off their backs and cheering when it is caught up and consumed.

He sees the women who row the boat carrying lighted torches and climbing down the pathway

407

to the slip. They untie the currachs and touch fire to them, launching them to burn on top of the sea. Saint Brigid did that, long ago, once she was settled there, sent all the boats away, set them on fire so no one would ever be able to leave. He will tell his mother this, when he finds her. She will not be amused.

He moves through the spinning bodies of islanders and every once in a while they catch his arm and turn him around, cheering when he gives in to the instinctive tap and shuffle of his feet. He doesn't want to dance, or swallow the dripping fruit that is being passed around, or kiss in the way they all seem to be, opening their mouths like they are feeding on each other. All he wants is to find his mother; he won't accept a morsel until she tells him he can have it. He wants to be small enough to fit in her lap again, and drink from the very heart of her, milk that, if he closes his eyes and remembers, he can still taste. Warmer and sweeter than the tea which replaced it.

He spins through the crowd and something starts to change, the sky grows dark, the fire climbs, the faces around him seep with shadows that look like spilled ink. Their features warp and twist from familiar to vicious and unrecognisable. Their voices are all wrong, high-pitched, frantic, like impatient birds. The women are naked and have babies, half-formed and horrible, growing out of them, a head between two breasts, a foot protruding from an abdomen, a tiny, wizened hand reaching out of someone's neck. He tries to scream, break free of the whirling crowd, but he has no voice. It's because he can't find his mother, she is holding his voice hostage, it's why she always puts her hand there, to her throat, as if she is checking on something she has swallowed and is not about to let it come back up. His mother has stolen his voice, his heart, his feet. He cannot join in anything until she gives it all back.

Then he sees her, she is on the other side of the fire. She looks so miserable, so lonely, so much like she has always looked, no matter how hard he tries to pull it away. He knows, he has known for a while now, that no matter how many times he kisses or hugs or pulls a palm across the screwed-up skin of her forehead, it will never be enough. She's too vigilant, she always has been, she will never let go of the fear of losing him long enough to actually take him in her arms.

He fights his way through the mob of dancing creatures, trying not to look as they grow more and more deformed. Brigid moves in front of him. She no longer has Rose's babies attached, she is moaning, she grabs his arm, lowers herself to a squat. Her colossal belly is transparent, and inside, coiled and writhing, an atrocious pig.

Niall pulls his arm away and stumbles backwards, right through the corner of the fire. He gets within the range of his mother's limited vision, coming upon her from the right so she will be able to see him with her only eye.

She spots him and for an instant she looks delighted, he has never seen her look so overjoyed, and he reaches out a hand to clasp the one she is raising to pull him in. She is holding something in front of her.

She is offering him something to drink.

410

26

Stones

When Emer gets there, his breath has just gone.

The doctor leans over him, listening at his mouth, pounding his chest, then putting his loose, foul lips over the sweet mouth of her child and blowing so hard his chest rises.

She tries to go to him, to knock the doctor back, the doctor who appears to be devouring her son's face, but someone stops her with a clawed hand on her arm.

''Tis the breath of life, sure,' her mother reassures her. Emer remembers that doctor's breath, so sharp it's like he's breathing petrol.

'Why are you doing that?' Emer says. 'Aren't you taking him to hospital?' The doctor doesn't even look at her but puts his cheek down, gentle as a mother, on to the warm pillow of Niall's chest. Listening. Emer and Niall do this in her bed, taking turns, she listening for Niall's heart, he listening for hers. *Mo chroí*, they whisper, my heart. It is one of their games.

The house is filled with people, island women, men from Muruch and the mainland, every one of them has at one time felt the bitterness that rises up from Emer's heart and pools like sweat in the palms of her hands. Everyone goes still, hushes, as if their silence will create the sound the doctor is hoping for. Not a breath comes to

411

them for one beat, two beats, three. The doctor's head rises, lowers, pauses, and then gives up and lifts again. He shakes his head. A collective island gasp and click of the palette, a sound that means surprise, anger, remorse and disapproval all in one. They all gasp and Emer begins to scream.

She tries it herself, before they pull her away. Puts her hands on him, her cruel hands that have only ever touched him with love, presses his heart, kisses his mouth, keens into the warm dirty hollow of his ear. She puts a hand under his nightshirt, to feel the familiar warmth of his back. Only his back is not warm. Not cold exactly, but no temperature at all. She is shaking his body, insisting he answer her, and then she is pulled away, her grip pried off, familiar voices speaking nonsense about collecting herself. The priest comes in with his vial of oil to administer the last rites.

'He's not in there,' she says to them, lashing out with the hands they cower away from even as they try to hold her down.

'That's not my son. They've taken him.'

★ ★ ★

Later, after a tablet and the pit of sleep where she can hear everything but say nothing, Rose is with her again, looking as if nothing has happened.

'Where's Niall?' Emer says, and Rose winces.

'Where's Brigid, then?'

'She's with the doctor.'

'She has to come for Niall. Put her hands on him.'

412

'She did, Emer.'

'She didn't. I've been waiting.'

'I watched her do it myself. It didn't do any good.'

'Where is my boy?' she asks again, and this time Rose answers her.

'He's laid out on the table, Emer.'

'We'll sit up tonight, Rose. We'll wait for him to come in and we'll snatch him back. He knows better than to eat with them. They won't be able to hold on. We'll wait here and he'll come. He will.'

'Emer, love,' Rose says. She has to look away from Rose's face. There is too much in there, she wants to slash at it. But she needs her sister to wait with her.

'You'll stay and watch over him with me?' Emer says.

Rose gives her another tablet, and Emer takes it because sleep seems more welcome than life ever has to her.

'You'll wake me with the moon, won't you, Rose?'

'I will, Emer. Hush now.'

'Don't leave him alone. We don't want them stealing the body as well.'

'I won't, Emer. I won't leave you alone.'

★ ★ ★

In the middle of the night, Emer gets up and sits by the table where they have laid out the small, still body of her son. His face has been leached of colour, like someone has made a mould of him and left the outer layer unpainted. In the

413

candlelight she can deceive herself into seeing rosy cheeks and a red mouth still moist with breathing and she can almost imagine she is waiting for him to wake up. That she is stealing the few, sweet moments she gets watching him sleep. How still he is in sleep, often it is a relief to her, after a long wet day alone in the house, to feel the moment he switches, from a twitchy, talkative boy to a gently breathing pile upon the bedclothes. She regrets that now. That wanting of stillness. She would slash herself to the bone for the chance to never watch him sleep again.

Rose sits with her for a while, the older girls left with the babies, but she keeps leaking milk and fussing around and asking if Emer needs anything and finally Emer sends her away. She prefers to be alone in the moment he comes back through the door.

The story that is going around in her head is this:

A woman died in childbirth, but a fairy told her husband she was only snatched, and if he waited up by her body in the moonlight he could take her back. So he waited, his wife's body laid out on one side of him, the cradle with the newborn baby and a set of tongs across the rim on the other. In the night, her spirit came in the door, and moved to peek in the cradle. When she did he threw some holy water at her and grabbed her by the wrists and held on and wouldn't let go, the baby shrieking like a storm the whole time. She fell back into her body then, the spell broken, and sat up to soothe the baby at her leaking breasts.

414

Emer waits for her son to come through the door, so she can grab on to him so tight she can squeeze away death, and never, for the rest of her days, let go of him again.

★ ★ ★

'Emer, come to bed.'
'I'm waiting, Rose.'
'You're asleep on your feet, pet.'
'I'll wait for him to come back to me.'
'Emer, you'll be waiting a lifetime. He's gone, love.'
'I'll wait regardless.'

★ ★ ★

Nothing the first night. During the day the islanders file in to weep and speak in low tones and kiss him until she wants to chase them all out with the broom. A second night of waiting. Her body has never done anything so precisely determined in her life. She waits with every cell and fibre of her flesh. She waits, burning up with it, slowly consumed by every moment he doesn't come, like a sod of turf eaten by fire. By the end there is nothing left of her. You could blow at her and she'd scatter, like the ash of a fire let to go out.

★ ★ ★

On the third morning there is a row over whether to bury him. The priest has come

415

over for it, bringing a small coffin from the mainland, and Emer bars the door with a cupboard. The men have to break through, knocking over the press she pinned against the door, all the delph crashing into shards on the stone floor. They grab on to her, screaming and writhing and electrified with pure sorrow. A few of the men who take turns holding her end up getting sick outside. No man or woman who touches Emer that day will ever forget the vileness that emerges, wave after wave of it, like a hive of evil broken open and raging with revenge.

In the end, the doctor has to give her a shot and she is not there when they bury her child.

★   ★   ★

Rose cannot watch as they say their prayers and begin to shovel wet earth on to the absurdly small coffin. She turns and walks away to soothe Wee Emer who is squawking in her arms. This is the fussiest child she has ever had; she wants to be held twenty-four hours a day. The baby's cries and the wind almost drown out the vicious sound of wet earth on wood. The graveyard stands just above the quay, on the jutting circle of land where they burn their signal bonfires. Mostly it's children who are here, jagged purplish stone marking the graves of babies and toddlers from a time when women had so many and lost most of them. They say children never died when Saint Brigid was here, but when she was gone, the families that were left lost them, one after the other, to typhoid, tetanus, smallpox. Siblings who never met nestled together under rough grey stone. Children don't die as often nowadays. Rose can't imagine that even when it was common it was any less of a blasphemy. The first thing you see when you row a boat to this island is all the children who have already gone.

27

Currach

Brigid sits very still, holding the mound of her belly as the doctor listens to it with a stethoscope.

'What's all this talk now, of burning and witches?'

'Just Emer panicking. She was out of her senses with the boy ill.' Dying, she corrects herself, he was dying. She mustn't think of it. She must keep this from splitting her apart at the seams. The only way she can help Niall now is to leave.

'I heard the women called up to you.'

'Not at all.'

The doctor raises a weedy eyebrow and looks around. The floor is still a wreck of muddy treads, and the place reeks of something burned, meat that has gone off but is cooked nonetheless.

Brigid's back has healed. It smoothed itself as soon as Emer turned away. Emer is too grief-stricken to hurt her any more. But she is going anyway.

'They burned your mother, they say. They're a superstitious lot.'

'I'd like to go back to the mainland,' Brigid says. 'I'll get a lift to Galway from there.'

'We can call in to the guards. Have charges brought against them. There's a smell of burnt flesh in here that would sicken you.'

'They did nothing. I want to have my baby in hospital is all. I'm afraid of what might happen out here.'

'And you the midwife. Didn't you insist I wasn't needed?'

'I've changed my mind.'

'After all your talk of staying you'll go as soon as it suits you.'

'I didn't know,' Brigid says.

'Didn't know that a boy could die with nothing but a fire calling for help? It's pathetic.'

'What's pathetic,' Brigid says, 'is that they weren't given a telephone. Or a radio.'

'So they could send a distress signal and still wait for the sea to swallow their boats? Don't be daft, woman. They should take the land being offered to them and be done with this rock. The government isn't to blame. The sea will do what it likes. It always has. At least they've a choice. Not like some.'

He stops when he sees that Brigid is shaking so hard her pretty white teeth are rattling in her head.

'I'll take you across,' he says. 'Are you sure you don't want to stop at the guards in town?'

'Positive.'

'I'll have some of the lads up to carry your things.'

'There's no need,' Brigid says, her voice quavering. She sounds more like an islander than ever. 'I'm leaving it to the birds.'

★ ★ ★

419

She considers bringing the cradle. Whether it was hand-carved by a saint or an ancestor doesn't matter; it was where her mother and grandmother were laid, where Brigid herself would have slept if her mother had been let to stay.

The man who held on to them both in that lighthouse was not her father after all. He was just a man her mother asked to save her, whom she couldn't leave. Brigid can see why now. Nuala confused violence with love. She thought she only had magic enough for one life-changing swim across the sea. And she didn't want to run any more.

She leaves the cradle behind, in plain sight in the bedroom for whoever dares to steal it. She won't need it. This baby will sleep in her arms.

* * *

Rose comes once more to the house, leaving Emer asleep and the body of Niall, bathed by island women, in the newly turned ground.

'How is she?' Brigid asks. Rose can't even say it, holds a hand to her mouth to keep from spitting out a wail.

'I'm so sorry,' Brigid says. They are silent for a while, while Rose makes tea. Nothing is so unbearable that they won't stop to make tea.

'When I think of what they did to you,' Rose says when the tea is poured, 'it makes me sick, it does.'

'They were afraid.'

'Did you heal yourself? The way your mother could?'

'Something like that.'

420

'You couldn't heal Niall.'

Some part of Brigid feels like she is not even there. She is standing on the edge of the cliffs, screaming all her terror and remorse into the wind. She has been there too many times before.

'No.'

'Does it make you a witch, then?'

'It's only what I am. Same as Emer. Doesn't amount to much in the end.'

'Where will you have the baby?'

'I don't know. Somewhere safe.'

'Where's that?'

'I'm wondering myself.'

'We won't stay here, anyways. Emer was right about that. Sure, it won't be much comfort to her now.'

'You'll miss it.'

'Every day of my life, I suspect. Not as much . . . ' but she doesn't finish, though they both say the words in their minds.

Not as much as you'd miss a child.

Rose pours the tea into the two stained mugs Brigid has always thought of as hers and Emer's.

'She's nothing without him,' Rose says.

'She'll have to be. You'll keep an eye on her.'

'I will. I will, of course.'

★ ★ ★

They leave in the early morning, the sun still crawling its way above the mountains on the mainland. Brigid stops at the graveyard, finds the disturbed spot, lets the wet of it seep into her knees, staining them the colour of bog.

421

The doctor has summoned Muruch men come to collect them; the women with whom she learned to row will not be there to see her off.

'I'm bringing the dog with me,' Brigid says to the doctor at the quay.

'Have you taken leave of your senses, woman?'

'I can't leave her behind.'

'You can't take a dog like that off the island. It'll be chasing cars and get itself killed.'

'I won't go without her.'

'Jesus, you Yanks. The notion. You're after being persecuted and all you care about is that bleeding animal. It's yourself and that baby you should be thinking of now.'

'I can think of more than one thing at a time.'

He cocks his head, lets air gust through his teeth.

'Fair enough,' he sighs. 'Put a rope on the thing at least.'

At the quay the dog hesitates, pulling away from her.

'Rua?' she says. The dog sits obediently and looks up. She puts the rope over her neck, and pulls on it, but she doesn't budge. It's as if the rope or the future has frozen her in place. Brigid yanks harder and says, 'come,' trying to sound firm. Rua looks penitent, but still won't budge. Something opens up in Brigid, something she imagines could swallow her whole.

'Rua,' she says softly, trying not to cry. She feels as close to feral, incessant tears as a girl. A girl who hasn't learned to deter them yet. She crouches down, and whispers, begs, to something more than just the dog.

'If you want to be with us, you need to get in the boat.' There is a pause where she thinks Rua will deny her and she won't have an idea what to do next. She does not know if she will ever be let back here to retrieve her. Then the dog sighs, stands up, and walks to the lip of the quay, where she allows herself, with as much dignity as she can muster, to be lifted and placed kindly into the belly of the currach.

She holds on to the dog the whole trip. With her scarf pulled over her head in a protective veil and her face pressed into warm fur, she barely sees the green rock of the island moving away. Of her leaving she will remember only the hiss of the oars, the list and promise of the boat as it moves over the sea.

28

Vigil

February, March, 1960

While she is sleeping, her son is still alive. She struggles to stay down beneath it, under the ground that is her slumber, where she can still smell him. He fills her nostrils first, then she can feel his body warm and wiggly and so tall he has to fold himself to fit in her lap. She holds tight, inhales and he murmurs to her in Irish. *A chuisle mo chroí.* You are the pulse of my heart. His voice comes out all wrong, it is the gravelled voice of an old man. It shocks her awake, he is ripped away, and all she can smell is the bread Rose brought going stale under a towel, the damp that lives on everything, the turf smoke backing up from the quiet chimney. All the odours of her life, choking her.

For the first few days she believed he would come back in. That a shadow of him, a Niall-shaped light, would come in to look at her while she was sitting up with his body and she would be able to snatch him back. That her greatest fear, her son stolen, has finally occurred, and she only needs to believe in his being returned to her. That he will get away, just as she told him how, just as she did, and come home.

But after they bury him, she knows that she

424

shouldn't have worried about him being stolen. That wasn't anywhere near the worst thing, not at all. She was so afraid of him being stolen by fairies it had never occurred to her that his life, like anyone else's, could simply end. That, like all those children before him, he would die.

When she hears about Brigid leaving, she is livid, raging until she falls upon her bed and cries like a disappointed girl. At all the things she should have said, so that none of it would have happened. She spends most of her time now spinning it all in her head, changing what she did so the direction shifts and she saves her son. The night with Austin, the cursing stone, lying down with Brigid on her bed. Bringing the women into Brigid's home to burn her. Take away all of them, any of them, and fate could be reshuffled so he is not doomed.

Now of course she wants Austin's baby back. Wants it as fiercely as she wants her son to be alive. She didn't realise until now that the baby that Austin put in her was part of Niall as well.

She thinks often now of the way her mother sat by the fire after her son died, as if there was no life in her, as if she were already dead but her body still insisted on beating her heart and filling her lungs. Emer feels like this now. Buried inside herself but with skin so warm and flushed and healthy it insults her to be inside of it. She drugs herself to sleep only to have her child returned and taken away all over again.

Emer's neck doesn't plague her any more. There is no pressure there, no threat; her breath comes in and out so easily it is offensive. There is nothing left for her to be afraid of.

★ ★ ★

She sleeps through the springtime. She is in Rose's house now, on the hearth bed. Rose puts her there on purpose, so Emer is forced to be aware of life going on around her as she lies like an invalid in the corner. Tea is set beside her, a bun, a bowl of spuds with new butter. Sometimes she sits up to eat, often she does not.

The weather barely lifts. The plans for evacuation seem to be divided between a voice for leaving at the beginning of the summer and those who want to stay to the end. They decide to abandon the sowing they've started and get it over with. None of them want to be lulled into optimism by another glorious summer. In years to come, they will talk as if this island was a paradise, but the truth was, to live there required faith, courage and sheer stupid luck. As well as the knowledge that all of them might fail you.

The bees, Fiona and Eve report before Rose can shush them, Brigid's bees are awake again. They are busy making babies and comb and honey, but there is no one left who dares to approach them and pilfer a cup of sweetness from their home.

On the handful of days that give them a reprieve, Rose forces Emer to sit on a stool in the sun, her back propped against the stone wall of the house. The sunlight is insulting and she soon crawls back inside, where it remains damp and cool and dark no matter what.

They won't leave her alone. Either Rose is there, or the other women, or worse, her own mother like a carcass of disappointment wrapped in a woollen shawl. She can't even look at her, her mother, with her cruel, satisfied face, as if she is glad that this new generation has finally lost something. Emer would like to blame her for it all, but she barely has the energy to keep upright in her chair. She begs for sleep, deep and blackened sleep, and barely swims to the surface to open her eyes, see that nothing has changed, and close them again. She doesn't dream of him now. Only when she is first awake, the split second before she opens her eyes, like when you're sleeping in a strange bed but have forgotten and are expecting the particular view from yours, does her heart leap, first in hope, then plunge down again, so hard she thinks it will stop altogether. But it doesn't, so she must roll over to a cooler spot on her pillow and listen to the same wind and rain she's heard all her life, flinging at the windows like a child in a tantrum, and dig her way back down into the underworld beneath her consciousness.

After they have all gone to bed, when the house is dark and silent, she rises and sits by the glowing fire. She doesn't bother to try the door, padlocked from the inside by Rose who sleeps with the key. She sits for hours, her head aching and swimming with the effort of being upright, watching the fire as it slowly burns into the earth, trying with all its might to stay lit. She sits and pokes the fire and waits. She hasn't given up on him, but he never comes.

★ ★ ★

She fools the girls in the end. Fiona and Eve, dumbed by grief themselves, are told to run after their Mammy if they see Emer get up. She waits until Fiona goes out to milk the cows. Her mother is napping with the babies. Teresa and Bernie are minding the toddlers by the shore. She moves silently getting her clothes on, not bothering with shoes, and puts a finger to her lips to signal Eve that she shouldn't say a thing.

'I'm to tell Mam when you wake up.'

'I'm only going to get your mother. Which way is she?'

Eve, as gullible as Rose before her, looks relieved and says her mother has gone to move the sheep to the back field. Fiona would be more vigilant.

'I'll meet her on the road,' Emer says. 'Wait here, child, and wet the tea.'

Emer walks the other way, unsteady on legs that haven't held her up in a fortnight. The wind has gone; the island is preternaturally calm, as if the whole place is listening. The fog is close; she can't see the next house on the road let alone the mainland. Emer slips into the fog easily, following the green road at her feet, and no one comes after her.

She walks towards Brigid's house, meeting no one, not even a dog. She wonders where they all are, then remembers it is Sunday, and in sea this

428

calm they'll have gone over to Mass before the fog. The fog will keep them now. For all she knows it is only herself and Rose and the girls on the island, the rest of them meeting with the priest and the government official about the evacuation. She overheard something, stretches of conversation floated into her as she lay, heavy as a stone in her bed. Plans that once would have left her jubilant with success. She won't be going with them.

At Brigid's house the door opens without resistance and she slips inside. It still smells of her, and of the dog. Emer heard she took the dog with her, tying a rope to its neck and dragging it into a boat. The priest had spoken of it, of how the doctor was annoyed but Brigid had insisted. She loved that stupid creature as if it were her own child and not a dog at all.

Brigid has left the house as if she had merely gone for a walk. There are dirty dishes in the basin. A pair of knickers on the floor of the bedroom. The fire has burned without disturbance into ghost ash still holding the form of turf sods. She left the same way others left before her. Some tidied like they were merely going on holiday, others dropped it all where they stood and ran. If they were able to return, their lives would still be there for them. If not, what was the use of any of it? On the mainland, things could be procured easily, there were shops and post offices and trains and buses and butchers, and no need for the things you desperately hoarded on a remote island. There'd be nothing you couldn't replace if you wanted it dearly enough.

There is nothing here that Emer needs. A book of Yeats's poetry lies by her bedside, scraps of paper marking multiple pages. Emer flicks through bright clothing, sticks her finger into the face cream that Brigid once smoothed on to Emer's lips, which were chapped and happy from a long, brutal session of kissing.

She never should have left him alone. Not for an instant. Not to seduce his uncle, not to drown his father, not to come to this house and plunge herself into the body of another woman. She shouldn't have left him to milk the cows. All those moments she stole away from him were now stolen from her. In one of them, in any one of those thieving moments, she might have been let to keep him.

She lies down on Brigid's soft bed. She wants to sleep again. Sleep and sleep until her body forgets how to wake up. Except the problem is it keeps remembering. And will every day for the rest of her life. Which seems so unbearably long and yet empty, like an enormous sea with no land to row towards. The bed doesn't work, every time she wakes up it seems bigger, all of this emptiness, than it did before. So she makes her legs stand up, weak and heavy as if the whole of her is a vessel filled with stone, and leaves by the back door and climbs through grass and bracken, so steep that every few moments she must grab on to a rock the colour of jutting bone and pull herself forwards.

★　★　★

She almost makes it to the top before Rose ruins it all. Huffing her way up the cliffs from the other side, calling Emer's name like a curse. Emer briefly hopes the fog will disguise her, but then Rose is there, her hand is on Emer's wrist, as tight and strong and full of hope as it was when she was a girl. As if she hasn't in all that time learned any better, doesn't know that faith will get her nowhere.

'Will you never leave me be, Rose,' Emer says.

'You're soaked to the bone with the mist. You need the fire, so you do. And a cup of tea.'

'I'll drown in any more tea,' Emer barks. 'Let go of my arm.'

They struggle a bit, but Rose has always been stronger, and is immune to the hands that fill everyone else with hopelessness. Emer sinks exhausted to the wet ground. All she can hear is her angry breathing, and Rose's breath, which is determined and smooth.

'I won't let go of you,' Rose says. 'Not in your lifetime.'

'You've no right.'

'You're my sister.'

'I AM NOTHING!' Emer screams, which startles Rose, but not enough to make her let go. 'He was the only good in me and now he's gone.'

'We'll leave the island, Emer. We'll start over. You'll have another child.'

'I don't want one. And you don't want to leave.'

'I don't mind, so long as we're together.'

'I killed Austin.'

'Ah, stop it, Emer.'

431

'And Patch.'

'That's enough. You didn't either.'

'I did, Rose. I went to the cursing stone to get rid of Austin's baby.'

Rose blinks, fine mist on her lashes. As if she can blink away anything that she does not want to see.

'Then it was Austin's fault,' Rose says. 'You didn't mean to. You didn't mean any of it.'

'I did. I meant every bit. There's a terrible thing in me, Rose. A dark thing. Any love that was in me died with him.'

'That's fear, Emer, nothing else. You've been scared witless for ages. Even as a girl, you were afraid of everything. Afraid of love.'

The strength of Rose's grip weakens, enough for Emer to stand and wrench free, pushing towards the wind, the diving birds, the merciless rock and sea. Rose dives after her, holding on to her leg like a stubborn toddler.

'Take me over so. Orphan my children.'

'Oh, for fuck's sake, Rose, let go!'

Rose gives a great yank and Emer falls, scraping her cheek on a stone, her face soaked by the wet grass and the onslaught of tears. Rose slides up to her and lays her whole self, heavy with milk and a lifetime of vigilant cheer, on top of Emer, like a wet woollen blanket, like the earth, like Austin, or Brigid, or Patch but with more desire, more loyalty, more regret, than all three of them put together.

Rose whispers, as angry as she gets, which is still, underneath, kinder than it should be, 'You'll break my heart so you will.'

And Emer knows this is true, even as she is enraged by it. That somehow it won't be Austin drowning or Brigid leaving or her children going to America or her nephew dying right in front of her, but her sister, who she's held on to all this time, her sister going over that cliff will be the thing that breaks Rose. That she loves wretched Emer more than the lot of them. A miracle. Blasphemous, but a miracle nonetheless.

'How will I go on without him?' she croaks.

'Emer,' Rose says, all semblance of optimism gone. 'He was never yours to begin with.'

Emer keens then, cries into the damp cushion of ground, into the yielding body of her twin. She wants to cry her life out. She won't even come close.

'I hate you, Rose,' Emer says. And that's when Rose says something so manipulative and cruel that Emer knows they are related after all. And it works.

'If you take your own life, you'll go straight to Hell. How will you ever see him then?'

29

Birth

April, 1960

One night, when the days have got so long it is nine o'clock before the purple leaves the sky, Emer, waiting by the fire, doesn't turn or start when she hears the door creak open behind her. It is not Niall but Brigid who steps into the light of the hearth. Emer has spent so much time sleeping, her dreams bleed into waking life with ease. She thinks this is another dream.

Brigid is in labour. She is pacing the room, grunting, one hand below her massive belly, the other pressing her lower back, stopping to squat and moan. Her movements and noises are crude, feral, like an animal, a cow giving birth in a field rather than a woman in a house.

'Emer,' she pants between pains, and to Emer it is a breath of memory, Brigid lying beneath her and crying her name. 'Emer, help me.'

And though if she came to Emer in the daytime, in the world, Emer might scratch her eyes out, right now she does the only thing she can. Brigid holds her hand out and Emer takes it.

She leads her out the back door, not into the dark island night, but into a corridor. They walk on cold floors and enter a room full of women labouring, separated by linen partitions, so they each have a hell of their own. Nuns move back and forth in white habits, their faces pinched and void of emotion. The collective moan is deafening. It is the hospital on the mainland where she had Niall.

'In here,' Brigid says, and she pulls Emer through a door into a white chamber with round brick walls, a spiral metal staircase in the middle leading up to a revolving light. A small oval window looks out on a violent sea.

'Where are we?' Emer asks.

There is a single bed with a metal frame and Brigid grabs hold of it and squats again. This time she screams. She is so drenched with sweat it looks as though she has gone swimming in her nightgown. Her features are distorted with fear and pain.

'Emer,' she pants, when she can. 'You'll need to catch the baby.'

'I'll get a nun,' Emer says.

'No,' Brigid says. 'They want to gas me. I need you to do it.'

'You can't have your baby in a lighthouse,' Emer says. She almost laughs at how ridiculous this sounds.

'Please, Emer.' Her breath is quickening again, her short break is over; another pain rising in her like a lethal wave.

'I can't! My hands. I'll hurt the baby'

Brigid roars this time, head back, hair dark and tangled, she howls towards the sky. She looks like some old druid warrior, queens who birthed babies standing in their castle bedrooms

435

then ran downstairs with their swords to join the fight.

'Now, Emer!' she thunders, and Emer darts forwards. Brigid is lying half on the bed, her feet on the floor, her legs spread, thighs trembling from the effort. Emer lifts her nightgown and crouches in front of that dark, deep cavern between her legs and as Brigid screams again, screams like she's being murdered, a glistening wet mound slides out into Emer's waiting hands.

'It's in the caul,' Emer whispers, and Brigid slumps on to the mattress, gulping for breath and sobbing and reaching out all at once. Emer lifts the silver sac, warm, jiggling like a jellyfish she has picked up from the sand, and hands it to Brigid. Brigid tears it open with her finger, liquid gushes out, and she peels the veil away from the tranquil face of a sleeping baby.

Not Niall. Not a monster or a saint or a changeling. Just a newborn baby, like any other. Except to Brigid, who looks at it as if it is a marvel.

Brigid lies back on the bed, wiping at the baby's face with her nightgown, pulling its arms and legs out of the pouch where it has grown. It's a girl. Brigid is crying and laughing at the same time. The baby breathes, opens its eyes, looks intently at her mother, then to Emer, as if waiting for instructions.

'Thank you,' Brigid whispers, and Emer, who has no rage left, only regret, leans over and kisses her lover gently on her full, smiling mouth. She puts her hand out and cups the warm little head, so warm it is like she is made of soft skin and fire. She can hardly believe that Niall's head was once this size, that it fit so delicately in the palm of her cursed hand. That he was, however briefly, hers.

'Isn't she beautiful?' Brigid whispers.

Just before she wakes, sweaty and panting from the strange and vivid dream, Brigid wraps the silver mantle, the womb that was lent to her, in a piece of blue flannel, and gives it to Emer like a gift.

'There's no one left to save,' Emer says.

'There's you,' Brigid whispers. And then she is gone.

★　★　★

Emer wakes in bed, realising she fell asleep before ever getting up to go to the fire at all. She peels back the blankets and looks around, but there is nothing, only damp sheets left from her thrashing, and a fierce hunger like she hasn't had in weeks. She eats the dinner Rose left for her and boils and eats six eggs, one after the other, spooning them hot and runny straight into her ravenous mouth. When her mother and Rose wake up, they find Emer has made the tea and a loaf and already gone to the hens to replace the eggs she stole in the night-time.

'You're up, so you are,' their mother slurs.

'For all it's worth,' Emer counters.

'You were always a keen little thing,' her mother says.

This is not how Emer thinks of herself, not at all.

Rose has told Emer how their mother broke down at Niall's burial, how she wept as if it were her precious child laid to rest all over again. Emer doesn't know what to do with this. It is too late, for a lot of things.

She pulls a chair out for the woman as she always does, and sits with them, her mother, her sister, her nieces, and they pour the tea.

★　★　★

After that she is upright, anyway. Not agreeable, not overly useful, but upright. She does some household chores, stays hidden from the sun. On a close day she might walk down to the quay and back, a look of concentrated bearing on her face, as if she is walking off a cramp. There is nothing left of her that is fearsome. Her hands are as mild and scarred with life as the next woman's. Any power she once had over people's minds has gone inward. She keeps her hands close, wrapped around her waist under a shawl, and her one eye looking down. She is far from pleasant. But there's always Rose, by her side at every instant, for the smiling.

★　★　★

In April, the weather continues its desperate course, barely a breath between storms, battering the island with swells and wind. The sea rages, pummelling the rock, great chunks of green earth slide into the waves as it retreats. As though the island itself is trying to strip away

438

generations of anger and remorse, holding them hostage at the same time that it laments their leaving.

30

Evacuation

May, 1960

On the first of May, on the feast of Bealtaine that marks the beginning of summer, one beautiful day is blown across the island as if from Heaven. The sun shines high and bright, the water that has been rushing off the houses and stone walls into dykes dug by nuns long ago slows to a steady drip. The sea is as calm as glass. Islanders emerge, squinty as moles in the sunlight. The children run barefoot down to the water to greet the procession of boats.

All morning, while they empty their homes, they talk of the council houses that await them. With running water, toilets, electricity, gas cookers instead of a fire. Each family will be given a bicycle to go to the shops and pub only three miles up the road. The land is poor but they won't be as dependent on it. Their animals will have to learn to get out of the way of cars on the road.

The children squirm with excitement while they trap their pets in covered pots. The women tear up at every pause. The one old man lights his pipe and turns his face to the sea. They all wipe at their eyes and continue packing.

The children tell their mothers what they heard from the teacher: There will be dances, every Saturday at the hall in Cois Cuain.

Sure, they say, sounding like old immigrants already, *haven't island people always been great ones for the dancing.*

They wonder now if they ever truly had a say in it, whether they were let to stay or made to go. It may not have been the fairies or the saints, but the island itself that was in charge all along.

Before they go, most women take water from Saint Brigid's well. This has been done for generations, anyone leaving for work or war or marriage takes some of the holy water with them. Should they crave the blessings of home they only need to pour a little out. If they have their babies far away, they can be sprinkled in it, just as they would be dipped on the island. Before Brigid came with her hands, the water had been the only one to ease things. It has flowed in the driest weather for as long as anyone can remember. They each take a swallow of it with them to ease their way into the world. Even the women who don't believe in it fill a bottle with this promise and seal it with wax. With superstition, it is better to stick to the thing than to stray. Better it doesn't work than you lose your chance at saving yourself altogether.

★ ★ ★

When Rose finishes cleaning and almost everything is gone from the house, she ties up the mattress on Emer's bed into a roll for the men to bring down. It is made of the feathers of sea birds and would be expensive to replace. Under the

441

mattress, wedged beneath the corner of the bed frame, she finds a small scrap of blue flannel, wrapped up and tied with butcher's string. She goes to open it then decides not to. It isn't hers, it must belong to Emer. She'll bring it down to her at the boats, and let Emer decide what to do with it.

As she closes the door for the last time, she whispers their names: *Austin, Niall, Brigid*. She believes she is saying goodbye.

She walks down in the direction of the quay where chaos reigns. Men are still carrying bedsteads and bureaus, transferring them to currachs that bring them to bigger boats waiting in the sea. She has never in her life seen so many boats in their water at once. They say one time when the fish were plenty, boats came from all over Europe, but most of them went to the harbour of Inis Muruch. There wasn't anything here for them. Brigid was the only tourist they'd ever had. It's like a regatta or a fair, all the excitement. There is far too much happiness surrounding their leaving. She'd like to smack the smiles off the faces of her children. As this is not a usual turn of her mind, she shakes it away and tries to lift her chin high and walk as if she knows which way she's going in the sunshine.

In the boat, ignoring the photographer feverishly snapping pictures of all the twins, she hands the flannel pouch to her sister. Emer stiffens, the little bit of colour she has managed to gain drains instantly from her face. Like the worst moment of her life has just seared across her vision again.

'What is it?' Rose asks.

'Brigid gave this to me,' Emer says. 'I thought it was a dream.'

Emer hands Rose the baby. Then she stands so quickly the boat threatens to tip. A man shouts at her to sit her bloody self down.

'Let me out,' Emer says. 'I've left something.'

Rose tries to pull her back, the babies start crying, a sudden swell pitches the currach, one of the toddlers almost tumbles out of the boat. Finally, a man plucks Emer up by her armpits and plops her impatiently on the quay. She runs away from them all, up the green road and beyond. Rose has to negotiate and distribute children before she can be lifted out as well, her polite approach is not as immediately effective. By the time she's out, Emer has disappeared over the hill that leads to the cliffs. Rose follows after her.

Emer stumbles down the cliff path with no regard for the sheer drop. She ducks into the shrine and kneels at the opening to the well, her heart rising like it might leap out her throat any moment. She unwraps the flannel and finds a shrivelled, vile, gorgeous thing, dried and brown and empty, a pouch knit out of blood and seaweed. It's bigger than a partial veil, it's the entire container, an enormous version of the mermaid's purses they collected from the coves as girls. Abandoned sacs where basking sharks grow before they break out one end and swim away.

She holds Brigid's caul just where the water flows thickest, until the sides of it soften and bellow out, until the sac where Brigid's child was formed is full again. Then she places it like a holy relic on top of the flannel and sets the offering in the cushion of grass and blue flowers. Flowers so tiny they've never, in all her life, seemed to belong to the human world. Fairy flowers, they called them as girls. A gift the good people presented to the blue-cloaked saint that came to their island. Emer lets go and holds her breath.

Inside the pouch, something moves. Thrashes and stretches, like a fish caught in a net. Then it swells and the whole thing grows, expands beyond its proportions, and Rose is there, her sister is beside her and Emer hasn't breathed yet, she mustn't breathe yet though her lungs are crying for it, and finally, when she thinks her chest might burst holding it in, a hand tears at the membrane and tries to pull itself, slow and sticky and human, out of the place where it has grown.

Images rush at her, swarming, merciless. All those hands. The turnip stump and the curled-up lichen remains of a miniature hand, her sister's fingers dripping with dangerous honey, her child swiping regret from her forehead, Brigid pulling her clothes away and dropping them, heavy as armour, to the ground. Her own hands and their insertion of misery, like a blade hidden in her palm.

The hand claws at the sides of the sac, and she can see the panic, the body behind it trapped in something so thick it cannot be pulled away. Emer has to go for her knife and slice it right

444

down the middle, allowing what is within to straighten itself, and the husk of the membrane to fall away.

He is there, naked and fish-white and smeared with afterbirth, hot blue eyes opening to look at his mother whom he will, after this, always remember as smiling.

'Will you look at him,' Rose hisses, and she crosses herself. 'Saints alive.'

Emer grabs hold of Niall, the whole slimy length of him, folding him almost in half to fit inside her arms. She wipes at his face and his eyes with her shawl, cleaning the clots off, kissing his skin and inhaling, he smells of salt and blood and milk and, underneath it all, his glorious self.

'I didn't drink, Mammy. Not a drop.'

'Good lad.' She barely trusts herself to speak.

'It was Brigid,' he says. 'She told them to let me go.'

'I know,' Emer shushes him. 'She gave me the caul.'

'Not that Brigid.'

Another hand returns to her, the first one, that woman, all those years ago, who peeled the curtain back to show her the world. Who held a scrap of blue fabric out to her like a gift, or a warning. Emer had thought she was something else altogether.

He is ice-cold from the water, so she wraps him in her shawl and they climb, stumbling up again into the sun, to warm him.

'Mammy,' he says, blinking in the unaccustomed brightness. He is looking beyond her towards the site of the evacuation.

'Look at all the boats in our sea.'

She holds him for ages, murmuring the same way she did the day he was born the first time, *a leanbh, a leanbh, a leanbh*. My child. He doesn't mind it, he lets her hold him for as long as she needs to, before they must rise and meet the boats and their new life on the other side. Where this day will fade in Niall's memory until all he recalls is a fevered dream. He won't even remember the woman who saved him, after first allowing him to die. Perhaps they will go further than they planned, take their new bicycles and ride until they reach a place they have never seen, safe from the fairies, and themselves, where Emer's hands will be mild and forgettable, away from the opinions of the women who would rather she be punished than forgiven.

Go on, Emer's heart whispers, *go on. Find out where she has gone.*

Emer knows it as well as any of them. She doesn't deserve this. She who murdered their husbands and drove off the closest thing they had to a saint, who used her hands to insert hopelessness into any soul that seemed the slightest bit happier than she was. She who took their island away from them with the same vicious disregard as a fairy who steals a child right out of its mother's arms.

She doesn't deserve it — doesn't deserve a saint's absolution or a fairy's surrender, or the forgiveness of a woman scorned — and she will not be allowed to keep him, he will grow up and away from her, already on that walk down she can imagine his small hand letting go, but still she gets him back, her son, her bones, her soul, her pulse.

Mercy. He is given back to her, all the same.

Acknowledgements

I suspect no one aside from writers and people who hope to be mentioned by writers read the acknowledgements. But I always do, so I will try to make these as long and boring as possible. If I forget to thank you, please forgive me. It took five years, three countries, and two colonies to write this book, so chalk it up to age-related memory loss rather than ingratitude.

I am indebted to my fabulous agents, Grainne Fox and Christy Fletcher, for believing in me even when everyone else in the publishing world had forgotten me, as well as my editors, Arzu Tahsin and Jillian Verrillo, who saw my book for what it was and helped make it even more so. Thanks to the fabulous teams on both sides of the Atlantic who guided me patiently through the process of publishing again, especially Jennifer Kerslake with her keen (much keener than mine) editorial eye. Also, Veronica Goldstein at Fletcher & Co, keeper of all the things I can't manage to keep, and Nuala Ni Chonchúir for the fadas.

I am profoundly grateful to the entire population of Inishbofin, Ireland, many of whom have housed me, fed me, shuttled me back and forth, answered my ignorant questions, and always greeted me and my son with love. For housing and feeding us: The Doonmore Hotel, The Beach Bar, Caroline Coyne, and Lorraine

MacLean. Ann Prendergast for slagging my boy until he understood it, and, along with Claire. Veronica and countless babysitters, for making him feel safe when his mother had to work. Cliodhna Hallissey for pirate stories under the picnic table; Michael Joe and Robbie for the bodhrán lessons; Orla, Bernie and Lalage for *all that wine*; Padraic and Lisa McIntyre and their children for the craic; Julie for sweetness and light; Tommy Burke for tours and history on Shark and Bofin; Tara, Audrey and the staff at the Community Centre for everything else. Thanks most of all to my dearest, oldest friends on the island: Susan and Joanne Elliott, who helped edit the final draft for inappropriate American phrases and ignorant farming details, and Desmond O'Halloran, who was always available for emergency lattes.

Kieran Concannon's film, *Death of an Island*, was the initial inspiration for the prologue of this book, and I will always be grateful for it, and to Kieran for smuggling me a copy meant for someone else. Thank you to the people of Inishark for sharing their stories, and Teresa Lacey for not packing her delph; I hope they forgive me for manipulating something that was all too real in their lives in the name of fiction.

Thanks to The MacDowell Colony, where I began this novel, and all the staff and office folk who make the running of a paradise appear effortless. Special thanks to Blake, for telling me about the women and their knives, and hanging a graduation balloon on my door after I finished the first draft.

I am grateful to the Virginia Center for the Creative Arts, where I wrestled with many later drafts, to Craig and Sheila Pleasants, Bea Booker and everyone in the office and staff, to all the artists who inspired me and made me laugh, in particular the ones who also let me cry: Priyanka Champaneri and Kathryn Levy.

To my early readers: Gary Miller for tossing the hammer that stunned the poor pig, Sandra Miller for the popovers and truth telling, and Lacy Berman for loving Emer and reminding me to read poetry.

Thank you to the people of Kaçs, Turkey, for giving my family a home while we wrote, worked and studied, especially Zühre, who gave Tim and Liam a classroom at Sofa, and Engin, Arife, and Burcu for all those afternoons in çay bahçesi that made me feel like a local.

I am indebted to my friends in Maine, especially Aja Stephan and Beth O'Malley, for remaining my friends even though I escape to residencies and abroad and don't talk to them for months at a time. Thanks to Breakwater School teachers and parents (especially Mr Jim, Michelle Littlefield, Alicia Amy, Kathy Fisher, Shannon Thomas, Ellie Falby, Janette Hough, and Kate Hanify), for the reassurance that my son is with a family that loves him, even when I am not at home. Special kudos goes to Lucy and Caroline Green for their jaunt to Inishbofin to share the magic. For the friends I've had for so long they are part of my soul: you know who you are and you've heard this all before.

I am thankful for my parents and my extended

family; they have always supported my choice to be a writer, even when it means I am useless at calling them back.

Last and best: Tim, who made it possible for me to go away and write, and Liam, who forgave me for leaving. I am grateful every day for my little family. You have made me happier than I ever suspected I would be.

The Story Behind *The Stolen Child*

Abandoned village, Inishark,
Saint Leo's Church, 2012

Inishbofin — an island off the west coast of Ireland — is a place I have returned to countless times since my first stay in 1995. During that initial visit I researched my first novel, and based my fictional island on the landscape there. My second novel was also set on an island, this time in Maine. So by the time I went to write my fifth

I had absolutely *no* intention of writing anything set on an island, certainly not one in Ireland. I safely could have said that's exactly what I *wouldn't* be writing. If every writer has only one story in them that they get to tell over and over again, then mine appears to be surrounded by water.

Fifteen years later, I visited Inishbofin with my four-year-old son. We met a group of American archaeologists who had a six-year-old, and they were kind enough to share their babysitter. One night, this allowed me the time to watch a documentary, *Death of an Island*, by a local man named Kieran Concannon. It was about the evacuation of a smaller neighbouring island, Inishark, which was once home to hundreds of families. The combined blows of the famine, two world wars, and Irish emigration dwindled the population down to twenty-three residents by 1960. Inishbofin, with its natural harbour and sandy beaches, attracted sailboats and visitors and would eventually build a thriving tourism business. But Inishark's harbour was a dangerous cove that could only be navigated during the right tide by experienced locals. It had no electricity, phone lines, or doctors, and was on its own in an emergency. The government, which often provided social welfare to poor Irish villages, wanted to clear people off Inishark, and so refused to set up the island with modern conveniences. What the government did offer were houses on the mainland if the islanders agreed to leave. After the sea killed three young men on their way back from Mass on Easter

Sunday, the islanders had too few men to handle their boats. They left for a mainland village that overlooked their old home, and no one has lived on Inishark since. The documentary interviews people who have remembered the island in their dreams their entire lives.

Not all novels come to you in a shivering flash, like a dream. This one did. I knew I would write about a community's final year on an Irish island, though my characters would not be the kind, generous, respectable people of that documentary, because, let's face it, I don't write characters like that. I would take the real evacuation and replace the community with one from my imagination. But the documentary remains, in my Prologue, as a tribute to the real residents of Inishark.

I always say I don't start a novel with one idea. I have to have at least five, all of which could be different novels and none of which have much in common. One woman from the documentary, whom I later met myself, told how she did not want to leave and refused to pack until the last minute. I started to imagine two sisters, one who hated her life on the island, and the other who loved it. For some reason I had the Salem witch persecutions on my brain at the time, and imagined an outsider frightening the islanders into something similar. I was reading *Walk the Blue Fields* by Claire Keegan, one of my favourite Irish authors, about a female healer who moved into a desolate house in the West of Ireland. Her new home was next door to a bachelor who lived with a goat, and she ended

Liam and mates, West Quarter, Inishbofin, 2014

up having his child. I couldn't get this character out of my mind, and she was my first inspiration for Brigid. I was also reading a book about Maine lighthouses and the families who lived in them before the lights were automated. I was reading Irish myths of changelings and stolen children to my son. Finally, I had an idea — leftover from when I was researching my second novel — about a torrid affair between the Irish saints Patrick and Brigid. (I never worked out the details of this, thank goodness.)

So there I had it: evacuated islands, sisters, witch burning, healers, lighthouses, fairies, and saints. At least seven ideas, and many more that either ended up on the cutting-room floor or never made it in there in the first place. Then, while writing the first draft, Emer and Brigid rejected my plans for friendship and became lovers. I hate it when writers talk about characters doing things on their own, because for me writing is extremely difficult and not one bit of it feels like it is being written by anyone else but miserable me, but in this case, they really did. I had to write it, but they told me to.

The Stolen Child is not an autobiographical novel; my abandoned memoir is proof that I fail when I try to write about myself. I kept a few things from my memoir: my lovely Irish dog, and a baby who couldn't breastfeed. While writing it I was quite sure it had little to do with me, because the story was so difficult to manage and get a proper hold on. I have no healing powers, and I've never lived in a lighthouse, an orphanage, or anywhere without electricity and plumbing. I don't believe in fairies and I am not a lesbian. I wrote an entire draft that built towards one ending, then changed my mind while writing the last chapter and had to go back and redo the whole thing about five more times. But once I neared the final draft, and read the entire story out loud. I was shocked. It may not be about me or my life, but its themes, particularly motherhood and all its backstories and consequences — pregnancy, miscarriage, abortion, love, loneliness, worship and resentment, the inability to live in the moment because you're too busy missing something else — had been in my life for years. So don't believe it when I say my books aren't about me. They are nothing about me, and everything at the same time. Because, as my son said recently. 'You are

Liam, West Quarter, Inishbofin, 2016

only able to have one perspective your whole life. Doesn't that make you the centre of the universe?'

But still, it is other people's worlds that I fall in love with. I have been to Inishark every summer since I first saw the film, going for day trips in a local boat that drops you off and picks you up according to the tide. You have to leap off the boat while it's still running, just at the moment where it rises with a wave. There are only sheep there now, and sunbathing seals, and rabbits, and occasionally that group of archaeologists, who camp there for two weeks every year no matter what the weather. It is one of the most beautiful places I have ever seen, yet I know, from being trapped on Bofin in a storm, how desolate it must have been at times. The houses are still there, their roofs fallen in, and if you visit with a local they will tell you the families that lived in each abandoned building, because they still remember. You can almost hear the children in the school playground, or the bells announcing Mass in the church. Two years ago a series of winter storms tore in half what remained of the cement quay that lined the cove. The graveyard, set perilously on a cliff side, is beginning to release the bones of its ancestors as the land succumbs to erosion.

I never saw Shark when it was populated, but I have visited its sister, Inishbofin, as well as their neighbour Inishturk, countless times over the last twenty-one years. I have been welcomed again and again by the wild landscape and the generous people; learned to understand the accents that required subtitles in the documentary; watched the babies from my first trip become adults manning the boat, serving Guinness, or playing music in the bar. I have spent lazy days sitting outside the pub, watching the silhouette of my son run back and forth on the hillside against a sunset that lasts for hours. Although I have only seen Inishark as an abandoned village, I can imagine how heartbreaking it was to leave it, and I can see precisely what life would be like there now, if it weren't for the dangers of nature and the limited imagination of the outsiders who were in charge.

We do hope that you have enjoyed reading this large print book.

Did you know that all of our titles are available for purchase?

We publish a wide range of high quality large print books including:
Romances, Mysteries, Classics
General Fiction
Non Fiction and Westerns

Special interest titles available in large print are:
The Little Oxford Dictionary
Music Book
Song Book
Hymn Book
Service Book

Also available from us courtesy of Oxford University Press:
Young Readers' Dictionary
(large print edition)
Young Readers' Thesaurus
(large print edition)

For further information or a free brochure, please contact us at:
Ulverscroft Large Print Books Ltd.,
The Green, Bradgate Road, Anstey,
Leicester, LE7 7FU, England.
Tel: (00 44) 0116 236 4325
Fax: (00 44) 0116 234 0205

Other titles published by Ulverscroft:

CONFESSIONS OF A WILD CHILD

Jackie Collins

Lucky Santangelo is powerful and charismatic — but how did she become the woman she is today? This is the story of the teenage Lucky as she discovers boys and love, and fights her father, the infamous Gino Santangelo, to forge her own individual and strong road to success. Even at 15, Lucky follows her own path — and it's a crazy ride, from a strict girls' school in Switzerland to an idyllic Greek island, a Bel Air estate, a New York penthouse, and a luxurious villa in the south of France. Nobody can control Lucky. She knows what she wants — and she goes for it with no holds barred . . .

THE AWARD

Danielle Steel

France, 1940: When the German army invades, sixteen-year-old Gaëlle de Barbet loses her family, and her closest friend is sent to a detention camp. Joining the Resistance, Gaëlle takes terrifying risks to fearlessly deliver Jewish children to safety, and later to help save France's art treasures. But when the war draws to a close, she is falsely accused of collaboration, and flees to Paris in disgrace. There, she begins a new life that eventually takes her to New York, from a career as a Dior model to marriage and motherhood, unbearable loss, and mature, lasting love when she returns to France. No matter where she goes, however, her label as a collaborator remains ? until her granddaughter, a respected political journalist, embarks on a journey to see Gaëlle recognized as the war hero she was.

CITY OF FRIENDS

Joanna Trollope

The day Stacey Grant loses her job feels like the last day of her life. For who was she if not a City high-flyer, senior partner at one of the top private equity firms in London? As Stacey starts to reconcile her old life with the new — one without professional achievements or meetings, but instead long days at home with her dog and ailing mother, waiting for her successful husband to come home — she at least has the girls to fall back on. Now women, they had all been best friends from the early days of university right through their working lives, and for all the happiness and heartbreaks in between. But when Stacey's redundancy forces a betrayal to emerge that was supposed to remain secret, their long-cherished friendships will be pushed to their limits . . .

LOST HORIZON

GOODBYE, MR. CHIPS

and Other Stories

LOST HORIZON

GOODBYE, MR. CHIPS

and Other Stories

JAMES HILTON

THE WORLD'S BEST READING

The Reader's Digest Association Limited, London

LOST HORIZON, GOODBYE, MR. CHIPS *and* OTHER STORIES

This Reader's Digest edition contains the complete text
of James Hilton's *Lost Horizon*, first published in 1933 by Macmillan & Co. Ltd.,
Goodbye, Mr. Chips, first published in 1934 by Hodder and Stoughton Ltd.,
and *To You, Mr. Chips*, first published in 1938 by Hodder and Stoughton Ltd.

Illustrations for *Lost Horizon* by Robert Andrew Parker.
Illustrations for *Goodbye, Mr. Chips and Other Stories* by David Frankland.

Printed in the United States of America by R.R. Donnelley & Sons Company.

Contents

LOST HORIZON
page 9

GOODBYE, MR. CHIPS
and *Other Stories*
page 179

Afterword by Leonée Ormond
page 333

LOST HORIZON

Englishmen in a foreign capital could have brought us together, and I had already reached the conclusion that the slight touch of priggishness which I remembered in Wyland Tertius had not diminished with years and an M.V.O. Rutherford I liked better; he had ripened well out of the skinny, precocious infant whom I had once alternately bullied and patronized. The probability that he was making much more money and having a more interesting life than either of us gave Wyland and me our only shared emotion—a touch of envy.

The evening, however, was far from dull. We had a good view of the big Lufthansa machines as they arrived at the aerodrome from all parts of Central Europe, and towards dusk, when arc flares were lighted, the scene took on a rich, theatrical brilliance. One of the planes was English, and its pilot, in full flying kit, strolled past our table and saluted Wyland, who did not at first recognize him. When he did so there were introductions all round, and the stranger was invited to join us. He was a pleasant, jolly youth named Sanders. Wyland made some apologetic remark about the difficulty of identifying people when they were all dressed up in Sibleys and flying helmets; at which Sanders laughed and answered: "Oh, rather, I know that well enough. Don't forget I was at Baskul." Wyland laughed also, but less spontaneously, and the conversation then took other directions.

Sanders made an attractive addition to our small company, and we all drank a great deal of beer together. About ten o'clock Wyland left us for a moment to speak to someone at a table nearby, and Rutherford, into the sudden hiatus of talk, remarked: "Oh, by the way, you mentioned Baskul just now. I know the place slightly. What was it you were referring to that happened there?"

Sanders smiled rather shyly. "Oh, just a bit of excitement we had once when I was in the Service." But he was a youth who could not long refrain from being confidential. "Fact is, an Afghan or an Afridi or somebody ran off with one of our buses, and there was the very devil to pay afterwards, as you can imagine. Most impudent thing I ever heard of. The blighter waylaid the pilot, knocked him out, pinched his kit, and climbed into the cockpit without a soul spotting him. Gave the mechanics the proper signals, too, and was up and away in fine style. The trouble was, he never came back."

Rutherford look interested. "When did this happen?"

"Oh—must have been about a year ago. May, thirty-one. We were evacuating civilians from Baskul to Peshawar owing to the revolution—perhaps you remember the business. The place was in a bit of an upset, or I don't suppose the thing could have happened. Still, it *did* happen—and it goes some way to show that clothes make the man, doesn't it?"

Rutherford was still interested. "I should have thought you'd have had more than one fellow in charge of a plane on an occasion like that?"

"We did, on all the ordinary troop carriers, but this machine was a special one, built for some maharajah originally—quite a stunt kind of outfit. The Indian Survey people had been using it for high-altitude flights in Kashmir."

"And you say it never reached Peshawar?"

"Never reached there, and never came down anywhere else, so far as we could discover. That was the queer part about it. Of course, if the fellow was a tribesman he might have made for the hills, thinking to hold the passengers for ransom. I suppose they all got killed, somehow. There are heaps of places on the frontier where you might crash and not be heard of afterwards."

"Yes, I know the sort of country. How many passengers were there?"

"Four, I think. Three men and some woman missionary."

"Was one of the men, by any chance, named Conway?"

Sanders looked surprised. "Why, yes, as a matter of fact. 'Glory' Conway—did you know him?"

"He and I were at the same school," said Rutherford a little self-consciously, for it was true enough, yet a remark which he was aware did not suit him.

"He was a jolly fine chap, by all accounts of what he did at Baskul," went on Sanders.

Rutherford nodded. "Yes, undoubtedly . . . but how extraordinary . . . extraordinary . . . ." He appeared to collect himself after a spell of mind-wandering. Then he said: "It was never in the papers, or I think I should have read about it. How was that?"

Sanders looked suddenly rather uncomfortable, and even, I imagined, was on the point of blushing. "To tell you the truth," he replied, "I seem to have let out more than I should have. Or perhaps it doesn't matter now—it must be stale news in every mess, let alone in the bazaars. It was hushed up, you see—I mean, about the way the thing happened. Wouldn't have sounded well. The government people merely gave out that one of their machines was missing, and mentioned the names. Sort of thing that didn't attract an awful lot of attention among outsiders."

At this point Wyland rejoined us, and Sanders turned to him half apologetically. "I say, Wyland, these chaps have been talking about 'Glory' Conway. I'm afraid I spilled the Baskul yarn—I hope you don't think it matters?"

Wyland was severely silent for a moment. It was plain that he was reconciling the claims of compatriot courtesy and official rectitude. "I can't help feeling," he said at length, "that it's a pity to make a mere anecdote of it. I always thought you air fellows were put on your honour not to tell tales out of school." Having thus snubbed the youth, he turned, rather more graciously, to Rutherford. "Of course, it's all right in your case, but I'm sure you realize that it's sometimes necessary for events up on the frontier to be shrouded in a little mystery."

"On the other hand," replied Rutherford dryly, "one has a curious itch to know the truth."

"It was never concealed from anyone who had any real reason for wanting to know it. I was at Peshawar at the time, and I can assure you of that. Did you know Conway well—since schooldays, I mean?"

"Just a little at Oxford, and a few chance meetings since. Did *you* come across him much?"

"At Angora, when I was stationed there, we met once or twice."

"Did you like him?"

"I thought he was clever, but rather slack."

Rutherford smiled. "He was certainly clever. He had a most exciting university career—until war broke out. Rowing Blue and a leading light at the Union and prizeman for this, that, and the other—also I reckon him the best amateur pianist I ever heard. Amazingly many-sided fellow, the kind, one feels, that Jowett would have tipped for a future premier. Yet, in point of fact, one never heard much about him after those Oxford days. Of course the War cut into his career. He was very young and I gather he went through most of it."

"He was blown up or something," responded Wyland, "but nothing very serious. Didn't do at all badly, got a D.S.O. in France. Then I believe he went back to Oxford for a spell as a sort of don. I know he went east in twenty-one. His Oriental languages got him the job without any of the usual preliminaries. He had several posts."

Rutherford smiled more broadly. "Then, of course, that accounts for everything. History will never disclose the amount of sheer brilliance wasted in the routine of decoding F.O. chits and handing round tea at legation bun fights."

"He was in the Consular Service, not the Diplomatic," said Wyland loftily. It was evident that he did not care for the chaff, and he made no protest when, after a little more badinage of a similar kind, Rutherford rose to go. In any case it was getting late, and I said I would go, too. Wyland's attitude as we made our farewells was still one of official propriety suffering in silence, but Sanders was very cordial and he said he hoped to meet us again some time.

I was catching a transcontinental train at a very dismal hour of the early morning, and, as we waited for a taxi, Rutherford asked me if I would care to spend the interval at his hotel. He had a sitting room, he said, and we could talk. I said it would suit me excellently, and he answered: "Good. We can talk about Conway, if you like, unless you're completely bored with his affairs."

I said that I wasn't at all, though I had scarcely known him. "He left at the end of my first term, and I never met him afterwards. But he was extraordinarily kind to me on one occasion. I was a new boy and there was no earthly reason why he should have done what he did. It was only a trivial thing, but I've always remembered it."

Rutherford assented. "Yes, I liked him a good deal too, though I also saw surprisingly little of him, if you measure it in time."

And then there was a somewhat odd silence, during which it was evident that we were both thinking of someone who had mattered to us far more than might have been judged from such casual contacts. I have often found since then that others who met Conway, even quite formally and for a moment, remembered him afterwards with great vividness. He was certainly remarkable as a youth, and to me, at the hero-worshipping age when I saw him, his memory is still quite romantically distinct. He was tall and extremely good-looking, and not only excelled at games but walked off with every conceivable kind of school prize. A rather sentimental headmaster once referred to his exploits as "glorious," and from that arose his nickname. Perhaps only he could have survived it. He gave a Speech Day oration in Greek, I recollect, and was outstandingly first-rate in school theatricals. There was something rather Elizabethan about him—his casual versatility, his good looks, that effervescent combination of mental with physical activities. Something a bit Philip-Sidney-ish. Our civilization doesn't often breed people like that nowadays. I made a remark of this kind to Rutherford, and he replied: "Yes, that's true, and we have a special word of disparagement for them—we call them dilettanti. I suppose some people must have called Conway that, people like Wyland, for instance. I don't much care for Wyland. I can't stand his type—all that primness and mountainous self-importance. And the complete head-prefectorial mind, did you notice it? Little phrases about 'putting people on their honour' and 'telling tales out of school'—as though the bally Empire was the fifth form at St. Dominic's! But, then, I always fall foul of these sahib diplomats."

We drove a few blocks in silence, and then he continued: "Still, I wouldn't have missed this evening. It was a peculiar experience for me, hearing Sanders tell that story about the affair at Baskul. You see, I'd heard it before, and hadn't properly believed it. It was part of a much more fantastic story, which I saw no reason to believe at all—or, well, only one very slight reason, anyway. *Now* there are *two* very slight reasons. I daresay you can guess that I'm not a particularly gullible person. I've spent a good deal of my life travelling about, and I know there are queer things in the world—if you see them yourself, that is, but not so often if you hear of them second-hand. And yet . . . ."

He seemed suddenly to realize that what he was saying could not mean very much to me, and broke off with a laugh. "Well, there's one thing certain—I'm not likely to take Wyland into my confidence. It would be like trying to sell an epic poem to *Tit-Bits*. I'd rather try my luck with you."

"Perhaps you flatter me," I suggested.

"Your book doesn't lead me to think so."

I had not mentioned my authorship of that rather technical work (after all, a neurologist's is not everybody's "shop"), and I was agreeably surprised that Rutherford had even heard of it. I said as much, and he answered: "Well, you see, I was interested, because amnesia was Conway's trouble at one time."

We had reached the hotel and he had to get his key at the bureau. As we went up to the fifth floor he said: "All this is mere beating about the bush. The fact is, Conway isn't dead. At least he wasn't a few months ago."

This seemed beyond comment in the narrow space and time of a lift ascent. In the corridor a few seconds later I responded: "Are you sure of that? How do you know?"

And he responded, unlocking his door: "Because I travelled with him from Shanghai to Honolulu in a Jap liner last November." He did not speak again till we were settled in armchairs and had fixed ourselves with drinks and cigars. "You see, I was in China in the autumn on a holiday. I'm always wandering about. I hadn't seen Conway for years. We never corresponded, and I can't say he was often in my thoughts, though his was one of the few faces that have always come to me quite effortlessly if I tried to picture it. I had been visiting a friend in Hankow and was returning by the Pekin express. On the train I chanced to get into conversation with a very charming Mother Superior of some French sisters of charity. She was travelling to Chung-Kiang, where her convent was, and, because I knew a little French, she seemed to enjoy chattering to me about her work and affairs in general. As a matter of fact, I haven't much sympathy with ordinary missionary enterprise, but I'm prepared to admit, as many people are nowadays, that the Romans stand in a class by themselves, since at least they work hard and don't pose as commissioned officers in a world full of other ranks. Still, that's by the by. The point is that this lady, talking to me about the mission hospital at Chung-Kiang, mentioned a fever case that had been brought in some weeks back, a man who they thought must be a European, though he could give no account of himself and had no papers. His clothes were native, and of the poorest kind, and when taken in by the nuns he had been very ill indeed. He spoke fluent Chinese, as well as pretty good French, and my train companion assured me that before he realized the nationality of the nuns, he had also addressed them in English with a refined accent. I said I couldn't imagine such a phenomenon, and chaffed her gently about being able to detect a refined accent in a language she didn't know. We joked about these and other matters, and it ended by her inviting me to visit the mission if ever I happened to be thereabouts. This, of course, seemed then as unlikely as that I should climb Everest, and when the train reached Chung-Kiang I shook hands with genuine regret that our chance contact had come to an end. As it happened, though, I was back in Chung-Kiang within a few hours. The train broke down a mile or two farther on, and with much difficulty pushed us back to the station, where we learned that a relief engine could not possibly arrive for twelve hours. That's the sort of thing that often happens on Chinese railways. So there was half a day to be lived through in Chung-Kiang—which made me decide to take the good lady at her word and call at the mission.

"I did so, and received a cordial, though naturally a somewhat astonished, welcome. I suppose one of the hardest things for a non-Catholic to realize is how easily a Catholic can combine official rigidity with non-official broad-mindedness. Is that too complicated? Anyhow, never mind, those mission people made quite delightful company. Before I'd been there an hour I found that a meal had been prepared, and a young Chinese Christian doctor sat down with me to it and kept up a conversation in a jolly mixture of French and English. Afterwards, he and the Mother Superior took me to see the hospital, of which they were very proud. I had told them I was a writer, and they were simple-minded enough to be aflutter at the thought that I might put them all into a book. We walked past the beds while the doctor explained the cases. The place was spotlessly clean and looked to be very competently run. I had forgotten all about the mysterious patient with the refined English accent till the

Mother Superior reminded me that we were just coming to him. All I could see was the back of the man's head; he was apparently asleep. It was suggested that I should address him in English, so I said 'Good afternoon,' which was the first and not very original thing I could think of. The man looked up suddenly and said 'Good afternoon' in answer. It was true; his accent was educated. But I hadn't time to be surprised at that, for I had already recognized him, despite his beard and altogether changed appearance and the fact that we hadn't met for so long. He was Conway. I was certain he was, and yet, if I'd paused to think about it, I might well have come to the conclusion that he couldn't possibly be. Fortunately I acted on the impulse of the moment. I called out his name and my own, and though he looked at me without any definite sign of recognition, I was positive I hadn't made any mistake. There was an odd little twitching of the facial muscles that I had noticed in him before, and he had the same eyes that at Balliol we used to say were so much more of a Cambridge blue than an Oxford. But besides all that, he was a man one simply didn't make mistakes about—to see him once was to know him always. Of course the doctor and the Mother Superior were greatly excited. I told them that I knew the man, that he was English, and a friend of mine, and that if he didn't recognize me, it could only be because he had completely lost his memory. They said yes, in a rather amazed way, and we had a long consultation about the case. They weren't able to make any suggestions as to how Conway could possibly have arrived at Chung-Kiang in the state he was.

"To make the story brief, I stayed there over a fortnight, hoping that somehow or other I might induce him to remember things. I didn't succeed, but he regained his physical health, and we talked a good deal. When I told him quite frankly who I was and who he was, he was docile enough not to argue about it. He was quite cheerful, even, in a vague sort of way, and seemed glad enough to have my company. To my suggestion that I should take him home, he simply said that he didn't mind. It was a little unnerving, that apparent lack of any personal desire. As soon as I could I fixed up our departure. I made a confidant of an acquaintance in the consular office at Hankow, and thus the necessary passport and so on were made out without the fuss there might otherwise have been. Indeed, it seemed to me that for Conway's sake the whole business had better be kept free from publicity and newspaper headlines, and I'm glad to say I succeeded in that. It would have been jam, of course, for the press.

"Well, we made our exit from China in quite a normal way. We sailed down the Yangtze to Nanking, and then took a train for Shanghai. There was a Jap liner leaving for 'Frisco that same night, so we made a great rush and got on board."

"You did a tremendous lot for him," I said.

Rutherford did not deny it. "I don't think I should have done quite as much for anyone else," he answered. "But there was something about the fellow, and always had been—it's hard to explain, but it made one enjoy doing what one could."

"Yes," I agreed. "He had a peculiar charm, a sort of winsomeness that's pleasant to remember even now when I picture it, though, of course, I think of him still as a schoolboy in cricket flannels."

"A pity you didn't know him at Oxford. He was just brilliant—there's no other word. After the War people said he was different. I think myself he was. But I can't help feeling that with all his gifts he ought to have been doing bigger work. All that Britannic Majesty stuff isn't my idea of a great man's career. And Conway was—or should have been—*great*. You and I have both known him, and I don't think I'm exaggerating when I say it's an experience we shan't ever forget. And even when he and I met in the middle of China, with his mind a blank and his past a mystery, there was still that queer core of attractiveness in him."

Rutherford paused reminiscently and then continued: "As you can imagine, we renewed our old friendship on the ship. I told him as much as I knew about himself, and he listened with an attention that might almost have seemed a little absurd. He remembered everything quite clearly since his arrival at Chung-Kiang, and another point that may interest you is that he hadn't forgotten languages. He told me, for instance, that he knew he must have had something to do with India, because he could speak Hindostani.

"At Yokohama the ship filled up, and among the new passengers was Sieveking, the pianist, en route for a concert tour in the States.

He was at our dining table and sometimes talked with Conway in German. That will show you how outwardly normal Conway was. Apart from his loss of memory, which didn't show in ordinary intercourse, there couldn't have seemed much wrong with him.

"A few nights after leaving Japan, Sieveking was prevailed upon to give a piano recital on board, and Conway and I went to hear him. He played well, of course, some Brahms and Scarlatti, and a lot of Chopin. Once or twice I glanced at Conway and judged that he was enjoying it all, which appeared very natural, in view of his own musical past. At the end of the programme the show lengthened out into an informal series of encores which Sieveking bestowed, very amiably, I thought, upon a few enthusiasts grouped round the piano. Again he played mostly Chopin; he rather specializes in it, you know. At last he left the piano and moved towards the door, still followed by admirers, but evidently feeling that he had done enough for them. In the meantime a rather odd thing was beginning to happen. Conway had sat down at the keyboard and was playing some rapid, lively piece that I didn't recognize, but which drew Sieveking back in great excitement to ask what it was. Conway, after a long and rather strange silence, could only reply that he didn't know. Sieveking exclaimed that it was incredible, and grew more excited still. Conway then made what appeared to be a tremendous physical and mental effort to remember, and said at last that the thing was a Chopin study. I didn't think myself it could be, and I wasn't surprised when Sieveking denied it absolutely. Conway, however, grew suddenly quite indignant about the matter—which startled me, because up to then he had shown so little emotion about anything. 'My dear fellow,' Sieveking remonstrated, 'I know everything of Chopin's that exists, and I can assure you that he never wrote what you have just played. He might well have done so, because it's utterly his style, but he just didn't. I challenge you to show me the score in any of the editions.' To which Conway replied at length: 'Oh, yes, I remember now, it was never printed. I only know it myself from meeting a man who used to be one of Chopin's pupils . . . . Here's another unpublished thing I learned from him.'"

Rutherford studied me with his eyes as he went on: "I don't know if you're a musician, but even if you're not, I daresay you'll be able to imagine something of Sieveking's excitement, and mine, too, as Conway continued to play. To me, of course, it was a sudden and quite mystifying glimpse into his past, the first clue of any kind that had escaped. Sieveking was naturally engrossed in the musical problem, which was perplexing enough, as you'll realize when I remind you that Chopin died in 1849.

"The whole incident was so unfathomable, in a sense, that perhaps I should add that there were at least a dozen witnesses of it, including a California university professor of some repute. Of course, it was easy to say that Conway's explanation was chronologically impossible, or almost so; but there was still the music itself to be explained. If it wasn't what Conway said it was, then what *was* it? Sieveking assured me that if those two pieces were published, they would be in every virtuoso's repertoire within six months. Even if this is an exaggeration, it shows Sieveking's opinion of them. After much argument at the time, we weren't able to settle anything, for Conway stuck to his story, and as he was beginning to look fatigued, I was anxious to get him away from the crowd and off to bed. The last episode was about making some gramophone records. Sieveking said he would fix up all arrangements as soon as he reached America, and Conway gave his promise to play before the microphone. I often feel it was a great pity, from every point of view, that he wasn't able to keep his word."

Rutherford glanced at his watch and impressed on me that I should have plenty of time to catch my train, since his story was practically finished. "Because that night—the night after the recital—he got back his memory. We had both gone to bed and I was lying awake, when he came into my cabin and told me. His face had stiffened into what I can only describe as an expression of overwhelming sadness—a sort of universal sadness, if you know what I mean—something remote or impersonal, a *Wehmut* or *Weltschmerz*, or whatever the Germans call it. He said he could call to mind everything, that it had begun to come back to him during Sieveking's playing, though only in patches at first. He sat for a long while on the edge of my bed, and I let him take his own time and make his own method of telling me.

I said that I was glad his memory had returned, but sorry if he already wished that it hadn't. He looked up then and paid me what I shall always regard as a marvellously high compliment. 'Thank God, Rutherford,' he said, 'you are capable of imagining things.' After a while I dressed and persuaded him to do the same, and we walked up and down the boat deck. It was a calm night, starry and very warm, and the sea had a pale, sticky look, like condensed milk. Except for the vibration of the engines, we might have been pacing an esplanade. I let Conway go on in his own way, without questions at first. Somewhere about dawn he began to talk consecutively, and it was mid-morning and hot sunshine when he had finished. When I say 'finished' I don't mean that there was nothing more to tell me after that first confession. He filled in a good many important gaps during the next twenty-four hours. He was very unhappy, and couldn't have slept, so we talked almost constantly. About the middle of the following night the ship was due to reach Honolulu. We had drinks in my cabin the evening before; he left me about ten o'clock, and I never saw him again."

"You don't mean—" I had a picture in mind of a very calm, deliberate suicide I once saw on the mail boat from Holyhead to Kingstown.

Rutherford laughed. "Oh, Lord, no—he wasn't that sort. He just gave me the slip. It was easy enough to get ashore, but he must have found it hard to avoid being traced when I set people searching for him, as of course I did. Afterwards I learned that he'd managed to join the crew of a banana boat going south to Fiji."

"How did you get to know that?"

"Quite straightforwardly. He wrote to me, three months later, from Bangkok, enclosing a draft to pay the expenses I'd been put to on his account. He thanked me and said he was very fit. He also said he was about to set out on a long journey—to the northwest. That was all."

"Where did he mean?"

"Yes, it's pretty vague, isn't it? A good many places lie to the northwest of Bangkok. Even Berlin does, for that matter."

Rutherford paused and filled up my glass and his own. It had been a queer story—or else he had made it seem so; I hardly knew which.

The music part of it, though puzzling, did not interest me so much as the mystery of Conway's arrival at that Chinese mission hospital; and I made this comment. Rutherford answered that in point of fact they were both parts of the same problem. "Well, how *did* he get to Chung-Kiang?" I asked. "I suppose he told you all about it that night on the ship?"

"He told me something about it, and it would be absurd for me, after letting you know so much, to be secretive about the rest. Only, to begin with, it's a longish sort of tale, and there wouldn't be time even to outline it before you'd have to be off for your train. And besides, as it happens, there's a more convenient way. I'm a little diffident about revealing the tricks of my dishonourable calling, but the truth is, Conway's story, as I pondered over it afterwards, appealed to me enormously. I had begun by making simple notes after our various conversations on the ship, so that I shouldn't forget details; later, as certain aspects of the thing began to grip me, I had the urge to do more—to fashion the written and recollected fragments into a single narrative. By that I don't mean that I invented or altered anything. There was quite enough material in what he told me: he was a fluent talker and had a natural gift for communicating an atmosphere. Also, I suppose, I felt I was beginning to understand the man himself." He went to an attaché case, and took out a bundle of typed manuscript. "Well, here it is, anyhow, and you can make what you like of it."

"By which I suppose you mean that I'm not expected to believe it?"

"Oh, hardly so definite a warning as that. But mind, if you *do* believe, it will be for Tertullian's famous reason—you remember? *quia impossibile est.* Not a bad argument, maybe. Let me know what you think, at all events."

I took the manuscript away with me and read most of it on the Ostend express. I intended returning it with a long letter when I reached England, but there were delays, and before I could post it I got a short note from Rutherford to say that he was off on his wanderings again and would have no settled address for some months. He was going to Kashmir, he wrote, and thence "east." I was not surprised.

Chapter 1

URING THAT THIRD WEEK of May the situation in Baskul had become much worse and, on the 20th, air force machines arrived by arrangement from Peshawar to evacuate the white residents. These numbered about eighty, and most were safely transported across the mountains in troop carriers. A few miscellaneous aircraft were also employed, among them being a cabin machine lent by the maharajah of Chandrapur. In this, about 10 A.M., four passengers embarked: Miss Roberta Brinklow, of the Eastern Mission; Henry D. Barnard, a US citizen; Hugh Conway, H.M. Consul; and Captain Charles Mallinson, H.M. Vice-Consul.

These names are as they appeared later in Indian and British newspapers.

CONWAY WAS THIRTY-SEVEN. He had been at Baskul for two years, in a job which now, in the light of events, could be regarded as a persistent backing of the wrong horse. A stage of his life was finished; in a few weeks' time, or perhaps after a few months' leave in England, he would be sent somewhere else. Tokyo or Tehran, Manila or Muscat; people in his profession never knew what was coming. He had been ten years in the Consular Service, long enough to assess his own chances as shrewdly as he was apt to do those of others. He knew that the plums were not for him; but it was genuinely consoling, and not merely sour grapes, to reflect that he had no taste for plums. He preferred the less formal and more picturesque jobs that were on offer, and as these were often not good ones, it had doubtless seemed to others that he was playing his cards rather badly. Actually, to suit his own tastes, he felt he had played them rather well; he had had a varied and moderately enjoyable decade.

He was tall, deeply bronzed, with brown short-cropped hair and slate-blue eyes. He was inclined to look severe and brooding until he laughed, and then (but it happened not so very often) he looked boyish. There was a slight nervous twitch near the left eye which was usually noticeable when he worked too hard or drank too much, and as he had been packing and destroying documents throughout the whole of the day and night preceding the evacuation, the twitch was very conspicuous when he climbed into the aeroplane. He was tired out, and overwhelmingly glad that he had contrived to be sent in the maharajah's luxurious airliner instead of in one of the crowded troop carriers. He spread himself indulgently in the basket seat as the plane soared aloft. He was the sort of man who, being used to major hardships, expected minor comforts by way of compensation. Cheerfully he might endure the rigours of the road to Samarkand, but from London to Paris he would spend his last tenner on the Golden Arrow.

It was after the flight had lasted more than an hour that Mallinson said he thought the pilot wasn't keeping a straight course. Mallinson sat immediately in front. He was a youngster in his middle twenties, pink-cheeked, intelligent without being intellectual, beset with public-school limitations, but also with their excellences. Failure to pass an examination was the chief cause of his being sent to Baskul, where Conway had had six months of his company and had grown to like him.

But Conway did not want to make the effort that an aeroplane conversation demands. He opened his eyes drowsily and replied that whatever the course taken, the pilot presumably knew best.

Half an hour later, when weariness and the drone of the engine had lulled him nearly to sleep, Mallinson disturbed him again. "I say, Conway, I thought Fenner was piloting us?"

"Well, isn't he?"

"The chap turned his head just now and I'll swear it wasn't him."

"It's hard to tell, through that glass panel."

"I'd know Fenner's face anywhere."

"Well, then, it must be someone else. I don't see that it matters."

"But Fenner told me definitely that he was taking this machine."

"They must have changed their minds and given him one of the others."

"Well, who is this man, then?"

"My dear boy, how should I know? You don't suppose I've memorized the face of every flight lieutenant in the air force, do you?"

"I know a good many of them, anyway, but I don't recognize this fellow."

"Then he must belong to the minority whom you don't know.' Conway smiled and added: "When we arrive in Peshawar very soon you can make his acquaintance and ask him all about himself."

"At this rate we shan't get to Peshawar at all. The man's right off his course. And I'm not surprised, either—flying so damned high he can't see where he is."

Conway was not bothering. He was used to air travel, and took things for granted. Besides, there was nothing particular he was eager to do when he got to Peshawar, and no one particular he was eager to see; so it was a matter of complete indifference to him whether the journey took four hours or six. He was unmarried; there would be no tender greetings on arrival. He had friends, and a few of them would probably take him to the club and stand him drinks; it was a pleasant prospect, but not one to sigh for in anticipation.

Nor did he sigh retrospectively when he viewed the equally pleasant but not wholly satisfying vista of the past decade. Changeable, fair intervals, becoming rather unsettled; it had been his own meteorological summary during that time, as well as the world's. He thought of Baskul, Pekin, Macao, and other places—he had moved about pretty often. Remotest of all was Oxford, where he had had a couple of years of donhood after the war, lecturing on Oriental history, breathing dust in sunny libraries, cruising down the High on a push bicycle. The vision attracted, but did not stir him; there was a sense in which he felt that he was still a part of all that he might have been.

A familiar gastric lurch informed him that the plane was beginning to descend. He felt tempted to rag Mallinson about his fidgets, and would perhaps have done so had not the youth risen abruptly, bumping his head against the roof and waking Barnard, the American, who had been dozing in his seat at the other side of the narrow gangway. "My God!" Mallinson cried, peering through the window. "Look down there!"

Conway looked. The view was certainly not what he had expected, if, indeed, he had expected anything. Instead of the trim, geometrically laid-out cantonments and the larger oblongs of the hangars, nothing was visible but an opaque mist veiling an immense, sun-brown desolation. The plane, though descending rapidly, was still at a height unusual for ordinary flying. Long, corrugated mountain ridges could be picked out, perhaps a mile or so closer than the cloudier smudge of the valleys. It was typical frontier scenery, though Conway had never viewed it before from such an altitude. It was also, which struck him as odd, nowhere that he could imagine near Peshawar. "I don't recognize this part of the world," he commented. Then, more privately, for he did not wish to alarm the others, he added into Mallinson's ear: "Looks as if you're right. The man's lost his way."

The plane was swooping down at a tremendous speed, and as it did so, the air grew hotter; the scorched earth below was like an oven with the door suddenly opened. One mountaintop after another lifted itself above the horizon in craggy silhouette; now the flight was along a curving valley, the base of which was strewn with rocks and the debris of dried-up watercourses. It looked like a floor littered with nutshells. The plane bumped and tossed in air pockets as uncomfortably as a rowing boat in a swell. All four passengers had to hold on to their seats.

"Looks like he wants to land!" shouted the American hoarsely.

"He can't!" Mallinson retorted. "He'd be simply mad if he tried to! He'll crash and then—"

But the pilot did land. A small cleared space opened by the side of a gully, and with considerable skill the machine was jolted and heaved to a standstill. What happened after that, however, was more puzzling and less reassuring. A swarm of bearded and turbaned tribesmen came forward from all directions, surrounding the machine and effectively preventing anyone from getting out of it except the pilot. The latter clambered to earth and held excited colloquy with them, during which proceeding it became clear that, so far from being Fenner, he was not an Englishman at all, and possibly not even a European. Meanwhile cans of petrol were fetched from a dump close by, and emptied into the exceptionally capacious tanks. Grins and disregarding silence met the shouts of the four imprisoned passengers, while the slightest attempt to alight provoked a menacing movement from a score of rifles. Conway, who knew a little Pushtu, harangued the tribesmen as well as he could in that language, but without effect; while the pilot's sole retort to any remarks addressed him in any language was a significant flourish of his revolver. Midday sunlight, blazing on the roof of the cabin, grilled the air inside till the occupants were almost fainting with the heat and with the exertion of their protests. They were quite powerless; it had been a condition of the evacuation that they should carry no arms.

When the tanks were at last screwed up, a petrol can filled with tepid water was handed through one of the cabin windows. No questions were answered, though it did not appear that the men were personally hostile. After a further parley the pilot climbed back into the cockpit, a Pathan clumsily swung the propeller, and the flight was resumed. The takeoff, in that confined space and with the extra petrol load, was even more skilful than the landing. The plane rose high into the hazy vapours; then turned east, as if setting a course. It was mid-afternoon.

A MOST EXTRAORDINARY and bewildering business! As the cooler air refreshed them, the passengers could hardly believe that it had really happened; it was an outrage to which none could recall any parallel, or suggest any precedent, in all the turbulent records of the frontier. It would have been incredible, indeed, had they not been victims of it themselves. It was quite natural that high indignation should follow incredulity, and anxious speculation only when indignation had worn itself out. Mallinson then developed the theory which, in the absence of any other, they found easiest to accept. They were being kidnapped for ransom. The trick was by no means new in itself, though this particular technique must be regarded as original. It was a little more comforting to feel that they were not making entirely virgin history; after all, there had been kidnappings before, and a good many of them had ended up all right. The tribesmen kept you in some lair in the mountains till the government paid up and you were released. You were treated quite decently, and as the money that had to be paid wasn't your own, the whole business was only unpleasant while it lasted. Afterwards, of course, the Air people sent a bombing squadron, and you were left with one good story to tell for the rest of your life. Mallinson enunciated the proposition a shade nervously; but Barnard, the American, chose to be heavily facetious. "Well, gentlemen, I daresay this is a cute idea on somebody's part, but I can't exactly see that your air force has covered itself with glory. You Britishers make jokes about the holdups in Chicago and all that, but I don't recollect any instance of a gunman running off with one of Uncle Sam's aeroplanes. And I should like to know, by the way, what this fellow did with the real pilot. Sandbagged him, I should reckon." He yawned. He was a large, fleshy man, with a hard-bitten face in which good-humoured wrinkles were not quite offset by pessimistic pouches. Nobody in Baskul had known much about him except that he had arrived from Persia, where it was presumed he had something to do with oil.

Conway meanwhile was busying himself with a very practical task. He had collected every scrap of paper that they all had, and was composing messages in various languages to be dropped to earth at intervals. It was a slender chance, in such sparsely populated country, but worth taking.

The fourth occupant, Miss Brinklow, sat tight-lipped and straight-backed, with few comments and no complaints. She was a small, rather leathery woman, with an air of having been compelled to attend a party at which there were goings-on that she could not wholly approve.

Conway had talked less than the two other men, for translating SOS messages into dialects was a mental exercise requiring concentration. He had, however, answered questions when asked, and had agreed, tentatively, with Mallinson's kidnapping theory. He had also agreed, to some extent, with Barnard's strictures on the air force. "Though one can see, of course, how it may have happened. With the place in commotion as it was, one man in flying kit would look very much like another. No one would think of doubting the bona fides of any man in the proper clothes who looked as if he knew his job. And this fellow *must* have known it—the signals, and so forth.

Pretty obvious, too, that he knows how to fly . . . still, I agree with you that it's the sort of thing that someone ought to get into hot water about. And somebody will, you may be sure, though I suspect he won't deserve it."

"Well, sir," responded Barnard, "I certainly do admire the way you manage to see both sides of the question. It's the right spirit to have, no doubt, even when you're being taken for a ride."

Americans, Conway reflected, had the knack of being able to say patronizing things without being offensive. He smiled tolerantly, but did not continue the conversation. His tiredness was of a kind that no amount of possible peril could stave off. Towards late afternoon, when Barnard and Mallinson, who had been arguing, appealed to him on some point, it appeared that he had fallen asleep.

"Dead beat," Mallinson commented. "And I don't wonder at it, after these last few weeks."

"You're his friend?" queried Barnard.

"I've worked with him at the Consulate. I happen to know that he hasn't been in bed for the last four nights. As a matter of fact, we're damned lucky in having him with us in a tight corner like this. Apart from knowing the languages, he's got a sort of way with him in dealing with people. If anyone can get us out of this mess, he'll do it. He's pretty cool about most things."

"Well, let him have his sleep, then," agreed Barnard.

Miss Brinklow made one of her rare remarks. "I think he *looks* like a very brave man," she said.

CONWAY WAS FAR less certain that he *was* a very brave man. He had closed his eyes in sheer physical fatigue, but without actually sleeping. He could hear and feel every movement of the plane, and he heard also, with mixed feelings, Mallinson's eulogy of himself. It was then that he had his doubts, recognizing a tight sensation in his stomach which was his own bodily reaction to a disquieting mental survey. He was not, as he knew well from experience, one of those persons who love danger for its own sake. There was an aspect of it which he sometimes enjoyed, an excitement, a purgative effect upon sluggish emotions, but he was far from fond of risking his life. Twelve years earlier he had grown to hate the perils of trench warfare in France, and had several times avoided death by declining to attempt valorous impossibilities. Even his D.S.O. had been won, not so much by physical courage, as by a certain hardly developed technique of endurance. And since the War, whenever there had been danger ahead, he had faced it with increasing lack of relish unless it promised extravagant dividends in thrills.

He still kept his eyes closed. He was touched, and a little dismayed, by what he had heard Mallinson say. It was his fate in life to have his equanimity always mistaken for pluck, whereas it was actually something much more dispassionate and much less virile. They were all in a damnably awkward situation, it seemed to him, and so far from being full of bravery about it, he felt chiefly an enormous distaste for whatever trouble might be in store. There was Miss Brinklow, for instance. He foresaw that in certain circumstances he would have to act on the supposition that because she was a woman she mattered far more than the rest of them put together, and he shrank from a situation in which such disproportionate behaviour might be unavoidable.

Nevertheless, when he showed signs of wakefulness, it was to Miss Brinklow that he spoke first. He realized that she was neither young nor pretty—negative virtues, but immensely helpful ones in such difficulties as those in which they might soon find themselves. He was also rather sorry for her, because he suspected that neither Mallinson nor the American liked missionaries, especially female ones. He himself was unprejudiced, but he was afraid she would find his open mind a less familiar and therefore an even more disconcerting phenomenon. "We seem to be in a queer fix," he said, leaning forward to her ear, "but I'm glad you're taking it calmly. I don't really think anything dreadful is going to happen to us."

"I'm certain it won't if you can prevent it," she answered; which did not console him.

"You must let me know if there is anything we can do to make you more comfortable."

Barnard caught the word. "Comfortable?" he echoed raucously. "Why, of course we're comfortable. We're just enjoying the trip. Pity we haven't a pack of cards—we could make up a bridge four."

Conway welcomed the spirit of the remark, though he disliked bridge. "I don't suppose Miss Brinklow plays," he said, smiling.

But the missionary turned round briskly to retort: "Indeed I do, and I could never see any harm in cards at all. There's nothing against them in the Bible."

They all laughed, and seemed obliged to her for providing an excuse. At any rate, Conway thought, she wasn't hysterical.

ALL AFTERNOON the plane had soared through the thin mists of the upper atmosphere, far too high to give clear sight of what lay beneath. Sometimes, at longish intervals, the veil was torn for a moment, to display the jagged outline of a peak, or the glint of some unknown stream. The direction could be determined roughly from the sun; it was still east, with occasional twists to the north; but whither it had led depended on the speed of travel, which Conway could not judge with any accuracy. It seemed likely, though, that the flight must already have exhausted a good deal of the petrol; though that again depended on uncertain factors. Conway had no technical knowledge of aircraft, but he was sure that the pilot, whoever he might be, was altogether an expert. That halt in the rock-strewn valley had demonstrated it, and also other incidents since. And Conway could not repress a feeling that was always his in the presence of any superb and indisputable competence. He was so used to being appealed to for help that mere awareness of someone who would neither ask nor need it was slightly tranquillizing, even amidst the greater perplexities of the future. But he did not expect his companions to share such a tenuous emotion. He recognized that they were likely to have far more personal reasons for anxiety than he had himself. Mallinson, for instance, was engaged to a girl in England; Barnard might be married; Miss Brinklow had her work, vocation, or however she might regard it. Mallinson, incidentally, was by far the least composed; as the hours passed he showed himself increasingly excitable—apt, also, to resent to Conway's face the very coolness which he had praised behind his back. Once, above the roar of the engine, a sharp storm of argument arose. "Look here," Mallinson shouted angrily, "are we bound to sit here twiddling our thumbs while this maniac does everything he damn well wants? What's to prevent us from smashing that panel and having it out with him?"

"Nothing at all," replied Conway, "except that he's armed and we're not, and that in any case, none of us would know how to bring the machine to earth afterwards."

"It can't be very hard, surely. I daresay you could do it."

"My dear Mallinson, why is it always *me* you expect to perform these miracles?"

"Well, anyway, this business is getting hellishly on my nerves. Can't we *make* the fellow come down?"

"How do you suggest it should be done?"

Mallinson was becoming more and more agitated. "Well, he's *there*, isn't he? About six feet away from us, and we're three men to one! Have we got to stare at his damned back all the time? At least we might force him to tell us what the game is."

"Very well, we'll see." Conway took a few paces forward to the partition between the cabin and the pilot's cockpit, which was situated in front and somewhat above. There was a pane of glass, about six inches square and made to slide open, through which the pilot, by turning his head and stooping slightly, could communicate with his passengers. Conway tapped on this with his knuckles. The response was almost comically as he had expected. The glass panel slid sideways and the barrel of a revolver obtruded. Not a word; just that. Conway retreated without arguing the point, and the panel slid back again.

Mallinson, who had watched the incident, was only partly satisfied. "I don't suppose he'd have dared to shoot," he commented. "It's probably bluff."

"Quite," agreed Conway, "but I'd rather leave you to make sure."

"Well, I do feel we ought to put up some sort of a fight before giving in tamely like this."

Conway was sympathetic. He recognized the convention, with all its associations of red-coated soldiers and school history books, that Englishmen fear nothing, never surrender, and are never defeated. He said: "Putting up a fight without a decent chance of winning is a poor game, and I'm not that sort of hero."

"Good for you, sir," interposed Barnard heartily. "When some-body's got you by the short hairs you may as well give in pleasantly and admit it. For my part I'm going to enjoy life while it lasts and have a cigar. I hope you don't think a little bit of extra danger mat-ters to us?"

"Not so far as I'm concerned, but it might bother Miss Brinklow."

Barnard was quick to make amends. "Pardon me, madam, but do you very much object if I smoke?"

"Not at all," she answered graciously. "I don't do so myself, but I just love the smell of a cigar."

Conway felt that of all the women who could possibly have made such a remark, she was easily the most typical. Anyhow, Mallinson's excitement had calmed a little, and to show friendliness he offered him a cigarette, though he did not light one himself. "I know how you feel," he said gently. "It's a bad outlook, and it's all the worse, in some ways, because there isn't much we can do about it."

"And all the better, too, in other ways," he could not help adding to himself. For he was still immensely fatigued. There was also in his nature a trait which some people might have called laziness, though it was not quite that. No one was capable of harder work, when it had to be done, and few could better shoulder responsibility; but the facts remained that he was not passionately fond of activity, and did not enjoy responsibility at all. Both were included in his job, and he made the best of them, but he was always ready to give way to any-one else who could function as well or better. It was partly this, no doubt, that had made his success in the Service less striking than it might have been. He was not ambitious enough to shove his way past others, or to make an important parade of doing nothing when there was really nothing doing. His dispatches were sometimes laconic to the point of curtness, and his calm in emergencies, though admired, was often suspected of being too sincere. Authority likes to feel that a man is imposing some effort on himself, and that his apparent non-chalance is only a cloak to disguise an outfit of well-bred emotions. With Conway the dark suspicion had sometimes been current that he really was as unruffled as he looked, and that whatever happened, he did not give a damn. But this, too, like the laziness, was an imperfect interpretation. What most observers failed to perceive in him was something quite bafflingly simple—a love of quietness, contemplation, and being alone.

Now, since he was so inclined and there was nothing else to do, he leaned back in the basket chair and went definitely to sleep. When he woke he noticed that the others, despite their various anxieties, had likewise succumbed. Miss Brinklow was sitting bolt upright with her eyes closed, like some rather dingy and outmoded idol; Mallinson had lolled forward in his place with his chin in the palm of a hand. The American was even snoring. Very sensible of them all, Conway thought; there was no point in wearying themselves with shouting. But immediately he was aware of certain physical sensations in himself—slight dizziness and heart-thumping and a tendency to inhale sharply and with effort. He remembered similar symptoms once before—in Switzerland.

Then he turned to the window and gazed out. The surrounding sky had cleared completely, and in the light of late afternoon there came to him a vision which, for the instant, snatched the remaining breath out of his lungs. Far away, at the very limit of distance, lay range upon range of snow peaks, festooned with glaciers, and floating, in appearance, upon vast levels of cloud. They compassed the whole arc of the circle, merging towards the west in a horizon that was fierce, almost garish in colouring, like an impressionist backdrop done by some half-mad genius. And meanwhile, the plane, on that stupendous stage, was droning over an abyss in face of a sheer white wall that seemed part of the sky itself until the sun caught it. Then, like a dozen piled-up Jungfraus seen from Mürren, it flamed into superb and dazzling incandescence.

Conway was not apt to be easily impressed, and as a rule he did not care for "views," especially the more famous ones for which thoughtful municipalities provide garden seats. Once, on being taken to Tiger Hill, near Darjeeling, to watch the sun rise on Everest, he had found the highest mountain in the world a definite disappointment. But this fearsome spectacle beyond the windowpane was of different calibre; it had no air of posing to be admired. There was something raw and monstrous about those uncompromising ice cliffs, and a certain sublime impertinence in approaching them thus. He pondered, envisaging maps, calculating distances, estimating times and speeds. Then he became aware that Mallinson had wakened also. He touched the youth on the arm.

Chapter 2

T WAS TYPICAL OF CONWAY that he let the others waken for themselves, and made small response to their exclamations of astonishment; yet later, when Barnard sought his opinion, gave it with something of the detached fluency of a university professor elucidating a problem. He thought it likely, he said, that they were still in India; they had been flying east for several hours, too high to see much, but probably the course had been along some river valley—one stretching roughly east and west. "I wish I hadn't to rely on memory, but my impression is that the valley of the upper Indus fits in well enough. That would have brought us by now to a very spectacular part of the world, and, as you see, so it has."

"You recognize where we are, then?" Barnard interrupted.

"Well, no—I've never been anywhere near here before, but I wouldn't be surprised if that mountain is Nanga Parbat, the one Mummery lost his life on. In structure and general layout it seems in accord with all I've heard about it."

"You are a mountaineer yourself?"

"In my younger days I was keen. Only the usual Swiss climbs, of course."

Mallinson intervened peevishly: "There'd be more point in discussing where we're going to. I wish to God somebody could tell us."

"Well, it looks to me as if we're heading for that range yonder," said Barnard. "Don't you think so, Conway? You'll excuse me calling you that, but if we're all going to have a little adventure together, it's a pity to stand on ceremony."

Conway thought it very natural that anyone should call him by his own name, and found Barnard's apologies for so doing a trifle needless. "Oh, certainly," he agreed, and added: "I think that range must be the Karakorams. There are several passes if our man intends to cross them."

"Our man?" exclaimed Mallinson. "You mean our maniac! I reckon it's time we dropped the kidnapping theory. We're far past the frontier country by now—there aren't any tribes living around here. The only explanation I can think of is that the fellow's a raving lunatic. Would anybody except a lunatic fly into this sort of country?"

"I know that nobody except a damn fine airman *could*," retorted Barnard. "I never was great at geography, but I understand that these are reputed to be the highest mountains in the world, and if that's so, it'll be a pretty first-class performance to cross them."

"And also the will of God," put in Miss Brinklow unexpectedly.

Conway did not offer his opinion. The will of God or the lunacy of man—it seemed to him that you could take your choice, if you wanted a good enough reason for most things. Or, alternatively (and he thought of it as he contemplated the small orderliness of the cabin against the window background of such frantic natural scenery), the will of man and the lunacy of God. It must be satisfying to be quite certain which way to look at it. Then, while he watched and pondered, a strange transformation took place. The light turned to bluish over the whole mountain, with the lower slopes darkening to violet. Something deeper than his usual aloofness rose in him—not quite excitement, still less fear, but a sharp intensity of expectation. He said: "You're quite right, Barnard, this affair grows more and more remarkable."

"Remarkable or not, I don't feel inclined to propose a vote of thanks about it," Mallinson persisted. "We didn't ask to be brought here, and heaven knows what we shall do when we get *there*, wherever *there* is. And I don't see that it's any less of an outrage because the fellow happens to be a stunt flyer. Even if he is, he can be just as much a lunatic. I once heard of a pilot going mad in midair. This fellow must have been mad from the beginning. That's my theory, Conway."

Conway was silent. He found it irksome to be continually shouting above the roar of the machine, and after all, there was little point in arguing possibilities. But when Mallinson pressed for an opinion, he said: "Very well-organized lunacy, you know. Don't forget the landing for petrol, and also that this was the only machine that could climb to such a height."

"That doesn't prove he isn't mad. He may have been mad enough to arrange everything."

"Yes, of course, that's possible."

"Well, then, we've got to decide on a plan of action. What are we going to do when he comes to earth? If he doesn't crash and kill us all, that is. What are we going to *do*? Rush forward and congratulate him on his marvellous flight, I suppose."

"Not on your life," answered Barnard. "I'll leave you to do all the rushing forward."

Again Conway was loth to prolong the argument, especially since the American, with his level-headed banter, seemed quite capable of handling it himself. Already Conway found himself reflecting that the party might have been far less fortunately constituted. Only Mallinson was inclined to be cantankerous, and that might partly be due to the altitude. Rarefied air had different effects on people; Conway, for instance, derived from it a combination of mental clarity and physical apathy that was not unpleasant. Indeed, he breathed the clear cold air in little spasms of content. The whole situation, no doubt, was appalling, but he had no power at the moment to resent anything that proceeded so purposefully and with such captivating interest.

And there came over him, too, as he stared at that superb mountain-piece, a glow of satisfaction that there were such places still left on earth, distant, inaccessible, as yet unhumanized. The icy rampart of the Karakorams was now more striking than ever against the northern sky, which had become mouse-coloured and sinister; the peaks had a chill gleam; utterly majestic and remote, their very namelessness had dignity. Those few thousand feet by which they fell short of the known giants might save them eternally from the climbing expedition; they offered a less tempting lure to the record-breaker. Conway was the antithesis of such a type; he was inclined to see vulgarity in the Western ideal of superlatives, and "the utmost for the highest" seemed to him a less reasonable and perhaps more common-place proposition than "the much for the high." He did not, in fact, care for excessive striving, and he was bored by mere exploits.

While he was still contemplating the scene, twilight fell, steeping the depths in a rich, velvet gloom that spread upwards like a dye. Then the whole range, much nearer now, paled into fresh splendour; a full moon rose, touching each peak in succession like some celestial lamplighter, until the long horizon glittered against a blue-black sky. The air grew cold and a wind sprang up, tossing the machine uncom-fortably. These new distresses lowered the spirits of the passengers; it had not been reckoned that the flight could go on after dusk, and now the last hope lay in the exhaustion of petrol. That, however, was bound to come soon. Mallinson began to argue about it, and Conway, with some reluctance, for he really did not know, gave as his estimate that the utmost distance might be anything up to a thousand miles, of which they must already have covered most. "Well, where would that bring us?" queried the youth miserably.

"It's not easy to judge, but probably some part of Tibet. If these are the Karakorams, Tibet lies beyond. One of the crests, by the way, must be K2, which is generally counted the second highest mountain in the world."

"Next on the list after Everest," commented Barnard. "Gee, this is some scenery."

"And from a climber's point of view much stiffer than Everest. The Duke of Abruzzi gave it up as an absolutely impossible peak."

"*Oh, God!*" muttered Mallinson testily, but Barnard laughed. "I guess you must be the official guide on this trip, Conway, and I'll allow that if only I'd got a flask of café cognac I wouldn't care if it's Tibet or Tennessee."

"But what are we going to do about it?" urged Mallinson again. "Why are we here? What can be the point of it all? I don't see how you can make jokes about it."

"Well, it's as good as making a scene about it, young feller. Besides, if the man *is* a loonie, as you've suggested, there probably *isn't* any point."

A full moon rose, touching each peak in succession

"He *must* be mad. I can't think of any other explanation. Can you, Conway?"

Conway shook his head.

Miss Brinklow turned round, as she might have done during the interval of a play. "As you haven't asked my opinion, perhaps I oughtn't to give it," she began, with shrill modesty, "but I should like to say that I agree with Mr. Mallinson. I'm sure the poor man can't be quite right in his head. The pilot, I mean, of course. There would be no excuse for him, anyhow, if he were *not* mad." She added, shouting confidentially above the din: "And do you know, this is my first trip in the air! My very first! Nothing would ever induce me to do it before, though a friend of mine tried her very best to persuade me to fly from London to Paris."

"And now you're flying from India to Tibet instead," said Barnard. "That's the way things happen."

She went on: "I once knew a missionary who had been to Tibet. He said the Tibetans were very odd people. They believe we are descended from monkeys."

"Real smart of 'em."

"Oh dear no, I don't mean in the modern way. They've had the belief for hundreds of years—it's only one of their superstitions. Of course I'm against all of it myself, and I think Darwin was far worse than any Tibetan. I take my stand on the Bible."

"Fundamentalist, I suppose?"

But Miss Brinklow did not appear to understand the term. "I used to belong to the L.M.S.," she shrieked, "but I disagreed with them about infant baptism."

Conway continued to feel that this was a rather comic remark long after it had occurred to him that the initials were those of the London Missionary Society. Still picturing the inconveniences of holding a theological argument at Euston Station, he began to think that there was something slightly fascinating about Miss Brinklow. He even wondered if he could offer her any article of his clothing for the night, but decided at length that her constitution was probably wirier than his. So he huddled up, closed his eyes, and went quite easily and peacefully to sleep. And the flight proceeded.

SUDDENLY THEY WERE all wakened by a lurch of the machine. Conway's head struck the window, dazing him for the moment; a returning lurch sent him floundering between the two tiers of seats. It was much colder. The first thing he did, automatically, was to glance at his watch; it showed half-past one—he must have been asleep for some time. His ears were full of a loud, flapping sound, which he took to be imaginary until he realized that the engine had been shut off and that the plane was rushing against a gale. Then he stared through the window and could see the earth quite close, vague and snail-grey, scampering underneath. "He's going to land!" Mallinson shouted; and Barnard, who had also been flung out of his seat, responded with a saturnine: "If he's lucky." Miss Brinklow, whom the entire commotion seemed to have disturbed least of all, was adjusting her hat as calmly as if Dover Harbour were just in sight.

Presently the plane touched ground. But it was a bad landing this time—"Oh, my God, damned bad, *damned* bad!" Mallinson groaned as he clutched at his seat during ten seconds of crashing and swaying. Something was heard to strain and snap, and one of the tyres exploded. "That's done it," he added in tones of anguished pessimism. "A broken tailskid—we'll have to stay where we are now, that's certain."

Conway, never talkative at times of crisis, stretched his stiffened legs and felt his head where it had banged against the window. A bruise, nothing much. He must do something to help these people. But he was the last of the four to stand up when the plane came to rest. "Steady," he called out as Mallinson wrenched open the door of the cabin and prepared to make the jump to earth; and eerily, in the comparative silence, the youth's answer came: "No need to be steady—this looks like the end of the world—there's not a soul about, anyhow."

A moment later, chilled and shivering, they were all aware that this was so. With no sound in their ears save the fierce gusts of wind and their own crunching footsteps, they felt themselves at the mercy of something dour and savagely melancholy—a mood in which both earth and air were saturated. The moon looked to have disappeared behind clouds, and starlight illumined a tremendous emptiness heaving with wind. Without thought or knowledge, one could have guessed that this bleak world was mountain-high, and that the mountains rising from it were mountains on top of mountains. A range of them gleamed on a far horizon like a row of dog-teeth.

Mallinson, feverishly active, was already making for the cockpit. "I'm not scared of the fellow on land, whoever he is," he cried. "I'm going to tackle him right away . . . ."

The others watched apprehensively, hypnotized by the spectacle of such energy. Conway sprang after him, but too late to prevent the investigation. After a few seconds, however, the youth dropped down again, gripping his arm and muttering in a hoarse, sobered staccato: "I say, Conway, it's queer . . . I think the fellow's ill or dead or something . . . I can't get a word out of him. Come up and look . . . I took his revolver, at any rate."

"Better give it to me," said Conway, and though still rather dazed by the recent blow on his head, he nerved himself for action. Of all times and places and situations on earth, this seemed to him to combine the most hideous discomforts. He hoisted himself stiffly into a position from which he could see, not very well, into the enclosed cockpit. There was a strong smell of petrol, so he did not risk striking a match. He could just discern the pilot, huddled forward, his head sprawling over the controls. He shook him, unfastened his helmet, and loosened the clothes round his neck. A moment later he turned round to report: "Yes, there's something happened to him. We must get him out." But an observer might have added that something had happened to Conway as well. His voice was sharper, more incisive; no longer did he sound to be hovering on the brink of some profound doubtfulness. The time, the place, the cold, his fatigue, were now of less account; there was a job that simply had to be done, and the more conventional part of him was uppermost and preparing to do it.

With Barnard and Mallinson assisting, the pilot was extracted from his seat and lifted to the ground. He was unconscious, not dead. Conway had no particular medical knowledge, but, as to most men who have lived in outlandish places, the phenomena of illness were mostly familiar. "Possibly a heart attack brought on by the high altitude," he diagnosed, stooping over the unknown man. "We can do very little for him out here—there's no shelter from this infernal wind. Better get him inside the cabin, and ourselves too. We haven't any idea where we are, and it's hopeless to make a move until daylight."

The verdict and the suggestion were both accepted without dispute. Even Mallinson concurred. They carried the man into the cabin and laid him full length along the gangway between the seats. The interior was no warmer than outside, but offered a screen to the flurries of wind. It was the wind, before much time had passed, that became the central preoccupation of them all—the leitmotif, as it were, of the whole mournful night. It was not an ordinary wind. It was not merely a strong wind or a cold wind. It was somehow a frenzy that lived all around them, a master stamping and ranting over his own domain. It tilted the loaded machine and shook it viciously, and when Conway glanced through the windows it seemed as if the wind were whirling splinters of light out of the stars.

The stranger lay inert, while Conway, with difficulty in the dimness and confined space, made what examination he could by the light of matches. But it did not reveal much. "His heart's faint," he said at last, and then Miss Brinklow, after groping in her handbag, created a small sensation. "I wonder if this would be any use to the poor man," she proffered condescendingly. "I never touch a drop myself, but I always carry it with me in case of accidents. And this *is* a sort of accident, isn't it?"

"I should say it was," replied Conway with grimness. He unscrewed the bottle, smelt it, and poured some of the brandy into the man's mouth. "Just the stuff for him. Thanks." After an interval the slightest movement of eyelids was visible under the match-flame. Mallinson suddenly became hysterical. "I can't help it," he cried, laughing wildly. "We all look such a lot of damn fools striking matches over a corpse . . . . And he isn't much of a beauty, is he? Chink, I should say, if he's anything at all."

"Possibly." Conway's voice was level and rather severe. "But he's not a corpse yet. With a bit of luck we may bring him round."

"Luck! It'll be his luck, not ours."

"Don't be too sure. And shut up for the time being, anyhow."

There was enough of the schoolboy still in Mallinson to make him respond to the curt command of a senior, though he was obviously in poor control of himself. Conway, though sorry for him, was more concerned with the immediate problem of the pilot, since he, alone of them all, might be able to give some explanation of their plight. Conway had no desire to discuss the matter further in a merely speculative way; there had been enough of that during the journey. He was uneasy now beyond his continuing mental curiosity, for he was aware that the whole situation had ceased to be excitingly perilous and was threatening to become a trial of endurance ending in catastrophe. Keeping vigil throughout that gale-tormented night, he faced facts none the less frankly because he did not trouble to enunciate them to the others. He guessed that the flight had progressed far beyond the western range of the Himalayas towards the less-known heights of the Kuen-Luns. In that event they would by now have reached the loftiest and least hospitable part of the earth's surface, the Tibetan plateau, two miles high even in its lowest valleys, a vast, uninhabited, and largely unexplored region of windswept upland. Somewhere they were, in that forlorn country, marooned in far less comfort than on most desert islands. Then abruptly, as if to answer his curiosity by increasing it, a rather awe-inspiring change took place. The moon, which he had thought to be hidden by clouds, swung over the lip of some shadowy eminence and, whilst still not showing itself directly, unveiled the darkness ahead. Conway could see the outline of a long valley, with rounded, sad-looking low hills on either side, not very high from where they rose, and jet-black against the deep electric blue of the night sky. But it was to the head of the valley that his eyes were led irresistibly, for there, soaring into the gap, and magnificent in the full shimmer of moonlight, appeared what he took to be the loveliest mountain on earth. It was an almost perfect cone of snow, simple in outline as if a child had drawn it, and impossible to classify as to size, height, or nearness. It was so radiant, so serenely poised, that he wondered for a moment if it were real at all. Then, while he gazed, a tiny puff clouded the edge of the pyramid, giving life to the vision before the faint rumble of the avalanche confirmed it.

He had an impulse to rouse the others to share the spectacle, but decided after consideration that its effect might not be tranquillizing. Nor was it so, from a commonsense viewpoint; such virgin splendours merely emphasized the facts of isolation and danger. There was quite a probability that the nearest human settlement was hundreds of miles away. And they had no food; they were unarmed except for one revolver; the aeroplane was damaged and almost fuel-less, even if anyone had known how to fly. They had no clothes suited to the terrific chills and winds; Mallinson's motoring coat and his own ulster were quite inadequate, and even Miss Brinklow, woollied and muffled as for a polar expedition (ridiculous, he had thought, on first beholding her), could not be feeling happy. They were all, too, except himself, affected by the altitude. Even Barnard had sunk into melancholy under the strain. Mallinson was muttering to himself; it was clear what would happen to him if these hardships went on for long. In face of such distressful prospects Conway found himself quite unable to restrain an admiring glance at Miss Brinklow. She was not, he reflected, a normal person; no woman who taught Afghans to sing hymns could be considered so. But she was, after every calamity, still normally abnormal, and he was deeply obliged to her for it. "I hope you're not feeling too bad?" he said sympathetically, when he caught her eye.

"The soldiers during the War had to suffer worse things than this," she replied.

The comparison did not seem to Conway a very valuable one. In point of fact, he had never spent a night in the trenches quite so thoroughly unpleasant, though doubtless many others had. He concentrated his attention on the pilot, now breathing fitfully and sometimes slightly stirring. Probably Mallinson was right in guessing the man Chinese. He had the typical Mongol nose and cheekbones, despite his successful impersonation of a British flight lieutenant. Mallinson had called him ugly, but Conway, who had lived in China, thought him a fairly passable specimen, though now, in the burnished circle of match-flame, his pallid skin and gaping mouth were not pretty.

The night dragged on, as if each minute were something heavy and tangible that had to be pushed to make way for the next. Moonlight faded after a time, and with it that distant spectre of the mountain; then the triple mischiefs of darkness, cold, and wind increased until dawn. As at its signal, the wind dropped, leaving the world in compassionate quietude. Framed in the pale triangle ahead, the mountain showed again, grey at first, then silver, then pink as the earliest sun rays caught the summit. In the lessening gloom the valley itself took shape, revealing a floor of rock and shingle sloping upwards. It was not a friendly picture, but to Conway, as he surveyed, there came a queer perception of fineness in it, of something that had no romantic appeal at all, but a steely, almost an intellectual quality. The white pyramid in the distance compelled the mind's assent as passionlessly as a Euclidean theorem, and when at last the sun rose into a sky of deep delphinium blue, he felt only a little less than comfortable again.

As the air grew warmer the others wakened, and he suggested carrying the pilot into the open, where the sharp dry air and the sunlight might help to revive him. This was done, and they began a second and pleasanter vigil. Eventually the man opened his eyes and began to speak convulsively. His four passengers stooped over him, listening intently to sounds that were meaningless except to Conway, who occasionally made answers. After some time the man became weaker, talked with increasing difficulty, and finally died. That was about mid-morning.

CONWAY THEN TURNED to his companions. "I'm sorry to say he told me very little—little, I mean, compared with what we should like to know. Merely that we are in Tibet, which is obvious. He didn't give any coherent account of why he had brought us here, but he seemed to know the locality. He spoke a kind of Chinese that I don't understand very well, but I think he said something about a lamasery near here—along the valley, I gathered—where we could get food and shelter. Shangri-La, he called it. *La* is Tibetan for mountain pass. He was most emphatic that we should go there."

"Which doesn't seem to me any reason at all why we should," said

46

Mallinson. "After all, he was probably off his head. Wasn't he?"

"You know as much about that as I do. But if we don't go to this place, where else are we to go?"

"Anywhere you like, I don't care. All I'm certain of is that this Shangri-La, if it's in that direction, must be a few extra miles from civilization. I should feel happier if we were lessening the distance, not increasing it. Damnation, man, aren't you going to get us back?"

Conway replied patiently: "I don't think you properly understand the position, Mallinson. We're in a part of the world that no one knows very much about, except that it's difficult and dangerous even for a fully equipped expedition. Considering that hundreds of miles of this sort of country probably surround us on all sides, the notion of walking back to Peshawar doesn't strike me as very hopeful."

"I don't think I could possibly manage it," said Miss Brinklow seriously.

Barnard nodded. "It looks as if we're darned lucky, then, if this lamasery *is* just round the corner."

"Comparatively lucky, maybe," agreed Conway. "After all, we've no food, and as you can see for yourselves, the country isn't the kind it would be easy to live on. In a few hours we shall all be famished. And then tonight, if we were to stay here, we should have to face the wind and the cold again. It's not a pleasant prospect. Our only chance, it seems to me, is to find some other human beings, and where else should we begin looking for them except where we've been told they exist?"

"And what if it's a trap?" asked Mallinson, but Barnard supplied an answer. "A nice warm trap," he said, "with a piece of cheese in it, would suit me down to the ground."

They laughed, except Mallinson, who looked distraught and nerve-racked. Finally, Conway went on: "I take it, then, that we're all more or less agreed? There's an obvious way along the valley; it doesn't look too steep, though we shall have to take it slowly. In any case, we could no nothing here. We couldn't even bury this man without dynamite. Besides, the lamasery people may be able to supply us with porters for the journey back. We shall need them. I suggest we start at once, so that if we don't locate the place by late

47

afternoon we shall have time to return for another night in the cabin."

"And supposing we *do* locate it?" queried Mallinson, still intransigent. "Have we any guarantee that we shan't be murdered?"

"None at all. But I think it is a less, and perhaps also a preferable, risk to being starved or frozen to death." He added, feeling that such chilly logic might not be entirely suited for the occasion: "As a matter of fact, murder is the very last thing one would expect in a Buddhist monastery. It would be rather less likely than being killed in an English cathedral."

"Like Saint Thomas of Canterbury," said Miss Brinklow, nodding an emphatic agreement, but completely spoiling his point. Mallinson shrugged his shoulders and responded with melancholy irritation: "Very well, then, we'll be off to Shangri-La. Wherever and whatever it is, we'll try it. But let's hope it's not half-way up that mountain."

The remark served to fix their glances on the glittering cone towards which the valley pointed. Sheerly magnificent it looked in the full light of day; and then their gaze turned to a stare, for they could see, far away and approaching them down the slope, the figures of men. "Providence!" whispered Miss Brinklow.

Chapter 3

 ART OF CONWAY was always an onlooker, however active might be the rest. Just now, while waiting for the strangers to come nearer, he refused to be fussed into deciding what he might or mightn't do in any number of possible contingencies. And this was not bravery, or coolness, or any especially sublime confidence in his own power to make decisions on the spur of the moment. It was, if the worst view be taken, a form of indolence, an unwillingness to interrupt his mere spectator's interest in what was happening.

As the figures moved down the valley they revealed themselves to be a party of a dozen or more, carrying with them a hooded chair.

In this, a little later, could be discerned a person robed in blue. Conway could not imagine where they were all going, but it certainly seemed providential, as Miss Brinklow had said, that such a detachment should chance to be passing just there and then. As soon as he was within hailing distance he left his own party and walked ahead, though not hurriedly, for he knew that Orientals enjoy the ritual of meeting and like to take their time over it. Halting when a few yards off, he bowed with due courtesy. Much to his surprise the robed figure stepped from the chair, came forward with dignified deliberation, and held out his hand. Conway responded, and observed an old or elderly Chinese, grey-haired, clean-shaven, and rather pallidly decorative in a silk embroidered gown. He in his turn appeared to be submitting Conway to the same kind of reckoning. Then, in precise and perhaps too accurate English, he said: "I am from the lamasery of Shangri-La."

Conway bowed again, and after a suitable pause began to explain briefly the circumstances that had brought him and his three companions to such an unfrequented part of the world. At the end of the recital the Chinese made a gesture of understanding. "It is indeed remarkable," he said, and gazed reflectively at the damaged aeroplane. Then he added: "My name is Chang, if you would be so good as to present me to your friends."

Conway managed to smile urbanely. He was rather taken with this latest phenomenon, a Chinese who spoke perfect English and observed the social formalities of Bond Street amidst the wilds of Tibet. He turned to the others, who had by this time caught up and were regarding the encounter with varying degrees of astonishment. "Miss Brinklow . . . Mr. Barnard, who is an American . . . Mr. Mallinson . . . and my own name is Conway. We are all glad to see you, though the meeting is almost as puzzling as the fact of our being here at all. Indeed, we were just about to make our way to your lamasery, so it is doubly fortunate. If you could give us directions for the journey—"

"There is no need for that. I shall be delighted to act as your guide."

"But I could not think of putting you to such trouble. It is

49

exceedingly kind of you, but if the distance is not far—"

"It is not far, but it is not easy, either. I shall esteem it an honour to accompany you and your friends."

"But really—"

"I must insist."

Conway thought that the argument, in its context of place and circumstance, was in some danger of becoming ludicrous. "Very well," he responded. "I'm sure we are all most obliged."

Mallinson, who had been sombrely enduring these pleasantries, now interposed with something of the shrill acerbity of the barrack square. "Our stay won't be long," he announced curtly. "We shall pay for anything we have, and we should like to hire some of your men to help us on our journey back. We want to return to civilization as soon as possible."

"And are you so very certain that you are away from it?"

The query, delivered with much suavity, only stung the youth to further sharpness. "I'm quite sure I'm far away from where I want to be, and so are we all. We shall be grateful for temporary shelter, but we shall be more grateful still if you'll provide means for us to return. How long do you suppose the journey to India will take?"

"I really could not say at all."

"Well, I hope we're not going to have any trouble about it. I've had some experience of hiring native porters, and we shall expect you to use your influence to get us a square deal."

Conway felt that most of all this was rather needlessly truculent, and he was just about to intervene when the reply came, still with immense dignity: "I can only assure you, Mr. Mallinson, that you will be honourably treated and that ultimately you will have no regrets."

"*Ultimately?*" Mallinson exclaimed, pouncing on the word, but there was greater ease in avoiding a scene since wine and fruit were now on offer, having been unpacked by the marching party, stocky Tibetans in sheepskins, fur hats, and yak-skin boots. The wine had a pleasant flavour, not unlike a good hock, while the fruit included mangoes, perfectly ripened and almost painfully delicious after so many hours of fasting. Mallinson ate and drank with incurious relish; but Conway, relieved of immediate worries and reluctant to cherish distant ones, was wondering how mangoes could be cultivated at such an altitude. He was also interested in the mountain beyond the valley; it was a sensational peak, by any standards, and he was surprised that some traveller had not made much of it in the kind of book that a journey in Tibet invariably elicits. He climbed it in mind as he gazed, choosing a route by col and couloir until an exclamation from Mallinson drew his attention back to earth; he looked round then and saw that the Chinese had been earnestly regarding him. "You were contemplating the mountain, Mr. Conway?" came the enquiry.

"Yes. It's a fine sight. It has a name, I suppose?"

"It is called Karakal."

"I don't think I ever heard of it. Is it very high?"

"Over twenty-eight thousand feet."

"Indeed? I didn't realize there would be anything on that scale outside the Himalayas. Has it been properly surveyed? Whose are the measurements?"

"Whose would you expect, my dear sir? Is there anything incompatible between monasticism and trigonometry?"

Conway savoured the phrase and replied: "Oh, not at all—not at all." Then he laughed politely. He thought it a poorish joke, but one perhaps worth making the most of. Soon after that the journey to Shangri-La was begun.

ALL MORNING THE CLIMB proceeded, slowly and by easy gradients; but at such height the physical effort was considerable, and none had energy to spare to talk. The Chinese travelled luxuriously in his chair, which might have seemed unchivalrous had it not been absurd to picture Miss Brinklow in such a regal setting. Conway, whom the rarefied air troubled less than the rest, was at pains to catch the occasional chatter of the chair-bearers. He knew a very little Tibetan, just enough to gather that the men were glad to be returning to the lamasery. He could not, even had he wished, have continued to converse with their leader, since the latter, with eyes closed and face half hidden behind curtains, appeared to have the knack of instant and well-timed sleep.

Meanwhile the sun was warm; hunger and thirst had been appeased, if not satisfied; and the air, clean as from another planet, was more precious with every intake. One had to breathe consciously and deliberately, which, though disconcerting at first, induced after a time an almost ecstatic tranquillity of mind. The whole body moved in a single rhythm of breathing, walking, and thinking; the lungs, no longer discrete and automatic, were disciplined to harmony with mind and limb. Conway, in whom a mystical strain ran in curious consort with scepticism, found himself not unhappily puzzled over the sensation. Once or twice he spoke a cheerful word to Mallinson, but the youth was labouring under the strain of the ascent. Barnard also gasped asthmatically, while Miss Brinklow was engaged in some grim pulmonary warfare which for some reason she made efforts to conceal. "We're nearly at the top," Conway said encouragingly.

"I once ran for a train and felt just like this," she answered.

So also, Conway reflected, there were people who considered cider was just like champagne. It was a matter of palate.

He was surprised to find that beyond his puzzlement he had few misgivings, and none at all on his own behalf. There were moments in life when one opened wide one's soul just as one might open wide one's purse if an evening's entertainment were proving unexpectedly costly but also unexpectedly novel. Conway, on that breathless morning in sight of Karakal, made just such a willing, relieved, yet not excited response to the offer of new experience. After ten years in various parts of Asia he had attained to a somewhat fastidious valuation of places and happenings; and this he was bound to admit promised unusually.

About a couple of miles along the valley the ascent grew steeper, but by this time the sun was overclouded and a silvery mist obscured the view. Thunder and avalanches resounded from the snowfields above; the air took chill, and then, with the sudden changefulness of mountain regions, became bitterly cold. A flurry of wind and sleet drove up, drenching the party and adding immeasurably to their discomfort; even Conway felt at one moment that it would be impossible to go much farther. But

The journey to Shangri=La was begun

shortly afterwards it seemed that the summit of the ridge had been reached, for the chair-bearers halted to readjust their burden. The condition of Barnard and Mallinson, who were both suffering severely, led to continued delay; but the Tibetans were clearly anxious to press on, and made signs that the rest of the journey would be less fatiguing.

After these assurances it was disappointing to see them uncoiling ropes. "Do they mean to hang us already?" Barnard managed to exclaim, with desperate facetiousness; but the guides soon showed that their less sinister intention was merely to link the party together in ordinary mountaineering fashion. When they observed that Conway was familiar with rope-craft, they became much more respectful and allowed him to dispose the party in his own way. He put himself next to Mallinson, with Tibetans ahead and to the rear, and with Barnard and Miss Brinklow and more Tibetans farther back still. He was prompt to notice that the men, during their leader's continuing sleep, were inclined to let him deputize. He felt a familiar quickening of authority; if there were to be any difficult business he would give what he knew was his to give—confidence and command. He had been a first-class mountaineer in his time, and was still, no doubt, pretty good. "You've got to look after Barnard," he told Miss Brinklow, half jocularly, half meaning it; and she answered, with the coyness of an eagle: "I'll do my best, but you know, I've never been roped before."

But the next stage, though occasionally exciting, was less arduous than he had been prepared for, and a relief from the lung-bursting strain of the ascent. The track consisted of a traverse cut along the flank of a rock wall whose height above them the mist obscured. Perhaps mercifully it also obscured the abyss on the other side, though Conway, who had a good eye for heights, would have liked to see where he was. The path was scarcely more then two feet wide in places, and the manner in which the bearers manoeuvred the chair at such points drew his admiration almost as strongly as did the nerves of the occupant who could manage to sleep through it all. The Tibetans were reliable enough, but they seemed happier when the path widened and became slightly downhill. Then they began to

54

sing amongst themselves, lilting barbaric tunes that Conway could imagine orchestrated by Massenet for some Tibetan ballet. The rain ceased and the air grew warmer. "Well, it's quite certain we could never have found our way here by ourselves," said Conway, intending to be cheerful, but Mallinson did not find the remark very comforting. He was, in fact, acutely terrified, and in more danger of showing it now that the worst was over. "Should we be missing much?" he retorted bitterly. The track went on, more sharply downhill, and at one spot Conway found some edelweiss, the first welcome sign of more hospitable levels. But this, when he announced it, consoled Mallinson even less. "Good God, Conway, d'you fancy you're pottering about the Alps? What sort of hell's kitchen are we making for, that's what I'd like to know? And what's our plan of action when we get to it? *What are we going to do?*"

Conway said quietly, "If you'd had all the experiences I've had, you'd know that there are times in life when the most comfortable thing is to do nothing at all. Things happen to you and you just let them happen. The War was rather like that. One is fortunate if, as on this occasion, a touch of novelty seasons the unpleasantness."

"You're too confoundedly philosophic for me. That wasn't your mood during the trouble at Baskul."

"Of course not, because then there was a chance that I could alter events by my own actions. But now, for the moment at least, there's no such chance. We're here because we're here, if you want a reason. I've usually found it a soothing one."

"I suppose you realize the appalling job we shall have to get back by the way we've come. We've been slithering along the face of a perpendicular mountain for the last hour—I've been taking notice."

"So have I."

"Have you?" Mallinson coughed excitedly. "I daresay I'm being a nuisance, but I can't help it. I'm suspicious about all this. I feel we're doing far too much what these fellows want us to. They're getting us into a corner."

"Even if they are, the only alternative was to stay out of it and perish."

"I know that's logical, but it doesn't seem to help. I'm afraid I don't find it as easy as you do to accept the situation. I can't forget that two days ago we were in the Consulate at Baskul. To think of all that has happened since is a bit overwhelming to me. I'm sorry. I'm overwrought. It makes me realize how lucky I was to miss the War; I suppose I should have got hysterical about things. The whole world seems to have gone completely mad all round me. I must be pretty wild myself to be talking to you like this."

Conway shook his head. "My dear boy, not at all. You're twenty-four years old, and you're somewhere about two and a half miles up in the air: those are reasons enough for anything you may happen to feel at the moment. I think you've come through a trying ordeal extraordinarily well, better than I should at your age."

"But don't *you* feel the madness of it all? The way we flew over those mountains, and that awful waiting in the wind, and the pilot dying, and then meeting these fellows—doesn't it all seem nightmarish and incredible when you look back on it?"

"It does, of course."

"Then I wish I knew how you manage to keep so cool about everything."

"Do you really wish that? I'll tell you if you like, though you'll perhaps think me cynical. It's because so much else that I can look back on seems nightmarish too. This isn't the only mad part of the world, Mallinson. After all, if you *must* think of Baskul, do you remember just before we left how the revolutionaries were torturing their captives to get information? An ordinary washing mangle, quite effective, of course, but I don't think I ever saw anything more comically dreadful. And do you recollect the last message that came through before we were cut off? It was a circular from a Manchester textile firm asking if we knew of any trade openings in Baskul for the sale of corsets! Isn't that mad enough for you? Believe me, in arriving here the worst that can have happened is that we've exchanged one form of lunacy for another. And as for the War, if you'd been in it you'd have done the same as I did, learned how to funk with a stiff lip."

They were still conversing when a sharp but brief ascent robbed them of breath, inducing in a few paces all their earlier strain. Presently the ground levelled, and they stepped out of the mist into clear, sunny air. Ahead, and only a short distance away, lay the lamasery of Shangri-La.

To CONWAY, seeing it first, it might have been a vision fluttering out of that solitary rhythm in which lack of oxygen had encompassed all his faculties. It was, indeed, a strange and half-incredible sight. A group of coloured pavilions clung to the mountainside with none of the grim deliberation of a Rhineland castle, but rather with the chance delicacy of flower petals impaled upon a crag. It was superb and exquisite. An austere emotion carried the eye upward from milk-blue roofs to the grey rock bastion above, tremendous as the Wetterhorn above Grindelwald. Beyond that, in a dazzling pyramid, soared the snow slopes of Karakal. It might well be, Conway thought, the most terrifying mountainscape in the world, and he imagined the immense stress of snow and glacier against which the rock functioned as a gigantic retaining wall. Some day, perhaps, the whole mountain would split, and a half of Karakal's icy splendour come toppling into the valley. He wondered if the slightness of the risk combined with its fearfulness might even be found agreeably stimulating.

Hardly less an enticement was the downward prospect, for the mountain wall continued to drop, nearly perpendicularly, into a cleft that could only have been the result of some cataclysm in the far past. The floor of the valley, hazily distant, welcomed the eye with greenness; sheltered from winds, and surveyed rather than dominated by the lamasery, it looked to Conway a delightfully favoured place, though if it were inhabited its community must be completely isolated by the lofty and sheerly unscalable ranges on the farther side. Only to the lamasery did there appear to be any climbable egress at all. Conway experienced, as he gazed, a slight tightening of apprehension; Mallinson's misgivings were not, perhaps, to be wholly disregarded. But the feeling was only momentary, and soon merged in the deeper sensation, half mystical, half visual, of having reached at last some place that was an end, a finality.

He never exactly remembered how he and the others arrived at the lamasery, or with what formalities they were received, unroped, and ushered into the precincts. That thin air had a dream-like texture, matching the porcelain blue of the sky; with every breath and every glance he took in a deep anaesthetizing tranquillity that made him impervious alike to Mallinson's uneasiness, Barnard's witticisms, and Miss Brinklow's portrayal of a lady well prepared for the worst. He vaguely recollected surprise at finding the interior spacious, well warmed, and quite clean; but there was no time to do more than notice these qualities, for the Chinese had left his hooded chair and was already leading the way through various antechambers. He was quite affable now. "I must apologize," he said, "for leaving you to yourselves on the way, but the truth is, journeys of that kind don't suit me, and I have to take care of myself. I trust you were not too fatigued?"

"We managed," replied Conway with a wry smile.

"Excellent. And now, if you will come with me, I will show you to your apartments. No doubt you would like baths. Our accommodation is simple, but I hope adequate."

At this point Barnard, who was still affected by shortness of breath, gave vent to an asthmatic chuckle. "Well," he gasped, "I can't say I like your climate yet—the air seems to stick on my chest a bit—but you've certainly got a darned fine view out of your front windows. Do we all have to line up for the bathroom, or is this an American hotel?"

"I think you will find everything quite satisfactory, Mr. Barnard."

Miss Brinklow nodded primly. "I should hope so, indeed."

"And afterwards," continued the Chinese, "I should be greatly honoured if you will all join me at dinner."

Conway replied courteously. Only Mallinson had given no sign of his attitude in the face of these unlooked-for amenities. Like Barnard, he had been suffering from the altitude, but now, with an effort, he found breath to exclaim: "And afterwards, also, if you don't mind, we'll make our plans for getting away. The sooner the better, so far as I'm concerned."

Chapter 4

S O YOU SEE," Chang was saying, "we are less barbarian than you expected . . . ."

Conway, later that evening, was not disposed to deny it. He was enjoying that pleasant mingling of physical ease and mental alertness which seemed to him, of all sensations, the most truly civilized. So far, the appointments of Shangri-La had been all that he could have wished, certainly more than he could ever have expected. That a Tibetan monastery should possess a system of central heating was not, perhaps, so very remarkable in an age that supplied even Lhasa with telephones; but that it should combine the mechanics of Western hygiene with so much that was Eastern and traditional, struck him as exceedingly singular. The bath, for instance, in which he had recently luxuriated, had been of a delicate green porcelain, a product, according to inscription, of Akron, Ohio. Yet the native attendant had valeted him in Chinese fashion, cleansing his ears and nostrils, and passing a thin silk swab under his lower eyelids. He had wondered at the time if and how his three companions were receiving similar attentions.

Conway had lived for nearly a decade in China, not wholly in the bigger cities; and he counted it, all things considered, the happiest part of his life. He liked the Chinese, and felt at home with Chinese ways. In particular he liked Chinese cooking, with its subtle undertones of taste; and his first meal at Shangri-La had therefore conveyed a welcome familiarity. He suspected, too, that it might have contained some herb or drug to relieve respiration, for he not only felt a difference himself, but could observe a greater ease among his fellow guests. Chang, he noticed, ate nothing but a small portion of green salad, and took no wine. "You will excuse me," he had explained at the outset, "but my diet is very restricted: I am obliged to take care of myself."

It was the reason he had given before, and Conway wondered by what form of invalidism he was afflicted. Regarding him now more closely, he found it difficult to guess his age; his smallish and somehow undetailed features, together with the moist clay texture of his skin, gave him a look that might either have been that of a young man prematurely old or of an old man remarkably well preserved. He was by no means without attractiveness of a kind; a certain formalized courtesy hung about him in a fragrance too delicate to be detected till one had ceased to think about it. In his embroidered gown of blue silk, with the usual side-slashed skirt and tight-ankled trousers, all the hue of water-colour skies, he had a cool metallic charm which Conway found pleasing, though he knew it was not everybody's taste.

The atmosphere, in fact, was Chinese rather than specifically Tibetan; and this in itself gave Conway an agreeable sensation of being at home, though again it was one that he could not expect the others to share. The room, too, pleased him; it was admirably proportioned, and sparingly adorned with tapestries and one or two fine pieces of lacquer. Light was from paper lanterns, motionless in the still air. He felt a soothing comfort of mind and body, and his renewed speculations as to some possible drug were hardly apprehensive. Whatever it was, if it existed at all, it had relieved Barnard's breathlessness and Mallinson's truculence; both had dined well, finding satisfaction in eating rather than talk. Conway also had been hungry enough, and was not sorry that etiquette demanded gradualness in approaching matters of importance. He had never cared for hurrying a situation that was itself enjoyable, so that the technique well suited him. Not, indeed, until he had begun a cigarette did he give a gentle lead to his curiosity; he remarked then, addressing Chang: "You seem a very fortunate community, and most hospitable to strangers. I don't imagine, though, that you receive them often."

"Seldom indeed," replied the Chinese, with measured stateliness. "It is not a travelled part of the world."

Conway smiled at that. "You put the matter mildly. It looked to me, as I came, the most isolated spot I ever set eyes on. A separate culture might flourish here without contamination from the outside world."

"Contamination, would you say?"

"I use the word in reference to dance bands, cinemas, electric signs, and so on. Your plumbing is quite rightly as modern as you can get it—the only certain boon, to my mind, that the East can take from the West. I often think that the Romans were fortunate; their civilization reached as far as hot baths without touching the fatal knowledge of machinery."

Conway paused. He had been talking with an impromptu fluency which, though not insincere, was chiefly designed to create and control an atmosphere. He was rather good at that sort of thing. Only a willingness to respond to the superfine courtesy of the occasion prevented him from being more openly curious.

Miss Brinklow, however, had no such scruples. "Please," she said, though the word was by no means submissive, "will you tell us about the monastery?"

Chang raised his eyebrows in very gentle deprecation of such immediacy. "It will give me the greatest of pleasure, madam, so far as I am able. What exactly do you wish to know?"

"First of all, how many are there of you here, and what nationality do you belong to?" It was clear that her orderly mind was functioning no less professionally than at the Baskul mission house.

Chang replied: "Those of us in full lamahood number about fifty, and there are a few others, like myself, who have not yet attained to complete initiation. We shall do so in due course, it is to be hoped. Till then we are half-lamas, postulants, you might say. As for our racial origins, there are representatives of a great many nations among us, though it is perhaps natural that Tibetans and Chinese make up the majority."

Miss Brinklow would never shirk a conclusion, even a wrong one. "I see. It's really a native monastery, then. Is your head lama a Tibetan or a Chinese?"

"No."

"Are there any English?"

"Several."

"Dear me, that seems very remarkable." Miss Brinklow paused only for breath before continuing: "And now, tell me what you all believe in."

Conway leaned back with somewhat amused expectancy. He had always found pleasure in observing the impact of opposite mentalities; and Miss Brinklow's girl-guide forthrightness applied to Lamaistic philosophy promised to be entertaining. On the other hand, he did not wish his host to take fright. "That's rather a big question," he said, temporizingly.

But Miss Brinklow was in no mood to temporize. The wine, which had made the others more reposeful, seemed to have given her an extra liveliness. "Of course," she said with a gesture of magnanimity, "I believe in the true religion, but I'm broad-minded enough to admit that other people—foreigners, I mean—are quite often sincere in their views. And naturally in a monastery I wouldn't expect to be agreed with."

Her concession evoked a formal bow from Chang. "But why not, madam?" he replied in his precise and flavoured English. "Must we hold that because one religion is true, all others are bound to be false?"

"Well, of course, that's rather obvious, isn't it?"

Conway again interposed. "Really, I think we had better not argue. But Miss Brinklow shares my own curiosity about the motive of this unique establishment."

Chang answered rather slowly and in scarcely more than a whisper: "If I were to put it into a very few words, my dear sir, I should say that our prevalent belief is in moderation. We inculcate the virtue of avoiding excess of all kinds—even including, if you will pardon the paradox, excess of virtue itself. In the valley which you have seen, and in which there are several thousand inhabitants living under the control of our order, we have found that the principle makes for a considerable degree of happiness. We rule with moderate strictness, and in return we are satisfied with moderate obedience. And I think I can claim that our people are moderately sober, moderately chaste, and moderately honest."

Conway smiled. He thought it well expressed, besides which it made some appeal to his own temperament. "I think I understand. And I suppose the fellows who met us this morning belonged to your valley people?"

"Yes. I hope you had no fault to find with them during the journey?"

"Oh, no, none at all. I'm glad they were more than moderately surefooted, anyhow. You were careful, by the way, to say that the rule of moderation applied to *them*—am I to take it that it does not apply to your priesthood also?"

But at that Chang could only shake his head. "I regret, sir, that you have touched upon a matter which I may not discuss. I can only add that our community has various faiths and usages, but we are most of us moderately heretical about them. I am deeply grieved that at the moment I cannot say more."

"Please don't apologize. I am left with the pleasantest of speculations." Something in his own voice, as well as in his bodily sensations, gave Conway a renewed impression that he had been very slightly doped. Mallinson appeared to have been similarly affected, though he seized the present chance to remark: "All this has been very interesting, but I really think it's time we began to discuss our plans for getting away. We want to return to India as soon as possible. How many porters can we be supplied with?"

The question, so practical and uncompromising, broke through the crust of suavity to find no sure foothold beneath. Only after a longish interval came Chang's reply: "Unfortunately, Mr. Mallinson, I am not the proper person to approach. But in any case, I hardly think the matter could be arranged immediately."

"But something has *got* to be arranged! We've all got our work to return to, and our friends and relatives will be worrying about us. We simply *must* return. We're obliged to you for receiving us like this, but we really can't slack about here doing nothing. If it's at all feasible, we should like to set out not later than tomorrow. I expect there are a good many of your people who would volunteer to escort us—we should make it well worth their while, of course."

Mallinson ended nervously, as if he had hoped to be answered before saying so much; but he could extract from Chang no more than a quiet and almost reproachful: "But all this, you know, is scarcely in my province."

"Isn't it? Well, perhaps you can do *something*, at any rate. If you could get us a large-scale map of the country, it would help. It looks as if we shall have a long journey, and that's all the more reason for making an early start. You have maps, I suppose?"

"Yes, we have a great many."

"We'll borrow some of them, then, if you don't mind. We can return them to you afterwards. I suppose you must have communications with the outer world from time to time. And it would be a good idea to send messages ahead, also, to reassure our friends. How far away is the nearest telegraph line?"

Chang's wrinkled face seemed to have acquired a look of infinite patience, but he did not reply.

Mallinson waited a moment and then continued: "Well, where do you send to when you want anything? Anything civilized, I mean." A touch of scaredness began to appear in his eyes and voice. Suddenly he thrust back his chair and stood up. He was pale, and passed his hand wearily across his forehead. "I'm so tired," he stammered, glancing round the room. "I don't feel that any of you are really trying to help me. I'm only asking a simple question. It's obvious you must know the answer to it. When you had all these modern baths installed, how did they get here?"

There followed another silence.

"You won't tell me, then? It's part of the mystery of everything else, I suppose. Conway, I must say I think you're damned slack. Why don't *you* get at the truth? I'm all in, for the time being—but— tomorrow, mind—we *must* get away tomorrow—it's essential—"

He would have slid to the floor had not Conway caught him and helped him to a chair. Then he recovered a little, but did not speak.

"Tomorrow he will be much better," said Chang gently. "The air here is difficult for the stranger at first, but one soon becomes acclimatized."

Conway felt himself waking from a trance. "Things have been a little trying for him," he commented with rather rueful mildness. He added, more briskly: "I expect we're all feeling it somewhat. I think we'd better adjourn this discussion and go to bed. Barnard, will you look after Mallinson? And I'm sure *you're* in need of sleep too, Miss Brinklow." There had been some signal given, for at that moment a servant appeared. "Yes, we'll get along—good night—good night—I

64

shall soon follow." He almost pushed them out of the room, and then, with a scantness of ceremony that was in marked contrast with his earlier manner, turned to his host. Mallinson's reproach had spurred him.

"Now, sir, I don't want to detain you long, so I'd better come to the point. My friend is impetuous, but I don't blame him, he's quite right to make things clear. Our return journey has to be arranged, and we can't do it without help from you or from others in this place. Of course, I realize that leaving tomorrow is impossible, and for my own part I hope to find a minimum stay quite interesting. But that, perhaps, is not the attitude of my companions. So if it's true, as you say, that you can do nothing for us yourself, please put us in touch with someone else who can."

The Chinese answered: "You are wiser than your friends, my dear sir, and therefore you are less impatient. I am glad."

"That's not an answer."

Chang began to laugh—a jerky high-pitched chuckle so obviously forced that Conway recognized in it the polite pretence of seeing an imaginary joke with which the Chinese "saves face" at awkward moments. "I feel sure you have no cause to worry about the matter," came the reply, after an interval. "No doubt in due course we shall be able to give you all the help you need. There are difficulties, as you can imagine, but if we all approach the problem sensibly, and without undue haste—"

"I'm not suggesting haste. I'm merely seeking information about porters."

"Well, my dear sir, that raises another point. I very much doubt whether you will easily find men willing to undertake such a journey. They have their homes in the valley, and they don't care for leaving them to make long and arduous trips outside."

"They can be prevailed upon to do so, though, or else why and where were they escorting you this morning?"

"This morning? Oh, that was quite a different matter."

"In what way? Weren't you setting out on a journey when I and my friends chanced to come across you?"

There was no response to this, and presently Conway continued in a quieter voice: "I understand. Then it was *not* a chance meeting. I had wondered all along, in fact. So you came there deliberately to intercept us. That suggests you must have known of our arrival beforehand. And the interesting question is, *How?*"

His words laid a note of stress amidst the exquisite quietude of the scene. The lantern-light showed up the face of the Chinese; it was calm and statuesque. Suddenly, with a small gesture of the hand, Chang broke the strain; pulling aside a silken tapestry, he undraped a window leading to a balcony. Then, with a touch upon Conway's arm, he led him into the cold crystal air. "You are clever," he said dreamily, "but not entirely correct. For that reason I should counsel you not to worry your friends by these abstract discussions. Believe me, neither you nor they are in any danger at Shangri-La."

"But it isn't danger we're bothering about. It's delay."

"I realize that. And of course there *may* be a certain delay, quite unavoidably."

"If it's only for a short time, and genuinely unavoidable, then naturally we shall have to put up with it as best we can."

"How very sensible, for we desire nothing more than that you and your companions should enjoy your stay here."

"That's all very well, and as I told you, in a personal sense I can't say I shall mind a great deal. It's a new and interesting experience, and in any case, we need some rest."

He was gazing upward to the gleaming pyramid of Karakal. At that moment, in bright moonlight, it seemed as if a hand reached high might just touch it; it was so brittle-clear against the blue immensity beyond.

"Tomorrow," said Chang, "you may find it even more interesting. And as for rest, if you are fatigued, there are not many better places in the world."

Indeed, as Conway continued to gaze, a deeper repose overspread him, as if the spectacle were as much for the mind as for the eye. There was hardly any stir of wind, in contrast to the upland gales that had raged the night before; the whole valley, he perceived, was a landlocked harbour, with Karakal brooding over it, lighthouse-fashion. The smile grew as he considered it, for there was actually light on the summit, an ice-blue gleam that matched the splendour it reflected. Something prompted him then to enquire the literal interpretation of the name, and Chang's answer came as a whispered echo of his own musing. "Karakal, in the valley patois, means Blue Moon," said the Chinese.

CONWAY DID NOT PASS on his conclusion that the arrival of himself and party at Shangri-La had been in some way expected by its inhabitants. He had had it in mind that he must do so, and he was aware that the matter was important; but when morning came his awareness troubled him so little, in any but a theoretical sense, that he shrank from being the cause of greater concern in others. One part of him insisted that there was something distinctly queer about the place, that the attitude of Chang on the previous evening had been far from reassuring, and that the party were virtually prisoners unless and until the authorities chose to do more for them. And it was clearly his duty to compel them to action. After all, he was a representative of the British government, if nothing else; it was iniquitous that the inmates of a Tibetan monastery should refuse him any proper request . . . . That, no doubt, was the normal official view that would be taken; and part of Conway was both normal and official. No one could better play the strong man on occasions; during those final difficult days before the evacuation he had behaved in a manner which (he reflected wryly) should earn him nothing less than a knighthood and a Henty school-prize novel entitled *With Conway at Baskul.* To have taken on himself the leadership of some scores of mixed civilians, including women and children, to have sheltered them all in a small consulate during a hot-blooded revolution led by anti-foreign agitators, and to have bullied and cajoled the revolutionaries into permitting a wholesale evacuation by air—it was not, he felt, a bad achievement. Perhaps by pulling wires and writing interminable reports, he could wangle something out of it in the next New Year Honours. At any rate it had won him Mallinson's fervent admiration. Unfortunately, the youth must now be finding him so much more of a disappointment. It was a pity, of course, but Conway had grown used to people liking him only because they misunderstood him. He was not genuinely one of those resolute, strong-jawed, hammer-and-tongs empire-builders; the semblance he had given was merely a little one-act play, repeated from time to time by arrangement with fate and the Foreign Office, and for a salary which anyone could turn up in the pages of Whitaker.

The truth was, the puzzle of Shangri-La, and of his own arrival there, was beginning to exercise over him a rather charming fascination. In any case he found it hard to feel any personal misgivings. His official job was always liable to take him into odd parts of the world, and the odder they were, the less, as a rule, he suffered from boredom; why, then, grumble because accident instead of a chit from Whitehall had sent him to this oddest place of all?

He was, in fact, very far from grumbling. When he rose in the morning and saw the soft lapis blue of the sky through his window, he would not have chosen to be elsewhere on earth—either in Peshawar or Piccadilly. He was glad to find that on the others, also, a night's repose had had a heartening effect. Barnard was able to joke quite cheerfully about beds, baths, breakfasts, and other hospitable amenities. Miss Brinklow admitted that the most strenuous search of her apartment had failed to reveal any of the drawbacks she had been well prepared for. Even Mallinson had acquired a touch of half-sulky complacency. "I suppose we shan't get away today after all," he muttered, "unless somebody looks pretty sharp about it. Those fellows are typically Oriental, you can't get them to do anything quickly and efficiently."

Conway accepted the remark. Mallinson had been out of England just under a year; long enough, no doubt, to justify a generalization which he would probably still repeat when he had been out for twenty. And it was true, of course, in some degree. Yet to Conway it did not appear that the Eastern races were abnormally dilatory, but rather that Englishmen and Americans charged about the world in a state of continual and rather preposterous fever-heat. It was a point of view that he hardly expected any fellow Westerner to share, but he was more faithful to it as he grew older in years and experience. On the other hand, it was true enough that Chang was a subtle quibbler and that there was much justification for Mallinson's impatience. Conway had a slight wish that he could feel impatient too; it would have been so much easier for the boy.

He said: "I think we'd better wait and see what today brings. It was perhaps too optimistic to expect them to do anything last night."

Mallinson looked up sharply. "I suppose you think I made a fool of myself, being so urgent? I couldn't help it; I thought that Chinese fellow was damned fishy, and I do still. Did you succeed in getting any sense out of him after I'd gone to bed?"

"We didn't stay talking long. He was rather vague and non-committal about most things."

"We shall jolly well have to keep him up to scratch today."

"No doubt," agreed Conway, without marked enthusiasm for the prospect. "Meanwhile this is an excellent breakfast." It consisted of pomelo, tea, and chapatties, perfectly prepared and served. Towards the finish of the meal Chang entered and with a little bow began the exchange of politely conventional greetings which, in the English language, sounded just a trifle unwieldy. Conway would have preferred to talk in Chinese, but so far he had not let it be known that he spoke any Eastern tongue; he felt it might be a useful card up his sleeve. He listened gravely to Chang's courtesies, and gave assurances that he had slept well and felt much better. Chang expressed his pleasure at that, and added: "Truly, as your national poet says, 'Sleep knits up the ravelled sleeve of care.'"

This display of erudition was not too well received. Mallinson answered with that touch of scorn which any healthy-minded young Englishman must feel at the mention of poetry. "I suppose you mean Shakespeare, though I don't recognize the quotation. But I know another one that says 'Stand not upon the order of your going, but go at once.' Without being impolite, that's rather what we should all like to do. And I want to hunt round for those porters right away—this morning, if you've no objection."

The Chinese received the ultimatum impassively, replying at length: "I am sorry to tell you that it would be of little use. I fear we have no men available who would be willing to accompany you so far from their homes."

"But good God, man, you don't suppose we're going to take that for an answer, do you?"

"I am sincerely regretful, but I can suggest no other."

"You seem to have figgered it all out since last night," put in Barnard. "You weren't nearly so dead sure of things then."

"I did not wish to disappoint you when you were so tired from your journey. Now, after a refreshing night, I am in hope that you will see matters in a more reasonable light."

"Look here," intervened Conway briskly, "this sort of vagueness and prevarication won't do. You know we can't stay here indefinitely. It's equally obvious that we can't get away by ourselves. What, then, do you propose?"

Chang smiled with a radiance that was clearly for Conway alone. "My dear sir, it is a pleasure to make the suggestion that is in my mind. To your friend's attitude there was no answer, but to the demand of a wise man there is always a response. You may recollect that it was remarked yesterday—again by your friend, I believe—that we are bound to have occasional communication with the outside world. That is quite true. From time to time we require certain things from distant entrepôts, and it is our habit to obtain them in due course, by what methods and with what formalities I need not trouble you. The point of importance is that such a consignment is expected to arrive shortly, and as the men who make delivery will afterwards return, it seems to me that you might manage to come to some arrangement with them. Indeed I cannot think of a better plan, and I hope, when they arrive—"

"When *do* they arrive?" interrupted Mallinson bluntly.

"The exact date is, of course, impossible to forecast. You have yourself had experience of the difficulty of movement in this part of the world. A hundred things may happen to cause uncertainty, hazards of weather—"

Conway again intervened. "Let's get this clear. You're suggesting that we should employ as porters the men who are shortly due here with some goods. That's not a bad idea as far as it goes, but we must know a little more about it. First, as you've already been asked, when are these people expected? And second, where will they take us?"

"That is a question you would have to put to them."

"Would they take us to India?"

"It is hardly possible for me to say."

"Well, let's have an answer to the other question. When will they be here? I don't ask for a date, I just want some idea whether it's likely to be next week or next year."

"It might be about a month from now. Probably not more than two months."

"Or three, four, or five months," broke in Mallinson hotly. "And you think we're going to wait here for this convoy or caravan or whatever it is to take us God knows where at some completely vague time in the distant future?"

"I think, sir, the phrase 'distant future' is hardly appropriate. Unless something unforeseen occurs, the period of waiting should not be longer than I have said."

"But *two months*! Two months in this place! It's preposterous! Conway, you surely can't contemplate it! Why, two weeks would be the limit!"

Chang gathered his gown about him in a little gesture of finality. "I am sorry. I did not wish to offend. The lamasery continues to offer all of you its utmost hospitality for as long as you have the misfortune to remain. I can say no more."

"You don't need to," retorted Mallinson furiously. "And if you think you've got the whip hand over us, you'll soon find you're damn well mistaken! We'll get all the porters we want, don't worry. You can bow and scrape and say what you like—"

Conway laid a restraining hand on his arm. Mallinson in a temper presented a child-like spectacle; he was apt to say anything that came into his head, regardless alike of point and decorum. Conway thought it readily forgivable in one so constituted and circumstanced, but he feared it might affront the more delicate susceptibilities of a Chinese. Fortunately Chang had ushered himself out, with admirable tact, in good time to escape the worst.

Chapter 5

HEY SPENT THE REST of the morning discussing the matter. It was certainly a shock for four persons who in the ordinary course should have been luxuriating in the clubs and mission houses of Peshawar to find themselves faced instead with the prospect of two months in a Tibetan monastery. But it was in the nature of things that the initial shock of their arrival should have left them with slender reserves either of indignation or astonishment; even Mallinson, after his first outburst, subsided into a mood of half-bewildered fatalism. "I'm past arguing about it, Conway," he said, puffing at a cigarette with nervous irritability. "You know how I feel. I've said all along that there's something queer about this business. It's crooked. I'd like to be out of it this minute."

"I don't blame you for that," replied Conway. "Unfortunately, it's not a question of what any of us would like, but of what we've all got to put up with. Frankly, if these people say they won't or can't supply us with the necessary porters, there's nothing for it but to wait till the other fellows come. I'm sorry to admit that we're so helpless in the matter, but I'm afraid it's the truth."

"You mean we've got to stay here for two months?"

"I don't see what else we can do."

Mallinson flicked his cigarette ash with a gesture of forced nonchalance. "All right, then. Two months it is. And now let's all shout hooray about it."

Conway went on: "I don't see why it should be much worse than two months in any other isolated part of the world. People in our jobs are used to being sent to odd places, I think I can say that of us all. Of course, it's bad for those of us who have friends and relatives. Personally, I'm fortunate in that respect, I can't think of anyone who'll worry over me acutely, and my work, whatever it might have been, can easily be done by somebody else."

He turned to the others as if inviting them to state their own cases. Mallinson proffered no information, but Conway knew roughly how he was situated. He had parents and a girl in England; it made things hard.

Barnard, on the other hand, accepted the position with what Conway had learned to regard as an habitual good humour. "Well, I guess I'm pretty lucky, for that matter, two months in the penitentiary won't kill me. As for the folks in my hometown, they won't bat an eye. I've always been a bad letter-writer."

"You forget that our names will be in the papers," Conway reminded him. "We shall all be posted missing, and people will naturally assume the worst."

Barnard looked startled for a moment; then he replied, with a slight grin: "Oh, yes, that's true, but it don't affect me, I assure you."

Conway was glad it didn't, though the matter remained a little puzzling. He turned to Miss Brinklow, who till then had been remarkably silent; she had not offered any opinion during the interview with Chang. He imagined that she too might have comparatively few personal worries. She said brightly: "As Mr. Barnard says, two months here is nothing to make a fuss about. It's all the same, wherever one is, when one's in the Lord's service. Providence has sent me here. I regard it as a call."

Conway thought the attitude a very convenient one, in the circumstances. "I'm sure," he said encouragingly, "you'll find your mission society pleased with you when you *do* return. You'll be able to give much useful information. We'll all of us have had an experience, for that matter. That should be a small consolation."

The talk then became general. Conway was rather surprised at the ease with which Barnard and Miss Brinklow had accommodated themselves to the new prospect. He was relieved, however, as well; it left him with only one disgruntled person to deal with. Yet even Mallinson, after the strain of all the arguing, was experiencing a reaction; he was still perturbed, but more willing to look at the brighter side of things. "Heaven knows what we shall find to do with ourselves," he exclaimed, but the mere fact of making such a remark showed that he was trying to reconcile himself.

"The first rule must be to avoid getting on each other's nerves," replied Conway. "Happily, the place seems big enough, and by no means overpopulated. Except for servants, we've only seen one of its inhabitants so far."

Barnard could find another reason for optimism. "We won't starve, at any rate, if our meals up to now are a fair sample. You know, Conway, this place isn't run without plenty of hard cash. Those baths, for instance, they cost real money. And I can't see that any-body earns anything here, unless those chaps in the valley have jobs, and even then, they wouldn't produce enough for export. I'd like to know if they work any minerals."

"The whole place is a confounded mystery," responded Mallinson. "I daresay they've got pots of money hidden away, like the Jesuits. As for the baths, probably some millionaire supporter presented them. Anyhow, it won't worry me, once I get away. I must say, though, the view *is* rather good, in its way. Fine winter sport centre if it were in the right spot. I wonder if one could get any skiing on some of those slopes up yonder?"

Conway gave him a searching and slightly amused glance. "Yesterday, when I found some edelweiss, you reminded me that I wasn't in the Alps. I think it's my turn to say the same thing now. I wouldn't advise you to try any of your Wengen-Scheidegg tricks in this part of the world."

"I don't suppose anybody here has ever seen a ski jump."

"Or even an ice-hockey match," responded Conway banteringly. "You might try to raise some teams. What about 'Gentlemen *v.* Lamas'?"

"It would certainly teach them to play the game," Miss Brinklow put in with sparkling seriousness.

Adequate comment upon this might have been difficult, but there was no necessity, since lunch was about to be served and its character and promptness combined to make an agreeable impression. After-wards, when Chang entered, there was small disposition to continue the squabble. With great tactfulness the Chinese assumed that he was still on good terms with everybody, and the four exiles allowed the assumption to stand. Indeed, when he suggested that they might care to be shown a little more of the lamasery buildings, and that if so, he would be pleased to act as guide, the offer was readily accepted. "Why, surely," said Barnard. "We may as well give the place the once-over while we're here. I reckon it'll be a long time before any of us pay a second visit."

Miss Brinklow struck a more thought-giving note. "When we left Baskul in that aeroplane I'm sure I never dreamed we should ever get to a place like this," she murmured as they all moved off under Chang's escort.

"And we don't know yet why we have," answered Mallinson unforgetfully.

CONWAY HAD NO RACE or colour prejudice, and it was an affectation for him to pretend, as he sometimes did in clubs and first-class railway carriages, that he set any particular store on the "whiteness" of a lobster-red face under a toupee. It saved trouble to let it be so assumed, especially in India, and Conway was a conscientious trouble-saver. But in China it had been less necessary; he had had many Chinese friends, and it had never occurred to him to treat them as inferiors. Hence, in his intercourse with Chang, he was sufficiently unpreoccupied to see in him a mannered old gentleman who might not be entirely trustworthy, but who was certainly of high intelligence. Mallinson, on the other hand, tended to regard him through the bars of an imaginary cage; Miss Brinklow was sharp and sprightly, as with the heathen in his blindness; while Barnard's wise-cracking bonhomie was of the kind he would have cultivated with a butler.

Meanwhile the grand tour of Shangri-La was interesting enough to transcend these attitudes. It was not the first monastic institution Conway had inspected, but it was easily the largest and, apart from its situation, the most remarkable. The mere procession through rooms and courtyards was an afternoon's exercise, though he was aware of many apartments passed by, indeed, of whole buildings into which Chang did not offer admission. The party were shown enough, however, to confirm the impressions each one of them had formed already. Barnard was more certain than ever that the lamas were rich;

Miss Brinklow discovered abundant evidence that they were immoral. Mallinson, after the first novelty had worn off, found himself no less fatigued than on many sight-seeing excursions at lower altitudes; the lamas, he feared, were not likely to be his heroes.

Conway alone submitted to a rich and growing enchantment. It was not so much any individual thing that attracted him as the gradual revelation of elegance, of modest and impeccable taste, of harmony so fragrant that it seemed to gratify the eye without arresting it. Only indeed by a conscious effort did he recall himself from the artist's mood to the connoisseur's, and then he recognized treasures that museums and millionaires alike would have bargained for— exquisite pearl-blue Sung ceramics, paintings in tinted inks preserved for more than a thousand years, lacquers in which the cold and lovely detail of fairyland was not so much depicted as orchestrated. A world of incomparable refinements still lingered tremulously in porcelain and varnish, yielding an instant of emotion before its dissolution into purest thought. There was no boastfulness, no striving after effect, no concentrated attack upon the feelings of the beholder. These delicate perfections had an air of having fluttered into existence like petals from a flower. They would have maddened a collector, but Conway did not collect; he lacked both money and the acquisitive instinct. His liking for Chinese art was an affair of the mind; in a world of increasing noise and hugeness, he turned in private to gentle, precise, and miniature things. And as he passed through room after room, a certain pathos touched him remotely at the thought of Karakal's piled immensity over against such fragile charms.

The lamasery, however, had more to offer than a display of Chinoiserie. One of its features, for instance, was a very delightful library, lofty and spacious, and containing a multitude of books so retiringly housed in bays and alcoves that the whole atmosphere was more of wisdom than of learning, of good manners rather than seriousness. Conway, during a rapid glance at some of the shelves, found much to astonish him; the world's best literature was there, it seemed, as well as a great deal of abstruse and curious stuff that he could not appraise. Volumes in English, French, German, and Russian abounded, and there were vast quantities of Chinese and other Eastern scripts. A section which interested him particularly was devoted to Tibetiana, if it might be so called; he noticed several rarities, among them the *Novo Descubrimento de grao catayo ou dos Regos de Tibet*, by Antonio de Andrada (Lisbon, 1626); Athanasius Kircher's *China* (Antwerp, 1667); Thevenot's *Voyage à la Chine des Pères Grueber et d'Orville*; and Beligatti's *Relazione Inedita di un Viaggio al Tibet*. He was examining the last named when he noticed Chang's eyes fixed on him in suave curiosity. "You are a scholar, perhaps?" came the enquiry.

Conway found it hard to reply. His period of donhood at Oxford gave him some right to assent, but he knew that the word, though the highest of compliments from a Chinese, had yet a faintly priggish sound for English ears, and chiefly out of consideration for his companions he demurred to it. He said: "I enjoy reading, of course, but my work during recent years hasn't supplied many opportunities for the studious life."

"Yet you wish for it?"

"Oh, I wouldn't say all that, but I'm certainly well aware of its attractions."

Mallinson, who had picked up a book, interrupted: "Here's something for your studious life, Conway. It's a map of the country."

"We have a collection of several hundreds," said Chang. "They are all open to your inspection, but perhaps I can save you trouble in one respect. You will not find Shangri-La marked on any."

"Curious," Conway made comment. "I wonder why?"

"There is a very good reason, but I am afraid that is all I can say."

Conway smiled, but Mallinson looked peevish again. "Still piling up the mystery," he said. "So far we haven't seen much that anyone need bother to conceal."

Suddenly Miss Brinklow came to life out of a mute, processional stupor. "Aren't you going to show us the lamas at work?" she fluted, in the tone which one felt had intimidated many a Cook's man. One felt, too, that her mind was probably full of hazy visions of native handicrafts—prayer-mat weaving, or something picturesquely primitive that she could talk about when she got home. She had an extraordinary knack of never seeming very much surprised, yet of always seeming very slightly indignant, a combination of fixities which was not in the least disturbed by Chang's response: "I am sorry to say it is impossible. The lamas are never, or perhaps I should say only very rarely, seen by those outside the lamahood."

"I guess we'll have to miss 'em then," agreed Barnard. "But I do think it's a real pity. You've no notion how much I'd like to have shaken the hand of your headman."

Chang acknowledged the remark with benign seriousness. Miss Brinklow, however, was not yet to be sidetracked. "What do the lamas do?" she continued.

"They devote themselves, madam, to contemplation and to the pursuit of wisdom."

"But that isn't *doing* anything."

"Then, madam, they do nothing."

"I thought as much." She found occasion to sum up. "Well, Mr. Chang, it's a pleasure being shown all these things, I'm sure, but you won't convince me that a place like this does any real good. I prefer something more practical."

"Perhaps you would like to take tea?"

Conway wondered at first if this were intended ironically, but it soon appeared not; the afternoon had passed swiftly, and Chang, though frugal in eating, had the typical Chinese fondness for tea-drinking at frequent intervals. Miss Brinklow, too, confessed that visiting art galleries and museums always gave her a touch of headache. The party, therefore, fell in with the suggestion, and followed Chang through several courtyards to a scene of quite sudden and unmatched loveliness. From a colonnade steps descended to a garden, in which by some tender curiosity of irrigation a lotus pool lay entrapped, the leaves so closely set that they gave an impression of a floor of moist green tiles. Fringing the pool were posed a brazen menagerie of lions, dragons, and unicorns, each offering a stylized ferocity that emphasized rather than offended the surrounding peace. The whole picture was so perfectly proportioned that the eye was entirely unhastened from one part to another; there was no vying or vanity, and even the summit of Karakal, peerless above the blue-tiled roofs, seemed to have surrendered within the framework of an exquisite artistry.

"Pretty little place," commented Barnard, as Chang led the way into an open pavilion which, to Conway's further delight, contained a harpsichord and a modern grand piano. He found this in some ways the crowning astonishment of a rather astonishing afternoon. Chang answered all his questions with complete candour up to a point; the lamas, he explained, held Western music in high esteem, particularly that of Mozart; they had a collection of all the great European compositions, and some were skilled executants on various instruments.

Barnard was chiefly impressed by the transport problem. "D'you mean to tell me that this pi-anno was brought here by the route we came along yesterday?"

"There is no other."

"Well, that certainly beats everything! Why, with a gramophone and a radio you'd be all fixed complete! Perhaps, though, you aren't yet acquainted with up-to-date music?"

"Oh, yes, we have had reports, but we are advised that the mountains would make wireless reception impossible, and as for a gramophone, the suggestion has already come before the authorities, but they have felt no need to hurry in the matter."

"I'd believe that even if you hadn't told me," Barnard retorted. "I guess that must be the slogan of your society—'No hurry.'" He laughed loudly and then went on: "Well, to come down to details, suppose in due course your bosses decide that they *do* want a gramophone, what's the procedure? The makers wouldn't deliver here, that's a sure thing. I figger you have an agent in Pekin or Shanghai or somewhere, and I'll bet everything costs a mighty lot of dollars by the time you handle it."

But Chang was no more to be drawn than on a previous occasion. "Your surmises are intelligent, Mr. Barnard, but I fear I cannot discuss them."

So there they were again, Conway reflected, edging the invisible borderline between what might and might not be revealed. He thought he could soon begin to map out that line in imagination, though the impact of a new surprise deferred the matter. For servants were already bringing in the shallow bowls of scented tea, and along with the agile, lithe-limbed Tibetans there had also entered, quite inconspicuously, a girl in Chinese dress. She went directly to the harpsichord and began to play a gavotte by Rameau. The first bewitching twang stirred in Conway a pleasure that was beyond amazement; those silvery airs of eighteenth-century France seemed to match in elegance the Sung vases and exquisite lacquers and the lotus pool beyond; the same death-defying fragrance hung about them, lending immortality through an age to which their spirit was alien. Then he noticed the player. She had the long, slender nose, high cheekbones, and eggshell pallor of the Manchu; her black hair was drawn tightly back and braided; she looked very finished and miniature. Her mouth was like a little pink convolvulus, and she was quite still, except for her long-fingered hands. As soon as the gavotte was ended, she made a little obeisance and went out.

Chang smiled after her and then, with a touch of personal triumph, upon Conway. "You are pleased?" he queried.

"Who is she?" asked Mallinson, before Conway could reply.

"Her name is Lo-Tsen. She has much skill with Western keyboard music. Like myself, she has not yet attained the full initiation."

"I should think not, indeed!" exclaimed Miss Brinklow. "She looks hardly more than a child. So you have women lamas, then?"

"There are no sex distinctions among us."

"Extraordinary business, this lamahood of yours," Mallinson commented loftily, after a pause. The rest of the tea-drinking proceeded without conversation; echoes of the harpsichord seemed still in the air, imposing a strange spell. Presently, leading the departure from the pavilion, Chang ventured to hope that the tour had been enjoyable. Conway, replying for the others, seesawed with the customary courtesies. Chang then assured them of his own equal enjoyment, and hoped they would consider the resources of the music room and library wholly at their disposal throughout their stay. Conway, with some sincerity, thanked him again. "But what about the lamas?" he added. "Don't they ever want to use them?"

"They yield place with much gladness to their honoured guests."

"Well, that's what I call real handsome," said Barnard. "And what's more, it shows that the lamas do really know we exist. That's a step forward, anyhow, makes me feel much more at home. You've certainly

She was quite still, except for her long-fingered hands

got a swell outfit here, Chang, and that little girl of yours plays the pi-anno very nicely. How old would she be, I wonder?"

"I am afraid I cannot tell you."

Barnard laughed. "You don't give away secrets about a lady's age, is that it?"

"Precisely," answered Chang with a faintly shadowing smile.

THAT EVENING, after dinner, Conway made occasion to leave the others and stroll out into the calm, moon-washed courtyards. Shangri-La was lovely then, touched with the mystery that lies at the core of all loveliness. The air was cold and still; the mighty spire of Karakal looked nearer, much nearer than by daylight. Conway was physically happy, emotionally satisfied, and mentally at ease; but in his intellect, which was not quite the same thing as mind, there was a little stir. He was puzzled. The line of secrecy that he had begun to map out grew sharper, but only to reveal an inscrutable background. The whole amazing series of events that had happened to him and his three chance companions swung now into a sort of focus; he could not yet understand them, but he believed they were somehow to be understood.

Passing along a cloister, he reached the terrace leaning over the valley. The scent of tuberose assailed him, full of delicate associations; in China it was called "the smell of moonlight." He thought whimsically that if moonlight had a sound also, it might well be the Rameau gavotte he had heard so recently; and that set him thinking of the little Manchu. It had not occurred to him to picture women at Shangri-La; one did not associate their presence with the general practice of monasticism. Still, he reflected, it might not be a disagreeable innovation; indeed, a female harpsichordist might be an asset to any community that permitted itself to be (in Chang's words) "moderately heretical."

He gazed over the edge into the blue-black emptiness. The drop was phantasmal; perhaps as much as a mile. He wondered if he would be allowed to descend it and inspect the valley civilization that had been talked of. The notion of this strange culture pocket, hidden amongst unknown ranges, and ruled over by some vague kind of theocracy, interested him as a student of history, apart from the curious though perhaps cognate secrets of the lamasery.

Suddenly, on a flutter of air, came sounds from far below. Listening intently, he could hear gongs and trumpets and also (though perhaps only in imagination) the massed wail of voices. The sounds faded on a veer of the wind, then returned to fade again. But the hint of life and liveliness in those veiled depths served only to emphasize the austere serenity of Shangri-La. Its forsaken courts and pale pavilions simmered in repose from which all the fret of existence had ebbed away, leaving a hush as if moments hardly dared to pass. Then, from a window high above the terrace, he caught the rose-gold of lantern-light; was it there that the lamas devoted themselves to contemplation and the pursuit of wisdom, and were those devotions now in progress? The problem seemed one that he could solve merely by entering at the nearest door and exploring through gallery and corridor until the truth were his; but he knew that such freedom was illusory, and that in fact his move-ments were watched. Two Tibetans had padded across the terrace and were idling near the parapet. Good-humoured fellows they looked, shrugging their coloured cloaks negligently over naked shoulders. The whisper of gongs and trumpets uprose again, and Conway heard one of the men question his companion. The answer came: "They have buried Talu." Conway, whose knowledge of Tibetan was very slight, hoped they would continue talking; he could not gather much from a single remark. After a pause the ques-tioner, who was inaudible, resumed the conversation, and obtained answers which Conway overheard and loosely understood as follows:

"He died outside."

"He obeyed the high ones of Shangri-La."

"He came through the air over the great mountains with a bird to hold him."

"Strangers he brought, also."

"Talu was not afraid of the outside wind, nor of the outside cold."

"Though he went outside long ago, the valley of Blue Moon remembers him still."

Nothing more was said that Conway could interpret, and after waiting for some time he went back to his own quarters. He had heard enough to turn another key in the locked mystery, and it fitted so well that he wondered he had failed to supply it by his own deductions. It had, of course, crossed his mind, but a certain initial and fantastic unreasonableness about it had been too much for him. Now he perceived that the unreasonableness, however fantastic, was to be swallowed. That flight from Baskul had *not* been the meaningless exploit of a madman. It had been something planned, prepared, and carried out at the instigation of Shangri-La. The dead pilot was known by name to those who lived there; he had been one of them, in some sense; his death was mourned. Everything pointed to a high directing intelligence bent upon its own purposes; there had been, as it were, a single arch of intention spanning the inexplicable hours and miles. But what *was* that intention? For what possible reason could four chance passengers in a British government aeroplane be whisked away to these trans-Himalayan solitudes?

Conway was somewhat aghast at the problem, but by no means wholly displeased with it. It challenged him in the only way in which he was readily amenable to challenge—by touching a certain clarity of brain that only demanded a sufficient task. One thing he decided instantly: the cold thrill of discovery must not yet be communicated, neither to his companions, who could not help him, nor to his hosts, who doubtless would not.

Chapter 6

 RECKON SOME FOLKS have to get used to worse places," Barnard remarked towards the close of his first week at Shangri-La, and it was doubtless one of the many lessons to be drawn. By that time the party had settled themselves into something like a daily routine, and with Chang's assistance the boredom was no more acute than on many a planned holiday. They had all become acclimatized to the atmosphere, finding it quite invigorating so long as heavy exertion was avoided. They had learned that the days were warm and the nights cold, that the lamasery was almost completely sheltered from winds, that avalanches on Karakal were most frequent about midday, that the valley grew a good brand of tobacco, that some foods and drinks were more pleasant than others, and that each one of themselves had personal tastes and peculiarities. They had, in fact, discovered as much about each other as four new pupils of a school from which everyone else was mysteriously absent. Chang was tireless in his efforts to make smooth the rough places. He conducted excursions, suggested occupations, recommended books, talked with his slow, careful fluency whenever there was an awkward pause at meals, and was on every occasion benign, courteous, and resourceful. The line of demarcation was so marked between information willingly supplied and politely declined that the latter ceased to stir resentment, except fitfully from Mallinson. Conway was content to take note of it, adding another fragment to his constantly accumulating data. Barnard even "jollied" the Chinese after the manner and traditions of a Middle West rotary convention. "You know, Chang, this is a damned bad hotel. Don't you have newspapers sent here ever? I'd give all the books in your library for this morning's *Herald Tribune*." Chang's replies were always serious, though it did not necessarily follow that he took every question seriously. "We have the files of *The Times*, Mr. Barnard, up to a few years ago. But only, I regret to say, the London *Times*."

Conway was glad to find that the valley was not to be "out of bounds," though the difficulties of the descent made unescorted visits impossible. In company with Chang they all spent a whole day inspecting the green floor that was so pleasantly visible from the cliff edge, and to Conway, at any rate, the trip was of absorbing interest. They travelled in bamboo sedan chairs, swinging perilously over precipices while their bearers in front and to the rear picked a way nonchalantly down the steep track. It was not a route for the squeamish, but when at last they reached the lower levels of forest and foothill the supreme good fortune of the lamasery was everywhere to be realized. For the valley was nothing less than an enclosed paradise of amazing fertility, in which the vertical difference of a few thousand feet spanned the whole gulf between temperate and tropical. Crops of unusual diversity grew in profusion and contiguity, with not an inch of ground untended. The whole cultivated area stretched for perhaps a dozen miles, varying in width from one to five, and, though narrow, it had the luck to take sunlight at the hottest part of the day. The atmosphere, indeed, was pleasantly warm even out of the sun, though the little rivulets that watered the soil were ice-cold from the snows. Conway felt again, as he gazed up at the stupendous mountain wall, that there was a superb and exquisite peril in the scene; but for some chance-placed barrier, the whole valley would clearly have been a lake, nourished continually from the glacial heights around it. Instead of which, a few streams dribbled through to fill reservoirs and irrigate fields and plantations with a disciplined conscientiousness worthy of a sanitary engineer. The whole design was almost uncannily fortunate, so long as the structure of the frame remained unmoved by earthquake or landslide.

But even such vaguely future fears could only enhance the total loveliness of the present. Once again Conway was captivated, and by the same qualities of charm and ingenuity that had made his years in China happier than others. The vast encircling massif made perfect contrast with the tiny lawns and weedless gardens, the painted teahouses by the stream, and the frivolously toy-like houses. The inhabitants seemed to him a very successful blend of Chinese and Tibetan; they were cleaner and handsomer than the average of either race, and looked to have suffered little from the inevitable inbreeding of such a small society. They smiled and laughed as they passed the chaired strangers, and had a friendly word for Chang; they were good-humoured and mildly inquisitive, courteous and carefree, busy at innumerable jobs but not in any apparent hurry over them. Altogether Conway thought it one of the pleasantest communities he had ever seen, and even Miss Brinklow, who had been watching for symptoms of pagan degradation, had to admit that everything looked very well "on the surface." She was relieved to find the natives "completely" clothed, even though the women did wear ankle-tight

Chinese trousers; and her most imaginative scrutiny of a Buddhist temple revealed only a few items that could be regarded as somewhat doubtfully phallic. Chang explained that the temple had its own lamas, who were under loose control from Shangri-La, though not of the same order. There were also, it appeared, a Taoist and a Confucian temple farther along the valley. "The jewel has facets," said the Chinese, "and it is possible that many religions are moderately true."

"I agree with that," said Barnard heartily. "I never did believe in sectarian jealousies. Chang, you're a philosopher, I must remember that remark of yours: 'Many religions are moderately true.' I reckon you fellows up on the mountain must be a lot of wise guys to have thought that out. You're right, too, I'm dead certain of it."

"But we," responded Chang dreamily, "are only *moderately* certain."

Miss Brinklow could not be bothered with all that, which seemed to her a sign of mere laziness. In any case she was preoccupied with an idea of her own. "When I get back," she said with tightening lips, "I shall ask my society to send a missionary here. And if they grumble at the expense, I shall just bully them until they agree."

That, clearly, was a much healthier spirit, and even Mallinson, little as he sympathized with foreign missions, could not forbear his admiration. "They ought to send *you*," he said. "That is, of course, if you'd like a place like this."

"It's hardly a question of *liking* it," Miss Brinklow retorted. "One wouldn't like it, naturally—how could one? It's a matter of what one feels one ought to do."

"I think," said Conway, "if I were a missionary I'd choose this rather than quite a lot of other places."

"In that case," snapped Miss Brinklow, "there would be no merit in it, obviously."

"But I wasn't thinking of merit."

"More's the pity, then. There's no good in doing a thing because you like doing it. Look at these people here!"

"They all seem very happy."

"*Exactly*," she answered with a touch of fierceness. She added:

"Anyhow, I don't see why I shouldn't make a beginning by studying the language. Can you lend me a book about it, Mr. Chang?"

Chang was at his most mellifluous. "Most certainly, madam, with the greatest of pleasure. And, if I may say so, I think the idea an excellent one."

When they ascended to Shangri-La that evening he treated the matter as one of immediate importance. Miss Brinklow was at first a little daunted by the massive volume compiled by an industrious nineteenth-century German (she had more probably imagined some slighter work of a "Brush up your Tibetan" type), but with help from the Chinese and encouragement from Conway she made a good beginning and was soon observed to be extracting grim satisfaction from her task.

CONWAY, TOO, FOUND much to interest him, apart from the engrossing problem he had set himself. During the warm, sunlit days he made full use of the library and music room, and was confirmed in his impression that the lamas were of quite exceptional culture. Their taste in books was catholic, at any rate: Plato in Greek touched Omar in English; Nietzsche partnered Newton; Thomas More was there, and also Hannah More, Thomas Moore, George Moore, and even Old Moore. Altogether Conway estimated the number of volumes at between twenty and thirty thousand; and it was tempting to speculate upon the method of selection and acquisition. He sought also to discover how recently there had been additions, but he did not come across anything later than a cheap reprint of *Im Western Nichts Neues*. During a subsequent visit, however, Chang told him that there were other books published up to about the middle of 1930 which would doubtless be added to the shelves eventually; they had already arrived at the lamasery. "We keep ourselves fairly up-to-date, you see," he commented.

"There are people who would hardly agree with you," replied Conway with a smile. "Quite a lot of things have happened in the world since last year, you know."

"Nothing of importance, my dear sir, that could not have been foreseen in 1920, or that will not be better understood in 1940."

"You're not interested, then, in the latest developments of the world crisis?"

"I shall be very deeply interested—in due course."

"You know, Chang, I believe I'm beginning to understand you. You're geared differently, that's what it is. Time means less to you than it does to most people. If I were in London I wouldn't always be eager to see the latest hour-old newspaper, and you at Shangri-La are no more eager to see a year-old one. Both attitudes seem to me quite sensible. By the way, how long is it since you last had visitors here?"

"That, Mr. Conway, I am unfortunately unable to say."

It was the usual ending to a conversation, and one that Conway found less irritating than the opposite phenomenon from which he had suffered much in his time—the conversation which, try as he would, seemed never to end. He began to like Chang rather more as their meetings multiplied, though it still puzzled him that he met so few of the lamasery personnel; even assuming that the lamas themselves were unapproachable, were there not other postulants besides Chang?

There was, of course, the little Manchu. He saw her sometimes when he visited the music room; but she knew no English, and he was still unwilling to disclose his own Chinese. He could not quite determine whether she played merely for pleasure, or was in some way a student. Her playing, as indeed her whole behaviour, was exquisitely formal, and her choice lay always among the more patterned compositions—those of Bach, Corelli, Scarlatti, and occasionally Mozart. She preferred the harpsichord to the pianoforte, but when Conway went to the latter she would listen with grave and almost dutiful appreciation. It was impossible to know what was in her mind; it was difficult even to guess her age. He would have doubted her being over thirty or under thirteen; and yet, in a curious way, such manifest unlikelihoods could neither of them be ruled out as wholly impossible.

Mallinson, who sometimes came to listen to the music for want of anything better to do, found her a very baffling proposition. "I can't think what she's doing here," he said to Conway more than once.

"This lama business may be all right for an old fellow like Chang, but what's the attraction in it for a girl? How long has she been here, I wonder?"

"I wonder too, but it's one of those things we're not likely to be told."

"Do you suppose she *likes* being here?"

"I'm bound to say she doesn't appear to *dis*like it."

"She doesn't appear to have feelings at all, for that matter. She's like a little ivory doll more than a human being."

"A charming thing to be like, anyhow."

"As far as it goes."

Conway smiled. "And it goes pretty far, Mallinson, when you come to think about it. After all, the ivory doll has manners, good taste in dress, attractive looks, a pretty touch on the harpsichord, and she doesn't move about a room as if she were playing hockey. Western Europe, so far as I recollect it, contains an exceptionally large number of females who lack these virtues."

"You're an awful cynic about women, Conway."

Conway was used to the charge. He had not actually had a great deal to do with the other sex, and during occasional leaves in Indian hill stations the reputation of cynic had been as easy to sustain as any other. In truth he had had several delightful friendships with women who would have been pleased to marry him if he had asked them—but he had not asked them. He had once got nearly as far as an announcement in the *Morning Post*, but the girl did not want to live in Pekin and he did not want to live at Tunbridge Wells, mutual reluctances which proved impossible to dislodge. So far as he had had experience of women at all, it had been tentative, intermittent, and somewhat inconclusive. But he was not, for all that, a cynic about them.

He said with a laugh: "I'm thirty-seven—you're twenty-four. That's all it amounts to."

After a pause Mallinson asked suddenly: "Oh, by the way, how old should you say Chang is?"

"Anything," replied Conway lightly, "between forty-nine and a hundred and forty-nine."

SUCH INFORMATION, however, was less trustworthy than much else that was available to the new arrivals. The fact that their curiosities were sometimes unsatisfied tended to obscure the really vast quantity of data which Chang was always willing to outpour. There were no secrecies, for instance, about the customs and habits of the valley population, and Conway, who was interested, had talks which might have been worked up into a quite serviceable degree thesis. He was particularly interested, as a student of affairs, in the way the valley population was governed; it appeared, on examination, to be a rather loose and elastic autocracy operated from the lamasery with a benevolence that was almost casual. It was certainly an established success, as every descent into that fertile paradise made more evident. Conway was puzzled as to the ultimate basis of law and order; there appeared to be neither soldiers nor police, yet surely some provision must be made for the incorrigible? Chang replied that crime was very rare, partly because only serious things were considered crimes, and partly because everyone enjoyed a sufficiency of everything he could reasonably desire. In the last resort the personal servants of the lamasery had power to expel an offender from the valley—though this, which was considered an extreme and dreadful punishment, had only very occasionally to be imposed. But the chief factor in the government of Blue Moon, Chang went on to say, was the inculcation of good manners, which made men feel that certain things were "not done," and that they lost caste by doing them. "You English inculcate the same feeling," said Chang, "in your public schools, but not, I fear, in regard to the same things. The inhabitants of our valley, for instance, feel that it is 'not done' to be inhospitable to strangers, to dispute acrimoniously, or to strive for priority amongst one another. The idea of enjoying what your English headmasters call the mimic warfare of the playing field would seem to them entirely barbarous—indeed, a sheerly wanton stimulation of all the lower instincts."

Conway asked if there were never disputes about women.

"Only very rarely, because it would not be considered good manners to take a woman that another man wanted."

"Supposing somebody wanted her so badly that he didn't care a damn whether it was good manners or not?"

"Then, my dear sir, it would be good manners on the part of the other man to let him have her, and also on the part of the woman to be equally agreeable. You would be surprised, Conway, how the application of a little courtesy all round helps to smooth out these problems."

Certainly during visits to the valley Conway found a spirit of goodwill and contentment that pleased him all the more because he knew that of all the arts, that of government has been brought least to perfection. When he made some complimentary remark, however, Chang responded: "Ah, but you see, we believe that to govern perfectly it is necessary to avoid governing too much."

"Yet you don't have any democratic machinery—voting, and so on?"

"Oh, no. Our people would be quite shocked by having to declare that one policy was completely right and another completely wrong."

Conway smiled. He found the attitude a sufficiently congenial one.

MEANWHILE, MISS BRINKLOW derived her own kind of satisfaction from a study of Tibetan; meanwhile, also, Mallinson fretted and groused, and Barnard persisted in an equanimity which seemed almost equally remarkable, whether it were real or simulated.

"To tell you the truth," said Mallinson, "the fellow's cheerfulness is just about getting on my nerves. I can understand him trying to keep a stiff lip, but that continual joke-over of his begins to upset me. He'll be the life and soul of the party if we don't watch him."

Conway too had once or twice wondered at the ease with which the American had managed to settle down. He replied: "Isn't it rather lucky for us he *does* take things so well?"

"Personally, I think it's damned peculiar. What do you *know* about him, Conway? I mean who he is, and so on."

"Not much more than you do. I understood he came from Persia and was supposed to have been oil-prospecting. It's his way to take things easily—when the air evacuation was arranged I had quite a job to persuade him to join us at all. He only agreed when I told him that an American passport wouldn't stop a bullet."

"By the way, did you ever see his passport?"

"Probably I did, but I don't remember. Why?"

Mallinson laughed. "I'm afraid you'll think I haven't exactly been minding my own business. Why should I, anyhow? Two months in this place ought to reveal all our secrets, if we have any. Mind you, it was a sheer accident, in the way it happened, and I haven't let slip a word to anyone else, of course. I didn't think I'd tell even you, but now we've got on to the subject I may as well."

"Yes, of course, but I wish you'd let me know what you're talking about."

"Just this. Barnard was travelling on a forged passport and he isn't Barnard at all."

Conway raised his eyebrows with an interest that was very much less than concern. He liked Barnard, so far as the man stirred him to any emotion at all; but it was quite impossible for him to care intensely who he really was or wasn't. He said: "Well, who do you think he is, then?"

"He's Chalmers Bryant."

"The deuce he is! What makes you think so?"

"He dropped a pocketbook this morning and Chang picked it up and gave it to me, thinking it was mine. I couldn't help seeing it was stuffed with newspaper clippings—some of them fell out as I was handling the thing, and I don't mind admitting that I looked at them. After all, newspaper clippings aren't private, or shouldn't be. They were all about Bryant and the search for him, and one of them had a photograph which was absolutely like Barnard except for a moustache."

"Did you mention your discovery to Barnard himself?"

"No, I just handed him his property without any comment."

"So the whole things rest on your identification of a newspaper photograph?"

"Well, so far, yes."

"I don't think I'd care to convict anyone on that. Of course you might be right—I don't say he couldn't *possibly* be Bryant. If he were, it would account for a good deal of his contentment at being here— he could hardly have found a better place to hide."

Mallinson seemed a trifle disappointed by this casual reception of news which he evidently thought highly sensational. "Well, what are you going to do about it?" he asked.

Conway pondered a moment and then answered: "I haven't much of an idea. Probably nothing at all. What *can* one do, in any case?"

"But dash it all, if the man *is* Bryant—"

"My dear Mallinson, if the man were Nero it wouldn't have to matter to us for the time being! Saint or crook, we've got to make what we can of each other's company as long as we're here, and I can't see that we shall help matters by striking any attitudes. If I'd suspected who he was at Baskul, of course, I'd have tried to get in touch with Delhi about him—it would have been merely a public duty. But now I think I can claim to be *off* duty."

"Don't you think that's rather a slack way of looking at it?"

"I don't care if it's slack so long as it's sensible."

"I suppose that means your advice to me is to forget what I've found out?"

"You probably can't do that, but I certainly think we might both of us keep our own counsel about it. Not in consideration for Barnard or Bryant or whoever he is, but to save ourselves the deuce of an awkward situation when we get away."

"You mean we ought to let him go?"

"Well, I'll put it a bit differently and say we ought to give somebody else the pleasure of catching him. When you've lived quite sociably with a man for a few months, it seems a little out of place to call for the handcuffs."

"I don't think I agree. The man's nothing but a large-scale thief—I know plenty of people who've lost their money through him."

Conway shrugged his shoulders. He admired the simple black-and-white of Mallinson's code; the public-school ethic might be crude, but at least it was downright. If a man broke the law, it was everyone's duty to hand him over to justice—always provided that it was the kind of law one was not allowed to break. And the law pertaining to cheques and shares and balance sheets was decidedly that kind. Bryant had transgressed it, and though Conway had not taken much interest in the case, he had an impression that it was a fairly bad one of its kind. All he knew was that the failure of the giant Bryant group in New York had resulted in losses of about a hundred million dollars—a record crash, even in a world that exuded records. In some way or other (Conway was not a financial expert) Bryant had been monkeying on Wall Street, and the result had been a warrant for his arrest, his escape to Europe, and extradition orders against him in half a dozen countries.

Conway said finally: "Well, if you take my tip you'll say nothing about it—not for his sake but for ours. Please yourself, of course, so long as you don't forget the possibility that he mayn't be the fellow at all."

BUT HE WAS, and the revelation came that evening after dinner. Chang had left them; Miss Brinklow had turned to her Tibetan grammar; the three male exiles faced each other over coffee and cigars. Conversation during the meal would have languished more than once but for the tact and affability of the Chinese; now, in his absence, a rather unhappy silence supervened. Barnard was for once without jokes. It was clear to Conway that it lay beyond Mallinson's power to treat the American as if nothing had happened, and it was equally clear that Barnard was shrewdly aware that something *had* happened.

Suddenly the American threw away his cigar. "I guess you all know who I am," he said.

Mallinson coloured like a girl, but Conway replied in the same quiet key: "Yes, Mallinson and I think we do."

"Darned careless of me to leave those clippings lying about."

"We're all apt to be careless at times."

"Well, you're mighty calm about it, that's something."

There was another silence, broken at length by Miss Brinklow's shrill voice: "I'm sure *I* don't know who you are, Mr. Barnard, though I must say I guessed all along you were travelling incognito." They all looked at her enquiringly and she went on: "I remember when Mr. Conway said we should all have our names in the papers, you said it didn't affect you. I thought then that Barnard probably wasn't your real name."

The culprit gave a slow smile as he lit himself another cigar. "Madam," he said eventually, "you're not only a smart detective, but you've hit on a really polite name for my present position. I'm travelling incognito. You've said it, and you're dead right. As for you boys, I'm not sorry in a way that you've found me out. So long as none of you had an inkling, we could all have managed, but considering how we're fixed it wouldn't seem very neighbourly to play the high hat with you now. You folks have been so darned nice to me that I don't want to make a lot of trouble. It looks as if we are all going to be joined together for better or worse for some little time ahead, and it's up to us to help one another out as far as we can. As for what happens afterwards, I reckon we can leave that to settle itself."

All this appeared to Conway so eminently reasonable that he gazed at Barnard with considerably greater interest, and even—though it was perhaps odd at such a moment—a touch of genuine appreciation. It was curious to think of that heavy, fleshy, good-humoured, rather paternal-looking man as the world's hugest swindler. He looked far more the type that, with a little extra education, would have made a popular headmaster of a prep school. Behind his joviality there were signs of recent strains and worries, but that did not mean that the joviality was forced. He obviously was what he looked—a "good fellow" in the world's sense, by nature a lamb and only by profession a shark.

Conway said: "Yes, that's very much the best thing, I'm certain."

Then Barnard laughed. It was as if he possessed even deeper reserves of good humour which he could only now draw upon. "Gosh, but it's mighty queer," he exclaimed, spreading himself in his chair. "The whole darned business, I mean. Right across Europe, and on through Turkey and Persia to that little one-horse burg! Police after me all the time, mind you—they nearly got me in Vienna! It's pretty exciting at first, being chased, but it gets on your nerves after a bit. I got a good rest at Baskul, though—I thought I'd be safe in the midst of a revolution."

"And so you were," said Conway with a slight smile, "except from bullets."

"Yeah, and that's what bothered me at the finish. I can tell you it was a mighty hard choice—whether to stay in Baskul and get plugged, or accept a trip in your government's aeroplane and find the bracelets waiting at the other end. I wasn't exactly keen to do either."

"I remember you weren't."

Barnard laughed again. "Well, that's how it was, and you can figger it out for yourself that the change of plan which brought me here don't worry me an awful lot. It's a first-class mystery, I'll allow, but for me, speaking personally, there couldn't have been a better one. It ain't my way to grumble so long as I'm satisfied."

Conway's smile became more definitely cordial. "A very sensible attitude, though I think you rather overdid it. We were all beginning to wonder how you managed to be so contented."

"Well, I *was* contented. This ain't a bad place, when you get used to it. The air's a bit nippy at first, but you can't have everything. And it's nice and quiet for a change. Every fall I go down to Palm Beach for a rest cure, but they don't give you it, those places—you're on the racket just the same. But here I guess I'm having just what the doctor ordered, and it certainly feels grand to me. I'm on a different diet, I can't look at the tape, and my broker can't get me on the telephone."

"I daresay he wishes he could."

"Sure. There'll be a tidy-sized mess to clear up, I've no doubt."

He said this with such simplicity that Conway could not help responding: "I'm not much of an authority on what people call high finance."

It was a lead, and the American accepted it without the slightest reluctance. "High finance," he said, "is mostly a lot of bunk."

"So I've often suspected."

"Look here, Conway, I'll put it like this. A feller does what he's been doing for years, and what lots of other fellers have been doing, and suddenly the market goes against him. He can't help it, but he braces up and waits for the turn. But somehow the turn don't come as it always used to, and when he's lost ten million dollars or so he reads in some paper that a Swede professor thinks it's the end of the world. Now I ask you, does that sort of thing help markets? Of course, it gives him a bit of a shock, but he still can't help it. And there he is till the cops come—if he waits for 'em. I didn't."

"You claim it was all just a run of bad luck, then?"

"Well, I certainly had a large packet."

"You also had other people's money," put in Mallinson sharply.

"Yeah, I did. And why? Because they all wanted something for nothing and hadn't the brains to get it for themselves."

"I don't agree. It was because they trusted you and thought their money was safe."

"Well, it wasn't safe. It couldn't be. There isn't safety anywhere, and those who thought there was were like a lot of saps trying to hide under an umbrella in a typhoon."

Conway said pacifyingly: "Well, we'll all admit you couldn't help the typhoon."

"I couldn't even pretend to help it—any more than you could help what happened after we left Baskul. The same thing struck me then as I watched you in the aeroplane keeping dead calm while Mallinson here had the fidgets. You knew you couldn't do anything about it, and you weren't caring two hoots. Just like I felt myself when the crash came."

"That's nonsense!" cried Mallinson. "Anyone can help swindling. It's a matter of playing the game according to the rules."

"Which is a darned difficult thing to do when the whole game's going to pieces. Besides, there isn't a soul in the world who knows what the rules are. All the professors of Harvard and Yale couldn't tell you 'em."

Mallinson replied rather scornfully: "I'm referring to a few quite simple rules of everyday conduct."

"Then I guess your everyday conduct doesn't include managing trust companies."

Conway made haste to intervene. "We'd better not argue. I don't object in the least to the comparison between your affairs and mine. No doubt we've all been flying blind lately, both literally and in other ways. But we're here now, that's the important thing, and I agree with you that we could easily have had more to grumble about. It's curious, when you come to think about it, that out of four people picked up by chance and kidnapped a thousand miles, three should be able to find some consolation in the business. *You* want a rest cure and a hiding place; Miss Brinklow feels a call to evangelize the heathen Tibetan."

"Who's the third person you're counting?" Mallinson interrupted. "Not me, I hope?"

"I was including myself," answered Conway. "And my own reason is perhaps the simplest of all—I just rather like being here."

Indeed, a short time later, when he took what had come to be his usual solitary evening stroll along the terrace or beside the lotus pool, he felt an extraordinary sense of physical and mental settle- ment. It was perfectly true; he just rather liked being at Shangri-La. Its atmosphere soothed while its mystery stimulated, and the total sensation was agreeable. For some days now he had been reaching, gradually and tentatively, a curious conclusion about the lamasery and its inhabitants; his brain was still busy with it, though in a deeper sense he was unperturbed. He was like a mathematician with an abstruse problem—worrying over it, but worrying very calmly and impersonally.

As for Bryant, whom he decided he would still think of and address as Barnard, the question of his exploits and identity faded instantly into the background, save for a single phrase of his—"the whole game's going to pieces." Conway found himself remembering and echoing it with a wider significance than the American had probably intended; he felt it to be true of more than American banking and trust-company management. It fitted Baskul and Delhi and London, war-making and empire-building, consulates and trade concessions and dinner parties at Government House; there was a reek of dissolu- tion over all that recollected world, and Barnard's cropper had only, perhaps, been better dramatized than his own. The whole game *was* doubtless going to pieces, but fortunately the players were not as a rule put on trial for the pieces they had failed to save. In that respect financiers were unlucky.

But here, at Shangri-La, all was in deep calm. In a moonless sky the stars were lit to the full, and a pale blue sheen lay upon the dome of Karakal. Conway realized then that if by some change of plan the porters from the outside world were to arrive immediately, he would not be completely overjoyed at being spared the interval of waiting. And neither would Barnard, he reflected with an inward smile. It was amusing, really; and then suddenly he knew that he still liked Barnard, or he wouldn't have found it amusing. Somehow the loss of a hundred million dollars was too much to bar a man for; it would have been easier if he had only stolen one's watch. And after all, how *could* anyone lose a hundred millions? Perhaps only in the sense in which a cabinet minister might airily announce that he had been "given India."

And then again he thought of the time when he would leave Shangri-La with the returning porters. He pictured the long, arduous journey, and that eventual moment of arrival at some planter's bungalow in Sikkim or Baltistan—a moment which ought, he felt, to be deliriously cheerful, but which would probably be slightly disappointing. Then the first hand-shakings and self-introduction; the first drinks on clubhouse verandas; sun-bronzed faces staring at him in barely concealed incredulity. At Delhi, no doubt, interviews with the viceroy and the C.I.C.; salaams of turbaned menials; endless reports to be prepared and sent off. Perhaps even a return to England and Whitehall; deck games on the P. & O.; the flaccid palm of an under-secretary; newspaper interviews; hard, mocking, sex-thirsty voices of women—"And is it really true, Mr. Conway, that when you were in Tibet . . .?" There was no doubt of one thing: he would be able to dine out on his yarn for at least a season. But would he enjoy it? He recalled a sentence penned by Gordon during the last days at Khartoum—"I would sooner live like a dervish with the Mahdi than go out to dinner every night in London." Conway's aversion was less definite—a mere anticipation that to tell his story in the past tense would bore him a great deal as well as sadden him a little.

Abruptly, in the midst of his reflections, he was aware of Chang's approach. "Sir," began the Chinese, his slow whisper slightly quickening as he spoke, "I am proud to be the bearer of important news. . . ."

So the porters *had* come before their time, was Conway's first thought; it was odd that he should have been thinking of it so recently. And he felt the pang that he was half prepared for. "Well?" he queried.

Chang's condition was as nearly that of excitement as seemed physically possible for him. "My dear sir, I congratulate you," he continued. "And I am happy to think that I am in some measure responsible—it was after my own strong and repeated recommendations that the High Lama made his decision. He wishes to see you immediately."

Conway's glance was quizzical. "You're being less coherent than usual, Chang. What has happened?"

"The High Lama has sent for you."

"So I gather. But why all the fuss?"

"Because it is extraordinary and unprecedented—even I who urged it did not expect it to happen yet. A fortnight ago you had not arrived, and now you are about to be received by *him*! Never before has it occurred so soon!"

"I'm still rather fogged, you know. I'm to see your High Lama—I realize that all right. But is there anything else?"

"Is it not enough?"

Conway laughed. "Absolutely, I assure you—don't imagine I'm being discourteous. As a matter of fact, something quite different was in my head at first. However, never mind about that now. Of course, I shall be both honoured and delighted to meet the gentleman. When is the appointment?"

"Now. I have been sent to bring you to him."

"Isn't it rather late?"

"That is of no consequence. My dear sir, you will understand many things very soon. And may I add my own personal pleasure that this interval—always an awkward one—is now at an end. Believe me, it has been irksome to me to have to refuse you information on so many occasions—extremely irksome. I am joyful in the knowledge that such unpleasantness will never again be necessary."

"You're a queer fellow, Chang," Conway responded. "But let's be going—don't bother to explain any more. I'm perfectly ready and I appreciate your nice remarks. Lead the way."

Chapter 7

ONWAY WAS QUITE UNRUFFLED, but his demeanour covered an eagerness that grew in intensity as he accompanied Chang across the empty courtyards. If the words of the Chinese meant anything, he was on the threshold of discovery; soon he would know whether his theory, still half formed, were less impossible than it appeared.

Apart from this, it would doubtless be an interesting interview. He had met many peculiar potentates in his time; he took a detached interest in them, and was shrewd as a rule in his assessments. Without self-consciousness he had also the valuable knack of being able to say polite things in languages of which he knew very little indeed. Perhaps, however, he would be chiefly a listener on this occasion. He noticed that Chang was taking him through rooms he had not seen before, all of them rather dim and lovely in lantern-light. Then a spiral staircase climbed to a door at which the Chinese knocked, and which was opened by a Tibetan servant with such promptness that Conway suspected he had been stationed behind it. This part of the lamasery, on a higher storey, was no less tastefully embellished than the rest, but its most immediately striking feature was a dry, tingling warmth, as if all the windows were tightly closed and some kind of steam-heating plant were working at full pressure. The airlessness increased as he passed on, until at last Chang paused before a door which, if bodily sensation could have been trusted, might well have admitted to a Turkish bath.

"The High Lama," whispered Chang, "will receive you alone." Having opened the door for Conway's entrance, he closed it afterwards so silently that his own departure was almost imperceptible. Conway stood hesitant, breathing an atmosphere that was not only sultry, but full of dusk, so that it was several seconds before he could accustom his eyes to the gloom. Then he slowly built up an

He was a little old man in Chinese dress

impression of a dark-curtained, low-roofed apartment, simply furnished with table and chairs. On one of these sat a small, pale, and wrinkled person, motionlessly shadowed and yielding an effect as of some fading, antique portrait in chiaroscuro. If there were such a thing as presence divorced from actuality, here it was, adorned with a classic dignity that was more an emanation than an attribute. Conway was curious about his own intense perception of all this, and wondered if it were dependable or merely his reaction to the rich, crepuscular warmth; he felt dizzy under the gaze of those ancient eyes, took a few forward paces, and then halted. The occupant of the chair grew now less vague in outline, but scarcely more corporeal; he was a little old man in Chinese dress, its folds and flounces loose against a flat, emaciated frame. "You are Mr. Conway?" he whispered in excellent English.

The voice was pleasantly soothing, and touched with a very gentle melancholy that fell upon Conway with strange beatitude; though once again the sceptic in him was inclined to hold the temperature responsible.

"I am," he answered.

The voice went on. "It is a pleasure to see you, Mr. Conway. I sent for you because I thought we should do well to have a talk together. Please sit down beside me and have no fear. I am an old man and can do no one any harm."

Conway answered: "I feel it a signal honour to be received by you."

"I thank you, my dear Conway—I shall call you that, according to your English fashion. It is, as I said, a moment of great pleasure for me. My sight is poor, but believe me, I am able to see you in my mind, as well as with my eyes. I trust you have been comfortable at Shangri-La since your arrival?"

"Extremely so."

"I am glad. Chang has done his best for you, no doubt. It has been a great pleasure to him also. He tells me you have been asking many questions about our community and its affairs?"

"I am certainly interested in them."

"Then if you can spare me a little time, I shall be pleased to give you a brief account of our foundation."

"There is nothing I should appreciate more."

"That is what I had thought—and hoped . . . . But first of all, before our discourse . . . ."

He made the slightest stir of a hand, and immediately, by what technique of summons Conway could not detect, a servant entered to prepare the elegant ritual of tea-drinking. The little eggshell bowls of almost colourless fluid were placed on a lacquered tray; Conway, who knew the ceremony, was by no means contemptuous of it. The voice resumed: "Our ways are familiar to you, then?"

Obeying an impulse which he could neither analyse nor find desire to control, Conway answered: "I lived in China for some years."

"You did not tell Chang?"

"No."

"Then why am I so honoured?"

Conway was rarely at a loss to explain his own motives, but on this occasion he could not think of any reason at all. At length he replied: "To be quite candid, I haven't the slightest idea, except that I must have wanted to tell you."

"The best of all reasons, I am sure, between those who are to become friends . . . . Now tell me, is this not a delicate aroma? The teas of China are many and fragrant, but this, which is a special product of our own valley, is in my opinion their equal."

Conway lifted the bowl to his lips and tasted. The savour was slender, elusive, and recondite, a ghostly bouquet that haunted rather than lived on the tongue. He said: "It is very delightful, and also quite new to me."

"Yes, like a great many of our valley herbs, it is both unique and precious. It should be tasted, of course, very slowly—not only in reverence and affection, but to extract the fullest degree of pleasure. This is a famous lesson that we may learn from Kou Kai Tchou, who lived some fifteen centuries ago. He would always hesitate to reach the succulent marrow when he was eating a piece of sugarcane, for, as he explained—'I introduce myself gradually into the region of delights.' Have you studied any of the great Chinese classics?"

Conway replied that he was slightly acquainted with a few of them. He knew that the allusive conversation would, according to etiquette, continue until the tea bowls were taken away; but he found it far from irritating, despite his keenness to hear the history of Shangri-La. Doubtless there was a certain amount of Kou Kai Tchou's reluctant sensibility in himself.

At length the signal was given, again mysteriously, the servant padded in and out, and with no more preamble the High Lama of Shangri-La began:

"Probably you are familiar, my dear Conway, with the general outline of Tibetan history. I am informed by Chang that you have made ample use of our library here, and I doubt not that you have studied the scanty but exceedingly interesting annals of these regions. You will be aware, anyhow, that Nestorian Christianity was widespread throughout Asia during the Middle Ages, and that its memory lingered long after its actual decay. In the seventeenth century a Christian revival was impelled directly from Rome through the agency of those heroic Jesuit missionaries whose journeys, if I may permit myself the remark, are so much more interesting to read of than those of St. Paul. Gradually the Church established itself over an immense area, and it is a remarkable fact, not realized by many Europeans today, that for thirty-eight years there existed a Christian mission in Lhasa itself. It was not, however, from Lhasa but from Pekin, in the year 1719, that four Capuchin friars set out in search of any remnants of the Nestorian faith that might still be surviving in the hinterland.

"They travelled southwest for many months, by Lanchow and the Koko-Nor, facing hardships which you will well imagine. Three died on the way, and the fourth was not far from death when by accident he stumbled into the rocky defile that remains today the only practical approach to the valley of Blue Moon. There, to his joy and surprise, he found a friendly and prosperous population who made haste to display what I have always regarded as our oldest tradition—that of hospitality to strangers. Quickly he recovered health and began to preach his mission. The people were Buddhists, but willing to hear him, and he had considerable success. There was an ancient lamasery existing then on this same mountain shelf, but it was in a state of decay both physical and spiritual, and as the Capuchin's harvest increased, he conceived the idea of setting up

106

on the same magnificent site a Christian monastery. Under his surveillance the old buildings were repaired and largely reconstructed, and he himself began to live here in the year 1734, when he was fifty-three years of age.

"Now let me tell you more about this man. His name was Perrault, and he was by birth a Luxembourger. Before devoting himself to Far Eastern missions he had studied at Paris, Bologna, and other universities; he was something of a scholar. There are few existing records of his early life, but it was not in any way unusual for one of his age and profession. He was fond of music and the arts, had a special aptitude for languages, and before he was sure of his vocation he had tasted all the familiar pleasures of the world. Malplaquet was fought when he was a youth, and he knew from personal contact the horrors of war and invasion. He was physically sturdy; during his first years here he laboured with his hands like any other man, tilling his own garden, and learning from the inhabitants as well as teaching them. He found gold deposits along the valley, but they did not tempt him; he was more deeply interested in local plants and herbs. He was humble and by no means bigoted. He deprecated polygamy, but he saw no reason to inveigh against the prevalent fondness for the *tangatse* berry, to which were ascribed medicinal properties, but which was chiefly popular because its effects were those of a mild narcotic. Perrault, in fact, became somewhat of an addict himself; it was his way to accept from native life all that it offered which he found harmless and pleasant, and to give in return the spiritual treasure of the West. He was not an ascetic; he enjoyed the good things of the world, and was careful to teach his converts cooking as well as catechism. I want you to have an impression of a very earnest, busy, learned, simple, and enthusiastic person who, along with his priestly functions, did not disdain to put on a mason's overall and help in the actual building of these very rooms. That was, of course, a work of immense difficulty, and one which nothing but his pride and steadfastness could have overcome. Pride, I say, because it was undoubtedly a dominant motive at the beginning—the pride in his own Faith that made him decide that if Gautama could inspire men to build a temple on the ledge of Shangri-La, Rome was capable of no less.

"But time passed, and it was not unnatural that this motive should yield place gradually to more tranquil ones. Emulation is, after all, a young man's spirit, and Perrault, by the time his monastery was well established, was already full of years. You must bear in mind that he had not, from a strict point of view, been acting very regularly; though some latitude must surely be extended to one whose ecclesiastical superiors are located at a distance measurable in years rather than miles. But the folk of the valley and the monks themselves had no misgivings; they loved and obeyed him, and as years went on, came to venerate him also. At intervals it was his custom to send reports to the Bishop of Pekin; but often they never reached him, and as it was to be presumed that the bearers had succumbed to the perils of the journey, Perrault grew more and more unwilling to hazard their lives, and after about the middle of the century he gave up the practice. Some of his earlier messages, however, must have got through, and a doubt of his activities have been aroused, for in the year 1769 a stranger brought a letter written twelve years before, summoning Perrault to Rome.

"He would have been over seventy had the command been received without delay; as it was, he had turned eighty-nine. The long trek over mountain and plateau was unthinkable; he could never have endured the scouring gales and fierce chills of the wilderness outside. He sent, therefore, a courteous reply explaining the situation, but there is no record that his message ever passed the barrier of the great ranges.

"So Perrault remained at Shangri-La, not exactly in defiance of superior orders, but because it was physically impossible for him to fulfil them. In any case he was an old man, and death would probably soon put an end both to him and his irregularity. By this time the institution he had founded had begun to undergo a subtle change. It might be deplorable, but it was not really very astonishing; for it could hardly be expected that one man unaided should uproot permanently the habits and traditions of an epoch. He had no Western colleagues to hold firm when his own grip relaxed; and it had perhaps been a mistake to build on a site that held such older and differing memories. It was asking too much; but was it not asking even more to expect a white-haired veteran, just entering the nineties, to realize the mistake that he had made? Perrault, at any rate, did not then realize it. He was far too old and happy. His followers were devoted even when they forgot his teaching, while the people of the valley held him in such reverent affection that he forgave with ever-increasing ease their lapse into former customs. He was still active, and his faculties had remained exceptionally keen. At the age of ninety-eight he began to study the Buddhist writings that had been left at Shangri-La by its previous occupants, and his intention was then to devote the rest of his life to the composition of a book attacking Buddhism from the standpoint of orthodoxy. He actually finished this task (we have his manuscript complete), but the attack was very gentle, for he had by that time reached the round figure of a century—an age at which even the keenest acrimonies are apt to fade.

"Meanwhile, as you may suppose, many of his early disciples had died, and as there were few replacements, the number resident under the rule of the old Capuchin steadily diminished. From over eighty at one time, it dwindled to a score, and then to a mere dozen, most of them very aged themselves. Perrault's life at this time grew to be a very calm and placid waiting for the end. He was far too old for disease and discontent; only the everlasting sleep could claim him now, and he was not afraid. The valley people, out of kindness, supplied food and clothing; his library gave him work. He had become rather frail, but still kept energy to fulfil the major ceremonial of his office; the rest of the tranquil days he spent with his books, his memories, and the mild ecstasies of the narcotic. His mind remained so extraordinarily clear that he even embarked upon a study of certain mystic practices that the Indians call yoga, and which are based upon various special methods of breathing. For a man of such an age the enterprise might well have seemed hazardous, and it was certainly true that soon afterwards, in that memorable year 1789, news descended to the valley that Perrault was dying at last.

"He lay in his room, my dear Conway, where he could see from the window the white blur that was all his failing eyesight gave him of Karakal; but he could see with his mind also; he could picture the clear and matchless outline that he had first glimpsed half a century before. And there came to him, too, the strange parade of all his many experiences, the years of travel across desert and upland, the great crowds in Western cities, the clang and glitter of Marlborough's troops. His mind had straitened to a snow-white calm; he was ready, willing, and glad to die. He gathered his friends and servants round him and bade them all farewell; then he asked to be left alone a while. It was during such a solitude, with his body sinking and his mind lifted to beatitude, that he had hoped to give up his soul . . . but it did not happen so. He lay for many weeks without speech or movement, and then he began to recover. He was a hundred and eight."

The whispering ceased for a moment, and to Conway, stirring slightly, it appeared that the High Lama had been translating, with fluency, out of a remote and private dream. At length he went on:

"Like others who have waited long on the threshold of death, Perrault had been granted a vision of some significance to take back with him into the world; and of this vision more must be said later. Here I will confine myself to his actions and behaviour, which were indeed remarkable. For instead of convalescing idly, as might have been expected, he plunged forthwith into rigorous self-discipline somewhat curiously combined with narcotic indulgence. Drug-taking and deep-breathing exercises—it could not have seemed a very death-defying regimen; yet the fact remains that when the last of the old monks died, in 1794, Perrault himself was still living.

"It would almost have brought a smile had there been anyone at Shangri-La with a sufficiently distorted sense of humour. The wrinkled Capuchin, no more decrepit than he had been for a dozen years, persevered in a secret ritual he had evolved, while to the folk of the valley he soon became veiled in mystery, a hermit of uncanny powers who lived alone on that formidable cliff. But there was still a tradition of affection for him, and it came to be regarded as meritorious and luck-bringing to climb to Shangri-La and leave a simple gift, or perform some manual task that was needed there. On all such pilgrims Perrault bestowed his blessing—forgetful, it might be, that they were lost and straying sheep. For 'Te Deum Laudamus' and 'Om Mane Padme Hum' were now heard equally in the temples of the valley.

"As the new century approached, the legend grew into a rich and fantastic folklore—it was said that Perrault had become a god, that he worked miracles, and that on certain nights he flew to the summit of Karakal to hold a candle to the sky. There is a paleness always on the mountain at full moon; but I need not assure you that neither Perrault nor any other man has ever climbed there. I mention it, even though it may seem unnecessary, because there is a mass of unreliable testimony that Perrault did and could do all kinds of impossible things. It was supposed, for instance, that he practised the art of self-levitation, of which so much appears in accounts of Buddhist mysticism; but the more sober truth is that he made many experiments to that end, but entirely without success. He did, however, discover that the impairment of ordinary senses could be somewhat offset by a development of others; he acquired skill in telepathy which was perhaps remarkable, and though he made no claim to any specific powers of healing, there was a quality in his mere presence that was helpful in certain cases.

"You will wish to know how he spent his time during these unprecedented years. His attitude may be summed up by saying that, as he had not died at a normal age, he began to feel that there was no discoverable reason why he either should or should not do so at any definite time in the future. Having already proved himself abnormal, it was as easy to believe that the abnormality might continue as to expect it to end at any moment. And that being so, he began to behave without care for the imminence with which he had been so long preoccupied; he began to live the kind of life that he had always desired, but had so rarely found possible; for he had kept at heart and throughout all vicissitudes the tranquil tastes of a scholar. His memory was astonishing; it appeared to have escaped the trammels of the physical into some upper region of immense clarity; it almost seemed that he could now learn *everything* with far greater ease than during his student days he had been able to learn *anything*. He was soon, of course, brought up against a need for books, but there were a few he had had with him from the first, and they included, you may be interested to hear, an English grammar and dictionary and Florio's translation of Montaigne. With these to work on he contrived to master the intricacies of your language, and we still possess in our library the manuscript of one of his first linguistic exercises—a translation of Montaigne's essay on Vanity into Tibetan—surely a unique production."

Conway smiled. "I should be interested to see it some time, if I might."

"With the greatest of pleasure. It was, you may think, a singularly unpractical accomplishment, but recollect that Perrault had reached a singularly unpractical age. He would have been lonely without some such occupation—at any rate until the fourth year of the nineteenth century, which marks an important event in the history of our foundation. For it was then that a second stranger from Europe arrived in the valley of Blue Moon. He was a young Austrian named Henschell who had soldiered against Napoleon in Italy—a youth of noble birth, high culture, and much charm of manner. The wars had ruined his fortunes, and he had wandered across Russia into Asia with some vague intention of retrieving them. It would be interesting to know how exactly he reached the plateau, but he had no very clear idea himself; indeed, he was as near death when he arrived here as Perrault himself had once been. Again the hospitality of Shangri-La was extended, and the stranger recovered—but there the parallel breaks down. For Perrault had come to preach and proselytize, whereas Henschell took a more immediate interest in the gold deposits. His first ambition was to enrich himself and return to Europe as soon as possible.

"But he did not return. An odd thing happened—though one that has happened so often since that perhaps we must now agree that it cannot be very odd after all. The valley, with its peacefulness and its utter freedom from worldly cares, tempted him again and again to delay his departure, and one day, having heard the local legend, he climbed to Shangri-La and had his first meeting with Perrault.

"That meeting was, in the truest sense, historic. Perrault, if a little beyond such human passions as friendship or affection, was yet endowed with a rich benignity of mind which touched the youth as water upon a parched soil. I will not try to describe the association that sprang up between the two; the one gave utmost adoration, while the other shared his knowledge, his ecstasies, and the wild dream that had now become the only reality left for him in the world."

There was a pause, and Conway said very quietly, "Pardon the interruption, but that is not quite clear to me."

"I know." The whispered reply was completely sympathetic. "It would be remarkable indeed if it were. It is a matter which I shall be pleased to explain before our talk is over, but for the present, if you will forgive me, I will confine myself to simpler things. A fact that will interest you is that Henschell began our collections of Chinese art, as well as our library and musical acquisitions. He made a remarkable journey to Pekin and brought back the first con-signment in the year 1809. He did not leave the valley again, but it was his ingenuity which devised the complicated system by which the lamasery has ever since been able to obtain anything needful from the outer world."

"I suppose you found it easy to make payment in gold?"

"Yes, we have been fortunate in possessing supplies of a metal which is held in such high esteem in other parts of the world."

"Such high esteem that you must have been very lucky to escape a gold rush."

The High Lama inclined his head in the merest indication of agreement. "That, my dear Conway, was always Henschell's fear. He was careful that none of the porters bringing books and art treasures should ever approach too closely; he made them leave their burdens a day's journey outside, to be fetched afterwards by our valley folk themselves. He even arranged for sentries to keep constant watch on the entrance to the defile. But it soon occurred to him that there was an easier and more final safeguard."

"Yes?" Conway's voice was guardedly tense.

"You see, there was no need to fear invasion by an army. That will never be possible, owing to the nature and distances of the country. The most ever to be expected was the arrival of a few half-lost wan-derers who, even if they were armed, would probably be so weakened as to constitute no danger. It was decided, therefore, that hencefor-ward strangers might come as freely as they chose—with but one important proviso.

"And, over a period of years, such strangers did come. Chinese merchants, tempted into the crossing of the plateau, chanced occasionally on this one traverse out of so many others possible to them. Nomad Tibetans, wandering from their tribes, strayed here sometimes like weary animals. All were made welcome, though some reached the shelter of the valley only to die. In the year of Waterloo two English missionaries, travelling overland to Pekin, crossed the ranges by an unnamed pass and had the extraordinary luck to arrive as calmly as if they were paying a call. In 1820 a Greek trader, accompanied by sick and famished servants, was found dying at the topmost ridge of the pass. In 1822 three Spaniards, having heard some vague story of gold, reached here after many wanderings and disappointments. Again, in 1830, there was a larger influx. Two Germans, a Russian, an Englishman, and a Swede made the dreaded crossing of the Tian-Shans, impelled by a motive that was to become increasingly common—scientific exploration. By the time of their approach a slight modification had taken place in the attitude of Shangri-La towards its visitors—not only were they now welcomed if they chanced to find their way into the valley, but it had become customary to meet them if they ever ventured within a certain radius. All this was for a reason I shall later discuss, but the point is of importance as showing that the lamasery was no longer hospitably indifferent; it had already both a need and a desire for new arrivals. And indeed in the years to follow it happened that more than one party of explorers, glorying in their first distant glimpse of Karakal, encountered messengers bearing a cordial invitation—and one that was rarely declined.

"Meanwhile the lamasery had begun to acquire many of its present characteristics. I must stress the fact that Henschell was exceedingly able and talented, and that the Shangri-La of today owes as much to him as to its founder. Yes, quite as much, I often think. For his was the firm yet kindly hand that every institution needs at a certain stage of its development, and his loss would have been altogether irreparable had he not completed more than a lifework before he died."

Conway looked up to echo rather than question those final words. *"He died!"*

"Yes. It was very sudden. He was killed. It was in the year of your Indian Mutiny. Just before his death a Chinese artist had sketched him, and I can show you that sketch now—it is in this room."

The slight gesture of the hand was repeated, and once again a servant entered. Conway, as a spectator in a trance, watched the man withdraw a small curtain at the far end of the room and leave a lantern swinging amongst the shadows. Then he heard the whisper inviting him to move, the whisper that had already become a familiar music.

He stumbled to his feet and strode across to the trembling circle of light. The sketch was small, hardly more than a miniature in coloured inks, but the artist had contrived to give the flesh-tones a waxwork delicacy of texture. The features were of great beauty, almost girlish in modelling, and Conway found in their winsomeness an instantly personal appeal, even across the barriers of time, death, and artifice. But the strangest thing of all was one that he realized only after his first gasp of admiration: the face was that of a young man.

He stammered as he moved away: "But—you said—this was done just before his death?"

"Yes. It is a very good likeness."

"Then if he died in the year you said—"

"He did."

"And he came here, you told me, in 1803, when he was a youth?"

"Yes."

Conway did not answer for a moment; presently, with an effort, he collected himself to say: "And he was killed, you were telling me?"

"Yes. An Englishman shot him. It was a few weeks after the Englishman had arrived at Shangri-La. He was another of those explorers."

"What was the cause of it?"

"There had been a quarrel—about some porters. Henschell had just told him of the important proviso that governs our reception of guests. It was a task of some difficulty, and ever since, despite my own enfeeblement, I have felt constrained to perform it myself."

The High Lama made another and longer pause, with just a hint of enquiry in his silence; when he continued, it was to add: "Perhaps you are wondering, my dear Conway, what that proviso may be?"

Conway answered slowly and in a low voice: "I think I can already guess."

"Can you indeed? And can you guess anything else after this long and curious story of mine?"

Conway dizzied in brain as he sought to answer the question; the room was now a whorl of shadows with that ancient benignity at its centre. Throughout the narrative he had listened with an intentness that had perhaps shielded him from realizing the fullest implications of it all; now, with the mere attempt at conscious expression, he was flooded over with amazement, and the gathering certainty in his mind was almost stifled as it sprang to words. "It seems impossible," he stammered. "And yet I can't help thinking of it—it's astonishing—and extraordinary—and quite incredible—and yet not *absolutely* beyond my powers of belief—"

"What is, my son?"

And Conway answered, shaken with an emotion for which he knew no reason and which he did not seek to conceal: *"That you are still alive, Father Perrault."*

Chapter 8

HERE HAD BEEN A PAUSE, imposed by the High Lama's call for further refreshment; Conway did not wonder at it, for the strain of such a long recital must have been considerable. Nor was he himself ungrateful for the respite. He felt that the interval was as desirable from an artistic as from any other point of view, and that the bowls of tea, with their accompaniment of conventionally improvised courtesies, fulfilled the same function as a cadenza in music. This reflection brought out (unless it were mere coincidence) an odd example of the High Lama's telepathic powers, for he immediately began to talk about music and to express pleasure that Conway's taste in that direction had not been entirely unsatisfied at Shangri-La. Conway answered with suitable politeness and added that he had been surprised to find the lamasery in possession of such a complete library of European composers. The compliment was acknowledged between slow sips of tea. "Ah, my dear Conway, we are fortunate in that one of our number is a gifted musician—he was, indeed, a pupil of Chopin's—and we have been happy to place in his hands the entire management of our salon. You must certainly meet him."

"I should like to. Chang, by the way, was telling me that your favourite Western composer is Mozart."

"That is so," came the reply. "Mozart has an austere elegance which we find very satisfying. He builds a house which is neither too big nor too little, and he furnishes it in perfect taste."

The exchange of comments continued until the tea bowls were taken away; by that time Conway was able to remark quite calmly: "So, to resume our earlier discussion, you intend to keep us? That, I take it, is the important and invariable proviso?"

"You have guessed correctly, my son."

"In other words, we are to stay here for ever?"

"I should greatly prefer to employ your excellent English idiom and say that we are all of us here 'for good.'"

"What puzzles me is why we four, out of all the rest of the world's inhabitants, should have been chosen."

Relapsing into his earlier and more consequential manner, the High Lama responded: "It is an intricate story, if you would care to hear it. You must know that we have always aimed, as far as possible, to keep our numbers in fairly constant recruitment—since, apart from any other reasons, it is pleasant to have with us people of various ages and representative of different periods. Unfortunately, since the recent European War and the Russian Revolution, travel and exploration in Tibet have been almost completely held up; in fact, our last visitor, a Japanese, arrived in 1912, and was not, to be candid, a very valuable acquisition. You see, my dear Conway, we are not quacks or charlatans; we do not and cannot guarantee success; some of our visitors derive no benefit at all from their stay here; others merely live to what might be called a normally advanced age and then die from some trifling ailment. In general we have found that Tibetans, owing to their being inured to both the altitude and other conditions, are much less sensitive than outside races; they are charming people, and we have admitted many of them, but I doubt if more than a few will pass their hundredth year. The Chinese are a little better, but even among them we have a high percentage of failures. Our best subjects, undoubtedly, are the Nordic and Latin races of Europe; perhaps the Americans would be equally adaptable, and I count it our great good fortune that we have at last, in the person of one of your companions, secured a citizen of that nation. But I must continue with the answer to your question. The position was, as I have been explaining, that for nearly two decades we had welcomed no newcomers, and as there had been several deaths during that period, a problem was beginning to arise. A few years ago, however, one of our number came to the rescue with a novel idea; he was a young fellow, a native of our valley, absolutely trustworthy and in fullest sympathy with our aims; but, like all the valley people, he was denied by nature the chance that comes more fortunately to those from a distance. It was he who suggested that he should leave us, make his way to some surrounding country, and bring us additional colleagues by a method which would have been impossible in an earlier age. It was in many respects a revolutionary proposal, but we gave our consent after due consideration. For we must move with the times, you know, even at Shangri-La."

"You mean that he was sent out deliberately to bring someone back by air?"

"Well, you see, he was an exceedingly gifted and resourceful youth, and we had great confidence in him. It was his own idea, and we allowed him a free hand in carrying it out. All we knew definitely was that the first stage of his plan included a period of tuition at an American flying school."

"But how could he manage the rest of it? It was only by chance that there happened to be that aeroplane at Basku—"

"True, my dear Conway—many things are by chance. But it happened, after all, to be just the chance that Talu was looking for. Had he not found it, there might have been another chance in a year or two—or perhaps, of course, none at all. I confess I was surprised when our sentinels gave news of his descent on the plateau. The progress of aviation is rapid, but it had seemed likely to me that much more time would elapse before an average machine could make such a crossing of the mountains."

"It wasn't an average machine. It was a rather special one, made for mountain flying."

"Again by chance? Our young friend was indeed fortunate. It is a pity that we cannot discuss the matter with him—we were all grieved at his death. You would have liked him, Conway."

Conway nodded slightly; he felt it very possible. He said, after a silence: "But what's the idea behind it all?"

"My son, your way of asking that question gives me infinite pleasure. In the course of a somewhat long experience it has never before been put to me in tones of such calmness. My revelation has been greeted in almost every conceivable manner—with indignation, distress, fury, disbelief, and hysteria—but never until this night with mere interest. It is, however, an attitude that I most cordially welcome. Today you are interested; tomorrow you will feel concern; eventually, it may be, I shall claim your devotion."

"That is more than I should care to promise."

"Your very doubt pleases me—it is the basis of profound and significant faith . . . . But let us not argue. You are interested, and that, from you, is much. All I ask in addition is that what I tell you now shall remain, for the present, unknown to your three companions."

Conway was silent.

"The time will come when they will learn, like you, but that moment, for their own sakes, had better not be hastened. I am so certain of your wisdom in this matter that I do not ask for a promise; you will act, I know, as we both think best . . . . Now let me begin by sketching for you a very agreeable picture. You are still, I should say, a youngish man by the world's standards; your life, as people say, lies ahead of you; in the normal course you might expect twenty or thirty years of only slightly and gradually diminishing activity. By no means a cheerless prospect, and I can hardly expect you to see it as I do—as a slender, breathless, and far too frantic interlude. The first quarter-century of your life was doubtless lived under the cloud of being too young for things, while the last quarter-century would normally be shadowed by the still darker cloud of being too old for them; and between those two clouds, what small and narrow sunlight illumines a human lifetime! But you, it may be, are destined to be more fortunate, since by the standards of Shangri-La your sunlit years have scarcely yet begun. It will happen, perhaps, that decades hence you will feel no older than you are today—you may preserve, as Henschell did, a long and wondrous youth. But that, believe me, is only an early and superficial phase. There will come a time when you will age like others, though far more slowly, and into a condition infinitely nobler; at eighty you may still climb to the pass with a young man's gait, but at twice that age you must not expect the whole marvel to have persisted. We are not workers of miracles; we have made no conquest of death or even of decay. All we have done and can sometimes do is to slacken the tempo of this brief interval that is called life. We do this by methods which are as simple here as they are impossible elsewhere; but make no mistake: the end awaits us all.

"Yet it is, nevertheless, a prospect of much charm that I unfold for you—long tranquillities during which you will observe a sunset as men in the outer world hear the striking of a clock, and with far less care. The years will come and go, and you will pass from fleshly enjoyments into austerer but no less satisfying realms; you may lose the keenness of muscle and appetite, but there will be gain to match your loss; you will achieve calmness and profundity, ripeness and wisdom, and the clear enchantment of memory. And, most precious of all, you will have Time—that rare and lovely gift that your Western countries have lost the more they have pursued it. Think for a moment. You will have time to read—never again will you skim pages to save minutes, or avoid some study lest it prove too engrossing. You have also a taste for music—here, then, are your scores and instruments, with Time, unruffled and unmeasured, to give you their richest savour. And you are also, we will say, a man of good fellowship—does it not charm you to think of wise and serene friendships, a long and kindly traffic of the mind from which death may not call you away with his customary hurry? Or, if it is solitude that you prefer, could you not employ our pavilions to enrich the gentleness of lonely thoughts?"

The voice made a pause which Conway did not seek to fill.

"You make no comment, my dear Conway. Forgive my elo-quence—I belong to an age and a nation that never considered it bad form to be articulate . . . . But perhaps you are thinking of wife, par-ents, children, left behind in the world? Or maybe ambitions to do this or that? Believe me, though the pang may be keen at first, in a decade from now even its ghost will not haunt you. Though in point of fact, if I read your mind correctly, you have no such griefs."

Conway was startled by the accuracy of the judgment. "That's so," he replied. "I'm unmarried; I have few close friends and no ambitions."

"No ambitions? And how have you contrived to escape those wide-spread maladies?"

For the first time Conway felt that he was actually taking part in a conversation. He said: "It always seemed to me in my profession that a good deal of what passed for success would be rather disagreeable, apart from needing more effort than I felt called upon to make. I was in the Consular Service—quite a subordinate post, but it suited me well enough."

"Yet your soul was not in it?"

"Neither my soul nor my heart nor more than half my energies. I'm naturally rather lazy."

The wrinkles deepened and twisted till Conway realized that the High Lama was very probably smiling. "Laziness in doing certain things can be a great virtue," resumed the whisper. "In any case, you will scarcely find us exacting in such a matter. Chang, I believe, explained to you our principle of moderation, and one of the things in which we are always moderate is activity. I myself, for instance, have been able to learn ten languages; the ten might have been twenty had I worked immoderately. But I did not. And it is the same in other directions; you will find us neither profligate nor ascetic. Until we reach an age when care is advisable, we gladly accept the pleasures of the table, while—for the benefit of our younger col-leagues—the women of the valley have happily applied the principle of moderation to their own chastity. All things considered, I feel sure you will get used to our ways without much effort. Chang, indeed, was very optimistic—and so, after this meeting, am I. But there is, I admit, an odd quality in you that I have never met in any of our visitors hitherto. It is not quite cynicism, still less bitterness; perhaps it is partly disillusionment, but it is also a clarity of mind that I should not have expected in anyone younger than—say, a century or so. It is, if I had to put a single word to it, passionlessness."

Conway answered: "As good a word as most, no doubt. I don't know whether you classify the people who come here, but if so, you can label me '1914–18.' That makes me, I should think, a unique specimen in your museum of antiquities—the other three who arrived along with me don't enter the category. I used up most of my passions and energies during the years I've mentioned, and though I don't talk much about it, the chief thing I've asked from the world since then is to leave me alone. I find in this place a certain charm and quietness that appeals to me, and no doubt, as you remark, I shall get used to things."

"Is that all, my son?"

"I hope I am keeping well to your own rule of moderation."

"You are clever—as Chang told me, you are very clever. But is there nothing in the prospect I have outlined that tempts you to any stronger feeling?"

Conway was silent for an interval and then replied: "I was deeply impressed by your story of the past, but to be candid, your sketch of the future interests me only in an abstract sense. I can't look so far ahead. I should certainly be sorry if I had to leave Shangri-La tomorrow or next week, or perhaps even next year; but how I shall feel about it if I live to be a hundred isn't a matter to prophesy. I can face it, like any other future, but in order to make me keen it must have a point. I've sometimes doubted whether life itself has any; and if not, long life must be even more pointless."

"My friend, the traditions of this building, both Buddhist and Christian, are very reassuring."

"Maybe. But I'm afraid I still hanker after some more definite reason for envying the centenarian."

"There *is* a reason, and a very definite one indeed. It is the whole reason for this colony of chance-sought strangers living beyond their years. We do not follow an idle experiment, a mere whimsy. We have a dream and a vision. It is a vision that first appeared to old Perrault when he lay dying in this room in the year 1789. He looked back then on his long life, as I have already told you, and it seemed to him that all the loveliest things were transient and perishable, and that war, lust, and brutality might some day crush them until there were no more left in the world. He remembered sights he had seen with his own eyes, and with his mind he pictured others; he saw the nations strengthening, not in wisdom, but in vulgar passions and the will to destroy; he saw their machine power multiplying until a single-weaponed man might have matched a whole army of the Grand Monarque. And he perceived that when they had filled the land and sea with ruin, they would take to the air . . . . Can you say that his vision was untrue?"

"True indeed."

"But that was not all. He foresaw a time when men, exultant in the technique of homicide, would rage so hotly over the world that every precious thing would be in danger, every book and picture and harmony, every treasure garnered through two millenniums, the small, the delicate, the defenceless—all would be lost like the lost books of Livy, or wrecked as the English wrecked the Summer Palace in Pekin."

"I share your opinion of that."

"Of course. But what are the opinions of reasonable men against iron and steel? Believe me, that vision of old Perrault will come true. And that, my son, is why *I* am here, and why *you* are here, and why we may pray to outlive the doom that gathers around on every side."

"To outlive it?"

"There is a chance. It will all come to pass before you are as old as I am."

"And you think that Shangri-La will escape?"

"Perhaps. We may expect no mercy, but we may faintly hope for neglect. Here we shall stay with our books and our music and our meditations, conserving the frail elegancies of a dying age, and seeking such wisdom as men will need when their passions are all spent. We have a heritage to cherish and bequeath. Let us take what pleasure we may until that time comes."

"And then?"

"Then, my son, when the strong have devoured each other, the Christian ethic may at last be fulfilled, and the meek shall inherit the earth."

A shadow of emphasis had touched the whisper, and Conway surrendered to the beauty of it; again he felt the surge of darkness around, but now symbolically, as if the world outside were already brewing for the storm. And then he saw that the High Lama of Shangri-La was actually astir, rising from his chair, standing upright like the half-embodiment of a ghost. In mere politeness Conway made to assist; but suddenly a deeper impulse seized him, and he did what he had never done to any man before: he knelt, and hardly knew he did.

"I understand you, Father,' he said.

He was not perfectly aware of how at last he took his leave; he was in a dream from which he did not emerge till long afterwards. He remembered the night air icy after the heat of those upper rooms, and Chang's presence, a silent serenity, as they crossed the starlit court-yards together. Never had Shangri-La offered more concentrated loveliness to his eyes; the valley lay imagined over the edge of the cliff, and the image was of a deep unrippled pool that matched the peace of his own thoughts. For Conway had passed beyond astonishments. The long talk, with its varying phases, had left him empty of all save a satisfaction that was as much of the mind as of the emotions, and as much of the spirit as of either; even his doubts were now no longer harassing, but part of a subtle harmony. Chang did not speak, and neither did he. It was very late, and he was glad that all the others had gone to bed.

Chapter 9

N THE MORNING he wondered if all that he could call to mind were part of a waking or a sleeping vision. He was soon reminded. A chorus of questions greeted him when he appeared at breakfast. "You certainly had a long talk with the boss last night," began the American. "We meant to wait up for you, but we got tired. What sort of a guy is he?"

"Did he say anything about the porters?" asked Mallinson eagerly.

"I hope you mentioned to him about having a missionary stationed here," said Miss Brinklow.

The bombardment served to raise in Conway his usual defensive armament. "I'm afraid I'm probably going to disappoint you all," he replied, slipping easily into the mood. "I didn't discuss with him the question of missions; he didn't mention the porters to me at all; and as for his appearance, I can only say that he's a very old man who speaks excellent English and is quite intelligent."

Mallinson cut in with irritation: "The main thing to us is whether he's to be trusted or not. Do you think he means to let us down?"

"He didn't strike me as a dishonourable person."

"Why on earth didn't you worry him about the porters?"

"It didn't occur to me."

Mallinson stared at him incredulously. "I can't understand you, Conway. You were so damned good in that Baskul affair that I can hardly believe you're the same man. You seem to have gone all to pieces."

"I'm sorry."

"No good being sorry. You ought to buck up and look as if you cared what happens."

"You misunderstand me. I meant that I was sorry to have disappointed you."

Conway's voice was curt, an intended mask to his feelings, which were, indeed, so mixed that they could hardly have been guessed by others. He had slightly surprised himself by the ease with which he had prevaricated; it was clear that he intended to observe the High Lama's suggestion and keep the secret. He was also puzzled by the naturalness with which he was accepting a position which his companions would certainly and with some justification think traitorous; as Mallinson had said, it was hardly the sort of thing to be expected of a hero. Conway felt a sudden half-pitying fondness for the youth; then he steeled himself by reflecting that people who hero-worship must be prepared for disillusionments. Mallinson at Baskul had been far too much the new boy adoring the handsome games captain, and now the games captain was tottering if not already fallen from the pedestal. There was always something a little pathetic in the smashing of an ideal, however false; and Mallinson's admiration might have been at least a partial solace for the strain of pretending to be what he was not. But pretence was impossible anyway. There was a quality in the air of Shangri-La—perhaps due to its altitude—that forbade one the effort of counterfeit emotion.

He said: "Look here, Mallinson, it's no use harping continually on Baskul. Of course I was different then—it was a completely different situation."

"And a much healthier one in my opinion. At least we knew what we were up against."

"Murder and rape—to be precise. You can call that healthier if you like."

The youth's voice rose in pitch as he retorted: "Well, I *do* call it healthier—in one sense. It's something I'd rather face than all this mystery business." Suddenly he added: "That Chinese girl, for instance—how did *she* get here? Did the fellow tell you?"

"No. Why should he?"

"Well, why shouldn't he? And why shouldn't you ask, if you had any interest in the matter at all? Is it usual to find a young girl living with a lot of monks?"

That way of looking at it was one that had scarcely occurred to Conway before. "This isn't an ordinary monastery," was the best reply he could give after some thought.

"My God, it isn't!"

There was a silence, for the argument had evidently reached a dead end. To Conway the history of Lo-Tsen seemed rather far from the point; the little Manchu lay so quietly in his mind that he hardly knew she was there. But at the mere mention of her Miss Brinklow had looked up suddenly from the Tibetan grammar which she was studying even over the breakfast table (just as if, thought Conway, with secret meaning, she hadn't all her life for it). Chatter of girls and monks reminded her of those stories of Indian temples that men missionaries told their wives, and that the wives passed on to their unmarried female colleagues. "Of course," she said between tightened lips, "the morals of this place are quite hideous—we might have

There was a silence, for the argument had evidently reached a dead end

expected that." She turned to Barnard as if inviting support, but the American only grinned. "I don't suppose you folks'd value my opinion on a matter of morals," he remarked dryly. "But I should say myself that quarrels are just as bad. Since we've gotter be here for some time yet, let's keep our tempers and make ourselves comfortable."

Conway thought this good advice, but Mallinson was still unplacated. "I can quite believe you find it more comfortable than Dartmoor," he said meaningly.

"Dartmoor? Oh, that's your big penitentiary?—I get you. Well, yes, I certainly never did envy folks in them places. And there's another thing too—it don't hurt when you chip me about it. Thick-skinned and tenderhearted, that's my mixture."

Conway glanced at him in appreciation, and at Mallinson with some hint of reproof; but then abruptly he had the feeling that they were all acting on a vast stage, of whose background only he himself was conscious; and such knowledge, so incommunicable, made him suddenly want to be alone. He nodded to them and went out into the courtyard. In sight of Karakal misgivings faded, and qualms about his three companions were lost in an uncanny acceptance of the new world that lay so far beyond their guesses. There came a time, he realized, when the strangeness of everything made it increasingly difficult to realize the strangeness of anything; when one took things for granted merely because astonishment would have been as tedious for oneself as for others. Thus far had he progressed at Shangri-La, and he remembered that he had attained a similar though far less pleasant equanimity during his years at the War.

He needed equanimity, if only to accommodate himself to the double life he was compelled to lead. Thenceforward, with his fellow exiles, he lived in a world conditioned by the arrival of porters and a return to India; at all other times the horizon lifted like a curtain; time expanded and space contracted and the name Blue Moon took on a symbolic meaning, as if the future, so delicately plausible, were of a kind that might happen once in a blue moon only. Sometimes he wondered which of his two lives were the more real, but the problem was not pressing; and again he was reminded of the War, for during heavy bombardments he had had the same comforting sensation that he had many lives, only one of which could be claimed by death.

Chang, of course, now talked to him completely without reserve, and they had many conversations about the rule and routine of the lamasery. Conway learned that during his first five years he would live a normal life, without any special regimen; this was always done, as Chang said, "to enable the body to accustom itself to the altitude, and also to give time for the dispersal of mental and emotional regrets."

Conway remarked with a smile: "I suppose you're certain, then, that no human affection can outlast a five-year absence?"

"It can, undoubtedly," replied the Chinese, "but only as a fragrance whose melancholy we may enjoy."

After the probationary five years, Chang went on to explain, the process of retarding age would begin, and if successful, might give Conway half a century or so at the apparent age of forty—which was not a bad time of life at which to remain stationary.

"What about yourself?" Conway asked. "How did it work out in your case?"

"Ah, my dear sir, I was lucky enough to arrive when I was quite young—only twenty-two. I was a soldier, though you might not have thought it; I had command of troops operating against brigand tribes in the year 1855. I was making what I should have called a reconnaissance if I had ever returned to my superior officers to tell the tale, but in plain truth I had lost my way in the mountains, and of my men only seven out of over a hundred survived the rigours of the climate. When at last I was rescued and brought to Shangri-La I was so ill that only extreme youth and virility saved me."

"Twenty-two," echoed Conway, performing the calculation. "So you're now ninety-seven?"

"Yes. Very soon, if the lamas give their consent, I shall receive full initiation."

"I see. You have to wait for the round figure?"

"No, we are not restricted by any definite age limit, but a century is generally considered to be an age beyond which the passions and moods of ordinary life are likely to have disappeared."

"I should certainly think so. And what happens afterwards? How long do you expect to carry on?"

"There is reason to hope that I shall enter lamahood with such prospects as Shangri-La has made possible. In years, perhaps another century or more."

Conway nodded. "I don't know whether I ought to congratulate you—you seem to have been granted the best of both worlds, a long and pleasant youth behind you, and an equally long and pleasant old age ahead. When did you begin to grow old in appearance?"

"When I was over seventy. That is often the case, though I think I may still claim to look younger than my years."

"Decidedly. And suppose you were to leave the valley now, what would happen?"

"Death, if I remained away for more than a very few days."

"The atmosphere, then, is essential?"

"There is only one valley of Blue Moon, and those who expect to find another are asking too much of nature."

"Well, what would have happened if you had left the valley, say, thirty years ago, during your prolonged youth?"

Chang answered: "Probably I should have died even then. In any case, I should have acquired very quickly the full appearance of my actual age. We had a curious example of that some years ago, though there had been several others before. One of our number had left the valley to look out for a party of travellers who we had heard might be approaching. This man, a Russian, had arrived here originally in the prime of life, and had taken to our ways so well that at nearly eighty he did not look more than half as old. He should have been absent no longer than a week (which would not have mattered), but unfortunately he was taken prisoner by nomad tribes and carried away some distance. We suspected an accident and gave him up for lost. Three months later, however, he returned to us, having made his escape. But he was a very different man. Every year of his age was in his face and behaviour, and he died shortly afterwards, as an old man dies."

Conway made no remark for some time. They were talking in the library, and during most of the narrative he had been gazing through a window towards the pass that led to the outer world; a little wisp of cloud had drifted across the ridge. "A rather grim story, Chang," he commented at length. "It gives one the feeling that Time is like some baulked monster, waiting outside the valley to pounce on the slackers who have managed to evade him longer than they should."

"*Slackers?*" queried Chang. His knowledge of English was extremely good, but sometimes a colloquialism proved unfamiliar.

"'Slacker,'" explained Conway, "is a slang word meaning a lazy fellow, a good-for-nothing. I wasn't, of course, using it seriously."

Chang bowed his thanks for the information. He took a keen interest in languages and liked to weigh a new word philosophically. "It is significant," he said after a pause, "that the English regard slackness as a vice. We, on the other hand, should vastly prefer it to tension. Is there not too much tension in the world at present, and might it not be better if more people were slackers?"

"I'm inclined to agree with you," Conway answered with solemn amusement.

DURING THE COURSE of a week or so after the interview with the High Lama, Conway met several other of his future colleagues. Chang was neither eager nor reluctant to make the introductions, and Conway sensed a new and, to him, rather attractive atmosphere in which urgency did not clamour nor postponement disappoint. "Indeed," as Chang explained, "some of the lamas may not meet you for a considerable time—perhaps years—but you must not be surprised at that. They are prepared to make your acquaintance when it may so happen, and their avoidance of hurry does not imply any degree of unwillingness." Conway, who had often had similar feelings when calling on new arrivals at foreign consulates, thought it a very intelligible attitude.

The meetings he did have, however, were quite successful, and conversation with men thrice his age held none of the social embarrassments that might have obtruded in London or Delhi. His first encounter was with a genial German named Meister, who had entered the lamasery during the eighties, as the survivor of an exploring party. He spoke English well, though with an accent. A day or two later a second introduction took place, and Conway enjoyed his first talk with the man whom the High Lama had particularly mentioned—Alphonse Briac, a wiry, small-statured Frenchman who did not look especially old, though he announced himself as a pupil of Chopin. Conway thought that both he and the German would prove agreeable company. Already he was subconsciously analysing, and after a few further meetings he reached one or two general conclusions; he perceived that though the lamas he met had individual differences, they all possessed that quality for which agelessness was not an outstandingly good name, but the only one he could think of. Moreover, they were all endowed with a calm intelligence which pleasantly overflowed into measured and well-balanced opinions. Conway could give an exact response to that kind of approach, and he was aware that they realized it and were gratified. He found them quite as easy to get on with as any other group of cultured people he might have met, though there was often a sense of oddity in hearing reminiscences so distant and apparently so casual.

One white-haired and benevolent-looking person, for instance, asked Conway, after a little conversation, if he were interested in the Brontës. Conway said he was, to some extent, and the other replied: "You see, when I was a curate in the West Riding during the forties, I once visited Haworth and stayed at the Parsonage. Since coming here I've made a study of the whole Brontë problem—indeed, I'm writing a book on the subject. Perhaps you might care to go over it with me some time?"

Conway responded cordially, and afterwards, when he and Chang were left together, commented on the vividness with which the lamas appeared to recollect their pre-Tibetan lives. Chang answered that it was all part of the training. "You see, my dear sir, one of the first steps towards the clarifying of the mind is to obtain a panorama of one's own past, and that, like any other view, is more accurate in perspective. When you have been among us long enough you will find your old life slipping gradually into focus as through a telescope when the lens is adjusted. Everything will stand out still and clear, duly proportioned and with its correct significance. Your new acquaintance, for instance, discerns that the really big moment of his entire life occurred when he was a young man visiting a house in which there lived an old parson and his three daughters."

"So I suppose I shall have to set to work to remember my own big moments?"

"It will not be an effort. They will come to you."

"I don't know that I shall give them much of a welcome," answered Conway moodily.

BUT WHATEVER THE PAST might yield, he was discovering happiness in the present. When he sat reading in the library, or playing Mozart in the music room, he often felt the invasion of a deep spiritual emotion, as if Shangri-La were indeed a living essence, distilled from the magic of the ages and miraculously preserved against time and death. His talk with the High Lama recurred memorably at such moments; he sensed a calm intelligence brooding gently over every diversion, giving a thousand whispered reassurances to ear and eye. Thus he would listen while Lo-Tsen marshalled some intricate fugue rhythm, and wonder what lay behind the faint impersonal smile that stirred her lips into the likeness of an opening flower. She talked very little, even though she now knew that Conway could speak her language; to Mallinson, who liked to visit the music room sometimes, she was almost dumb. But Conway discerned a charm that was perfectly expressed by her silences.

Once he asked Chang her history, and learned that she came of royal Manchu stock.

"She was betrothed to a prince of Turkestan, and was travelling to Kashgar to meet him when her carriers lost their way in the mountains. The whole party would doubtless have perished but for the customary meeting with our emissaries."

"When did this happen?"

"In 1884. She was eighteen."

"Eighteen *then*?"

Chang bowed. "Yes, we are succeeding very well with her, as you may judge for yourself. Her progress has been consistently excellent."

"How did she take things when she first came?"

"She was, perhaps, a little more than averagely reluctant to accept the situation—she made no protest, but we were aware that she was troubled for a time. It was, of course, an unusual occurrence—to intercept a young girl on the way to her wedding . . . . We were all particularly anxious that she should be happy here." Chang smiled blandly. "I am afraid the excitement of love does not make for an easy surrender, though the first five years proved ample for their purpose."

"She was deeply attached, I suppose, to the man she was to have married?"

"Hardly that, my dear sir, since she had never seen him. It was the old custom, you know. The excitement of her affections was entirely impersonal."

Conway nodded, and thought a little tenderly of Lo-Tsen. He pictured her as she might have been half a century before, statuesque in her decorated chair as the carriers toiled over the plateau, her eyes searching the windswept horizons that must have seemed so harsh after the gardens and lotus pools of the East. "Poor child!" he said, thinking of such elegance held captive over the years. Knowledge of her past increased rather than lessened his content with her stillness and silence; she was like a lovely cold vase, unadorned save by an escaping ray.

He was also content, though less ecstatically, when Briac talked to him of Chopin, and played the familiar melodies with much brilliance. It appeared that the Frenchman knew several Chopin compositions that had never been published, and as he had written them down, Conway devoted pleasant hours to memorizing them himself. He found a certain piquancy in the reflection that neither Cortot nor Pachmann had been so fortunate. Nor were Briac's recollections at an end; his memory continually refreshed him with some little scrap of tune that the composer had thrown off or improvised on some occasion; he took them all down on paper as they came into his head, and some were very delightful fragments. "Briac," Chang explained, "has not long been initiated, so you must make allowances if he talks a great deal about Chopin. The younger lamas are naturally preoccupied with the past; it is a necessary step to envisaging the future."

"Which is, I take it, the job of the older ones?"

"Yes. The High Lama, for instance, spends almost his entire life in clairvoyant meditation."

Conway pondered a moment and then said: "By the way, when do you suppose I shall see him again?"

"Doubtless at the end of the first five years, my dear sir."

But in that confident prophecy Chang was wrong, for less than a month after his arrival at Shangri-La Conway received a second summons to that torrid upper room. Chang had told him that the High Lama never left his apartments, and that their heated atmosphere was necessary for his bodily existence; and Conway, being thus prepared, found the change less disconcerting than before. Indeed, he breathed easily as soon as he had made his bow and been granted the faintest answering liveliness of the sunken eyes. He felt kinship with the mind beyond them, and though he knew that this second interview following so soon upon the first was an unprecedented honour, he was not in the least nervous or weighed down with solemnity. Age was to him no more an obsessing factor than rank or colour; he had never felt debarred from liking people because they were too young or too old. He held the High Lama in most cordial respect, but he did not see why their social relations should be anything less than urbane.

They exchanged the usual courtesies, and Conway answered many polite questions. He said he was finding the life very agreeable and had already made friendships.

"And you have kept our secrets from your three companions?"

"Yes, up to now. It has proved awkward for me at times, but probably less so than if I had told them."

"Just as I surmised; you have acted as you thought best. And the awkwardness, after all, is only temporary. Chang tells me he thinks that two of them will give little trouble."

"I daresay that is so."

"And the third?"

Conway replied: "Mallinson is an excitable youth—he's pretty keen to get back."

"You like him?"

"Yes, I like him very much."

At this point the tea bowls were brought in, and talk became less serious between sips of the scented liquid. It was an apt convention, enabling the verbal flow to acquire a touch of that almost frivolous fragrance, and Conway was responsive. When the High Lama asked him whether Shangri-La was not unique in his experience, and if the Western world could offer anything in the least like it, he answered with a smile: "Well, yes—to be quite frank, it reminds me very slightly of Oxford, where I used to lecture. The scenery there is not so good, but the subjects of study are often just as impractical, and though even the oldest of the dons is not quite so old, they appear to age in a somewhat similar way."

"You have a sense of humour, my dear Conway," replied the High Lama, "for which we shall all be grateful during the years to come."

Chapter 10

XTRAORDINARY," CHANG SAID, when he heard that Conway had seen the High Lama again. And from one so reluctant to employ superlatives, the word was significant. It had never happened before, he emphasized, since the routine of the lamasery became established; never had the High Lama desired a second meeting until the five years' probation had effected a purge of all the exile's likely emotions. "Because, you see, it is a great strain on him to talk to the average newcomer. The mere presence of human passions is an unwelcome and, at his age, an almost unendurable unpleasantness. Not that I doubt his entire wisdom in the matter. It teaches us, I believe, a lesson of great value— that even the fixed rules of our community are only moderately fixed. But it is extraordinary, all the same."

To Conway, of course, it was no more extraordinary than anything else, and after he had visited the High Lama on a third and fourth occasion, he began to feel that it was not very extraordinary at all. There seemed, indeed, something almost preordained in the ease with which their two minds approached each other; it was as if in Conway all secret tensions were relaxed, giving him, when he came away, a sumptuous tranquillity. At times he had the sensation of being completely bewitched by the mastery of that central intelligence, and then, over the little pale blue tea bowls, the cerebration would contract into a liveliness so gentle and miniature that he had an impression of a theorem dissolving limpidly into a sonnet.

Their talks ranged far and fearlessly; entire philosophies were unfolded; the long avenues of history surrendered themselves for inspection and were given new plausibility. To Conway it was an entrancing experience, but he did not suspend the critical attitude, and once, when he had argued a point, the High Lama replied: "My son, you are young in years, but I perceive that your wisdom has the ripeness of age. Surely some unusual thing has happened to you?"

Conway smiled. "No more unusual than has happened to many others of my generation."

"I have never met your like before."

Conway answered after an interval: "There's not a great deal of mystery about it. That part of me which seems old to you was worn out by intense and premature experience. My years from nineteen to twenty-two were a supreme education, no doubt, but rather exhausting."

"You were very unhappy at the War?"

"Not particularly so. I was excited and suicidal and scared and reckless and sometimes in a tearing rage—like a few million others, in fact. I got mad drunk and killed and lechered in great style. It was the self-abuse of all one's emotions, and one came through it, if one did at all, with a sense of almighty boredom and fretfulness. That's what made the years afterwards so difficult. Don't think I'm posing myself too tragically—I've had pretty fair luck since, on the whole. But it's been rather like being in a school where there's a bad headmaster—plenty of fun to be got if you feel like it, but nerve-racking off and on, and not really very satisfactory. I think I found that out rather more than most people."

"And your education thus continued?"

Conway gave a shrug. "Perhaps the exhaustion of the passions is the beginning of wisdom, if you care to alter the proverb."

"That also, my son, is the doctrine of Shangri-La."

"I know. It makes me feel quite at home."

HE HAD SPOKEN no less than the truth. As the days and weeks passed he began to feel an ache of contentment uniting mind and body; like Perrault and Henschell and the others, he was falling under the spell. Blue Moon had taken him, and there was no escape. The mountains gleamed around in a hedge of inaccessible purity, from which his eyes fell dazzled to the green depths of the valley; the whole picture was incomparable, and when he heard the harpsichord's silver monotony across the lotus pool, he felt that it threaded the perfect pattern of sight and sound.

He was, and he knew it, very quietly in love with the little Manchu. His love demanded nothing, not even reply; it was a tribute of the mind, to which his senses added only a flavour. She stood for him as a symbol of all that was delicate and fragile; her stylized courtesies and the touch of her fingers on the keyboard yielded a completely satisfying intimacy. Sometimes he would address her in a way that might, if she cared, have led to less formal conversation; but her replies never broke through the exquisite privacy of her thoughts, and in a sense he did not wish them to. He had suddenly come to realize a single facet of the promised jewel: he had Time, Time for everything that he wished to happen, such Time that desire itself was quenched in the certainty of fulfilment. A year, a decade hence, there would still be Time. The vision grew on him, and he was happy with it.

Then, at intervals, he stepped into the other life to encounter Mallinson's impatience, Barnard's heartiness, and Miss Brinklow's robust intention. He felt he would be glad when they all knew as much as he; and, like Chang, he could imagine that neither the American nor the missionary would prove difficult cases. He was even amused when Barnard once said: "You know, Conway, I'm not sure that this wouldn't be a nice little place to settle down in. I thought at first I'd miss the newspapers and the movies, but I guess one can get used to anything."

"I guess one can," agreed Conway.

He learned afterwards that Chang had taken Barnard down to the valley, at his own request, to enjoy everything in the way of a "night out" that the resources of the locality could provide. Mallinson, when he heard of this, was rather scornful. "Getting tight, I suppose," he remarked to Conway, and to Barnard himself he commented: "Of course it's none of my business, but you'll want to keep yourself pretty fit for the journey, you know. The porters are due in a fortnight's time, and from what I gather, the return trip won't be exactly a joyride."

Barnard nodded equably. "I never figgered it would," he answered. "And as for keeping fit, I guess I'm fitter than I've been for years. I get exercise daily, I don't have any worries, and the speakeasies down in the valley don't let a feller go too far. Moderation, y'know—the motto of the firm."

"Yes, I've no doubt you've been managing to have a moderately good time," said Mallinson acidly.

"Certainly I have. This establishment caters for all tastes—some people like little Chink gels who play the pi-anno, isn't that so? You can't blame anybody for what they fancy."

Conway was not at all put out, but Mallinson flushed like a schoolboy. "You can send them to jail, though, when they fancy other people's property," he snapped, stung to fury that set a raw edge to his wits.

"Sure, if you can catch 'em." The American grinned affably. "And that leads me to something I may as well tell you folks right away, now we're on the subject. I've decided to give those porters a miss. They come here pretty regular, and I'll wait for the next trip, or maybe the next but one. That is, if the monks'll take my word that I'm still good for my hotel expenses."

"You mean you're not coming with us?"

"That's it. I've decided to stop over for a while. It's all very fine for you—you'll have the band playing when *you* get home, but all the welcome I'll get is from a row of cops. And the more I think about it, the more it don't seem good enough."

"In other words, you're just afraid to face the music?"

"Well, I never did like music, anyhow."

Mallinson said with cold scorn: "I suppose it's your own affair. Nobody can prevent you from stopping here all your life if you feel inclined." Nevertheless he looked round with a flash of appeal. "It's not what everybody would choose to do, but ideas differ. What do you say, Conway?"

"I agree. Ideas *do* differ."

Mallinson turned to Miss Brinklow, who suddenly put down her book and remarked: "As a matter of fact, I think I shall stay too."

"*What?*" they all cried together.

She continued, with a bright smile that seemed more an attachment to her face than an illumination of it: "You see, I've been thinking over the way things happened to bring us all here, and there's only one conclusion I can come to. There's a mysterious power working behind the scenes. Don't you think so, Mr. Conway?"

Conway might have found it hard to reply, but Miss Brinklow went on in a gathering hurry: "Who am I to question the dictates of Providence? I was sent here for a purpose, and I shall stay."

"Do you mean you're hoping to start a mission here?" Mallinson asked.

"Not only hoping, but fully intending. I know just how to deal with these people—I shall get my own way, never fear. There's no real grit in any of them."

"And you intend to introduce some?"

"Yes, I do, Mr. Mallinson. I'm strongly opposed to that idea of moderation that we hear so much about. You can call it broadmindedness if you like, but in my opinion it leads to the worst kind of laxity. The whole trouble with the people here is their so-called broad-mindedness, and I intend to fight it with all my powers."

"And they're so broad-minded that they're going to let you?" said Conway, smiling.

"Or else she's so strong-minded that they can't stop her," put in Barnard. He added with a chuckle: "It's just what I said—this establishment caters for all tastes."

"Possibly, if you happen to *like* prison," Mallinson snapped.

"Well, there's two ways of looking even at that. My goodness, if you think of all the folks in the world who'd give all they've got to be out of the racket and in a place like this, only they can't *get* out! Are *we* in the prison or are *they?*"

"A comforting speculation for a monkey in a cage," retorted Mallinson; he was still furious.

AFTERWARDS HE SPOKE to Conway alone. "That man still gets on my nerves," he said, pacing the courtyard. "I'm not sorry we shan't have him with us when we go back. You may think me touchy, but being chipped about that Chinese girl didn't appeal to my sense of humour."

Conway took Mallinson's arm. It was becoming increasingly clear to him that he was very fond of the youth, and that their recent weeks in company had deepened the feeling, despite jarring moods. He answered: "I rather took it that *I* was being ragged about her, not you."

"No, I think he intended it for me. He knows I'm interested in her. I am, Conway. I can't make out why she's here, and whether she really likes being here. My God, if I spoke her language as you do, I'd soon have it out with her."

"I wonder if you would. She doesn't say a great deal to anyone, you know."

"It puzzles me that you don't badger her with all sorts of questions."

"I don't know that I care for badgering people."

He wished he could have said more, and then suddenly the sense of pity and irony floated over him in a filmy haze; this youth, so eager and ardent, would take things very hardly. "I shouldn't worry about Lo-Tsen if I were you," he added. "She's happy enough."

THE DECISION OF BARNARD and Miss Brinklow to remain behind seemed to Conway all to the good, though it threw Mallinson and himself into an apparently opposite camp for the time being. It was an extraordinary situation, and he had no definite plans for tackling it.

Fortunately there was no apparent need to tackle it at all. Until the two months were past, nothing much could happen; and afterwards there would be a crisis no less acute for his having tried to prepare himself for it. For this and other reasons he was disinclined to worry over the inevitable, though he did once say: "You know, Chang, I'm bothered about young Mallinson. I'm afraid he'll take things very badly when he finds out."

Chang nodded with some sympathy. "Yes, it will not be easy to persuade him of his good fortune. But the difficulty is, after all, only a temporary one. In twenty years from now our friend will be quite reconciled."

Conway felt that this was looking at the matter almost too philosophically. "I'm wondering," he said, "just how the truth's going to be broached to him. He's counting the days to the arrival of the porters, and if they don't come—"

"But they *will* come."

"Oh? I rather imagined that all your talk about them was just a pleasant fable to let us down lightly."

"By no means. Although we have no bigotry on the point, it is our custom at Shangri-La to be moderately truthful, and I can assure you that my statements about the porters were almost correct. At any rate, we are expecting the men at or about the time I said."

"Then you'll find it hard to stop Mallinson from joining them."

"But we should never attempt to do so. He will merely discover—no doubt by personal experiment—that the porters are reluctantly unable to take anyone back with them."

"I see. So that's the method? And what do you expect to happen afterwards?"

"Then, my dear sir, after a period of disappointment, he will—since he is young and optimistic—begin to hope that the next convoy of porters, due in nine or ten months' time, will prove more amenable to his suggestions. And this is a hope which, if we are wise, we shall not at first discourage."

Conway said sharply: "I'm not so sure that he'll do that at all. I should think he's far more likely to try an escape on his own."

"*Escape?* Is that *really* the word that should be used? After all, the pass is open to anyone at any time. We have no jailers, save those that Nature herself has provided."

Conway smiled. "Well, you must admit that she's done her job pretty well. But I don't suppose you rely on her in every case, all the same. What about the various exploring parties that have arrived here? Was the pass always equally open to *them* when they wanted to get away?"

It was Chang's turn now to smile. "Special circumstances, my dear sir, have sometimes required special consideration."

"Excellent. So you only allow people the chance of escape when you know they'd be fools to take it? Even so, I expect some of them do."

"Well, it has happened very occasionally, but as a rule the absentees are glad to return after the experience of a single night on the plateau."

"Without shelter and proper clothing? If so, I can quite understand that your mild methods are as effective as are stern ones. But what about the less usual cases that don't return?"

"You have yourself answered the question," replied Chang. "They do *not* return." But he made haste to add: "I can assure you, however, that there are few indeed who have been so unfortunate, and I trust your friend will not be rash enough to increase the number."

Conway did not find these responses entirely reassuring, and Mallinson's future remained a preoccupation. He wished it were possible for the youth to return by consent, and this would not be unprecedented, for there was the recent case of Talu, the airman. Chang admitted that the authorities were fully empowered to do anything that they considered wise. "But *should* we be wise, my dear sir, in trusting our future entirely to your friend's feelings of gratitude?"

Conway felt that the question was pertinent, for Mallinson's attitude left little doubt as to what he would do as soon as he reached India. It was his favourite theme, and he had often enlarged upon it.

But all that, of course, was in the mundane world that was gradually being pushed out of his mind by the rich, pervasive world of Shangri-La. Except when he thought about Mallinson, he was extraordinarily content; the slowly revealed fabric of this new environment continued to astonish him by its intricate suitability to his own needs and tastes.

Once he said to Chang: "By the way, how do you people here fit love into your scheme of things? I suppose it does sometimes happen that those who come here develop attachments?"

"Quite often," replied Chang with a broad smile. "The lamas, of course, are immune, and so are most of us when we reach the riper years, but until then we are as other men, except that I think we can claim to behave more reasonably. And this gives me the opportunity,

Mr. Conway, of assuring you that the hospitality of Shangri-La is of a comprehensive kind. Your friend Mr. Barnard has already availed himself of it."

Conway returned the smile. "Thanks," he answered dryly. "I've no doubt he has, but my own inclinations are not—at the moment—so assertive. It was the emotional more than the physical aspect that I was curious about."

"You find it easy to separate the two? Is it possible that you are falling in love with Lo-Tsen?"

Conway was somewhat taken aback, though he hoped he did not show it. "What makes you ask that?"

"Because, my dear sir, it would be quite suitable if you were to do so—always, of course, in moderation. Lo-Tsen would not respond with any degree of passion—that is more than you could expect—but the experience would be very delightful, I assure you. And I speak with some authority, for I was in love with her myself when I was much younger."

"Were you indeed? And did she respond then?"

"Only by the most charming appreciation of the compliment I paid her, and by a friendship which has grown more precious with the years."

"In other words, she didn't respond?"

"If you prefer it so." Chang added, a little sententiously: "It has always been her way to spare her lovers the moment of satiety that goes with all absolute attainment."

Conway laughed. "That's all very well in your case, and perhaps mine too—but what about the attitude of a hot-blooded young fellow like Mallinson?"

"My dear sir, it would be the best possible thing that could happen! Not for the first time, I assure you, would Lo-Tsen comfort the sorrowful exile when he learns that there is to be no return."

"*Comfort?*"

"Yes, though you must not misunderstand my use of the term. Lo-Tsen gives no caresses, except such as touch the stricken heart from her very presence. What does your Shakespeare say of Cleopatra?—'She makes hungry where she most satisfies.' A popular type, doubtless, among the passion-driven races, but such a woman, I assure you, would be altogether out of place at Shangri-La. Lo-Tsen, if I might amend the quotation, *removes* hunger where she *least* satisfies. It is a more delicate and lasting accomplishment."

"And one, I assume, which she has much skill in performing?"

"Oh, decidedly—we have had many examples of it. It is her way to calm the throb of desire to a murmur that is no less pleasant when left unanswered."

"In that sense, then, you could regard her as a part of the training equipment of the establishment?"

"*You* could regard her as that, if you wished," replied Chang with deprecating blandness. "But it would be more graceful, and just as true, to liken her to the rainbow reflected in a glass bowl, or to the dewdrops on the blossoms of the fruit tree."

"I entirely agree with you, Chang. That would be *much* more grace-ful." Conway enjoyed the measured yet agile repartees which his good-humoured ragging of the Chinese very often elicited.

But the next time he was alone with the little Manchu he felt that Chang's remarks had had a great deal of shrewdness in them. There was a fragrance about her that communicated itself to his own emo-tions, kindling the embers to a glow that did not burn, but merely warmed. And suddenly then he realized that Shangri-La and Lo-Tsen were quite perfect, and that he did not wish for more than to stir a faint and eventual response in all that stillness. For years his passions had been like a nerve that the world jarred on; now at last the aching was soothed, and he could yield himself to love that was neither a torment nor a bore. As he passed by the lotus pool at night he some-times pictured her in his arms, but the sense of time washed over the vision, calming him to an infinite and tender reluctance.

He did not think he had ever been so happy, even in the years of his life before the great barrier of the War. He liked the serene world that Shangri-La offered him, pacified rather than dominated by its single tremendous idea. He liked the prevalent mood in which feel-ings were sheathed in thoughts, and thoughts softened into felicity by their transference into language. Conway, whom experience had taught that rudeness is by no means a guarantee of good faith, was even less inclined to regard a well-turned phrase as a proof of insincerity. He liked the mannered, leisurely atmosphere in which talk was an accomplishment, not a mere habit. And he liked to realize that the idlest things could now be freed from the curse of time-wasting, and the frailest dreams receive the welcome of the mind. Shangri-La was always tranquil, yet always a hive of unpursuing occupations; the lamas lived as if indeed they had time on their hands, but time that was scarcely a featherweight. Conway met no more of them, but he came gradually to realize the extent and variety of their employments; besides their knowledge of languages, some, it appeared, took to the full seas of learning in a manner that would have yielded big surprises to the Western world. Many were engaged in writing manuscript books of various kinds; one (Chang said) had made valuable researches into pure mathematics; another was co-ordinating Gibbon and Spengler into a vast thesis on the history of European civilization. But this kind of thing was not for them all, nor for any of them always; there were many tideless channels in which they dived in mere waywardness, retrieving, like Briac, fragments of old tunes, or, like the English ex-curate, a new theory about *Wuthering Heights*. And there were even fainter impracticalities than these. Once, when Conway made some remark in this connection, the High Lama replied with a story of a Chinese artist in the third century B.C. who, having spent many years in carving dragons, birds, and horses upon a cherrystone, offered his finished work to a royal prince. The prince could see nothing in it at first except a mere stone, but the artist bade him "have a wall built, and make a window in it, and observe the stone through the window in the glory of the dawn." The prince did so, and then perceived that the stone was indeed very beautiful. "Is not that a charming story, my dear Conway, and do you not think it teaches a very valuable lesson?"

Conway agreed; he found it pleasant to realize that the serene purpose of Shangri-La could embrace an infinitude of odd and apparently trivial employments, for he had always had a taste for such things himself. In fact, when he regarded his past, he saw it strewn with images of tasks too vagrant or too taxing ever to have been accomplished; but now they were all possible, even in a mood of idleness. It was delightful to contemplate, and he was not disposed to sneer when Barnard confided in him that he too envisaged an interesting future at Shangri-La.

It seemed that Barnard's excursions to the valley, which had been growing more frequent of late, were not entirely devoted to drink and women. "You see, Conway, I'm telling you this because you're different from Mallinson—he's got his knife into me, as probably you've gathered. But I feel you'll be better at understanding the position. It's a funny thing—you British officials are so darned stiff and starchy at first, but you're the sort a fellow can put his trust in, when all's said and done."

"I wouldn't be too sure," replied Conway, smiling. "And anyhow, Mallinson's just as much a British official as I am."

"Yes, but he's a mere boy. He don't look at things reasonably. You and me are men of the world—we take things as we find them. This joint here, for instance—we still can't understand all the ins and outs of it, and why we've been landed here, but then, isn't that the usual way of things? Do we know why we're in the world at all, for that matter?"

"Perhaps some of us don't, but what's all this leading up to?"

Barnard dropped his voice to a rather husky whisper. "Gold, my lad," he answered with a certain ecstasy. "Just that, and nothing less. There's tons of it—literally—in the valley. I was a mining engineer in my young days and I haven't forgotten what a reef looks like. Believe me, it's as rich as the Rand, and ten times easier to get at. I guess you thought I was on the loose whenever I went down there in my little armchair. Not a bit of it. I knew what I was doing. I'd figgered it out all along, you know, that these guys here couldn't get all their stuff sent in from outside without paying mighty high for it, and what else could they pay with except gold or silver or diamonds or something? Only logic, after all. And when I began to scout round, it didn't take me long to discover the whole bag of tricks."

"You found it out on your own?" asked Conway.

"Well, I won't say that, but I made my guess, and then I put the matter to Chang—straight, mind you, as man to man. And believe me, Conway, that Chink's not as bad a fellow as we might have thought."

147

"Personally, I never thought him a bad fellow at all."

"Of course, I know you always took to him, so you won't be surprised at the way we got on together. We certainly did hit it off famously. He showed me all over the workings, and it may interest you to know that I've got the full permission of the authorities to prospect in the valley as much as I like and make a comprehensive report. What d'you think of that, my lad? They seemed quite glad to have the services of an expert, especially when I said I could probably give 'em tips on how to increase output."

"I can see you're going to be altogether at home here," said Conway.

"Well, I must say I've found a job, and that's something. And you never know how a thing'll turn out in the end. Maybe the folks at home won't be so keen to jail me when they know I can show 'em the way to a new goldfield. The only difficulty is—would they take my word about it?"

"They might. It's extraordinary what people *will* believe."

Barnard nodded with enthusiasm. "Glad you get the point, Conway. And that's where you and I can make a deal. We'll go fifty-fifty in everything, of course. All you've gotter do is to put your name to my report—British Consul, you know, and all that. It'll carry weight."

Conway laughed. "We'll have to see about it. Make your report first."

It amused him to contemplate a possibility so unlikely to happen, and at the same time he was glad that Barnard had found something that yielded such immediate comfort.

So also was the High Lama, whom Conway began to see more and more frequently. He often visited him in the late evening and stayed for many hours, long after the servants had taken away the last bowls of tea and had been dismissed for the night. The High Lama never failed to ask him about the progress and welfare of his three companions, and once he enquired particularly as to the kind of careers that their arrival at Shangri-La had so inevitably interrupted.

Conway answered reflectively: "Mallinson might have done quite well in his own line—he's energetic and has ambitions. The two others—" He shrugged his shoulders. "As a matter of fact, it happens to suit them both to stay here—for a while, at any rate."

He noticed a flicker of light at the curtained window; there had been mutterings of thunder as he crossed the courtyard on his way to the now familiar room. No sound could be heard, and the heavy tapestries subdued the lightning into mere sparks of pallor.

"Yes," came the reply, "we have done our best to make both of them feel at home. Miss Brinklow wishes to convert us, and Mr. Barnard would also like to convert us—into a limited liability company. Harmless projects—they will pass the time quite pleasantly for them. But your young friend, to whom neither gold nor religion can offer solace, how about *him*?"

"Yes, he's going to be the problem."

"I am afraid he is going to be *your* problem."

"Why mine?"

There was no immediate answer, for the tea bowls were introduced at that moment, and with their appearance the High Lama rallied a faint and desiccated hospitality. "Karakal sends us storms at this time of the year," he remarked, feathering the conversation according to ritual. "The people of Blue Moon believe they are caused by demons raging in the great space beyond the pass. The 'outside,' they call it— perhaps you are aware that in their patois the word is used for the entire rest of the world. Of course they know nothing of such countries as France or England or even India—they imagine the dread altiplano stretching, as it almost does, illimitably. To them, so snug at their warm and windless levels, it appears unthinkable that anyone inside the valley should ever wish to leave it; indeed, they picture all unfortunate 'outsiders' as passionately desiring to enter. It is just a question of viewpoint, is it not?"

Conway was reminded of Barnard's somewhat similar remarks, and quoted them. "How very sensible!" was the High Lama's comment. "And he is our first American, too—we are truly fortunate."

Conway found it piquant to reflect that the lamasery's fortune was to have acquired a man for whom the police of a dozen countries were actively searching; and he would have liked to share the piquancy but for feeling that Barnard had better be left to tell his own story in due course. He said: "Doubtless he's quite right, and there are many people in the world nowadays who would be glad enough to be here."

"*Too* many, my dear Conway. We are a single lifeboat riding the seas in a gale; we can take a few chance survivors, but if all the shipwrecked were to reach us and clamber aboard we should go down ourselves . . . . But let us not think of it just now. I hear that you have been associating with our excellent Briac. A delightful fellow countryman of mine, though I do not share his opinion that Chopin is the greatest of all composers. For myself, as you know, I prefer Mozart. . ."

Not till the tea bowls were removed and the servant had been finally dismissed did Conway venture to recall the unanswered question. "We were discussing Mallinson, and you said he was going to be *my* problem. Why mine, particularly?"

Then the High Lama replied very simply: "Because, my son, I am going to die."

It seemed an extraordinary statement, and for a time Conway was speechless after it. Eventually the High Lama continued: "You are surprised? But surely, my friend, we are all mortal—even at Shangri-La. And it is possible that I may still have a few moments left to me—or even, for that matter, a few years. All I announce is the simple truth that already I see the end. It is charming of you to appear so concerned, and I will not pretend that there is not a touch of wistfulness, even at my age, in contemplating death. Fortunately little is left of me that can die physically, and as for the rest, all our religions display a pleasant unanimity of optimism. I am quite content, but I must accustom myself to a strange sensation during the hours that remain—I must realize that I have time for only one thing more. Can you imagine what that is?"

Conway was silent.

"It concerns you, my son."

"You do me a great honour."

"I have in mind to do much more than that."

Conway bowed slightly, but did not speak, and the High Lama, after waiting a while, resumed: "You know, perhaps, that the frequency of

these talks has been unusual here. But it is our tradition, if I may permit myself the paradox, that we are never slaves to tradition. We
have no rigidities, no inexorable rules. We do as we think fit, guided
a little by the example of the past, but still more by our present wisdom, and by our clairvoyance of the future. And thus it is that I am
encouraged to do this final thing."

Conway was still silent.

"I place in your hands, my son, the heritage and destiny of
Shangri-La."

At last the tension broke, and Conway felt beyond it the power of
a bland and benign persuasion; the echoes swam into silence, till all
that was left was his own heartbeat, pounding like a gong. And then,
intercepting the rhythm, came the words:

"I have waited for you, my son, for quite a long time. I have sat in
this room and seen the faces of newcomers, I have looked into their
eyes and heard their voices, and always in hope that some day I
might find you. My colleagues have grown old and wise, but you who
are still young in years are as wise already. My friend, it is not an
arduous task that I bequeath, for our order knows only silken bonds.
To be gentle and patient, to care for the riches of the mind, to pre-
side in wisdom and secrecy while the storm rages without—it will all
be very pleasantly simple for you, and you will doubtless find great
happiness."

Again Conway sought to reply, but could not, till at length a vivid
lightning flash paled the shadows and stirred him to exclaim: "The
storm . . . this storm you talk of . . . ."

"It will be such a one, my son, as the world has not seen before.
There will be no safety by arms, no help from authority, no answer in
science. It will rage till every flower of culture is trampled, and all
human things are levelled in a vast chaos. Such was my vision when
Napoleon was still a name unknown; and I see it now, more clearly
with each hour. Do you say I am mistaken?"

Conway answered: "No, I think you may be right. A similar crash
came once before, and then there were the Dark Ages lasting five
hundred years."

"The parallel is not quite exact. For those Dark Ages were not really so very dark—they were full of flickering lanterns, and even if the light had gone out of Europe altogether, there were other rays, literally from China to Peru, at which it could have been rekindled. But the Dark Ages that are to come will cover the whole world in a single pall; there will be neither escape nor sanctuary, save such as are too secret to be found or too humble to be noticed. And Shangri-La may hope to be both of these. The airman bearing loads of death to the great cities will not pass our way, and if by chance he should, he may not consider us worth a bomb."

"And you think all this will come in my time?"

"I believe that you will live through the storm. And after, through the long age of desolation, you may still live, growing older and wiser and more patient. You will conserve the fragrance of our history and add to it the touch of your own mind. You will welcome the stranger, and teach him the rule of age and wisdom; and one of these strangers, it may be, will succeed you when you are yourself very old. Beyond that, my vision weakens, but I see, at a great distance, a new world stirring in the ruins, stirring clumsily but in hopefulness, seeking its lost and legendary treasures. And they will all be here, my son, hidden behind the mountains in the valley of Blue Moon, preserved as by miracle for a new Renaissance . . . ."

The speaking finished, and Conway saw the face before him full of a remote and drenching beauty; then the glow faded and there was nothing left but a mask, dark-shadowed, and crumbling like old wood. It was quite motionless, and the eyes were closed. He watched for a while, and presently, as part of a dream, it came to him that the High Lama was dead.

IT SEEMED NECESSARY to rivet the situation to some kind of actuality, lest it become too strange to be believed in; and with instinctive mechanism of hand and eye, Conway glanced at his wristwatch. It was a quarter-past midnight. Suddenly, when he crossed the room to the door, it occurred to him that he did not in the least know how or whence to summon help. The Tibetans, he knew, had all been sent away for the night, and he had no idea where to find Chang or anyone else. He stood uncertainly on the threshold of the dark corridor;

through a window he could see that the sky was clear, though the mountains still blazed in lightning like a silver fresco. And then, in the midst of the still-encompassing dream, he felt himself master of Shangri-La. These were his beloved things, all around him, the things of that inner mind in which he lived increasingly, away from the fret of the world. His eyes strayed into the shadows and were caught by golden pinpoints sparkling in rich, undulating lacquers; and the scent of tuberose, so faint that it expired on the very brink of sensation, lured him from room to room. At last he stumbled into the courtyards and by the fringe of the pool; a full moon sailed behind Karakal. It was twenty minutes to two.

Later, he was aware that Mallinson was near him, holding his arm and leading him away in a great hurry. He did not gather what it was all about, but he could hear that the boy was chattering excitedly.

Chapter 11

HEY REACHED THE BALCONIED ROOM where they had meals, Mallinson still clutching his arm and half dragging him along. "Come on, Conway we've till dawn to pack what we can and get away. Great news, man—I wonder what old Barnard and Miss Brinklow will think in the morning when they find us gone . . . . Still, it's their own choice to stay, and we'll probably get on far better without them . . . . The porters are about five miles beyond the pass—they came yesterday with loads of books and things . . . tomorrow they begin the journey back . . . . It just shows how these fellows here intended to let us down—they never told us—we should have been stranded here for God knows how much longer . . . . I say, what's the matter? Are you ill?"

Conway had sunk into a chair, and was leaning forward with elbows on the table. He passed his hand across his eyes. "Ill? No. I don't think so. Just—rather—tired."

"Probably the storm. Where were you all the while? I'd been waiting for you for hours."

"I—I was visiting the High Lama."

"Oh, *him*! Well, *that's* for the last time, anyhow, thank God."

"Yes, Mallinson, for the last time."

Something in Conway's voice, and still more in his succeeding silence, roused the youth to irascibility. "Well, I wish you wouldn't sound so deuced leisurely about it—we've got to get a considerable move on, you know."

Conway stiffened for the effort of emerging into keener consciousness. "I'm sorry," he said. Partly to test his nerve and the reality of his sensations he lit a cigarette. He found that both hands and lips were unsteady. "I'm afraid I don't quite follow . . . you say the porters . . . ."

"Yes, the porters, man—do pull yourself together."

"You're thinking of going out to them?"

"*Thinking* of it? I'm damn well certain—they're only just over the ridge. And we've got to start immediately."

"*Immediately?*

"Yes, yes—why not?"

Conway made a second attempt to transfer himself from one world into the other. He said at length, having partly succeeded: "I suppose you realize that it mayn't be quite as simple as it sounds?"

Mallinson was lacing a pair of knee-high Tibetan mountain boots as he answered jerkily: "I realize everything, but it's something we've got to do, and we shall do it, with luck, if we don't delay."

"I don't see how—"

"Oh, Lord, Conway, must you fight shy of everything? Haven't you any guts left in you at all?"

The appeal, half passionate and half derisive, helped Conway to collect himself.

"Whether I have or haven't isn't the point, but if you want me to explain myself, I will. It's a question of a few rather important details. Suppose you *do* get beyond the pass and find the porters there, how do you know they'll take you with them? What inducement can you offer? Hasn't it struck you that they mayn't be quite so willing as you'd like them to be? You can't just present yourself and demand to be escorted. It all needs arrangements, negotiations beforehand—"

"Or anything else to cause a delay," exclaimed Mallinson bitterly. "God, what a fellow you are! Fortunately I haven't you to rely on for arranging things. Because they *have* been arranged—the porters have been paid in advance, and they've agreed to take us. And here are clothes and equipment for the journey, all ready. So your last excuse disappears. Come on, let's *do* something."

"But—I don't understand . . . ."

"I don't suppose you do, but it doesn't matter."

"Who's been making all these plans?"

Mallinson answered brusquely: "Lo-Tsen, if you're really keen to know. She's with the porters now. She's waiting."

"Waiting?"

"Yes. She's coming with us. I assume you've no objection?"

AT THE MENTION of Lo-Tsen the two worlds touched and fused suddenly in Conway's mind. He cried sharply, almost contemptuously: "That's nonsense. It's impossible."

Mallinson was equally on edge. "Why is it impossible?"

"Because . . . well, it is. There are all sorts of reasons. Take my word for it; it won't do. It's incredible enough that she should be out there now—I'm astonished at what you say has happened—but the idea of her going any farther is just preposterous."

"I don't see that it's preposterous at all. It's as natural for her to want to leave here as for me."

"But she doesn't want to leave. That's where you make the mistake."

Mallinson smiled tensely. "You think you know a good deal more about her than I do, I daresay," he remarked. "But perhaps you don't, for all that."

"What do you mean?"

"There are other ways of getting to understand people without learning heaps of languages."

"For heaven's sake, what *are* you driving at?" Then Conway added more quietly: "This is absurd. We mustn't wrangle. Tell me, Mallinson, what's it all about? I still don't understand."

"Then why are you making such an almighty fuss?"

"Tell me the truth, *please* tell me the truth."

"Well, it's simple enough. A kid of her age shut up here with a lot of queer old men—naturally she'll get away if she's given a chance. She hasn't had one up to now."

"Don't you think you may be imagining her position in the light of your own? As I've always told you, she's perfectly happy."

"Then why did she say she'd come?"

"She said that? How could she? She doesn't speak English."

"I asked her—in Tibetan—Miss Brinklow worked out the words. It wasn't a very fluent conversation, but it was quite enough to—to lead to an understanding." Mallinson flushed a little. "Damn it, Conway, don't stare at me like that—anyone would think I'd been poaching on *your* preserves."

Conway answered: "No one would think so at all, I hope, but the remark tells me more than you were perhaps intending me to know. I can only say that I'm very sorry."

"And why the devil should you be?"

Conway let the cigarette fall from his fingers. He felt tired, bothered, and full of deep conflicting tenderness that he would rather not have had aroused. He said gently: "I wish we weren't always at such cross-purposes. Lo-Tsen is very charming, I know, but why should we quarrel about it?"

"*Charming?*" Mallinson echoed the word with scorn. "She's a good bit more than that. You mustn't think everybody's as cold-blooded about these things as you are yourself. Admiring her as if she were an exhibit in a museum may be your idea of what she deserves, but mine's more practical, and when I see someone I like in a rotten position I try and *do* something."

"But surely there's such a thing as being too impetuous? Where do you think she'll go to if she does leave?"

"I suppose she must have friends in China or somewhere. Anyhow, she'll be better off than here."

"How can you possibly be so sure of that?"

"Well, I'll see that she's looked after myself, if nobody else will. After all, if you're rescuing people from something quite hellish, you don't usually stop to enquire if they've anywhere else to go to."

"And you think Shangri-La is hellish?"

"Definitely, I do. There's something dark and evil about it. The whole business has been like that, from the beginning—the way we were brought here, without reason at all, by some madman—and the way we've been detained since, on one excuse or another. But the most frightful thing of all—to me—is the effect it's had on you."

"On *me?*"

"Yes, on you. You've just mooned about as if nothing mattered and you were content to stay here for ever. Why, you even admitted you liked the place . . . . Conway, what *has* happened to you? Can't you manage to be your real self again? We got on so well together at Baskul—you were absolutely different in those days."

"My *dear* boy!"

Conway reached his hand towards Mallinson's, and the answering grip was hot and eagerly affectionate. Mallinson went on: "I don't suppose you realize it, but I've been terribly alone these last few weeks. Nobody seemed to be caring a damn about the only thing that was really important—Barnard and Miss Brinklow had reasons of a kind, but it was pretty awful when I found *you* against me."

"I'm sorry."

"You keep on saying that, but it doesn't help."

Conway replied, on sudden impulse: "Then let me help, if I can, by telling you something. When you've heard it, you'll understand, I hope, a great deal of what now seems very curious and difficult. At any rate, you'll realize why Lo-Tsen can't possibly go back with you."

"I don't think anything would make me see that. And do cut it as short as you can, because we really haven't time to spare."

Conway then gave, as briefly as he could, the whole story of Shangri-La, as told him by the High Lama, and as amplified by the conversation both with the latter and with Chang. It was the last thing he had ever intended to do, but he felt that in the circumstances it was justified and even necessary; it was true enough that Mallinson *was* his problem, to solve as he thought fit. He narrated rapidly and easily, and in doing so came again under the spell of that strange, timeless world; its beauty overwhelmed him as he spoke of it, and more than once he felt himself reading from a page of memory, so clearly had ideas and phrases impressed themselves. Only one thing he withheld—and that to spare himself an emotion he could not yet grapple with—the fact of the High Lama's death that night and of his own succession.

When he approached the end he felt comforted; he was glad to have got it over, and it was the only solution, after all. He looked up calmly when he had finished, confident that he had done well.

But Mallinson merely tapped his fingers on the tabletop and said, after a long wait: "I really don't know what to say, Conway . . . except that you must be completely mad . . . ."

There followed a long silence, during which the two men stared at each other in far differing moods—Conway withdrawn and disappointed, Mallinson in hot, fidgeting discomfort. "So you think I'm mad?" said Conway at length.

Mallinson broke into a nervous laugh. "Well, I should damn well say so, after a tale like that. I mean . . . well, really . . . such utter nonsense . . . it seems to me rather beyond arguing about."

Conway looked and sounded immensely astonished. "You think it's nonsense?"

"Well . . . how else can I look at it? I'm sorry, Conway—it's a pretty strong statement—but I don't see how any sane person could be in any doubt about it."

"So you still hold that we were brought here by blind accident—by some lunatic who made careful plans to run off with an aeroplane and fly it a thousand miles just for the fun of the thing?"

Conway offered a cigarette, and the other took it. The pause was one for which they both seemed grateful. Mallinson answered eventually: "Look here, it's no good arguing the thing point by point. As a matter of fact, your theory that the people here sent someone vaguely into the world to decoy strangers, and that this fellow deliberately learned flying and bided his time until it happened that a suitable machine was due to leave Baskul with four passengers . . . well, I won't say that it's literally impossible, though it does seem to me ridiculously far-fetched. If it stood by itself, it might just be worth considering, but when you tack it on to all sorts of other things that are *absolutely* impossible—all this about the lamas being hundreds of years old, and having discovered a sort of elixir of youth, or whatever you'd call it . . . well, it just makes me wonder what kind of microbe has bitten you, that's all."

Conway smiled. "Yes, I daresay you find it hard to believe. Perhaps I did myself at first—I scarcely remember. Of course it *is* an extraordinary story, but I should think your own eyes have had enough evidence that this is an extraordinary place. Think of all that we've actually seen, both of us—a lost valley in the midst of unexplored mountains, a monastery with a library of European books—"

"Oh, yes, and a central heating plant, and modern plumbing, and afternoon tea, and everything else—it's all very marvellous, I know."

"Well, then, what do you make of it?"

"Damn little, I admit. It's a complete mystery. But that's no reason for accepting tales that are physically impossible. Believing in hot baths because you've had them is different from believing in people hundreds of years old just because they've told you they are." He laughed again, still uneasily. "Look here, Conway, it's got on your nerves, this place, and I really don't wonder at it. Pack up your things and let's quit. We'll finish this argument a month or two hence after a jolly little dinner at Maiden's."

Conway answered quietly: "I've no desire to go back to that life at all."

"What life?"

"The life you're thinking of . . . dinners . . . dances . . . polo . . . and all that. . . ."

"But I never said anything about dances and polo! Anyhow, what's wrong with them? D'you mean that you're not coming with me? You're going to stay here like the other two? Then at least you shan't stop *me* from clearing out of it!" Mallinson threw down his cigarette and sprang towards the door with eyes blazing. "You're off your head!" he cried wildly. "You're mad, Conway, that's what's the matter with you! I know you're always calm, and I'm always excited, but I'm sane, at any rate, and you're not! They warned me about it before I joined you at Baskul, and I thought they were wrong, but now I can see they weren't—"

"What did they warn you of?"

"They said you'd been blown up in the War, and you'd been queer at times ever since. I'm not reproaching you—I know it was nothing you could help—and heaven knows I hate talking like this . . . . Oh, I'll go. It's all frightful and sickening, but I must go. I gave my word."

"To Lo-Tsen?"

"Yes, if you want to know."

Conway got up and held out his hand. "Goodbye, Mallinson."

"For the last time, you're not coming?"

"I can't."

"Goodbye, then."

They shook hands, and Mallinson left.

CONWAY SAT ALONE in the lantern-light. It seemed to him, in a phrase engraved on memory, that all the loveliest things were transient and perishable, that the two worlds were finally beyond reconciliation, and that one of them hung, as always, by a thread. After he had pondered for some time he looked at his watch; it was ten minutes to three.

He was still at the table, smoking the last of his cigarettes, when Mallinson returned. The youth entered with some commotion, and on seeing him, stood back in the shadows as if to gather his wits. He was silent, and Conway began, after waiting a moment: "Hello, what's happened? Why are you back?"

The complete naturalness of the question fetched Mallinson forward; he pulled off his heavy sheepskins and sat down. His face was ashen and his whole body trembled. "I hadn't the nerve," he cried, half sobbing. "That place where we were all roped—you remember? I got as far as that . . . I couldn't manage it. I've no head for heights, and in moonlight it looked fearful. Silly, isn't it?" He broke down completely and was hysterical until Conway pacified him. Then he added: "They needn't worry, these fellows here—nobody will ever threaten them by land. But, my God, I'd give a good deal to fly over with a load of bombs!"

"Why would you like to do that, Mallinson?"

"Because the place wants smashing up, whatever it is. It's

unhealthy and unclean—and for that matter, if your impossible yarn were true, it would be more hateful still! A lot of wizened old men crouching here like spiders for anyone who comes near . . . it's filthy . . . who'd want to live to an age like that, anyhow? And as for your precious High Lama, if he's half as old as you say he is, it's time some-one put him out of his misery . . . . Oh, why *won't* you come away with me, Conway? I hate imploring you for my own sake, but damn it all, I'm young and we've been pretty good friends together—does my whole life mean nothing to you compared with the lies of these awful creatures? And Lo-Tsen, too—*she's* young—doesn't *she* count at all?"

"Lo-Tsen is not young," said Conway.

Mallinson looked up and began to titter hysterically. "Oh no, not young—not young at all, of course. She looks about seventeen, but I suppose you'll tell me she's really a well-preserved ninety."

"Mallinson, she came here in 1884."

"You're raving, man!"

"Her beauty, Mallinson, like all other beauty in the world, lies at the mercy of those who do not know how to value it. It is a fragile thing that can only live where fragile things are loved. Take it away from this valley and you will see it fade like an echo."

Mallinson laughed harshly, as if his own thoughts gave him confi-dence. "I'm not afraid of that. It's here that she's only an echo, if she's one anywhere at all." He added after a pause: "Not that this sort of talk gets us anywhere. We'd better cut out all the poetic stuff and come down to realities. Conway, I want to help you—it's all the sheerest nonsense, I know, but I'll argue it out if it'll do you any good. I'll pretend it's something possible that you've told me, and that it really does need examining. Now tell me, seriously, what evidence have you for this story of yours?"

Conway was silent.

"Merely that someone spun you a fantastic rigmarole. Even from a thoroughly reliable person whom you'd known all your life, you wouldn't accept that sort of thing without proof. And what proofs have you in this case? None at all, so far as I can see. Has Lo-Tsen ever told you her history?"

"No, but—"

"Then why believe it from someone else? And all this longevity business—can you point to a single outside fact in support of it?"

Conway thought a moment and then mentioned the unknown Chopin works that Briac had played.

"Well, that's a matter that means nothing to me—I'm not a musician. But even if they're genuine, isn't it possible that he could have got hold of them in some way without his story being true?"

"Quite possible, no doubt."

"And then this method that you say exists—of preserving youth and so on. What is it? You say it's a sort of drug—well, I want to know *what* drug? Have you ever seen it or tried it? Did anyone ever give you any positive facts about the thing at all?"

"Not in detail, I admit."

"And you never asked for details? It didn't strike you that such a story needed any confirmation at all? You just swallowed it whole?" Pressing his advantage, he continued: "How much do you actually know of this place, apart from what you've been told? You've seen a few old men—that's all it amounts to. Apart from that, we can only say that the place is well fitted up, and seems to be run on rather highbrow lines. How and why it came into existence we've no idea, and why they want to keep us here, if they do, is equally a mystery, but surely all that's hardly an excuse for believing any old legend that comes along! After all, man, you're a critical sort of person—you'd hesitate to believe all you were told even in an English monastery— I really can't see why you should jump at everything just because you're in Tibet!"

Conway nodded. Even in the midst of far keener perceptions he could not restrain approval of a point well made. "That's an acute remark, Mallinson. I suppose the truth is that when it comes to believing things without actual evidence, we all incline to what we find most attractive."

"Well, I'm dashed if I can see anything attractive about living till you're half-dead. Give me a short life and a gay one, for choice. And this stuff about a future war—it all sounds pretty thin to me. How does anyone know when the next war's going to be or what it'll be like? Weren't all the prophets wrong about the last war?" He added, when Conway did not reply: "Anyhow, I don't believe in saying things are inevitable. And even if they were, there's no need to get into a funk about them. Heaven knows I'd most likely be scared stiff if I had to fight in a war, but I'd rather face up to it than bury myself here."

Conway smiled. "Mallinson, you have a superb knack of misunderstanding me. When we were at Baskul you thought I was a hero—now you take me for a coward. In point of fact, I'm neither—though of course it doesn't matter. When you get back to India you can tell people, if you like, that I decided to stay in a Tibetan monastery because I was afraid there'd be another war. It isn't my reason at all, but I've no doubt it'll be believed by the people who already think me mad."

Mallinson answered rather sadly: "It's silly, you know, to talk like that. Whatever happens, I'd never say a word against you. You can count on that. I don't understand you—I admit that—but—but—I wish I did. Oh, I wish I did. Conway, can't I possibly help you? Isn't there anything I can say or do?"

There was a long silence after that, which Conway broke at last by saying: "There's just a question I'd like to ask—if you'll forgive me for being terribly personal."

"Yes?"

"Are you in love with Lo-Tsen?"

The youth's pallor changed quickly to a flush. "I daresay I am. I know you'll say it's absurd and unthinkable, and probably it is, but I can't help my feelings."

"I don't think it's absurd at all."

The argument seemed to have sailed into a harbour after many buffetings, and Conway added: "I can't help *my* feelings either. You and that girl happen to be the two people in the world I care most about . . . though you may think it odd of me." Abruptly he got up and paced the room. "We've said all we *can* say, haven't we?"

"Yes, I suppose we have." But Mallinson went on, in a sudden rush of eagerness: "Oh, what stupid nonsense it all is—about her not being young! And foul and horrible nonsense, too. Conway, you *can't* believe it! It's just too ridiculous. How can it really mean anything?"

"How can you really know that she's young?"

Mallinson half turned away, his face lit with a grave shyness. "Because I *do* know . . . . Perhaps you'll think less of me for it . . . but I *do* know. I'm afraid you never properly understood her, Conway. She was cold on the surface, but that was the result of living here—it had frozen all the warmth. But the warmth was there."

"To be unfrozen?"

"Yes . . . that would be one way of putting it."

"And she's *young*, Mallinson—you are so *sure* of that?"

Mallinson answered softly: "God, yes—she's just a girl. I was terribly sorry for her, and we were both attracted, I suppose. I don't see that it's anything to be ashamed of. In fact in a place like this I should think it's about the decentest thing that's ever happened . . . ."

Conway went to the balcony and gazed at the dazzling plume of Karakal; the moon was riding high in a waveless ocean. It came to him that a dream had dissolved, like all too lovely things, at the first touch of reality; that the whole world's future, weighed in the balance against youth and love, would be light as air. And he knew, too, that his mind dwelt in a world of its own, Shangri-La in microcosm, and that this world also was in peril. For even as he nerved himself, he saw the corridors of his imagination twist and strain under impact; the pavilions were toppling; all was about to be in ruins. He was only partly unhappy, but he was infinitely and rather sadly perplexed. He did not know whether he had been mad and was now sane, or had been sane for a time and was now mad again.

When he turned, there was a difference in him; his voice was keener, almost brusque, and his face twitched a little; he looked much more the Conway who had been a hero at Baskul. Clenched for action, he faced Mallinson with a sudden new alertness. "Do you think you could manage that tricky bit with a rope if I were with you?" he asked.

Mallinson sprang forward. "*Conway!*" he cried chokingly. "You mean you'll *come*? You've made up your mind at last?"

THEY LEFT AS SOON as Conway had prepared himself for the journey. It was surprisingly simple to leave—a departure rather than an

They halted breathlessly and saw the last of Shangri-La

escape; there were no incidents as they crossed the bars of moonlight and shadow in the courtyards. One might have thought there was no one there at all, Conway reflected; and immediately the idea of such emptiness became an emptiness in himself; while all the time, though he hardly heard him, Mallinson was chattering about the journey. How strange that their long argument should have ended thus in action, that this secret sanctuary should be forsaken by one who had found in it such happiness! For indeed, less than an hour later, they halted breathlessly at a curve of the track and saw the last of Shangri-La. Deep below them the valley of Blue Moon was like a cloud, and to Conway the scattered roofs had a look of floating after him through the haze. Now, at that moment, it was farewell. Mallinson, whom the steep ascent had kept silent for a time, gasped out: "Good man, we're doing fine—carry on!"

Conway smiled, but did not reply; he was already preparing the rope for the knife-edge traverse. It was true, as the youth had said, that he had made up his mind; but it was only what was left of his mind. That small and active fragment now dominated; the rest comprised an absence hardly to be endured. He was a wanderer between two worlds and must ever wander; but for the present, in a deepening inward void, all he felt was that he liked Mallinson and must help him; he was doomed, like millions, to flee from wisdom and be a hero.

Mallinson was nervous at the precipice, but Conway got him over in traditional mountaineering fashion, and when the trial was past, they leaned together over Mallinson's cigarettes. "Conway, I must say it's damned good of you . . . . Perhaps you guess how I feel . . . I can't tell you how glad I am . . . ."

"I wouldn't try, then, if I were you."

After a long pause, and before they resumed the journey, Mallinson added: "But I *am* glad—not only for my own sake, but for yours as well. . . . It's fine that you can realize now that all that stuff was sheer nonsense . . . it's just wonderful to see you your real self again."

"Not at all," responded Conway, with a wryness that was for his own private comforting.

Towards dawn they crossed the divide, unchallenged by sentinels, even if there were any; though it occurred to Conway that the route, in the true spirit, might only be moderately well watched. Presently they reached the plateau, picked clean as a bone by roaring winds, and after a gradual descent the encampment of porters came in sight. Then all was as Mallinson had foretold; they found the men ready for them, sturdy fellows in furs and sheepskins, crouching under the gale and eager to begin the journey to Tatsien-Fu—eleven hundred miles eastward on the China border.

"He's coming with us!" Mallinson cried excitedly when they met Lo-Tsen. He forgot that she knew no English; but Conway translated.

It seemed to him that the little Manchu had never looked so radiant. She gave him a most charming smile, but her eyes were all for the boy.

Epilogue

T was in Delhi that I met Rutherford again. We had been guests at a Viceregal dinner party, but distance and ceremonial kept us apart until the turbaned flunkeys handed us our hats afterwards. "Come back to my hotel and have a drink," he invited.

We shared a cab along the arid miles between the Lutyens still-life and the warm, palpitating cinematograph of Old Delhi. I knew from the newspapers that he had just returned from Kashgar. His was one of those well-groomed reputations that get the most out of everything; any unusual holiday acquires the character of an exploration, and though the explorer takes care to do nothing really original, the public does not know this, and he capitalizes the full value of a hasty impression. It had not seemed to me, for instance, that Rutherford's journey, as reported in the press, had been particularly epoch-making; the buried cities of Khotan were old stuff, if anyone remembered Stein and Sven Hedin. I knew Rutherford well enough to chaff him about this, and he laughed: "Yes, the truth would have made a better story," he admitted cryptically.

We went to his hotel room and drank whisky. "So you *did* search for Conway?" I suggested when the moment seemed propitious.

"Search is much too strong a word," he answered. "You can't search a country half as big as Europe for one man. All I can say is that I have visited places where I was prepared to come across him or to get news of him. His last message, you remember, was that he had left Bangkok for the northwest. There were traces of him up-country for a little way, and my own opinion is that he probably made for the tribal districts on the Chinese border. I don't think he'd have cared to enter Burma, where he might have run up against British officials. Anyhow, the definite trail, you may say, peters out somewhere in Upper Siam, but of course I never expected to follow it far that end."

"You thought it might be easier to look for the valley of Blue Moon?"

"Well, it did seem as if it might be a more fixed proposition. I suppose you glanced at that manuscript of mine?"

"Much more than glanced at it. I should have returned it, by the way, but you left no address."

Rutherford nodded. "I wonder what you made of it?"

"I thought it very remarkable—assuming, of course, that it's all quite genuinely based on what Conway told you."

"I give you my solemn word for that. I invented nothing at all—indeed, there's even less of my own language in it than you might think. I've got a good memory, and Conway always had a way of describing things. Don't forget that we had about twenty-four hours of practically continuous talk."

"Well, as I said, it's all very remarkable."

He leaned back and smiled. "If that's all you're going to say, I can see I shall have to speak for myself. I suppose you consider me a rather credulous person. I don't really think I am. People make mistakes in life through believing too much, but they have a damned dull time if they believe too little. I was certainly taken with Conway's story—in more ways than one—and that was why I felt interested enough to put as many tabs on it as I could—apart from the chance of running up against the man himself."

He went on, after lighting a cigar: "It meant a good deal of odd journeying, but I like that sort of thing, and my publishers can't object to a travel book once in a while. Altogether I must have done some thousands of miles—Baskul, Bangkok, Chung-Kiang, Kashgar— I visited them all, and somewhere inside the area between them the mystery lies. But it's a pretty big area, you know, and all my investigations didn't touch more than the fringe of it—or of the mystery either, for that matter. Indeed, if you want the actual downright facts about Conway's adventures, so far as I've been able to verify them, all I can tell you is that he left Baskul on the twentieth of May and arrived in Chung-Kiang on the fifth of October. And the last we know of him is that he left Bangkok again on the third of February. All the rest is probability, possibility, guesswork, myth, legend, whatever you like to call it."

"So you didn't find anything in Tibet?"

"My dear fellow, I never got into Tibet at all. The people up at Government House wouldn't hear of it; it's as much as they'll do to sanction an Everest expedition, and when I said I thought of wandering about the Kuen-Luns on my own, they looked at me rather as if I'd suggested writing a life of Gandhi. As a matter of fact, they knew more than I did. Strolling about Tibet isn't a one-man job; it needs an expedition properly fitted out and run by someone who knows at least a word or two of the language. I remember when Conway was telling me his story I kept wondering why there was all that fuss about waiting for porters—why didn't they all simply walk off? I wasn't very long in discovering. The government people were quite right—all the passports in the world couldn't have got me over the Kuen-Luns. I actually went as far as seeing them in the distance, on a very clear day—perhaps fifty miles off. Not many Europeans can claim even that."

"Are they so very forbidding?"

"They looked just like a white frieze on the horizon, that was all. At Yarkand and Kashgar I questioned everyone I met about them, but it was extraordinary how little I could discover. I should think they must be the least explored range in the world. I had the luck to meet an American traveller who had once tried to cross them, but he'd been unable to find a pass. There *are* passes, he said, but they're terrifically high and unmapped. I asked him if he thought it possible for a valley to exist of the kind Conway described, and he said he wouldn't call it impossible, but he thought it not very likely—on geological grounds, at any rate. Then I asked if he had ever heard of a cone-shaped mountain almost as high as the highest of the Himalayas, and his answer to that was rather intriguing. There was a legend, he said, about such a mountain, but he thought himself there could be no foundation for it. There were even rumours, he added, about mountains actually higher than Everest, but he didn't himself give credit to them. 'I doubt if any peak in the Kuen-Luns is more than twenty-five thousand feet, if that,' he said. But he admitted that they had never been properly surveyed.

"Then I asked him what he knew about Tibetan lamaseries—he'd been in the country several times—and he gave me just the usual accounts that one can read in all the books. They weren't beautiful places, he assured me, and the monks in them were generally corrupt and dirty. 'Do they live long?' I asked, and he said, yes, they often did, if they didn't die of some filthy disease. Then I went boldly to the point and asked if he'd ever heard legends of extreme longevity among the lamas. 'Heaps of them,' he answered; 'it's one of the stock yarns you hear everywhere, but you can't verify them. You're told that some foul-looking creature has been walled up in a cell for a hundred years, and he certainly looks as if he might have been, but of course you can't demand his birth certificate.' I asked him if he thought they had any occult or medicinal way of prolonging life or preserving youth, and he said they were supposed to have a great deal of very curious knowledge about such things, but he suspected that if you came to look into it, it was rather like the Indian rope trick—always something that somebody else had seen. He did say, however, that the lamas appeared to have odd powers of bodily control. 'I've watched them,' he said, 'sitting by the edge of a frozen lake, stark naked, with a temperature below zero and in a tearing wind, while their servants break the ice and wrap sheets round them that have been dipped in the water. They do this a dozen times or more, and the lamas dry the sheets on their own bodies. Keeping warm by willpower, so one imagines, though that's a poor sort of explanation.'"

Rutherford helped himself to more drink. "But of course, as my American friend admitted, all that had nothing much to do with longevity. It merely showed that the lamas had sombre tastes in self-discipline . . . . So there we were, and probably you'll agree with me that all the evidence, so far, was less than you'd hang a dog on."

I said it was certainly inconclusive, and asked if the names Karakal and Shangri-La had meant anything to the American.

"Not a thing—I tried him with them. After I'd gone on questioning him for a time, he said: 'Frankly, I'm not keen on monasteries—indeed, I once told a fellow I met in Tibet that if I went out of my way at all, it would be to avoid them, not pay them a visit.' That chance remark of his gave me a curious idea, and I asked him when this meeting in Tibet had taken place. 'Oh, a long time ago,' he answered, 'before the War—in nineteen-eleven, I think it was.' I badgered him for further details, and he gave them, as well as he could remember. It seemed that he'd been travelling then for some American geographical society, with several colleagues, porters, and so on—in fact, a pukka expedition. Somewhere near the Kuen-Luns he met this other man, a Chinese who was being carried in a chair by native bearers. The fellow turned out to speak English quite well, and strongly recommended them to visit a certain lamasery in the neighbourhood—he even offered to be the guide there. The American said they hadn't time and weren't interested, and that was that." Rutherford went on, after an interval: "I don't suggest that it means a great deal. When a man tries to remember a casual incident that happened twenty years ago, you can't build *too* much on it. But it offers an attractive speculation."

"Yes, though if a well-equipped expedition had accepted the invitation, I don't see how they could have been detained at the lamasery against their will."

"Oh, quite. And perhaps it wasn't Shangri-La at all."

We thought it over, but it seemed too hazy for argument, and I went on to ask if there had been any discoveries at Baskul.

"Baskul was hopeless, and Peshawar was worse. Nobody could tell me anything, except that the kidnapping of the aeroplane did

171

undoubtedly take place. They weren't keen even to admit that—it's an episode they're not proud of."

"And nothing was heard of the plane afterwards?"

"Not a word or a rumour, or of its four passengers either. I verified, however, that it was capable of climbing high enough to cross the ranges. I also tried to trace that fellow Barnard, but I found his past history so mysterious that I wouldn't be at all surprised if he really were Chalmers Bryant, as Conway said. After all, Bryant's complete disappearance in the midst of the big hue and cry was rather amazing."

"Did you try to find anything about the actual kidnapper?"

"I did. But again it was hopeless. The air force man whom the fellow had knocked out and impersonated had since been killed, so one promising line of enquiry was closed. I even wrote to a friend of mine in America who runs an aviation school, asking if he had had any Tibetan pupils lately, but his reply was prompt and disappointing. He said he couldn't differentiate Tibetans from Chinese, and he had had about fifty of the latter—all training to fight the Japs. Not much chance there, you see. But I did make one rather quaint discovery— and one which I could have made just as easily without leaving London. There was a German professor at Jena about the middle of the last century who took to globe-trotting and visited Tibet in 1887. He never came back, and there was some story about him having been drowned in fording a river. His name was Friedrich Meister."

"Good heavens—one of the names Conway mentioned!"

"Yes—though it may only have been coincidence. It doesn't prove the whole story, by any means, because the Jena fellow was born in 1845. Nothing very exciting about that."

"But it's odd," I said.

"Oh, yes, it's odd enough."

"Did you succeed in tracing any of the others?"

"No. It's a pity I hadn't a longer list to work on. I couldn't find any record of a pupil of Chopin's called Briac, though of course that doesn't prove that there wasn't one. Conway was pretty sparing with his names, when you come to think about it—out of fifty-odd lamas supposed to be on the premises he only gave us one or two. Perrault and Henschell, by the way, proved equally impossible to trace."

"How about Mallinson?" I asked. "Did you try to find out what happened to him? And the girl—the Chinese girl?"

"My dear fellow, of course I did. The awkward part was, as you perhaps gathered from the manuscript, that Conway's story ended at the moment of leaving the valley with the porters After that he either couldn't or wouldn't tell me what happened—perhaps he might have done, mind you, if there'd been more time. I feel that we can guess at some sort of tragedy. The hardships of the journey would be perfectly appalling, apart from the risk of brigandage or even treachery among their own escorting party. Probably we shall never know exactly what did occur, but it seems tolerably certain that Mallinson never reached China. I made all sorts of enquiries, you know. First of all I tried to trace details of books, et cetera, sent in large consignments across the Tibetan frontier, but at all the likely places, such as Shanghai and Pekin, I drew complete blanks. That, of course, doesn't count for much, since the lamas would doubtless see that their methods of importation were kept secret. Then I tried at Tatsien-Fu. It's a weird place, a sort of world's-end market town, deuced difficult to get at, where the Chinese coolies from Yunnan transfer the loads of tea to the Tibetans. You can read about it in my new book when it comes out. Europeans don't often get as far. I found the people quite civil and courteous, but there was absolutely no record of Conway's party arriving at all."

"So how Conway himself reached Chung-Kiang is still unexplained?"

"The only conclusion is that he wandered there, just as he might have wandered anywhere else. Anyhow, we're back in the realm of hard facts when we get to Chung-Kiang, that's something. The nuns at the mission hospital were genuine enough, and so, for that matter, was Sieveking's excitement on the ship when Conway played that pseudo-Chopin." Rutherford paused and then added reflectively: "It's really an exercise in the balancing of probabilities, and I must say the scales don't bump very emphatically either way. Of course, if you don't accept Conway's story, it means that you doubt either his veracity or his sanity—one may as well be frank."

He paused again, as if inviting a comment, and I said: "As you know, I never saw him after the War, but people said he was a good deal changed by it."

Rutherford answered: "Yes, he certainly was, there's no denying the fact. You can't subject a mere boy to three years of intense physical and emotional stress without tearing something to tatters. People would say, I suppose, that he came through without a scratch. But the scratches were there—on the inside."

We talked for a little time about the War and its effects on various people, and at length he went on: "But there's just one more point that I must mention—and perhaps in some ways the oddest of all. It came out during my enquiries at the mission. They all did their best for me there, as you can guess, but they couldn't recollect much, especially as they'd been so busy with a fever epidemic at the time. One of the questions I put was about the manner Conway had reached the hospital first of all—whether he had presented himself alone, or had been found ill and been taken there by someone else. They couldn't exactly remember—after all, it was a long while back—but suddenly, when I was on the point of giving up the cross-examination, one of the nuns remarked quite casually, 'I think the doctor said he was brought here by a woman.' That was all she could tell me, and as the doctor himself had left the mission, there was no confirmation to be had on the spot.

"But having got so far, I wasn't in any mood to give up. It appeared that the doctor had gone to a bigger hospital in Shanghai, so I took the trouble to get his address and call on him there. It was just after the Jap air-raiding, and things were pretty grim. I'd met the man before during my first visit to Chung-Kiang, and he was very polite, though terribly overworked—yes, *terribly*'s the word, for, believe me, the air raids on London by the Germans were just nothing to what the gaps did to the native parts of Shanghai. Oh, yes, he said instantly, he remembered the case of the Englishman who had lost his memory. Was it true he had been brought to the mission hospital by a woman? I asked. Oh, yes, certainly, by a woman, a Chinese woman. Did he remember anything about her? Nothing, he answered, except that she had been ill of the fever herself, and had died almost immediately . . . . Just then there was an interruption—a batch of wounded were carried in and packed on stretchers in the corridors—the wards were all full—and I didn't care to go on taking up the man's time, especially as the thudding of the guns at Woosung was a reminder that he would still have plenty to do. When he came back to me, looking quite cheerful even amidst such ghastliness, I just asked him one final question, and I daresay you can guess what it was. 'About that Chinese woman,' I said. 'Was she young?'"

Rutherford flicked his cigar as if the narration had excited him quite as much as he hoped it had me. Continuing, he said: "The little fellow looked at me solemnly for a moment, and then answered in that funny clipped English that the educated Chinese have—'Oh, no, she was most old—most old of anyone I have ever seen.'"

We sat for a long time in silence, and then talked again of Conway as I remembered him, boyish and gifted and full of charm, and of the war that had altered him, and of so many mysteries of time and age and of the mind, and of the little Manchu who had been "most old," and of the strange ultimate dream of Blue Moon. "Do you think he will ever find it?" I asked.

WOODFORD GREEN
APRIL, 1933

GOODBYE, MR. CHIPS

and Other Stories

Goodbye, Mr. Chips ◆ PAGE 179

A Chapter of Autobiography ◆ PAGE 233

Gerald and the Candidate ◆ PAGE 256

Young Waveney ◆ PAGE 285

Mr. Chips Takes a Risk ◆ PAGE 291

Mr. Chips Meets a Sinner ◆ PAGE 300

Mr. Chips Meets a Star ◆ PAGE 310

Merry Christmas, Mr. Chips ◆ PAGE 319

GOODBYE, MR. CHIPS

Chapter 1

WHEN YOU ARE GETTING ON IN YEARS (but not ill, of course), you get very sleepy at times, and the hours seem to pass like lazy cattle moving across a landscape. It was like that for Chips as the autumn term progressed and the days shortened till it was actually dark enough to light the gas before call-over. For Chips, like some old sea-captain, still measured time by the signals of the past; and well he might, for he lived at Mrs. Wickett's, just across the road from the School.

He had been there more than a decade, ever since he finally gave up his mastership; and it was Brookfield far more than Greenwich time that both he and his landlady kept. "Mrs. Wickett," Chips would sing out, in that jerky, high-pitched voice that had still a good deal of sprightliness in it, "you might bring me a cup of tea before prep, will you?"

When you are getting on in years it is nice to sit by the fire and drink a cup of tea and listen to the School bell sounding dinner, call-over, prep, and lights-out. Chips always wound up the clock after that last bell; then he put the wire guard in front of the fire, turned out the gas, and carried a detective novel to bed. Rarely did he read more than a page of it before sleep came swiftly and peacefully, more like a mystic intensifying of perception than any changeful entrance into another world. For his days and nights were equally full of dreaming.

He was getting on in years (but not ill, of course); indeed, as Doctor Merivale said, there was really nothing the matter with him. "My dear fellow, you're fitter than I am," Merivale would say, sipping a glass of sherry when he called every fortnight or so. "You're past the age when people get these horrible diseases; you're one of the few lucky ones who're going to die a really natural death. That is, of course, if you die at all. You're such a remarkable old boy that one never knows." But when Chips had a cold or when east winds roared over the fenlands, Merivale would sometimes take Mrs. Wickett aside in the lobby and whisper: "Look after him, you know. His chest . . . it puts a strain on his heart. Nothing really wrong with him—only anno domini, but that's the most fatal complaint of all, in the end."

Anno domini . . . by Jove, yes. Born in 1848, and taken to the Great Exhibition as a toddling child—not many people still alive could boast a thing like that. Besides, Chips could even remember Brookfield in Wetherby's time. A phenomenon, that was. Wetherby had been an old man in those days—1870—easy to remember because of the Franco-Prussian War. Chips had put in for Brookfield after a year at Melbury, which he hadn't liked, because he had been ragged there a good deal. But Brookfield he *had* liked, almost from the beginning. He remembered that day of his preliminary interview—sunny June, with the air full of flower scents and the plick-plock of cricket on the pitch. Brookfield was playing Barnhurst, and one of the Barnhurst boys, a chubby little fellow, made a brilliant century. Queer that a thing like that should stay in the memory so clearly. Wetherby himself was very fatherly and courteous; he must have been ill then, poor chap, for he died during the summer vacation, before Chips began his first term. But the two had seen and spoken to each other, anyway.

Chips often thought, as he sat by the fire at Mrs. Wickett's: I am probably the only man in the world who has a vivid recollection of old Wetherby .... Vivid, yes; it was a frequent picture in his mind, that summer day with the sunlight filtering through the dust in Wetherby's study. "You are a young man, Mr. Chipping, and Brookfield is an old foundation. Youth and age often combine well. Give your enthusiasm to Brookfield, and Brookfield will give you something in return. And don't let anyone play tricks with you. I—er—gather that discipline was not always your strong point at Melbury?"

"Well, no, perhaps not, sir."

"Never mind; you're full young; it's largely a matter of experience. You have another chance here. Take up a firm attitude from the beginning—that's the secret of it."

Perhaps it was. He remembered that first tremendous ordeal of taking prep; a September sunset more than half a century ago; Big Hall full of lusty barbarians ready to pounce on him as their legitimate prey. His youth, fresh-complexioned, high-collared, and side-whiskered (odd fashions people followed in those days), at the mercy of five hundred unprincipled ruffians to whom the baiting of new masters was a fine art, an exciting sport, and something of a tradition. Decent little beggars individually, but, as a mob, just pitiless and implacable. The sudden hush as he took his place at the desk on the dais; the scowl he assumed to cover his inward nervousness; the tall clock ticking behind him, and the smells of ink and varnish; the last blood-red rays slanting in slabs through the stained-glass windows. Someone dropped a desk lid—quickly, he must take everyone by surprise; he must show that there was no nonsense about him. "You there in the fifth row—you with the red hair— what's your name?" "Colley, sir." "Very well, Colley, you have a hundred lines." No trouble at all after that. He had won his first round.

And years later, when Colley was an alderman of the City of London and a baronet and various other things, he sent his son (also red-haired) to Brookfield, and Chips would say: "Colley, your father was the first boy I ever punished when I came here twenty-five years ago. He deserved it then, and you deserve it now." How they all laughed; and how Sir Richard laughed when his son wrote home the story in next Sunday's letter!

And again, years after that, many years after that, there was an even better joke. For another Colley had just arrived—son of the Colley who was a son of the first Colley. And Chips would say, punctuating his remarks with that little "umph-um" that had by then become a habit with him: "Colley, you are—umph—a splendid example of—umph—inherited traditions. I remember your grandfather—umph—he could never grasp the Ablative Absolute. A stupid fellow, your grandfather. And your father, too—umph—I remember him—he used to sit at that far desk by the wall—he wasn't much better, either. But I do believe—my dear Colley—that you are—umph—the biggest fool of the lot!" Roars of laughter.

A great joke, this growing old—but a sad joke, too, in a way. And as Chips sat by his fire with autumn gales rattling the windows, the waves of humour and sadness swept over him very often until tears fell, so that when Mrs. Wickett came in with his cup of tea she did not know whether he had been laughing or crying. And neither did Chips himself.

Chapter 2

ACROSS THE ROAD BEHIND a rampart of ancient elms lay Brookfield, russet under its autumn mantle of creeper. A group of eighteenth-century buildings centred upon a quadrangle, and there were acres of playing fields beyond; then came the small dependent village and the open fen country. Brookfield, as Wetherby had said, was an old foundation; established in the reign of Elizabeth, as a grammar school, it might, with better luck, have become as famous as Harrow. Its luck, however, had been not so good; the School went up and down, dwindling almost to nonexistence at one time, becoming almost illustrious at another. It was during one of these latter periods, in the reign of the first George, that the main structure had been rebuilt and large additions made. Later, after the Napoleonic Wars and until mid-Victorian days, the School declined again, both in numbers and in repute. Wetherby, who came in 1840, restored its fortunes somewhat; but its subsequent history never raised it to front-rank status. It was, nevertheless, a good school of the second rank. Several notable families supported it; it supplied fair samples of the history-making men of the age—judges, Members of Parliament, colonial administrators, a few peers and bishops. Mostly, however, it turned out merchants, manufacturers, and professional men, with a good sprinkling of country squires and parsons. It was the sort of school which, when mentioned, would sometimes make snobbish people confess that they rather thought they had heard of it.

But if it had not been this sort of school it would probably not have taken Chips. For Chips, in any social or academic sense, was just as respectable, but no more brilliant, than Brookfield itself.

It had taken him some time to realize this, at the beginning. Not that he was boastful or conceited, but he had been, in his early twenties, as ambitious as most other young men at such an age. His dream had been to get a headship eventually, or at any rate a senior mastership in a really first-class school; it was only gradually, after repeated trials and failures, that he realized the inadequacy of his qualifications. His degree, for instance, was not particularly good, and his discipline, though good enough and improving, was not absolutely reliable under all conditions. He had no private means and no family connections of any importance. About 1880, after he had been at Brookfield a decade, he began to recognize that the odds were heavily against his being able to better himself by moving elsewhere; but about that time, also, the possibility of staying where he was began to fill a comfortable niche in his mind. At forty, he was rooted, settled, and quite happy. At fifty, he was the doyen of the staff. At sixty, under a new and youthful Head, he *was* Brookfield—the guest of honour at Old Brookfeldian dinners, the court of appeal in all matters affecting Brookfield history and traditions. And in 1913, when he turned sixty-five, he retired, was presented with a cheque and a writing-desk and a clock, and went across the road to live at Mrs. Wickett's. A decent career, decently closed; three cheers for old Chips, they all shouted, at that uproarious end-of-term dinner.

Three cheers, indeed; but there was more to come, an unguessed epilogue, an encore played to a tragic audience.

Chapter 3

I T WAS A SMALL but very comfortable and sunny room that Mrs. Wickett let to him. The house itself was ugly and pretentious; but that didn't matter. It was convenient—that was the main thing. For he liked, if the weather were mild enough, to stroll across to the playing fields in an afternoon and watch the games. He liked to smile and exchange a few words with the boys when they touched their caps to him. He made a special point of getting to know all the new boys and having them to tea with him during their first term. He always ordered a walnut cake with pink icing from Reddaway's, in the village, and during the winter term there were crumpets, too—a little pile of them in front of the fire, soaked in butter so that the bottom one lay in a little shallow pool. His guests found it fun to watch him make tea—mixing careful spoonfuls from different caddies. And he would ask the new boys where they lived, and if they had family connections at Brookfield. He kept watch to see that their plates were never empty, and punctually at five, after the session had lasted an hour, he would glance at the clock and say: "Well—umph—it's been very delightful—umph—meeting you like this—umph—I'm sorry—umph—you can't stay. . . ." And he would smile and shake hands with them in the porch, leaving them to race across the road to the School with their comments. "Decent old boy, Chips. Gives you a jolly good tea, anyhow, and you *do* know when he wants you to push off. . . ."

And Chips also would be making his comments—to Mrs. Wickett when she entered his room to clear away the remains of the party. "A most—umph—interesting time, Mrs. Wickett. Young Branksome tells me—umph—that his uncle was Major Collingwood—the Collingwood we had here in—umph—nought-two, I think it was. Dear me, I remember Collingwood very well. I once thrashed him—umph—for climbing on to the gymnasium roof—to get a ball out of the gutter. Might have—umph—broken his neck, the young fool. Do you remember him, Mrs. Wickett? He must have been in your time."

Mrs. Wickett, before she saved money, had been in charge of the linen room at the School.

"Yes, I knew 'im, sir. Cheeky, 'e was to me, gener'ly. But we never 'ad no bad words between us. Just cheeky-like. 'E never meant no harm. That kind never does, sir. Wasn't it 'im that got the medal, sir?"

"Yes, a D.S.O."

"Will you be wanting anything else, sir?"

"Nothing more now—umph—till Chapel time. He was killed—in Egypt, I think. . . . Yes—umph—you can bring my supper about then."

"Very good, sir."

A pleasant, placid life, at Mrs. Wickett's. He had no worries; his pension was adequate, and there was a little money saved up besides. He could afford everything and anything he wanted. His room was furnished simply and with schoolmasterly taste: a few bookshelves and sporting trophies; a mantelpiece crowded with fixture cards and signed photographs of boys and men; a worn Turkey carpet; big easy chairs; pictures on the wall of the Acropolis and the Forum. Nearly everything had come out of his old housemaster's room in School House. The books were chiefly classical, the classics having been his subject; there was, however, a seasoning of history and belles-lettres. There was also a bottom shelf piled up with cheap editions of detective novels. Chips enjoyed these. Sometimes he took down Virgil or Xenophon and read for a few moments, but he was soon back again with Doctor Thorndyke or Inspector French. He was not, despite his long years of assiduous teaching, a very profound classical scholar; indeed, he thought of Latin and Greek far more as dead languages from which English gentlemen ought to know a few quotations than as living tongues that had ever been spoken by living people. He liked those short leading articles in *The Times* that introduced a few tags that he recognized. To be among the dwindling number of people who understood such things was to him a kind of secret and valued freemasonry; it represented, he felt, one of the chief benefits to be derived from a classical education.

So there he lived, at Mrs. Wickett's, with his quiet enjoyments of reading and talking and remembering; an old man, white-haired and only a little bald, still fairly active for his years, drinking tea, receiving callers, busying himself with corrections for the next edition of the Brookfeldian Directory, writing his occasional letters in thin, spidery, but very legible script. He had new masters to tea, as well as new boys. There were two of them that autumn term, and as they were leaving after their visit one of them commented: "Quite a character, the old boy, isn't he? All that fuss about mixing the tea—a typical bachelor, if ever there was one."

Which was oddly incorrect; because Chips was not a bachelor at all. He had married; though it was so long ago that none of the staff at Brookfield could remember his wife.

Chapter 4

*T*HERE CAME TO HIM, stirred by the warmth of the fire and the gentle aroma of tea, a thousand tangled recollections of old times. Spring—the spring of 1896. He was forty-eight—an age at which a permanence of habits begins to be predictable. He had just been appointed housemaster; with this and his classical forms, he had made for himself a warm and busy corner of life. During the summer vacation he went up to the Lake

District with Rowden, a colleague; they walked and climbed for a week, until Rowden had to leave suddenly on some family business. Chips stayed on alone at Wasdale Head, where he boarded in a small farmhouse.

One day, climbing on Great Gable, he noticed a girl waving excitedly from a dangerous-looking ledge. Thinking she was in difficulties, he hastened towards her, but in doing so slipped himself and wrenched his ankle. As it turned out, she was not in difficulties at all, but was merely signalling to a friend farther down the mountain; she was an expert climber, better even than Chips, who was pretty good. Thus he found himself the rescued instead of the rescuer; and neither role was one for which he had much relish. For he did not, he would have said, care for women; he never felt at home or at ease with them; and that monstrous creature beginning to be talked about, the New Woman of the nineties, filled him with horror. He was a quiet, conventional person, and the world, viewed from the haven of Brookfield, seemed to him full of distasteful innovations; there was a fellow named Bernard Shaw who had the strangest and most reprehensible opinions; there was Ibsen, too, with his disturbing plays; and there was this new craze for bicycling which was being taken up by women equally with men. Chips did not hold with all this modern newness and freedom. He had a vague notion, if he ever formulated it, that nice women were weak, timid, and delicate, and that nice men treated them with a polite but rather distant chivalry. He had not, therefore, expected to find a woman on Great Gable; but, having encountered one who seemed to need masculine help, it was even more terrifying that she should turn the tables by helping him. For she did. She and her friend had to. He could scarcely walk, and it was a hard job getting him down the steep track to Wasdale.

Her name was Katherine Bridges; she was twenty-five—young enough to be Chips's daughter. She had blue, flashing eyes and freckled cheeks and smooth straw-coloured hair. She too was staying at a farm, on holiday with a girl-friend, and as she considered herself responsible for Chips's accident, she used to bicycle along

He found himself the rescued instead of the rescuer

the side of the lake to the house in which the quiet, middle-aged, serious-looking man lay resting.

That was how she thought of him at first. And he, because she rode a bicycle and was unafraid to visit a man alone in a farmhouse sitting room, wondered vaguely what the world was coming to. His sprain put him at her mercy, and it was soon revealed to him how much he might need that mercy. She was a governess out of a job, with a little money saved up; she read and admired Ibsen; she believed that women ought to be admitted to the universities; she even thought they ought to have a vote. In politics she was a radical, with leanings towards the views of people like Bernard Shaw and William Morris. All her ideas and opinions she poured out to Chips during those summer afternoons at Wasdale Head; and he, because he was not very articulate, did not at first think it worthwhile to contradict them. Her friend went away, but she stayed; what *could* you do with such a person? Chips thought. He used to hobble with sticks along a footpath leading to the tiny church; there was a stone slab on the wall, and it was comfortable to sit down, facing the sunlight and the green-brown majesty of the Gable and listening to the chatter of—well, yes, Chips had to admit it—a very beautiful girl.

He had never met anyone like her. He had always thought that the modern type, this "new woman" business, would repel him; and here she was, making him positively look forward to the glimpse of her safety bicycle careering along the lakeside road. And she, too, had never met anyone like *him*. She had always thought that middle-aged men who read *The Times* and disapproved of modernity were terrible bores; yet here he was, claiming her interest and attention far more than youths of her own age. She liked him, initially, because he was so hard to get to know, because he had gentle and quiet manners, because his opinions dated from those utterly impossible seventies and eighties and even earlier—yet were, for all that, so thoroughly honest; and because—because his eyes were brown and he looked charming when he smiled. "Of course, *I* shall call you Chips, too," she said, when she learned that was his nickname at school.

Within a week they were head over heels in love; before Chips could walk without a stick, they considered themselves engaged; and they were married in London a week before the beginning of the autumn term.

Chapter 5

W HEN CHIPS, dreaming through the hours at Mrs. Wickett's, recollected those days, he used to look down at his feet and wonder which one it was that had performed so signal a service. That, the trivial cause of so many momentous happenings, was the one thing of which details evaded him. But he resaw the glorious hump of the Gable (he had never visited the Lake District since), and the mouse-grey depths of Wastwater under the Screes; he could resmell the washed air after heavy rain, and refollow the ribbon of the pass across to Sty Head. So clearly it lingered, that time of dizzy happiness, those evening strolls by the waterside, her cool voice and her gay laughter. She had been a very happy person, always.

They had both been so eager, planning a future together; but he had been rather serious about it, even a little awed. It would be all right, of course, her coming to Brookfield; other housemasters were married. And she liked boys, she told him, and would enjoy living among them. "Oh, Chips, I'm so glad you are what you are. I was afraid you were a solicitor or a stockbroker or a dentist or a man with a big cotton business in Manchester. When I first met you, I mean. Schoolmastering's so different, so important, don't you think? To be influencing those who are going to grow up and matter to the world. . . ."

Chips said he hadn't thought of it like that—or, at least, not often. He did his best; that was all anyone could do in any job.

"Yes, of course, Chips. I do love you for saying simple things like that."

And one morning—another memory gem-clear when he turned to

it—he had for some reason been afflicted with an acute desire to depreciate himself and all his attainments. He had told her of his only mediocre degree, of his occasional difficulties of discipline, of the certainty that he would never get a promotion, and of his complete ineligibility to marry a young and ambitious girl. And at the end of it all she had laughed in answer.

She had no parents and was married from the house of an aunt in Ealing. On the night before the wedding, when Chips left the house to return to his hotel, she said, with mock gravity: "This is an occasion, you know—this last farewell of ours. I feel rather like a new boy beginning his first term with you. Not scared, mind you—but just, for once, in a thoroughly respectful mood. Shall I call you 'sir'—or would 'Mr. Chips' be the right thing? 'Mr. Chips,' I think. Goodbye, then—goodbye, Mr. Chips. . . ."

(A hansom clop-clopping in the roadway; green-pale gas lamps flickering on a wet pavement; newsboys shouting something about South Africa; Sherlock Holmes in Baker Street.)

"Goodbye, Mr. Chips. . . ."

Chapter 6

T HERE HAD FOLLOWED then a time of such happiness that Chips, remembering it long afterwards, hardly believed it could ever have happened before or since in the world. For his marriage was a triumphant success. Katherine conquered Brookfield as she had conquered Chips; she was immensely popular with boys and masters alike. Even the wives of the masters, tempted at first to be jealous of one so young and lovely, could not long resist her charms.

But most remarkable of all was the change she made in Chips. Till his marriage he had been a dry and rather neutral sort of person; liked and thought well of by Brookfield in general, but not of the stuff that makes for great popularity or that stirs great affection.

He had been at Brookfield for over a quarter of a century, long enough to have established himself as a decent fellow and a hard worker; but just too long for anyone to believe him capable of ever being much more. He had, in fact, already begun to sink into that creeping dry-rot of pedagogy which is the worst and ultimate pitfall of the profession; giving the same lessons year after year had formed a groove into which the other affairs of his life adjusted themselves with insidious ease. He worked well; he was conscientious; he was a fixture that gave service, satisfaction, confidence, everything except inspiration.

And then came this astonishing girl-wife whom nobody had expected—least of all Chips himself. She made him, to all appearances, a new man; though most of the newness was really a warming to life of things that were old, imprisoned, and unguessed. His eyes gained sparkle; his mind, which was adequately if not brilliantly equipped, began to move more adventurously. The one thing he had always had, a sense of humour, blossomed into a sudden richness to which his years lent maturity. He began to feel a greater sureness; his discipline improved to a point at which it could become, in a sense, less rigid; he became more popular. When he had first come to Brookfield he had aimed to be loved, honoured, and obeyed—but obeyed, at any rate. Obedience he had secured, and honour had been granted him; but only now came love, the sudden love of boys for a man who was kind without being soft, who understood them well enough, but not too much, and whose private happiness linked him with their own. He began to make little jokes, the sort that schoolboys like—mnemonics and puns that raised laughs and at the same time imprinted something in the mind. There was one that never failed to please, though it was only a sample of many others. Whenever his Roman History forms came to deal with the *Lex Canuleia*, the law that permitted patricians to marry plebeians, Chips used to add: "So that, you see, if Miss Plebs wanted Mr. Patrician to marry her, and he said he couldn't, she probably replied: 'Oh yes, you can, you liar!'" Roars of laughter.

And Kathie broadened his views and opinions, also, giving him an outlook far beyond the roofs and turrets of Brookfield, so that he saw his country as something deep and gracious to which Brookfield was but one of many feeding streams. She had a cleverer brain than his, and he could not confute her ideas even if and when he disagreed with them; he remained, for instance, a Conservative in politics, despite all her radical Socialist talk. But even where he did not accept, he absorbed; her young idealism worked upon his maturity to produce an amalgam very gentle and wise.

Sometimes she persuaded him completely. Brookfield, for example, ran a mission in East London, to which boys and parents contributed generously with money but rarely with personal contact. It was Katherine who suggested that a team from the mission should come up to Brookfield and play one of the School's elevens at soccer. The idea was so revolutionary that from anyone but Katherine it could not have survived its first frosty reception. To introduce a group of slum boys to the serene pleasances of better-class youngsters seemed at first a wanton stirring of all kinds of things that had better be left untouched. The whole staff was against it, and the School, if its opinion could have been taken, was probably against it too. Everyone was certain that the East End lads would be hooligans, or else that they would be made to feel uncomfortable; anyhow, there would be "incidents," and everyone would be confused and upset. Yet Katherine persisted.

"Chips," she said, "they're wrong, you know, and I'm right. I'm looking ahead to the future, they and you are looking back to the past. England isn't always going to be divided into officers and 'other ranks.' And those Poplar boys are just as important—to England—as Brookfield is. You've got to have them here, Chips. You can't satisfy your conscience by writing a cheque for a few guineas and keeping them at arm's length. Besides, they're proud of Brookfield—just as you are. Years hence, maybe, boys of that sort will be coming here—a few of them, at any rate. Why not? Why ever not? Chips, dear, remember this is eighteen *ninety*-seven—not *sixty*-seven, when you were up at Cambridge. You got your ideas well stuck in those days, and good ideas they were too, a lot of them. But a few—just a few, Chips—want unsticking. . . ."

Rather to her surprise, he gave way and suddenly became a keen advocate of the proposal, and the *volte-face* was so complete that the authorities were taken unawares and found themselves consenting to the dangerous experiment. The boys from Poplar arrived at Brookfield one Saturday afternoon, played soccer with the School's second team, were honourably defeated by seven goals to five, and later had high tea with the School team in the Dining Hall. They then met the Head and were shown over the School, and Chips saw them off at the railway station in the evening. Everything had passed without the slightest hitch of any kind, and it was clear that the visitors were taking away with them as fine an impression as they had left behind.

They took back with them also the memory of a charming woman who had met them and talked to them; for once, years later, during the War, a private stationed at a big military camp near Brookfield called on Chips and said he had been one of that first visiting team. Chips gave him tea and chatted with him, till at length, shaking hands, the man said: "And 'ow's the missus, sir? I remember her very well."

"Do you?" Chips answered, eagerly. "Do you remember her?"

"Rather. I should think anyone would."

And Chips replied: "They don't, you know. At least, not here. Boys come and go; new faces all the time; memories don't last. Even masters don't stay for ever. Since last year—when old Gribble retired—he's—um—the School butler—there hasn't been anyone here who ever saw my wife. She died, you know, less than a year after your visit. In ninety-eight."

"I'm real sorry to 'ear that, sir. There's two or three o' my pals, anyhow, who remember 'er clear as anything, though we did only see 'er that wunst. Yes, we remember 'er, all right."

"I'm very glad. . . . That was a grand day we all had—and a fine game, too."

"One o' the best days that I ever 'ad in me life. Wish it was then and not nah—straight, I do. I'm off to Frawnce tomorrer."

A month or so later Chips heard that he had been killed at Passchendaele.

Chapter 7

AND SO IT STOOD, a warm and vivid patch in his life, casting a radiance that glowed in a thousand recollections. Twilight at Mrs. Wickett's, when the School bell clanged for call-over, brought them back to him in a cloud—Katherine scampering along the stone corridors, laughing beside him at some "howler" in an essay he was marking, taking the cello part in a Mozart trio for the School concert, her creamy arm sweeping over the brown sheen of the instrument. She had been a good player and a fine musician. And Katherine furred and muffed for the December house matches, Katherine at the Garden Party that followed Speech Day Prize-giving, Katherine tendering her advice in any little problem that arose. Good advice, too—which he did not always take, but which always influenced him.

"Chips, dear, I'd let them off if I were you. After all, it's nothing very serious."

"I know. I'd like to let them off, but if I do I'm afraid they'll do it again."

"Try telling them that, frankly, and give them the chance."

"I might."

And there were other things, occasionally, that *were* serious.

"You know, Chips, having all these hundreds of boys cooped up here is really an unnatural arrangement, when you come to think about it. So that when anything does occur that oughtn't to, don't you think it's a bit unfair to come down on them as if it were their own fault for being here?"

"Don't know about that, Kathie, but I do know that for everybody's sake we have to be pretty strict about this sort of thing. One black sheep can contaminate others."

"After he himself has been contaminated to begin with. After all, that's what probably *did* happen, isn't it?"

"Maybe. We can't help it. Anyhow, I believe Brookfield is better than a lot of other schools. All the more reason to keep it so."

"But this boy, Chips . . . you're going to sack him?"

"The Head probably will, when I tell him."

"And you're going to tell the Head?"

"It's a duty, I'm afraid."

"Couldn't you think about it a bit . . . talk to the boy again . . . find out how it began. . . . After all—apart from this business—isn't he rather a nice boy?"

"Oh, he's all right."

"Then, Chips dear, don't you think there ought to be some other way?"

And so on. About once in ten times he was adamant and wouldn't be persuaded. In about half of these exceptional cases he afterwards rather wished he had taken her advice. And years later, whenever he had trouble with a boy, he was always at the mercy of a softening wave of reminiscence; the boy would stand there, waiting to be told his punishment, and would see, if he were observant, the brown eyes twinkle into a shine that told him all was well. But he did not guess that at such a moment Chips was remembering something that had happened long before he was born; that Chips was thinking: Young ruffian, I'm hanged if *I* can think of any reason to let him off, but I'll bet *she* would have done!

But she had not always pleaded for leniency. On rather rare occasions she urged severity where Chips was inclined to be forgiving. "I don't like his type, Chips. He's too cocksure of himself. If he's looking for trouble I should certainly let him have it."

What a host of little incidents, all deep-buried in the past—problems that had once been urgent, arguments that had once been keen, anecdotes that were funny only because one remembered the fun. Did any emotion really matter when the last trace of it had vanished from human memory; and if that were so, what a crowd of emotions clung to him as to their last home before annihilation! He must be kind to them, must treasure them in his mind before their long sleep. That affair of Archer's resignation, for instance—a queer business, that was. And that affair about the rat that Dunster put in the organ

"Chips dear, don't you think there ought to be some other way?"

loft while old Ogilvie was taking choir practice. Ogilvie was dead and Dunster drowned at Jutland; of others who had witnessed or heard of the incident, probably most had forgotten. And it had been like that, with other incidents, for centuries. He had a sudden vision of thousands and thousands of boys, from the age of Elizabeth onwards; dynasty upon dynasty of masters; long epochs of Brookfield that had left not even a ghostly record. Who knew why the old fifth-form room was called "the Pit"? There was probably a reason, to begin with; but it had since been lost—lost like the lost books of Livy. And what happened at Brookfield when Cromwell fought at Naseby, nearby? How did Brookfield react to the great scare of the "Forty-Five"? Was there a whole holiday when news came of Waterloo? And so on, up to the earliest time that he himself could remember—1870, and Wetherby saying, by way of small talk after their first and only interview: "Looks as if we shall have to settle with the Prussians ourselves one of these fine days, eh?"

When Chips remembered things like this he often felt that he would write them down and make a book of them; and during his years at Mrs. Wickett's he sometimes went even so far as to make desultory notes in an exercise book. But he was soon brought up against difficulties—the chief one being that writing tired him, both mentally and physically. Somehow, too, his recollections lost much of their flavour when they were written down; that story about Rushton and the sack of potatoes, for instance—it would seem quite tame in print, but Lord, how funny it had been at the time! It was funny, too, to remember it; though perhaps if you didn't remember Rushton . . . and who would, anyway, after all those years? It was such a long time ago . . . Mrs. Wickett, did you ever know a fellow named Rushton? Before your time, I daresay . . . went to Burma in some government job . . . or was it Borneo? . . . Very funny fellow, Rushton. . . .

And there he was, dreaming again before the fire, dreaming of times and incidents in which he alone could take secret interest. Funny and sad, comic and tragic, they all mixed up in his mind, and some day, however hard it proved, he *would* sort them out and make a book of them. . . .

Chapter 8

AND THERE WAS ALWAYS in his mind that spring day in ninety-eight when he had paced through Brookfield village as in some horrifying nightmare, half struggling to escape into an outside world where the sun still shone and where everything had happened differently. Young Faulkner had met him there in the lane outside the School. "Please, sir, may I have the afternoon off? My people are coming up."

"Eh? What's that? Oh yes, yes. . . ."

"Can I miss Chapel, too, sir?"

"Yes . . . yes. . . ."

"And may I go to the station to meet them?"

He nearly answered: "You can go to blazes for all I care. My wife is dead and my child is dead, and I wish I were dead myself."

Actually he nodded and stumbled on. He did not want to talk to anybody or to receive condolences; he wanted to get used to things, if he could, before facing the kind words of others. He took his fourth form as usual after call-over, setting them grammar to learn by heart while he himself stayed at his desk in a cold, continuing trance. Suddenly someone said: "Please, sir, there are a lot of letters for you."

So there were; he had been leaning his elbows on them; they were all addressed to him by name. He tore them open one after the other, but each contained nothing but a blank sheet of paper. He thought in a distant way that it was rather peculiar, but he made no comment; the incident gave hardly an impact upon his vastly greater preoccupations. Not till days afterwards did he realize that it had been a piece of April foolery.

THEY HAD DIED on the same day, the mother and the child just born; on April 1st, 1898.

Chapter 9

CHIPS CHANGED HIS MORE commodious apartments in School House for his old original bachelor quarters. He thought at first he would give up his housemastership, but the Head persuaded him otherwise; and later he was glad. The work gave him something to do, filled up an emptiness in his mind and heart. He was different; everyone noticed it. Just as marriage had added something, so did bereavement; after the first stupor of grief he became suddenly the kind of man whom boys, at any rate, unhesitatingly classed as "old." It was not that he was less active; he could still knock up a half-century on the cricket field; nor was it that he had lost any interest or keenness in his work. Actually, too, his hair had been greying for years; yet now, for the first time, people seemed to notice it. He was fifty. Once, after some energetic fives, during which he had played as well as many a fellow half his age, he overheard a boy saying: "Not half bad for an old chap like him."

Chips, when he was over eighty, used to recount that incident with many chuckles. "Old at fifty, eh? Umph—it was Naylor who said that, and Naylor can't be far short of fifty himself by now. I wonder if he still thinks that fifty's such an age? Last I heard of him, he was lawyering, and lawyers live long—look at Halsbury—umph—Chancellor at eighty-two, and died at ninety-nine. There's an—umph—age for you! Too old at fifty—why, fellows like that are too *young* at fifty . . . . I was myself . . . a mere infant. . . ."

And there was a sense in which it was true. For with the new century there settled upon Chips a mellowness that gathered all his developing mannerisms and his oft-repeated jokes into a single harmony. No longer did he have those slight and occasional disciplinary troubles, or feel diffident about his own work and worth. He found that his pride in Brookfield reflected back, giving him cause for pride in himself and his position. It was a service that gave him freedom to

He could still knock up a half-century

be supremely and completely himself. He had won, by seniority and ripeness, an uncharted no-man's-land of privilege; he had acquired the right to those gentle eccentricities that so often attack schoolmasters and parsons. He wore his gown till it was almost too tattered to hold together; and when he stood on the wooden bench by Big Hall steps to take call-over, it was with an air of mystic abandonment to ritual. He held the School List, a long sheet curling over a board; and each boy, as he passed, spoke his own name for Chips to verify and then tick off on the list. That verifying glance was an easy and favourite subject of mimicry throughout the School—steel-rimmed spectacles slipping down the nose, eyebrows lifted, one a little higher than the other, a gaze half rapt, half quizzical. And on windy days, with gown and white hair and School List fluttering in uproarious confusion, the whole thing became a comic turn sandwiched between afternoon games and the return to classes.

Some of those names, in little snatches of a chorus, recurred to him ever afterwards without any effort of memory. "Ainsworth, Attwood, Avonmore, Babcock, Baggs, Barnard, Bassenthwaite, Battersby, Beccles, Bedford-Marshall, Bentley, Best. . . ."

Another one:

". . . Unsley, Vailes, Wadham, Wagstaff, Wallington, Waters Primus, Waters Secundus, Watling, Waveney, Webb. . . ."

And yet another that comprised, as he used to tell his fourth-form Latinists, an excellent example of a hexameter:

". . . Lancaster, Latton, Lemare, Lytton-Bosworth, MacGonigall, Mansfield. . . ."

Where had they all gone to, he often pondered; those threads he had once held together, how far had they scattered, some to break, others to weave into unknown patterns? The strange randomness of the world beguiled him, that randomness which never would, so long as the world lasted, give meaning to those choruses again.

And behind Brookfield, as one may glimpse a mountain behind another mountain when the mist clears, he saw the world of change and conflict; and he saw it, more than he realized, with the remembered eyes of Kathie. She had not been able to bequeath him all her mind, still less the brilliance of it; but she had left him with a calmness and a poise that accorded well with his own inward emotions. It was typical of him that he did not share the general jingo bitterness against the Boers. Not that he was a pro-Boer—he was far too traditional for that, and he disliked the kind of people who *were* pro-Boers; but still, it did cross his mind at times that the Boers were engaged in a struggle that had a curious similarity to those of certain English history-book heroes—Hereward the Wake, for instance, or Caractacus. He once tried to shock his fifth form by suggesting this, but they only thought it was one of his little jokes.

However heretical he might be about the Boers, he was orthodox about Mr. Lloyd George and the famous Budget. He did not care for either of them. And when, years later, L. G. came as the guest of honour to a Brookfield Speech Day, Chips said, on being presented to him: "Mr. Lloyd George, I am nearly old enough—umph—to remember you as a young man, and—umph—I confess that you seem to me—umph—to have improved—umph—a great deal." The Head, standing with them, was rather aghast; but L. G. laughed heartily and talked to Chips more than to anyone else during the ceremonial that followed.

"Just like Chips," was commented afterwards. "He gets away with it. I suppose at that age anything you say to anybody is all right. . . ."

Chapter 10

IN 1900 OLD MELDRUM, who had succeeded Wetherby as Head and had held office for three decades, died suddenly from pneumonia; and in the interval before the appointment of a successor, Chips became Acting Head of Brookfield. There was just the faintest chance that the Governors might make the appointment a permanent one; but Chips was not really disappointed when they brought in a youngster of thirty-seven, glittering with Firsts and Blues and with the kind of personality that could reduce Big Hall to silence by the mere lifting of an eyebrow.

Chips was not in the running with that kind of person; he never had been and never would be, and he knew it. He was an altogether milder and less ferocious animal.

Those years before his retirement in 1913 were studded with sharply remembered pictures.

A May morning; the clang of the School bell at an unaccustomed time; everyone summoned to assemble in Big Hall. Ralston, the new Head, very pontifical and aware of himself, fixing the multitude with a cold, presaging severity. "You will all be deeply grieved to hear that His Majesty King Edward the Seventh died this morning. . . . There will be no school this afternoon, but a service will be held in the Chapel at four-thirty."

A summer morning on the railway line near Brookfield. The railway men were on strike, soldiers were driving the engines, stones had been thrown at trains. Brookfield boys were patrolling the line, thinking the whole business great fun. Chips, who was in charge, stood a little way off, talking to a man at the gate of a cottage. Young Cricklade approached. "Please, sir, what shall we do if we meet any strikers?"

"Would you like to meet one?"

"I—I don't know, sir."

God bless the boy—he talked of them as if they were queer animals out of a zoo! "Well, here you are, then—umph—you can meet Mr. Jones—he's a striker. When he's on duty he has charge of the signal box at the station. You've put your life in his hands many a time."

Afterwards the story went round the School. There was Chips, talking to a striker. Talking to a striker. Might have been quite friendly, the way they were talking together.

Chips, thinking it over a good many times, always added to himself that Kathie would have approved, and would also have been amused.

Because always, whatever happened and however the avenues of politics twisted and curved, he had faith in England, in English flesh and blood, and in Brookfield as a place whose ultimate worth depended on whether she fitted herself into the English scene with dignity and without disproportion. He had been left a vision that grew clearer with each year—of an England for which days of ease were nearly over, of a nation steering into channels where a hair's breadth of error might be catastrophic. He remembered the Diamond Jubilee; there had been a whole holiday at Brookfield, and he had taken Kathie to London to see the procession. That old and legendary lady, sitting in her carriage like some crumbling wooden doll, had symbolized impressively so many things that, like herself, were nearing an end. Was it only the century, or was it an epoch?

And then that frenzied Edwardian decade, like an electric lamp that goes brighter and whiter just before it burns itself out.

Strikes and lockouts, champagne suppers and unemployed marchers, Chinese labour, tariff reform, HMS *Dreadnought*, Marconi, Home Rule for Ireland, Doctor Crippen, suffragettes, the lines of Chatalja. . . .

An April evening, windy and rainy; the fourth form construing Virgil, not very intelligently, for there was exciting news in the papers; young Grayson, in particular, was careless and preoccupied. A quiet, nervous boy.

"Grayson, stay behind—umph—after the rest."

Then:

"Grayson, I don't want to be—umph—severe, because you are generally pretty good—umph—in your work, but today—you don't seem—umph—to have been trying at all. Is anything the matter?"

"N-no, sir."

"Well—umph—we'll say no more about it, but—umph—I shall expect better things next time."

Next morning it was noised around the School that Grayson's father had sailed on the *Titanic*, and that no news had yet come through as to his fate.

Grayson was excused lessons; for a whole day the School centred emotionally upon his anxieties. Then came news that his father had been among those rescued.

Chips shook hands with the boy. "Well—umph—I'm delighted, Grayson. A happy ending. You must be feeling pretty pleased with life."

"Y-yes, sir."

A quiet, nervous boy. And it was Grayson Senior, not Junior, with whom Chips was destined later to condole.

Chapter 11

ND THEN THE ROW WITH RALSTON. Funny thing, Chips had never liked him; he was efficient, ruthless, ambitious, but not, somehow, very likeable. He had, admittedly, raised the status of Brookfield as a school, and for the first time in memory there was a longish waiting list. Ralston was a live wire; a fine power transmitter, but you had to beware of him.

Chips had never bothered to beware of him; he was not attracted by the man, but he served him willingly enough and quite loyally. Or, rather, he served Brookfield. He knew that Ralston did not like him, either; but that didn't seem to matter. He felt himself sufficiently protected by age and seniority from the fate of other masters whom Ralston had failed to like.

Then suddenly, in 1908, when he had just turned sixty, came Ralston's urbane ultimatum. "Mr. Chipping, have you ever thought you would like to retire?"

Chips stared about him in that book-lined study, startled by the question, wondering why Ralston should have asked it. He said, at length: "No—umph—I can't say that—umph—I have thought much about it—umph—yet."

"Well, Mr. Chipping, the suggestion is there for you to consider. The Governors would, of course, agree to your being adequately pensioned."

Abruptly Chips flamed up. "But—umph—I don't want—to retire. I don't—umph—need to consider it."

"Nevertheless, I suggest that you do."

"But—umph—I don't see—why—I should!"

"In that case, things are going to be a little difficult."

"Difficult? Why—difficult?"

And then they set to, Ralston getting cooler and harder, Chips getting warmer and more passionate, till at last Ralston said, icily: "Since you force me to use plain words, Mr. Chipping, you shall have them. For some time past, you haven't been pulling your weight here. Your methods of teaching are slack and old-fashioned; your personal habits are slovenly; and you ignore my instructions in a way which, in a younger man, I should regard as rank insubordination. It won't do, Mr. Chipping, and you must ascribe it to my forbearance that I have put up with it so long."

"But—" Chips began, in sheer bewilderment; and then he took up isolated words out of that extraordinary indictment. "*Slovenly—* umph—you said—?"

"Yes, look at the gown you're wearing. I happen to know that that gown of yours is a subject of continual amusement throughout the School."

Chips knew it, too, but it had never seemed to him a very regrettable matter.

He went on: "And—you also said—umph—something about—*insubordination—?*"

"No, I didn't. I said that in a younger man I should have regarded it as that. In your case it's probably a mixture of slackness and obstinacy. This question of Latin pronunciation, for instance—I think I told you years ago that I wanted the new style used throughout the School. The other masters obeyed me; you prefer to stick to your old methods, and the result is simply chaos and inefficiency."

At last Chips had something tangible that he could tackle. "Oh, *that!*" he answered scornfully. "Well, I—umph—I admit that I don't agree with the new pronunciation. I never did. Umph—a lot of nonsense, in my opinion. Making boys say 'Kickero' at school when—umph—for the rest of their lives they'll say 'Cicero'—if they ever—umph—say it at all. And instead of 'vicissim'—God bless my soul—you'd make them say, 'We kiss 'im'! Umph-umph!" And he chuckled momentarily, forgetting that he was in Ralston's study and not in his own friendly form room.

"Well, there you are, Mr. Chipping—that's just an example of what I complain of. You hold one opinion and I hold another, and, since you decline to give way, there can't very well be any alternative. I aim to make Brookfield a thoroughly up-to-date school. I'm a science man myself, but for all that I have no objection to the classics—provided that they are taught efficiently. Because they are dead languages is no reason why they should be dealt with in a dead educational technique. I understand, Mr. Chipping, that your Latin and Greek lessons are exactly the same as they were when I began here ten years ago?"

Chips answered, slowly and with pride: "For that matter—umph—they are the same as when your predecessor—Mr. Meldrum—came here, and that—umph—was thirty-eight years ago. We began here, Mr. Meldrum and I—in—umph—in 1870. And it was—um—Mr. Meldrum's predecessor, Mr. Wetherby—who first approved my syllabus. 'You'll take the Cicero for the fourth,' he said to me. Cicero, too—not Kickero!"

"Very interesting, Mr. Chipping, but once again it proves my point—you live too much in the past, and not enough in the present and future. Times are changing, whether you realize it or not. Modern parents are beginning to demand something more for their three years' school fees than a few scraps of languages that nobody speaks. Besides, your boys don't learn even what they're supposed to learn. None of them last year got through the Lower Certificate."

And suddenly, in a torrent of thoughts too pressing to be put into words, Chips made answer to himself. These examinations and certificates and so on—what did they matter? And all this efficiency and up-to-dateness—what did *that* matter, either? Ralston was trying to run Brookfield like a factory—a factory for turning out a snob culture based on money and machines. The old gentlemanly traditions of family and broad acres were changing, as doubtless they were bound to; but instead of widening them to form a genuine inclusive democracy of duke and dustman, Ralston was narrowing them upon the single issue of a fat banking account. There never had been so many rich men's sons at Brookfield. The Speech Day Garden Party was like Ascot. Ralston met these wealthy fellows in London clubs and persuaded them that Brookfield was *the* coming school, and, since they couldn't buy their way into Eton or Harrow, they greedily swallowed the bait. Awful fellows, some of them—though others were decent enough. Financiers, company promoters, pill manufacturers. One of them gave his son five pounds a week pocket money. Vulgar . . . ostentatious . . . all the hectic rotten-ripeness of the age. . . . And once Chips had got into trouble because of some joke he had made about the name and ancestry of a boy named Isaacstein. The boy wrote home about it, and Isaacstein *père* sent an angry letter to Ralston. Touchy, no sense of humour, no sense of proportion—that was the matter with them, these new fellows . . . . No sense of proportion. And it was a sense of proportion, above all things, that Brookfield ought to teach—not so much Latin or Greek or Chemistry or Mechanics. And you couldn't expect to test that sense of proportion by setting papers and granting certificates. . . .

All this flashed through his mind in an instant of protest and indignation, but he did not say a word of it. He merely gathered his tattered gown together and with an "umph-umph" walked a few paces away. He had had enough of the argument. At the door he turned and said: "I don't—umph—intend to resign—and you can—umph—do what you like about it!"

Looking back upon that scene in the calm perspective of a quarter of a century, Chips could find it in his heart to feel a little sorry for Ralston. Particularly when, as it happened, Ralston had been in such complete ignorance of the forces he was dealing with. So, for that matter, had Chips himself. Neither had correctly estimated the toughness of Brookfield tradition, and its readiness to defend itself and its defenders. For it had so chanced that a small boy, waiting to see Ralston that morning, had been listening outside the door during the whole of the interview; he had been thrilled by it, naturally, and had told his friends. Some of these, in a surprisingly short time, had told their parents; so that very soon it was common knowledge that Ralston had insulted Chips and had demanded his resignation. The amazing result was a spontaneous outburst of sympathy and partisanship such as Chips, in his wildest dreams, had never envisaged. He found, rather to his astonishment, that Ralston was thoroughly unpopular; he was feared and respected, but not liked; and in this issue of Chips the dislike rose to a point where it conquered fear and demolished even respect. There was talk of having some kind of public riot in the School if Ralston succeeded in banishing Chips. The masters, many of them young men who agreed that Chips was hopelessly old-fashioned, rallied round him nevertheless because they hated Ralston's slave-driving and saw in the old veteran a likely champion. And one day the Chairman of the Governors, Sir John Rivers, visited Brookfield, ignored Ralston, and went direct to Chips. "A fine fellow, Rivers," Chips would say, telling the story to Mrs. Wickett for the dozenth time. "Not—umph—a very brilliant boy in class. I remember he could never—umph—master his verbs. And now—umph—I see in the papers—they've made him—umph—a baronet. It just shows you—umph—it just shows you."

Sir John had said, on that morning in 1908, taking Chips by the arm as they walked round the deserted cricket pitches: "Chips, old boy, I hear you've been having the deuce of a row with Ralston. Sorry to hear about it, for your sake—but I want you to know that the Governors are with you to a man. We don't like the fellow a great deal. Very clever and all that, but a bit too clever, if you ask me. Claims to have doubled the School's endowment funds by some monkeying on the Stock Exchange. Daresay he has, but a chap like that wants watching. So if he starts chucking his weight about with you, tell him very politely he can go to the devil. The Governors don't want you to resign. Brookfield wouldn't be the same without you, and they know it. We all know it. You can stay here till you're a hundred if you feel like it—indeed, it's our hope that you will."

And at that—both then and often when he recounted it afterwards—Chips broke down.

Chapter 12

S O HE STAYED ON AT BROOKFIELD, having as little to do with Ralston as possible. And in 1911 Ralston left, "to better himself"; he was offered the headship of one of the greater public schools. His successor was a man named Chatteris, whom Chips liked; he was even younger than Ralston had been—thirty-four. He was supposed to be very brilliant; at any rate, he was modern (Natural Sciences Tripos), friendly, and sympathetic.

Recognizing in Chips a Brookfield institution, he courteously and wisely accepted the situation.

In 1913 Chips had had bronchitis and was off duty for nearly the whole of the winter term. It was that which made him decide to resign that summer, when he was sixty-five. After all, it was a good, ripe age; and Ralston's straight words had, in some ways, had an effect. He felt that it would not be fair to hang on if he could not decently do his job. Besides, he would not sever himself completely. He would take rooms across the road, with the excellent Mrs. Wickett who had once been linen-room maid; he could visit the School whenever he wanted, and could still, in a sense, remain a part of it.

At that final end-of-term dinner, in July 1913, Chips received his farewell presentations and made a speech. It was not a very long speech, but it had a good many jokes in it, and was made twice as long, perhaps, by the laughter that impeded its progress. There were several Latin quotations in it, as well as a reference to the Captain of the School, who, Chips said, had been guilty of exaggeration in speaking of his (Chips's) services to Brookfield. "But then—umph— he comes of an—umph—exaggerating family. I—um—remember— once—having to thrash his father—for it. [Laughter.] I gave him one mark—umph—for a Latin translation, and he—umph—exaggerated the one into a seven! Umph-umph!" Roars of laughter and tumultuous cheers! A typical Chips remark, everyone thought.

And then he mentioned that he had been at Brookfield for forty-two years, and that he had been very happy there. "It has been my life," he said, simply. "*O mihi praeteritos referat si Jupiter annos. . . .* Umph—I need not—of course—translate. . . ." Much laughter. "I remember lots of changes at Brookfield. I remember the—um—the first bicycle. I remember when there was no gas or electric light and we used to have a member of the domestic staff called a lamp-boy— he did nothing else but clean and trim and light lamps throughout the School. I remember when there was a hard frost that lasted for seven weeks in the winter term—there were no games, and the whole School learned to skate on the fens. Eighteen eighty-something, that was. I remember when two thirds of the School went down with German measles and Big Hall was turned into a hospital ward. I remember the great bonfire we had on Mafeking night. It was lit too near the pavilion and we had to send for the fire brigade to put it out. And the firemen were having their own celebrations and most of them were—um—in a regrettable condition. [Laughter.] I remember Mrs. Brool, whose photograph is still in the tuck-shop; she served there until an uncle in Australia left her a lot of money. In fact, I remember so much that I often think I ought to write a book. Now what should I call it? 'Memories of Rod and Lines'—eh? [Cheers and laughter. That was a good one, people thought—one of Chips's best.] Well, well, perhaps I shall write it, some day. But I'd rather tell you about it, really. I remember . . . I remember . . . but chiefly I remember all your faces. I never forget them. I have thousands of faces in my mind—the faces of boys. If you come and see me again in years to come—as I hope you all will—I shall try to remember those older faces of yours, but it's just possible I shan't be able to—and then some day you'll see me somewhere and I shan't recognize you and you'll say to yourself, 'The old boy doesn't remember me.' [Laughter.] But I *do* remember you—as you are *now*. That's the point. In my mind you never grow up at all. Never. Sometimes, for instance, when people talk to me about our respected Chairman of the Governors, I think to myself, 'Ah yes, a jolly little chap with hair that sticks up on top—and absolutely no idea whatever about the difference between a Gerund and a Gerundive.' [Loud laughter.] Well, well, I mustn't go on—umph— all night. Think of me sometimes as I shall certainly think of you. *Hæc olim meminisse juvabit* . . . again I need not translate." Much laughter and shouting and prolonged cheers.

August 1913. Chips went for a cure to Wiesbaden, where he lodged at the home of the German master at Brookfield, Herr Staefel, with whom he had become friendly. Staefel was thirty years his junior, but the two men got on excellently. In September, when term began, Chips returned and took up residence at Mrs. Wickett's. He felt a great deal stronger and fitter after his holiday, and almost wished he had not retired. Nevertheless, he found plenty to do. He had all the new boys to tea. He watched all the important matches on the

Brookfield ground. Once a term he dined with the Head, and once also with the masters. He took on the preparation and editing of a new Brookfeldian Directory. He accepted presidency of the Old Boys' Club and went to dinners in London. He wrote occasional articles, full of jokes and Latin quotations, for the Brookfield terminal magazine. He read his *Times* every morning—very thoroughly; and he also began to read detective stories—he had been keen on them ever since the first thrills of Sherlock. Yes, he was quite busy, and quite happy, too.

A year later, in 1914, he again attended the end-of-term dinner. There was a lot of war talk—civil war in Ulster, and trouble between Austria and Serbia. Herr Staefel, who was leaving for Germany the next day, told Chips he thought the Balkan business wouldn't come to anything.

Chapter 13

HE WAR YEARS.

The first shock, and then the first optimism. The Battle of the Marne, the Russian steamroller, Kitchener. "Do you think it will last long, sir?"

Chips, questioned as he watched the first trial game of the season, gave quite a cheery answer. He was, like thousands of others, hopelessly wrong; but, unlike thousands of others, he did not afterwards conceal the fact. "We ought to have—um—finished it—um—by Christmas. The Germans are already beaten. But why? Are you thinking of—um—joining up, Forrester?"

Joke—because Forrester was the smallest new boy Brookfield had ever had—about four feet high above his muddy football boots. (But not so much a joke, when you came to think of it afterwards; for he was killed in 1918—shot down in flames over Cambrai.) But one didn't guess what lay ahead. It seemed tragically sensational when the first Old Brookfeldian was killed in action—in September. Chips thought, when that news came: A hundred years ago boys from the School were fighting *against* the French. Strange, in a way, that the sacrifices of one generation should so cancel out those of another. He tried to express this to Blades, the Head of School House; but Blades, eighteen years old and already in training for a cadetship, only laughed. What had all that history stuff to do with it, anyhow? Just old Chips with one of his queer ideas, that's all.

1915. Armies clenched in deadlock from the sea to Switzerland. The Dardanelles. Gallipoli. Military camps springing up quite near Brookfield; soldiers using the playing fields for sports and training; swift developments of Brookfield O.T.C. Most of the younger masters gone or in uniform. Every Sunday night, in the Chapel after evening service, Chatteris read out the names of old boys killed, together with short biographies. Very moving; but Chips, in the back pew under the gallery, thought: They are only names to him; he doesn't see their faces as I do. . . .

1916. The Somme Battle. Twenty-three names read out one Sunday evening.

Towards the close of that catastrophic July, Chatteris talked to Chips one afternoon at Mrs. Wickett's. He was overworked and over-worried and looked very ill. "To tell you the truth, Chipping, I'm not having too easy a time here. I'm thirty-nine, you know, and unmar-ried, and lots of people seem to think they know what I ought to do. Also, I happen to be diabetic, and couldn't pass the blindest M.O., but I don't see why I should pin a medical certificate on my front door."

Chips hadn't known anything about this; it was a shock to him, for he liked Chatteris.

The latter continued: "You see how it is. Ralston filled the place up with young men—all very good, of course—but now most of them have joined up and the substitutes are pretty dreadful, on the whole. They poured ink down a man's neck in prep one night last week—silly fool—got hysterical. I have to take classes myself, take prep for fools like that, work till midnight every night, and get cold-shouldered as a slacker on top of everything. I can't stand it much longer. If things don't improve next term I shall have a breakdown."

"I do sympathize with you," Chips said.

"I hoped you would. And that brings me to what I came here to ask you. Briefly, my suggestion is that—if you felt equal to it and would care to—how about coming back here for a while? You look pretty fit, and, of course, you know all the ropes. I don't mean a lot of hard work for you—you needn't take anything strenuously—just a few odd jobs here and there, as you choose. What I'd like you for more than anything else is not for the actual work you'd do—though that, naturally, would be very valuable—but for your help in other ways—in just *belonging* here. There's nobody ever been more popular than you were, and are still—you'd help to hold things together if there were any danger of them flying to bits. And perhaps there *is* that danger. . . ."

Chips answered, breathlessly and with a holy joy in his heart: "I'll come. . . ."

Chapter 14

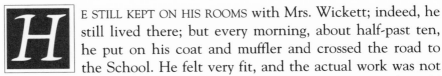

E STILL KEPT ON HIS ROOMS with Mrs. Wickett; indeed, he still lived there; but every morning, about half-past ten, he put on his coat and muffler and crossed the road to the School. He felt very fit, and the actual work was not taxing. Just a few forms in Latin and Roman History—the old lessons—even the old pronunciation. The same joke about the *Lex Canuleia*—there was a new generation that had not heard it, and he was absurdly gratified by the success it achieved. He felt a little like a music-hall favourite returning to the boards after a positively last appearance.

They all said how marvellous it was that he knew every boy's name and face so quickly. They did not guess how closely he had kept in touch from across the road.

He was a grand success altogether. In some strange way he did, and they all knew and felt it, help things. For the first time in his life he felt *necessary*—and necessary to something that was nearest his heart.

There is no sublimer feeling in the world, and it was his at last.

He made new jokes, too—about the O.T.C. and the food-rationing system and the anti-air-raid blinds that had to be fitted on all the windows. There was a mysterious kind of rissole that began to appear on the School menu on Mondays, and Chips called it *abhorrendum*—"meat to be abhorred." The story went round—heard Chips's latest?

Chatteris fell ill during the winter of seventeen, and again, for the second time in his life, Chips became Acting Head of Brookfield. Then in April Chatteris died, and the Governors asked Chips if he would carry on "for the duration." He said he would, if they would refrain from appointing him officially. From that last honour, within his reach at last, he shrank instinctively, feeling himself in so many ways unequal to it. He said to Rivers: "You see, I'm not a young man and I don't want people to—um—expect a lot from me. I'm like all these new colonels and majors you see everywhere—just a wartime fluke. A ranker—that's all I am really."

1917. 1918. Chips lived through it all. He sat in the headmaster's study every morning, handling problems, dealing with plaints and requests. Out of vast experience had emerged a kindly, gentle confidence in himself. To keep a sense of proportion, that was the main thing. So much of the world was losing it; as well keep it where it had, or ought to have, a congenial home.

On Sundays in Chapel it was he who now read out the tragic list, and sometimes it was seen and heard that he was in tears over it. Well, why not, the School said; he was an old man; they might have despised anyone else for the weakness.

One day he got a letter from Switzerland, from friends there; it was heavily censored, but conveyed some news. On the following Sunday, after the names and biographies of old boys, he paused a moment and then added:

"Those few of you who were here before the War will remember Max Staefel, the German master. He was in Germany, visiting his home, when war broke out. He was popular while he was here, and made many friends. Those who knew him will be sorry to hear that he was killed last week, on the Western Front."

He was a little pale when he sat down afterwards, aware that he had done something unusual. He had consulted nobody about it, anyhow; no one else could be blamed. Later, outside the Chapel, he heard an argument:

"On the Western Front, Chips said. Does that mean he was fighting for the Germans?"

"I suppose it does."

"Seems funny, then, to read his name out with all the others. After all, he was an *enemy*."

"Oh, just one of Chips's ideas, I expect. The old boy still has 'em."

Chips, in his room again, was not displeased by the comment. Yes, he still had 'em—those ideas of dignity and generosity that were becoming increasingly rare in a frantic world. And he thought: Brookfield will take them, too, from me; but it wouldn't from anyone else.

Once, asked for his opinion of bayonet practice being carried on near the cricket pavilion, he answered, with that lazy, slightly asthmatic intonation that had been so often and so extravagantly imitated: "It seems—to me—umph—a very vulgar way of killing people."

The yarn was passed on and joyously appreciated—how Chips had told some big brass hat from the War Office that bayonet fighting was vulgar. Just like Chips. And they found an adjective for him—an adjective just beginning to be used: he was pre-War.

Chapter 15

AND ONCE, ON A NIGHT of full moonlight, the air-raid warning was given while Chips was taking his lower fourth in Latin. The guns began almost instantly, and, as there was plenty of shrapnel falling about outside, it seemed to Chips that they might just as well stay where they were, on the ground floor of School House. It was pretty solidly built and made as good a dugout as Brookfield could offer; and as for a direct hit, well, they could not expect to survive that, wherever they were.

So he went on with his Latin, speaking a little louder amid the reverberating crashes of the guns and the shrill whine of anti-aircraft shells. Some of the boys were nervous; few were able to be attentive. He said, gently: "It may possibly seem to you, Robertson—at this particular moment in the world's history— umph—that the affairs of Cæsar in Gaul some two thousand years ago—are—umph—of somewhat secondary importance—and that— umph—the irregular conjugation of the verb *tollo* is—umph—even less important still. But believe me—umph—my dear Robertson— that is not really the case." Just then there came a particularly loud explosion—quite near. "You cannot—umph—judge the importance of things—umph—by the noise they make. Oh dear me, no." A lit-tle chuckle. "And these things—umph—that have mattered—for thousands of years—are not going to be—snuffed out—because some stink merchant—in his laboratory—invents a new kind of mischief." Titters of nervous laughter; for Buffles, the pale, lean, and medically unfit science master, was nicknamed the Stink Merchant. Another explosion—nearer still. "Let us—um—resume our work. If it is fate that we are soon to be—umph—interrupted, let us be found employing ourselves in something—umph—really appropri-ate. Is there anyone who will volunteer to construe?"

Maynard, chubby, dauntless, clever, and impudent, said: "I will, sir."

"Very good. Turn to page forty and begin at the bottom line."

The explosions still continued deafeningly; the whole building shook as if it were being lifted off its foundations. Maynard found the page, which was some way ahead, and began, shrilly:

"*Genus hoc erat pugnae*—this was the kind of fight—*quo se Germani exercuerant*—in which the Germans busied themselves. Oh, sir, that's good—that's really very funny indeed, sir—one of your very best—"

Laughing began, and Chips added: "Well—umph—you can see— now—that these dead languages—umph—can come to life again sometimes—eh? Eh?"

Afterwards they learned that five bombs had fallen in and around Brookfield, the nearest of them just outside the School grounds. Nine persons had been killed.

The story was told, retold, embellished. "The dear old boy never turned a hair. Even found some old tag to illustrate what was going on. Something in Cæsar about the way the Germans fought. You wouldn't think there were things like that in Cæsar, would you? And the way Chips laughed . . . you know the way he *does* laugh . . . the tears all running down his face . . . never seen him laugh so much . . . ."

He was a legend.

With his old and tattered gown, his walk that was just beginning to break into a stumble, his mild eyes peering over the steel-rimmed spectacles, and his quaintly humorous sayings, Brookfield would not have had an atom of him different.

November 11th, 1918.

News came through in the morning; a whole holiday was decreed for the School, and the kitchen staff were implored to provide as cheerful a spread as wartime rationing permitted. There was much cheering and singing, and a bread fight across the Dining Hall. When Chips entered in the midst of the uproar there was an instant hush, and then wave upon wave of cheering; everyone gazed on him with eager, shining eyes, as on a symbol of victory. He walked to the dais, seeming as if he wished to speak; they made silence for him, but he shook his head after a moment, smiled, and walked away again.

It had been a damp, foggy day, and the walk across the quadrangle to the Dining Hall had given him a chill. The next day he was in bed with bronchitis, and stayed there till after Christmas. But already, on that night of November 11th, after his visit to the Dining Hall, he had sent in his resignation to the Board of Governors.

When school reassembled after the holidays he was back at Mrs. Wickett's. At his own request there were no more farewells or presentations, nothing but a handshake with his successor and the word "Acting" crossed out on official stationery. The "duration" was over.

Chapter 16

ND NOW, FIFTEEN YEARS after that, he could look back upon it all with a deep and sumptuous tranquillity. He was not ill, of course—only a little tired at times, and bad with his breathing during the winter months. He would not go abroad—he had once tried it, but had chanced to strike the Riviera during one of its carefully unadvertised cold spells. "I prefer—um—to get my chills—umph—in my own country," he used to say, after that. He had to take care of himself when there were east winds, but autumn and winter were not really so bad; there were warm fires, and books, and you could look forward to the summer. It was the summer that he liked best, of course; apart from the weather, which suited him, there were the continual visits of old boys. Every weekend some of them motored up to Brookfield and called at his house. Sometimes they tired him, if too many came at once; but he did not really mind; he could always rest and sleep afterwards. And he enjoyed their visits—more than anything else in the world that was still to be enjoyed. "Well, Gregson—umph—I remember you— umph—always late for everything—eh—eh? Perhaps you'll be late in growing old—umph—like me—umph—eh?" And later, when he was alone again and Mrs. Wickett came in to clear away the tea things: "Mrs. Wickett, young Gregson called—umph—you remember him, do you? Tall boy with spectacles. Always late. Umph. Got a job with the—umph—League of Nations—where—I suppose—his—um— dilatoriness—won't be noticeable—eh?"

And sometimes, when the bell rang for call-over, he would go to the window and look across the road and over the School fence and see, in the distance, the thin line of boys filing past the bench. New times, new names . . . but the old ones still remained . . . Jefferson, Jennings, Jolyon, Jupp, Kingsley Primus, Kingsley Secundus, Kingsley Tertius, Kingston . . . where are you all, where have you all gone to? . . . Mrs. Wickett, bring me a cup of tea just before prep, will you, please?

The post-War decade swept through with a clatter of change and maladjustments; Chips, as he lived through it, was profoundly disappointed when he looked abroad. The Ruhr, Chanak, Corfu; there was enough to be uneasy about in the world. But near him, at Brookfield, and even, in a wider sense, in England, there was something that charmed his heart because it was old—and had survived. More and more he saw the rest of the world as a vast disarrangement for which England had sacrificed enough—and perhaps too much. But he was satisfied with Brookfield. It was rooted in things that had stood the test of time and change and war. Curious, in this deeper sense, how little it *had* changed. Boys were a politer race; bullying was nonexistent; there was more swearing and cheating. There was a more genuine friendliness between master and boy—less pomposity on the one side, less unctuousness on the other. One of the new masters, fresh from Oxford, even let the sixth call him by his Christian name. Chips didn't hold with that; indeed, he was just a little bit shocked. "He might as well—umph—sign his terminal reports—umph—'yours affectionately'—eh—eh?" he told somebody.

During the General Strike of 1926, Brookfield boys loaded motor vans with foodstuffs. When it was all over, Chips felt stirred emotionally as he had not been since the War. Something had happened, something whose ultimate significance had yet to be reckoned. But one thing was clear: England had burned her fire in her own grate again. And when, at a Speech Day function that year, an American visitor laid stress on the vast sums that the strike had cost the country, Chips answered: "Yes, but—umph—advertisement—always *is* costly."

"Advertisement?"

"Well, wasn't it—umph—advertisement—and very fine advertisement—too? A whole week of it—umph—and not a life lost—not a shot fired! Your country would have—umph—spilt more blood in—umph—raiding a single liquor saloon!"

Laughter . . . laughter . . . wherever he went and whatever he said, there was laughter. He had earned the reputation of being a great jester, and jests were expected of him. Whenever he rose to speak at a meeting, or even when he talked across a table, people prepared their minds and faces for the joke. They listened in a mood to be amused and it was easy to satisfy them. They laughed sometimes before he came to the point. "Old Chips was in fine form," they would say, afterwards. "Marvellous the way he can always see the funny side of things. . . ."

After 1929, Chips did not leave Brookfield—even for Old Boys' dinners in London. He was afraid of chills, and late nights began to tire him too much. He came across to the School, however, on fine days; and he still kept up a wide and continual hospitality in his room. His faculties were all unimpaired, and he had no personal worries of any kind. His income was more than he needed to spend, and his small capital, invested in gilt-edged stocks, did not suffer when the slump set in. He gave a lot of money away—to people who called on him with a hard-luck story, to various School funds, and also to the Brookfield mission. In 1930 he made his will. Except for legacies to the mission and to Mrs. Wickett, he left all he had to found an open scholarship to the School.

1931. . . . 1932. . . .

"What do you think of Hoover, sir?"

"Do you think we shall ever go back to gold?"

"How d'you feel about things in general, sir? See any break in the clouds?"

"When's the tide going to turn, Chips, old boy? You ought to know, with all your experience of things."

They all asked him questions, as if he were some kind of prophet and encyclopædia combined—more even than that, for they liked their answer dished up as a joke. He would say:

"Well, Henderson, when I was—umph—a much younger man— there used to be someone who—um—promised people ninepence for fourpence. I don't know that anybody—umph—ever got it, but umph—our present rulers seem—um—to have solved the problem how to give—umph—fourpence for ninepence."

Laughter.

Sometimes, when he was strolling about the School, small boys of

222

the cheekier kind would ask him questions, merely for the fun of getting Chips's "latest" to retail.

"Please, sir, what about the Five-Year Plan?"

"Sir, do you think Germany wants to fight another war?"

"Have you been to the new cinema, sir? I went with my people the other day. Quite a grand affair for a small place like Brookfield. They've got a Wurlitzer."

"And what—umph—on earth—is a Wurlitzer?"

"It's an organ, sir—a cinema organ."

"Dear me . . . . I've seen the name on the hoardings, but I always—umph—imagined—it must be some kind of—umph—sausage."

Laughter. . . . Oh, there's a new Chips joke, you fellows, a perfectly lovely one. I was gassing to the old boy about the new cinema, and . . . .

Chapter 17

H E SAT IN HIS FRONT PARLOUR at Mrs. Wickett's on a November afternoon in thirty-three. It was cold and foggy, and he dared not go out. He had not felt too well since Armistice Day; he fancied he might have caught a slight chill during the Chapel service. Merivale had been that morning for his usual fortnightly chat. "Everything all right? Feeling hearty? That's the style—keep indoors this weather—there's a lot of flu about. Wish I could have your life for a day or two."

His life . . . and what a life it had been! The whole pageant of it swung before him as he sat by the fire that afternoon. The things he had done and seen: Cambridge in the sixties; Great Gable on an August morning; Brookfield at all times and seasons throughout the years. And, for that matter, the things he had *not* done, and would never do now that he had left them too late—he had never travelled by air, for instance, and he had never been to a talkie show. So that he was both more and less experienced than the youngest new boy at the School might well be; and that, that paradox of age and youth, was what the world called progress.

Mrs. Wickett had gone out, visiting relatives in a neighbouring village; she had left the tea things ready on the table, with bread and butter and extra cups laid out in case anybody called. On such a day, however, visitors were not very likely; with the fog thickening hourly outside, he would probably be alone.

But no. About a quarter to four a ring came, and Chips, answering the front door himself (which he oughtn't to have done), encountered a rather small boy wearing a Brookfield cap and an expression of anxious timidity. "Please, sir," he began, "does Mr. Chips live here?"

"Umph—you'd better come inside," Chips answered. And in his room a moment later he added: "I am—umph—the person you want. Now what can I—umph—do for you?"

"I was told you wanted me, sir."

Chips smiled. An old joke—an old leg-pull, and he, of all people, having made so many old jokes in his time, ought not to complain. And it amused him to cap their joke, as it were, with one of his own; to let them see that he could keep his end up, even yet. So he said, with eyes twinkling: "Quite right, my boy. I wanted you to take tea with me. Will you—umph—sit down by the fire? Umph—I don't think I have seen your face before. How is that?"

"I've only just come out of the sanatorium, sir—I've been there since the beginning of term with measles."

"Ah, that accounts for it."

Chips began his usual ritualistic blending of tea from the different caddies; luckily there was half a walnut cake with pink icing in the cupboard. He found out that the boy's name was Linford, that he lived in Shropshire, and that he was the first of his family at Brookfield.

"You know—umph—Linford—you'll like Brookfield—when you get used to it. It's not half such an awful place—as you imagine. You're a bit afraid of it—um, yes—eh? So was I, my dear boy—at first. But that was—um—a long time ago. Sixty-three years ago—umph—to be precise. When I—um—first went into Big Hall and—um—I saw all those boys—I tell you—I was quite scared. Indeed—umph—I don't think I've ever been so scared in my life. Not even when—umph—the Germans bombed us—during the War. But—umph—it didn't last long—the scared feeling, I mean. I soon made myself—um—at home."

"Were there a lot of other new boys that term, sir?" asked Linford shyly.

"Eh? But—God bless my soul—I wasn't a boy at all—I was a man—a young man of twenty-two! And the next time you see a young man—a new master—taking his first prep in Big Hall—umph—just think—what it feels like!"

"But if you were twenty-two then, sir—"

"Yes? Eh?"

"You must be—very old—now, sir."

Chips laughed quietly and steadily to himself. It was a good joke.

"Well—umph—I'm certainly—umph—no chicken."

He laughed quietly to himself for a long time.

Then he talked of other matters, of Shropshire, of schools and school life in general, of the news in that day's papers. "You're growing up into—umph—a very cross sort of world, Linford. Maybe it will have got over some of its—umph—crossness—by the time you're ready for it. Let's hope so—umph—at any rate. . . . Well . . . ." And with a glance at the clock he delivered himself of his old familiar formula. "I'm—umph—sorry—you can't stay. . . ."

At the front door he shook hands.

"Goodbye, my boy."

And the answer came, in a shrill treble: "Goodbye, Mr. Chips. . . ."

Chips sat by the fire again, with those words echoing along the corridors of his mind. "Goodbye, Mr. Chips. . . ." An old leg-pull, to make new boys think that his name was really Chips; the joke was almost traditional. He did not mind. "Goodbye, Mr. Chips. . . ." He remembered that on the eve of his wedding day Kathie had used that same phrase, mocking him gently for the seriousness he had had in those days. He thought: Nobody would call me serious today, that's very certain. . . .

Suddenly the tears began to roll down his cheeks—an old man's

225

"Goodbye, Mr. Chips"

failing; silly, perhaps, but he couldn't help it. He felt very tired; talking to Linford like that had quite exhausted him. But he was glad he had met Linford. Nice boy. Would do well.

Over the fog-laden air came the bell for call-over, tremulous and muffled. Chips looked at the window, greying into twilight; it was time to light up. But as soon as he began to move he felt that he couldn't; he was too tired; and, anyhow, it didn't matter. He leaned back in his chair. No chicken—eh, well—that was true enough. And it had been amusing about Linford. A neat score off the jokers who had sent the boy over. Goodbye, Mr. Chips . . . odd, though, that he should have said it just like that. . . .

Chapter 18

HEN HE AWOKE, for he seemed to have been asleep, he found himself in bed; and Merivale was there, stooping over him and smiling. "Well, you old ruffian—feeling all right? That was a fine shock you gave us!"

Chips murmured, after a pause, and in a voice that surprised him by its weakness: "Why—um—what—what has happened?"

"Merely that you threw a faint. Mrs. Wickett came in and found you—lucky she did. You're all right now. Take it easy. Sleep again if you feel inclined."

He was glad someone had suggested such a good idea. He felt so weak that he wasn't even puzzled by the details of the business—how they had got him upstairs, what Mrs. Wickett had said, and so on. But then, suddenly, at the other side of the bed, he saw Mrs. Wickett. She was smiling. He thought: God bless my soul, what's she doing up here? And then, in the shadows behind Merivale, he saw Cartwright, the new Head (he thought of him as "new," even though he had been at Brookfield since 1919), and old Buffles, commonly called "Roddy." Funny, the way they were all here. He felt: Anyhow, I can't be bothered to wonder why about anything. I'm going to go to sleep.

But it wasn't sleep, and it wasn't quite wakefulness, either; it was a sort of in-between state, full of dreams and faces and voices. Old scenes and old scraps of tunes: a Mozart trio that Kathie had once played in—cheers and laughter and the sound of guns—and, over it all, Brookfield bells, Brookfield bells. "So you see, if Miss Plebs wanted Mr. Patrician to marry her . . . yes, you can, you liar. . . ." Joke . . . . Meat to be abhorred. . . . Joke . . . . That you, Max? Yes, come in. What's the news from the Fatherland? . . . *O mihi praeteritos.* . . . Ralston said I was slack and inefficient—but they couldn't manage without me . . . . *Obile heres ago fortibus es in aro.* . . . Can you translate that, any of you? . . . It's a joke. . . .

Once he heard them talking about him in the room.

Cartwright was whispering to Merivale. "Poor old chap—must have lived a lonely sort of life, all by himself."

Merivale answered: "Not always by himself. He married, you know."

"Oh, did he? I never knew about that."

"She died. It must have been—oh, quite thirty years ago. More, possibly."

"Pity. Pity he never had any children."

And at that, Chips opened his eyes as wide as he could and sought to attract their attention. It was hard for him to speak out loud, but he managed to murmur something, and they all looked round and came nearer to him.

He struggled, slowly, with his words. "What—was that—um—you were saying—about me—just now?"

Old Buffles smiled and said: "Nothing at all, old chap—nothing at all—we were just wondering when you were going to wake out of your beauty sleep."

"But—umph—I heard you—you *were* talking about me—"

"Absolutely nothing of any consequence, my dear fellow—really, I give you my word. . . ."

"I thought I heard you—one of you—saying it was a pity—umph—a pity I never had—any children . . . eh? . . . But I have, you know . . . I have. . . ."

The others smiled without answering, and after a pause Chips began a faint and palpitating chuckle.

"Yes—umph—I have," he added, with quavering merriment. "Thousands of 'em . . . thousands of 'em . . . and all boys."

And then the chorus sang in his ears in final harmony, more grandly and sweetly than he had ever heard it before, and more comfortingly too . . . Pettifer, Pollett, Porson, Potts, Pullman, Purvis, Pym-Wilson, Radlett, Rapson, Reade, Reaper, Reddy Primus . . . come round me now, all of you, for a last word and a joke . . . Harper, Haslett, Hatfield, Hatherley . . . my last joke . . . did you hear it? . . . Did it make you laugh? . . . Bone, Boston, Bovey, Bradford, Bradley, Bramhall-Anderson . . . wherever you are, whatever has happened, give me this moment with you . . . this last moment . . . my boys . . . .

And soon Chips was asleep.

He seemed so peaceful that they did not disturb him to say good night; but in the morning, as the School bell sounded for breakfast, Brookfield had the news. "Brookfield will never forget his lovableness," said Cartwright, in a speech to the School. Which was absurd, because all things are forgotten in the end. But Linford, at any rate, will remember and tell the tale: "I said goodbye to Chips the night before he died. . . ."

A Note on the Short Stories in this Volume

When *Goodbye, Mr. Chips* was published for the first time, over sixty years ago, readers around the world took the curmudgeonly schoolmaster to their hearts. Some even claimed that they had been taught by the original Mr. Chips. It was not long before James Hilton's publisher asked him to resurrect the character, even though in *Goodbye, Mr. Chips* the schoolteacher had died peacefully in his sleep. Pleased that his character had given rise to such affection, the author was happy to create six short stories featuring Mr. Chips at various stages of his life. First published in a collection entitled *To You, Mr. Chips*, these delightful tales are reprinted here.

THE EDITORS

A CHAPTER OF
AUTOBIOGRAPHY

I F I USE THE WORD "I" a good deal in these pages, it is not from self-importance, but because I would rather talk about my own schooldays than generalize about schools. Schooling is perhaps the most universal of all experiences, but it is also one of the most individual. (Here I am, generalizing already!) No two schools are alike, but more than that—a school with two hundred pupils is really two hundred schools, and among them, almost certainly, are somebody's long-remembered heaven and somebody else's hell. So that I must not conceal, but rather lay stress on the first personal pronouns. The schools I write of were *my* schools; to others at the same schools at the same time, everything may have been different.

I went to three schools altogether—an elementary school, a grammar school, and a public school. I matriculated at London University and spent four years at Christ's College, Cambridge. Thus, from the age of six, when my mother led me through suburban streets for presentation to the headmistress of the nearest Infants' Department, up to the age of twenty-three, when I left Cambridge supposedly equipped for the world and its problems, the process called my education was going on. Seventeen years—quite a large slice out of a life, when you come to think about it. And yet the ways I have earned my living since—by writing newspaper articles, novels, and film scenarios—were not taught me at any of these schools and colleges. Furthermore, though I won scholarships and passed examinations, I do not think I now remember more than twenty per cent of all I learned during these seventeen years, and I do not think I could now scrape through any of the examinations I passed after the age of twelve.

Nor was there any sort of co-ordination between my three schools and the university. For this, nobody was to blame in a free country. To some extent, I learned what I liked; to a greater extent, my teachers taught me what they liked. In my time I "took," as they say, practically every subject takable. At the elementary school, for instance, I spent an hour a week on "Botany," which was an excuse for wandering through Epping Forest in charge of a master who, in his turn, regarded the hour as an excuse for a pleasant smoke in the open air. The result is that Botany to me today stands for just a few words like "calyx," "stamen," and "capillary attraction," plus the memory of lovely hours amidst trees and bracken. I do not complain.

Again, at the grammar school I spent six hours a week for three years at an occupation called "Chemistry," and all these hours have left me with nothing but a certain skill in blowing glass tubes into various shapes. In Mathematics I went as far as the calculus, but I do not think I could be quite sure nowadays of solving a hard quadratic equation. Of languages I learned (enough to pass examinations in them) Latin, Greek, French, and German. I suppose I could still read

Virgil or Sophocles with the help of a dictionary, but I do not do so, because it would give me no pleasure. My French and German are of the kind that is understood by sympathetic Frenchmen and Germans who know English.

The only school-learning of which I remember a good deal belongs to English Literature, History, and Music; but even in these fields my knowledge is roving rather than academic, and I could no longer discuss with any degree of accuracy the debt of Shakespeare to Saxo-Grammaticus or the statute *De Heretico Comburendo*. In fact, although I am, in the titular sense, a Scholar of my college, I do not feel myself to be very scholarly. But give me a new theory about Emily Brontë or read me a pamphlet about war and peace, and I will tell you whether, in my view, the author is worth listening to. To make up for all I have forgotten, there is this that I have acquired, and I call it sophistication since it is not quite the same thing as learning. It is the flexible armour of doubt in an age when too many people are certain.

What all this amounts to, whether my seventeen years were well spent, whether I am a good or a bad example of what schooling can do, whether I should have been a better citizen if I had gone to work at fourteen, I cannot say. I can only reply in the manner of the youth who, on being asked if he had been educated at Eton, replied: "That is a matter of opinion."

The elementary school was in one of the huge dormitory suburbs of northeast London—a suburb which people from Hampstead or Chelsea would think entirely characterless, but which, if one lived in it for twenty years as I did, revealed a delicate and by no means unlikeable quality of its own. I am still a young man, and I suppose that for the next twenty years people will go on calling me "one of our younger novelists"; but whenever nowadays I pass by that elementary school, I realize what an age it is since I breathed its prevalent smell of ink, strong soap, and wet clothes. Just over a quarter of a century, to be precise, but it cannot be measured by that reckoning. The world today looks back on the pre-War world as a traveller may look back through a railway tunnel to the receding pinpoint of light in the distance. It is more than the past; it is already a legend.

To this legend my earliest recollections of school life belong. My father was the headmaster of another school in the same town, and I was a good deal petted and favoured by his colleagues. There were quite a few dirty and ragged boys in the class of seventy or so; the school itself was badly heated and badly lit; schoolbooks were worn and smeary because every boy had to follow the words with his finger as he read—an excusable rule, for it was the only way the teacher could see at a glance if his multitude were all paying attention. He was certainly not to blame because I found his reading lessons a bore. At the time that I was spelling out "cat-sat-on-the-mat" stuff at school, I was racing through Dickens, Thackeray, and Jules Verne at home.

The school curriculum had its oddities. Mathematics was divided into Arithmetic, Algebra, and Mensuration. (Why this last had a special name and subdivision, I have no idea.) Geography consisted largely of learning the special names of capes, bays, counties, and county towns. When a teacher once told me that Cardigan Bay was the largest in Great Britain, I remember asking him promptly what was the smallest. He was somewhat baffled. But I have always been interested in miniature things, and perhaps I was right in supposing that England's smallest bay, were it to be identified, would be worth knowing. This teacher gave me full marks, however, because I attained great proficiency in copying maps with a fine-nibbed pen— a practice which enabled me to outline all the coasts with what appeared to be a fringe of stubbly hairs.

I was not so good at History because, in the beginning, I could not make head or tail of most of it. When I read that So-and-so "gathered his army and laid waste to the country," I could not imagine what it meant. I had heard of gathering flowers and laying an egg, but these other kinds of gathering and laying were more mystifying, and nobody bothered to explain them to me. They remained just phrases that one had to learn and repeat. I was also puzzled by the vast number of people in history who were put to death because they would not change their religion; indeed, the entire fuss about religion throughout history was inexplicable to a boy whose father played the organ at a Congregational Church during the reign of Edward the Seventh.

Since then I have helped to write school history books and have found out for myself the immense difficulty of teaching the subject to children. It is not the words only that have to be simplified, but the ideas—and if you oversimplify ideas, you often falsify them. Hence the almost inevitable perversion of history into a series of gags, anecdotes, labels—that So-and-so was a "good" king, that Henry the Eighth had six wives and Cromwell a wart on his nose, that the messenger came to Wolfe crying "They run, they run" and that Nelson clapped the glass to his sightless eye. When later I studied history seriously for a university scholarship, I was continually amazed by the discovery that historical personages behaved, for the most part, with reasonable motivation for their actions and not like the Marx Brothers in a costume-play.

"Scripture" was another subject I did not excel at. It consisted of a perfunctory reading of a daily passage from the Bible; and our Bibles were always dirty, ragged, and bound in black. They left me with an impression of a book I did not want to handle, much less to read; it is only during the past ten years that I have read the Bible for pleasure. Our school Bibles also suffered from too small print; some of the words in the text were in italics and nobody explained to me that the reason for this concerned scholars more than schoolboys. Not long ago I heard a local preacher who seemed to me, when reading from the Psalms, to give certain sentences an unusual rhythm, and on enquiry I found that he had always imagined that the words in italics had to be accented! Why not print an abridged and large-print Bible for schools, consolidating groups of verses into paragraphs, and finally binding the whole as attractively as any other book? Maybe this has been done, and I am out of date for suggesting it.

Another oddity of my early schooldays was something called a free-arm system of handwriting—it consisted of holding the wrist rigid and moving the pen by means of the forearm muscle. I can realize now that somebody got his living by urging this fad on schoolmasters who liked to be thought modern or were amenable to sales-talk; I thought it nonsense at the time and employed some resolution in not learning it.

Perhaps the chief thing I *did* learn at my first school was that my father (then earning about six pounds a week) was a rich man. When, later on, I went to schools at which he seemed (in the same comparative sense) a poor man, I had the whole social system already sketch-mapped in my mind, and I did not think it perfect.

The school was perhaps a better-than-average example, both structurally and educationally, of its type; so I can only conjecture what conditions were like at the worst schools in the worst parts of London. I do know that there have been tremendous improvements since those days; that free meals and medical inspections have smoothed down the rougher differences between the poor man's child and others; that, under Hitler and Stalin and Neville Chamberlain alike, the starved and ragged urchin has become a rarity. Such a trend is common throughout the world and we need not be complacent about it, since its motive is as much militaristic as humanitarian. But it does remain, intrinsically, a mighty good thing. I believe I would have benefited a lot from the improved elementary school of today. I might not have learned any more, but I should probably have had better teeth.

From the elementary school I went to a grammar school in the same suburb. It was an old foundation (as old as Harrow), but it had come down in the world. I had the luck to have for a form-master a man who was very deaf. I call it "luck," because he was an excellent teacher and would probably have attached himself to a much better school but for his affliction. As it was, his discipline was the best in the school—with the proviso, of course, that his eyes had to do vigilance for his ears. The result was that, in addition to Latin, English, and History, I gained in his class another proficiency that has never been of the slightest use to me since—ventriloquism.

I was devoted to that man (and I am sure he never guessed it). His frown could spoil my day, his rare slanting smile could light it up. I was conceited enough to think that he took some special interest in me, just because he read out my essays publicly to the class; and after I sent him in an essay I used to picture the excitement he must feel on reading it. It did not occur to me that, like most good professionals (as opposed to amateurs), he did his job conscientiously but without hysterical enthusiasm, and that during out-of-school hours he would rather have a drink and a chat with a friend than read the best schoolboy's essay ever written.

Once he wrote on the blackboard some sentences for parsing and analysis. Among them was: "Dreams such as thine pass now like evening clouds before me; when I think how beautiful they seem, 'tis but to feel how soon they fade, how fast the night shuts in." I was so struck with this that I sat for a long time thinking of it; and presently, noticing my idleness, he asked me rather sharply why I wasn't working. I couldn't tell him, partly because I hardly knew, partly because my answer would have had to be shouted at the top of my voice on account of his deafness. I let him think I was just lazy, yet in my heart I never forgave him for not understanding.

Children are merciless—as much in what they expect as in what they offer. Not only will they bait unmercifully a schoolmaster who lacks the power to discipline them, but they lavish the most fantastic and unreasonable adorations. The utmost bond of lover and mistress is less than the comprehension a boy expects from a schoolmaster whom he has singled out for worship.

I cannot imagine any more desperate situation for a school than the one in which this grammar school found itself. (It has since moved to another site, so nothing I say can bear any current reflection.) Flanked on one side by a pickle-factory, it shared its other aspects between the laundry of the municipal baths and a busy thoroughfare lined by market-stalls. Personally I rather liked the rococo liveliness of such surroundings. I grew used to the pervading smell of chutney and steaming bath-towels, to the cries of costers selling oranges and cough-drops, and it was fun to step out of the classroom on winter evenings and search a book-barrow lit by naphtha-flares, or listen to a Hindu peddling a corn-cure. And there was a roaring music-hall nearby, with jugglers and Little Tich and Gertie Gitana; and on Friday nights outside the municipal baths a strange-eyed long-haired soap-boxer talked anarchism. Somehow it was all rather like Nijni Novgorod, though I have never seen Nijni Novgorod.

I probably learned more in the street than I did in the school, but the latter did leave me with a good grammatical foundation in Latin, as well as a certain facility in the use of woodworking tools. (Since then I have usually made my own bookshelves.) One of the teachers made us learn three solid pages of Sir Walter Scott's prose from *The Talisman* (a passage, I still remember, beginning—"Beside his couch stood Thomas de Vaux, in face, attitude and manner the strongest possible contrast to the suffering monarch"); the intention, I suppose, was that we might somehow learn to write a bit more like Scott; but as I did not want to write like Scott at all, the effort of memory was rather wasted.

I worked hard at this grammar school, chiefly because homework was piled on by various masters acting independently of each other. I was a quick worker, but often I did not finish till nearly midnight, and how the slower workers managed I can only imagine. I have certainly never worked so hard in my life since, and it has often struck me as remarkable that an age that restricts the hours of child-employment in industry should permit the much harder routine of schoolwork by day and homework in the evenings. A twelve-hour shift is no less harmful for a boy or girl because it is spent over books; indeed, the overworked errand-boy is less to be pitied. Unless conditions have changed (and I know that in some schools they haven't), there are still many thousands of child-slaves in this country.

The chief reason for such slavery is probably the life-and-death struggle for examination distinctions in which most schools are compelled to take part. And that again is based on the whole idea of pedagogy which has survived, with less change than one might think, from the Middle Ages. It is perhaps a pity that the average school curriculum fits a pupil for one profession better than any other—that of schoolmastering. It is a pity because the clever schoolboy is tempted into the only profession in which his store of knowledge is of immediate practical value in getting him a job, and is then tempted to emphasize the value of passing on precisely that same knowledge to others. He is somewhat in the position of a shopkeeper whose aim is less to sell people what they need than to get rid of what he has in stock. The circle is vexatious, but I would not call it vicious, because I do not think that the whole or even the chief value of a school-master can be measured by the knowledge he imparts. Much of that knowledge will be forgotten, anyway, and far more easily than the influence of a cultured and liberal-minded personality. Indeed, in a world in which the practical people are so busy doing things that had better not be done at all, there may even be some advantage in the sheer mundane uselessness of a classical education. Better the vagaries of "*tollo*" than those of a new poison gas; better to learn and forget our Latin verbs than to learn and remember our experimental chemistry; better by far we should forget and smile than that we should remember and be sad.

So I defend (somewhat tepidly) a classical education for the very reason that so many people attack it. It is of small practical value in a world whose practical values are mostly wrong; it is "waste time" in a world whose time had better be wasted than spent in most of its present activities. My Mr. Chips, who went on with his Latin lesson while the Zeppelins were dropping bombs, was aware that he was "wasting" the possibly last moments of himself and his pupils, but he believed that at any rate he was wasting them with dignity and without malice.

The War broke out while I was still at the suburban grammar school; during that last lovely June of the pre-War era, I had won a scholarship to a public school in Hertfordshire. I remember visiting a charming little country town and being quartered there at a temperance hotel in company with other entrants. The school sent its German master to look after us—a pleasant, sandy-haired, kind-faced man with iron-rimmed spectacles and a guttural accent—almost the caricatured Teuton whom, two months later, we were all trying to hate. I forget his name, and as I never saw him or the school again, I do not know what happened to him.

I never saw the place again because my father, poring over the prospectus, discovered that the school possessed both a rifle-range and an Officers' Training Corps—symbols of the War that, above all things, he hated. He had been a pacifist long before he ever called himself one (indeed, he never liked the term), and it is literally true to say that he would not hurt a fly—for my mother could never use a fly-swat if he were in the same room. Yet I know that if anyone had broken into our house and attacked my mother or me—the kind of problem put two years later by truculent army officers to nervous

241

conscientious objectors—it would have been no problem at all to my father; he would have died in battle. He was no sentimentalist. When a bad disciplinarian on his teaching staff once asked him what he (my father) would say if a boy squirted ink at him, my father answered promptly: "It isn't what I'd *say*, it's what I'd *do*." And he would have—though I cannot imagine that he ever had to. Boys in his presence always gave an impression of enjoying liberty without taking liberties. He was a strong man, physically—a good swimmer, a good cricketer, nothing of the weakling about him; and to call him a pacifist is merely to exemplify his fighting capacity for lost causes. It never occurred to me then, and it rarely occurs to me now, that any of his ideas were fundamentally wrong. He was and happily is still a mixture of Cobbett and Tagore with a dash of aboriginal John Bull.

I was just fourteen then—the age at which most boys in England leave school and go to work. It was the first autumn of the War, when our enthusiasm for the Russian steamroller led us to deplore the fact that we could not read Dostoievski in the original; so with this idea in mind, I began to learn Russian and tried for a job in a Russian bank in London. Worse still, I nearly got it. If I had, it is excitingly possible that I should have been sent to Russia and been there during the Revolution; but far more probable that I should have added figures in a City office until the bank eventually went out of business.

My father, however, was beginning to dally again with the idea of a public school for me, and soon conceived the idea that since he could not make up his mind, I should choose a school for myself. So I toured England on this eccentric but interesting quest and learned how to work out train journeys from York to Cheltenham and from Brighton to Sherborne, how to pick good but cheap hotels in small towns, and how to convince a headmaster that if I didn't get a good impression of his school, I should unhesitatingly cross it off my list. When I look back upon these visits, I am inclined to praise my father for a stroke of originality of which both he and I were altogether unaware. It would, perhaps, be a good thing if boys were given more say in choosing their own schools. It certainly would be a good thing if headmasters cared more about the impressions they made on boys and less about the impressions they made on parents. Only a few of the headmasters to whom I explained my mission were elaborately sarcastic and refused to see me.

Eventually I spent a weekend at Cambridge and liked the town and university atmosphere so much that I finally made the choice, despite the fact that the school there possessed both the rifle-range and the cadet corps. Relying on the fact that my father was both forgetful and unobservant, I said nothing about this at home, got myself entered for the school, and joined it half-way through the summer term of 1915.

You will here remark that your sympathies are entirely with the headmasters who were sarcastic, and that I must have been an exceptionally priggish youngster. I shall not disagree, except to remark that, prig or not, I am grateful to those pedagogues who showed me over their establishments with as much bored and baffled courtesy as they might have accorded to a foreign general or the wife of a Speech Day celebrity.

Not so long ago I read a symposium contributed by various young and youngish writers about their own personal experiences at public schools. These experiences ranged from the mildly tolerable to the downright disgusting; indeed, the whole effect of the book was to create pity for any sensitive, intelligent youngster consigned to such environment. I do not for a moment dispute the sincerity of this symposium. I am prepared to believe almost any specific detail about almost any specific school. Of my own school I could say, for instance, that some of its hygienic conditions would have aroused the indignation of every Socialist M.P. if only they had been found in a Durham or a South Wales mining village. I could specify, quite truthfully, that the main latrines were next to the dining room; that we were apt to find a drowned rat in the bath-tub if we left the water to stand overnight; that in winter the moisture ran down walls that had obviously been built without a dampcourse; that the school sanatorium was an incredible Victorian villa at the other end of the town, hopelessly unsuited to its purpose. These things have been remedied since, but they were true enough in my time—and what of it? Their enumeration cannot present a true impression of my school or of any school, because a school is something more than the buildings of which it is composed.

I know that a visiting American would have been sheerly horrified by the plumbing and drainage, but no more horrified than I am when, having duly admired some magnificent million-dollar scholastic outfit on the plains of the Middle West, I learn that it offers a degree in instalment-selling and pays its athletic coach twice as much as its headmaster. This seems to me the worst kind of modern lunacy. Better to have rats in the bath-tub than bats in the belfry.

I am, as I said just now, prepared to believe almost any specific detail about almost any specific school. But a book or even a page of specific details must be considered with due allowance for the age and character of the writer. Many men after middle-life remember nothing but good about their schools. Their prevalent mood by that time has become so nostalgic for past youth that anything connected with it acquires a halo, so that even a beating bitterly resented at the time becomes, in retrospect, a rather jolly business. (Most of the "jolly" words for corporal punishment—"spank," "whack," etc., were, I suspect, invented by sentimentalists of over forty.) The kind of man who feels like this is often the kind that makes a material success of life and whose autobiography, written or ghost-written, exudes the main idea that "school made him what he was"—than which, of course, he can conceive no higher praise.

On the other hand, in reading the school reminiscences of youths who have just left it, one should remember that the typical schoolboy is inarticulate, and that by putting any such reminiscences on paper the writer is proving himself, *ipso facto*, to be untypical. In other words, recollection of schools are apt to be written either by elderly successful men who remember nothing but good, or by youths who, by their very skill in securing an audience at such an early age, argue themselves to have been unlike the average schoolboy.

There is nothing for it, therefore, but to be frankly personal and leave others to make whatever allowances they may think necessary.

I am thirty-seven years of age. I do not think I am old enough yet to feel that school was a good place because I was young in it, or self-satisfied enough to feel that school was a good place because it "made me what I am." (In any case, I do not think it did make me what I am, whatever that may be.) But I enjoyed my schooldays, on the whole, and if I had a son I daresay I would send him to my old school, if only because I would not know what else to do with him.

I was not a typical schoolboy, and the fact that I was happy at (shall we say?) Brookfield argues that the school tolerated me even more generously than I tolerated it. Talking to other men about their schooldays, I have often thought that Brookfield must have been less rigid than many schools in enforcing conformity to type. Perhaps the fact that it was, in the religious sense, a Nonconformist school helped to distil a draught of personal freedom that even wartime could not dissipate. At any rate, I did not join the almost compulsory Officers' Training Corps, despite the fact that the years were 1914–1918. My reasons for keeping out (which I did not conceal) were simply that I disliked military training and had no aptitude for it. Lest anyone should picture my stand as a heroic one, I should add that it was really no stand at all; nobody persecuted me—if they had, no doubt I should have joined.

When later I was called up for military service I responded, chiefly because my friends were in the army and I guessed I should be happier with them there than on committees of anti-war societies with people whose views I mainly held. If this seems an illogical reason, I shall agree, with the proviso that it is also a more civilized reason than a desire to kill Germans.

I did not conceal my views about the War, but I did conceal my general feeling about games. I was, in this respect, a complete hypocrite. I have never been able to take the slightest interest in most games, partly because I am no good at them myself; I like outdoor pursuits such as walking, sea-bathing, and mountaineering, but the competitive excitements of cup-finals and test matches bore me to exasperation. The only contest even remotely athletic into which I ever entered with zest was the saying of the Latin grace at my Cambridge college; it was a long grace, and I was told (how accurately I cannot say) that I lowered the all-time speed record from sixteen to fourteen and a fifth seconds. At Brookfield, however, grace was said by the masters, so that my prowess in this field remained unsuspected, even by myself. The craze for clipping fifths of seconds raged elsewhere. Most of my friends were tremendously concerned about "the hundred yards" and the various School and House matches, and I would not for the world have let them know that I cared nothing about such things at all. Sometimes, if there was absolutely no one else left to fill the team, I took part in some very junior House match, and I always hoped that my side would lose, because then I should not have to play in any subsequent game. Outwardly, however, I pretended to share all the normal enthusiasms over victory and despairs over defeat; and I think I carried it off pretty well. There is always some ultimate thing you must do when you are in Rome, even if the Romans are exceptionally broad-minded.

I never received corporal punishment at Brookfield; I was never bullied; I never had a fight with anybody; and the only trouble I got into was for breaking bounds. I used to enjoy lazy afternoons at the Orchard, Grantchester, with strawberries and cream for tea; I liked to attend Evensong at King's College Chapel; I liked to smoke cigarettes in cafés. Most of these diversions were against school rules, and I have an idea that often when I was seen breaking them, the observer tactfully closed an eye. Perhaps it was realized that my desire for personal freedom did not incline me to foment general rebellion. Many things that I care about do not attract others at all, and awareness of this has always made me reluctant to exalt my own particular cravings into the dimensions of a crusade. On the whole, I thought the school discipline reasonable, if occasionally irksome, and when I transgressed I did so without either resentment or regret.

Strangely, perhaps, since I was not "the type," I was quite happy at Brookfield. The very things I disliked (games, for instance) brightened some days by darkening others; I have rarely been so happy in my life as when, taking a hot bath after a football game in which I hardly touched the ball, I reflected that no one would compel me to indulge in such preposterous pseudo-activity for another forty-eight hours. I had many acquaintances, and a few close friends with whom my relationship was as unselfish as any I have experienced since in my life. I do not think I had any particular enemies, and I got on well enough with authority. Despite the sexual aberrations that are supposed to thrive at boarding-schools, I never succumbed to any, nor was I ever tempted. I played the piano dashingly rather than accurately at Speech Day concerts, breakfasted with the Head once a term, argued for or against capital punishment (I forget which) in the school debating society, and cycled many windy miles along the fenland lanes.

The magic of youth is in the sudden unfolding of vistas, the lifting of mists from the mile-high territory of manhood. It sometimes falls to me nowadays to read a fine new book by a new writer, but never to discover a whole shelf of new books at once—as happened after I had first read *Clayhanger*. New worlds are for the young to explore; later one is glad of a new room or even of a view from a new window. That the worlds were not seen in proper focus, while the room or the view may be, does not entirely compensate for the slowing of excitement—for the loss of a mood in which one hid *The New Machiavelli* inside the Chapel hymn-book, or read *Major Barbara* by flashlight under the bedclothes. To such ecstasies youth could add a passionate awareness of being alive, and—during the years 1914–1918—of being alive by a miracle.

Looking back on those days I see that they had an epic quality, and that, after all, the school experiences of my generation were unique. Behind the murmur of genitive plurals in dusty classrooms and the plick-plock of cricket balls in the summer sunshine, there was always the rumble of guns, the guns that were destroying the world that Brookfield had made and that had made Brookfield. Sometimes these guns were actually audible, or we fancied they were; every weekday there was a rush to the newspapers, every Sunday a batch of names read out to stilled listeners. The careful assessments of schoolmasters were blotted out by larger and wilder markings; a boy who had been expelled returned as a hero with medals; those whose inability to conjugate *avoir* and *être* seemed likely in 1913 to imperil a career were to conquer France's enemies better than they did her language; offenders gated for cigarette-smoking in January were dropping bombs from the sky in December. It was a frantic world; and we knew it even if we did not talk about it. Slowly, inch by inch, the tide of war lapped to the gates of our seclusion; playing fields were ploughed up for trenches and drill grounds; cadet-corps duties took precedence over classroom studies; the school that had prepared so many beloved generations for life was preparing this one, equally beloved, for death.

When I said just now that I disliked military training and had no aptitude for it, I was putting the matter mildly. I dislike regimentation of any kind, and I loathe war, not only for its pain and misery and life wastage, but for its enthronement of the second-rate—in men, standards, and ideals. In the declension of spirit in which England fought, it is correct to say that we began with Rupert Brooke and ended with Horatio Bottomley. But at Brookfield the loftier mood prevailed even when it was no more than a Cellophane illusion separating us from the visible darkness without.

On Sundays we attended Chapel and heard sermons that, as often as not, preached brotherly love and forgiveness of our enemies. On Mondays we watched cadets on the football field bayoneting sacks with special aim for vital parts of the human body. This paradox did not, I am sure, affect most Brookfield boys as it did me. To be frank, it obsessed me; I would wonder endlessly whether Sunday's or Monday's behaviour were the more hypocritical. I have changed my attitude since. That Brookfield declined to rationalize warfare into its code of ethics while at the same time sending its sons to fight and die, seems to me now to have been pardonably illogical and creditably inconsistent; looking round on the present-day world of 1938, I can see that countries where high ideals are preached but not practised are at least better off than countries in which low ideals are both preached *and* practised.

Many of us at Brookfield, like myself, were too young—*just* too young—to see actual service in the War; yet during our last school years we lived under the shadow, for we knew or took for granted that if the War lasted we should be illogical and inconsistent in the same English way. Such tragic imminence hardly worried us, but it gave a certain sharpness to all the joys and a certain comfort for all the trivial hardships of school life—gave also, in my own case, the clearest focus for memory. There is hardly a big event of those years that I do not associate with a Brookfield scene; Kitchener's death reminds me of cricketers hearing the news as they fastened pads in the pavilion; the Russian Revolution gives me the voice of a man, now dead, who talked about it instead of giving his usual Geography lesson; the *Lusitania* sinking reminds me of early headlines, read hastily over a master's shoulder at breakfast. I composed a sonnet on the Russian Revolution, which my father had the temerity to send to Mr. A. G. Gardiner, eliciting from him the comment that it "showed merit." I also wrote a poem on the *Lusitania* which appeared in the *Cambridge Magazine*, a pacifist weekly run by Mr. C. K. Ogden, who has since distinguished himself by the invention of Basic English. These things I recount, not for vainglory (for they were not particularly good poems), but to reveal something of the mood of Brookfield, in which a boy could be eccentric enough to write poetry and subversive enough to write pacifist and revolutionary poetry without being either persecuted or ostracized. As a matter of fact, I was editor of the school magazine, and wrote for it articles, stories, and poems of all kinds and in all moods. Nobody tried to censor them; nobody tried to depose or harass me. Looking back on this genial indifference, it seems to me that Brookfield in wartime was not only less barbarian than the world outside it, but also less barbarian than many institutions in what we have since chosen to call peacetime. Is there a school in Soviet Russia where a student may offer even the mildest printed criticism of Stalin? Is there a debating society throughout all Nazi Germany that would dare to allow a Socialist to defend his faith? I suspect that nowadays the boys of Brookfield, members predominantly of the despised bourgeois-capitalist class, are nevertheless free to be Marxian or Mosleyite if they like, and no doubt a few of them are writing wild stuff which in twenty years' time they will either forget or regret. Let us hope, however, that they will not forget the spirit of tolerance which today is in such grave peril because it is in the very nature of tolerance to take tolerance for granted.

I do not know whether this spirit obtained at other schools besides Brookfield. Probably at some it did and at others it didn't. But I stress it because the quality of any institution can be tested by the extent to which it withstands attack without compromising too much with the attacker. Granted that during the War all civilized institutions were subtly contaminated, which of them passed such a test most creditably? Perhaps we can say that England as a whole, though suffering vast changes, has survived more recognizably than any other country. She is more than the ghost of her former self—she has a good deal still left of the substance. Alone among the countries that participated substantially in the War, her national life is still reasonably well anchored. Mr. Chips, if he were alive (and I have reason to believe he is, in a few schools), could still give the same lessons as in 1908 (not an ideal educational programme, but one that at least attests the durability of a tradition), could still make the same jokes to a new generation that still understands them, could still offer himself in the kindly role of jester, critic, mentor, and friend. No upstart authority has yet compelled him to click his heels and begin the day with juju incantations of *Heils* and *Vivas*. He can still say, without fear of rubber truncheons: "Umph . . . Mr. Neville Chamberlain . . . umph . . . I used to know his father when he was the wild man of Born—I mean Birmingham . . . but his sons have turned—umph—respectable. . . ."

This spirit of free criticism, even if it expresses itself no more momentously than as a classroom squib, is the sort of thing that makes English Conservatives liberal and keeps English Socialists conservative. It is the spirit that made Baldwin protest against Fascist brutality at the Albert Hall, that gives Citrine misgivings about Russia, and that united ninety per cent of Englishmen in fervent if soon-forgotten admiration of Dimitrov. It is the spirit that made Mr. Chips protest amidst the bomb explosions: "These things that have mattered for thousands of years are not going to be snuffed out because some stink merchant invents a new kind of mischief."

Unfortunately, it looks as if they *are* going to be snuffed out. Mr. Chips was too valiant an optimist to face the tragic impasse of the twentieth century—the fact that civilization, because in its higher manifestations it is essentially organized for peace, cannot long survive war—even a war supposedly undertaken on its behalf. There can be no war to end wars, because all wars begin other wars. There can be no such thing as a war to save democracy, because all wars destroy democracy. There could have been a peace to save what was left of democracy, but the chance of that came and went in 1919—the saddest year in all the martyrdom of man.

Here the reader may protest that much of the above arguments depends on the assumption that England and our institutions deserve to survive. There was a time when I would not by any means have taken this for granted. It was possible, then, to feel that the pre-War world, having encouraged or permitted a system that led to catastrophe, might as well be destroyed completely to make way for newer and better things. (It was possible, then, to say "newer and better" as glibly as one says "spick and span.") It was possible, then, to decry the public schools as the bulwark of a system that had had its day, to attack them for their creation of a class snobbery, to lampoon their play-the-game fetish and their sedate philistinism. That these attacks were partly justified one may as well admit. The public schools *do* create snobbery, or at any rate the illusion of superiority; you cannot train a ruling class without such an illusion. My point is that the English illusion has proved, on the whole, humaner and more endurable, even by its victims, than the current European illusions that are challenging and supplanting it; that the public-school Englishmen who flock to a Noël Coward revue to join in laughs against themselves are patterned better than the polychromed shirt-wearers of the Continent who not only cannot laugh but dare not allow laughter. Granted that the long afternoon of English imperialism is over, that dusk is falling on a dominion wider if less solid than Rome's. Granted that the world is tired of us and our solar topees and our faded *kiplingerie*, that it will not raise a finger to save us from eclipse. Time will bring regrets, if any. For myself, I do not object to being called a sentimentalist because I acknowledge the passing of a great age with something warmer than a sneer.

But the accusation of sentimentality comes oddly from those who extol the Russian collectivist as Rousseau extolled the noble savage. In some circles today it is even fashionable to decry the more literate occupations altogether and to redress the undoubted middle-class overweight in pre-War art by refusing hallmarks to anything modern that cannot call itself "proletarian." This forces me to a confession (snobbish if you insist) that in my opinion a man need not be ashamed of having been educated—even at Brookfield and Cambridge. When I reflect on the manner in which the Gadarene pace of 1938 is being set by an ex-house-painter, I do not need to apologize for being an ex-public schoolboy (comic phrase though it is), and I can even turn with relief to the visionary ideals of a man whose reputation, faded today, will bloom again as we remember him more and more wistfully in the years ahead. And Woodrow Wilson was an ex-schoolmaster.

Let history write the epitaph—England, liberalism, democracy were not so bad—not so good, either, on all occasions, but better, maybe, in a longer retrospect. Some of us may even survive to make such a retrospect. All over the world today the theme and accents of barbarism are being orchestrated, while the technique of mass-hypnotism, as practised by controlled press and radio, is being schooled to construct a façade of justification for any and every excess. The English illusion is dying; "on dune and headland sinks the fire." But there are other and fiercer fires. It is remarkable (if only a coincidence) that the first victims of the new ferocities have been countries in which there is a long tradition of cruelty (Chinese tortures, Ethiopian mutilations, Spanish bull-rings); one is almost tempted to a belief that the soil can be soured by ancestral lusts, and that English freedom from actual warfare within her own territories for two centuries has been, in effect, a cleansing and a purification. Perhaps this is too mystical for proof; perhaps it is just nonsense, anyway. But it is true that violence begets violence, that delight in the infliction of suffering is a poison in the bloodstream of nations as well as of individuals, and that soon we may be faced with the prospect of a world impelled to its doom by sadists and degenerates. In the next war (that is to say, in the war that has already begun) there will be no heroes charging splendidly to death because "someone has blundered," but grey-faced *morituri*, prone in their steel coffins, diving to kill and be killed because, in the reckoning of authority, no one has blundered at all.

Do not think I am blind to the faults of the age of which Mr. Chips and his type were the product as well as the makers. Its imperialism was, at its worst, smug, hypocritical, and predatory. Its *laissez-faire* capitalism resulted in such horrors as child-slavery in factories. Its vices were as solid as its virtues. But one fact does emerge from any critical analysis of the period beginning, roughly, with the

Queen's accession and ending with her death—that it was possible, during this time, for an intelligent man in Western Europe to look around his world and believe that it was getting better. He could see the spread of freedom, in thought and creed and speech, and—even more important—the spread of the belief that such an increase of freedom was an ultimate goal, even if it could not be immediately conceded. He could watch the transplantation of parliamentary government into lands where, though it might not wholly suit the soil, few doubted it would eventually flourish. He could believe that mechanical inventions were spreading civilization because the chief mechanical invention of the time, the railway, was not (like the aeroplane) diabolically apt for use in warfare. He could observe each year new sunderings of barriers between lands until traveller and student could roam through Europe more freely than at any time since the break-up of Christendom.

True that the boy Dickens toiled in a blacking-factory, but he grew up free to scarify the system that had forced him to it; he had been a child-slave, but he was never a man-slave. True that Huxley was attacked for teaching that men and monkeys were somewhat the same; but he was never exiled for refusing to teach that Jews and Gentiles were altogether different. Scientists may have incurred the wrath of bishops for spreading what the latter considered to be evolutionary nonsense; they were never ordered by government to teach what every acknowledged authority considers to be Aryan nonsense. And while Karl Marx laboriously constructed his time-bomb to explode the bourgeoisie, his victims rewarded him with a ticket to the British Museum instead of a Leipzig trial, and a peaceful grave in Highgate Cemetery instead of a trench in front of a firing-squad.

Occasionally throughout the ages, the clouds of history show a rift and through it the sun of human betterment shines out for a few deceptive moments over a limited area. The Greece of Pericles was one such time and place; parts of China under certain dynasties offered the spectacle of another; Paraguay under the Jesuit Communists was perhaps a third. These few have little in common save a crust of security over the prevalent turbulence of mankind; the crust was thin and its promise of permanence false. But Victorian

England sealed the volcano more stoutly than it had ever been sealed before, so that a man and his son and his son's son might live and die in the belief that the world would not witness certain things again. The crust, indeed, was such that even after the first shattering its debris is something to cling to—until the next.

All of which may sound a huge digression in a book dedicated to the memory of an old schoolmaster. But for me it is not so. I cannot think of my schooldays without the image of that incredible background—Zeppelins droning over sleeping villages, Latin lessons from which boys stepped into the brief lordliness of a second-lieutenancy on the Somme. I cannot forget the little room where my friends and I fried sausages over a gas-ring and played George Robey records on the gramophone, and how, in that same little room with the sausages frying and the gramophone playing, one of us received a telegram with bad news in it, and how we all tried to sympathize, yet in the end arrived at no better idea than to open a hoarded tin of pineapple chunks to follow the sausages. I cannot forget cycling so often over the ridge of the Gogmagogs (which, as Mr. Chips always informed us, was the highest land between Brookfield and the Ural Mountains), and the soft fenland rain beginning to fall on Cambridge streets at dusk, with old men fumbling in and out of bookshops, and young men, spent after route-marches, scampering over ancient quadrangles. Those days were history, but most of us were too young to be historians, too young to disassociate the trivial from the momentous—gnarled desks and war-headlines, photogravure generals and the school butler who stood at the foot of the dormitory staircase and at lights-out warned sepulchrally—"Time, Gentlemen, Time." It was Time in a way that so many of us could not realize. That warning marked the days during which, on an average, ten thousand men were killed.

MR. CHIPS WOULD WALK between the lines of beds in the dormitory and turn out the lights. He was an old man then, and it was impossible to think he had ever been much younger. He seemed already ageless, beyond the reach of any time that could be called. Schooldays are a microcosm of life—the boy is born the day he enters the school and dies the day he leaves it; in between are youth, middle age, and the elderly respectability of the sixth form. But outside this cycle stands the schoolmaster, watching the three-year lifetimes as they pass him by, remembering faces and incidents as a god might remember history. An old schoolmaster, if he is well liked and has dignity, is rather like a god. You can joke about him behind his back, but you must acknowledge him to his face while you love him a little carelessly in your hearts. This has been the relationship of good men and good gods since the world began.

THERE WAS NO SINGLE schoolmaster I ever knew who was entirely Mr. Chips, but there were several who had certain of his attributes and achieved that best reward of a well-spent life—to grow old beloved. One of them was my father. He did not train aristocrats to govern the Empire or plutocrats to run their fathers' businesses, but he employed his wise and sweetening influence just as valuably among the thousands of elementary schoolboys who knew and know him still in a London suburb.

GERALD AND THE CANDIDATE

GERALD WAS EIGHT WHEN HE first went to stay with Uncle Richard. He had no parents, and the frequent prep-school holidays had to be filled up somehow; that was the reason. He was a quiet boy, full of dreams. For weeks during the winter term at Grayshott (which was the prep school for Brookfield) he had talked to Martin Secundus about the visit: "I say, Martin, I'll have to go into training—Uncle Richard always takes people such long walks when they go and stay with him. He's a great explorer, you know. Once he was nearly killed in the jungle by a tiger. He can climb any mountain there is. And he lives in an old castle with a moat round it, and before you can get in you have to give the password."

Actually Gerald had never seen Uncle Richard or where he lived. Everything was new to him—the house and the town and the kind of country, the journey there in the train that went "You-can-if-you-like—You-can-if-you-like," and not just "No, you mustn't—No, you mustn't," like the local train to Grayshott; and the first meeting at twilight on Browdley station platform with Uncle Richard. The platform was made of wooden planks, and as Gerald walked along it the thump, thump, thump made him think of his second favourite "pretend"—that he was a great general, marching at the head of soldiers—"Follow me, my men!" But he was soon back at his chief and almost permanent "pretend"—that he was the engine-driver of the Scotch express, which was half an hour late with the King and Queen on board, and the King had said to the stationmaster: "My good fellow, I *must* arrive in time," and the stationmaster had answered: "Well, your Majesty, that's going to be a difficult matter, but we have one man, Gerald Holloway, whom we can try. If anyone can get you there, he will." Steadily, steadily, throughout the night, a hand always on the throttle-lever, eyes peering ahead . . . that was how it went on. Very often the King knighted him as the station clock struck the hour at which the train was due to arrive.

But this time Gerald hadn't a chance to think as far as that, because of Uncle Richard.

"Well, my boy," said Uncle Richard, in a very loud, gruff voice. Then he arranged with a porter about having Gerald's trunk and tuck-box sent on, and after that began to walk away towards the ticket-barrier. Gerald was sorry to be whisked off the platform so soon; he rather wanted to look at the engine—it was a Four-Four-Nought. None of the grown-up people he knew had any idea what a Four-Four-Nought was; but Gerald considered it quite everyday knowledge.

"So, you're Gerald," said Uncle Richard, when they came to the street.

Gerald said he was.

"You'll have to speak up a bit, my boy—I'm a little deaf. Gerald, eh? Well, you've come here at a lively time, and no mistake." And he made a noise in his throat which Gerald thought was like something, if he could only think what. It sounded like "wuff-wuff." "Yes, a right-down lively time. Better make a good start, young shaver, and wear your colours."

Whereat Uncle Richard halted under a lamp and fished in his pocket, producing after some search a large red rosette which he stooped and pinned to the lapel of Gerald's overcoat. Gerald looked up at him with an interest that suddenly quickened to excitement. Was it possible that here, at last, was a grown-up who knew the things that really mattered in the world? From that moment, at any rate, he was aware that Uncle Richard was not to be classed with any other people. He smiled, privately to himself, and then with open friendliness at the big face that overtopped his own.

"There you are, my boy. Red's for Liberal. Consequently is, the folks'll know what you are."

Gerald did not understand this at all, but he was quite contented as he trotted along. He knew he was going to like Uncle Richard.

Uncle Richard lived at Number 2, The Parade, which was the best house in Browdley's best street—a double pre-eminence signalized by the fact that none of the other streets in Browdley had front gardens, and none of the other front gardens in the Parade was as big as Uncle Richard's. His, indeed, was about the size of a railway waiting-room, and nothing grew in it except some evergreens that were really ever-black. Nevertheless, the social gulf proclaimed by them and by their cindery soil was immense. They made the Parade the Park Lane of Browdley. Uncle Richard's was the end house of a row of twelve—grimy, bay-windowed, and ornamented in the most florid mid-Victorian style; and Browdley, in point of fact, was just a Northern industrial town of some eight or ten thousand inhabitants, mostly employed in the local industries of iron-founding and calico-printing. In the junior geography form at Grayshott, noisy with talk of capes and bays and county towns and what belonged to whom, the word "Browdley" was unknown. It was the sort of place that nobody ever went to and that nobody had ever heard of.

But that, if he had known anything about it when he was eight, would have seemed to Gerald just a part of the vast grown-up con-spiracy to avoid seeing things as they really were. As he and Uncle

Richard walked through the streets from the station to the Parade, he was quite sure about Browdley and equally sure about himself in it. With that red rosette in his coat-lapel he was a knight, flaunting his banner and about to do something heroic; and Uncle Richard was clearly another knight; and Browdley was the beautiful and mysterious place where they both had to do whatever it was. The streets of that magic city were glittering with bright windows, and Gerald's eyes, as he walked along, could just peer over the sills and sometimes under the drawn blinds. Wonderful sights—an old man leaning over a fire; a woman peeling potatoes at a table covered with dishes; a little girl sitting on a high stool in front of a piano. Such people might have been seen elsewhere, but they would not have been the same; and that was because he was with Uncle Richard and they were both wearing those red rosettes.

Soon they came to the house. It had a street lamp outside it that shone a green light, and whenever afterwards Gerald mentioned this and Aunt Lavinia said (as she sometimes did): "What nonsense, Gerald! Did anyone ever see a street lamp with a green light!"— Gerald used to reply: "Well, it *was* a green light, and it made the house look wonderful. And there was a dragon on the front door." Whereupon Aunt Lavinia would usually say: "Don't take any notice of him, Mrs. So-and-so. He *romances*." But there *was* this green light, and the dragon on the front door was the brass knocker, which seemed to Gerald exactly like a dragon.

Uncle Richard unlocked the door with a key and guided Gerald down a dark passage-way, along which there were other doors with strips of light under them, and the sound of voices beyond. Suddenly Uncle Richard opened one. "Well, here's the young criminal!" he said, weighing his hand down on Gerald's shoulder.

Then Gerald looked up and saw what a huge, red face his uncle had, and how hair grew in tufts out of his nose and ears, how thick his fingers were, and how, when he spoke, the light in the room seemed to blink. And then suddenly he knew what the "wuff-wuff" was really like—it was like the bark of a big black dog. "Well, well, here we are, my boy. This is your Aunt Flo. She'll get you a bite of supper, and then off you go to bed."

Gerald was rather dashed at that; surely bed could not be part of this new and marvellous existence? But Aunt Flo, who wore glasses, smiled and patted his cheek. "You look tired after your journey," she said, but Gerald, who felt anything but tired, did not reply. Then she shouted to Uncle Richard: "He says he's tired after his journey"; which was really not true at all. By that time, however, Gerald was staring round the room and at everything in it. It was a very warm red room, with a crackling fire and a brass rail stretching the whole length of the mantelpiece over the fireplace. To one side stood a long dresser, scrubbed white, and on this there was a queer, dome-shaped object covered with a dark cloth. "That's Polly," said Aunt Flo. "She's gone to bed now and we mustn't wake her. A parrot, Gerald—have you never seen a parrot before?"

Of course he had; he had been to the Zoo. "Does it talk?" he asked.

"Yes, she can say 'Give me a nut.' You'll see tomorrow."

Gerald was a little awed at the prospect of seeing Polly, though he didn't think "Give me a nut" was much of a thing to say, even for a parrot. Then he noticed that the room had two windows, only one of which had a blind drawn over it; the other looked through into another sort of room. Now this was a peculiar thing—so peculiar that he could not help being rude (for Aunt Lavinia had always assured him that it was rude to ask questions). "Where does that lead to, Uncle Richard?" he said.

"He wants to know what's out there!" shouted Aunt Flo.

"Out there, my boy? Wuff-wuff. Why, that's the greenhouse. Only we don't use it as a greenhouse now. It's where I keep my tricycle."

"Tricycle?"

"Never seen a tricycle?"

"I've seen a parrot, but I've never seen a tricycle," answered Gerald; so Uncle Richard beckoned him nearer to the window, and there it was, quite plainly—a tricycle. And on the handlebars, as on the lapels of Gerald's and Uncle Richard's coats, there was a red rosette.

Gerald went to bed that night in a whirl of excitement that made him forget to be frightened because of the dark. Once he heard a lot of talking downstairs and Uncle Richard wuff-wuffing in the passage.

Then he closed his eyes and thought of Polly and the tricycle, and the King walked up to the engine-cab and said: "Rise, Sir Gerald," and pinned on his coat the biggest red rosette in the world.

In the morning, that first morning at Uncle Richard's, Gerald awoke with a half-fear that it would all be different. But no; when he came downstairs, Uncle Richard was there, looking just as big in the daylight. "Good morning," he began. "I hope you slept with your colours pinned to your nightshirt." Now this was exactly what Gerald had done, but he had not been going to tell anybody. Marvellous that Uncle Richard should have guessed! "Yes, of course," answered Gerald, and Uncle Richard laughed loudly and then went to look at something on the wall and blew his nose like a trumpet. "Glass is rising—consequently is, my boy, we'll have some fine days for you."

All at once Gerald looked across the room and saw Polly. She was perched inside the cage on a wooden bar, with her head cocked side-ways as if she were listening carefully. Oh, what a beautiful parrot! He ran towards her and she began to squawk and ruffle her feathers, which were bright green, with little patches of red and yellow. "Don't frighten Polly," said Aunt Flo. "When she gets to know you she'll let you stroke her, but don't try yet—she might nip." Gerald felt cross at being squawked at; after all, he had only meant to be friendly. So, when Aunt Flo and Uncle Richard were both looking away, he took a pencil out of his pocket and pushed it through the bars of the cage. This made the bird squawk more than ever, but Gerald had time to withdraw and hide the pencil before anyone saw him.

"Now that's very naughty of Polly," said Aunt Flo, coming over and putting her head against the cage. "Gerald's come to see you and you're being very rude, so you shall just go back to bed again." And she grabbed the piece of dark cloth and pulled it down over the cage. "She deserves it," Aunt Flo added, "for being in such a bad humour."

Nobody ever knew that Gerald had poked the parrot with a pencil. It was a secret for as long as the world should last.

There was porridge and a brown egg for breakfast and afterwards a girl came into the room. Uncle Richard said: "Aha, the gathering of the clans. We must introduce you . . . Olive . . . and Gerald . . . .

We're going to put you to work this morning—both of you."

She looked about the same age as Gerald and had straight yellow hair and blue eyes. He did not like girls as a rule, but he noticed that she was wearing the same kind of red rosette, and immediately he saw what it all meant in a flash—it was a secret society, and they were all sworn to help one another, even girls. So he said politely: "Hello."

Then Uncle Richard told them what he wanted them both to do. It was a grand adventure. They had to walk along the neighbouring streets and put a red bill through every letter-box, giving a double-knock afterwards, like a postman. Gerald had often practised being a postman, so he was overjoyed. If a house hadn't got a letter-box, then they would have to push the bill under the front door. It was all most important work, and they must wear their red rosettes all the time.

So they went out with the bills and began along the Parade. How beautiful the Parade was in the lovely sunshine! Some people asked them inside the houses and gave them sweets and pennies, which only proved to Gerald that real life wasn't a bit like the silly make-believe of being at school. And some day, when he left Grayshott, there would be real life all the time. He was so busy knocking like a postman that he hardly spoke to Olive, except once, when a whistle in the distance reminded him to ask: "Have you ever been faster than sixty miles an hour?"

"We have a horse that can run as fast as that," Olive said.

"A horse as fast as a train?" echoed Gerald scornfully, but he was a little perturbed as well. He just answered, very off-hand: "Oh, a race-horse—that doesn't count"—and let the conversation lapse.

When they had finished giving out the bills they went back to Uncle Richard's, and there another odd thing happened. A very old lady was in the passage-way talking to Uncle Richard and Aunt Flo, and as Gerald and Olive came in she lifted her spotty veil and stared. "Yours?" she said, and Aunt Flo shouted: "She's asking who they belong to, Richard!"

Uncle Richard answered: "My nephew, this is—wuff-wuff—and this"—pointing to Olive—"is the Candidate's little girl."

That was the first time that Gerald had ever heard of the Candidate.

THE BROWDLEY BY-ELECTION was what the newspapers called "closely contested." Sir Thomas Barton, a cotton magnate, was opposed by Mr. Courtenay Beale, a young London barrister with a superfluity of brains and bounce. Sir Thomas, wealthy, middle-aged, and a widower, liked to play the democrat on these occasions; and as, in any case, there were no good hotels in Browdley, he found it convenient to lodge with Uncle Richard during the campaign. In another sense, of course, he found it highly inconvenient; Number 2, The Parade, seemed a strange habitation after his baronial mansion a hundred miles away. In his own mind he saw Uncle Richard's house as "just an ordinary small house in a row"—he totally failed to perceive the immense social significance of the front garden. And Uncle Richard himself he thought a decent, well-meaning fellow, with some local influence, no doubt—a retired tradesman, wasn't he?—something of the sort. His wife, too, a good woman—fortunately, too, a good cook. Everything spotlessly clean, of course. And no children—only a little boy staying with them, a nephew—very quiet—one hardly knew he was there. Useful, too, as a playmate for Olive.

All this was remote from the world that Gerald lived in, and however much he probed it by questioning he could not really make it his own.

"Uncle Richard, what is a Candidate?"

"He wants to know who the Candidate is, Richard!"

"Oho—taking an interest in politics already, eh? Wuff-wuff! Why, he's a Liberal—that's why we're trying to get him in."

"Get in where?"

"He wants to know all about him, Richard, I do believe!"

"You mean his name? Well, my boy, he's called Sir Thomas Barton. Do you know what 'Sir' means?"

This time it was Gerald's turn to shout. "Yes, it means he's a knight."

"Right to a T, my boy. Knighted by the King—consequently is, you have to call him 'Sir.' Be careful of that, mind, if you should ever happen to meet him on the stairs."

All of which was tremendous confirmation of something that Gerald had long suspected—that he and Uncle Richard were real people, knowing real things. A knight, indeed! And on the stairs! That was how you were liable to meet knights, but no grown-up except Uncle Richard had ever seemed to realize it.

"You see," added Uncle Richard, pointing along the passage towards the closed door of the front parlour, "that's *his* room. Never you go making a noise outside of it, because you might disturb him when he's at work."

"At work?"

"Yes, my goodness, and plenty of it. Didn't I tell you, my boy, he's trying to Get In? And you and me and your aunt have all got to help him, otherwise the Other Candidate'll Get In!"

This was the first time that Gerald had ever heard of the Other Candidate.

Marvellous, mysterious days. Every morning when he came down-stairs Gerald found Uncle Richard still up, and every night when he went to bed Uncle Richard was still down. Was it possible that he never had to go to bed at all? And every morning he tapped the barometer (Gerald knew all about that now) and made some queer remark that was supposed to be funny; at any rate, it made Uncle Richard himself laugh. One morning he said: "Fine day for the race," and Gerald pricked up his ears and said: "What race?"

Then Uncle Richard's face crinkled up suddenly. "The human race," he answered. He went on laughing at that until Aunt Flo said: "Come and have some breakfast and stop plaguing the boy."

But Gerald wasn't plagued at all. He smiled at Uncle Richard to show that he appreciated the joke, whatever it was, and that, any-how, he and Uncle Richard were on the same side in the great battle.

The joy of being sure of this sharpened the joy of giving out bills and knocking at doors; there was also a song that the boys from the streets round about would sing:

"*A Li-ber-al Tom Barton is,*
And Li-ber-als are we,
We'll vote for Barton, all of us,
And make him our M.P."

Gerald liked this because he knew the tune (it was "Auld Lang Syne"), but he couldn't understand all the words. However, the words of songs never mattered. But he did know that "Tom Barton" was really wrong, so he always sang "Sir Thomas," very quietly to himself, so that he should be right without anyone hearing him.

(And afterwards, when the Candidate had Got In, he would tell people that he owed it all to one person—someone who had helped him by handing out bills, and who had called him by his proper name all the time; moreover, he had a most important engagement in London, and though there was a special train with steam up waiting for him at Browdley station, no one would undertake to drive it fast enough to reach London in time. So Gerald cried out: "I will, Sir Thomas . . ." and Uncle Richard waved to him from the platform, as the huge engine—a Pacific Four-Six-Two, by the way—gathered speed. . . .)

"Is the Other Candidate a knight?" he once asked Uncle Richard.

"Eh, what's that? Wuff-wuff—young Beale a knight? God bless my soul, no. A little jumped-up carpet-bagger, that's all he is."

The strangest things were happening all the time in that enchanted city of Browdley. Houses were decked with blue and red flags (blue, Gerald learned, was the Other Candidate's colour); windows were full of bills and cards; at every street corner in the evenings groups of people gathered, and sometimes a man got up and shouted at them, waving his arms about. Excitement filled the market-place and ran along the streets; the little brown houses, doors wide open on to the pavements, were alive with eagerness and gossip and the knowledge of something about to happen. Gerald, walking about with Uncle Richard, could sniff the battle of Good and Evil in the air.

"Well, Dick. D'ye think he'll get in?"

"We're doing our best, Tom."

"It'll be a touch-and-go with him, anyway. T'other Candidate's gaining ground."

"A carpet-bagger, Tom, if ever there was one—a carpet-bagger."

"They do say he's got one o' them motor-cars."

"He would have. Anything to make a noise."

In the morning the rumour was confirmed. The Other Candidate had a motor-car, and it was one of the very first motor-cars to appear in most of the streets of Browdley. Gerald, in secret, would not have minded looking at it; but because it belonged to the Other Candidate he pictured himself driving an express train and overtaking it, along a parallel road, so quickly that he could hardly see it at all. But, no, perhaps that was too easy. He was riding Uncle Richard's tricycle instead, and even *that* overtook it. And the Other Candidate scowled and shouted after him: "Who will rid me" (like Henry II and Thomas à Becket in the history book) "of this turbulent young man who rides a tricycle so fast that I cannot catch him up in my motor-car?" (Eight knights sprang forward and ran after Gerald, but they could not catch him.)

Actually Gerald spent most of his time in the streets near Uncle Richard's house. Sometimes, if it were raining, he played in the greenhouse; there were red and blue panes of glass in the greenhouse door. If you looked through the red, everything was hot and stormy; if you looked through the blue, it was like night-time. That was very wonderful.

One day he had a tremendous adventure. Browdley lies in a valley, and beyond the town, steepening as it rises, there is a green-brown lazy-looking mountain called Mickle. A few scattered farms occupy the lower slopes, and at one of these, Jones's Farm, it had been arranged that Gerald and Olive should leave some bills. A pony-cart drew up outside Uncle Richard's house soon after breakfast, and the journey began at a steady trot through street after street that Gerald had never been in before. The horse swished its tail from side to side, waving a red rosette tied on to it; big posters decorated the cart. The man who drove was called Fred. It was a lovely blue sunshiny morning, and when they had climbed a little way and looked back, they could see all Browdley flat below them, covered with a thin smoke-cloud, the factory chimneys sticking out of it like pins in a pincushion. Above them, very big now, the mountain lifted up. Gerald had never been close to a mountain before. He felt madly happy. The lane narrowed to a stony track where Fred had to get down several times to open gates. At last they reached the farm-house where Mrs. Jones lived. She was standing at the doorway wiping her arms on an apron and smiling at them; she was very fat and had hair piled up on top of her head. When Gerald and Olive got down from the cart she hugged them. "Well . . . well . . . well . . . ." she began, leading them inside the house; and just as they got into the kitchen a tabby cat suddenly moved from the hearthrug towards Gerald, tail erect. Gerald loved cats and stooped to stroke it, but he hadn't to stoop far, because (so the thought came to him) the cat was quite as large as a dog. Then he reflected that that wasn't a very sensible comparison, because dogs could be of all sizes, whereas cats had only one size, whatever size they were. Was that the way to put it? Anyway, Mrs. Jones's cat was a monster. It lifted up its head and met his hand in a warm, eager pressure that was beautiful to him. "Isn't she a big pussy?" said Mrs. Jones, standing with her fists at "hips firm," as they called it at Grayshott.

"She's a big cat," said Gerald gravely.

"Her name's Nib," continued Mrs. Jones, and began to say "Nibby, Nibby, Nibby," in a high-pitched voice. But the cat, after one shrewd upward glance, knew that this was all nonsense, and continued to heave up to Gerald's hand. While Gerald was thus entranced, Olive remembered the bills they had brought and handed them over. "Lawks-a-mussy," said Mrs. Jones, glancing at them, "it's Jones as'll read these, not me. A Liberal 'e is, that's very sure, even if it was his dyin' day."

Then she waddled away to a farther room, the cat abruptly following her, and presently returned with pieces of cake, glasses, and a jug. "Nettle-drink," she said. The cat was purring loudly. "Sup it up—it'll do you good."

Gerald was looking at the mountain through the doorway. In the sunlight it looked as if it were moving towards him.

"Is it the highest mountain in England?" he asked.

"Nay, that I can't say for certain—it'll happen not be as high as some on 'em."

"Isn't it the highest mountain of anywhere?" asked Gerald desperately; but neither Mrs. Jones nor Fred seemed to understand. Fred said: "'Tis only Mickle—I wouldn't call it much of a mountain at all."

All at once Gerald realized that it didn't matter how they answered: it *was* the highest mountain, the highest in the world, and he was going to climb it, like the men in the snowstorm in his geography book.

He put down his glass and walked to the doorway. "I'm going up there," he said.

"Nay, you can't, you'd get lost on Mickle," said Mrs. Jones.

"But I want to see what's over the other side," Gerald went on.

"Take 'em both up, Fred, if they want," Mrs. Jones then said. "It'll be a bit o' fresh air for 'em."

Fred nodded and began to trudge slowly up the steep track, Gerald and Olive following. But after a little while Gerald scampered ahead, because he liked to think that nobody had ever climbed the mountain before. It was a dangerous thing to do, and only he, the famous mountaineer and engine-driver, dare risk it. Up, up, scrambling through bracken and heather; there were tigers, too, that you had to watch out for. His blood was racing as he reached the smooth green summit. The earth was at his feet, the whole earth, and over the other side, which he had been so curious about, a further mountain was to be seen—doubtless the second highest mountain in the world. Far below he could make out the tower of Browdley Church, with a tramcar crawling beside it like a red beetle.

Suddenly he saw a halfpenny lying on the ground. "Look what I've found!" he cried, triumphantly; then he lay down in the cool blue air and waited for the others to come up.

Fred smoked in silence while Gerald talked to Olive.

"What makes your father a Candidate?"

"Because there's an election."

"But what's that?"

"It means he has to get in."

"Where does he get in?"

"In the house."

"Can't anybody get in?"

"Only if you're a Candidate."

"Does he ever have a special train?"

"A special train? I—I don't know."

"Don't know what a special train is? Do you like trains? When I came here there was a Four-Four-Nought on our train. Bet you don't know what that means."

No answer.

"Are you afraid to touch a snail?"

"No. And I'm not afraid to touch a bee, either. Even a bumble-bee. I don't suppose you've ever seen a bumble-bee."

"Oh yes, I have. It's like a piece of flying cat. I wouldn't be afraid to touch one. But I'll bet you'd be afraid to stand on the edge of the platform while the Scotch express dashed through at sixty miles an hour. I did that once. I stood right on the edge."

"Why?"

"It was a test. None of the others could do it. My father couldn't. Or Uncle Richard. Even the stationmaster couldn't."

"Why not?"

"Because the train was going too fast. It was really going at eighty miles an hour, not sixty."

Then there was a long silence, while Gerald lay back staring at the sky. He was very, very happy.

When you are a child, everything you think and dream of has a piercing realness that never happens again; there is no blurred background to that stereoscopic clarity, no dim perspective to drag at the heart's desire. That little world you live in is the widest, the loveliest, and the sweetest; it can be the bitterest also.

To Gerald, alone in his own vivid privacy, everything seemed miraculously right except the Other Candidate, who was miraculously wrong. The warm red room with the brass rail over the fireplace, and the greenhouse with the tricycle in it, and the parrot who never forgave him and whom he never forgave, were part of a secret intimacy in which Uncle Richard and Olive and Aunt Flo were partners (in descending order of importance), and over which, only a little lower than the angels, loomed the Candidate. Gerald could never catch a glimpse of the Candidate, though, after Uncle Richard's hint, he always looked out for him on the stairs. He knew that the Candidate lived in Uncle Richard's house, working in the front parlour with the door always closed, and sleeping in the front bedroom over it; yet he could never (and it must have been pure chance) see him entering or leaving the house, or passing from one room to another. Partly, of course, this was because of Aunt Flo's continual fidgeting. "Mind now, Gerald, be very quiet, and no playing in the passage—the

Candidate'll be in any minute." Or: "Gerald, time for bed now—must have you out of the way before the Candidate comes in!" Long after she had put him to bed and turned out the light, Gerald would lie awake, thinking and listening; often he *heard* the Candidate, but it was never any words—just the mix-up of footsteps and talk. Once he said to Uncle Richard: "Can't I ever *see* the Candidate?"—and Uncle Richard answered: "Not now, my boy—he's far too busy. But I'll take you out tonight and you'll see him then."

So that night Uncle Richard took Gerald to the market-place, which was full of a great crowd of people. Uncle Richard hoisted him on to his shoulder so that he could see; and far away, over all the cloth caps, a man was standing on a cart and shouting something. Gerald could not hear what it was he was shouting, because people round about were shouting much louder. "Aha, we're in good time," said Uncle Richard, in Gerald's ear. "That's only old Burstall—don't you take any notice of *him*. He'll only go on till the Candidate comes, that's all. Watch out—you'll soon see the Candidate!"

The talking and shouting went on, and Gerald, perched on Uncle Richard's shoulder, began to feel very sleepy. Everyone seemed to be smoking pipes and cigarettes, and the smoke rose in a cloud and got into his eyes, so that it became hard to keep them open. The man on the cart continued to talk, but he wasn't interesting either to watch or listen to . . . and still the Candidate didn't come . . . . Then suddenly, with a jerk, Gerald felt himself being lowered to the ground and Uncle Richard was stooping and shaking him. All around were the legs of people hurrying past. "Why," exclaimed Uncle Richard, "I do believe you've been asleep! Didn't you see the Candidate?"

Then Gerald realized what had happened. Uncle Richard laughed heartily. "Well, I don't know—you are a rum fellow, and no mistake! Badgering me all the time to see him, and then when he does come you drop off to sleep!"

"I couldn't help it," answered Gerald miserably. "I didn't know . . . . Why didn't you nudge me?"

"Nudge you? God bless my soul, I thought you were wide awake!" Uncle Richard went on laughing as if it were a great joke instead of something very sad. "Well, my boy, you missed something good, I can tell you. The Candidate's a treat—a fair treat!"

DAYS WENT BY, and the chance did not come again. All the commotion of shouting and singing and waving red rosettes was reaching some kind of climax that Gerald, even without understanding it, could clearly sense; every morning the magic was renewed, and Uncle Richard tapped the barometer with more zest for the day ahead.

In Gerald the desire to see the Candidate had grown into a great longing. It coloured all Browdley in a glow of excitement, for, as Uncle Richard had said: "You'll see him, my boy, if you keep your eyes open! Ha, ha—if you keep your eyes open, eh? That hits the mark, eh? Wuff-wuff . . . . He's everywhere in Browdley—you're bound to see him. But mind, now, no hanging about the passage—that would only annoy him. He's putting up a hard fight—we've all got to help."

That was so, of course, and it was for that reason he and Olive kept on putting bills in letter-boxes. It was like the Secret Service, where you did things you didn't properly understand because the King ordered you to; though you never really saw the King till afterwards, when the danger was all past and he received you at the Palace and conferred on you the Most Noble and Distinguished Order of the Red Rosette.

So Gerald wandered about, eager and happy and preoccupied, full of thoughts of his mission and stirred by wild hopes that some time, any time, on the stairs or at the corner of the street, the Candidate might suddenly appear. A vision! It was terribly exciting to think of—quite the most exciting thing since Martin Secundus had measles and went to the sanatorium, and Gerald used to wait about outside thinking that Martin would probably die and would want to give him a last message from his deathbed.

One afternoon Gerald was alone in the house, reading the Yearly Report of the Browdley and District Friendly and Co-operative Society, which he had found under the cushion of a chair, and which seemed to him, for the moment, of engrossing interest. There was a picture in it of the first train entering Browdley station in 1853, and beside it, a picture of the first shop opened by the Browdley and District Friendly and Co-operative Society in the same year. A long, long time ago, before Uncle Richard was born. Gerald began to think about a long, long time ago, but it was hard to think like that. He was relieved when the tinkle of a bell in the street outside reminded him of his unique position—he was alone in the house, and the bell belonged to the ice-cream cart that visited the Parade every afternoon. Gerald had a passion for ice-cream, and one of his constant puzzlements was that grown-ups, who had pockets full of money and complete freedom to do anything they liked, didn't eat ice-cream all day long. Aunt Flo, for example, would nibble at a spoonful and say she "didn't care for it much—it's too cold" (what a ridiculous thing to say!) and Uncle Richard wouldn't have any at all. Profound mystery of human behaviour! Sometimes, however, they had allowed Gerald to go out into the street with a cup and buy a halfpennyworth. Now, with a sudden consciousness of his great chance, Gerald reached down from the dresser the largest cup he could find and took two pennies carefully out of his purse. Then he ran down the passage and out at the front door. The ice-cream cart, drawn by a little donkey, stood in the middle of the roadway, with the ice-cream man sitting perched up inside it. It was a beautiful cart, covered with coloured pictures and gilt lettering, and with four bright brass pillars holding up a flat roof. It made the ice-cream man, whose name was Ulio, look like a king on his throne. "Two pennyworth," said Gerald, a little nervously, lest Mr. Ulio should see into his inmost heart. But Mr. Ulio just jabbed at his ice-cream and scooped a few slices into the cup—and not very much more, Gerald thought, than he had formerly got for a halfpenny.

Gerald ran back into the house and began to eat the ice-cream in a great hurry, because it was "waste" when it melted, and it always did, towards the bottom of the cup. The parrot squawked and pattered up and down the bars of the cage; she always demanded a share of anything that people were eating. Gerald, however, took no notice of her, partly because of their long-standing feud, but chiefly because he would not have given away even a fraction of his ice-cream to anybody. While he was eating ice-cream he was transfixed with greed; mind and body were united in the fulfilment of desire.

When the cup was empty he became his more usual self again; his passions became more mystical, more closely intertwined with thought. He was not sure what he would do next, but he ran into the greenhouse and stared for a time through the blue glass, which he liked better than the red. He was excitingly alone. The Candidate was out, Uncle Richard was out on his tricycle, Olive and Aunt Flo were "round the corner" on some errand. Suddenly a knock came at the front door and Gerald ran back to open it, hoping beyond hope that the Candidate might have returned unexpectedly and that he would say, when they had shaken hands: "Gerald, in all Browdley you are the man I have most of all been wanting to meet. I have heard of you, of course. Come into my parlour and let us talk. Has Mr. Ulio gone out of the street? I hope not, for I should like you to join me in a large dish of his excellent ice-cream. . . .' But no; it was an ordinary man, just an ordinary man, wanting to see the Candidate. Gerald said he was out.

"Hasn't he come back yet? There's this letter for him. He's been up at the farms on Mickle this morning, so they say, but I reckoned he'd be back by now. Will you give him this letter when he comes?"

"Is it very important?"

"Oh, no, it'll do when he has a minute to spare. No particular hurry."

Gerald gave his promise, but as soon as the man was gone he came to the conclusion that the letter *was* very important, and that the man had only said it wasn't because it really was. Secret Service people did things like that. And since it was very important, and if the Candidate were still at the farms on Mickle, why should not Gerald go up there himself, immediately, and deliver it to the Candidate in person? They would meet, perhaps, in Mrs. Jones's kitchen. "Where is the young man who brought this message? He has saved my life. *What?* He lives with Uncle Richard? And I never knew it! How can I ever forgive myself! . . . Mrs. Jones, bring us some of your nettle-drink—we will all quaff together."

Gerald left the house, walked to the centre of the town, crossed the market-place, and took the turning up the hill. The day was not so fine as when he had set out for Mickle before, and the mountain itself looked heavy and dark; but Gerald did not mind that—he had too many exciting thoughts. At one place where the street narrowed and two factories faced each other, he imagined that the walls were leaning over, and that if he didn't hurry they would fall on him. So he broke into a scamper till the danger was past, and then stood panting and not quite sure whether he was really afraid or only pretending. Then he took the Candidate's letter out of his pocket and looked at it solemnly; it reminded him of what he had to do. He hurried on. Presently he came to the end of the houses; the lane twisted and became steeper; a few drops of rain fell. He thought of the warm red room at Uncle Richard's with Aunt Flo making potato-cakes as she probably would be by this time, and just beginning to wonder where he was; the clatter of cups and the kettle singing, the parrot squawking for a spoonful of tea. Would it not be safer to go back? But no; no; he must climb up and up and deliver the letter to the Candidate. He came to a line of high trees; if there were an odd number of them, perhaps he would go back, but if there were an even number he would keep on. There were twelve. He often settled difficult problems by this kind of method, though he never told anybody about it, except Martin Secundus, who understood. He began to walk faster uphill. You cannot do it, they all cried, mocking him as he passed by; it is too dangerous to climb this mountain; no one has ever done it and come back alive. It is my duty, he answered proudly, as he swept on.

Then he began to see that the sky was darkening, not with rain only, but with twilight; the top of Mickle lay in a little cloud, as if someone had drawn the outline of the mountain in ink and then smudged it. He felt tired and his legs trembled. Soon the rain began to fall faster, until there was no mountain to see at all—only a grey curtain covering it; but he knew he was on the right path, because of the steepness. Never, remarked the famous engine-driver, do I remember such a night of wind and rain. . . .

He walked on and on, climbing all the time, till the rain had soaked through all his clothes, and was clammy-cold against his skin.

Suddenly he heard a noise, a strange noise, a kind of rumbling and

muttering from the road ahead. He stopped, scared a little, listening
to it above the swishing of the rain and the whine of the wind in the
telegraph wires. The noise grew louder, and all at once two bright yellow lights poked round a corner and came rushing at him. He ran for
safety to the side of the road, and there slipped on some mud and fell.
The next he knew was that the rumbling noise had halted somehow
beside him, and had changed and lowered its key. Someone was holding him up and feeling his arms.

"No bones broken, Roberts. I'm sure we didn't touch him—he just
slipped and fell over. We'd best take him along with us, anyhow."

"Yes, sir."

Gerald found himself lifted off his feet with his face pressing
against something rain-drenched and fluffy. A ray of yellow light
caught it, and he saw then that it was a rosette fastened to a man's
overcoat.

A blue rosette.

Blue.

Once again the truth besieged him in an overpowering rush. This
man who was holding him must be the Other Candidate . . . and the
noise-making Thing nearby must be the motor-car. There could be
no doubt about it. And he was shaken. He felt fear, horror, and the
simple presence of evil. "Let me go!" he shouted desperately, wriggling and twisting and hitting the man's face with his fists.

"Here, what's the matter, youngster?"

"Let me go—let me go!"

"What's all the fuss about? You aren't hurt, are you? Better get him
in the car, Roberts."

"No! No, no!"

"Well, what the devil *do* you want?"

Now that the man had used a swear, like that, Gerald was more
certain than ever that he must be the Other Candidate. And knowing that he was the Other Candidate, it was easy to see what a
wicked face he had. Terrible eyes and a curving nose and a sneery
mouth, like pictures of pirates. And what he wanted to do, undoubtedly, was to steal the Candidate's letter that Gerald was carrying.
Gerald looked around wildly. The man had put him down to earth

again, that was something; but both the men seemed so huge above him, and the falling rain seemed to enclose the darkness through which lay his only chance of escape.

"Come on," said the man roughly. "This is no place to hang about all night. We'd better make sure and take him along with us, Roberts."

"Very good, sir."

"No!" screamed Gerald. "You carpet-bagger!" And with that and a quick bound into the middle of the darkness, he ran down the hill, leaving the two men standing by the motor-car. He heard them laughing; then he heard them shouting after him and to each other; then he heard them beginning to run after him. He plunged sideways into a hedge, scratching his face and arms and bruising his eye against a thick branch. At last he managed to struggle through the long wet grasses of a field. He could hear the two men running down the hill; they passed within a few yards of him on the other side of the hedge; they passed by. As soon as he had gained breath he began to stumble farther across the field. They should not take him alive, and they should not find the Candidate's letter. So he tore it up into very little pieces and let go a few of them whenever there came a big gust of wind. When they were all gone he felt brave again and wished he had some other papers to tear up and throw away.

It was ten o'clock at night when Gerald, in charge of a policeman, arrived at Number 2, The Parade. The Candidate was out, but Uncle Richard and Aunt Flo were waiting up, worried and anxious and by no means reassured by Gerald's first appearance. For he was nearly speechless with exhaustion; his clothes were drenched and mud-plastered; his arms and face were streaked with scratches, and he had an unmistakable black eye. All the policeman could say was that he had found him fast asleep in a shop doorway along the Mickle road, and that he had been incapable of giving any account of what had happened to him—only the fact that he lived at Number 2, The Parade.

Uncle Richard fetched the doctor; meanwhile Aunt Flo rubbed Gerald with towels, gave him some Benger's Food, and put him to bed with three hot bricks wrapped round with pieces of blanket. He was fast asleep again long before the doctor came.

In the morning he felt much better except for a certain dazedness, aches in most of his limbs, and an eye which he could hardly open. Uncle Richard and Aunt Flo were beside his bed when he woke up. He smiled at them, because they were Good, and he was Good, and Uncle Richard's house was a Good House. They began to ask him what had happened, and when he was awake enough he launched into the full story of how he had been walking along the road when suddenly. . . .

"What road?"

"The road to Mrs. Jones's Farm."

"Jones's Farm!" shouted Aunt Flo, repeating the words in a loud voice so that Uncle Richard, who was deafer than usual some mornings, could hear. "But what on earth were you doing along that road?"

Gerald dared not mention the letter to the Candidate, because it was a Secret Document, and Secret Documents were not to be divulged even to one's best friends. So he said, in a casual way which he hoped would sound convincing: "I wanted to see Mrs. Jones and Nibby."

"Nibby?"

"The cat. A very big cat." He remembered with disfavour how Mrs. Jones had called it "a big pussy."

"Mrs. Jones and her cat!" shouted Aunt Flo. "He says he was going to see Mrs. Jones and her cat! The Mrs. Jones at Jones's Farm! Did you ever hear such a story!"

"Wuff-wuff," said Uncle Richard.

"Go on," said Aunt Flo, warningly. "And let's have the whole truth, mind. We know you bought some ice-cream off Ulio's cart when he came round in the afternoon, because Mrs. Silberthwaite saw you."

Gerald did not know who Mrs. Silberthwaite was, but he felt that it had been none of her business, anyhow. He went on, reproachfully: "You see, a motor-car came down the hill."

"A motor-car!" shouted Aunt Flo, in great excitement. "Richard, listen to that! He says a motor-car met him along the road! It would be Beale's motor-car, for certain—there's only the one! Beale in his motor-car knocked him down!"

Now this was not what Gerald had said at all, but he thought it an interesting variant of what had really happened, and he was just picturing it in his mind when Uncle Richard let out one of his biggest and most emphatic "wuffs."

"God bless my soul, that young carpet-bagger knocked him down! Knocked the boy down with his new-fangled stinking contraption! Knocked the boy down—God bless my soul! We'll have the law on him, *that* we will—it'll cost him something—wuff-wuff—knocked the boy down in the public highway! Goodness gracious, the Candidate must know immediately! Wuff—immediately! When Browdley hears of all this, young Beale won't stand a chance! It'll turn the election—mark my words—"

And Uncle Richard began capering out of the room and down the stairs with more agility than Gerald had ever seen him employ before. Gerald was excited. His mind was racing to catch the flying threads of a hundred possibilities; meanwhile Aunt Flo was rushing about to "tidy up" the room; for the Candidate was like the doctor in this, that it would never do to let him catch sight of a crooked picture or a hole in the counterpane.

After a few moments footsteps climbed the stairs, slowly and creakingly; Uncle Richard was talking loudly; another voice, rather tired and hoarse, was answering.

And so, after those many wonderful days of waiting and dreaming, Gerald at last met the Candidate face to face; and because he knew he was the Candidate he saw what a kind and beautiful face it was, the face of a real knight. Overwhelmed with many thoughts, transfigured with worship, Gerald smiled, and the Candidate smiled back and touched the boy's forehead. Gerald thrilled to that touch as he had never thrilled to anything before, not even when he had first seen the Bassett-Lowke shop in London.

"Better now?" asked the Candidate.

Gerald slowly nodded. He could not speak for a moment, he was so happy; it was so marvellously what he had longed for, to have the Candidate talking to him kindly like that.

"Tell the gentleman what happened," said Aunt Flo, on guard at the foot of the bed.

"Yes, do, please," said the Candidate, still with that gentle, comforting smile.

"I will," answered Gerald, gulping hard or he would have begun to cry. And he added, in a whisper: "Sir Thomas."

They all smiled at that; which was odd, Gerald thought, for there could really be no joke in calling the Candidate by his proper name. He went on: "You see, the motor-car came straight at me—"

"He says the motor-car charged straight into him!" shouted Aunt Flo, for Uncle Richard's benefit.

"Let the boy tell his own story," said the Candidate.

That calmed them, and also, in a queer way, it gave Gerald calmness of his own. He continued: "The motor-car came charging into me and knocked me over—"

"Was it going fast?"

"It was going *very* fast," answered Gerald, and added raptly: "Nearly as fast as the Scotch express."

"He's all trains," said Aunt Flo. "Never thinks of anything else."

But the Candidate showed an increasing unwillingness to listen to her. "So the motor-car was travelling fast," he said to Gerald quietly, "and I suppose you were knocked down because you couldn't get away in time. Is that it?"

"Yes, sir—Sir Thomas."

"And what happened then?"

"The motor-car stopped and two men got out and came up to me. One of them was wearing a blue badge."

"Beale!" cried Aunt Flo. "Didn't I say so? Richard, he says one of them was Beale himself!"

"Please go on," said the Candidate.

Gerald said after a pause: "They picked me up and stared at me."

"Stared at you?"

"Yes. That's what they did."

"And what after that?"

What, indeed? Gerald could not, for the moment, remember just how everything had happened. But suddenly the answer came.

"They laughed," he said.

"They *what?*" asked the Candidate, leaning forward nearer to Gerald.

"He says they jeered at him!" shouted Aunt Flo.

"They laughed," continued Gerald, with gathering confidence. "And one of them said it was all my fault for being in the way. He hit me." Pause. "He hit me in the eye. I ran away then and they both chased me, but they couldn't catch me." He sighed proudly. "I ran too fast."

"Richard—Richard—just listen to that—would you believe it—he says they hit him!"

"Wuff-wuff—my goodness—wuff—just wait—scandalous—wuff—"

"Tell me now," said the Candidate, still quietly. "You say one of the men hit you and gave you this black eye. You're sure he hit you?"

"He hit me," answered Gerald, with equal quietness, "*twice.*"

GERALD STAYED IN BED for several days after that, for it seemed that despite all the doctoring and hot bricks, he was destined to catch the thoroughly bad cold that he deserved. For a time his temperature was high—high enough to swing the hours along in an eager, throbbing trance, invaded by consciousness of strange things happening in the rooms below and in the streets outside. Voices and footsteps grew noisier and more continual, shouting and singing waved distantly over the roof-tops. Aunt Flo brought him jellies and beef-tea, and Uncle Richard sometimes came up for a cheery word; but for the most part Gerald was left alone, while the rest of the house abandoned itself to some climax of activity. He could feel all that, as he lay huddled up under the bedclothes. But he was not unhappy to be left alone, because he felt the friendliness of the house like a warm animal all around him, something alive and breathing and lovely to be near. There had been nothing in his life like this before. He could not remember his father and mother (they had both died when he was a baby); and Aunt Lavinia, who usually took charge of him during the school holidays, lived in a dull, big house in a dull, small place where nothing ever happened—nothing, at any rate, like this magic of Browdley streets and Ulio's ice-cream and climbing right to the very top of Mickle.

But the most wonderful thing of all had been when the Candidate bent over him and touched his forehead. As he lay feverishly in bed and thought of it, it all happened over again, but with more detail—with every possible detail.

"Gerald Holloway, I owe everything to you. If that letter had been discovered . . ." And suddenly Gerald thought of a big improvement: the Candidate was really his father, who hadn't actually died but had somehow got lost, but now here he was, found again, and they were both going to be together for always. They would live in the Parade, quite near to Uncle Richard, and Gerald need never go back to Grayshott except to see Martin Secundus and ask him to come and stay with them. "Father . . . this is Martin . . ."

And when he grew up he would go on serving his father in the Secret Service, because he was more than an ordinary father. He was a Loving Father, like the Father people talked about in church.

The clock on the mantelpiece ticked through Gerald's dreaming, ticking on the seconds to the time when he should be grown up and a man. What a long time ahead, but it was passing; he was eight already, and he could remember as far back as when he was four and Aunt Lavinia hit him for blowing on his rice pudding to make it cold.

But why "*Our* Father"? My father, he said to himself proudly, remembering how the Candidate had smiled.

So the hours passed in that shabby little back bedroom at Uncle Richard's; but Gerald never noticed the shabbiness, never noticed that the furniture was cheap and the wallpaper faded, never realized from such things that Uncle Richard and Aunt Flo were poor people compared with rich Aunt Lavinia in her dull, big house. All he felt was the realness here, and the unrealness of everywhere else in the world.

One morning the doctor pronounced him better and fit to get up. "His school begins again on Tuesday," said Aunt Flo. "Will he be able to go?"

"Good gracious, yes," replied the doctor. "Good gracious, yes."

Till then Gerald had had hopes that somehow the cloud of Grayshott on the horizon might be lifted, that the holidays would not end as all other holidays had done; but now, hearing that most clinching "Good gracious, yes," he felt a pinpoint of misery somewhere inside the middle of him, and it grew and grew with every minute of thinking about it.

That night was very quiet and there were no footsteps or voices, and in the morning, when he got up and dressed and went downstairs, he saw that the door of the parlour was wide open.

"Well," said Uncle Richard, tapping the barometer as usual, "so here you are again, young shaver."

There was a difference somewhere. Something had happened. After breakfast he began to ask, as he had so often begun: "Can Olive and I—" and Uncle Richard said: "Eh, what's that? Olive's not here any more—wuff-wuff—she's gone away with her father."

"Gone away? The Candidate's gone away?"

Uncle Richard laughed loudly. "Don't you go calling him the Candidate any more, my boy. Because he isn't. He's the Member now."

"What's the Member?"

"It means he's Got In. Margin of twenty-three—narrow squeak—but that doesn't matter. Still, it shows he wouldn't have done but for young Beale's behaviour with that motor-car of his—perfectly scandalous thing—as I said at the time—perfectly scandalous—wuff-wuff—and consequently was—as I said—it turned the scale. Turned the scale—wuff-wuff—didn't I say it would?"

All this was nothing that Gerald could understand much about, except that the Candidate had gone. "Uncle Richard," he said slowly, and then paused. Aunt Flo shouted: "Richard, why don't you answer the boy? He wants to ask you something!"

Uncle Richard put his hand to his ear. "Ask away, my boy."

"Uncle Richard—will it—all—ever—happen—again?"

"Eh, what? Happen again? Will what happen again?"

Then Gerald knew it was no use; even Uncle Richard couldn't understand. He ran away into the greenhouse and stared through the red glass.

The next morning Aunt Flo wakened him early and gave him a brown egg for breakfast, because he had "a journey in front of him."

Then he kissed her and said goodbye, and looked at the tricycle in the greenhouse for the last time. Uncle Richard took him to the station and told the guard about his luggage and where he was going. Thump, thump, thump, along the wooden platform; the train came in, actually drawn by a Four-Six-Nought, but Gerald had hardly the heart to notice it.

"Goodbye, my boy. Wuff-wuff. Don't forget to change at Crewe— the guard will put you right. And here you are—this is to buy yourself some sweets when you get back to school."

Fancy, thought Gerald, Uncle Richard didn't know that you weren't allowed to buy sweets at school; still, a shilling would be useful; perhaps he would buy some picture-postcards of railway engines. "Oh, thank you, Uncle Richard . . . goodbye . . . goodbye."

"Goodbye, my boy."

Gerald kept his head out of the window and waved his hand till the train curved out of sight of the station. Then, as the wheels gathered speed, they began to say things . . . Grayshott tonight, Grayshott tonight. . . . This time a week ago. . . . This time two weeks ago . . . . Oh dear, how sad that was . . . . The train entered a tunnel and Gerald decided: If I can hold my breath until the end of this tunnel, then it means that I shall soon go to Uncle Richard's again and the Candidate will be there and Olive too, and we shall all climb Mickle together and see Mrs. Jones and Nibby . . . . He held his breath till he felt his ears singing and his eyes pricking . . . then he had to give way while the train was still in the tunnel. That was an awful thing to have had to do. He took out of his pocket the pencil he had poked Polly with (that first morning, how far away!) and began to write his name on the cardboard notice that forbade you to throw bottles on the line. "Gerald," he wrote; but then, more urgently, it occurred to him to black out the "p" in "Spit," so that it read "Please do not Sit." Very funny, that was; he must tell Martin Secundus about that, because Martin had his own train-joke when there was nobody else in the compartment; he used to cross out the "s" in "To Seat Five," so that it read "To Eat Five." Gerald did not think this was quite as funny as "Please do not Sit." But suddenly in the midst of thinking about it, a wave of misery came over him at having to leave Uncle Richard's, and he threw himself into a corner seat and hid his face in the cushions.

ALL THIS HAPPENED a long time ago. Gerald never stayed with Uncle Richard again.

Uncle Richard is dead, but Aunt Flo is still living, an old woman, in a small cottage on the outskirts of Browdley—for Number 2, The Parade, has been pulled down to make room for Browdley's biggest super-cinema. The parrot, too, still lives—as parrots will. Just the two of them, in that small cottage.

The Candidate is dead, and Olive is married—to somebody in India, not such a good match, folks say.

The Other Candidate, however, has done pretty well for himself, as you would realize if you heard his name. He is in Parliament, of course, but not as Member for Browdley. Indeed, if he ever thinks of Browdley, it is with some natural distaste for a town whose slanderous gossip circulated the most fantastic stories about him once, delaying his career, he reckons, by three whole years. He is very popular and a fine after-dinner speaker.

And Gerald grew up to be happy and miserable like any other boy. He passed from Grayshott to Brookfield, where he became head of Chips's house; then he went to Cambridge and took a double first. But it is true to say that the world was never more wonderful to him than during that holiday at Uncle Richard's when he was eight, and never afterwards was he as miserable (not even during the War) as in the train going back to Grayshott; never did he adore anyone quite so purely as he adored the Candidate, or hate so fiercely as he hated the Other Candidate.

And never afterwards did he tell such a downright thumping lie, nor was there a time ever again when right and wrong seemed to him so simply on this side and on that. A little boy then, and a man now if he had lived; he was killed on July 1st, 1916. When Chips read out his name in Brookfield Chapel that week, his voice broke and he could not go on.

YOUNG
WAVENEY

W HEN WAVENEY HAD BEEN AT BROOKFIELD for a month he
was moved up into the lower fourth, Mr. Pearson's form;
which was a pity, because he did not like Mr. Pearson.
Nor, to be quite frank, did Mr. Pearson like him. For
Waveney was everything that Mr. Pearson was not; he was young,
he was attractive, and he possessed an inexhaustible vitality. Mr.
Pearson, on the other hand, was no longer young; he had never
been particularly attractive, and he had lately become exceedingly
tired. Actually he was forty-three, and owing to a weak heart that
made him ineligible for the army, he had come to Brookfield as a
wartime deputy.

How a schoolmaster must envy a boy who is obviously going to grow up into a man of much superior personality to his own, and how easily that envy can turn to loathing if the boy senses it and is cruel!

Waveney was not cruel, but he was a passionate hater of injustice, and before he had been in Mr. Pearson's class for a week, that passionate hatred was aroused.

For Mr. Pearson had a *system*. The system, which had served well enough at his previous school, was new to Brookfield; and it was as follows. If anyone in his class talked or fooled about while his back was turned, Mr. Pearson would swing round to try to catch him, but if (being rather short-sighted) he failed to do so, he would say: "Stand up, the boy who did that." Nobody would respond, of course, because there was a feeling at Brookfield that a schoolmaster had no *right* to ask such a question. He ought to spot offenders for himself, or else leave them unspotted. For, after all, as young Waveney eloquently remarked, if you ride your bicycle on the footpath, you may be copped, but you aren't expected to go to the police station and give yourself up; and all life was rather like that, one way and another.

Wherefore it was manifestly unjust for Mr. Pearson, when nobody made a confession, to pull out a large gunmetal watch, hold it dramatically in one hand, and say: "Very well, if the boy who did it doesn't own up within twenty seconds, I shall detain the whole form for half an hour after morning school. . . . Five . . . Ten . . . Fifteen . . . Very well, then, you will all meet me here again at twelve-thirty."

Partly by its detestable novelty, the system worked after a few preliminary trials, and Mr. Pearson's class remained fairly free from ragging. Which, doubtless, may be held to justify the system; for Mr. Pearson knew from long experience that, in matters of class discipline, he was such stuff as screams are made of.

Now young Waveney, who was about as clever as an eleven-year-old can well be without achieving something absolutely insufferable, had declared war on Mr. Pearson right from the first day, when in answer to a question in a History test paper—"What do you know about the Star Chamber?"—he had written: "Nothing"; and had afterwards claimed full marks, because, as he said, it was a perfectly correct answer. "It wasn't *my* fault, sir, that you framed the question badly—what you *meant* to say, sir, was 'Write what you know about the Star Chamber'—we like to be accurate about these things at Brookfield, you know, sir." Mr. Pearson did not give him full marks, but he mentally catalogued him as a boy to beware of; and Waveney mentally catalogued *him* as a poor sort of fish, anyway.

"The system," however, brought matters to a head. As Waveney urged afterwards to an excited mass meeting of fourth-formers—"Can't you see that the whole thing's just beastly unfair on everybody? He can't keep order himself, and he expects us to do the job for him. If we don't own up, we're supposed to be letting other people down—sort of honour-bright business—pretty convenient for him, when you come to think about it. Well, anyhow, I warn you, I'm going to make a stand, and I advise all you others to do the same. In future, let's arrange not to own up—ever—when he tries his little game. Let him spot us himself, if he wants to—why should we save him trouble? And if he keeps us in after hours, then let's all put up with it for a time until he gets tired. He soon will. Mind now, not another confession from anybody—we'll soon break his rotten system!"

As it happened, Waveney was himself the first to make the experiment. On the following day, he threw a piece of inky paper while Mr. Pearson's back was turned, refused to confess himself the thrower when the gunmetal watch was brought out, and became thus the cause of a detention for the whole class. The detention took place, and at the end of it Mr. Pearson said: "Some coward among you has allowed you all to suffer rather than confess his own trivial misdeed. I will give him another chance to declare himself, failing which I shall have no alternative but to repeat this detention every day until Conscience has done its work."

Afterwards, in rising fury, Waveney told his companions: "Well, if *that's* his game, we'll see who can stick it out the longest! Only, mind, you fellows have got to back me up! It's hard luck on you for the time being, but I'm breaking the system for you, don't forget that!"

Another detention followed on the next day, and another after that. Young Waveney became more and more tight-lipped about it; he was certainly not enjoying himself, though he was sustained by the feeling that he was leading a moral crusade. After the third detention Mr. Pearson said: "I am truly sorry for the hardship that some unspeakable coward is inflicting on you all, and if you should happen to know who he is, I don't for a moment suggest that you should tell me, but I have no doubt that you will let *him* know—in your own way—what you think of his behaviour." It became disappointingly clear, moreover, that Mr. Pearson did not greatly mind the detentions; he read a novel all the time, and as he was a lonely man with few social engagements an extra half-hour a day did not much matter to him.

Unfortunately the fourth form had many social engagements—in particular the annual match against Barnhurst, of which one of the detentions compelled them to miss the beginning. Ladbroke, a keen cricketer (which Waveney was not), said, rather curtly: "Pity you chose this week of all weeks for your stunt, Waveney."

After the fourth detention someone said: "Waveney daren't own up now, he's in too much of a funk—so I suppose we'll all get kept in for ever."

After the fifth detention Waveney found himself suddenly unpopular, and he hated it. "Bit of a swine, young Waveney, the way he's carrying on—pity he hasn't got more guts, he'd have owned up long since. Pearson says it's a cowardly thing to do, and I reckon it is, too."

After the sixth detention Waveney went to Mr. Pearson in his room and confessed.

"Ah," said Mr. Pearson, who was not essentially an unkind man (especially when his enemy was humbled), "so you are the culprit, eh?"

"Yes."

"And it is for you that your classmates have already suffered so much—and so undeservedly?"

"Yes, I did it."

"And you found you could not go on, eh? The pangs of Conscience became too acute—the still, small voice that spoke inside you, telling you it was a mean thing to have done, a cowardly thing—isn't that what it told you, Waveney—isn't that why the tears are in your eyes?"

"No," answered Waveney, nearly howling with rage. "I think it's nothing but a dirty trap, and it's your rotten system that's really the mean and cowardly thing, and—and—"

Mr. Pearson faced Waveney with a glassy stare. His moment was spoilt. "Waveney, you forget yourself! And you will go to the head-master for being intolerably impudent—impudence, sir, is a thing I will *not* put up with. . . ."

So young Waveney was summoned to Chips's study that same evening. Chips was seventy then, recalled from a well-earned retirement to assume the temporary headship of Brookfield during the War years. He had been at Brookfield for nearly half a century, and he had known boys rather like young Waveney before. He had also known masters rather like Mr. Pearson before. There was not much, indeed, that Chips had not known before; only the details, the patterned configurations of events, were apt to rearrange themselves.

"Well—umph?" he said, peering over his spectacles across the desk and giving his characteristic chuckle.

"Mr. Pearson sent me, sir."

"Umph—yes—you're Waveney, yes—umph—Mr. Pearson sent me a little note about you. Some little—umph—misunderstanding— eh? Suppose you—umph—tell me about it—in your own words?"

Waveney launched into a concise account of exactly what had happened (he was really a very clear-minded boy), while Chips listened with an occasional twitching of the eyes and face. When the tale was told, Chips sat for a moment in silence, looking at Waveney. At length he said: "Bless me, boy, what a chatterer you are—you take after your father—umph—he was president of the debating society—talked the biggest—umph—nonsense—I ever heard! And now he's—umph—in Parliament—well, well, I'm not surprised. . . ."

After a pause he went on:

"But you know, Waveney—umph—you're not fair to Mr. Pearson. You'd make his life a misery—umph—if you could—and you blame him because—umph—he's found a way of stopping you! Come, come—he's got to protect himself against all you fourth-form ruffians—umph—eh?"

"But it's the system, sir."

"Systems, my boy, are hard things to fight. I warn you of that. . . . Well, I must do something with you—umph—I suppose. What do you—umph—suggest?"

"I—I don't know, sir."

"The—umph—usual?"

"If you like, sir."

"Umph—as if I care—so long as *you're* satisfied—umph . . . but there's one thing, Waveney. . . ."

"Yes, sir?"

"Be—be *kind*, my boy."

"*Kind*, sir?"

"Yes—umph—even when you're fighting systems. Because there are—umph—human beings—behind those systems . . . . And now—umph—run along."

Chips watched the boy's receding figure as he walked to the door across the study carpet; then, with a half-smile to himself, he called out: "Oh, Waveney—"

"Yes, sir?"

"What—umph—are you going to be when you grow up?"

"I don't know, sir."

"Well—umph—I think I can tell you. You're going to be either—umph—a great man or—umph—a confounded nuisance . . . . Or—umph—both . . . as so many of 'em are . . . . Remember that. . . . Goodbye, my boy. . . ."

After Waveney had gone, Chips sat for a time at his desk, thinking about the boy; then he wrote a note asking Mr. Pearson to come and see him.

MR. CHIPS
TAKES A RISK

I T IS THE WISE MAN who is often wise enough not to know too much, and in his eighty-second year Mr. Chips had grown to be very wise indeed. Living in peaceful retirement after more than half a century of schoolmastering, it was possible for him to enter his old school well aware that, in mere items of knowledge, most Brookfield boys could teach him quite as much as they could learn from him. "What is a straight eight?" he might ask, innocently, and when a dozen young voices had finished explaining, he would reply, with the characteristic chuckle that everyone at Brookfield had imitated for years: "Umph—umph—I see. I just wondered how an eight—

umph—could possibly be straight—umph—that was all. I thought
perhaps—umph—Mr. Einstein had changed—umph—even the shape
of the figures. . . ."

He was always apt to joke about mathematics, partly because (as he
freely confessed) he had never understood "all this—umph—$x^2 + y^2$
business." Nor, with such an attitude, was it surprising that he
regarded High Finance with something of the bewilderment (but
none of the adoration) with which a South Sea Islander regards a
sewing machine. Indeed he once said: "Few people understand High
Finance, and—umph—the higher it goes, the fewer!" He was certainly not of the few, and whenever he had any small capital to
invest he put it prudently, if unadventurously, into British government securities. Only once did he stray from this orthodox path, and
that was when (on the advice of a new and excessively plausible bank
manager) he bought a few shares in National and International Trust
Limited, a corporation which, in the early spring of 1929, seemed as
reliable as its name.

One April morning of that year Chips found the following letter
on his breakfast table:

"DEAR OLD CHIPS—Just to remind you that we don't seem to
have met for years. Do you remember me? You once thrashed me
for climbing on the roof of the Big Hall—that was way back in
1903, which is a long time ago. If you are ever in town nowadays, do please have lunch with me at the St. Swithin's Club. I
should enjoy a chat over old times.
Yours ever,
Charles E. Menvers."

Which was just the sort of letter from an Old Brookfield boy that
Chips delighted to receive. He replied that very morning, in his neat
and very minute handwriting:

"DEAR MENVERS—Of course I remember you, and you will
doubtless be glad to know that your roof exploit still holds
the Brookfield record for impudence and foolhardiness. I

happen to be visiting London next Thursday, so I will lunch with you then with pleasure. . . ."

So it came about that Mr. Chips entered the luxurious precincts of the St. Swithin's Club for the first time in his life and was welcomed by a handsome, fresh-complexioned man of middle age, who had once been a boy with keen eyes and a mischievous face. The eyes were still keen, and to Chips it even seemed that the look of mischief had not disappeared entirely.

"Hello, Chips! Fine to see you again. You don't look a day older!"

They all said that. Chips answered: "I can't—umph—return the compliment. You look *many* days older!"

Menvers laughed and took the old man's arm affectionately as they entered the famous St. Swithin's dining room.

"Never been here before, Chips? Ah, well, I don't suppose business often takes you into the City. This is the Cathedral of High Finance, y'know. Why, I reckon there are a dozen millionaires having lunch in this room at the present moment. . . . And I'm one of 'em. Did you know *that?*"

No, Chips hadn't known that. "I'm afraid—umph—I never had much of a head for figures."

Menvers laughed again. There was nothing of the conventional caricatured financier about him. He was not fat, bloated, or truculent in manner. He did not wear a heavy gold watch chain—merely an inconspicuous silver wristwatch. And he did not smoke cigars—just ordinary cigarettes. Except for a veneer of self-display that was more flamboyant than really boastful, he had still the boyish charm that Chips so well remembered. And also (as he proudly confided) he had a pretty wife and one child, a boy. "Hope to put him into Brookfield in September, Chips. Keep an eye on him, won't you?"

Chips reminded him that he had long retired from schoolmastering and took no active part in the life of the modern Brookfield, but Menvers brushed the implication aside. "Nonsense, Chips. My spies report that your footsteps are heard on dark nights pacing up and down the old familiar corridors . . . . What was that tag in Virgil you used to teach us—begins *Quadrupedante putrem*—ah yes, I remember now—

Quadrupedante putrem sonitu quatit ungula campum. Have I got it right?"

"Perfectly right," answered Chips, "except that—umph—I am not yet—umph—a ghost, and I was never—umph—a horse . . . . But I'm glad to find you still keep up your classical knowledge. It was never—umph—so considerable as to be—umph—a burden to you."

So they talked and joked together throughout a simple but exquisitely expensive meal. Chips found that he still liked Menvers, and neither more nor less because the fellow was a millionaire. Nor, in his innocence, did it occur to him as in the least remarkable that a wealthy City magnate should devote two hours of a busy day to reminiscing with an octogenarian schoolmaster. Finally, when they were on the point of shaking hands and wishing each other the best of luck, Menvers said:

"Oh, by the way, Chips, I happen to be on the board of National and International Trust, and I saw your name on our register the other day . . . . Hardly the sort of investment for *you*, I should have thought. Quite safe, mind you—don't think there's anything wrong about it. But what's the matter with War Loan for a staid old buffer like yourself?"

Chips explained about his bank manager's recommendation, to which Menvers listened with, it seemed, a touch of exasperation. "Those fellows shouldn't take chances—why can't they leave that sort of thing to those in the game? . . . Not, mind you, that I want to give you a false impression. The stock's sound enough . . . . Fact is, I want as much of it for myself as I can get hold of. What did you pay for your packet?"

And Chips, of course, having no head for figures, couldn't remember. But by the time he reached his house at Brookfield that evening a long and (he thought) quite unnecessarily costly telegram awaited him. It ran:

AFTER YOUR DEPARTURE I FOUND OUT PRICE YOU PAID FOR NATS AND INTERNATS STOP OFFER YOU DOUBLE IF YOU WILL SELL STOP BEG YOU TO DO SO AND DEVOTE PROFIT IF YOU WISH TO SCHOOL MISSION OR ANY SIMILAR RACKET REGARDS CHARLES THE ROOFWALKER.

Now Chips, had he been a shrewd thinker in financial matters, would have argued: This man wants my stock so urgently that he is apparently willing to pay twice the market price for it. Ergo, since he is a financier and in the know, there must be something especially promising about it, and I should do better to refuse his offer and hold on. But Chips was not a shrewd thinker of this kind. He was simple enough to feel that acceptance of the offer was an easy way of obliging Menvers and at the same time benefiting a deserving charity. So he wrote (not telegraphed) an acceptance; and that was that.

April, remember. In June, as you probably won't need to remember, National and International Trust crashed into spectacular bankruptcy. When Chips saw the newspaper headlines his immediate reaction made him write to Menvers a sympathetic note in which he said:

"I feel that your generous purchase of my shares was so recent that I cannot possibly allow you to bear any extra loss, however small, that would otherwise have fallen on me. I am therefore enclosing my cheque for the full amount. . . ."

By return came a scribbled postcard enclosed in an envelope:

"I have torn up your cheque. Don't be a damned fool. I could see this coming and I wanted to get you out in time. If you must help me, pray for me. . . ."

Two days later the arrest of Charles E. Menvers on serious and complicated charges of fraud provided the City with its biggest sensation for years.

Chips, as I have stressed all along, did not understand High Finance. His business code, so far as he had any, was simple—to sell things fairly (though in point of fact he never sold anything in his life except old books to a second-hand dealer), to pay all debts promptly (which was easy for him, as he never owed anything but gas and lighting bills), and to give generously to the needy (which was also easy for him, as he was in the habit of living well within his income). Simple—yes, simple as his life. He didn't understand the money axis on which the lives of so many people revolve—or stop revolving.

What he *did* understand, however, was the notion that any one of his old boys never ceased to be *his*, no matter what happened ... no matter *what* happened ... and therefore, though he was old enough to find such a duty arduous, he attended every session of the four-day trial of Charles Menvers.

He sat for hours in one of the back rows of the public gallery at the Old Bailey, listening to expositions by counsel, long arguments by accounting experts, judicial rulings on incomprehensible issues, and (the only really interesting interludes) the prisoner's evidence under cross-examination. For Menvers, in that stuffy courtroom, provided the sole focus of anything even remotely aligned to humanity. The rest of the proceedings—long discussions as to the interpretation of abstruse points in company law—passed beyond Chips's intelligence as effortlessly as had the $x^2 + y^2$ of his algebra lessons seventy years before. All he gathered was that Menvers had done something (or perhaps many things) he shouldn't have done, but in a game so complicated that it must (Chips could not help feeling) be extremely difficult to know what should be done at all. Only one incident contributed much to the old man's understanding, and that was when the Crown Prosecuting Counsel asked Menvers why he had done something or other. Then had followed:

Menvers: Well, I took a chance.

C.P.C.: You mean a risk?

Menvers: A risk, if you prefer the word.

C.P.C.: And what you risked was other people's money?

Menvers: They gave it to me to risk.

C.P.C.: Why do you suppose they did that?

Menvers: Because they were greedy for the big profits that can only be obtained by taking risks, and they didn't know how to take risks themselves.

C.P.C.: I see. That is your opinion?

Menvers: Yes.

C.P.C.: You admit, then, that your policy has always been to take risks?

Menvers: Yes, always.

Chips smiled a little at that. But two hours later he did not smile when, after the verdict of "Guilty on all counts," the Judge began: "Charles Menvers, you have been found guilty of a crime which deeply stains the honour of the City of London as well as brings ruin into the lives of thousands of innocent persons who trusted you. . . . A man of intelligence, educated at a school whose traditions you might better have absorbed, you deliberately chose to employ your gifts for the exploitation rather than for the enrichment of society. . . . It is my sad duty to sentence you to imprisonment for twelve years. . . ."

Chips paled at the words, was startled by them, could hardly believe them for a moment. And then (such was his respect for English law and its implacable impartiality) he told himself, as he shuffled out of the court: Well, I suppose it must have been something pretty serious, or they wouldn't have come down on him so hard. . . .

He had asked for permission to see Menvers during the trial, but it had not been granted; in lieu of that, he intended to offer what help he could to Mrs. Menvers, and with this object planned to intercept her as she left the court. It had not occurred to him that some scores of journalists would have the same idea, plus a greater knack in carrying it out. He did, however, contrive a meeting at her house that evening. He introduced himself and she seemed relieved to talk to him. "Twelve years!" she kept repeating. "Twelve years!"

He stayed with her for an hour, and between them, during that time, there grew a warm and gentle friendliness. "Charles was a good man," she told him, simply; and he answered: "Yes—umph—I know he was, the young rascal!"

"*Young?*" she echoed, and then again came the terror: "Twelve years! Oh, my God, what will he be like in twelve years?"

And Chips, touching her arm with a movement rather than a contact of sympathy, murmured: "My dear, I am eighty-one," which might have seemed irrelevant, yet was somehow the most comforting thing he could think of.

Later she said: "He's worried about the boy. We were to have sent him to Brookfield next term. Of course that's impossible now . . . the disgrace . . . everybody knowing who he is . . . that was the only thing Charles really worried about. . . ."

"Tell him not to worry," said Chips.

THE NEXT DAY, from Brookfield, he wrote to the prisoner in Pentonville Jail:

"MY DEAR MENVERS—I understand that you always take risks—even on behalf of others. Take another risk, then, and send your boy to Brookfield as you had intended. . . ."

YOUNG MENVERS arrived on the first September day of the following school term, by which time his father had already served a month of the sentence. The boy was a nice-looking youngster, with more than a touch of the same eager charm that had lured thousands of profit-seekers to their doom.

On those first nights of term, despite his age and the fact that he was no longer on the official staff of the School, Chips would often take prep in substitution for some other master who had not yet arrived. He rather enjoyed being asked to do so; and the boys were equally satisfied. It relieved the misery of term-beginning to see old Chips sitting there at the desk on the platform, goggling over his spectacles, introducing new boys, and sometimes making jokes about them. Of course there was no real work done on such an evening, and it was an understood thing that one could rag the old man very gently and that he rather liked it.

But that evening there was an especial sensation—young Menvers. "I say, d'you see the fellow at the end of the third row—new boy—his name's Menvers—his father's in prison!" "No? Really?" "Yes—doing twelve years for fraud—didn't you read about it in the papers?" "Gosh, I wonder what it feels like to have your old man in quod!" "Mine said it served him right—we lost a packet through him. . . ." And so on.

And suddenly Chips, following his age-old custom, rose from his chair, his hand trembling a little as it held the typewritten sheet.

"We have—umph—quite a number of newcomers this term. . . .

Umph-umph .... Astley ... your uncle was here, Astley—umph—he exhibited—umph—a curious reluctance to acquire even the rudiments of a classical education ... umph-umph.... Brooks Secundus.... These Brooks seem—umph—to have adopted the—umph—Tennysonian attribute of—umph—going on for ever .... Dunster ... an unfortunate name, Dunster ... but perhaps you will claim benefit of the *lucus a non lucendo* theory ... umph-umph ... eh?"

Laughter ... laughter ... the usual laughter at the usual jokes.... And then, in its due alphabetical order:

"Menvers. . . ."

Chips said:

"Menvers ... umph ... your father was here ... umph ... I well remember him ... umph ... I hope you will be more careful than he has been—umph—lately ... [Laughter.] He was always a crazy fellow ... and once he did the craziest thing that ever was known at Brookfield ... climbed to the roof of the hall to rescue a kitten ... the kitten—umph—had more sense—didn't need rescuing—so this—umph—crazy fellow—umph—in sheer petulance, I suppose—climbed to the top of the belfry—umph—and tied up the weathervane with a Brookfield tie .... When you go out, take a look at the belfry and think what it meant—umph—crazy fellow, your father, Menvers—umph-umph—I hope you won't take after him. . . ."

Laughter.

And afterwards, alone in his sitting room across the road from the school, Chips wrote again to the prisoner in Pentonville:

"MY DEAR MENVERS—I took a risk too, and it was well taken. . . ."

MR. CHIPS MEETS
A SINNER

WHEN CHIPS WENT on his annual climbing holidays he never told people he was a schoolmaster and always hoped that there was nothing in his manner or behaviour that would betray him. This was not because he was ashamed of his profession (far from it); it was just a certain shyness about his own personal affairs plus a disinclination to exchange "shop" talk with other schoolmasters who might more openly reveal themselves. For when Chips was on holiday he didn't want to talk about his job—he didn't even want to think about it. Examination papers, class lists, terminal reports—all could dissolve into the thin air of the mountains, leaving not a wrack behind.

But he could never quite lose his interest in boys. And when, one September morning in 1917 in the English mountain town of Keswick, he saw an eager-faced freckled youngster of about eleven or twelve swinging astride a hotel balcony reading a book, he couldn't help intervening: "I'd be careful of that rail, if I were you. It doesn't look too safe."

The boy looked up, got up, looked down at the rail, then shook it. As if to prove Chips's point, it obligingly collapsed and set them both laughing. "So there you are," said Chips. "A minute more and you'd have been over the edge."

"Don't tell Father, that's all," answered the boy. "I'd never hear the end of it. I once cut my head open doing the same thing. See here?" And he tilted his head as he pointed to an inch-long scar above his right temple.

"What's the book?" Chips asked, thinking it better not to admire such an obviously valued trophy.

The boy then showed the book—an anthology of poems, open at Macaulay's ballad about the coming of the Spanish Armada. "See," cried the boy, with gathering enthusiasm, "it says—'The red glare on Skiddaw roused the burglars of Carlisle.' Where's Carlisle?"

"Burghers, not burglars. Carlisle's a town about thirty miles away."

"And that's Skiddaw, isn't it?" The boy pointed to the green and lovely mountain that rose up at the back of the hotel.

"Yes, that's it."

"And who were the burglars—burghers?"

"Oh, they were just citizens of the town. When they saw the bonfires on top of Skiddaw they knew it as the signal that the Spanish Armada had been sighted."

"Oh, you know the poem, then?"

Considering that Chips had read it to his class at Brookfield for thirty years or more, he was justified in the slight smile that played over his face as he answered: "Yes, I know it."

"You like poetry?"

"Yes. Do you?"

"Yes . . . I wish you'd come in the hotel and meet my father. We're staying here, you know. I want to climb Skiddaw, but he says it's too much for him at his age, and he won't let me go by myself because he says I'd break my neck over a precipice."

"You probably would," said Chips, "if there *were* any precipices. But there aren't—on Skiddaw. It's a very safe mountain."

"Oh, do come along and tell him that. . . ."

So CHIPS, almost before he realized what was happening, found himself piloted inside the breakfast room and presented to Mr. Richard Renshaw, a squat, pasty-faced, pompous-mannered heavyweight of fifty or thereabouts. One glance at him was enough to explain his reluctance to climb Skiddaw, and one moment of his conversation was enough to suggest that the boy's love of poetry would awake no answering sympathy in the father. "I'm a plain man," began Mr. Renshaw, expounding himself with great vigour in a strong Lancashire accent. "Just an ordinary plain businessman—I don't claim to be anything else. I'm here because my doctor said I needed a rest cure—and there's no rest cure to me in pushing myself up the side of a mountain. So David must just stay down with me and make the best of it. Especially as it's due to him—very largely—that I *need* the rest cure."

He glanced at the boy severely, but the latter made no comment and showed no embarrassment. Presently David moved away and left the two men together. "That boy's a terror," continued Mr. Renshaw, pointing after him.

"He's not mine, understand—he's my second wife's by an earlier marriage. My lad's quite different—fine young chap of twenty-five—accountant in Birmingham—settled down very nicely, *he* has. But David . . . well, it's my belief there's bad blood in him somewhere."

Chips went on listening—there was nothing else to do.

"Been sacked from two schools already . . . a proper good-for-nothing, if you ask me."

Chips hadn't asked him, but now he did ask, with the beginnings of interest: "What was he sacked for?"

"Well, from the first school it was for breaking into the matron's bedroom in the middle of the night and scaring her out of her wits . . . and the second school sacked him for an outrageous piece of hooliganism in the school chapel during Sunday service. Isn't that enough?"

"Quite enough," agreed Chips. "But what's the position now? What are you going to do with him?"

"I'm damned if I know. What can *anybody* do with him? If schoolmasters themselves . . . but it's my belief they don't try. I've not a lot of faith in schoolmasters."

"Neither have I—sometimes," said Chips.

During the days that followed, Chips would have had more and better chances to get to know David if Mr. Renshaw himself had been less obtrusive. He seemed a lonely, unhappy sort of man, and, having found in Chips a tolerant listener, he made the most of his opportunities. Chips could hardly get rid of the fellow at the hotel, and was heartily glad that he was no mountaineer. It was not that there was anything especially unpleasant about him—merely that he was a loud-voiced nuisance, and the more Chips saw and talked with him the more he felt that David, with or without bad blood, could not have found life very harmonious with such a stepfather. Chips wondered why such an ill-assorted pair chose to take their holidays together. The answer came in Renshaw's own words. "Y'see, Chipping, there's nowhere else for him to go. The rest of the family wouldn't take him as a gift—and you can't blame 'em. So he has to stay with me whether he likes it or not. I'm here for my health and he's here for his sins."

Chips smiled. "I only hope my own sins will never take me to a worse place."

"Oh, Keswick's all right, I know. Quite a nice spot for a holiday. But the boy isn't satisfied with a stroll in the afternoon—he's restless all the time—restless as a monkey. Only the other day one of the waiters caught him in the hotel kitchen tasting all the food out of the pans . . . of course I had to give the fellow a tip to say nothing about it. The boy's incorrigible, I tell you. Hasn't even the sense to see what's to his own advantage. He knows that his whole future depends on what I decide to do with him during the next few days."

"Oh?"

"Well, y'see, I promised that if he was a good boy I'd overlook his disgraceful behaviour at school and put him under a private tutor for a couple of years—then after that, if he still behaved well, my son in Birmingham—the accountant, y'know—might take him into his office. . . . Wonderful chance, that, for a boy who's had to leave school under a cloud . . . . You'd think it would make him turn over a new leaf, wouldn't you? But it doesn't . . . he doesn't seem to care."

Which was true enough. David's efforts to impress his stepfather with any appearance of remorse or future good intentions were, Chips could see, so vagrant as to be almost imperceptible. Once Chips gave the boy a lead to discuss the matter by saying, during a casual conversation in the hotel lobby: "By the way, your father says there's a chance of your becoming an accountant . . . . It's a good profession, if you like it."

"I wouldn't like it," answered David, with decision.

"What do you want to be, then?"

"An explorer."

Chips smiled. "That's not a very easy thing to be, nowadays."

"I once explored some caves in Scotland. It was easy enough. It was Father who made all the fuss about it."

"Oh?"

"Just because the tide came up and I had to sit on a ledge all night and wait for it to go down again. But I didn't find any gems."

"Any gems? What do you mean?"

"Well, it said in the poem, you know—'Full many a gem of purest ray serene the dark unfathomed caves of ocean bear.' . . . But I didn't find any."

Towards mid-September, as the beginning of term at Brookfield approached, Chips began to feel the familiar willingness to be back at work. His strenuous month of walking and climbing had made him feel immensely fit for his years; even Renshaw's conversations couldn't spoil such a holiday, despite their tendency to become less restrained and more repetitive. They dealt largely with the trials and tribulations of family and business life; Renshaw had not been a happy man, nor—quite evidently—had he possessed the knack of making others happy. It seemed that he had lost a great deal of money owing to the War. He couldn't forget it, and Chips, for whom money meant little and for whom the War (then in its third year) was a continuing nightmare, was scarcely interested to hear in great detail how certain properties of his in Germany had been confiscated. "There never was anything like it," said Renshaw, mournfully philosophizing. "And I'd put so much into them. That's what the War does."

Chips could have told him of other and perhaps worse things that the War did, but he refrained.

"And it's nearly as bad over here, Chipping, the way the export trade's going to pieces," Renshaw continued. "I'm in cotton, and I know." And he added, putting the direct question: "What are you in?"

"I'm in clover," answered Chips, almost to himself.

Renshaw looked puzzled. "What's that? ... Oh, I see—I suppose you mean you sold out in time and can sit back on the profits? ... Lucky fellow—I wish I had."

"Yes, I think I've been pretty lucky," agreed Chips, leading the conversation gently astray.

THERE CAME THE LAST evening. Both Chips and the Renshaws were to leave the following morning—in different directions, Chips was not sorry to realize. As a kindly gesture towards someone whom he did not definitely dislike (though he was aware that they had little in common), he agreed to visit Renshaw's room after dinner for a final drink and chat. He did this dutifully, listening in patience to the man's renewed plaints against the state of trade and affairs in general; about ten o'clock he thought he could decently take his leave. "I don't suppose we'll meet in the morning," he said. "I'd like to have said goodbye to David, but I suppose he's in bed by now."

"Not he," answered Renshaw. "I packed him off to the pictures to keep him out of the way while we had our talk. There's Chaplin on or something .... He can't get into much mischief in a cinema. Ought to be back any minute now."

"Well, say goodbye to him for me," said Chips, shaking hands.

But about midnight he was awakened by a tapping at his room

door. Renshaw, in nightshirt and dressing gown, stood outside. "I say, Chipping . . . sorry to wake you up . . . but David hasn't come back yet. What do you suppose I ought to do about it? Call the police?"

They adjourned to Renshaw's room to discuss the situation further. It was a night of bright moonlight and Chips, standing by the window, could see the full curve of Skiddaw outlined against a blue-black sky. He thought he had never seen the mountain look more beautiful, and he remembered, with a sharp ache of longing, his first meeting with his wife on another mountain not many miles away—the lovely girl whose marriage and death had taken place twenty years before, yet whose memory still lay as fresh as moonlight in his heart. And he knew, in some ways, that it was David as well as the mountain that had made him think of her, for she would have liked David, would have known how to deal with him—she had always known how to deal with boys, and whatever he himself had learned of that difficult art, the most had been from her.

He said quietly: "I'd give him a bit more time before calling the police, if I were you. After all, it's a nice night—he may have gone for a walk."

"Gone for a walk? At midnight? Are you crazy?"

"No . . . but *he* may be . . . a little. . . . In fact. . . ." And then suddenly Chips, turning his eyes to the mountain again, saw at the very tip of the summit a strange phenomenon—a faintly pinkish glow that might almost have been imagined, yet—on the other hand—might almost not have been. "Yes," he added, "I think he *is* a little crazy. . . . Do you mind if I go out and look for him? . . . I have an idea . . . well, let me look for him, anyway. And you wait here . . . don't call for help . . . till I come back. . . ."

CHIPS DRESSED and hurriedly left the hotel, walked through the deserted streets, and then, at the edge of the town, turned to the sidetrack that led steeply up the flank of the mountain. He knew his way; the night was brilliant; he had climbed Skiddaw many times before. A certain eagerness of heart, a feeling almost of youth, infected him as he climbed—an eagerness to find out if his guess were true, and a gladness to find that he could still climb a three-thousand-foot

mountain without utter exhaustion. He clambered on, till at last the
town lay beneath in spectral panorama, its roofs like pebbles in a
silver pool. Life was strange and mysterious, nearer perhaps to the
heart of a boy than to the account books of a man. . . . And presently,
reaching the rounded hump that was the summit, Chips heard a
voice, a weak, rather scared, treble voice that cried: "Hello—hello!"

"Hello, David," said Chips. "What are you doing up here?"

(Quite naturally, without excitement or indignation, just as if it
were the most reasonable thing in the world for a boy to be on top of
Skiddaw at two in the morning.)

"I've been trying to make a bonfire," David replied, sadly. "I
wanted to rouse the burglars of Carlisle. But the wind kept blowing it
out . . . and I'm tired and cold. . . ."

"You'd better come down with me," said Chips, taking the boy's
arm. A few half-burned newspapers at their feet testified to the
attempt that had been made. "And you needn't worry about the
burghers of Carlisle—burghers, not burglars—they're all fat, elderly
gentlemen who're so fast asleep at this time of night that they
wouldn't see anything even if you'd set the whole mountain on
fire . . . . So come on down."

David laughed. "Are burghers like that? They sound like Father."

"Oh no. He's anything but fast asleep. He's worried about where
you've got to."

"Don't tell him you found me up here. Please don't tell him. Say I
just went for a walk and got lost and you found me."

"Why don't you want me to tell him the truth?"

"He wouldn't understand. . . ."

"And do you think I do?"

"I don't know. Somehow . . . I think you do in a way . . . . There's
something about you that makes it easy for me to tell you things. . . .
Do you know what I mean?"

On the way down the mountain Chips talked to David quite a lot,
and David, thus encouraged, gave his own versions of the escapades
that had led to his expulsion from two schools.

"You see, Mr. Chipping . . . it was a line from one of Browning's
poems—I'm like that about poetry, you know—a line gets hold of me

sometimes—I can't help it . . . sort of makes me do things—crazy things . . . . Well, anyway, this was a line about trees bent by the wind over the edge of a lake . . . it said they bent over 'as wild men watch a sleeping girl' . . . I just couldn't forget that, somehow . . . it thrilled me . . . I wanted to act being a wild man . . . but I didn't know any sleeping girl . . . so I dressed up in a blanket and blacked my face and climbed in through the matron's window . . . of course, she wasn't exactly a girl, but she was asleep, anyway . . . . Oh, she was asleep all right . . . but she woke up while I was watching her . . . and my goodness, how she screamed."

"And that's what you were expelled for?"

"Yes."

"I suppose she didn't believe your explanation?"

"Nobody did."

"Well . . . tell me about the other school . . . . What did they expel you for there?"

"Oh, that was different . . . . You see, there was a preacher who used to visit us regularly and he always used to pray something about the weather—if there was a drought he'd pray for rain, and if there were floods he'd pray for the rain to stop, and so on. Seemed to me he just did it as a matter of course—so I thought it would be fun to find out if he'd really be surprised to have a prayer answered right away. . . . There was a sort of trapdoor in the chapel roof just over the pulpit, and one Sunday during the summer term, after there'd been no rain for a month, I guessed he'd start praying for it, and he did . . . so I just opened the trapdoor and tippled a bucket of water over him . . . . I thought he might think I was God. . . ."

WHEN CHIPS AND DAVID reached the hotel, the first glimmer of dawn lay over the mountain horizon. Renshaw was pacing up and down in his room, perplexed, alarmed, and—as soon as he saw David—in a furious rage. Chips tried, and eventually was able, to pacify him somewhat. They all breakfasted together a few hours later—David, very tired and subdued, half dozing over ham and eggs. Renshaw was still—and perhaps not without reason—in a grumbling mood.

"I'm damned if I know *what* to do with him," he said, glancing distastefully at his stepson, and careless whether the boy heard his words or not. "If only schoolmasters were any use I'd try to send him to another place, but they won't have him, y'know, when they find out he's been sacked twice already. Damned lazy fellows, schoolmasters—take your money and then say the job's too hard for them. After all, that's what they're paid for, to deal with boys— even with bad boys—why do they shirk it? ... I tell you, I've no patience with schoolmasters—too easy a life, too many holidays— they don't know what real work is .... What's your opinion, Chipping?"

Chips smiled. "Perhaps it's a prejudiced one, Mr. Renshaw," he answered. "You see, I *am* a schoolmaster."

"*What?* Oh ... I didn't mean . . . ."

"Don't apologize—I'm not offended. . . . I should never have told you except that ... well, I wonder if you'd consider sending David to Brookfield ... he could be—umph—directly under my—I won't say 'control'—let's call it 'guidance' . . . ."

"Do you really mean it?"

"Yes."

"Well, I'm sure it's very generous of you. . . ."

"Not at all. It's just that—as you say—schoolmasters oughtn't to shirk their jobs."

At this point David looked up from his dozing and Renshaw turned to him. "David—did you hear that? Mr. Chipping is a school-master ... how would you like to go to his school?"

David stared at Chips and Chips looked at David and they both began to smile. Then David said: "*What?* You a schoolmaster? I don't believe it!"

"I take that as a compliment," answered Chips.

MR. CHIPS MEETS A STAR

"COMING OUT OF THE ROYAL HOTEL the other day, who should I espy but Randolph Renny . . ." wrote Miss Lydia Jones ambiguously, ungrammatically, but in substance correctly. For it really was Randolph Renny himself, and by identifying him she made the scoop of a lifetime. A pretty long lifetime, too, for she had been doing an unpaid-for social gossip column for the *Brookfield Gazette* for over thirty years. Prim and spinsterish, she knew the exact difference (if any) between a pianoforte solo "tastefully rendered" and one "brilliantly performed"; and three times a year, at the Brookfield School end-of-term concert, she sat in the front row, notebook and pencil in hand, fully aware of herself as Brookfield's critical and social arbiter.

She had occupied this position so long that only one person could clearly remember her as an eager, ambitious girl, hopeful about her first and never-published novel; and that person was Chips. She had been a friend of his wife's, which was something he could never forget. As she grew primmer and more spinsterish with the years, he sometimes meditated on the strange chemistry of the sexes that so often enabled a man to ripen with age where a woman must only wither; and when she withered out of her fifties into her sixties, and Brookfield began to laugh at her and the *Gazette* to print fewer and fewer of her contributions, then Chips's attitude became even more gentle and benevolent. Poor old thing—she meant no harm, and she loved her work. He would always stop for a chat if he met her in the village, and he only smiled when, from time to time, she referred to him as "the doyan [sic] of the Brookfield staff."

Indeed, it was Chips who had given her the scoop about Randolph Renny—a scoop which many a bright young man from Fleet Street would have paid good money for. But Chips chose to give it to Miss Lydia Jones, of the *Brookfield Gazette,* and Miss Jones, faced with something far outside her customary world of whist drives and village concerts, could only deal with it in the way she dealt with most things ... that is to say, ambiguously, ungrammatically, but in substance correctly.

This is how it had all happened. One August evening Chips had been returning by train from London to Brookfield. The School was on summer vacation, and though he had long since retired from active teaching work (he was over eighty), he still experienced, during vacations, a sense of being on holiday himself. Travelling back after an enjoyable weekend with friends, he had been somewhat startled by the invasion of his compartment at the last moment by a youngish, almost excessively handsome, and certainly excessively well-dressed fellow, who slumped down into a corner seat breathlessly, mopped his forehead with a silk handkerchief, and absurdly overtipped a porter who threw in after him some items of very rich and strange luggage.

Now it was Chips's boast that he never forgot the faces of his old

boys, that somehow their growing up into manhood made no difference to his powers of recognition. That was mainly true; but as he
grew older he was apt to err in the other direction, to recognize too
often, to accost a stranger by name and receive the bewildered reply
that there must be some mistake, the stranger had never been to
Brookfield School, had never even heard of Brookfield, and so on.
And on such occasions, a little sad and perhaps also a little bothered,
Chips would mumble an apology and wonder why it was that his
memory could see so much more clearly than his eyes.

And now, in the train, memory tempted him again—this time with
the vision of a good-looking twelve-year-old who had almost established a record for the minimum amount of Latin learnable during a
year in Chips's classical form. So he leaned forward after a few
moments and said to the still breathless intruder: "Well—umph—
Renny . . . how are you?"

The young man looked up with a rather scared expression. "I beg
you, sir, not to give me away . . ." he stammered.

"Give you away . . . umph . . ." Some joke, obviously—Renny had
always been one for jokes. "What is it you've been up to this time—
umph?"

"I'm trying to get away from the crowd—I thought I'd actually succeeded . . . . I chose this compartment because—if you'll pardon me
for saying it—I noticed you were reading the paper through double
spectacles—so I guessed—I hoped—"

"I may be—umph—a little short-sighted, Renny—but I assure
you—umph—I never forget a Brookfield face. . . ."

"Brookfield? Why, that's where I'm going to. What sort of a place
is it?"

Chips looked astonished. Surely this was carrying a joke too far.
"Much the same—umph—as when you were there fifteen years ago,
my boy."

Then the young man looked astonished. "I? . . . But—but I've
never been there before in my life—this is my first visit to England,
even . . . . I don't understand."

Neither did Chips understand, though he certainly—now that the
other had suggested it—detected an accent from across the sea. He

said: "But—your name—it's Charles Renny . . . isn't it?"

"Renny, yes, but not Charles . . . Randolph—that's my name—Randolph Renny. I thought you recognized me."

"I thought so, too. I—umph—must apologize."

"Well, I hope you won't give me away now that I've told you."

"Give you away? I—umph—I don't know what you're driving at."

"My being Randolph Renny—that's what I mean. I'm travelling incognito."

"Mr. Renny, I'm afraid I still don't understand."

"You mean you don't recognize my name?"

"I fear not . . . . My own name—since you have been good enough to introduce yourself—is Chipping."

"Well, Mr. Chipping . . . you fairly beat the band. I reckon you must be the only person on this train who hasn't seen one or other of my pictures."

"Pictures? You are an artist?"

"I should hope so . . . . Oh, I get you—you mean a painter? . . . No, not that sort of artist. I'm on the films. Don't you ever go to the cinema?"

Chips paused; then he answered, contemplatively: "I went on one occasion only—umph—and that was ten years ago. I am given to understand—umph—that there have been certain improvements since then . . . but the—umph—poster-advertising outside has never—umph—tempted me to discover how far that is true."

Renny laughed. "So that's why you've never heard my name? My goodness, wouldn't I like to show you round Hollywood! . . . I suppose you're not interested in acting?"

"Indeed, yes. In my young days I was a great admirer of Henry Irving and Forbes-Robertson and—umph—Sarah Bernhardt—and the immortal Duse—"

"I guess none of them ever got three thousand fan letters a week—as I do."

"*Fan* letters?"

"Letters from admirers—total strangers—all over the world—who write to me."

Chips was bewildered. "You mean—umph—you have to read three thousand letters a week?"

"Well, I don't read 'em. But my secretary counts 'em."

"Dear me—umph—how extraordinary. . . ." And after a little pause for thought, Chips added: "You know, Mr. Renny, I feel—umph—somewhat in the mood of the late Lord Balfour when he was taken to see the sights of New York. He was shown the—umph—I think it is called the Woolworth Building—and when—umph—the boast was made to him that it was completely fireproof, all he could reply was—'What a pity!' "

"Good yarn—I must remember it. Tell me something about this place Brookfield."

"It's just a small English village. A pleasant place, I have always thought."

"You know it well?"

"Yes, I think I can say I do . . . . But why—if I may ask—are you going there?"

"Darned if I know myself, really. Matter of fact, it's my publicity man's idea, not mine. Fellow named McElvie—smart man . . . . You see, Mr. Chipping, your English public—bless their hearts—have fussed over me so much during the last few weeks that I'm all in—gets on your nerves after a time—signing autographs and being mobbed everywhere . . . so I said to McElvie, I'm going to take a real rest cure, get away to some little place and hide myself, travel incognito . . . just some little place in the country—must be lots of places like that in England . . . and then McElvie suddenly had one of his bright ideas. You see, I was born in Brooklyn, so he looks it up and finds there isn't a Brooklyn in England, but there's a Brookfield. Sort of sentimental association . . . you see?"

"I see," answered Chips, without seeing at all.

He could not really understand why a man born in Brooklyn should have a sentimental desire to visit Brookfield; he could not understand why letters should be counted instead of read; he could not understand why a man who wished to avoid publicity should travel around with the kind of luggage that would rivet the atten-tion of every fellow traveller and railway porter. These things were mysteries. But he said, with a final attempt to discover what man-ner of man this Randolph Renny might be: "In my young days we used—umph—to classify actors into two kinds—tragedians and comedians. Which kind are you, Mr. Renny?"

"I guess I'm not particularly either. Just an actor."

"But—umph—for what parts did you become—umph—famous?"

"Oh, heroes, you know—romantic heroes. Fact is . . . I guess it sounds stupid, but I can't help it . . . I've sometimes been labelled the world's greatest lover."

Chips raised his eyebrows and answered: "I have a good memory for faces—umph—and also for names—umph—but in the circumstances, Mr. Renny, it seems fortunate that I—umph—easily forget reputations. . . ."

THUS THEY TALKED till the train arrived at Brookfield, by which time Chips had grown rather to like the elegant strange young man who seemed to have acquired the most fantastic renown by means of the most fantastic behaviour. For Chips, listening to Renny's descriptions of Hollywood life, could not liken it to anything he had ever experienced or read about. For instance, Renny had a son, and in Hollywood, so he said, the boy was taken to and from school every day in a limousine accompanied by an armed bodyguard—the reason being that Renny had received threatening letters from kidnappers. "To tell you the truth, Mr. Chipping, I almost thought of sending him to a school in England. D'you know of any good school?"

"Umph," replied Chips, thinking the matter over—or rather, not needing to think the matter over. "There is a school at Brookfield."

"A good school?"

"Well, I have—umph—some reason—to believe so."

"You were educated there yourself?"

Chips answered, with a slow chuckle: "Yes . . . umph . . . . I rather imagine I have picked up a little knowledge there during—umph—the past half-century or so. . . ."

By such exchanges of question and answer Chips and Hollywood's ace film star came to know each other and each to marvel at the strange world that the other inhabited. It was on Chips's advice that Renny tore some of the labels off his luggage and wrapped up his Fifth Avenue hatbox in brown paper and did a few other simple things to frustrate the publicity he was apparently fleeing from. And at the Royal Hotel (still taking Chips's advice) he registered as plain Mr. Read, of London, and was careful to ask for "tomahtoes," not "tomaitoes," and to refrain from asking for ice water at all. A few days later he rang up Chips on the telephone, said he was feeling a little bored, and suggested a further meeting. Chips asked him to tea at his rooms opposite the School, and afterwards showed him over the School buildings. Renny was horrified at the primitiveness of the School bathrooms, and was still more horrified when Chips told him they had just been modernized. But he was pleased and relieved when Chips told him that there had not been a single case of kidnapping at Brookfield for the past three hundred years. "Before that—umph—I cannot definitely say," added Chips. "There were very disturbed times—we had a headmaster hanged during the sixteenth century for preaching the wrong kind of sermon—yes—umph—we have had disturbed times, Mr. Renny."

"You talk about them, sir, as if they were only yesterday."

"So they were," replied Chips, "in the history of England. And Brookfield is a part of that."

"And you're a part of Brookfield, I guess?"

"I should like to think so," answered Chips, pouring himself tea.

The two men met again, several times. One afternoon they lazed in deck chairs on the deserted School playing fields; another day Chips took Renny to the local parish church, showed him the points of historic interest in it, and introduced him to the verger and the vicar as a visiting American. Renny seemed surprised that neither recognized him, and uttered a word of warning afterwards. "You know, Mr. Chipping, you're taking a big chance showing me round like that."

"No," replied Chips. "I think not. There are—umph—quite a number of people in England who—umph—have never heard of you, Mr. Renny. The vicar here, for instance, is much more familiar with the personalities of Rome during the age of Diocletian—he has written several books on the subject ... while our verger is so passionately devoted to the cultivation of roses that—umph—I doubt if he ever goes to the cinema at all .... So I think you may feel quite safe in Brookfield—nobody will annoy or molest you."

But after another few days had passed and there had been other meetings, a dark suspicion began to enter Chips's mind. Renny looked much better for his rest cure; idle days in sunshine and fresh air had soothed the tired nerves of an idol whose pedestal too often revealed him as merely a target. All the same, there was this dark suspicion—a suspicion that suggested itself most markedly whenever the two men walked about the streets of Brookfield. Just this—that though Renny was doubtless sincere in wanting to get away from crowds of autograph-hunting admirers, he did not altogether relish the ease with which in Brookfield he was doing so. There were moments when, perhaps, the success of his incognito peeved him just a trifle. It would have been truly awful if a mob of girls had torn the clothes off his back (they had done this several times in America), but when they didn't, then . . . well, there were moments when Renny's attitude might almost have been diagnosed as: Why the hell don't they try to, anyway? . . .

All of which came to a head in the sudden appearance of McElvie on the scene. This wiry little Scots-American arrived in Brookfield like a human tornado, expressed himself delighted with the improvement in Renny's health, demanded to meet the old gentleman with whom he had been spending so much time, wrung Chips's hand effusively, and opined (gazing across the road at the School buildings) that it certainly looked "a swell joint."

"And see," he added, taking Renny and Chips by the arm and drawing them affectionately together, "I've got a swell idea, too. . . . I'll work up a lot of phooey in the papers about your disappearance . . . . 'Where is Randolph Renny?'—'Has anybody seen him?'—'He's hiding somewhere—where is it?'—you know the sort of thing . . . and then, when all the excitement's just boiling over, we'll discover you here . . . spending a vacation with the old professor. . . ."

"I'm not a professor . . . ." protested Chips, feebly.

"Aw, it's the same thing . . . and you knew Irving, too . . . and Forbes-Robertson . . . Sarah Bernhardt . . . the immortal Dewser. . . ."

"I didn't know them," protested Chips, still feebly. "I only saw them act."

"Aw, what does that matter? . . . After all, you saw 'em and you're old enough to have known the whole bunch of 'em . . . they gave you tips about acting—and you took in what they said—and now you pass it all on to Renny here. . . . Oh, boy, what an idea—handing on the great tradition—Randolph Renny vacations secretly with Dewser's oldest friend—you were roommates, maybe, you and Dewser—"

"Hardly," answered Chips. "It was—umph—before the days of co-education. . . ."

"Oh, a woman?" replied McElvie, seizing the point with an alertness Chips could not but recognize and admire. "I beg your pardon, Mr. Chipping—no offence meant, I'm sure . . . . But you got the idea, haven't you?—why, it's stupendous—it's unique—I don't believe it's ever been thought of before—Oh, boy, it'll be the greatest scoop in the history of movie publicity. . . ."

WHICH WAS WHY, that same evening, Chips gave Miss Lydia Jones the news that Randolph Renny was staying in Brookfield at the Royal Hotel. He decided that if there were to be a scoop at all (whatever a scoop was), Brookfield, as represented by the *Brookfield Gazette* and by its social reporter, should have it. And thus it came about that Miss Jones began her column of gossip ambiguously, ungrammatically, yet in substance correctly with the words: "Coming out of the Royal Hotel the other day, who should I espy but Randolph Renny. . . ."

It only remains to add that the following term Renny's son began his career at Brookfield School, and, during a preliminary interview with Chips, remarked: "Of course you know who my father is, don't you, sir?"

"I do, my boy," Chips answered. "But—umph—you need have no fear—on *that* account. We all know—but at Brookfield—umph—we do not care. . . ."

MERRY CHRISTMAS, MR. CHIPS

*T*HEY SAY THAT OLD SCHOOLMASTERS get into a rut, that it takes a young man to supply new ideas. Perhaps so; and it is true enough that Chips, in his seventieth year, was giving pretty much the same Latin lessons as he had given in his fiftieth or his thirtieth. "The use of—umph—the Supine in 'u,' Richards," said Chips, from his desk in the fourth-form room, "seems to have escaped your notice—umph—and that—umph—can only be ascribed to the Supine in You!" Laughter . . . and if some young man could have done it better, let us give him a cheer, for he is probably doing it better, or trying to—at Brookfield now.

But in 1917, that desperate year darkening towards its close, there were no young men at Brookfield. There was a strange gap between boyhood and age, between the noisy challenge of fourth-formers and the weary glances of elderly overworked men; and only Chips, oldest and most overworked of them all, knew how to bridge that gap with something eternally boyish in himself.

Besides, ideas did come to him—once, for instance, as he was sitting at his desk in the Head's study, that more illustrious desk to which, after his retirement in 1913, he had been summoned as youths were being summoned elsewhere. (But his own service, he often said, was "acting" rather than "active"; and that, with the little "umph—umph" that had become a mannerism with him, was a joke at the expense of his official status of "acting headmaster.")

The idea came because a tall air-browned soldier knocked at the study door during the hour devoted to what Chips called his "acting," strode colossally over the threadbare carpet, and, with a mixture of extreme shyness and bursting cordiality, stood grinning in front of the desk. "Hello, sir. Thought I'd give you a call while I was hereabouts. And I'll bet you don't know who I am!"

And Chips, adjusting his spectacles in a room already dim with November fog, blinked a little, and—after five seconds—answered: "Oh yes . . . it's—umph—it's Greenaway, isn't it?"

"Well, I guess that's one on me! You've got it right first time, sir! How on earth d'you manage it—Pelmanism or something?"

Chips shook his head with a slow smile. "No . . . no . . . I just—umph—remember. . . . I just remember. . . ." But he was a little saddened, because he had never taken so long to remember before, and he wondered if it were his eyesight or his memory that was beginning to fail; but perhaps, after all, only his eyes, for he added: "You were here in—umph—let me see—in nineteen hundred, eh? Well, how are you, my boy? Umph—you won't mind if—umph—I call you that, will you? . . . Sit down and talk to me. I'm—umph—delighted to see you again. Still—umph—imitating the farmyard?"

"Goodness—you remember that, too? You're a wonder. . . . I've turned Canadian—went out there in nineteen-oh-seven—got my own ranch—found quite a lot of new animals to imitate. . . . Now

I'm over with the battalion, and by the freakiest chance we've been sent here to camp. Quite a thriving military centre, Brookfield, just now. I met another fellow the other day who used to be in your fourth form—English fellow named Wallingford."

"Wallingford . . . there was only one Wallingford. A quiet boy— umph—with red hair. . . ."

"That's right—it's still red, what's left of it. He asked me to remember him to you. Too shy to come around. I guess there's quite a few Brookfield men stationed here feel the same. School's a strange place when you've left it a dozen years—makes you feel your age when you don't come across a single face you can remember."

"Except mine—umph—eh?"

"Sure . . . and you don't look a day older. But I thought I saw in the papers you'd retired—quite a time ago?"

"So I had, my boy. . . . " And then came the little joke about the "acting service."

THE IDEA CAME LATER, when Greenaway, having stayed to lunch in the School Dining Hall, had returned to camp, and when Chips, pleased as he always was by such an encounter, was resting and musing over his afternoon cup of tea. The idea came to him with sudden breath-taking excitement, as a young man may realize that he is in love, or as a poet may think of a lovely line. He would have a party, a Christmas party; there should be no more of that shyness; the men who had once been to Brookfield should meet the boys who were still there; all should meet and mix in the School Hall for an end-of-term party . . . a supper, the best that wartime catering could provide . . . a few songs . . . nonsense for those who liked nonsense, talk and gossip for those who preferred it . . . a few simple toasts, perhaps, and no speeches; nothing formal; everything to make the occasion gay and happy . . . his own party, and his own idea of a party.

It grew bright in his eyes as he thought of it, the details assembled into a rich unity; and by the time he went back to his rooms at Mrs. Wickett's, across the road from the School, it was like good news that he could no longer keep to himself. "Mrs. Wickett," he said, when she came in with his evening meal, "I've had an idea. . . ."

She was rather less enthusiastic than he had hoped. "Mind ye don't tire yeself, that's all," she commented. "There'll be a lot of work arranging a thing of that sort, and if you was to ask me, sir, you're a bit past the age for giving parties!"

"Past it, Mrs. Wickett? Why—umph—I've only just reached it!"

And the smile he gave her faded, as it so often did, into the private smile of reminiscence; he was thinking that he was really the right age because, as a young man, he would have been far too scared and worried to tackle such an enterprise at all. How he had fidgeted, in those days, over whether he ought to put on a white tie or a black tie for some function, whether he ought to shake hands with Mr. So-and-so, whether he would say the right thing in his speech . . . but now, thank heaven, he didn't care, and one of the lovely joys of growing old was to add to this list of trivial things one didn't care about, so that one had more time to care for the things that were not trivial.

"I shall count on you—umph—to help me, Mrs. Wickett. . . . Some of your famous meat-and-potato pies—umph—eh?"

"With wartime flour and strict rations of meat!" answered Mrs. Wickett in pitying scorn. But there were ways and means, and Chips knew that neither wars nor governments would be allowed to frustrate Mrs. Wickett in her search for them. She was *that* sort of an ally.

THE NEXT MORNING the idea was still so strong in him that he dropped a hint to his favourite fourth form and within an hour the rumour was all over the School—"Old Chips is going to give a party!"—"Have you heard the latest—Chips is having a party on the last day of term—a Christmas party"—"Everybody's invited . . . and also some old boys from the camps." This last was added, if at all, as an afterthought; for schoolboys are not really interested in old boys, except on Speech Days or unless they happen to be brothers. Their lack of interest is part of their lack of worry over the future, which is a natural thing—and in 1917 a good thing, too. For then at Brookfield there were boys who were to die within a year; and they were quite happy, playing rugger and conjugating verbs and reading the War news, only half aware that the last concerned them any more than the second, or as much as the first.

So the idea of the party was launched upon a boisterously welcoming world, and in that welcome Chips found more than compensation for extra work; he found a secret sunshine that warmed and comforted him during those sad November days. Indeed, he tremendously enjoyed the planning and discussion and settlement of all the difficult details—the writing of personal invitations, the wheedling of tradesmen into promising precious food, the building up of the whole evening's programme into what, on paper and in anticipation, was already a huge success. And fourth-formers found it enticingly easy, as the term-end drew near, to switch over from conversation about such dull matters as *Cæsar's Gallic War* and the use of the Supine in "u." "*Ut omnes conjurarent.* . . . Oh, I say, sir, that reminds me, do you think we could have any conjuring at the party? I know a few tricks, sir. . . ."

"Tricks, eh, Wilmer? And evidently—umph—one of those tricks is—umph—not to prepare your work! *Conjuro* doesn't mean 'conjure' . . ."

"I know, sir, but it reminded me. Do you think I *could* do a few conjuring tricks?"

"Well, well—umph—"

And then of course the lesson was ruined and everyone began to talk about the party. But no—not ruined. It was the world, the world outside Brookfield, that was nearly in ruins. Beyond the quiet mists of the fen country, men in their millions were crouching in frozen mud, starving and thirsting in deserts, drowning in angry seas and swooping to death in midair, fretting in hospitals far from home. So that at Brookfield, even at Brookfield, the Supine in "u" lost ground as a subject of topical discussion; it gave up part of its ancient ghost, and into that place, unbidden but also unforbidden, came Chips's Christmas party. It was fun to talk about that, to plan more schemes about it, to lure Chips on to chatting, gossiping, telling you things about Brookfield that had happened years before, things you'd never have known about unless Chips had told you them.

"Do you think Jones Tertius could play his mouth organ at the party, sir? He's awfully good at it."

"I could fix the electric lights to make a sort of footlights, sir, in front of the piano—don't you think that would be a good idea?"

"My brother's got a farm, sir, he's promised to send us some real butter. . . ."

And as he sat there at his desk, with suggestions and offers pouring in on him faster than he could deal with them all, he felt that history was not only made by guns and conquests, but by every pleasant thing that stays in memory after it has once happened, and that his party would so stay, would be remembered at Brookfield as long as—say—the strange revisitation of Mr. Amberley, Mr. Amberley who came back from South America and gave every boy ten shillings to spend at the tuck-shop. "Umph—yes—Mr. Amberley—a good many years ago that was."

"Oh, do tell us about Mr. Amberley, sir."

"Well, you see—umph—Mr. Amberley was once a master here—quite a young man—and not, I fear, very good at dealing with your—umph—ruffianly predecessors. [Laughter] Your father, Marston, will remember Mr. Amberley—umph—because he once—umph—umph—inserted a small snake in the lining of Mr. Amberley's hat. . . . [Laughter] Quite a harmless variety, of course . . . and so—umph—was Mr. Amberley. . . . [Laughter] And then—after his first term—Mr. Amberley very wisely went to South America, where—umph—he was much more successful in forecasting the future price of—umph—nitrates, I think it was. So that when he came back to see us he was—umph—quite a rich man . . . . Bless me, there's the bell—we don't seem to have done very much—umph—this morning. . . ."

"But about the party, sir—do you think I *could* fix the electric lights, sir?"

"Well, Richards, if you'll undertake not to blow us all up—"

The day came nearer. Three weeks off. A fortnight off. Then "Wednesday week." And on the Thursday the School was to disperse for the Christmas holidays. Brookfield was on rising tiptoe with the pure eagerness of anticipation. When you grow older you miss that eagerness; life may be happy, you may have health and wealth and love and success, but the odds are that you never look forward as you once did to a single golden day, you never count the hours to it, you never see some moment ahead beckoning like a goddess across a fourth dimension. But Brookfield did, and does still; and so, as that autumn term dragged to an end, the tension rose; the Big Hall took on a faintly roguish air with its unusual embellishments of holly and paper festoons; mysterious sounds of practice and rehearsal came from the music rooms; eager discussions were held in the kitchens between staff and housekeeper and Chips.

Because it was so clearly going to be a grand success. Eleven old boys in the neighbouring military camps had accepted invitations, and four walking cases from local hospitals; fifteen representatives of the Brookfield that Chips remembered, chance-chosen by the hazards of war. And this timely meeting of boys and men, if Chips allowed himself to dream about it, became something epic in his vision, the closer knitting of a fabric stronger, because more lasting, than war. He could not have put much of this into words, and would not even if he could; but the feeling was in him, giving joy to every detail. And the details came crowding in. Richards had contrived an elaborate electrical dodge for lighting up the piano. Greenaway would give his celebrated farmyard imitations. And Chips himself told Mrs. Wickett to look over the dinner suit that he had not worn for years and that smelt of age and camphor.

AND THEN, on a certain Sunday morning in December, an odd thing happened during the School Chapel service—in the middle of a sermon about the disputed authorship of one of the books of the Old Testament. Brookfield, plainly, was not interested in the dispute and definitely declined to take sides in it; you could tell that from the rows of faces in the pews. But all at once, quite astonishingly, something happened that interested Brookfield a great deal; Attwood Primus, commonly called Longlegs, suddenly fainted and, after slipping to the floor with a reverberating crash, had to be dragged out by hastily roused prefects. During the last hymn conversation buzzed excitedly, and (to the tune of "For All the Saints") it was confidently rumoured that Attwood was dead.

Attwood, however, was not dead (and is not dead yet); but he was in the sickroom with a temperature of a hundred and two, and before lights-out that same Sunday evening five others had joined him. The next day came seventeen more. Chips, very calm in such an emergency, sat late in consultation with Merivale, the School doctor. With the result that on the following morning Brookfield was alive with the most intoxicating rumour that even a school can ever have.

"I say, heard the latest?—we're breaking up tomorrow instead of Thursday week—someone heard Chips talking to Merivale—"

"It's the flu—it's in all the army camps and Longlegs got it from his cousin, who's in one of them—good old Longlegs—"

"Special orders from the War Office—so they say—Nurse told me—"

"Chips has sent down to the bank for journey money—"

"I say—ten days' extra hols—what luck!"

And—in an instant—in less than an instant—the party was forgotten. Perhaps the conjurer and the mouth-organist gave it a passing thought, perhaps even a thought of wasted planning and unapplauded prowess; but even in them regret was swamped by the overmastering joy of Going Home. Which was only natural. Chips, whose home was Brookfield, knew how natural it was. And so, as he sat at his window in the early morning and watched the taxis curving to and fro through the gateway, he smiled.

HE SPENT CHRISTMAS, as he had so often done, in his rooms across the road. There were no visitors, but he was fairly busy. There had been a few details of cancellation to put in order; the promised gifts of food were transferred to hospitals; outside guests were notified that owing to . . . etc., etc., it was much regretted that the party could not be held. But the decorations remained in the Hall, half finished, and Richards's vaunted footlights, in an embryo stage of dangling flex, impeded the progress of anyone who might seek to mount the platform; but no one did. Then the last of the sickroom unfortunates recovered and went home, shaking hands with Chips as the latter doled out money for the train fare. "Happy Christmas, sir."

"Thank you, Tunstall—umph—and the same to you, my boy."

Christmas Eve brought rain in the late afternoon; it had been a cold day with grey scudding clouds. No School bell sounded across the air, and that to Chips gave a curious impression of timelessness, so that when he sat by the fire and read the paper the moments swam easily towards the dinner hour. "You'll join me, Mrs. Wickett, in— umph—a glass of wine?" he had said, and she had answered, with familiar reluctance: "Oh dear, I dunno as I ought, sir; it does go to me head so."

But she did, of course, and in that little room, with the old-fashioned Victorian furniture and the red and blue carpet and the photographs of School groups on the walls, Chips made light of any disappointment that was in him.

"Well, sir, if you was to ask me, I'd say it was proper Providence, it was, for it's my belief the fuss of it all would have knocked you up— that it would, and Doctor Merivale said the same, knowin' what a lively set-to them boys was going to make of it."

"*Were* they, Mrs. Wickett? Umph—umph—well, they're all enjoying their own parties—now—more than—umph—they'd have enjoyed anything here—umph—that's very certain!"

"Oh no, sir, I don't think that, sir."

"Mrs. Wickett—umph—no normal healthy-minded boy—umph— ever wants to stay at school a moment longer than he needs— umph—and I'm glad to say that my boys are—umph—almost *excessively* normal! When is it that they're due back—January 15th— umph—eh?"

"That's right, sir. Term begins on the 15th."

"Umph—three weeks more."

After dinner he decided to write some letters, and as he had left an address book in his school desk he walked across the road through the gusty rain and unlocked his way into the chilly rooms and corridors where his feet guided him unerringly. A strange place, an empty school. Full of ghosts, full of echoes of voices, full of that sad smell of stale ink, varnish, and the carbolic soap that the charwomen used. In every classroom a scrap of writing on the blackboard, words or figures, some last thing done before the world lost its inhabitants. And on a whitewashed wall in a deserted corridor Chips saw, roughly scrawled in pencil, what looked at first to be some odd mathematical calculation:

17
16
15
14
13
12
11
10
9

Which, of course, at second glance he perfectly understood; nay more, he could imagine the joy of the eager calculator when, after that memorable Sunday, the last eight digits of the progression had been spared him! And possibly that same calculator, at this very moment on Christmas Eve, was giving a rueful thought to the date that lay ahead—January 15th—"only three more weeks!" Boys were like that.

He found his book and relocked the doors; then, back in Mrs. Wickett's house again, he wrote his letters. Like most of his, they were written to old boys of the School, and like most letters to old boys they were now addressed to camps and armies throughout the world. Chips was not a particularly good letter-writer. His jokes came to him only in speech; in letters he was always very simple and direct and (if you thought so) rather dull. Indeed, one of their recipients (a much cleverer man than Chips) had once called them affectionately "the letters of a schoolmaster by a schoolboy." Just this sort of thing:

"DEAR BRADLEY—I am very glad to hear you are getting on well after your bad smash. We have had a pretty fair term, on the whole (beat Barnhurst twice at rugger), but an epidemic of flu attacked us near the end, interfering with the House matches and one or two other affairs. We broke up ten days early on account of this. Mr. Godley has been called up, despite his age and health, so we are understaffed again. We had an air raid in October, but no one at the School was hurt. If you get leave and can spare the time, do come and see me here. We begin term on January 15th. . . ."

Chips wrote several of these letters; then he sat by the fire over his evening cup of tea. All that he had not said, and could never say or write, flooded his mind at the thought of a world so full of bloodshed and peril; and then, in answer, came the thought of those boys who might, by happier chance, miss such peril as carelessly and as cheerfully as they had missed his party. And he prayed, seated and silent: God, bring peace on earth . . . goodwill to men and boys. . . .

"Will ye be wantin' anything more, sir?"

"No thank you, Mrs. Wickett."

"Happy Christmas to you, sir."

"And the same—umph—to you, Mrs. Wickett."

"Thank you, sir. It don't seem long, sir, since—"

Mrs. Wickett always had to say that it didn't seem long since last Christmas, or last Good Friday, or last Sports Day, or some other annual occasion. Chips smiled as she did so—a gentle smile, for there was something in his mind that was always tolerant of tradition. We have our ways, and if we are good folk our ways are fondly endured. "Time goes so quickly, sir, you 'ardly know where you are. Only another three weeks and we'll 'ave the beginning of term again. . . ."

"Yes—umph—only another three weeks," answered Chips. And that, of course, was probably what the boys were saying. But Chips, thinking of those lonely classrooms, meant it differently.

AFTERWORD

Afterword

AT FIRST SIGHT, THE TWO BOOKS in this volume might seem very different. *Lost Horizon* is a novel of adventure and romance, and the name of its lost kingdom, Shangri-La, has become a byword for retreat from the "rat-race" of the Western world. *Goodbye, Mr. Chips*, on the other hand, is a novel that explores memory, and the story is told through the recollections of Mr. Chipping, a retired schoolmaster in his eighties, who has spent his working life at Brookfield School. However, the themes of the two books are surprisingly similar: Shangri-La and Brookfield are both enclosed worlds, and are both threatened by the ugliness and violence of life outside, particularly the impact of the First World War.

To Brookfield the war brings constant bereavement, as the death of old boy after old boy is reported. Shangri-La, hidden behind a steep mountain pass, deeply attracts those who have suffered from the effects of war. This is especially true of the novel's central character, Hugh Conway, the British Consul in Baskul, who has been strikingly changed and possibly damaged by his experiences in the Great War. Hilton himself, born in 1900, had narrowly missed that war, and, through the character of Hugh Conway, he was able to explore the effects of that conflict on a survivor. Conway's deputy at the Consulate at Baskul, Charles Mallinson, is less than a decade his junior but, like Hilton, has missed the war. The relationship between the two men lies at the heart of the plot of *Lost Horizon*, their contrasting personalities defining the reader's reactions to Shangri-La. Conway, at thirty-seven, is passive and disillusioned, while Mallinson, at twenty-nine, is optimistic but has a tendency to act rather than to think.

One of the key descriptive terms in *Lost Horizon* is "slack" and in this respect the two men are very different. Mallinson accuses Conway, who is making no effort to leave Shangri-La, of being "damned slack" whereas Mallinson, who is no "slacker", is always concerned with the need to leave Shangri-La. When Conway explains to the novice lama, Chang, that slacker is "a slang word meaning a lazy fellow", Chang responds: "the English regard slackness as a vice. We, on the other hand, should vastly prefer it to tension." When Conway tells Mallinson the lamas can extend their lives beyond the natural span, the younger man responds with: "I'm dashed if I can see anything attractive about living till you're half dead." In the end, however, the differences between these two men are perhaps less important than their bond. Conway grows to like his deputy and this has much to do with his decision (later deeply regretted) to leave Shangri-La and to help Mallinson down the mountainside.

Two other Westerners enter Shangri-La at the same time as Conway and Mallinson: the missionary, Roberta Brinklow, and the American, Henry D. Barnard. From the beginning, these two minor characters are seen to have clearly outlined "agendas" of their own. Roberta Brinklow's mind is set on converting those with whom she comes into contact, whereas Barnard, a corrupt financier, knows that a return to the outer world will lead to a spell in prison. Their reasons for wanting to stay in Shangri-La may be the wrong ones, but it is these two who do stay there in the end, while Conway, who is ideally suited to the life of the lamasery, finds himself outside the valley, back in the world of "contamination".

Lost Horizon is part of a long tradition of Utopian fiction in which characters find themselves in a strange and idealized world. A large part of the interest in such stories comes from a preoccupation with outlandish places and people, but there is usually a deeper element of social commentary as well, allowing the author to explore some of the failings in his or her own society. In *Lost Horizon*, the paradise-like valley, under the benevolent leadership of the lamas, is almost free from crime. Moderation in all things is insisted upon, even when it comes to showing obedience to the rules of the kingdom. Unlike Aldous Huxley's *Brave New World* (1932), where the author turned the Utopian genre on its head, showing a nightmarish vision of the future, *Lost Horizon* suggests that there are still worthwhile ideals for society to pursue. Hilton's vision of a perfect world is not, however, wholly positive, because his concept of an ideal future is concentrated entirely within the limits of Shangri-La. When he turns to the outside world, whether in the valley or beyond, the problems inherent in his plot become apparent. For example, ordinary people of the valley is very indistinctly sketched, encouraging the reader to ask challenging questions about this seemingly perfect world.

Part of *Lost Horizon*'s popularity comes from the skilful way in which James Hilton is able to tell a suspenseful story, contrasting inactivity with passages of breathtaking action in order to retain the reader's wrapt attention. This effect is deepened through the use of a "frame" where the tale is told as a story within a story. After-dinner conversation between a group of men, including the narrator and a character called Rutherford, provides the setting for the Prologue to *Lost Horizon*. The narrator has been dining in Berlin when the conversation turns to his old school-fellow, Hugh Conway, and Rutherford gives the narrator his own account of Conway's story. The Epilogue returns us to these two characters as Rutherford describes his unsuccessful quest for Conway. The device of using these apparently reliable men to tell the story predisposes a reader to believe in the unbelievable.

Women are only marginally present in *Lost Horizon*, and, although there are said to be women initiates at Shangri-La, only two play a part in the story: Roberta Brinklow and Lo-Tsen, the aristocratic Manchu woman with whom Mallinson falls in love. Conway too loves Lo-Tsen, but apparently accepts the sexless romantic friendships of the lamasery.

Lo-Tsen came to Shangri-La when, in 1884, the party taking her to an arranged marriage lost its way. That Lo-Tsen is still "troubled" by her imprisonment becomes clear when she flees from the lamasery, seizing her one chance of love, even though she must know the price that she has to pay will be death. The story of Lo-Tsen lies at the heart of the equivocal morality of *Lost Horizon*. Like many of the inhabitants of Shangri-La, although she has been rescued from certain death on the Tibetan plateau outside, she *has* been confined against her will. From the time when Perrault, the monastery's founder, recognized that safety lay in allowing no one to leave Shangri-La, all comers have been held as prisoners and the lamas are forced to use violence in order to protect what they have achieved and also to recruit new members. Even the ideal world, it seems, must be bought at a heavy price.

Unlike the carefully plotted *Lost Horizon*, *Goodbye, Mr. Chips* is less a novel than a series of sketches, ranged in a roughly chronological pattern. It is only at the end of the novel that the reader can put together the sequence of events in Mr. Chips's life. The additional short stories, originally collected in a volume entitled *To You, Mr Chips*, deal with different aspects of the schoolmaster's life and give an insight into his character. A common theme is the broad-mindedness of Mr. Chips, set in opposition to the narrowness and lack of enlightenment of others.

The fixed point is Mr. Chips himself, drowsing by the fire in Mrs. Wickett's house, just across the road from the School, and recalling the thousands of boys he has taught. We slowly learn that he came to Brookfield in 1870 when he was twenty-two. In 1896, Chipping met and married Katherine Bridges, twenty-three years younger than himself. She died in childbirth two years later. Apart from his move out of retirement to serve as acting headmaster during the later years of the First World War, Chipping's working life was entirely spent as a Classics master at Brookfield, and by the time of his death, in November 1933, he has become almost synonymous with the school.

The Great War is obliquely foreseen from the close of the second chapter, where the narrator, speaking of Mr. Chips's first retirement in 1913, adds the tantalising comment: "but there was more to come, an unguessed epilogue, an encore played to a tragic audience". The theme continues to emerge at intervals. Descriptions of the boys at the school almost inevitably have the coda of their deaths in the war. This sense of fate, and of death preying on the youngest and brightest, gives an otherwise soothing book a dark undertow. Mr. Chips's liberalism shines out amidst the tragedy, when he dares to announce the death of the former German teacher, Max Staefel, among those of old Brookfield boys. His finest hour comes when he takes a Latin class while German bombs fall onto the surrounding area. Wit and wisdom guide Mr. Chips to a relevant passage from Caesar's *Gallic Wars*. He is ably seconded by "Maynard, chubby, dauntless, clever, and impudent", the boy who offers to translate: "this was the kind of fight . . . in which the Germans busied themselves—Oh, sir, that's good—that's really very funny indeed, sir—one of your very best—".

At the end of *Goodbye, Mr. Chips*, by means of a practical joke, a small boy, Linford, is sent round to tea. After the meal, Mr. Chips politely sends him away with:

> "Goodbye, my boy."
> And the answer came, in a shrill treble:
> "Goodbye, Mr. Chips . . . ."

The book's title alerts us to the importance of these words, and they also have a precise echo, as they are those with which Kathie, Mr. Chips's long dead wife, parted from him on the evening before their wedding. Linford provides the stimulus to Mr. Chips's final memory of Kathie, but this is superseded, as he slips into sleep, and then into death, by a last recollection of his pupils: "wherever you are, whatever has happened, give me this moment with you . . . this last moment . . . my boys . . . ."

Professor Leonée Ormond, MA
King's College, University of London

70-048-1